A.C. DONAUBAUER
Family Bonds – Book 5

Family Bonds - The Order: Book 5

A.C. Donaubauer

First published as ebook in July 2017
Paperback
2nd edition

Copyright © 2019
      Astrid Donaubauer-Grobner
      Waltenhofengasse 3/3/3302
      1100 Vienna, Austria

The author online:
      www.ac-donaubauer.com
      www.facebook.com/acdonaubauer

Cover: Biskerka Design

Editing: Jürgen Donaubauer
Proofreading: Philip Scott

Print: CreateSpace, an Amazon.com enterprise
February 2019

ISBN 978-3-904142-09-0

For Christa, my lizard in law, who is too small to be a dragon in law.

Thanks for your firstborn – I'm a great fan of your work!

CHAPTER 1

An Heir for House Velkim

"Why can't I block the pain?" Eryn hissed between clenched teeth as another contraction clamped her innards.

Valrad was standing next to her bed at the clinic, enduring her vice-like grip around his fingers in manly fashion. The tips already looked slightly bluish from reduced circulation.

"You should not because this pain is not supposed to be blocked," he explained patiently. "It is meant to guide you through the birth, to give you signals."

"I don't care about any signals! I want this to be over!" she moaned and blinked when a young woman entered the room. She was holding something long and golden in her hands. A belt.

"What exactly do you think you are doing with this?" Eryn shouted. "You will not take my magic away! Off you go! Out!" The last word was a vicious bark that, surprisingly, failed to impress the young healer. Very obviously so judging from her almost amused expression. This was clearly not the first moody woman on the verge of giving birth she had encountered.

"Valrad," the woman said gently, "either I will wrestle her into submission or you can put it on her."

"You can try that, dear," Eryn scowled at her, "but unless you are immune to magic or stronger than me, I would not recommend it. There is every chance that I am stronger than the both of you together, so don't even think about it!"

"But not stronger than me," a measured voice came from the door. Ram'an walked in and put aside the bag he had brought from the Aren residence for her.

"You wouldn't!" she snarled.

He took the belt from the healer's unresisting hands and stepped next to her. "Eryn, there is a very good reason for damping down a magician's power when she is about to give birth. And after what just happened at the Senate hall, I would think it is a rather obvious one."

"You are taking away my power to keep me from harming somebody? I won't, I promise! I will behave!" she pleaded.

1

He took her hand in his and pressed a kiss onto her knuckles. "I am sorry, but there is no avoiding it. I have no doubt that you have no intention of harming anybody or destroying anything, but neither had you at the Senate meeting, I am assuming. Great strain in the form of emotions or sensations such as pain can cause a magician to lose control. And in your case, my dear girl, that might easily mean unwittingly collapsing the entire clinic on top of us," he explained carefully. "And it is not as if you can heal away any of your pain, anyway. Your magic would be useless, and in addition to that pose a great danger to all around you."

"Eryn," Valrad implored her, "they will not let you stay or go anywhere near you as long as you are not wearing the belt. You are strong enough to endanger all the healers and patients here. And Ram'an is right. The magic would not even be of use you. This is no pain you can magic away just like that - it returns anew after each moment until the cause disappears. The child, in your case."

Eryn's glare became worried while she contemplated their words. She had not counted on being deprived of her magic. That was a nasty surprise. She didn't have fond memories of having her powers taken away; it had always left her feeling exposed, vulnerable. Yet their arguments were valid enough, especially considering that she had just collapsed the Senate roof little more than an hour ago...

She pressed her head against the pillow when another contraction took her breath away and left her shaking and immensely relieved once the wash of pain receded.

When she lifted her head, feeling exhausted, she realised that Ram'an had used the momentary distraction to fasten the golden belt around her chest. She hadn't even noticed the void inside her, the empty feeling that blocking her magic normally left. The space was obviously filled up with pain now. How convenient.

"You!" she glowered at him and was about to punch him angrily, but he stepped aside. "That was mean! You'd better be careful never to be helpless in my presence, because it's damn sure I will take advantage of it!"

"There is no other choice for you," he said and just shrugged.

"Maybe not. But I would have valued reaching that conclusion myself after a minute or two," she snapped.

"Making people's life a misery again?" Orrin said when he, Junar and Vern entered the room. Behind them Malhora followed, Téa sleeping peacefully in her arms.

"Oh, just shut up, will you?" she whispered exhaustedly. She even lacked the energy to express her frustration properly. That annoyed her even more.

"Oh my," said another voice from the direction of the door. "That is quite an assembly in here." A healer about Valrad's age made his way to the bed. "Greetings, Maltheá. I will assist you in delivering your child. I see you already have your belt on. Good."

She looked up into his far too cheerful face. But then why wouldn't he be in a good mood? He was not the one enduring the cramps, and from what she knew it would first get a lot worse before it became better.

The face was familiar - he was one of the many healers she had seen in the staff canteen. And this man had also offered a handsome price for Vern's painting, if she remembered correctly.

"Noril," Valrad nodded. "A good day to you."

"And to you, Valrad. Now, there are too many people in here. You will cause more stress to Maltheá..."

"Eryn", she interrupted him, sending him a warning look. "Don't oppose me on that detail right now, because I am convinced that I can still do quite a lot of damage even without magic."

Noril nodded slowly. "You know, I have no doubt that you could. Ignoring a threat coming from an Aren woman does not generally end well for the one who is ignoring. Eryn, then..."

"Very true," Malhora smiled, clearly satisfied that their frightful reputation seemingly reached everywhere.

"Let us return to the matter at hand," the healer insisted. "Which one of you will stay with... ah... Eryn for the birth in her companion's stead?"

Three variations of "me" were proffered almost in unison by the three men around her.

Noril blinked. "Well, that number is a little above average," he said, careful when dealing with two Heads of Houses and a warrior known for his lack of impulse control when it came to protecting his loved ones.

They turned when they heard an exasperated sigh. Junar elbowed her way to Eryn's side, then pointed at Orrin.

"Inappropriate. You are another woman's companion, and even though I know that your feelings for her are more of the fatherly kind, I don't want you to get quite that intimate with her. I mean it." Then she turned to Valrad. "Inappropriate as well. You are her father and have been for only a few months! What makes you think she would be comfortable with you around for this occasion?" Her glare moved on to Ram'an.

"Inappropriate?" he ventured before she could open her mouth.

"You bet!" she nodded. "You pursued her relentlessly, tried to make her exchange Enric for you! A birth is something very intimate where you have to show sides of yourself normally only the person closest to you is allowed to see, both internal and external ones." She turned to the healer. "I will stay with her. You can kick out the rest."

* * *

"What do you mean, she has gone into labour?" Vran'el exclaimed. He had dragged Enric away from the road to be under a tree where he was able to lean against the trunk. "It is several weeks too early for that!"

"Thank you for pointing that bit out," Enric panted, glad that the immediate pain had relented for now.

"Are you sure?"

"Vran," he sighed and cringed under another assault, "honestly – these are contractions. I read about them. The interval is getting shorter, the pain is excruciating and fades after a few seconds only to return again little later. That's a pretty clear case, I would say."

"Alright, alright. You said she was angry before, did you not? I wonder if that was what has tipped her into premature labour."

Enric was breathing heavily, tiny beads of sweat forming on his forehead. "I will find out about that. Depend on it."

"Why do you not just shield against this? Do not tell me this sharing of pain is supposed to be some sentimental proof of love she does not even see, or a romantic notion of going through the birth with her? Because in this you may safely trust me – being there is something completely different than just having waves of pain bring you to your knees," Vran'el urged him.

"I can't shield against it! I couldn't even block out her anger when it was at its peak. This is too intense, this exceeds what the barrier is capable of holding back, especially as she is not shielding and her own emotions and sensations are sent out with their full intensity."

The lawyer raked the fingers of both hands through his hair agitatedly. "You bloody fool! Do you see now what your urge to control everything got you into? What am I to do with you now?" Then a thought occurred to him. "I can knock you out! Then you will just sleep through this whole thing!"

"You will do no such thing," Enric gasped through the pain and raised a shield between them. "I need to know if everything is alright."

"You really want to live through this?" Vran'el wrung his hands helplessly. "Idiot! Really! And I am stuck with you! Damn!" he cursed, then took a few calming breaths before adding more quietly, "Alright, I will not do it. You can lower the shield. I promise!" he added exasperatedly when Enric sent him a doubtful glance.

The lawyer shook his head and watched the other man groaning under another wave of pain. "I would never have thought that I would one day experience a birth without a woman being present. It is certainly less messy."

"So glad to accommodate you," Enric grunted. "How long did your daughter's birth take?"

"Six hours. And that was quick. I have heard about babies that took an entire day to be born."

"That is not helping me right now!" the blond magician exclaimed, the horror plain on his face. "Rather tell me how Intrea handled the whole matter back then."

"Admirably. She is the serene type; nothing can throw her off balance. She was very considerate and more worried about me than herself, I think. She kept sending people around to fetch me water, repeatedly told me that everything was going to be alright and that I was doing great."

They looked at each other for a moment, then Enric said slowly, "That is definitely not how Eryn will be treating those around her right now."

Vran'el nodded. "I tend to agree with you on that."

When Enric braved another surge of agony, he tried to imagine who was with her right now. It should have been him. He hoped that Valrad, Junar or Malhora would be helping her through this. Not Orrin. And definitely not Ram'an.

Ram'an might have accepted that he couldn't have her, but having her in his city without her companion and helping her through something as painful and intimate as a birth might give him ideas. But neither Valrad nor Orrin would permit such a thing, would they?

Vran'el spent the next ten hours sitting on the grass next to Enric, distracting him with stories about his childhood with Pe'tala, his years of studying the law, stupid pranks he had played as a boy and the day when he had decided to tell his family that he preferred men to women as partners.

Enric's skin was pale and clammy, sweat running down his face and throat. Vran'el urged him to drink water and maybe even eat something to keep up his strength, but while Enric accepted the water gladly, eating was not something he seemed keen on.

When the sun started disappearing behind the horizon, the lawyer unpacked their belongings and prepared a spot for the night. They had originally planned to spend it in the city of Kar, but they were unable to reach there in Enric's current condition. They would go to the city once this was over and they were both well rested.

It was around midnight when Enric released a last agonised cry and then he slowly tipped over towards the ground.

"Enric?"

"It's over," he breathed, his face awash with relief, elation and exhaustion. He couldn't even tell how much of it was his own and how much Eryn's.

"And? How does she feel?"

"Relieved. And happy. So everything is alright." And he gave in to the peaceful blackness that welcomed him like a warm, numbing embrace.

*   *   *

Eryn forced her heavy lids open when somebody shook her shoulder softly. It was Junar, holding a small bundle in her arms. It whimpered softly.

"Your son is hungry," she smiled. "Better feed him quickly. My own breasts have started leaking at his smell and the sounds he is making."

Eryn clumsily tried to pull the shirt they had put on her over her head, but her friend sighed and shook her head. "No, Eryn, this is why they gave you something to wear you just have to open at one side. See? There is a button at your side and you can flip the front open without undressing completely."

Junar waited patiently until Eryn had slipped out one breast and pushed the pillow in her back higher up so she could sit. Then she carefully placed the baby in his mother's arm.

Eryn was suddenly wide awake and stared down at the tiny creature. Her son. She had seen him a few moments after the birth, but at that time he had been covered in blood and gloop. When they had him cleaned up she was already drifting off to sleep. The last impressions she remembered before succumbing to the exhaustion were a warm bundle that was placed on her chest and an overwhelming feeling of relief, gratitude and contentment.

"He has my dark hair," she murmured and let her index finger glide over the surprisingly dense, downy strands. His eyes were blue, but that didn't say much in the first few months.

She adjusted her grip so that the tiny head lay in the crook of her arm and was thus positioned ideally for accessing his food supply.

"Come on, pet, the milk-bar is open." Teasing his lips open with her nipple, she watched him close them around the tip of her breast. She frowned when he didn't start sucking. "The convenient days were the feeding didn't require any effort on your part are over, my boy. Go on." She looked at Junar. "And now?"

"Try squeezing a drop or two out and into his mouth. He doesn't seem to be aware yet that this is his meal, not just a nice, cushy means to calm him," Junar suggested.

Eryn did so and watched the little mouth taste and swallow when the new diet seemed to pass muster. Only then did she feel a weak pull that quickly turned into something more determined, almost greedy.

She looked up in surprise. "He certainly learns fast." Then her gaze returned to him and she took the time to look him over thoroughly for the very first time. Looking at him inside her belly with magic was different than truly laying eyes on him now.

His eyes were closed as he suckled, obviously content with the world. He had her hair, but the rest of him certainly looked a lot like his father.

She swallowed at the thought of Enric who had sped off to save Malriel, leaving his pregnant companion here to fend for herself. Funny, how eager he had been to rush off towards the great unknown and even to dissolve their third level bond when hardly more than a year ago he had seemed so desperate to enter into it with her.

Junar pressed a kiss on her temple. "Don't worry about him, Eryn. He will be back really soon. I am sure of it."

"I don't care," the magician replied calmly. "I don't need him. I managed to get through this without him, didn't I? Right through uncovering Sanaf's evil games and then the birth. And I will continue to."

"You don't mean that, do you?" Junar swallowed hard and frowned.

Eryn's gaze remained on the face against her skin, the little fist that rested against her breast. "He made his choice. And choosing Malriel meant giving up our son. And me."

"You can't mean it!" the seamstress exclaimed, her eyes wide. "He didn't choose your mother over you - he is trying to intervene to stop a war!"

"This is not what it seemed like to me when he forced the bond off me."

"I am not going to fight about this with you, but what I am telling you is that you are being utterly and completely inconsiderate. I understand your anger at being deserted by him like this, but you completely misjudge his intentions. And I can imagine his reaction when you accuse him of pining for Malriel. Really now!"

"Bickering already?" Orrin's voice said from the door. He had an arm around Vern's shoulders, the other rested against the cloth with which his daughter was slung across his chest.

"She thinks Enric has gone after Malriel because he fancies her," Junar said accusingly.

Both men stared at her, then Orrin smiled and Vern rolled his eyes.

"That is the most ridiculous thing I ever heard," the warrior chuckled. "I look forward to hearing Enric's reply to that."

"That's what I said," Junar huffed.

Vern lifted a drawing pad and pen. "Do you mind if I make a drawing of this? It's the first time you are feeding him, after all."

Eryn grimaced. "If you must. I imagine I don't make a very pretty picture right now, though."

"Vain womenfolk," the boy sighed in mock exasperation and propped the pad up against a chair, kneeling in front of it.

Orrin stepped closer to the bed, looking down at the baby. "He has fallen asleep over breakfast. I imagine you will have to make more of an effort next time," he joked.

"Hilarious," she deadpanned and lifted her son to hand him to Junar so she could cover herself again. Her fingers touched the golden belt she was still wearing. "They forgot to take this blasted thing off. Orrin, be so good and take it off me, will you?"

"I am afraid that is not something I can do," he grimaced. "I am told that you need to wear it for another six weeks."

"What?" she barked angrily and flinched when she heard both babies start crying.

"Great," Junar groaned and rolled her eyes before pressing the boy into his mother's hands and lifting her daughter out of the sling her father was carrying her in to rock her gently.

"Oh my, what a noisy welcome," Valrad remarked while entering the room and walking towards them. "How is my grandson doing? Apart from making use of his lung capacity, that is. Has he had some milk yet?"

"He is doing great. And so am I, thank you for asking," she sighed.

"I know that you are, my child. I examined you myself after the birth."

"I thought we agreed on your not using magic on me without my permission again after you drugged me with fake bliss the first time I came here? We need to discuss certain boundaries here. Yet again."

Valrad shrugged in an unperturbed way as he lifted the gurgling little bundle from her arm. "Your permission was implied from where I stand. If you do not want to be examined, you had better avoid passing out in my presence from now on."

"So glad you dropped by," she huffed. "Now talk to me. Orrin just told me that I am supposed to wear this belt for six weeks? Tell me that he misunderstood something here and the term is six hours instead?"

"I am afraid he is right. The problem, you see, is that magicians in general and healers in particular might be tempted to speed along the recovery process of their body - which is not advisable. But it might be over earlier. Some women only take four weeks, very few are done in no more than two. Six weeks is the longest."

"But this is just about healing the open internal wounds and vulnerable spots! I dare say speeding that along a bit is hardly..."

Her father interrupted her. "You know very well that magical healing, no matter whether it is done by yourself or somebody else, diminshes your body's resources more rapidly than you can restore them in your current condition - even if you spent the entire day doing nothing but eating and sleeping. What happens if a human body loses a lot of blood in a short time?"

"Weakness, dizziness, coldness and in some cases even unconsciousness," Vern offered chirpily from behind his drawing pad.

"Why do we want to avoid this in particular in case of a woman who has just given birth?" Valrad went on.

Vern was ready again. "Because she needs her strength to recover from the birth. Finally and equally as important is she will be recovering more slowly anyway due to the lack of sleep resulting from the frequent feeding at the beginning. It means the ability to take care of the child might suffer which will, if delegated to another person, make forming a bond between mother and child more difficult. If the mother cares for the child despite her diminished physical strength, this might result in accidents and thereby endanger the child's well-being from a medical point of view."

Four pairs of eyes stared down at him. He didn't notice it at first as he was still busy with his drawing. When the silence stretched on, he looked up and blinked.

"What?" he asked in confusion. "That was right, wasn't it? If I have just made a fool of myself, I blame that book in the medical library."

Valrad, still rocking his grandson in his arms, slowly walked closer, all the time looking down at Vern thoughtfully.

"That was a very impressive demonstration of knowledge, especially while concentrating on this completely different task with your hands," the healer said slowly. "I do not suppose you would consider staying here and completing your training in Takhan anything interesting, would you?"

"You just wait a moment!" Orrin growled angrily before Vern could reply. "He is not yet of consenting age, and even if he considered it a good idea, I certainly do not! You have no right to offer this to him, he is in no position to accept it and I will not allow it."

Eryn gave a deep sigh at the drama unfolding in front of her. Vern's eyes had first widened with surprise and excitement, then narrowed with anger and resentment at having this chance presented to him only to have it whisked away again only a moment later.

"I think," Junar said with a disapproving expression and a frown at both men, "that you'd better take this discussion elsewhere. This is hardly the time or place."

"I apologise," Valrad said stiffly. "It was not my place to make the offer, you are right. I just got carried away a little. I fully understand your reluctance to leave your son in another country for that long."

Orrin nodded once, but remained silent.

"I am tired. Please don't be offended, but I would very much like to sleep for a few hours if you don't mind," Eryn spoke up, tired of the tension and longing for a bit of peace and quiet.

"Of course not," Junar assured her.

They waited for Valrad to hand the baby back to his daughter, then they left. Orrin's simmering anger was visible in his tense posture, Vern looked miserable and sulky, and Valrad seemed a little fretful and disappointed.

Eryn exhaled with relief when they were gone and lay back in her bed, placing the baby so that he was nestled between her arm and her side. This was the first time she had been alone with her son.

Her son. That made her a mother, definitively and finally. She'd had many months to get used to the thought, but only now that she was able to touch, smell and see him, the understanding of that tremendous change started on a deeper, more elemental level than the superficial intellectual one. She had sparked another human being into life. He would always be a part of her, all his life. And he depended on her. The way he would turn out would be a result of the values she passed on to him, the role model she was.

What an enormous responsibility, a gigantic challenge. But an Aren never shirked a challenge, and that was one of the things he would learn from her.

Vedric of House Vel'kim, she thought. Welcome to this exhausting family of yours.

CHAPTER 2

Arrival in Kar

Enric stirred when his subconscious reacted to the aroma of food. He opened his eyes to bright daylight and found Vran'el crouching not far from him in front of an impromptu fireplace.

"Fish?" he mumbled, pleasantly surprised.

The last two days they had lived solely off their dried travel provisions. They might be nourishing and easy to keep, but from a culinary point of view they were not satisfying. It was a means to survive, and survival didn't require liking the fare, but knowing that the alternative would be an empty stomach.

"Look at that. Welcome back from your little timeout. How do you feel?"

Enric took quick stock the way Eryn had showed him. The weak magical impulse he sent through his body provided him with all he needed to know.

"Slightly dehydrated, hungry, my neck and shoulders hurt, but apart from that I am fine."

"I can offer a remedy against the first two and the others you can heal away. So no great problems from where I am," Vran'el chuckled and gently turned the fish baking over the fire. "Lunch will be ready in a few minutes, so there is time for you to have a wash. There is a stream nearby. It is where I caught the fish. Well, when I say caught I mean I stunned them with magic and then collected them."

Enric closed his eyes, healed away the pain and then smiled. "I figured as much. I dare say it is more efficient than hunting them with a spear or crafting a net for a single meal." He climbed to his feet, stretching with a loud yawn. "How long did I sleep for?"

"Quite a while. About twelve hours. But then a birth is an enormous strain I would imagine, even sharing it the way you did. No wonder you needed to rest."

His son's birth. Enric swallowed and tried to feel something, anything through the mind bond. But there was nothing. Which was in a way good as it meant that she was neither in pain, fearful or greatly worried. Yet he remembered his last sensations received before drifting off. They had been positive and powerful. He wouldn't have

11

minded a bit more of those right now to drown out the regret at not being with his companion and their new-born son.

But the reason he was far away in another country right now, he reminded himself, was to make it possible for the now two most important people in his life to live their lives in peace and freedom.

Enric found the stream without any problems. It was knee-deep and free of sediment and mud, so that he could see the stones in the stream bed and the fish that carefully flashed out of his way.

He took his time washing himself and waded around in the cold water for a little. He felt his energy returning as his blood circulation was stimulated by the low temperature.

When he came back to Vran'el, most of their belongings were already packed up neatly and he was handed a round metal travel plate with two fish on it, sliced open so they would cool more quickly.

"Thank you, Vran. This is exactly what I need. The dried stuff just wouldn't have worked for me at this moment."

"I thought as much. Eat up! We should leave soon; I dare say you are now even more eager to get this whole business behind us and return." The lawyer ate the last bites of his own meal, then set his plate aside. "Have you thought about how to go about tackling the trouble with Malriel? I know that Malhora thinks that she must have been tricked, but then she would hardly want to think badly of her own daughter. The accusations might actually turn out to be justified."

Enric shook his head. "I haven't known Malriel for as long as you, but she does not seem the type to force men into bed with her. She simply doesn't have to, from what I have seen. Or were there ever any accusations of that kind back in Takhan all these years?"

"No, never," Vran'el admitted. "But I like to be prepared for the worst. And if she is not guilty, a lie filter should have revealed that quickly enough, I would think."

"True. Provided that they know how to apply it. You said that magicians are not exactly held in high esteem by those without magic, so even if they know how to use it they might not be permitted to. Another possibility is that the magicians want the negotiations to fail. In this case they would not be willing to help Malriel, as there is a chance that they might be the ones trying to trick her."

"So they will also not believe us when we apply the lie filter and tell them she is innocent. They will accuse us of being biased. And rightly so," the lawyer added with a grimace. "So what we are hoping is basically that they are not yet aware of how a lie filter works, but will agree to let us show them how to use it. And of course that the ones able to apply it - namely the magicians, or priests - are not the ones sabotaging her chances."

"Exactly."

Vran'el frowned. "What if we manage to coax them into releasing her? Will we bring her back with us or leave her here to try and continue the negotiations?"

Enric had a pretty clear idea of what he was aiming for, namely bringing Malriel back to Takhan so that she could take her House back and with that enable him to return to Anyueel with his family.

Despite his motivation to protect his companion from the King's advances, something still pulled him back home, made him wistful when he thought of his own country. And if the monarch dared to make another inappropriate move on her ever again, he would not get away with a touch of throttling like last time.

"We will see about that," he said noncommittally. "It depends on whether they would still trust or respect her enough to negotiate with her after this muddle, even if she is cleared of the charges. Or if she would want to stay here." He rose when he had finished his meal. "I'll just go rinse our plates, then we can get on and leave."

Enric felt his whole body itching for action. He wanted to leave here, move on, do whatever was necessary to resolve this situation as quickly as possible, then return to Takhan.

They followed the road towards the city, using the two hours to repeat the information they had, the course of action they had agreed on and to practice how to introduce themselves. They also agreed to compile a list of all the people they would meet along with their full collection of names and titles. That way they could repeat them in the evening in the privacy of their rooms and so avoid angering these people, who seemed to set such great store by having their full importance acknowledged, by thoughtlessly addressing them incorrectly.

They had almost reached the bridge that would enable them to cross the broad river and enter the city. They could already see guards - soldiers or whatever they were - in blue and grey uniforms, standing straight and imposing in a line to block the way.

So they were already expected. A welcoming committee armed to their teeth. If that didn't inspire confidence.

* * *

Eryn looked down at her peacefully sleeping son in his cradle. He reposed in the room she herself had lived in when she had been a child. The daylight was dwindling away and the room itself became a little dimmer with every minute.

They had released her from the clinic today and she was immensely glad about it. Normally they didn't let new mothers leave that early, but Valrad had assured them that she and her son would be under his personal care. It was not usually recommended for healers to treat their own family members if it could be avoided, but his colleagues at the clinic had refrained from bringing up that little fact. Very determinedly so.

Valrad was too influential to be opposed in such a way; and in addition to that they were probably glad to be rid of the trying Aren woman in their midst. Eryn was well enough aware that neither patience nor suffering in silence and dignity were her strong sites. And she didn't care one bit about that.

She turned when Malhora appeared in the door, holding up a folded piece of paper for her. So it seemed it was time to return to being a Head of House again. With a last glance at the sleeping baby she turned and followed her grandmother to the main room.

"It is from the triarchy. I assume there is a faint chance they want to remind you about a roof you are expected to pay for," Malhora grinned.

Eryn accepted the message and studied the old woman. "You haven't said anything about that incident yet. But from your smile back then and your reaction now I assume that you are alright with it."

"I told you that I think of collapsing a building every now and then as a useful way of reminding people of how well-deserved our reputation is. The roof of the Senate was quite an interesting choice of target. A little showy, if you ask me, but certainly effective. People will talk about that one for generations. Believe me."

"You know that I didn't do this purposefully to uphold any family reputation, don't you? I didn't intend to impress anybody that day. It just happened. I really lost control. I endangered a great number of people," she ended glumly.

Malhora snorted. "With that many magicians around to shield people from falling chunks of the roof? Hardly."

The younger woman opened the seal and raised her brow in surprise. "That's how much repairing that bloody structure is going to cost? They have to be kidding me!"

Her grandmother leaned closer to have a look at the amount, then shrugged. "That was to be expected. It is a rather large dome you collapsed. Not easy to repair. And then there is the artwork that needs to be restored to its former state. But this is nothing to worry about, girl. House Aren can easily afford it. Consider it a useful investment. This will certainly make our negotiation partners and political opponents treat us with more care and means it will benefit the House in the long run."

"Then I had better sent them a message back and humbly agree to bear the costs as is due and proper," Eryn grimaced.

"No humility!" Malhora insisted. "You are not meant to be sorry about it but accept paying for the damage as a price for your pride. Do not show any regret; it would diminish the effect. Just write that you acknowledge their claim and will settle the bill for all repairs."

A knock came from the entrance door.

"Would you take care of this, Grandmother? Then I will write the message to the triarchy."

"This will be a visitor for you, child. So you had better stay here and take care of the reply later. You do not want to appear too eager, anyway."

Malhora descended the stairs to the entrance door and returned a few moments later with Ram'an.

"Eryn, dear," he greeted her and kissed her forehead. "I was at the clinic, but they told me that they had released you already." He chuckled. "I expect your father threw his weight around a little, did he not?"

"I admit he did, yes. His colleagues were not too happy about it, but found it more prudent not to oppose him. And I am glad about it - I would have gone spare lying in that bed all day long. The only thing that really annoys me now is this bloody belt. I suppose there is no chance...?" She looked up at him with a pleading expression.

"No, dear, none," he replied simply.

Malhora rolled her eyes. "She keeps trying to bribe or threaten people to take it off her. A few hours ago she ordered Orrin to do it. Good thing his approach to authority is a sensible one and he ignored her."

Eryn sent her a frosty glare. "I dare say when the people at your estate ignore your orders you would not term their attitude a very sensible one."

"No, of course not. But then I never give stupid orders that would harm myself."

"I am a healer! I wouldn't harm myself! I know what I am doing."

"Eryn," Ram'an sighed and cupped her cheeks, "there is no way any one of us is going to remove that belt before Valrad agrees to it. So stop bullying people around you, alright? Better show me this son of yours."

"He is asleep."

"Then we had better be quiet," he smiled, obviously not willing to accept the hint that now was not a good time to look at the baby.

Defeated, Eryn sighed and pressed the letter from the triarchy into Malhora's hand. "Why don't you prepare a reply to that? Then you may at least be sure the tone is right. I'll sign it later."

Ram'an followed her and entered the room after her. They stepped next to the cradle, looking down.

She turned when she heard him give a slightly lamenting sigh. "What?" she asked in a low murmur.

"He looks like Enric."

"Why do you sound sad about that?"

"I cannot help thinking, Theá, that had things been only a little different, he would have been our son. Yours and mine."

She swallowed and tried to take a step away from him, but felt his arm around her shoulders that kept her in place.

"No, please. I did not mean to make you uncomfortable. I will from now on keep such thoughts to myself."

Now she felt guilty. "I am sorry this whole situation is a burden to you still. And I don't want you to reign back your thoughts. Even if I am not always happy about them."

They stood side-by-side, looking down at the sleeping infant for a while without speaking.

"Theá, Enric asked me to take care of you in case he did not return."

Eryn slowly turned her head to face him. "Did he now? May I ask what taking care of me entails?" she asked coolly, feeling her heart beating in her throat. Had Enric appointed him as his successor in their companionship or some such?

"He asked me to raise his son as my own."

She stared up at him with narrowed eyes. "And what did he tell you to do with me? Make me your companion?"

"He did not say the words as such, but I believe that was the implication, yes," he replied carefully.

Eryn turned on her heel and left the room, not at all happy to have her suspicions confirmed. She heard Ram'an close the door quietly and then follow her to the main room and out into the garden.

"Why are you telling me this?" she snapped. "Did you receive message that he will not be returning? That he is…"

"No!" he interrupted her quickly and took her by the shoulders. "There was nothing of that kind, I promise you. What I wanted to tell you is that even if the worst occurs, you will never be alone. I will be there for you. You do not look happy, Theá, or not as happy as you should be. And of course I understand why. I want to lift at least one burden from your shoulders."

She covered her face with her hands. "You shouldn't do this, Ram'an. You shouldn't have agreed to this. What if he is stuck there for who knows how long? This might stop you from ever moving on, from finding a woman you could be happy with instead of waiting for me. Once again. It was not right of him to ask such a thing of you."

She felt Ram'an's arms wrap around her and pull her against him.

"I would not have left you to fend for yourself even if he had not asked me."

Eryn looked up at him, shaking her head. "You would take me as your companion and raise my son with me, despite the fact that I chose another man over you? That I would probably only agree for fear of being alone otherwise?"

"I would, yes." Then he smiled. "And I would soon make you see that I am the better choice anyway. My culinary skills are superior to Enric's, and my wine is better than his, too."

She laughed, relieved that the intensity was gone thanks to his joke. "I am trying very hard not to be insulted at how easily you think I can be won over."

"I am told confidence is always useful when dealing with an Aren woman." Then he released her from his embrace and instead took her hand to tug her across to a low stone bench and sit with him. "About your little... display of anger at the Senate two days ago."

"Yes?" She grimaced, only now wondering how it would affect her plans for opening an orphanage here. The Senate would probably not be too eager to support her now after she had almost collapsed their roof on them.

"It certainly did not fail to impress. Golir approached me and asked me to assist you in drawing up a detailed proposal with a cost estimate, legal considerations and a timeframe for your project. He said that he has no doubt that the idea with the tax relief you mentioned came from me, so he assumed that I was in favour of the whole matter."

Eryn exhaled. That was more than she had dared hoping for. "And what about the other senators?"

"A few are angry and maybe a bit cowered of you, but most have expressed a wish to support your idea. Probably for fear of having their residences collapse on them if not," he added dryly.

"I would very much like to be angry at you for that last statement, but I have no idea if it was a joke or not."

Ram'an pursed his lips. "Let us say it was an exaggeration, but not that far-fetched."

"So you will really work on this with me?" Touched, she took his hand and squeezed it. "You keep giving me the feeling that I don't deserve you. How can I ever repay you?"

He smiled. "We will find a way. For example, support in the Senate and cooperating with Arbil-owned businesses for the building and running of the orphanage."

Eryn laughed. "Good to see that you are not self-sacrificing to the extent that borders on stupidity. Can we start tomorrow? I am still quite exhausted from giving birth and sitting is not the most pleasant position for me. Unless you are willing to assist me with that minor issue..."

He sighed and rose, pulling her to her feet as well. "No. I am not going to remove your belt." He listened for a moment, then nodded towards the terrace door. "I think your son just woke and wants to be fed. Off you go."

She walked in and saw Malhora approaching them with Vedric on her arm.

Eryn frowned when she saw Ram'an take a seat on the seating cushions. "You want to stay? I mean, this is rather..." She trailed off, at a loss for words. She had done it before with others watching; only yesterday, when Orrin, Valrad, Junar and Vern had been in the same room with her. But baring her breasts in front of Ram'an somehow seemed... wrong. Strange. Inappropriate.

"Shy, Theá?" he grinned and patted the spot next to him. "I assure you there is no need for that. Watching a mother breastfeed her child is a very appealing picture, but hardly one to arouse any inappropriate feelings in a man. Quite the opposite, in fact. It is a reminder that your breasts were not initially evolved for us to enjoy, but for our offspring to be nourished by."

Eryn bit her lip, still unsure whether to insist on his leaving or not. She dimly remembered Enric saying something like that when he had watched Junar feeding her daughter many weeks ago. Still...

"Sit, Eryn," Malhora commanded. "He is right. In time, you will come to appreciate quiet spots to feed your child when you are out. The luxury of their being completely private is not one you will encounter too often."

She took a deep breath, then sat down. "Alright, let's do this then." With her former suitor who had just told her that he would take her as his companion if Enric didn't return, observing her.

Vern strolled in and smiled when he saw them. He picked up his drawing pad and pen that somehow always seemed to be lying around ready for use these days and took a seat opposite them.

"Didn't you draw such a scene already yesterday? How many of them to you need?" She narrowed her eyes. "You are not going to sell them, are you? If I am invited somewhere and see myself half naked on a wall there, I will bite your head off."

Vern just laughed and continued drawing, safe in the knowledge that he was the stronger magician for the next few weeks as long she would be wearing the belt.

* * *

Enric dismounted once only a few steps separated them from the guards and approached them, the message to the triarchy that invited them to send a representative to stand by Malriel ready in his hand.

There was one figure, a woman in her late thirties, dressed in what was either a short dress or a long tunic that reached down to her knees and with light brown hair twisted into a bun at her neck.

"Greetings to you," she spoke first. She, too, had this tendency to mostly use her teeth and the tip of her tongue to form words. She hardly seemed to open her mouth when she talked. "My name is Lam Ceiga, Reig of the Moraugns, minister of external affairs."

She looked at Enric, who she had clearly identified as the one in charge.

"And greetings to you, Lam Ceiga, Reig of the Moraugns, minister of external affairs. My name is Lord Enric, Reig of House Aren, second in command of the Order and senator in Takhan. This," he indicated the other man, "is Lam Vran'el, Reig of House Vel'kim, lawyer and senator in Takhan."

"Welcome to the both of you," Lam Ceiga said politely. "There are some formalities that must be taken care of before we can grant you access to the captive Malriel, Holm of House Aren, senator in Takhan. Your horses will be taken to the stables and your belongings will be taken to your rooms. If you would follow me now."

She turned and walked on without waiting for them to agree. They both quickly grabbed their bags containing documents and gold, handed the reins to the two uniformed men who had stepped forward, then hurried after the woman who had not once turned around to see if they could keep up.

"That is not exactly a very hearty welcome, is it?" Vran'el whispered.

"Not really, but considering the circumstances I wouldn't have expected them to be very enthusiastic about us."

They took in the large, unusually even cobblestones on the street, the houses with their steep-pitched roofs and colourful facades that were a mix of wood and plaster. Many a window sported boxes with flowers growing in them like miniature gardens. The colourful blossoms increased the strangely joyful effect of multi-coloured sobriety.

The people walking the streets, however, were far from displaying such an abundance of colour with their attires. They were dressed in a range that reached from off-white to brown, bright grey to black. Only occasional scarves or other small adornments such as belts or hats in more cheerful tones lightened the overall effect.

Vran'el's attire earned them quite a few glances, some curious, others cool or even hostile. Enric himself couldn't help but being glad at his own preference for black.

Interestingly, the hair colour and skin tone here seemed to vary and encompassed both Enric's pale complexion and blond hair and Vran'el's tanned skin and dark hair.

There were red-headed people with freckles, black-haired ones with both dark and light skin, blond and brown hair in all possible shades.

There seemed to be a general tendency towards wearing hats, caps or scarves for both men and women.

Enric didn't mind standing out too much, it had been his usual state of affairs for several months now. Vran'el, however, was clearly not used to being different, judging from his tense posture and clenched jaw.

They walked for no more than a few minutes before their guide stopped in front of a tall house of at least four stories. There was a large stone slate fixed to the wall next to the wide entrance door.

Enric looked at the letters that seemed only partly familiar. He couldn't decipher what they said. This could be either a cheerful prison or a rather sombre guest house. Anything was possible.

"This is where we will take your data for the purpose of registration and filing. After this I will conduct you to your rooms. They are not far from here, only a few more minutes towards the city centre," she explained without showing any emotion.

"When will it be possible for us to visit Malriel, Holm of House Aren, senator in Takhan?" Enric enquired politely.

"Once your passes have been issued. This will be the case after your information has been checked with regard to completeness and approved by the clerks in charge."

"How long does that usually take?"

"It can take up to a week but we appreciate that in your case particular promptness is in order," Lam Ceiga acknowledged generously, then preceded them into the building without offering any information as to how long a particularly prompt approach would take.

Enric exchanged an uneasy look with Vran'el, then followed the woman through the double doors.

CHAPTER 3

Visiting Malriel

Eryn grinned broadly as Kilan entered the Aren main room. "I cannot believe my own eyes! Look who has finally managed to visit me after all that time! And all it took to lure you here was having a baby!"

He chuckled. "I remember the last time I visited you. I ended up with being told to take care of your correspondence. I was simply dreading what else you might burden me with and that meant I thought it wiser to stay at a safe distance."

"Coward," she laughed and kept on massaging Vedric's belly.

"What are you doing there?"

"Rubbing his belly is a good stimulation for his internal organs and is supposed to help him digest his meals," she explained. "By the way, today in the morning several message birds with congratulations arrived from Anyueel. Among them one from the King. He wrote something about being more respectful in expressing my disapproval. I suppose you'd better apologise for whatever he thinks I wrote last time. Don't get me into trouble, do you hear me?"

Kilan exhaled and closed his eyes. "Eryn, I haven't written anything of that kind in your name. Ever."

She cursed. "That means he worked out that it was not me writing the damned messages." She sent Kilan a disapproving look. "That very likely means you were much too friendly, polite and compliant. He probably had no choice other than to question the messages' origins or my mental state."

"Good for you he chose the first one, then, eh? Now hand me that child, will you? I need to see who he resembles." He took a seat and let Eryn tenderly place the baby in his arms. "That's Enric's face, no doubt about that. If his parentage is ever in question, he will probably start looking for his mother, because it's plain enough who his father is."

"Very nice," Eryn growled. "Just what a woman wants to hear after squeezing a human being out of her: how little the kid resembles her."

"His hair is your colour, so there are traces of you in there somewhere as well," he acknowledged generously.

"You know what? I am beginning to wonder why I was sad about not seeing you more often. Somehow I failed to see it as the blessing it was," she huffed.

He grinned broadly and examined a tiny hand. "Glad to be of service."

* * *

Enric looked out the window of Vran'el's room, observing the horse-carts on the crowded street and the people crossing between the vehicles seemingly without any concerns for their own safety.

The rooms they had been allocated shortly after their arrival two days before were far from the accommodation he had been given in Takhan when he was first there in his function as ambassador. And back home in Anyueel they would never have slighted guests by putting them in such humble rooms. It was probably a none too subtle hint that they were not exactly welcomed here. Or just reflected a culture that was used to a more frugal lifestyle.

But at least their accommodation was clean and warm if not particularly comfortable. Or spacious. Or bright.

They had spent the last two days waiting, more or less. Waiting for their documents and information to be approved, passed on to a person higher up on the ladder of power to check and approve as well and then onward and upwards. Lam Ceiga had instructed them to remain indoors and not walk around the city since the papers allowing them to do so were not yet ready. But today the passes had been delivered to them, which meant an end to their restless confinement.

Enric turned away from the window to watch Vran'el, who was busy assembling all the different papers they would need to gain access to the prison where Malriel had been put. It would be the first time that they met her.

They'd had to fill in a number of different forms for who knew what purposes and had one day later been given a note that was to be presented upon demand. It stated their identity, their purpose for being in the city, the permission to be in the city in the first place and which areas they were permitted to move around in.

Vran'el had been unnerved by the load of paperwork and had repeatedly cursed this tiresome and in his opinion ridiculous level of bureaucracy, but Enric had studied the forms and come to admire the degree of organisation.

At least until he had found himself filling out the same information in four different forms. That was not organised, but simply redundant and a waste of time. But it was not like they'd had anything else to do but wait.

Then finally, after two days of pushing paper around and waiting, they were granted the permission to visit Malriel and talk to her.

When Vran'el had managed to put together all the paperwork they needed, he straightened up.

"Alright - I am ready. Let us go and visit Malriel in her lockup. I need to remember every detail about that. It will cheer Eryn up when I tell her about it," the lawyer said and smiled. "I wonder if we should address her with the title Eryn uses to refer to her? Queen of Darkness does sound rather impressive. Maybe they would appreciate it here?"

Enric rolled his eyes. "I should have known from the start that the two of you couldn't possibly be simply cousins. The same disturbing sense of humour that seems to go a lot deeper than mere upbringing can account for. Come on. Time to start our work here."

* * *

Intrea grinned broadly when Eryn placed the baby in her arms. "Look at that! He looks like his father!"

Eryn rolled her eyes. "Yes, thank you so much for noticing that."

The other woman ignored her and motioned for her daughter to come closer. "Obal, I may introduce you to your cousin Vedric of House Vel'kim."

The girl came closer, though carefully as if fearing some kind of nasty attack.

"He doesn't bite, you know," Eryn said mildly and added, "Not yet."

Obal shot her one of those unnerved glances a five-year-old girl should not yet be able to do and inspected the infant in her mother's arm thoroughly.

"He is very small. My other cousin was bigger," she stated matter-of-factly.

"Yes, he was born quite a bit sooner that he should have been," Eryn nodded.

Another devastating glare was sent her way.

"I didn't do it on purpose, you know," Eryn defended herself, wondering why that kid got to her like that.

Obal didn't comment on that and returned to staring at the boy for another minute.

"He is not doing anything. Boring. Where is Urban?"

"In the garden," Eryn told her quickly, glad at the prospect of getting rid of the girl for a while.

Intrea smiled at her knowingly. "She has that effect on people. I hope she will outgrow this general disdain for the people around her. It does not exactly make her popular with her peers. Or adults. My father tells me I was just like her as a child, so there might still be hope. By the way, that little package on the table is for you. It is a bath oil that protects his skin from the dry heat. If you have any dry patches on your own skin, you can use it for that as well."

Eryn thanked her and opened the thin fabric wrapping before uncorking the glass bottle to take a sniff. The clear, yellow liquid smelled of some kind of flower and spices.

Intrea leaned forward to see where her daughter had gone and then looked at the new mother.

"How are you doing, my dear? I am sorry that you had to go through the birth without Enric. But your friend Junar was with you, was she not? I suppose after having a child herself only a few months ago she was a great help to you."

Eryn made herself smile. "I am fine. And yes, Junar was great. Though they had to heal her hand afterwards. It seems I still have a rather potent grip even without any magic at my disposal."

Intrea laughed. "I have to say that volunteering to stay with an Aren woman during a birth certainly shows nerves of steel." She turned serious again and looked down at the baby in her arm. "I am sure there is no need to worry about them, you know," she said quietly. "Vran may seem like this carefree, joking, easy-going lad, but he is very good at being a lawyer. I have always found his seemingly effortless transition to his professional self disconcerting, as though he is a completely different person. All of a sudden he is so serious, demanding and analytical. And Enric, he is so formidable, an imposing man both in appearance and mind. How can those two not be successful?"

Eryn didn't reply to that but just wondered silently why Intrea sounded so worried if there was indeed so little reason for it.

"Though I have to tell you that Neval is rather worried," she went on and smiled. "He told me that he is not happy about his lover being alone with a man like Enric for such a long time. He is obviously afraid that Vran may take a liking to the blond, exotic type if unsupervised."

The two women looked at each other for a moment, then started giggling, glad that Obal was far enough away not to roll her eyes at them in that dismissive way she had.

* * *

The two men walked along the wide street their windows overlooked, careful not to bump into any moving vehicles.

"I feel a bit out of place in my attire," Vran'el murmured, looking around at the plain, simple clothes people were wearing.

"I hope to be gone from here quickly enough so it doesn't really pay for us to see a tailor," Enric remarked and looked around. "Do you see how clean everything here is?"

The lawyer nodded. "I have noticed that, yes. I wonder how often they sweep the streets here. Probably every night."

Enric watched the people passing them and marvelled once again that neither his own light hair nor Vran'el's dark hair was unique here. Neither the skin tone he currently sported due to the tan the omnipresent sun in the Western Territories had bestowed upon him, nor his usual paler complexion were out of place either.

He thought about Orrin's daughter and her brown hair. Would Anyueel look like this in a few decades after the return of the magic in females provided for more variety in people's appearance?

"What was that charmless woman's full name again?" Vran'el asked.

Enric pulled his little notebook out from an inside pocket and opened the first page. "Lam Ceiga, Reig of the Moraugns, minister of foreign affairs," he read out.

They were about to meet her in front of the prison they had been told was just at the end of the street. It would surely not hurt to avoid angering the only person they had so far been officially introduced to by addressing her thoughtlessly.

They passed shops with large display windows showing off merchandise. They couldn't understand the shop signs, but judging from the goods on display they were different kinds of craftspeople. Tailors, jewellers, glass-makers, potters, manufacturers of paper and so on.

Enric stopped in front of one window, staring down at a little toy that resembled some kind of four-legged animal and seemed to move of its own accord.

"How is this possible?" he murmured, watching the jerky movements of the colourfully painted wooden item.

"Magic?" Vran'el ventured, equally fascinated.

"I doubt that very much if the information about how they regard magic here is true." He wondered if there was a chance to buy that piece. Would they sell to him, the foreigner of a country they would maybe soon be at war with? Would they even accept his gold slips here?

A man stepped out from the shop door, a little bell tinkling above him when the door brushed it. He sported a large, curved moustache, bright brown flecked with grey, just like his temples. Around his rather impressive girth he wore an apron with two large pockets, the sleeves of his shirt rolled up and revealing chunky, hirsute forearms.

An incomprehensible stream of the local language with its many hissing sounds was unleashed on them. It did not sound unfriendly, but with that language and the studied blank expressions people here seemed to wear in public it was hard to tell.

"I am afraid we do not understand you," Enric said slowly.

The man pursed his lips and narrowed his eyes at them, clearly wondering what to do with them.

Enric waited patiently, hoping that their immediate future would not entail being chased away by the man but instead being invited into his shop.

"Come," he finally said as if granting them a privilege and ushered them in.

Enric obeyed gladly, curious to see more. Vran'el was less comfortable with following a stranger that had not seemed too enthusiastic about them into a building.

The man took another toy of the same make but resembling a different animal from a shelf and twirled a little wheel that stuck out from its rear with a strange metallic purring. When he released the wheel and put the toy on his wooden counter, it started moving around with the same jerky movements exactly like its sibling in the shop window.

Enric watched it, mesmerised by the unfamiliar device. He felt the urge to pick it up, turn it around and work out its secrets.

"How much?"

The man pointed to a small slate on the shelf that obviously displayed the price. Enric couldn't read it and raised his brow questioningly.

The man sighed and raised three fingers.

"Help me, Vran," Enric murmured. "How many of your gold slips was one unit of their local currency again?"

"About two and a half."

That meant about seven and a half gold slips or almost four Anyueel gold coins. That seemed rather pricey. But then he had no idea how costly or time-consuming producing this toy was. He considered negotiating for a lower price, but decided against it. It might do them more harm than good. Instead he reached into his purse and pulled out eight gold slips, showing them to the man.

That did not quite trigger the response he had hoped for. Looking down his nose as if considering something utterly disgusting the shopkeeper started waving his hands around to signal them to leave.

Back out in the street Vran'el shook his head in wonder. "Oh my, that was a rather hefty reaction."

"From what I have seen they are very keen on rules here. Accepting money that has not been approved might get him into trouble for all we know. We should find out how to exchange our money into local currency," Enric mused.

They walked on towards a large, grey building looming at the end of the street that was very probably their destination.

"You did not even try to haggle," Vran'el shook his head in disapproval.

"That's because we have no idea how they react to that here. In my country an attempt at lowering a given price on principle would not get you anywhere. My people's view is that if you are not willing to pay the price asked you'd better move on and get out of the way of those who are," Enric explained. "It was quite a challenge for me to adjust to that at first. I do see certain parallels to my own home here. Well, to some extent. We, too, like our lists and reports, but they have obviously turned it into some kind of art. Also their food. It's less rich in spices but more meat and vegetables that keep you feeling sated and warm for a while."

"Alright, no haggling here," Vran'el sighed.

"Exactly. It is better to appear easy to trick and a tad naïve than greedy and shifty. It tends to make people underestimate you."

They had now come close enough to make out a familiar figure. The bun at the back of the neck was the same, as was the style of her attire.

"Greetings, Lord Enric, Reig of House Aren, second in command of the Order and senator in Takhan and Lam Vran'el, Reig of House Vel'kim, lawyer and senator in Takhan," she spoke, making the s' sound like hisses and the ts like rapid hammer strokes.

"Lam Ceiga, Reig of the Moraugns, minister of external affairs," Enric and Vran'el said together, exchanging a relieved look when the woman nodded with satisfaction and then turned to walk ahead again. It was like having passed muster by a particularly strict teacher.

They walked along high-ceilinged corridors with a number of tall, semi-circular windows that afforded a view of the street they had just come along.

They approached double doors, which were guarded by four men in dark grey uniforms.

Nodding to the woman, they wordlessly accepted her identification, read it carefully before passing it back and then held out their hands to the two men in her company.

Vran'el handed over their documents to have them scrutinised, held up to the light and finally after several minutes handed back to them. These guards were thorough indeed.

They were waved through the door and continued their way only to be stopped again after less than a minute. A further four guards, the same procedure.

When they carried on, Enric suppressed a sigh when he spotted another door with four men in dark grey and wondered how many more of these doors they would have to pass and if there was a chance of seeing Malriel before the sun set in a few hours. He saw from Vran'el's expression that he was equally unenthusiastic about what was considered the appropriate level of security here.

When they had finally been permitted to pass the fourth door of this kind, they were led into another corridor with four much smaller doors that looked massive and sported small, barred windows at eye level. These seemed to be the prison cells. Compared to the dungeons and lockups back in Anyueel the surroundings here looked a lot more cheerful, bright and clean.

One of the guards walked past them to unlock one of the doors and nodded towards Lam Ceiga, who in turn motioned for the two visitors to go ahead of her.

Enric stepped into what looked like a small, but very neatly and not sparsely furnished room. There was one corner for personal sanitation, a bed with two blankets and two pillows upon it, a large wing chair and a small table with four wooden stools around it.

"Enric!" a familiar female voice cried out in surprise and a moment later he found himself in a tight hug before he was even able to take a proper look at Malriel. "I cannot tell you how immensely good it does me to see you! They told me that somebody had arrived, but they did not give me any name."

She clung to Enric for what had to be a full minute before releasing him and then pulled Vran'el close to kiss both his cheeks.

"Vran, my dear," she laughed and Enric saw how the corners of her eyes became slightly moist, "with the pair of you on my side, I know that this mistake will be cleared up soon."

"I will leave you for now. Do knock at the door when you wish to leave," Lam Ceiga announced from the door where she had stopped and watched the emotional welcome impassively.

Enric nodded. "Thank you, Lam Ceiga, Reig of the Moraugns, minister of foreign affairs."

Then he looked Malriel up and down, taking in her appearance and general state. She had adapted to the local style of clothing and he found the lack of bold colours on her particularly depressing, just like the hair she had pulled back into a bun instead of letting the dark waves cascade down her shoulders and back. She did not look haggard or worn out, but he still missed that certain radiance. Which was not entirely unexpected considering her confinement here. She looked healthy if a little pale after the months without the desert sun.

She took both men's hands and pulled them toward the small table to sit with her, holding on to them once they were settled as comfortably as the hard wooden stools permitted.

"Before we delve into this mess here, tell me how my daughter is doing," she demanded.

"She found accepting Valrad as her father rather difficult, but managed it after a while. She has in the meantime obtained the insignia and is now officially a fully trained and recognised healer," Enric explained in as few sentences as he could manage. There was no saying how much time they would be granted in here for now.

"How about her pregnancy, has everything been alright?"

"Our son was born yesterday."

Malriel blinked, then shook her head. "But... that is too soon!" She paused, obviously for a quick mental reckoning. "She should have been due in another six or seven weeks!"

Enric squeezed her hand. "Yes. But from what I can tell everything seems to be in order."

Malriel frowned at him for a moment, then her eyes went wide. "The mind bond! Do not tell me you left the commitment bond intact despite leaving Maltheá for such a long time?" She stood agitatedly, glaring down at him. "How could you subject her to that? She will suffer from your absence a lot more than necessary, and now she even has to take care of a child! I would not have expected a reckless thing like this from you!"

"Calm down, Malriel. I only kept my side of the bond intact. Eryn's bond was severed."

Malriel breathed in with relief and sank back onto her seat. "Oh, I see. I apologise. I should have known that you would not submit her

28

to unnecessary suffering. Though you do not seem to have extended the same consideration to yourself." She gasped when a thought hit her. "Does that mean you experienced the pain of her giving birth?"

"I did, yes," he confirmed calmly, shivering inside at the memory.

"So you left your pregnant companion to come and help me out of my troubles and have now even missed your son's birth," she sighed and closed her eyes for a moment. "I do not know how I am ever to repay you for that, Enric." Then another thought occurred to her. "Who is in charge of House Aren now?"

"Eryn is the current Head of House Aren."

Malriel sucked in a breath and looked distressed. "Malthéa in charge of House Aren?"

"She will do fine. Malhora is there and will help her handle that duty."

She let her tension go with the relief. "My mother is in the city?"

"Malhora is in Takhan, yes. Though she refused to take the House in my absence and prefers to be in a more advisory than active role."

"I was not sure if she would come," Malriel murmured. "It is a mother's duty to stand by her daughter when she has her children, and after they met under such unpleasant circumstances, I was not sure whether my mother would step in for me." She released an unsteady breath. "I am so relieved. And grateful. To all of you."

Enric watched his adoptive mother with interest. This was not strong, invincible, merciless Malriel, but a woman who had been alone in a foreign country for a long time and had come to treasure acts of kindness in her solitude. She kept both her hands on his and Vran'el's, maintaining physical contact to people known and familiar to her. The first people she had been with in quite some time where she didn't have to worry about their intentions but could trust them unconditionally.

"Vran, how is Valrad doing? Did Malthéa make it very hard for him to get her to accept him as her father?"

He nodded with a smile. "She did, yes. She resisted his every attempt with the stubborn defiance of a true Aren woman and made him use all the ingenuity and patience he could come up with." He squeezed her hand. "He was relentless, though, and she never had any real chance against him. Not when she wanted to work as a healer at what people still like to see as his clinic."

"And your own daughter, how is little Obal doing?"

"She is growing like a weed and has, like I suppose many children, an unerring instinct for picking up the exact wrong word to repeat it in situations which are as embarrassing for her poor parents as possible."

Enric smiled at Malriel's laugh. It sounded rather rusty, as if she hadn't used it in a while.

He would have loved to go on cheering her up, but he couldn't afford to. They had no idea how long they were allowed to stay here for now or when they would be permitted to return.

He reached inside his shirt and pulled out his notebook. "Malriel, we need to get you out of here quickly. So we had better get started with what exactly has happened so far."

"I know. And I thank you for indulging me that much already. This has done wonders for my soul, believe me." She straightened, taking her hands off the two men's before she began her account.

* * *

Half an hour later Vran'el pursed his lips and looked down at the notebook he had commandeered from Enric a while ago to make his own notes and add helpful remarks and annotations for later.

"Good, Malriel - now let me repeat this in my own words so we can see if I have understood everything correctly." He cleared his throat. "Alright. Shortly after you managed to have them talk to you about the chance of exchanging a waiver on the greater part of the mining rights in the mountains in exchange for more beneficial trading arrangements, you met a young man at one of the social events you had been invited to. In the course of the following two weeks you met up with him again several times, seemingly by accident. When you went to a pub to have a meal, at other social occasions or even when you were just strolling along the street. Have I got this correct so far?"

"Yes," she confirmed, waiting for him to go on.

"His name is..." Vran'el flipped a page and scanned it before continuing, "...Geloin Urnen, Legen of the Nords, third level aspirant of the Inner Cirle. Geloin being the lower of the two existing religious titles, and the Inner Circle the most powerful religious union or faith group of the five they have here. He would join you at every opportunity, sharing bits of information with you. He went on to tell you about the discrimination magicians have to endure here and how much he envied you your freedom to do as you pleased and even hold a position of civic power. He also gave you the impression of being attracted to you as a woman." He looked at Malriel for confirmation. "Still correct?"

"Yes, Vran," she sighed. "Just go on and I will interrupt you if something is wrong."

"As you wish." He turned another page and went on, "After another social gathering you were both invited to, he took you for a walk and then offered to show you the view over the city from the top level of the temple where he lived. You agreed and let him take you there. After you let him kiss you on the platform, you agreed to join him in his room at the temple for the night. You first had a drink and about what follows you say your memory becomes unclear. You remember taking his hand and walking to his bed, then you laid down and you recall nothing much from then on. When you next opened your eyes, somebody was shouting. It turned out to be your young man. He had been bound to the bed frame with golden chains, crying for help. Later he claimed he had been forced into bed and ravaged by you, which led to your being accused of forcible rape."

She nodded.

"You suspect that he mixed something into the drink he gave you to make you pass out, if I understand you correctly. And you further deduce that this was an attempt to stop you from concluding those trade negotiations successfully. You think that there might be a group interested in promoting a war between our country and Pirinkar, or at least stopping the current process of convergence."

"How far have the proceedings progressed so far?" Enric enquired now that they had established the essential facts around the charge.

"They listened to his accusations, wrote them down, presented people who testified as to his good character and his exemplary conduct in carrying out his temple duties. And the unlikeliness that he would lie about something as grave as this," she snorted angrily. "Then they questioned me. Unfortunately, I had no solemn looking, upstanding, grey-haired member of society to swear that my impeccable character would keep me from ever doing a thing like that."

Enric smiled faintly, thinking that it was probably less her impeccable character than her immense pride that would make a deed like that impossible for her.

"Now a very important question, Malriel." He leaned forward. "Are they familiar here with the concept of a lie filter?"

"No, they are not. I tried to show them how to use it, but they simply refused to, fearing I would unleash some outlandish mind-control spell or whatever on them to influence them into letting me leave." She rolled her eyes. "Idiots. If I wanted to leave here without considering the consequences, I would have done it more than a week ago." She nodded to the barred window. "This is a joke. Any magician could walk out of here without any trouble."

"Which they are either not aware of," Vran'el threw in, "or hope you will make use of and basically provide them with an admission of guilt."

"I know. This is why I have been waiting more or less patiently for the reinforcement I knew the triarchy would send." She leaned forward and put a hand on each of their shoulders. "And what they sent me exceeded my boldest expectations."

Enric took her hand and held it between the two of his. "Malriel, there is something I need to do that you will probably not appreciate."

She smiled knowingly. "Do your thing, Enric. Of course you need to be sure. I am ready when you are."

He squeezed her hand, then let a stream of magic flow from his hand to hers.

"Malriel of House Aren, did you force a priest into bed with you?"

"No, I did not."

"Did you impose your will on him in any other way?"

"No."

"Is there any aspect of the story you told us that did not happen the way you said it did?"

"No."

He nodded and released her hand. He had not expected any other result, but it was important to know beyond any doubt.

They looked up when the door opened and Lam Ceiga cleared her throat pointedly.

Malriel rose with the two men and hugged them both before she watched them leaving with an expression that showed her reluctance to part with them as well as her careful optimism.

CHAPTER 4

A Helpful Skill

Eryn yawned loudly and leaned back in the chair in Malriel's study. She had been sitting here with Ram'an, working on the proposal the triarchy wanted, for several hours now, not counting a few interruptions when her son wanted his meals.

She studied Ram'an's cost estimate for delivering food to the orphanage three times a day from his nearest teahouse. He planned to expand the location for that purpose.

"Say, the costs look reasonable, but I trust we are talking about good quality here, right? Not just meals laden with fat and sugar, providing no real nourishment?"

"Of course not," he murmured without looking up from the sums he was calculating. "Three quarters of each serving will consist of fruit and vegetables. I would not dare selling anything else to a healer. And now do be quiet for a minute. I need to get these figures right."

She grimaced and did as she was told. Being a Head of House was obviously no protection against being instructed to shut up. Well, at least it was somebody of equal importance doing the instructing. How would Enric have reacted to a command like that?

Cursing herself for letting her guard down enough for him to insinuate himself into her thoughts, she concentrated on the matter at hand. It was bad enough that there was no real protection against it at night when the mind pretty much did what it felt like without the five senses providing distracting input all the time. She didn't have to permit this during the day as long as there were other things to occupy herself with.

She looked up and saw Ram'an's gaze resting on her.

"You look as if you are engaged in a battle with yourself. And losing," he remarked, with a sympathetic smile. "I assume this is about Enric. Would you like to talk about it? Share your troubles with an understanding listener?"

"No, thank you. I'd rather not. I assume you are done with your calculations?"

"I am, yes. That means we are also pretty much done here for now. We still need to await the cost estimate from the builder, then we can present all of this to the Senate."

He leaned back, stretching his legs and crossing his ankles. His change in posture emphasised what his words had announced - that the working part of this meeting was over.

"So, my dear, how have you been adapting to your role as new mother? I am pleased to see that you have given up pestering people to remove your golden belt for now."

She shifted uncomfortably on the soft cushion on her chair. Sitting for longer periods was still a trial and she had to take a few steps every now and again to take away the pressure from the areas that needed to heal.

"I am glad that he is out in the world and no longer blocking my view of my feet," she chuckled. "Though I admit that his feeding schedule is rather demanding. I am exhausted. I very much look forward to the day when he finally sleeps through the nights. But then I really shouldn't complain. Malhora and Junar are a great help; I wouldn't know what to do without them. They take care of him when I need to work. Although I do need to be careful not to delegate raising my own child to others. It's something I have always criticised in others."

"Have you received any offers for companionship agreements for Vedric yet?"

She rolled her eyes and opened a drawer to pull out a few folded messages. "Three of them. I mean, the boy is just a few days old! And Valrad tells me he was sent five of them. I don't even understand why people send them to both of us. Who is even in charge of this, him or me?"

"That is not quite as easy, Theá. You are the Head of House Aren, which certainly makes you somebody to address directly for now. And in case Malriel and Enric do not return, even permanently."

"So you are saying that those who send their messages to me directly do not count on either of them returning? How nice. And the others who address Valrad are confident that I will give up my new position here because the Queen of Darkness and her entourage are coming back again and he will be my Head of House again."

"That is a reasonable assumption, yes," he nodded. "And? Are you considering any of those offers?"

She shot him a dark look. "What do you think?"

"My guess would be that you will dismiss all of them on account of rejecting the entire principle of forging companionship agreements for infants."

She smiled coldly. "You know me so well. I mean", she lifted one of the messages, "this particular one here is not even born yet. Another child is already ten years old. I talked to Valrad and he promised me not to make any decisions here."

"Of course he did," Ram'an chuckled. "He has only just managed to make you accept him as your father. Promising your child to another House after your own experiences with companionship agreements would quickly put an end to this. And after your reuniting his House with Aren and Arbil, he is not exactly in dire need of alliances right now. He can afford to indulge you."

"To be perfectly honest with you, I wouldn't care if he couldn't afford to," she stated calmly. "I have no intention of letting him push my son into any commitments that serve nothing more than increasing the wealth of one or two Houses."

"You remember of course that we do not force our children to enter into a commitment?" Ram'an asked carefully. "Even if you entered into such an agreement with another House, it does not mean that you have sold his future to the highest bidder."

She frowned at him. "I really wonder about such a statement coming from you of all people! You were waiting for me for an eternity and then fought for me with everything you had, only to lose. Would you really want that for your own child? I certainly do not."

"They will continue to approach you with offers if you do not accept one of them," he warned her. "If you refuse their first offer, they will send you another one with improved terms."

"Then I will take the floor at the next Senate meeting and tell them to leave me and my son in peace and stop pestering me as I will not under any circumstances bow to this ridiculous custom of yours."

"Careful, Theá. Do not anger your fellow senators and the triarchy by doing that. Disrespect for our culture and society is not something people take lightly. You are one of us to a certain degree, but not completely. If somebody born and raised here questions the system, this is one matter, but having an outsider do so will not be received well." He lifted a hand when she was about protest. "And however little you care what others might think about you, this is not a luxury you can afford in your position right now. Neither as a Head of House who depends on allies nor as somebody who wants to realise quite a revolutionary project here. A project not everybody is in favour of, as you know."

She exhaled, looking down at her hands on the desk. He was right, and she knew it. But she didn't have to like it.

"So you are proposing what exactly? For me to agree to a commitment agreement to show my goodwill?"

He laughed. "I know better than to suggest anything like that to you. No, just keep politely declining the offers. They will understand or give up in time without your offending them publicly."

"So we are back to diplomacy because honesty wouldn't be appreciated," she sighed.

He shrugged. "That is politics, my dear. I know you are aware of the principle of diplomacy and smart enough to apply it, but your pride and temper are in your way. I would recommend working on that, Theá. Even if you do not hold your current position for long, this is a skill that will be useful in dealing with your King and your Order."

"I know!" she moaned. "You are not the first one to tell me that I am my own worst enemy."

"Good. Then I look forward to watching your efforts at the next meeting."

She grimaced. "No pressure, eh?"

* * *

Enric sat on the bed in his room and stared at the wall, and had been doing so for one hour since his return from Malriel's place of confinement. There was a framed picture of a lake with trees at one side, done in colours that had probably been vibrant at one point but were now in a rather depressing state of being washed out. It was well-executed from a technical point of view but in its precision lacked any particular artistic appeal.

But right now he wasn't seeing it, he was staring right through it, pondering how to solve this whole muddle. He first needed to make sure he was introduced to the people in charge of the proceedings here, then he had to convince them to let him teach a priest how to apply the truth block. And after that he had to find some trustworthy priest who had not been involved in tricking Malriel into her current predicament. Somebody who had no interest in lying to the judges.

But that was the trouble. He had been here only three days, so there was no saying who was involved in any of this. It could be the faith community of the so-called Inner Circle as a whole, or maybe even all the religious organisations which were conspiring together. Or an underground group with members in all five of them.

But then he could always interrogate the chosen candidate with a truth block first before teaching him or her the skill. He mulled over the idea of teaching several of them. If three or four of them were able to verify that Malriel was innocent, it would certainly be more impressive. Or maybe even five of them, one from each faith group.

Then the five of them could question the young priest who claimed that he had been forced by Malriel to engage in the offending acts.

He nodded to himself. That sounded like an approach with some chance. He had to talk to Lam Ceiga about that. He hoped she was not involved in this in some way. That would render things quite a lot more difficult.

* * *

Vran'el consulted Enric's notebook while walking along the street in order to memorise the names and titles of the three judges and four members of the local government.

"Etor Altrud, Reig of the Weisens, first level counsel of Pirinkar," the lawyer murmured, "Etor Gart, Legen of the Durachts, first level counsel of Pirinkar... And these are only two of them! Well, at least we only need to remember two different kinds of titles here. They are either first level counsels or first level judges of Pirinkar."

"Exactly. That leaves only their titles, names, family names and positions in the family," Enric grimaced. He himself had spent about half an hour memorising the names before his usual sparse breakfast of a piece of some kind of bread with a hot drink. They could not afford to anger even a single one of those seven very important people they were about to meet.

Lam Ceiga had arranged for this surprisingly quickly, considering the level of approvals and bureaucracy every single action seemed to require here. But then this particular case surely warranted special attention. They were, after all, accusing a foreign dignitary of a heinous crime, one that more often than not would be punished with a death sentence. Or lifelong incarceration if they were lenient. Neither would serve to improve the tense relationship between the two countries.

They neared the building Malriel was kept in. This would also be where they would meet the representatives of both the legal and the governmental system.

"Gistor Noraske, Legen of the Weisens, first level judge of Pirinkar," Vran'el muttered, then sighed. "The Weisens. Clearly one of the more influential families here with two people on top in different areas. There are five of them according to Ram'an's notes, but he did not give too many particulars."

"They are not particularly forthcoming with information here. I would attribute this to our status as potential future enemies, but this attitude doesn't seem to have been very different in the past, either."

"They always gave us the impression that they tolerate us on their doorstep but nothing more. We always knew that we were not exactly welcome here," the lawyer muttered. "They were never shy in communicating that."

"Then I wonder how you have managed to gain a basic insight into their laws. Especially without knowledge of the local language."

"It was one of the areas our law students can choose in the course of their training. This is basically a collection of snippets we have managed to gather and first-hand experience whenever one of the few visitors slithered into any legal trouble by breaking laws and regulations he had not been aware of. That led to books being written about what to avoid here and how violations had been handled in the past. And that does give you an insight into their legal system. Also into their attitude as a community," Vran'el added darkly. "A country obsessed with rules, laws, regulations and protocols, having no flexibility whatsoever. No consideration if one particular case requires a different approach. It is within their understanding of equality; one law applies to all. And as the circumstances tend to differ from one case to the next, they just keep passing new laws all the time. I wonder if even their own lawyers know them all."

They had arrived at the gate.

"Then let us not break any rules for now," Enric murmured and fished out his pass to show it to the guards. They waited for Vran'el to do the same and then waved them through.

They passed through the massive entrance gate and walked a few steps before they were addressed by a familiar figure. Lam Ceiga.

"Greetings, Lord Enric, Reig of House Aren, second in command of the Order, senator in Takhan and Lam Vran'el, Reig of House Vel'kim, lawyer and senator in Takhan. Follow me. I will take you to the counsels and judges," she announced in her usual impassive manner and accepted their salutations in return before walking ahead of them.

They walked along another series of corridors that appeared to be exactly like the ones from the day before, when they had come to see Malriel.

"I hope I never have to find my way out of here alone," Vran'el whispered. "Everything looks the same!"

They climbed a broad flight of stairs, then another until they reached unornamented double doors that almost reached up to the lofty ceiling. Each wing of the doors looked heavy enough to crush an adult if the hinges gave way. Enric decided that he would certainly not be too comfortable around them without his magic.

Of course there were guards stationed exactly like in front of every other door they had seen in this building so far.

Lam Ceiga presented her pass and waited for Enric and Vran'el to do the same before she nodded to the uniformed men to heave open the doors for them.

Then she indicated for them to enter. "I will wait for you here until you are done. I wish you success in you endeavour."

The last bit had not sounded overly sincere, Enric couldn't help but notice. It was probably no more than a polite phrase to throw at people when they were about to face a challenge.

He nodded to her and then set forth and entered an immensely spacious hall that based its only claim to being impressive on its sheer grand volume. This room was built to intimidate, to make those who entered feel minute and insignificant. A suitable state of mind for those who were supposed to be justifying whatever infraction or crime they had committed.

The entire far end of the room was elevated and had one long, black table placed at its centre. Behind it four figures, three men and one woman, were seated. They were all attired in dark red robes and looked solemn and forbidding. These had to be the counsels.

On their left side another table was positioned - behind it the three judges, all female, in white robes with their hands neatly folded before them on the table.

None of those seated rose, but Enric knew that this was simply no part of their understanding of politeness, no deliberate slight. He had to stop himself from bowing. This, too, was not regarded as a polite gesture of greeting here.

Enric and Vran'el both stopped at what they considered an appropriate distance to the two tables and waited to be addressed, as was customary here, when it came to facing people with higher ranks. Though Enric's own position in the Order was probably a rank higher than that of most who were present here. But they wouldn't know that, so humility probably paid off here in favour of avoiding an insult.

One of the male counsels in red raised his chin and spoke.

"Lord Enric, Reig of House Aren, second in command of the Order and senator in Takhan, we greet you. And you, Lam Vran'el, Reig of House Vel'kim, lawyer and senator in Takhan. My name is Etor Liprolf, Legen of the Peverons, first level counsel of Pirinkar." He indicated another man to his left. "This is Lam Menreich, Holm of the Brughs, first level counsel of Pirinkar. My other two colleagues are Etor Altrud, Reig of the Weisens, first level counsel of Pirinkar and Etor Gart, Legen of the Durachts, first level counsel of Pirinkar. We represent the government in this matter."

Enric quickly memorised their most prominent detail so as to be able to address them accordingly next time. Etor Liprolf was almost completely bald, but sported an impressive, bushy moustache. They seemed to be in fashion here. He appeared to have a tendency to blink his eyes several times in quick succession, as if suffering a shortage in lubricating teardrops. He imagined what reaction an offer to heal it away could trigger. Probably not a very favourable one. He forced his thoughts back to the people in front of him.

Lam Menreich was a plain, unimposing man with short, dark hair almost as dark as Vran'el's. His only remarkable feature was a large mole on one cheek.

The next one was the woman, Etor Altrud. She was a stunning beauty in her late fifties, long blond hair that was artfully braided into a complicated looking plait that hung down one side over her shoulder. He would have no difficulties remembering her, Enric knew.

The last one, Etor Gart, was rather younger than his colleagues, maybe Vran'el's age, and had a piercing and intelligent look about him. He would surely have to be smart to reach such a formidable position at such a young age. And maintain it.

Now the judges introduced themselves. He wondered if it was a coincidence that they were all female or whether the law was a profession favoured more by women here.

Enric waited patiently until one of the judges had finished greeting him and Vran'el with their full names and titles and then moved on to introducing herself and her colleagues.

The speaker, Gistor Noraske, Legen of the Weisens, first level judge of Pirinkar, was just like the other two at her side also close in age to the older counsels. She had a monotonous voice, probably robbed of modulation after decades of quoting and reciting pages of dull law articles and sub-paragraphs.

Etor Wilmen, Reig of the Fenzens, first level judge of Pirinkar, was the only one of them who openly showed curiosity at the visitors. Her eyes kept wandering to Vran'el, and Enric wondered if she would appreciate exchanging knowledge and discuss legal points of view with a colleague from another country. He filed this away for later use.

Judge number three, Gistor Igelerm, Legen of the Brughs, first level judge of Pirinkar, was a petite woman with bright red hair and blue eyes, wrinkled in their corners, who regarded them rather suspiciously.

Enric waited for the introductions to finish, then took a deep breath and greeted each and every one of them with their full array of names, titles, functions and family positions. It took him a while, but the impressed expressions on a few of the faces showed him that the time used for memorising the names had been well spent.

"Lord Enric, Reig of House Aren, second in command of the Order and senator in Takhan," Etor Liprolf, the man who had spoken first, addressed him, "We hear you want to make a proposal that will aid an expeditious conclusion of the case involving Malriel, Holm of House Aren, senator in Takhan. We are listening."

Enric marvelled at this way of speaking in that clear, short style that was unencumbered by any softening or polite expressions. It was an interesting contrast to the custom of addressing individuals that extensively. Probably to compensate for lost time after greeting somebody. He would try to adapt to it.

He nodded. "Indeed. I wish to propose using a truth block. It is a technique for determining whether a person speaks the truth. Or what they consider the truth."

One of the judges, the one with the red hair, pursed her lips. "Malriel, Holm of House Aren, senator in Takhan has tried to convince us to utilise this method. We remain sceptical. Present your proposed course of action."

Enric cleared his throat, reminding himself not to use surplus words such as would and could. "I appreciate your scepticism at teaching a new magical skill to citizens not normally involved in the pursuit of justice. I thus propose instructing one respected member of each of the five belief groups, thereby reducing the risk of depending on one person alone."

"This technique can only be taught to priests. Is this correct?" the counsel with the mole enquired. He didn't look happy at the prospect of depending on a magician to conclude this important case.

"Yes. It is a skill that requires magic," Enric confirmed calmly.

"So we counsels and judges depend on the word of the priests in assessing the truth."

"Yes. This is why this requires choosing trustworthy persons." He refrained from pointing out that he had no doubt that they would be in a position to take care of this – he had a feeling that they would not react favourably to any attempts at flattering them.

"Are you willing to have the truth block, as you call it, applied to yourself to judge your own trustworthiness after it has been taught to our priests, Lord Enric, Reig of House Aren, second in command of the Order and senator in Takhan?" Etor Altrud, the only female counsel asked.

"I am. Not only that, I furthermore offer - and even advise - having the truth block employed on Malriel, Holm of House Aren, senator in Takhan, as well."

He could see how most of them remained sceptical.

"There is the risk that this truth block is able to be circumvented," Etor Wilmen, the judge who had showed interest in Vran'el, pointed out.

"I am not aware of such a risk and invite you to try it yourself. I shall apply the block on a volunteer and you may ask questions. The volunteer attempts to lie, allowing you to judge the effectiveness of the method," Enric offered.

"So it can be used on everybody, not just those who are able to apply it?" Etor Wilmen enquired.

"Yes."

The seven robed figures exchanged questioning looks between each other, then one after another gave assenting nods.

Gistor Igelerm, the red-haired judge, got to her feet and stepped down from the elevated area. "You will demonstrate this truth block with me. My colleagues will ask questions and decide if my answers are correct."

Enric nodded once and lifted his hand. The judge just stared at it and then looked up at him as if the prospect of touching him was nothing she was prepared to endure.

"This requires physical contact," he explained simply and watched the woman take a deep breath before lifting her hand for him to take. "You will feel warmth. Do not be alarmed, this is completely normal and will do you no harm. Are you ready?"

He waited for the curt nod, then let a low-level pulse of magic enter her body. She tensed slightly, but otherwise remained still.

"Your questions, please."

"How many provisions does the code of trade contain?"

Gistor Igelerm opened her mouth, but not a single syllable came out. She touched her throat, trying to form the words with her lips, but her vocal cords refused to obey her command. Her face showed a slightly panicky expression.

Enric caught her gaze and smiled reassuringly. "Just say the correct number now."

"Five hundred and seventy-tree," she blurted out, clearly relieved to see that she had not lost her ability to speak completely.

"What is the name of the accused party in this proceeding?" another question came from the table of counsels.

Another futile attempt at lying, then Gistor Igelerm exhaled and recited Malriel's name in full.

"How did you experience this limitation?" Etor Wilmen, the curious one, asked.

"A warm sensation on my arm, then I had problems articulating the wrong answers. My voice refused to cooperate. It was painless," Gistor Igelerm stated with a few short sentences while returning to her seat.

"We will discuss your proposal and inform you of our decision," Etor Liprolf, who had been the first one to talk to them, stated.

When they started low conversations amongst themselves without sparing their visitors another glance, Vran'el murmured, "I think we have been dismissed. Let us go."

They turned and left the hall, following Lam Ceiga, who had waited as she had told them she would, down to the exit of the building.

When they were back out on the street, Enric turned to her. "Is there any chance of exchanging my gold for your currency somewhere? There is a purchase I wish to make."

"You can do this at the building where I first took you after your arrival. You need to fill in forms and state the amount you wish to exchange, the purchases you wish to make and the reasons for said purchases."

He suppressed a sigh and just nodded. Of course there would be forms to fill in. Even for a minor thing as being allowed to spend his gold here. He thanked her and watched her walk off.

"Do not be annoyed, my friend," Vran'el patted his shoulder. "It is not as if we had anything else to do while we are waiting for them to arrive at their decision. At least they provide the forms in our language. That is thoughtful, is it not?" he said in mock cheerfulness.

"Just fabulous," Enric deadpanned.

CHAPTER 5

The Hearing

Eryn carried a small tub filled with water out into the garden. She had decided to bathe Vedric out there. It was still warm enough for him not to get chilled, but the sun had lost most of its destructive strength so that there was no great danger of burning his sensitive skin.

"What exactly are you doing?" Orrin asked and balanced her son on his arm while watching her.

"I am going to bathe him out here." She set down the vessel and turned to him. "Why? You don't think I should expose my son to the curious glances of the plants around us?" she smirked.

He rolled his eyes. "No. But I think you should keep your cat from drinking the water or there will be nothing left for you to bathe your son in."

Eryn turned and shooed the cat away. "It must be the oil Intrea brought me. Urban keeps following me around whenever I carry it. Just like with the soap she gave you for Téa. I need to ask her about the ingredients."

"Let's hope she doesn't go on to devour the boy when he smells of it then," the warrior commented dryly.

"Nonsense," she huffed, but eyed the mountain cat suspiciously before crouching down and scratching a furry cheek. "You wouldn't do that, would you? You know that I would skin you alive if you confused my son with a snack, don't you?"

Urban started sniffing her hand and then licked it with her rough tongue, removing drops of the oil that had splashed onto it when Eryn had prepared the bath.

"Alright," Eryn chuckled. "That re-establishes my trust in you. See?" She looked up at Orrin. "No bloodthirsty tendencies."

The warrior just shrugged and handed the baby to his mother when they heard a knock at the entrance door.

Eryn carefully sank down on the terrace floor and then lowered Vedric into the tub, holding on to his neck to keep it above the water.

Junar joined her a moment later, Téa sleeping peacefully in her arms.

"Valrad has just arrived," the seamstress murmured in a low voice with a tell-tale look.

Eryn grimaced. The two men had managed to get along fairly well after Valrad had got over his jealousy at her close friendship with Orrin. But her father's offer to Vern at the clinic did not sit well with Orrin, not at all.

Vern didn't talk much to his father these days. He of course was thrilled at the opportunity of staying here. And his own father denying it did not exactly make having both of them under the same roof a relaxing experience right now.

Valrad had apologised both to Orrin for making the offer to his son without clearing it with him first, and also to Vern for unjustly raising his hopes.

But Eryn had seen that the healer was not happy about having Orrin deny his very talented son the chance to develop in a way that was certainly not possible in Anyueel.

So the warrior and the healer treated each other with stilted politeness. And now she saw them both coming her way, their expressions clearly conveying how little they enjoyed each other's company.

"Hello Eryn," Valrad smiled and bent down to kiss the top of her head before turning to Junar and kissing her on the cheek. "How are the newest family members doing?"

"Téa seems to do nothing but sleep," Eryn chuckled. "She must be the most well-behaved baby in the world."

Junar snorted. "That's an outrageous exaggeration. She just prefers sleeping during the day so she has enough energy to keep me awake at night."

Vern stepped out onto the terrace, his drawing pad at the ready.

"You are in the mood for drawing, aren't you?" Eryn commented. "I hardly ever see you without pen and paper these days."

The boy greeted Valrad, ignored his father and shrugged at her before sitting on the floor, leaning against the house wall before propping the pad against his thighs.

"You look a little pale, Eryn," Valrad remarked and crouched down next to her. "How are you doing?"

"I am fine, thanks for asking," she replied.

"I know that having Enric up north and the matter with the commitment bond..."

"Stop, please," she asked quietly, relieved when he did. "I haven't been sleeping too well lately. During the few hours of sleep Vedric currently grants me I have lately been tossing and turning from nightmares."

"You have?" Orrin enquired worriedly, clearly not happy about hearing this by accident. "How long has this been going on?"

"Three nights now. But I am a big girl, I will get over it."

"What do you dream about, generally?" Valrad asked.

Eryn raised an eyebrow at him. "Don't tell me you are going to analyse my dreams and draw medical conclusions that way? I would seriously doubt your status as professional healer if you did."

"I was just wondering. So?"

Enric holding Malriel in his arms, looking at her and laughing loudly at the thought of her believing him even for a moment that he had ever loved her; Malriel joining the laughter with her deep, smoky voice.

Enric chained to a dungeon wall, bound in gold, blood trickling from deep wounds.

Enric returning to Anyueel without her, wondering where this indistinct feeling of having forgotten something came from.

Enric taking their son with him, leaving her behind and raising him together with Malriel to be the next Head of House Aren.

"Nothing particular, just indistinct pictures and feelings," she said lightly. "It's probably looking at papers all day long. Figures and contracts start pursuing me into my dreams. Being a Head of House probably doesn't agree with me. It is certainly no long-term perspective. I wonder at anybody doing this for decades."

When Valrad smiled she knew that the change of topic had been successful. "It is something to grow into, I admit."

Malhora appeared at the terrace door and pointed her finger first at Orrin, then at Valrad. "You and you. Food and tableware on the kitchen counter. Off you go."

When both men had marched off reluctantly, Eryn looked up at her grandmother and grimaced. "You just invited Valrad to have dinner with us. Not good. Haven't you noticed the tension between the two men?"

The old woman sneered. "Of course I have. I just find watching them entertaining. I wonder when Orrin will give in."

Vern's head jerked up. "You think he will?" he asked with wide eyes that were so full of hope that Eryn wanted to kick Malhora.

"Of course he will," the old woman shrugged. "Not doing so would be a crime. You are a precious anomaly with little chance of unfolding your full potential in that backward place you be from."

"Hey!" Eryn protested. "I happen to like this backward place!"

"I never said you could not. Just because you are attached to it does not mean that you should close your eyes to the limitations going back there means for your young friend here."

"I know," the younger woman sighed and watched the child in the tub moving happily in the warm water, wondering if it took him back to less trying times when in her womb. Would he return there if he could? He was still so small, pushed out into this world several weeks earlier than he should have. But Valrad said he was fully developed and sturdy.

"You could talk to my father," Vern suggested with a pleading look at her.

"That would just have the opposite effect, honestly. And I have no intention of poking around where I have no right to. This is his decision," she shook her head and lifted Vedric out of the tub to wrap him in a handy towel until only his face was visible at the top of the bundle. "And now we should go inside. I am starving. I don't feel comfortable leaving those two alone with my dinner. Who knows where it might end up."

Junar chuckled and rose as well. "You think they will start throwing food at each other? The noble warrior and the exalted healer?"

Eryn grimaced. "You are aware that the mighty and powerful in this country have taken a liking to chasing each other through the streets at night and throwing bolts at each other, are you not? Those two starting a food fight would slot nicely into that category."

Malhora nodded. "Good point. I have not spent an hour in the kitchen for nothing. Though watching them cleaning up the mess would certainly be adequate compensation. Vern could draw a picture of that."

"You are an evil woman," Eryn marvelled and shook her head.

"At times. And old enough not to be ashamed because of it," her grandmother grinned.

*   *   *

Enric climbed the narrow stairs to his room, careful to keep his new purchase from bumping against the wall or the handrail.

It had taken him about two and a half hours to finally get his hands on a few units of the local currency. There had been a lot of murmuring and twirling of moustaches when he had not been able to state exactly what he intended to spend the money on. Saying that he wanted to buy gifts for his companion and his son had been too vague for them. Explaining to them that one of the gifts would be a wooden toy with the ability to move on its own had been easy, but he'd had no idea whatsoever what to get Eryn. He had hoped to wander the streets and let inspiration strike him.

They had them handed him the coins for purchasing the toy and told him to come back for more as soon as he knew what else he wanted to buy. The intended purchase would then be assessed for its acceptability. Only if it were deemed so would he be given the amount necessary. And not more than that.

Enric shook his head. They really were immensely careful as to what they allowed to leave their country. The toy had seemed harmless enough, but the gifts for Eryn had led to quite some discussion.

He had indeed found something he knew would appeal to her. Trinkets such as jewellery, perfume and things of that kind were out of the question. She would probably throw them in this face, considering the way he had left her behind. The trick was to give her something she really wanted to throw in his face but wouldn't do so because she considered the value of the gift higher than the chance of hurting him with it. That was a challenge.

But then he had seen a bookshop and known that this was definitely a place worth looking around in. He had entered the shop and felt immediately lost. Loads of books around him, and he wasn't able to decipher a single title. He had wondered why he had even come in here. The chances of finding a book in his language were surely rather slim.

Fortunately, the man behind the counter, a short fellow of Enric's own age, had been more forthcoming and also more ready to use a foreign language than his counterpart at the toy shop.

Enric had explained to him what kind of books he was looking for. Something related to healing if possible, about herbs or illnesses.

The man had then brought a selection of books for Enric to look at. The magician had done so, but to little avail as he couldn't understand a single word they bore upon their pages. The shop owner had then taken pity on him and translated the table of contents so his potential customer had at least a basic idea what he was looking at.

They were going through the third book like that, when Enric lifted a hand. There was a book on illnesses and treatments that contained the sleeping sickness Eryn had been interested in when she had first heard about it during their first stay in Takhan. She had wanted to know why no expedition had ever been sent up north to investigate this phenomenon and then heard for the first time of the growing conflict between the Western Territories and Pirinkar.

Enric had stared at the book, knowing that this was certainly nothing she would risk damaging by throwing it after him. But there was one little matter that had held him back: it would be a torture to give her a book that contained interesting information that she had no chance of accessing when it was written in another language.

The man had just smiled and pushed another two books towards him. One contained instructions, exercises and explanations, and the shop owner went on to explain that this was what the locals used to learn the language that was spoken in that hot, sandy place down south to take care of the small amount of trade that had been happening these last two centuries. The second book was a collection of words with their equivalents in the other language.

Enric felt a tingle run along his spine when he looked at the three books before him. They comprised the perfect gift.

When he had tried to change more money, however, they told him that this was a rather sensitive choice as there was the difficulty of allowing knowledge about how to acquire their language to leave the country. That was problematic and needed to be adjudicated by a higher authority. They would pass on his request and the forms he had filled in and inform him of the outcome. They had not given him any understanding about how long such a thing might take.

He opened the door and drew in a breath when he beheld an envelope on the small desk under the window. They had obviously no qualms about entering a person's room in his absence. Clearly no false modesty when it came to privacy, he thought sourly, and was glad that he had taken to carrying whatever he was unwilling to lose or have uncovered in a search along with him at all times.

He picked up the message and opened it, holding his breath for a moment and releasing it when he read the words he had been hoping for. They had granted his request to teach the priests how to apply a truth block.

His relief was so profound that he had to sit down for a moment as his knees went weak. That meant that he would be able to conclude this distasteful case here fairly quickly. And then return to his family.

* * *

"You look pale and tired, my friend," Vran'el commented after they had left for the hearing that would, they hoped, clear Malriel once and for all.

"Nightmares," Enric murmured. "Almost every night of late."

"Really? I was not aware that what we are doing here burdened you that much," the lawyer frowned. "You always appear so stoically solid and unflappable. Who would have thought that it is an act?"

Enric stared at him for a moment, then shook his head. "What? No, not me. Eryn. She is anxious and panicky in the early morning hours, so I strongly suspect that she is having nightmares." While sleeping alone in her bed, without him to comfort her, hold her in his arms and promise her that everything would turn out for the best. And it wouldn't be an empty promise. He would make everything alright for her, no matter what the cost was.

"I am sorry to hear that. If we are lucky we can see Malriel is cleared of the charges soon and leave tomorrow morning. Then you will be reunited with Eryn in around one week."

Enric just nodded. A week seemed like an eternity when every hour was already too much. He felt the magic of the bond tugging at his soul, in addition to his own impulse to be reunited with her. He was itchy, restless, eager to be on the move, to reduce the distance between them.

They reached their destination and after presenting their documents they entered the building for the third time in as many days. Vran'el led the way up the two flights of stairs to the hall where they had requested the truth block to be considered a valid method of obtaining the unblemished facts in the case.

He and Vran'el had spent the prior evening with the five priests from the different faith groups and taught each of them how to apply the truth block. Every single one of them had been eager to learn it. From what Enric had gathered so far, they were not normally encouraged to increase their knowledge into other, new uses of magic. Quite the opposite.

Enric was still astonished about the striking contrast in how magic was obviously regarded within the different societies. While in both Anyueel and the Western Territories it was considered a privilege, a blessing that brought along rather a few advantages, it was a flaw, a blemish here. He would have loved to learn more about this country's history, about what had happened to make these magicians - who were basically in a stronger position - comply with and endure being treated in this subordinate way.

He forced his attention back to the main issue when they stood in front of the uncommonly tall doors and had the guards scrutinise their documents once again. He couldn't afford to let his thoughts stray now. This was his chance to achieve what he had come here to do: get Malriel out of trouble and then return to Takhan as quickly as his horse could carry him.

The guards hefted open the doors to let them enter. Enric noted that both the counsels and the judges were positioned on the exact same seats as yesterday, the first again in red robes, the latter in white.

This time, however, there was an additional table, though not on the elevated part of the room. It was for the five priests who were going to test the truth of the statements soon to be given. Of course being magicians, it meant they were not important enough for elevated seats, Enric thought grimly.

Vran'el walked with him to the front, where they stopped and waited to be addressed. After the extensive, full-length greetings had been exchanged first with the counsels, then with the judges and finally with the priests, the two foreign magicians were asked to take seats to one side of the room and advised to interrupt the proceedings only if there was a reason that truly justified such a serious breach of protocol.

As soon as they were seated, the doors groaned open once more and Malriel was brought in, around her four guards in dark grey. She could easily have overwhelmed them without even straining herself, but she walked between them obediently. She was led to where Enric and Vran'el had been standing only a minute ago and greeted all twelve people completely with name, titles and function, just as the two men had done before her.

Gistor Noraske, one of the judges, addressed her. "Malriel, Holm of House Aren, senator in Takhan, you are before us here today to give testimony in the case against you. You are charged with attacking a citizen of Pirinkar and subsequently forcing him to have sexual intercourse with you. The punishment for a despicable deed such as this is lifelong incarceration. As in your case there is another aspect to be considered - namely, the aggravating circumstance of using your powers to inflict bodily harm - this sentence would be converted into a death sentence."

Enric watched Malriel, noting her slightly stiffer posture at the judge's last words. Other than that she showed no sign of distress.

Which was quite an accomplishment, he thought, as she had not yet been informed of the good news of the truth block having been permitted as a means to clear up the uncertainties over witness testimony.

"Malriel, Holm of House Aren, senator in Takhan, are you willing to subject yourself to the technique that is known to us under the term truth block?" the judge then asked.

Malriel showed a reaction now. She slowly turned towards Enric and stared at him in wonderment for a few moments, before clearing her throat and announcing, "Yes, I am willing."

One of the priests, the one Enric remembered was the leader of the temple of the Inner Circle where Malriel's accuser also came from, got up and stepped towards her. She lifted her hand for him to take and closed her fingers around his when he did.

Now the petite, red-headed judge Gistor Igelerm took over and asked her first question. "Malriel, Holm of House Aren, senator in Takhan, did you have the intention of spending the night with Geloin Urnen, Legen of the Nords, third level aspirant of the Inner Circle, when you left the gathering to accompany him to the temple?"

"Yes," Malriel stated clearly.

Enric didn't like the way the counsels exchanged glances. She had not incriminated herself in any way, but it seemed that her intention to spend the night with a man did not show herself to them in a good light.

"Did you have the impression that Geloin Urnen, Legen of the Nords, third level aspirant of the Inner Circle had any intention of spending the night with you when he took you to the temple that night?"

"I did, yes."

"Did he at any time state this intention explicitly?"

"No, he did not," the accused admitted. "It was implied, though."

"Implied how?"

"He kissed me several times."

"How did you come to be in his room?" Gistor Igelerm asked on.

"He invited me there."

"What happened in his room?"

"He offered me a drink which I accepted. I have no memory of anything that happened afterwards. My next clear memory is being awoken by loud shouts, finding myself naked in the bed of Geloin Urnen, Legen of the Nords, third level aspirant of the Inner Circle and finding him naked and bound in gold to his own bed next to me."

"Malriel, Holm of House Aren, senator in Takhan, did you force Geloin Urnen, Legen of the Nords, third level aspirant of the Inner Circle to have sexual intercourse with you?"

"No," Malriel stated firmly, her head held high, her eye contact with the judge unwavering.

"Beld Abhert, Legen of the Sanderns, High Priest of the Inner Circle," the judge addressed the man applying the truth block, "has

Malriel, Holm of House Aren, senator in Takhan spoken the truth? Have you been able to use the technique you were taught only yesterday in a way that ensures that no untruth was spoken here?"

"Yes, Gistor Igelerm, Legen of the Brughs, first level judge of Pirinkar, I have been able to do that," he replied.

"Good. You may return to your seat," the judge granted and addressed the other four priests. "Now each of you will step forward, one after the other, and subject Malriel, Holm of House Aren, senator in Takhan to a truth block so each one of you may confirm that her words express nothing but the truth."

Enric leaned back and watched one priest followed by another take her hand and ask her to confirm that every single word she had spoken here had been nothing but the absolute truth without any falsehood or attempt at concealment. He had tested every single one of them and knew that none of them was involved in the plot to incriminate Malriel, yet he felt his relief deepen with every priest who confirmed that her testimony was honest.

"Malriel, Holm of House Aren, senator in Takhan, you may take a seat with your Reig while we proceed with our interrogation of Geloin Urnen, Legen of the Nords, third level aspirant of the Inner Circle," Gistor Noraske instructed her and motioned for the guards that had brought her here to summon the accuser from the corridor.

Enric gave Malriel a barely perceptible smile when she sank down next to him. He felt her cool, tense hand take his and squeezed it reassuringly. Now the interesting part was about to start.

The man the guards led in was in his late twenties with short bright brown hair and features as finely chiselled as a woman's, yet less fragile. A handsome man - one who would have no difficulty catching a woman's eye. Especially not when it came to the attentions of a woman who was known for her penchant for attractive young men.

Enric glanced at Malriel and wondered how she was coping with having her one known weakness used against her so very effectively. If she was anything like her daughter, she would curse herself for her own stupidity in the privacy of her own thoughts. Right now she was staring at the priest, with her eyes slightly narrowed and her lips pressed together. She reminded Enric of Eryn when she was about to lash out and held on to her hand to keep exactly such a thing from happening if necessary.

Geloin Urnen did not appear nervous, not in the least. He radiated righteous suffering to a degree that made Enric wonder if maybe he, too, had been administered the same drug that seemed to have been in Malriel's drink and had been made to believe himself raped by the woman in his bed. This would be immensely inconvenient, since it would throw them back to where they had been before the truth block: his word against hers.

He stifled an impatient sigh when the young priest started addressing every single person behind the tables.

"Geloin Urnen, Legen of the Nords, third level aspirant of the Inner Circle", Gistor Noraske asked again, "are you willing to subject yourself to a technique that allows us to determine the truth of the words you will speak?"

Enric straightened slightly at Geloin Urnen's reaction. His leader, Beld Abhert, had obviously followed the instruction of not mentioning the truth block. The young man was surprised and evidently at a loss about what to think of this new development. His gaze darted to Malriel for a moment and then back to the judges.

"This truth block, it could be a means to control my mind to make Malriel, Holm of House Aren, senator in Takhan appear innocent when she is clearly not. I do not trust these foreign men who are on her side and do thus not wish to be subjected to their technique, which would put me at their mercy," Geloin Urnen stated indignantly.

Enric kept the smile that tugged at his lips at bay. That had been a mistake. Had the priest claimed not to trust the technique itself instead of having it applied by him or Vran'el, it might have been considered a valid objection. But he had not taken into account the likelihood of his own countrymen's being able to use it. Unless he dared accusing them of being untrustworthy, he had little choice but to agree to it now. Or admit to lying.

Gistor Noraske nodded. "We duly note your objections and can reassure you that you do not have to concern yourself about our visitors' attempting at manipulating your thoughts in any way. The leading priests of the temples have been carefully instructed in the correct application of the technique."

The young priest swallowed audibly, his eyes wide while his gaze darted from one priest to the next.

"Are there any additional objections you have failed to mention as of yet or can we proceed with the interrogation, Geloin Urnen, Legen of the Nords, third level aspirant of the Inner Circle?" Gistor Noraske asked pointedly.

Geloin Urnen frowned and found himself the target of fifteen pairs of eyes staring at him in heightened suspicion. He took a deep breath and all of a sudden looked determined.

"Yes, we can proceed," he said, visibly steeling himself against whatever obstacle he had to brave now.

"The bloody fool has no idea what he is about to face," Malriel whispered almost inaudibly. "He thinks he can outsmart the lie filter."

Enric nodded slightly. Yes, that was indeed the impression he made. He seemed prepared for a desperate attempt at trying to lie his way out of this.

When the high priest of the Inner Circle took his hand, Geloin Urnen drew a breath, doubtlessly at the warm stream of magic along his arm.

"Geloin Urnen, Legen of the Nords, third level aspirant of the Inner Circle," the other judge, Gistor Igelerm took over again, "did you take

52

Malriel, Holm of House Aren, senator in Takhan to your room in the temple to have sexual intercourse with her?"

"No, I did not," the young priest said a tad too loudly and flinched at the echo's throwing his words back at him from different directions.

"Why did you take her to your room?"

Enric saw how Malriel next to him held her breath and felt her fingernails digging into his palm.

They watched Geloin Urnen take a breath, open his lips and... frown when his mouth failed to cooperate in producing the words he had intended to utter.

Enric felt the weight of the tension fall off him and triumph surge through him in its stead. That had been a recognisable attempt at lying under a truth block. And judging from the grim and angry expressions on the faces of the judges, counsels and priests, he was not the only one aware of it.

"Geloin Urnen, Legen of the Nords, third level aspirant of the Inner Circle," Gistor Igelerm barked, "did you take Malriel, Holm of House Aren, senator in Takhan to your room to trick her into being falsely accused of a serious crime?"

The young priest gripped his throat, desperate and at a loss to understand what was happening to him, trying to form words, but failing to release them.

"I cannot speak!" he finally managed to croak, relieved at having regained the ability to express himself verbally.

"This is how the technique works, Geloin Urnen, Legen of the Nords, third level aspirant of the Inner Circle," Etor Altrud, the only female counsel said acidly, "it prevents any lies from being articulated."

When Geloin Urnen opened his mouth, probably in an attempt to either cry out that he had not intended anything of that kind or to promise his innocence, again not a single syllable escaped his vocal cords.

The bald counsel with the large moustache, Etor Liprolf, got up from his seat, his voice cold and forbidding when he announced, "The evidence suggests that Geloin Urnen, Legen of the Nords, third level aspirant of the Inner Circle has repeatedly attempted to lie to this court. He will be questioned in more detail. Lord Enric, Reig of House Aren, second in command of the Order and senator in Takhan and Lam Vran'el, Reig of House Vel'kim, lawyer and senator in Takhan, you may leave now and return to your allocated accommodation. Malriel, Holm of House Aren, senator in Takhan may join you, instead of returning to her holding cell. You will all stay there and await our notification concerning the outcome of these proceedings."

The three of them all but jumped up from their chairs and turned to leave the large hall, leaving Geloin Urnen in the company of twelve obviously displeased people who became even more eager to hear him talk.

* * *

Malriel sat at the small desk in Enric's room, drumming her fingers against the surface, her fingernails making rhythmical clicking sounds on the wood.

"Three hours. What can be taking them so long? I mean, it was obvious that he was lying and that I was not!" she exclaimed. It was not for the first time she had uttered these words.

Enric was sitting on his bed, adding a few notes to Ram'an's book. "Don't worry too much, Malriel. If they still thought you were guilty they would hardly have permitted you to leave and wait here with us," he stated calmly without looking up.

"I know! Yet I cannot rely on their setting me free as long as there is no official judgement."

"Malriel, if they declare you innocent today, Vran'el and I will leave here tomorrow morning after breakfast. What are your plans? Will you stay here and continue your negotiations?"

She snorted. "Hardly, Enric. This stupid plot has destroyed almost everything I managed to achieve in those last few months here. They may prove that I am innocent, but how can people here trust me again after this? No, I will have to leave here with you. And I do not mind telling you that I am sick and tired of this place, anyway. I will have to return to Takhan in shame and humiliation," she murmured, her eyes on the floor. "But at least it will mean that I return alive."

"Do not fret on that account yet, Malriel. One thing after the other. First we shall get you out of here, then we need to consider what comes after that."

Malriel pushed back the chair and walked over to the bed, sitting down on it and clasping one of Enric's hands between both hers. She waited until he had lifted his face to look at her.

"Enric, however this will end, I want you to know that I am indebted to you for coming after me when I needed you. And that I deeply regret that it cost you the experience of seeing your son arriving in the world. Thank you for everything. For taking over my House, for being a companion worthy of an Aren woman to my daughter."

He nodded slowly. "You are Eryn's mother, however troubled your relationship with her is. That makes you family." He freed his hand from hers and cupped her face, pulling her a little closer so that she had no chance to turn away. "But there are two things I have been wanting to say to you for a while, and I think you are now in the mood to listen to them." His eyes narrowed. "I did not like your slipping Eryn that potion to allow her to be impregnated. Do not take me wrong, I am happy about my child, immensely so, but I would never have forced anything like that on her. I wanted to try and convince her that having children with me is not something to be afraid of, but that it would be a gift to bestow upon each other. This is the chance you stole from me for your own selfish reasons. But you will make up for it by being a supportive and loving grandmother, none of your Aren harshness and strictness with my son. Have I made myself understood?"

Malriel swallowed hard and nodded. "Yes. And the second thing?"

"When I accompanied you to Bonhet when you were on your way back to Takhan after visiting us, I saw you send a bird back to the King when we were at the inn. Doubtlessly to inform him that I had declined your invitation to come to Takhan for a while." His stare had turned cold. "I assume you are aware of the consequences this message of yours had?"

"His kiss that made you take her away from Anyueel," she murmured and grimaced. "I assure you that I had no idea what measures he would resort to. He just told me that he would manage to make you come to Takhan if I did not."

"And you didn't ask of him how he intended to accomplish this feat?" Enric asked bitterly.

Malriel closed her eyes. "No. I admit I did not want to know. I knew that he would not harm either of you, and that was all the luxury I could afford back then. I knew that he was attracted to her, but I had hoped he would not act in a way to cater to his own desires in this case. I am sorry that he did. I really am."

He studied her for a few moments, then pursed his lips. "If you ever again participate in or initiate a scheme like that to manipulate or provoke me into doing something I don't intend to do, I will make you pay for it. Severely so."

Only when Malriel nodded silently did he release her face and lean back.

Both froze when a weighty knock made the door rattle. Malriel slowly got back to her feet and opened the door, accepting the bundle of papers that was pressed into her hands before the messenger slipped away again.

Enric was on his feet a moment later, taking the sheets from her slightly unsteady hands. The first one was a message from the judges that officially acquitted Malriel, Holm of House Aren, senator in Takhan of all and any charges against her. He handed it to Malriel, who sank against the closest wall, sliding down to the floor when her knees gave up the power of support.

The next four papers were the forms he had filled in to have his application for exchanging money for the purchase of the three books granted. Every single one of them was signed and approved.

He smiled. That was quite a concession they were willing to make, considering that they tried to prevent knowledge of any kind from leaving their country. Very likely as small compensation for having had a member of their society try to incriminate the one person who had been sent here to avoid a war. This was a dangerous situation that might easily be interpreted as a hostile act, when all was said and done.

"There is a purchase I wish to make today," he told her. "I assume you have to return and collect your things and talk to a few people about your departure. Do you wish to leave with us tomorrow morning?"

She smiled feebly and nodded. "Yes. There is a thing or two I have to conclude before I leave. I will join you and Vran'el for breakfast tomorrow. Then we can leave here. At long last."

CHAPTER 6

Returning

Both magicians looked up when Malriel walked towards their table in the small, frugal dining room of the guest house they were staying at.

She was already clad in the clothes she would be wearing for the journey, a sturdy pair of dark leather trousers and a coarse linen tunic that almost reached to her knees.

"Good morning, my friends," she said calmly with a tense smile and took a seat on an unadorned wooden chair, which creaked slightly under her weight.

"And a good morning to you," Vran'el nodded. "I have to admit we were expecting you a little earlier."

"I had a final meeting with a few of the government representatives. There was a little something I had to take care of before leaving." At Enric's inquisitively raised eyebrow she continued, "I have managed to convince them to let us send another representative and continue the negotiations. They had little choice in the matter, considering that I am leaving here after one of their citizens tried to spring such a nasty trick on me. They owe it to us, especially, as we are mature enough not to treat this as an act of aggression against our country."

"That is excellent news," the blond magician nodded and took another slice of the rather dry bread from a round basket. It was not the most delicious fare but since he would have to make do with the dried travel rations in the next few days he was resigned, as it was still the last chance to eat something that did not expand its volume in his mouth while he was chewing.

"How about you, boys? Are you ready to leave after breakfast? I will admit I am eager to get on the road." She nodded at Enric. "And I dare say so are you."

"Everything is taken care of and packed," Enric confirmed. "As soon as we have finished eating we can mount our horses and be off. I have had ours saddled and brought here. Where is yours?"

"Tied to a pole next to yours."

"Do we have to consider any farewell rites before we are able to leave?" Vran'el enquired. "It seems rather strange to just ride off like that."

"We do not, no," Malriel shook her head. "We said our official goodbyes yesterday and this is as ceremonial as it is going to get. They are not exactly a very warm and emotional type of people here," she murmured, careful to make sure none of the other five guests could hear her.

Enric swallowed the last bite of his bread and pushed back his chair to get up. "I am ready if you are, then. Malriel, I assume you have already had breakfast?"

"I did, yes. About three hours ago. As far as I am concerned we can leave here."

They stepped outside through the narrow doorframe and walked the few steps to where their horses were waiting patiently with loads lashed to their saddles.

"Nobody came to see us off," Vran'el shook his head. "Incredible."

"I have learned that those rules of hospitality that go without saying in our country do not apply here," Malriel explained while mounting her horse. "In the Kingdom of Anyueel they are considered a matter of good manners, but still not as important as they are to us. Do not mistake it for an intentional slight, it is just their way of doing things here. This case was concluded, there is nothing more for now, so they see no need to make any additional effort with us. They are more concerned with using their resources sparingly, especially when there is nothing to be won by squandering them, as it were. As the chance that I am about to return here anytime soon is rather remote, there is no need to treat me in an overly friendly manner and make me want to come back."

"Perfectly heartless," Vran'el muttered and set his own horse into a gentle trot after Malriel's.

Enric followed them towards the bridge that would enable them to cross the broad river and thereby leave the city behind them. The colourfully clad guards that had blocked their way into the city only several days ago stood to one side and let them pass without any trouble or even a flicker of recognition.

He drew in a deep breath when they moved on, safe in the knowledge that every single step was bringing him a little closer to Eryn.

* * *

Eryn returned from the nursery after putting her son to bed and yawned, remembering in time that she was not alone in the Aren main room and covering her mouth with the back of her hand.

But from the four people that had been there only ten minutes ago, only one remained.

"Where is everyone?" Eryn frowned.

Ram'an smiled. "Junar and Orrin have retired, and Malhora said something about feeling the urgent need for some fresh air. She is roaming the gardens with your cat. And you, my dear, look like you had better go to bed as well."

She grimaced. "That's the one thing I dread every day: going to bed."

"So you are still suffering from these nightmares?" he enquired sympathetically.

"I am, yes. Every single night. Falling asleep has become easier since the birth, but on the whole my nights are even less restful than before. I wonder if I should just switch my rhythm and sleep during the day," she sighed.

"That might be quite a challenge considering that you are supposed to be available for any issues concerning your House. Preferably at a time when everybody else is awake," Ram'an smiled and got up from the seating cushions. "Come on."

Eryn frowned at the hand he held out to her. "Where?"

"To bed. I will tuck you in and treat you to a routine that worked nicely for me when I was a boy. I will first make sure there are no unpleasant creatures lurking under your bed and then tell you a bedtime story."

She couldn't help but grin. "A story? Don't you think I am a little old for that?"

"Nonsense. We are never too old for a good story. That is why we surround ourselves with them all the time. Every song tells a story, every picture we look at. Go out into that garden here, it tells you the story of generations of Aren leaders. The vaults of most Houses hold precious heirlooms that tell stories of deeds and practices long gone, as do our books." He took her hand when she just gave him a sceptical look. "And in a city where mighty politicians and venerated civic leaders run through the streets to play invasion, everything is possible, Theá. Even one Head of House telling a bedtime story to another one."

That made her laugh and she let herself be pulled along towards her bedroom. He opened the door and released her hand.

"Wait here. I will first make sure everything is safe," he whispered and entered the room cautiously, staring into every corner, behind the door and finally he went down on his knees to look under the bed.

Eryn watched him with folded arms while leaning against the doorframe, grinning and shaking her head. He really was a piece of work. Had she ever seen him that playful before?

"I am happy to report that the room is safe and you may enter without fear," he announced grandly. "I will step outside for a moment so you can change into your sleeping attire. Do not lie down without my being present, it has to be done the right way." He winked at her and walked out into the corridor, pulling the door shut behind him.

She quickly slipped out of her tunic and trousers and into a loose, opaque night gown.

"I am ready," she called out and a moment later Ram'an returned and stepped next to the bed to lift the blanket for her.

She lifted an eyebrow at him. "And I couldn't have done that without your help?"

"Do not question the routine, Theá," he admonished her and waited for her to slip under the blanket. Then he went around the bed and took off his shoes to lie down on what used to be Enric's side of the bed. She swallowed and frowned.

"You are not expecting me to stand or sit on the floor while I take the trouble of telling you a lengthy story, are you? I will be a perfect gentleman, I promise. Now make yourself comfortable and let me tell you the legend of how the city of Takhan came to exist and why it is situated at the exact spot where it is today."

She listened to him recount a story of elemental spirits of the river and mountains fighting over dominion of the land many thousand years before, the arrival of humans in these parts and how they forged an alliance with the powerful sun spirit to take the land as their own, founding their capital city at a place that granted both the river spirit and the nearby mountain spirit direct access and to it to console them into a peaceful coexistence. His soft, melodious voice painted pictures of fighting natural gods that used the elements of sand, water, earth and heat to try and subdue each other, of humans and their feeble understanding of magic that still helped them to gain the upper hand at the end.

She was captured by his lively and solemn style of relaying the story to her, wondering how a man like that could ever have ended up studying the law and being content with rules and regulations. But then he had also studied history, had he not? The discipline that dedicated all its resources to uncovering and preserving stories long told.

His low voice managed to speak of mighty earthquakes and floods without even raising the volume, but applied the principles of modulation so skilfully that she found her eyes glued to his lips while magnificent pictures were painted by his words. How could she ever have believed that one could be too old to be captured by a good story told by a man who turned out to be a masterful teller?

Eryn smiled when almost an hour later his eyes had finally closed. She had noticed that his lids had started getting heaver a while ago, but he had fought against the pull of sleep. It seemed that he had either given in now or lost the fight.

He was lying on top of the second blanket, so she couldn't use it to cover him to keep him from freezing. The thought of waking and sending him home didn't even occur to her.

She moved closer so her own blanket would cover both of them and bedded her head on his upper arm. The sensation of a warm body against her back was such a powerful relief that she had to swallow.

She would for just one night pretend that he was Enric, that she was no longer alone but that he was here in this room to hold and protect her, ward off bad dreams. She would indulge herself this one night. It would help her sleep, gather the strength she needed. And tomorrow she would go and see Iklan and ask him to help her leave the pain and longing behind.

It was time to get over Enric and concentrate on the new man in her life, the one to whom she would from now on dedicate all her strength: Vedric.

*   *   *

Enric exhaled and dismounted his horse in front of the Aren residence. Never would he have believed that this place - where Malriel had managed to summon him with trickery - would ever seem such a welcome sight. But it was no longer mere accommodation, a seat of office, it was the place Eryn was staying. And that made it home.

He turned towards Vran'el. "I assume you will ride on home right away?"

The lawyer smiled tiredly and shook his head. "No, I first want to have a peek at my nephew. And see how my sister reacts to the sight of you."

Enric nodded and looked at Malriel. She smiled wearily down at him from her elevated position.

"Do not worry, Enric, I promised you to behave, remember? If there is to be an escalation with three Aren women under one roof I will not be the one to cause it. Now go on in. I will lead the horses to the stables and take care of them. Vran, you can pick up yours tomorrow. It deserves to rest, just as we do."

Both men untied their bundles from the saddles and Enric opened the entrance door carefully while Malriel led away the horses. He lit a lamp and ascended the stairs into the main room, Vran'el close behind him.

"I will wait for you here. I dare say you will not want any witnesses to your reunion, whichever way it goes," Vran'el smiled and took a seat on the seating island, visibly enjoying the sensation of a soft bolster that didn't sway or rock for a change.

Enric nodded once and braved himself while continuing his way to the bedroom. He had no illusions about the kind of welcome he would receive. But that was something he was more than willing to brave in exchange for laying eyes on her again. He had felt how the pull of the commitment bond had grown in this last day. He would have expected the close proximity to ease the tension, but instead the impending reunion seemed to increase the sense of urgency. Or was that his own, personal longing that had nothing to do with the magic that bound him to her?

He stood in front of the bedroom, the lamp in one hand and carefully opened the door to step inside. And froze.

Of all the bad scenarios in his head when he had imagined his return, not a single one of them had prepared him for the sight right before his eyes.

Eryn lay on her side, her head bedded on Ram'an's upper arm while his other hand rested on her hip like he had every right to touch her wherever it pleased him.

Enric closed his eyes and leaned against the doorframe, fighting the cold fist that squeezed his heart and threatened to bring him to his knees.

He should never have trusted Ram'an. Not ever. How could he have been so naïve to even ask that man to look after her? The very man who had fought for her with everything at his disposal, who had been willing to give up his claim to power for her?

He stared at the strangely peaceful picture in front of him. She didn't look as if she had been forced into submission, but as if sleeping in his arms was pleasant instead of the disquiet she should have felt from where Enric stood. Had she given in to him to hurt her companion? To take revenge? Or had she done so out of desperation and loneliness? He remembered her pain at night through the mind bond. And that this was the first night he had received none. The night where he found her in Ram'an's arms, blissfully resting in his warm embrace.

He couldn't find it in him to reproach or accuse her for it. His gaze jumped to Ram'an who had started moving. This was where his anger, his fury belonged!

Ram'an slowly opened his eyes and blinked when he beheld the man watching them from the doorframe, clad in dusty travelling clothes and his face a stony mask, cold blue eyes staring daggers at him.

"Enric? You are back!" the lawyer whispered and looked down at the woman next to him. Only then did realisation seem to dawn on him. The picture they made, him holding this very man's companion in his arms while lying in his bed. "Wait, I can explain..."

"You treacherous mongrel," Enric hissed and slowly came closer. "You should at least have made sure that I didn't come back."

He saw Eryn move slightly before she opened her eyes and then stared at him in utter disbelief, her eyes wide, her mouth agape.

"Enric," Ram'an said urgently, getting up from the bed and lifting both his hands before him, palms facing towards the newcomer. "Please, we need to sit down and talk about this. Then you will see..."

The bolt hitting him right in the middle of his chest cut him off mid-sentence and sent him to the floor with a thud, unconscious.

Eryn's eyes were still glued to the figure in front of her that approached her slowly. This situation was so strange, so unreal that her brain was helpless to judge if this was just another one of her painful dreams or not.

"Eryn," she heard him whisper when he placed the lamp on her bedside table and sat on the bed next to her, his face contorted in agony. She could see tears building in front of his incredibly blue irises; something she had never seen before. His lips were dry and chapped in places, his face and hair covered with a thin patina of dust and sand.

A moment later she felt warm lips pressing onto hers and a tender hand at her neck to hold her close. His other hand circled her waist.

She was utterly lost in this absurd situation, unable to react in any way. And even if she could have responded, she wouldn't have been able to decide whether to push him away and escape the bitter sweet torture that his taste on her lips was, or hug him close.

He broke the contact and stared down at where his hand touched her hip. There was the outline of something solid under her nightgown.

"He put a golden belt on you?" Enric growled and touched the offending item to release her from it by sending a small pulse of magic through the fabric. "I am so sorry," he murmured and shook his head, still lost in the absurdity of finding her sleeping peacefully in the arms of a man who had gone to such measures to make her compliant.

Eryn slowly woke from the shock. A powerful surge of ire and pain finally ripped her from her inanimate demeanour. She saw him frown in utter incomprehension and spat, "As well you should be, Bastard!" before lifting her palm and releasing a powerful bolt of magic from her hand.

His eyes went wide in confusion before he sank back and slid to the floor.

A moment later she heard steps from the corridor running towards her before Vran'el appeared in the doorframe, staring bewildered at her, then at the two lifeless men on the floor, then back at her. He, too, looked exhausted and travel-worn.

It took him a few seconds to find his words. "What have you done now? And why was Ram'an in your bedroom at this time of night?"

He quickly bent down briefly to touch first Enric, then Ram'an to take stock. He squatted on his haunches and looked up at her, shaking his head.

"At least they are not dead", he sighed wearily and rubbed his face. "Which probably means that I should congratulate you on your restraint, sister."

She slowly shook her head. "No, dead they are not." Her gaze fell on Enric. "But one of them will probably soon wish he were."

*   *   *

Eryn was leaning against the wall with folded arms and watched the goings on in the main room impassively. It had to be a few hours after midnight.

Vran'el had carried first Enric and then Ram'an from her bedroom to the seating cushions and stood in front of them.

"Which one shall we awaken first?" he addressed Malhora next to him.

The old woman pursed her lips. "Arbil. If Enric has another go at him, he should at least be awake to defend himself. Not that it will help him much against a stronger magician, mind you. But maybe he will be quick enough to dodge."

Eryn straightened and walked towards them, wordlessly bending down to the man she legally speaking still had to consider her companion and fastened the golden belt he had taken off her only a few minutes ago around his waist.

"Alright," Vran'el nodded slowly. "That solves one problem."

They heard steps from the corridor to their left and then Orrin's astonished voice. "Vran'el! You are back!" Then his gaze shifted to the two recumbent men on the cushions. "Oh my word, what have you done now, Eryn?"

The second one to ask her that very question. She didn't bother with an answer but returned to her position against the wall. She felt oddly detached from this whole drama around her. This scene in front of her appeared still ridiculously unreal.

There he was - Enric, the man whose absence had fuelled her nightmares, had made her feel lost and lonely - and all she felt was this strange numbness now that the initial anger had abated. The healer in her wondered if she was dealing with some kind of shock reaction here.

Malhora answered the warrior in her granddaughter's stead. "Enric found Ram'an in her bed and knocked him out. And after freeing her from the belt, she repaid him in kind," she explained simply as if this reaction was the most natural one in the world.

Eryn could see that Orrin was about to speak again, probably to ask why Ram'an had even been in her bed to be found there by Enric, but changed his mind and just shook his head in wonder.

Vran'el bent down to touch the Head of House Arbil lightly on the forehead for a moment before straightening again. Ram'an's eyelids opened little later and it took him a few seconds to take in his surroundings and find back to reality.

He turned his head slightly and jumped up cursing when he found Enric close by, only relaxing after he realised that the tall magician was unconscious.

He exhaled slowly and looked at the other lawyer. "So you have returned."

"As you can see," Vran'el replied coldly. "What were you doing in my sister's bed?"

He sighed. "I fell asleep there after telling her a bedtime story. She has been suffering from nightmares for some time."

Vran'el nodded reluctantly. He at least knew the part with the nightmares to be true.

"Did you return alone?" Malhora asked carefully.

"No," a throaty, tired voice spoke from the terrace door, "they did not. Greetings, mother."

Eryn tensed and pressed her lips together at Malriel's sight, making no move towards or away from the travel-weary figure that entered the room and came to a halt a few paces away from Malhora.

"I am glad to see you are well, Malriel," the older woman said softly. "Not that I had much doubt that you would prevail," she added as an afterthought.

Malriel's smile was thin. "Of course not. It is good to see that you had not been worrying about me needlessly, mother."

Eryn could hear something swinging with the words, something unexpected. Hurt feelings at her own mother not worrying about her only daughter?

"Of course I was worried, you fool," Malhora retorted gently.

The two women stared at each other for several moments and Eryn wondered if they would embrace. They didn't and just stood there awkwardly, neither of them sure what to do. Eryn stared at them and thought what a burden being an Aren had to be if they couldn't even show their affection for each other, probably for fear of appearing weak. She swore to herself that this was not something she would ever allow between her son and herself.

Malriel nodded once and then turned towards her daughter. "Maltheá," she sighed and came closer. If she noticed the narrowed eyes and the frown, she had decided to ignore it and without a warning pulled her daughter into her arms, holding on tightly when the younger woman made to free herself.

"No," Malriel murmured, "Please indulge me for only a short moment, will you?"

Eryn blinked and stilled, surprised at the plea in her mother's voice. The time up north must have been a great strain on her to admit to a weakness like the need for an embrace.

Malriel released her again and then looked at Ram'an and Enric on the cushions. She sighed. "Was this really necessary? Did you really have to knock him out? And what are you doing here at this time of night, anyway?"

Ram'an's brow shot up. "I did not do this. Eryn did."

The older woman's gaze snapped back to her daughter. "You did? Not quite the welcome he would have wished for, I would imagine," she said, without a trace of irony.

"And yet the one he deserves," Eryn hissed and stepped away from her mother.

Vran'el sighed. "I had better send a messenger to my father to inform him that we have returned."

"Don't bother, I will fetch him," Orrin offered and descended the stairs without waiting for an answer.

"I would say we ought to wake him," Vran'el sighed. "Any volunteers for that honour?"

Eryn took a deep breath and stepped forward. "I will."

The other four gathered around her when she marched to the seating cushions and looked down at him. The sight of him gave her a stab, a mix of longing to touch him and pain at the thought that he had left her here to run after Malriel. Now he was back again and she had no idea how to deal with him. She had played scenarios through in her head. Admittedly, knocking him out had indeed featured in a few of them. But that was about as far as she had thought.

She remembered how he had touched her in the bedroom, the feeling of his rough lips on hers, the immense suffering clear from his eyes. Had his quest to free Malriel not brought him what he had hoped? Had she not sunk into his arms the way he had expected? Had he been counting on being welcomed by his companion now as if nothing had happened?

She felt warm anger rising inside her and squared her shoulders before touching his forehead just how Vran'el had done with Ram'an.

Enric stirred little later, opening his eyes and staring into Eryn's cool expression. His gaze snapped to Ram'an and he quickly climbed to his feet, realising only then that his magic was missing. He looked down at the golden belt and cursed. He lifted his index finger, pointing it at the Head of House Arbil.

"You will pay for this, I swear to you - I will make you pay as soon as I have my magic back!" he snarled.

Eryn lifted a finger and used a little magic to give Enric a push that sent him back onto the cushions.

"What is your problem, Enric?" she asked coldly. "Are you sick of Malriel already? Or is the thought of Ram'an getting the prize such a painful one? Are you embracing the Aren spirit of winning every time, no matter if the cause is worth it?"

"What?" Enric stared up at her, utterly astonished at the absurdity of her words. "What are you talking about?"

"I am talking about your forcing the commitment bond off me and running after Malriel - the damsel in distress. I take it she hasn't reciprocated your feelings so far?"

Eryn turned her head when she heard Malriel's low chuckle to her right. "Maltheá, you have completely got the wrong end of the stick here."

Enric's head had lolled back and he stared up at the ceiling. "You think I am in love with your mother?" he asked and pressed his thumb and index finger against the bridge of his nose. "Please tell me that this is a joke. One I do not at all find amusing," he added darkly when his gaze returned to her face.

"What else am I to believe?" Eryn hissed, her arms folded, her stance broad. "How could you run off like this with my being heavy with your child to stand by another woman? You dissolved the bloody bond! The one you pretended to be so very keen on entering into with me!"

Enric forced himself to breathe evenly. Why now? Why couldn't he have to deal with this when he was well-rested instead of exhausted and weary like now?

"I went after Malriel," he said slowly, "so you and I would be free again instead of being chained to Takhan. So that with her back as Head of House we would be able to return home. And to avoid a war that would have endangered your family here. I had the bond removed from you to spare you the pain of feeling drawn towards me through magic. I wanted to spare you any horrific experiences I might have gone through in Pirinkar. I had no idea what I was about to encounter up there. It might just as well have been torture and death."

He frowned when he felt a warm hand move to grip his wrist, and a moment later warm magic seeped through his skin. Eryn. She was applying a truth block.

"Do you feel attracted to Malriel of House Aren?"

"Not in any amorous way," he replied evenly, looking her straight in the eyes.

"In what way do you feel attracted to her?" Eryn asked tensely.

"I respect her and admire her strength, endurance and intelligence."

"Why did you go after her?"

"To keep my family safe. To preserve our freedom. To avoid a war, if possible. And to assist a family member in need," he replied tiredly.

Eryn swallowed and closed her eyes. Enric felt the mighty wave of relief washing over her through the mind bond and slowly shook his head. He freed his wrist from her grip and instead laid his palm against her cheek.

"How could you ever have doubted me like that?" he asked quietly, torn between anger at her for her lack of faith in him and sympathy for what she had needed to suffer because of it. "Is that why you gave in to Ram'an?"

Her eyes opened and she regarded him thoughtfully. "A bold question from the man who just reprimanded me for my lack of faith. I did not give in to Ram'an. And couldn't have, as he never ever once tried to take advantage of the situation, or of me. He has in these last few weeks been a great friend to me, a valuable ally. What you saw was his taking me to bed and falling asleep there after telling me a story to help me sleep."

Enric leaned back again. His head fell against the cushions behind him and he closed his eyes. A single tear ran down from the corner of one eye, leaving a wet streak across his cheek and then his jawline. He felt as if years had fallen off him. She was still his. The relief was so powerful, so mighty, that it was almost excruciating. He was glad that he was seated or it might have brought him to his knees.

"We will renew the bond as soon as possible," he smiled tiredly and looked at her. "I suppose I also owe Ram'an an apology."

She nodded slowly. "I agree with the second, but not with the first. Your motives may have been honourable, but I do not approve of your course of action." She lifted her chin. "For now there will be no third level bond between us. I first have some healing to do before I make myself that vulnerable ever again." She smiled thinly. "And to be honest, you wouldn't want to feel some of the things that are currently going on inside me."

Enric ground his teeth, feeling his stomach clench, but remained silent.

Vran'el next to Eryn cleared his throat audibly and sent him a pointed look. "I cannot help but feel that this is your cue for a little confession."

"I agree," Ram'an came to his colleague's aid and stepped next to the other lawyer. Both of them had their arms folded and looked down at him sternly, radiating disapproval.

Eryn's eyes narrowed. "What confession?"

Enric sighed deeply and let his head fall back once again. "I really need a bath and then a bed. Can't we deal with this tomorrow?"

"No," both lawyers agreed in unison and glared down at him.

"If you do not tell her, I will," Vran'el threatened. "I mean it!"

"Tell me what?" Eryn barked, wondering if it was even possible for this night to get any stranger.

"Alright," Enric gave in and straightened with an effort, bracing himself. "Eryn, the third level bond wasn't dissolved completely. My end was left intact. That also means the mind bond."

She stared down at him in utter shock, a part of her noting how the echo of the hot spear of wrath inside her made him wince.

"You bloody bastard," she hissed. "So you have been spying on my emotions all this time! On everything that was going on inside me without even letting me know! How could you? Now you want me to trust you enough to renew the bond? Are you even aware of how betrayed I feel?" The last sentence she had shouted.

Enric exhaled in relief. She had let go of her anger, showed it instead of locking it in. He had been afraid of her returning to her former strategy of keeping her feelings parcelled up. But there was clearly no danger of that right now.

She lifted her index finger at him. "You must have your side of the bond dissolved. This is an order!"

He folded his arms. "No."

"I am your Head of House and you will do exactly as I say!" she spat.

"The Head of House has no jurisdiction concerning personal matters such as commitment bonds, apart from granting them," he explained calmly.

Eryn turned to the two lawyers. "Is that true? Can he refuse just like that?"

Both of them nodded rather reluctantly, obviously unhappy that they had no choice but to confirm it.

"What can I do to make him comply? Apart from being his Head of House I am also his companion - I must have some rights there!"

"You could discuss this with the triarchy. They are the ones to permit and dissolve third level bonds. Though I imagine this is something of a unique situation. I have no idea what they would decide," Ram'an explained carefully. Vran'el nodded in agreement.

Eryn massaged her temples with the index fingers of both hands to release the tension knotted there, closing her eyes and cursing herself for ever entering into the stupid bond, cursing Enric for never relinquishing control no matter the cost, and the local laws that provided idiotic rules to cause her trouble but hardly any to help her out of it.

"Alright," she said slowly, forcing herself to be calm and reasonable. There was no sense in exploding here and now. "I will talk to the triarchy about it. I am sure there will be a Senate meeting tomorrow now that the three of you are back. I will ask them for a few minutes of their time afterwards."

They heard the entrance door downstairs opening and closing, and little later Valrad appeared on the top of the stairs, out of breath, his hair tousled, and a moment later he held his son in a firm embrace.

Both men stood there for almost a minute and Eryn thought that this was how family members were supposed to greet, not the way Malhora and Malriel had, with frosty words and restraint. How lucky she was to have escaped House Aren to be one of them instead.

Then Valrad stepped towards Enric, who had in the meantime clambered back to his feet, and grabbed his hand to pull him into an embrace as well.

When he had released the blond magician, the healer's gaze fell on the third one of the returnees.

"Malriel," he said softly.

Malriel's expression was determined, but her movements strangely awkward when she approached him.

"Valrad." She stopped in front of him, swallowed, took a deep breath and lifted her hand to his neck to pull him close and press her mouth on his in a kiss that was far from how old friends were supposed to greet each other.

Valrad went stiff from surprise for a moment, but then his arms wrapped around Malriel and he returned the kiss, fervently, hungrily.

Eryn's eyes bulged and she shook her head, unwilling to believe what she was seeing. She wanted to interfere, stop this horseplay somehow, but found that she couldn't move, was frozen into place.

After what seemed like an eternity, the two kissers released each other again.

Malriel smiled in wonder and lifted her hand to caress his cheek. "I cannot tell you how long I have wanted to do this but were afraid how you would react. When I was up there, locked in that dreadful cell, under threat of a death sentence, I swore to myself that I would, should some miracle help me to return here, finally go through with it and risk being pushed away."

Valrad closed his eyes and shook his head. "Fools, the both of us. I wish you had done this years ago. And I wish I had not been such a coward myself. An Aren woman is only conquered by a strong man, after all."

"You stop this right now!" Eryn whispered, wide-eyed and dumbfounded.

Malriel looked at her daughter and sighed. "I suppose I better spend the night at the Vel'kim residence tonight. I do not have the feeling that three Aren women under one roof is going to be a good idea right now. Mother, I trust I can rely on you to take care of Maltheá."

Malhora did not dignify that statement with an answer but just raised her brow.

Orrin stood at the top of the stairs with Vern, both of them hastily stepping aside when Valrad and Malriel walked past them hand in hand, smiling at each other.

"Can I stay here?" Vran'el grimaced. "I do not want to spend the night under the same roof as those two. I would say they will not take kindly to company tonight."

Malhora nodded briskly. "Orrin will show you to a spare guestroom."

Orrin nodded and followed the instruction he had just been given, preceding Vran'el and leading him to an empty guestroom close to Vern's.

"They just..." Eryn stammered and raised her hand towards where her parents had just disappeared. She shook her head and let herself sink back into the cushions, burying her face in her hands. This was her fault, she thought. She had wondered if this night could become any worse, and alas, an answer had been provided swiftly enough.

She looked up when Vern sat down next to her and squeezed her shoulder.

"Come on, Eryn. Having your parents reunited is not the worst thing that can happen to a woman," he ventured.

"Don't," she grimaced, "just don't. What are you even doing here? I thought you were supposed to be with your lover tonight."

"Father picked me up after he had roused Valrad. He probably thought that he would need reinforcements," he smiled, clearly only half-joking.

"Eryn?"

She looked up at Enric, waiting for him to go on.

"I would very much like to meet my son," he said quietly.

She stared into his eyes, blue, deep and calm like the sea on a pleasant day. She remembered the tear that he had shed tonight when she had told him that nothing untoward had happened between Ram'an and her. There was still a trace down his cheek on his dusty face.

He was back, truly. And he was still hers, even though he would soon enough find out that there was quite some way to go for him to make amends. He would have to work on repairing what he had damaged, and she would not make it any easier for him than it should be.

She nodded and accepted his hand to let herself be tugged up.

"You'd better go and wash your hands and face first. I will await you here with him when you return."

She watched him nod and turn to do what she had bidden. She found she had handled matters with extreme restraint considering the circumstances and the fact that she had only recently caused a large roof to collapse when she had lost control over herself.

At least so far nobody had thought of replacing the golden belt on her waist.

CHAPTER 7

At the Senate

Eryn blinked against the sunlight that teased her through closed lids from a slit between the curtains.

"Good morning, my love," Enric's voice came from the bed right next to her.

She swallowed and turned slowly. So it had not been a strange dream, he truly had returned.

There he sat, leaning against the headboard of the bed, holding his son in his arm, swaying him gently and looking down at him with a mix of awe and bliss.

"Good morning," she replied, still at a loss how to deal with him.

They had been separated for only three weeks, but so much had changed in the meantime that she had yet to find a place for him in there somewhere. There had been no child when he had left, for one. And she had not been Head of a House. Then there were her concerns over the orphanage she was in the middle of founding and which he didn't even know of yet. She had basically built up a whole new life in this brief period. And now she needed to work out how he fit in there somewhere.

She sat up awkwardly, wondering if permitting him to spend the night in what used to be their bed had been a good idea. He had not exactly told her that he would have spurned the alternative, but when he told her of how much he had suffered from their separation, both physically thanks to the third level bond and emotionally due to his love for her, it had been more or less implied that he would not agree to spending their first night under the same roof anywhere else than in the same bed as her.

He might have complied if she had insisted, she considered. But then the thought of spending the night close to him, for once not being lonely, had been so very tempting that she had not mastered the strength to deny it to herself. And true enough, there had not been any nightmares this time, though this might just as well have been the same if Ram'an had stayed with her instead, not necessarily due to Enric's actual presence. Pretending that Ram'an's arm had been Enric's had worked just as well. A woman just needed to know how to trick herself.

"He favours me," Enric smiled. "Apart from his hair colour, of course."

Eryn sighed and got up from the bed to open the curtains. "Yes, I know."

"You don't sound too happy about that," he ventured, his tone serious.

She looked out into the gardens, watching Urban dozing in a shady spot under a tree, and kept her back turned to him when she nodded.

"I wasn't. Looking at him reminded me of you. And thinking of you made me either angry or pained me."

She turned when he didn't reply.

His expression had turned sad and he was shaking his head slightly. "I am sorry you had to go through this. I love you."

"Don't. Please. I don't want to hear this when I am angry at you. This is not a magic spell you can use to get everything back to how it was. It is neither a justification, nor an excuse for going over my head like this."

He nodded and looked at her for an uncomfortably long time. "So I may say it again when you are not angry at me anymore?"

"I think, yes," she confirmed and then added briskly, "But do not expect this to be anytime soon. It may be quite a while until I am done being angry at you."

"I understand," he just said.

And he did. He knew he was lucky that she was even talking to him, let alone permitting him to sleep next to her.

Considering everything that had happened, especially yesterday night, or rather early this morning, she had been handling matters extremely well. Knocking him out after he had taken the belt off her had been a minor thing considering that she had been suspecting him of leaving her for Malriel. And then there had been the shock of seeing that Valrad and Malriel had obviously never really lost their deep affection for each other. She had only just managed to accept Valrad as her father, and now this was another blow. House Vel'kim had in the past always been a safe haven for her when Malriel had caused trouble. In the future, that would probably not be as easy.

"The triarchy has already sent out the invitations for the Senate meeting in the afternoon. Valrad has informed them of our return," Enric told her.

She nodded. "Alright, that doesn't leave us too much time. Will you hand him over? I better feed him now or there is little chance that he will behave while we are at the Senate."

Enric watched while she unbuttoned her nightshirt and then took the baby to place him with casual skill into the exact, perfect position to access her nipple. She had already got into a routine while Enric was gone.

He watched the tranquil picture and wondered what else he had missed apart from being at her side during the birth. There were so many things he wanted to tell her, to ask her, but he knew he had to hold back for now until she allowed him to get closer to her again.

Yet being near her, watching her, being able to smell and touch her even though there was currently a certain distance from her side was still infinitely preferable to being separated.

"There are a few things I should take care of before the meeting," she said into his thoughts. "Can you manage to look after your son for about two hours? I am sure Malhora and Junar will aid you if there are any difficulties. I need to see Ram'an."

"Of course. I would be delighted to."

"Or you could take a walk with him if you want. To the Vel'kim residence," she suggested casually. That way Malriel could have a look at her grandson without having to come over here today.

Judging from Enric's quiet smile he was guessing in what direction her thoughts were going.

* * *

Ram'an kissed her on both cheeks and handed her a moist towel before walking on ahead on his terrace and out into the garden.

"What is it I can do for you today, Theá? I admit I am rather surprised that you came here. I would have thought that you were enjoying the reunion with your companion."

She scowled. "I wish it were that simple. I am afraid I have not yet really forgiven him for abandoning me like that. And learning that he kept the bloody bond intact all the time didn't serve to make me more well-disposed towards him, either." Her eyes narrowed. "Which brings me to another little thing I couldn't help but wonder about. You were one of those to remove the bond from me, so you must have known that his end was still intact. And yet you didn't tell me!"

"You are right, I was aware of it. But Enric made us all swear not to inform you. Your brother was rather angry at him because of it. I assume that the beginning of their journey was not the most harmonious one."

Shaking her head, she leaned against a tall tree. "I didn't shield my emotions, so I inadvertently shared every private feeling with him, not aware that I was opening up a lot more than I would have wanted. That was not fair."

"Not, it was not," he confirmed calmly, then a small smile curved his lips. "But I dare say that you may consider yourselves even on that account at least."

She frowned. "Why?"

"He felt every strong emotion you experienced, including also pain."

"Yes, so what of it? So he knows now that I was heartbroken after he left. That has probably even flattered him."

He sighed. "Think! What was the most painful occasion you had to endure in these last three weeks?"

"Well, apart from the birth there was..." She sucked in a sharp breath. "The birth! Does that mean that he went through that too with me? All of it?"

"I would assume so, yes," Ram'an nodded. "So he may not have been with you, but he surely experienced his share of it."

Eryn exhaled deeply. The pain had been excruciating - that birth had been the most agonising occurrence in her life so far. Now she did begin to feel sympathy for him. She at least had been presented with a result afterwards. He had been stuck in another country without any visible reward afterwards that showed him that this torture had been worth enduring.

"I can see that you have just mellowed a little bit," the lawyer smiled. "Tell me why you are visiting me today. What can I do for you?"

She sat down on the grass, careful to stay in the shadow. "I need to hang on to my position of Head of House Aren for a bit longer. I need your help here. I didn't want to ask Malhora, I have no idea on whose side she is, mine or Malriel's."

"I take it this has something to do with the orphanage project? You probably want to make sure it cannot be stopped so easily once Malriel is back in charge."

"Exactly."

"Does Malriel know of this?"

"If she doesn't by now she will certainly learn of it before the Senate meeting. I sent Enric to the Vel'kim residence and I would be surprised if this matter remained unmentioned. Valrad surely wants to avoid that Malriel learns about it in the course of the Senate meeting and throws a fit there in front of everyone but rather in the privacy of his own home."

He raised an eyebrow at her. "So after she hears that you have committed to spending most of her savings she will at the meeting learn that you intend to hold on to the position she doubtlessly expects to take back today? I wonder if the newly repaired roof will be up to the challenge."

"There are enough magicians around to protect the people in the building, and House Aren can afford to pay for another reconstruction," she shrugged. "So, tell me what I can to do remain in power for the time being."

Ram'an pursed his lips while thinking the matter through. "You were given the responsibility by the last Head of House Aren, namely Enric. That means that the appointment is valid, especially as it has been done before the Senate and was officially acknowledged and confirmed. A Head of House cannot normally be stripped of their title without substantial reasons such as misconduct, criminal activity, betrayal, or for any other reason that would result in causing harm to the family - such as incompetence."

"I don't think that I could be accused of any of those. I never intentionally harmed House Aren or broke any laws. As for incompetence, I always made sure to consult you or Malhora if something important had to be decided. That means I shouldn't have made a mess of anything so far. Does that mean I am more or less immune to whatever means she will undoubtedly use to get rid of me?"

"From where I stand there are not many options for her. And considering that your father is the Head of House Vel'kim she needs to be careful not to do anything extreme that would anger him. Since they are apparently now also lovers she will surely be eager not to hurt him by attacking you."

Eryn smiled broadly. "This is excellent news, my friend. You know, now I am even looking forward to that Senate meeting."

"What will Enric think of your remaining in power? Do you know if he has any plans to return to Anyueel soon? With Malriel back he probably counted on being released from Takhan."

"To be honest with you, I don't care a lot about his plans right now. He is currently eager to accommodate me, so even if he is angry at me after that, I trust he won't be so for long." She chuckled. "You know, this is the very first time I have found myself in a position of authority when it comes to Enric. Now that he is not in the Order any longer, I am not subordinate to him. And I am his Head of House."

Ram'an grinned. "Devious, Theá. I bow to you. Yet there is one little matter you might want to take into consideration here. One that could thwart your plans quite effectively, after all."

She frowned. "Such as?"

"Your King. He still has a hold on you thanks to your second level commitment bond to his Kingdom. He might summon you to return now that Malriel is back. Especially if she asks him to do just that to make you give up your position."

"The King still owes me something for kissing me to provoke Enric into leaving Anyueel. I dare say a friendly message where I tell him that I would appreciate being granted another two months here should do the trick. Particularly if I promise to bring back Enric and to be a good girl after my return."

"A good girl?" Ram'an laughed. "I am sure King Folrin will not be able to resist an offer like that. Especially as refusing it would very likely result in your being a bad girl."

"I am confident that he won't. Especially as I am doing it for the purposes of what he likes to call political strategy."

They both looked up when Intrea stepped outside through the terrace door, barefoot, wearing nothing but a long, sleeveless shirt that reached her knees.

Eryn raised a brow at him. "You know, I still find it immensely disturbing that you are having sex with my brother's companion."

Intrea laughed and shook her head before sinking down on the grass. "But the thought of your brother having a very handsome lover himself is no problem at all for you, then?"

"It is, really. I have to fight the urge to shake Neval every time I see him, tell him to stop it all and remind him that my brother is in a companionship." She smirked. "Then I shall take a moment to return to reality and remember that the world is not quite as simple as that. Have you seen Vran'el yet, by the way?"

Intrea snorted. "What do you think? Of course I have. As soon as I heard that he was back I marched over to the Vel'kim residence and gave him an earful for not sending for me after his arrival. He gave me some petty excuse of not wanting to wake me in the middle of the night - but how ridiculous is that, I ask you? I would gladly have sacrificed a few hours of sleep in exchange for knowing that he was back safely. When something bad happens nobody hesitates when it comes to waking people, yet once there is a positive, joyous occasion suddenly there is consideration." She shrugged and rolled her eyes. "Men!" Then she grinned broadly. "Ram'an told me about your own reunion with Enric. How your companion found the two of you in one bed. Funny, really, how Ram'an has pursued you so relentlessly, and when he finally ends up in bed with you, nothing had even happened."

"Intrea," Ram'an sighed, "Eryn is no longer wearing the golden belt, in case you failed to notice this. Irritating her has become rather dangerous again."

"Nobody has put the belt back on you?" Intrea frowned. "But it has been a mere two weeks since the birth, has it not? You should still be wearing it from what I remember."

"Probably," Eryn smiled thinly. "Yet nobody was brave enough to try that. I wonder why. Are you volunteering, my dear?"

Intrea swallowed and shook her head. "You know, if Valrad has not seen fit to do it, who am I to question this course of action?"

Ram'an chuckled. "What a pity. I would have loved to see you try."

* * *

Enric followed Valrad and Malriel through the city towards the Senate hall, his son strapped across his chest with a length of colourful cloth. His head was still reeling from all the things he had heard from Valrad in these last two hours.

He had obviously missed quite a bit more than Vedric's birth. He had sat with Eryn's parents in the Vel'kim main room on the cushions and Valrad had told him and Malriel what had been going on in these last three weeks.

Malriel had cussed colourfully when she had learned about Sanaf's efforts to harm her daughter, and even more when Valrad had elaborated on the measures her friend Legara had seen as the appropriate punishment. What is more, it looked as if Legara had been the one to provoke Eryn enough to give birth more than a month too early. That woman was talented when it came to irking powerful people, one had to give her that.

Enric was of course immensely glad that this issue had finally been resolved, but as Ram'an had been instrumental in achieving it, he owed the Head of House Arbil now quite a lot more than a mere apology for knocking him out the night before.

Valrad had then talked about Eryn's discovering the shacks of the poor and what plans she had subsequently presented to the Senate to take care of things there. And how she intended to fund them. Malriel had gone pale at hearing that.

Enric had worked hard at appearing sympathetic. She would not have reacted well to the broad grin that had wanted to spread on his face. So Eryn had finally worked out a way to get back at her mother, and an immensely effective one, too. Elegant and in accordance with her own beliefs and values. He was truly impressed. And proud. She was slowly but steadily turning into a formidable opponent. If she continued like that, the King and Tyront would have to tread carefully around her. As would he himself.

Another detail that Malriel had not taken too well was that her mother and her daughter seemed to be getting along quite famously.

She had been sitting there for what must have been several minutes, not speaking a word, just staring ahead unseeingly, probably working on a strategy that would get her back in control somehow.

Finally she had looked up and demanded to hold her grandson. Enric had handed him over reluctantly, but holding her first and probably only grandchild was no unreasonable request. Yet he would have felt better if she had not just fought down very obvious urges to destroy something.

Holding the child in her arms had calmed her considerably, though. He had been surprised at that. Somehow the idea that a new-born child could have that effect on Malriel of House Aren had seemed absurd. He had remembered his demand to her back in Kar, when he had warned her not to treat his son in the typical Aren manner and wondered if she was planning to adhere to it, or if she was even able to.

They reached the steps to the Senate hall and saw Eryn and Ram'an approaching from the direction of the Arbil residence. She let Valrad greet her with a kiss on her forehead and nodded once to Malriel before stepping towards Enric.

"How did you manage with him?" she enquired and inspected her son as if taking inventory of all limbs still being attached correctly.

"I am happy to say that I braved the challenge masterfully, even if I do say so myself. I am surprised you have to ask," he replied good-naturedly, wondering how she would react if he kissed her here and now. It was probably better to try it at home instead of here in public before the last Senate meeting she had to attend as Head of House Aren.

When they ascended the stairs, Malriel hissed into her ear, "You and I, we will have to talk. I have heard of your plans with my savings. You will stop this frivolity at once, do you hear me?"

Eryn lifted one eyebrow and walked on without commenting. Malriel would see soon enough how good her chance of preventing the project was.

Once they had entered the hall Eryn couldn't help but look up at the ceiling. It had been repaired in record time. It clearly was an advantage to have magicians who were working in different professions. The only thing that was still missing was the artwork, and from what she had heard the two academies were competing for the privilege.

She waved to Vran'el who had already taken his seat next to where his father would sit. It was good to see him there again, it had been odd to see the place empty. Depressing. Worrying.

Malhora, too, was already waiting, comfortably settled in one of the chairs for the Aren senators. Eryn took a deep breath. She was curious to see how the old woman would react to watching her daughter being denied her position as Head of House.

"I dare say we may just as well walk on ahead to the triarchy," Malriel suggested. "As we are the reason for the meeting there is no other business they have to deal with today. We may just as well be ready to address the Senate."

Vern approached them from the area where a large number of watchers had assembled and cleared his throat, nodding at Vedric.

"Would you like me to take him for now as long as you address the Senate?"

Enric shook his head. He had no intention of parting with the warm, soft bundle against his chest, the tiny fist that rested on the fabric of his tunic.

"No, thank you, Vern. I would rather keep him close to me for a while longer. I feel I have to make up for the two weeks I lost with him."

Eryn swallowed when she caught the words and made herself look straight ahead instead of at her companion. If he continued like that she would be forgiving him a lot faster than she had intended to.

"I think this is the first time ever when somebody is to address the Senate with a child slung across their chest," Malhora chuckled. "But that is alright. Arens like to be the trendsetters in all areas."

The hall fell silent as the three triarchs mounted their pedestal and took their seats.

Torke'na was the one to speak, just as usual.

"Welcome back in Takhan, Malriel," she smiled faintly. "It is good to have you back in good health." Her gaze wandered to Vran'el who had decided to remain seated, and then to Enric. "And it is also a relief to have the two of you back after you rushed off so valiantly to aid Malriel in her hour of need. Malriel, we are all curious about what you have to tell us about your experiences in Pirinkar. And of course about the events that terminated your stay so abruptly, namely your being accused of a crime."

Malriel nodded and turned to address the Senate. The senators were clearly eager to learn of her stay in foreign parts. Not many had had that chance so far.

"A good day to all of you, my friends and colleagues! I cannot tell you how much good it does me to see you all, to be back among you," Malriel smiled.

Eryn was surprised to see that it was a genuine expression, not merely a polite one. She really was glad to be here.

She then started talking about her preparations for the negotiations, specifically settling down in Kar first of all, which had taken quite some time owing to the bureaucratic system there requiring a lot of administrative gymnastics. Then she had been introduced to the people who would be negotiating with her, which was a fairly large number as they had the custom of having each and every part taken care of by another expert in their particular area.

Eryn listened attentively, but found her gaze inadvertently drawn to the tall, blond man at the speaker's side. His eyes rested on her, a faint smile on his lips. One of his hands caressed the small head against his chest absentmindedly while he kept looking at her as if there was no other sight worth paying attention to in the hall.

She swallowed and looked away again, back at Malriel, but more than aware of his attention. Exhaling slowly, she forced herself to refrain from fidgeting. Why did he manage to make her nervous by merely looking at her?

Malriel's narrative had in the meantime arrived at that point of the night in question when a certain young priest had invited her to leave the social gathering they had both been attending in order to show her the view over the city of Kar from the temple where he worked and lived. After imparting how she had then been discovered naked in the man's bed with his being chained in gold to the very same, and subsequently being locked up and accused of using her magical powers to force a man to have sexual intercourse with her, she stopped and turned to Enric.

"I would ask you to continue from here, Enric. My role was from then on a rather passive one. You were the one to secure my release, after all."

He nodded and reluctantly tore away his gaze from Eryn to address the Senate and tell them about how he had managed to convince the judges and government representatives to let him teach five of their high priests how to apply a lie filter to be able to question both the young priest who had accused Malriel and also the accused herself. He continued with how the second hearing had revealed the man's attempt to obtain an unjust judgement for her and with Malriel's own testimony that had cleared her.

Malriel waited for him to finish, then turned back towards the triarchy.

"As you can see, I decided not to continue the negotiations on account of the damage it undoubtedly did to my reputation. I did, however, manage to make them agree to another delegate being sent there as my replacement who will continue where my efforts were interrupted. For now there is no imminent danger of war as they have agreed not to launch any hostile actions as long as both sides are still willing to find a diplomatic solution, a compromise, in the dispute. They have agreed to establishing a temporary ambassador in Kar. If the negotiations lead to a treaty, they will in the course of time send one of their own to Takhan."

Eryn exhaled in relief and saw most of the other senators and also the observers behind the last row of seats reacting in a similar manner. Malriel might not have been able to reach a final conclusion of things as such, but she had certainly avoided a war for the time being and had established promising conditions for whoever might go there next.

"As our neighbour's perception of magic is not quite as positive as our own, I would strongly recommend sending a non-magician to Kar. Somebody with diplomatic skills and experience in negotiating," Malriel concluded.

Eryn groaned inwardly when a person who fit those requirements most definitely came to her mind. Damn. But if she acted quickly, there might be something in it for herself.

"I vote against sending Erbál of House Feral to Kar," she suddenly announced unbidden and made all heads in the hall turn towards her.

Golir blinked. "I was not aware that we were voting on that. Or that there was even any proposal to send him there."

She shook her head impatiently. "Of course somebody will make that proposal! He is the most suitable and able candidate there is."

Golir looked at her indulgently. "Then I wonder, Maltheá, why you would be against offering him this position?"

"He is mine! I requested him and you granted him to me. And you owe me something after first sending Sanaf and all I had to endure because of him after I came here," she pointed out.

"So what you are asking us, Maltheá, is to decide in a way that would cater to your own personal preferences instead of following the path that would be most promising in establishing permanent peace with the country of Pirinkar?" Golir asked slowly, his expression making it clear that he was annoyed at such unthinking selfishness.

Enric frowned as well. This did appear rather clumsy, he couldn't help but think. She had managed to phrase this in a way that made sending Erbál the best solution and her being against it a matter of catering to her own whims. That didn't make her look good, and that she had to be aware of. He watched in fascination when a small smile curved her lips upwards.

"It does sound rather egoistic if you put it like that, doesn't it?" she admitted gently. "I wonder if there isn't another way to ensure that you may send the best person available to Kar, and that Anyueel still gets a more suitable ambassador than Erbál's predecessor."

Golir exhaled loudly and shook his head at her. "I see. And am I right in assuming that making certain of this by taking an active role in the selection of such a candidate would be acceptable to you, Maltheá of House Vel'kim?"

Eryn pretended to think for a moment, then nodded hesitantly. "Yes, I think I will accept your offer and thank you very much for taking my concerns into consideration. Only in the case there is such a motion about relocating the current ambassador to Anyueel, of course."

"I propose sending Erbál of House Feral to Kar to act as our temporary ambassador and continue the negotiations Malriel of House Aren was forced to cut short", Ram'an spoke up. "He is a trained diplomat and experienced negotiator, which makes him the most suitable candidate, in addition he is a member of one of the Houses. What is more, he meets the requirement of being a non-magician that Malriel has pointed out as an important consideration."

Enric smiled at the triumph he felt through the mind bond. He regretted that her end of the bond was not intact anymore and making her unable to feel how immensely proud and impressed he was right now.

Golir rolled his eyes. "Thank you so much, Head of House Arbil. This obviously means that we need to vote on this matter right here and now. Senators, show of hands who is in favour of the motion."

"Eighteen votes against nine in favour of offering the position to Erbál of House Feral," Torke'na announced.

Golir's attention returned to Eryn. "Is there any other business you wish to address before we conclude this meeting? Such as a request to renew your third level commitment bond, perhaps?"

She straightened. "That is indeed something I would very much like to discuss. Though I would prefer a less public setting for it if this is possible."

The triarch stared at her for a moment, then nodded. "We can talk about it following this meeting if you agree."

"Thank you, yes. I would like that very much."

"There is one minor issue I myself wish to take care of before we all leave," Malriel spoke up. "Maltheá, I thank you very much for taking over my House thereby enabling Enric to come and free me from my incarceration. I know that you never wished for this burden to be yours so I am all the more grateful for your taking it upon yourself. I would like to release you from the position and reassume my leadership of the Aren family."

Abrak, the third triarch who had so far not said a single word in the meeting, nodded. "The Senate herewith ackno..."

"Not so fast!" Eryn interrupted and leaned back in her chair, steepling her fingers the way Tyront back home liked to do. He probably knew that it tended to drive her crazy.

"I beg your pardon?" Abrak asked in confusion.

"I am not yet ready to give up my position as Head of House Aren," she announced, unruffled.

There were several seconds of utter silence before the murmurs and whispers exploded around her. She just smiled and observed Malriel, who was staring at her with narrowed eyes, her hands balled into fists.

"You step back this instant or I will make you pay," Malriel growled, her eyes shining with a dangerous glint.

"I don't think so, mother," she retorted, noticing Malhora's smile at the address in just the tone she herself had to endure from Malriel. "Your current lover wouldn't like it if you really threatened his daughter, would he now?"

She saw Valrad leaning forward and close his eyes, shaking his head. It seemed that this was not quite the way he had intended to make his involvement with Malriel public.

"I demand that Maltheá be removed from her current position," Malriel called out, staring at the triarchs one after the other.

"What do you accuse her of?" Torke'na asked simply.

"Accuse? Currently of usurping my position!"

Eryn grimaced in mock sympathy. "Dear me, I am afraid that is not quite enough. You see, I was appointed officially and with due consideration, confirmed by the Senate three weeks ago. To be removed from office would require a valid reason, I am told. A reason such as causing harm to my House intentionally or unintentionally through incompetence, for example. Or breaking the law in some way."

Malriel closed her eyes and breathed in and out several times, fighting to keep in whatever violent urges that were currently battling to get out.

Eryn saw a number of the senators glance up at the newly repaired ceiling as if to make sure that there were no cracks showing or dust floating down.

The people around her waited silently as if afraid to move and trigger some kind of reaction in her.

Malriel opened her eyes again a few moments later. Eryn had to give it to her - she certainly knew how to get herself under control again. She looked almost relaxed, and there was even a smile.

"Maltheá, as I am not aware of any misconduct on your side I have no valid argument to take away the position of Head of House Aren from you. You shall therefore remain in power. For now. Do not make any mistake about my efforts being of a short duration. I will get my House back. You may depend on it. Though there is certainly one point you can no longer deny: you clearly are an Aren, no matter how fervently you wish to distance yourself from your roots."

Eryn smiled back with the same lack of warmth, mirroring the expression on Malriel's face and making the resemblance even more stunningly obvious to those around them.

"I can disperse your concerns about that, mother. I am glad to say that since I have got to know my grandmother better, being of Aren blood has certainly lost most of its terror."

"The Senate is dismissed," Golir declared and rose from his seat.

Malriel turned on her heel and walked towards the closest exit, stopping when Legara of House Finran put a hand on her arm.

"Malriel, I am so glad you are back," Legara murmured. "And I am so sorry about Maltheá's conduct just now. If there is anything I can do to support you in returning to your..."

Her eyes bulged when Malriel's grip at her throat cut off the words.

"You listen very carefully to me, Legara," Malriel purred in a threatening, low voice that was nevertheless clearly audible thanks to the audience that had once more fallen completely silent and was watching in fascinated horror. "I would not even accept your help if I were stuck in the middle of the desert without water and about to die of thirst, you pathetic excuse for a Head of House. A member of your House wilfully endangered my guests' lives, among them my daughter and my grandson. And you found it suitable to petition for no more than a token punishment." Her fingers gripped Legara's throat a little tighter. "This is an insult to House Aren. And to me. This is not the kind of alliance I wish to continue as it lacks the respect and trust I offer my allies and ask of them in return." Then, having held Legara long enough in a throat clench for her eyes to show genuine fear for her life, she released her and walked on unperturbed, not bothering to look back but stepping outside into the bright afternoon light, taking a deep breath before descending the stairs.

The Senate hall emptied slowly after that, as if both the senators and the observers were reluctant to leave, greedy for more drama and wondering if whatever Maltheá of House Vel'kim, Head of House Aren had to discuss with the triarchy would qualify as such.

Once only Eryn, Enric, Valrad, Vran'el, Ram'an and the three triarchs were left, Golir lifted his hand and the three mighty double doors around them were pulled shut.

"What is it you wish to discuss, Maltheá?" he then asked.

"I know that you must be aware of the one-sided dissolution of the commitment bond between Enric and me," she stated and waited for his nod. "I demand for it to be removed from Enric as well. One side of the mind bond is still intact and he can still receive my feelings through the connection. I consider this a violation of privacy and want it rectified."

Golir nodded slowly. "And understandable sentiment. Enric? What do you have to say about this?"

Enric smiled thinly. "I wish for the third level bond to be restored completely to its former state."

All eyes were on Golir now, waiting for what he would decree. He stared at both of them, then turned his head to Ram'an.

"I do not remember any precedent of this kind. I cannot force one of them into the bond, and neither can I forcefully remove it from the other without good reason. Are you aware of any legal provisions to proceed in a case such as this?"

Ram'an slowly shook his head. "No, I am afraid I cannot help you here. You are right - there has not been any case like this that I can recall, especially considering the rather problematic additional aspect of a mind bond."

Eryn sighed heavily. "So I have no authority over Enric in this - neither as his Head of House nor as the wronged party in the commitment."

Ram'an grimaced. "No to both, Theá. Commitments are, as you were told before, not the Head's responsibility as soon as the third level bond has been granted. And as for your being the wronged party... that is a matter of perception, is it not? Enric wishes the bond to be re-established and may just as well call himself that. Legally speaking you are at an impasse here."

She swallowed and turned back to the triarchs. "How tightly are you bound to follow the laws when they fail to provide a solution for a particular situation? Are you at liberty to make a pronouncement in one party's favour here?"

Torke'na shook her head. "It would be to no avail, Maltheá. The other party would have powerful arguments to challenge the decision and invoke a Senate vote on it. This would undermine the triarchy's credibility."

"I am stuck in that half-bond now? So there is nothing you can do here?"

"Not as long as Enric is not willing to dissolve his side," Torke'na confirmed and looked at him questioningly.

Enric shook his head happily. "No, I have no intention whatsoever of doing so."

"We thus return the responsibility for finding a mutually satisfying agreement or compromise to you, Head of House Aren," Golir said pointedly, making it clear by using the title that he expected her to accept the decision as she was bound to.

"I am sorry, Maltheá," Torke'na said softly. "I wish there was a way for us to assist you in solving this."

She nodded in defeat. "Of course. I thank you for your time."

* * *

"What are you going to do now?" Vran'el asked after they had left the Senate hall.

Eryn shrugged dejectedly. "I have no idea." She looked up at Enric. "Any suggestions? Will we try to strong-arm each other into giving way for the months to come and see who will prevail?"

He shook his head and took her hand, glad that she didn't snatch it back, especially after the news just now. She was taking it amazingly well, he had to say.

"I respect that you do not want to re-enter into the bond with me for now. But my objective is to achieve just that, however long it may take. We will have to make a compromise here as neither of us is going to get what we want for now," he explained.

She narrowed her eyes. "I cannot help but think that your situation is a lot less unpleasant than mine. You still have access to my feelings, after all."

He raised an eyebrow. "To have you free of the magical commitment that pulls you back to me when we are apart is not something I value. You may thus rest safe in the knowledge that I, too, am dissatisfied enough with the current situation."

"Is there anything I can offer you to get you to dissolve your side as well?" she asked, without very much hope.

"Nothing at all. The connection to you, however painful at times, was what kept me upright when I was gone. I will not give it up. Is there in turn anything you might consider adequate compensation for joining me once again?"

"No, definitely not," she sighed and shook her head. "We truly are stuck."

He looked down at her. She looked resigned and unhappy. That was not what he wanted the connection to him to be like for her.

"Let me make you an offer." He waited for her to look up at him again. "You grant me six months, in the course of which I will do everything I can to make you want to join me again in the third level bond. After those six months there are three options and you may pick the one which appeals to you at that time. And I will accept your decision no matter what."

"Which options?" she asked suspiciously.

"You will either join me, ask me to dissolve my side of the bond, or leave things the way they are for another six months after which you will think about it again."

She stared at him, then nodded slowly. "Alright, that is a compromise I am willing to say yes to. And you will accept it should I decide to remove the bond? And comply without resisting?"

"I will," he promised solemnly. "Though I will first do my very best to convince you that this is not at all what you want. You are of course free to join me in the bond again earlier should the mood strike you," he smiled.

"Not that I do not trust you, Enric," Ram'an threw in before turning to Eryn, "but from a legal point of view I would recommend either a first level commitment or a written document to confirm this agreement."

Enric nodded and lifted his other hand up for her to take. "I have no objections."

Eryn swallowed. Accepting this offer would show a certain lack of trust, wouldn't it? Though she was tempted, there was no denying that. His proposal sounded almost too good to be true. She made herself shake her head and take a step back.

"No, that will not be necessary. You are known to be a man of your word and I trust you to keep your promise."

Ram'an shrugged. "Alright, I think the fact that you have three witnesses to confirm his promise means that should he decide to succumb to a sudden loss of memory and you drag him before the triarchy in six months it is still going to help your case."

Enric narrowed his eyes at him. "Why do I have the strong impression that you are against me?"

"Because you knocked me out last night without a valid reason and I have yet to receive an apology for it."

"You are right," the blond magician sighed. "This is overdue. Ram'an, please accept my apology for accusing you of taking advantage of my companion and knocking you out without giving you the chance to correct my impression last night. Especially as you were only trying to help Eryn to have a peaceful night. And in addition to this I wish to thank you for looking after her and assisting her in both looking after House Aren and finding the perpetrator of the attacks."

"Apology accepted," the lawyer replied grandly. "Now you need to excuse me, my brother has asked me to accompany him to a gathering."

"I think we'd better return," Eryn suggested with a look at the sky. "I don't want to expose Vedric to the sun for too long. Will the two of you be coming along, too?"

Vran'el shook his head. "I would rather return home if you do not mind."

Valrad put an arm around his son's shoulders. "Then I will come with you. We will have a glass of wine and celebrate that I have two of my three children back here in Takhan again."

They both kissed Eryn goodbye and went off towards their residences.

Enric set in motion, holding on to her hand she had still not withdrawn, linking his fingers with hers. He felt her hesitation for a short moment before her muscles relaxed again. It was frustrating to worry if his every touch would cause her to retreat, as if they were back in his quarters one and a half years ago when she was his prisoner.

But he had conquered her back then; he could do it again.

"Valrad told you about my newest venture, I imagine?" she said into his thoughts.

"He did, yes."

"This is my revenge on Malriel for the fertility potion."

"I gathered as much, yes."

"I need you to let me do this, even though you get along with her so well. I cannot have you siding with her or refunding the expenses."

"I wouldn't dream of it," he said simply.

She nodded, relieved. "Good. So I don't have to forbid it as your new Head of House."

He chuckled. "No, there is no need for that. About that little matter. How long are you planning to hold on to this position? You must be aware that the King and Tyront will not let us stay here much longer now that Malriel is available to take back her House."

"I know. I have written to the King to grant me another two months here. I want to make sure the orphanage is far enough along not to be stopped just like that anymore."

"You know that I will fund it in case she somehow manages to put a stop to the outlay from the House, don't you?" he asked softly.

She nodded without looking at him. "I had a feeling that you would. I feel there is quite a lot you would do right now."

He stopped and held on to her hand so that she had to half-turn and look at him. "This is nothing more than I would have done anyway, even without this whole conflict of interests."

Eryn sighed. She could see that even though his voice was calm, there was a faint trace of anger in the set of his jaw; it was recognisable even without the mind bond.

"I am sorry. I know. I didn't mean to imply that you were anything but generous. Ever. I am still getting used to this strangeness, this awkwardness between us now that you are back." She looked away again, resuming their walk. "I was ready to let go of you only last night when I thought that you wanted Malriel. I planned to see Iklan today to help me leave the pain behind me. And only several hours later we are walking along the street together. This is just a bit much."

He nodded wordlessly. It seemed he had returned just in time.

CHAPTER 8

Under One Roof

They heard two female voices exchanging angry words when they opened the door to the Aren residence.

"You brought this upon yourself, Malriel," they heard Malhora snap. "What did you expect?"

"I know that you must have showed her the vault! This is your fault, mother!" Malriel hissed back.

They both fell silent when the entrance door clicked shut.

When Eryn and Enric entered the main room a little later, both women had taken a seat on the seating cushions opposite each other, exchanging hostile glares.

"The two of you will either keep a civilised tone in my house or you leave. I have no intention of exposing my son to your bickering," Eryn stated and took a seat next to her grandmother before turning to Enric and unwrapping her shirt. "Hand him to me, will you? It's time for his feed. Well, one of them."

"Your house indeed," she heard Malriel growl and sent her a look from narrowed eyes.

"What was that? And what are you doing here, anyway? I had counted on your moving in with Valrad. Or was that a one-night thing between you?"

"I am here, Malthéa, because I happen to live here. Though it seems as though I have to make do with a guest room in my own house since my mother has commandeered my bedroom," Malriel replied, careful to keep her voice calm. "And no, this was not a one-night thing, as you like to put it so eloquently. Not that this is any of your business, mind you."

"It was my bedroom before it was yours," Malhora shrugged. "And Enric was so kind as to offer it to me when I came here."

Enric decided against joining them and leaned against a wall, choosing a spot where he could watch his companion and his son. He had no intention of being anything but an observer here. Yet with his son amidst three Aren women it was probably advisable to stay close in case he needed to be evacuated.

"Of course not, mother. Your affairs are your business entirely. Yet I can't help but take an interest in that particular one as he is my

Head of House and I am yours," she remarked lightly, delighted at the spark of annoyance her words caused.

"I want my House back, Maltheá," Malriel then spoke after several moments of silence.

"I was assuming you did," Eryn nodded unperturbed, noting the conspiratorial grin on Malhora's face.

"How long do you want to play this game?" her mother asked with a calm that was clearly forced.

"Until the orphanage is up and running, at the least. I don't want you hampering progress as soon as I am gone. And then we will see. I am starting to get comfortable in my new role. It affords me a position of authority over my companion for the very first time, after all. I might decide to enjoy it for a bit longer." She winced at a slightly painful tug on her nipple.

"I will write to Folrin to order you back," Malriel announced and all but jumped up.

"Let me save you the trouble, mother. I have written to him already and I am confident that he will grant my humble request before your message reaches him. By then he will not be able to comply with yours anymore as stepping back from a favour once granted would not look good for him, would it?"

"Stop calling me that!"

"Mother?" Eryn looked at her, all astonishment. "Why ever would you object to my addressing you as such when you kept telling everyone that a legal arrangement can never disrupt blood bonds?"

"You know what I mean! I want you to stop using that tone." Malriel's gaze came to rest on her mother. "That is your doing, I just know it! How did you get her to play your little game, mother? I hear you have taken to calling her Eryn. Was that her price to help you annoy me?"

Malhora just smiled malevolently.

"Let us talk like grown up people, alright? Theá, I have been saving this money for a long time to buy myself an estate when I retire from my position of Head of House and move to the countryside."

Eryn nodded. "I know. Yet after looking at the books I couldn't help but notice that we own quite a few estates already. You are very welcome to move to one of them. I don't see why it is necessary for you to acquire another one."

"This is a way to have something of my own that is not subject to the command of the new Head of House, but mine. And after my death it will become one of the Aren assets and thus increase the House's wealth," she explained with obvious self-control.

"That is unfortunate for you, then. I intend to put the money to good use by providing shelter and food for not only one person, but for many. And then you can start saving again as soon as you are back in office. I am confident that you will be able to afford a nice little plantation in another, say, twenty years. You know why I am doing this, don't you?"

Malriel didn't reply to that and just folded her arms.

"Do you or do you not know why I am doing this to you, mother?" Eryn repeated her last question. "I wouldn't want to think that you are not aware of the reason why I am taking revenge on you. Especially as it obviously hits you as hard as I was hoping it would. This is a little payback for slipping me that potion, in case you hadn't worked it out."

"What is to keep me from putting a stop to this nonsense as soon as you are gone from here? You will not hold this position for so very long, I am sure of it. Folrin will order you back sooner or later, and then your pet project will be at my mercy. What would stop me from closing it down again?" Malriel hissed.

"The reputation of House Aren, I would say," Eryn replied with a cool smile. "The thing is, you see, that I informed the Senate that House Aren would continue to fund the running of the orphanage as long as we are able to afford it. Your withdrawing the funding would imply that our financial standing is problematic. This might induce the Houses to think twice about whether doing business with us is advisable, and means the damage would very likely in the long run be greater than simply paying for food, clothes and education of the children, you see? Especially as House Aren has in turn been granted tax relief, which would go in addition to those decreasing profits."

She saw Enric grinning broadly at that. So obviously Valrad had not told them about that little detail so far.

Malriel closed her eyes for a moment, then nodded stiffly. "Well played, Malthéa, well played indeed. If you would excuse me now, I need to lie down for a bit."

* * *

Malriel removed the used dishes after everyone had finished their dinner and was leaning back, sated and relaxed. Téa on Junar's lap was happily sucking on her own fist and following the movements around her with big eyes.

Orrin got up to help Malriel, and Vern stood up as well and disappeared into the corridor that lead to his room, murmuring about having to fetch something.

When both of them had left the main room, Enric leaned closer to Eryn and whispered, "Is it only my impression or is there a certain coolness between Orrin and Vern?"

Eryn nodded. "Valrad has offered Vern a chance to stay here and continue his training in Takhan. And Orrin won't permit it. So Vern is angry at Orrin, Orrin is angry at Vern for wanting to stay here and also at Valrad for offering it in the first place. Valrad in turn is angry at Orrin for denying his son that chance."

Enric swallowed. As if having three generations of Aren women under one roof did not provide tension enough. It seemed as if Junar were currently the only one not angry at anybody.

Vern was the first to return, holding a drawing pad in one hand. He held it out for Enric to take.

"Here. This is for you."

"For me? What is it?"

"A few pictures I did. Things you missed," the boy explained and sat down next to Junar, lifting his sister from her lap to place her on his own instead and earning himself a smile from both mother and daughter.

Enric flipped the first page and laughed when he beheld the picture of smirking Malhora carrying a clearly unconscious Orrin over her shoulder like a sack, the Senate building in the background. Eryn, too, couldn't help but grin.

"That was after Golir and Ram'an made Sanaf admit to being behind all that trouble. Orrin was about to leap on him and I had to take him out. I suppose this picture is worse punishment than anything I could have done to him."

They turned the page and Eryn swallowed at that one. It showed herself in the centre of the Senate hall, looking lost and confused while staring up at the crumbling ceiling, Golir behind her on his pedestal, one hand lifted towards the ceiling where his shield kept the masonry from collapsing. Malhora and Valrad were visible as well, approaching her from different sides with worried expressions.

"That was when my waters broke." Eryn shook her head. "What a day."

Enric stared at her figure in different shades of grey and black on the paper. That must have been when he had received the first stab of panic through the mind bond.

He almost dreaded looking at the next picture. But it was a peaceful scene that showed her in what he assumed was a room at the clinic, holding Vedric in one arm, his tiny mouth wrapped around her nipple.

"The first time I fed him," she murmured next to him, touched at having this precious moment frozen in a way that would enable her to return to it and one day share it with her son when he was older.

The next drawing was again one of her feeding Vedric, though this time on the very cushions they were now sitting upon, Ram'an next to her with an expression that was both relaxed and a touch melancholic. Enric couldn't help but wonder if he had at that moment wished that it was his son she was holding like that.

Eryn flipped to the next page, uneasy about the picture that showed her with a bared breast next to Ram'an.

Again a drawing of her, this time in Malriel's study behind the sturdy desk, her chin propped on her fist, a loose strand of hair hanging down her cheek, her expression tired while she was looking at a sheet of paper in her hand.

Another picture showed Kilan with Vedric on his arm, slightly panicky as if afraid that he would break the baby if he wasn't careful enough.

Eryn smiled at the next one. Valrad holding his grandson on his arm, the other one around her shoulders, pressing her close, a blissful smile on his face.

"This is beautiful," Malriel's quiet voice said from behind them. She was looking over Enric's shoulder and swallowed. "I would be willing to pay handsomely for it."

Vern shrugged. "I gave them to Enric, they are his. But I can make you another one, if you like."

Malriel nodded. "I would very much like that, yes."

The next three pictures showed harmonious domestic scenes: Junar and Orrin, each of them holding a baby and grinning widely at each other; Malhora sitting in the garden with her great-grandson on her arm next to Eryn, who had her head tilted back to empty a glass of water, her shirt still half open to reveal the curve of one breast after feeding; Eryn bathing Vedric in the garden, Junar behind her with Téa sleeping in her arms, Orrin and Valrad exchanging a cool glance.

Enric smiled, at the same time glad for Eryn that she had experienced these peaceful moments, and sad that he himself had missed them.

"Go on," Eryn urged him. "I want to see the last one."

He obliged her and they looked at a picture of himself shortly after his return, sitting on the cushions, holding his son for the very first time, an expression of wonderment, of enchantment on his face, as if the world around him had ceased to exist and the small creature in his arm was the centre of all that was left.

Eryn stared down at the picture, swallowing hard. And a second time. She had stood behind him back then and had not seen his face. Had it not been for Vern's drawing, she would have missed it. That would have been a tragedy.

She lifted her hand to his chin and gently turned it towards her to press a kiss to his lips. Unlike when he had kissed her after his return, they were soft now; he had healed away the crusty scabs from the harsh climate in the meantime. She felt him exhale and lean into the kiss as if drinking in the simple, chaste touching of lips.

She leaned back after a few seconds, smiling and then nodding at the drawing pad.

"Vern," Enric said quietly and shook his head, for several moments at a loss for words. "This is incredible. A gift beyond value. I don't know what to say." He closed the pad again. "You have not only an amazing talent but the heart to use it to give such great joy to others. Should you ever find yourself in need of financial or any other support, I hope you will permit me to aid you however I can. It would be my honour. Withholding whatever chance for you to make use of your incredible potential would be a crime."

Their heads turned as one when Orrin pushed away from the wall he had been leaning against and turned without uttering a word to descend the stairs. A moment later they head the entrance door closing.

Eryn made to rise, but Enric took her hand and shook his head. "Let me. It should soon be time for Vedric, so you'd better stay."

It didn't take him long to catch up with the warrior on the street.

"What do you want?" Orrin growled at him without stopping or slowing his brisk pace.

"You bloody fool," Enric snapped at him. "What gives you the right to force Vern to come back with us when there is nothing for him in Anyueel?"

"There is enough for him in Anyueel!"

"What is there that can compare with the chance to learn both healing and the arts and anything else he is interested in?"

"There is me!" the warrior shouted and finally came to a halt, closing his eyes and breathing heavily. "This is my boy! How can I just leave him here?"

"There is hardly more than one more year until he comes of age. He will return here as soon as he is old enough not to depend on your acquiescence anymore. I can promise you that much. Will you drag him back to Anyueel to have him resent you for that final year that you manage to keep him with you, that year that you are stealing from him? That year that he would be able to finish his training here sooner and return home earlier?"

"This is too soon," Orrin whispered. "Too abrupt."

Enric sighed. "This is all about you, Orrin, not Vern. He is ready for this, ready to fly. Don't be the weight that drags him down. You have been doing incredibly well so far. You permitted him to be trained as a healer back home. As well as to explore drawing and put his talents to good use. You let him open these doors when you could have held them closed. This is where all of that finally led him. You can't start holding him back now; it would be cruel. You will have to let him go eventually. If you cling to him now, you might lose him."

"What do you know, Enric? You were clinging to Eryn, suffocating her at times."

"And I am learning my lessons," the younger man replied in a neutral tone. "In my case the consequences were a lot more immediate than they would be with you and Vern." He smiled wryly. "But I invite you to throw these words back at me one day when Vedric is on the verge of leaving the nest and I am trying to hold him back."

"Depend on it, I will. And now get out of my way. I need a drink. Alone."

* * *

Kilan smiled broadly when the servant led Enric into his study. He patted his visitor on the shoulder, careful not to shake the baby snoozing against his chest awake.

"You really did it, old friend. You went up there and brought Malriel back. Just like that." The ambassador snapped his fingers. "And don't tell me it wasn't quite that easy. I was at the Senate yesterday, and all the effort it required on your side was teaching them how to use a lie filter."

Enric grinned and took a seat, accepting a welcome glass of cool water. Kilan had obviously adopted the local expression instead of calling it a truth block like it was referred to in Anyueel. He was adapting well to his new home, and every now and then there was even a trace of a rolling r detectable when he spoke.

"What can I say? I am mightily persuasive."

"That you are indeed." He nodded at the sleeping infant. "You seem to have taken to your new role as father pretty quickly. Since you have returned nobody has seen you in public without your son."

"I have only been back for two days now."

"Still. Who would have thought that high and mighty old you would have turned out to be such a dedicated father?" Kilan shook his head. "But you are probably just showing him off because he looks like you. I remember that Eryn wasn't particularly happy about being told just that. How is she doing, by the way? That was quite a meeting at the Senate yesterday. Rely on that woman to liven up the usually so dull meetings there. Did you know that the number of observers has tripled since she took the position of Head of House? And she hardly ever disappoints when it comes to providing entertainment in the sacred halls of politics."

"She is fine so far. Though having her mother stay in the same house makes a bit of tension, especially considering that Malriel is restless and unhappy because she wants her House back. Finally and also most importantly there is the matter with her savings being used for the greater good while she would rather use them for her own purposes one day. Malhora's presence doesn't exactly make the whole arrangement any more harmonious. But at least she is on Eryn's side. She seems to think that Malriel's being subordinated to her daughter is a good joke. And you may imagine Malriel's reaction to that."

Kilan grimaced sympathetically. "Your life is never boring, is it? You remember that they are notorious for collapsing parts of their residence, right?"

"I trust that they will avoid that as long as Vedric is in there. He is their only chance to maintain their direct bloodline, after all," he concluded dryly.

"How did Eryn react when you returned in the middle of the night? I had the impression that she was mighty angry when you left."

Enric took another sip of water. "She knocked me out."

Kilan leaned back in his chair and laughed delightedly. "She did? Just like that? That was the first time she managed that, wasn't it?"

"I am glad to see that it amuses you."

"Oh, don't be squeamish, Enric!" the ambassador sniggered. "I dare say you are still several knockings-out ahead. So, are we to have another third level ceremony soon? I really want to see one, you know."

"No, she is refusing to renew the bond."

Kilan's eyes bulged. "No! Surely this cannot be true?" He whistled through his teeth. "Pretty angry still, your companion, isn't she?"

"Yes and no. There is anger, certainly, but not the explosive kind I would have expected. Yet I don't have the impression that she is holding back, I would feel that through the mind bond. It is more as if she is suddenly able to direct her anger somehow. I am used to her throwing a major fit and then things returning back to normal quite quickly. I just wonder if being a mother has brought about this change."

"Would that be bad?"

"Not as such, no. Just unusual. Though that control over her anger definitely makes her more dangerous. I remember that Golir said something like that about Malriel during our first visit here. That she is not most dangerous when her temper gets the better of her, but in the many cases where it doesn't and she is able to think properly before she reacts."

"So Eryn is growing more like her mother? I suppose you might want to refrain from pointing that out to her for now."

Enric shivered. "I had no intention of doing that. I am trying to make her like me again, after all. But now tell me what is going on at home. What did I miss?"

"Nothing much as far as I know. Though I think there will be quite a few messages arriving tomorrow to comment on your return. And probably even your call home."

"I am not so sure about that. Eryn has asked the King for another two months here and if he is smart, he will grant it."

"Good. I admit the thought of your returning to Anyueel depresses me somewhat. It's a lot more fun with you here. And you are a piece of home, after all." He frowned. "Say, there was this one thing... When Eryn mentioned something about Malriel's current lover - was she really talking about Valrad? Is that possible? Her mother is having an affair with her father?"

"Yes, so it would seem. To be honest, that was quite a surprise for all of us. I am curious to see where that will lead. I hope it does not burden Eryn's relationship with her father too much. They have only recently managed to make up again."

"Hey, wouldn't it be hilarious if they committed to each other? That would make you Eryn's brother and thus your son's uncle," Kilan mused.

"Yes, absolutely hilarious," Enric deadpanned.

* * *

Eryn and Junar looked up and both stared in surprise at the two men who had entered the main room from the direction of the entrance door. Orrin and Valrad, side by side without so much as an angry glance at each other.

"I must be dead and caught in some kind of really strange afterlife," Eryn murmured.

"Whatever killed you then must have been major because I think it did me in, too," Junar said slowly.

"Where is Vern?" Orrin asked instead of a greeting. "In his room?"

"Yes," Junar confirmed and lifted her cheek to have it kissed by Valrad after he had greeted his daughter, watching her companion walk towards his son's room.

"What is going on here?" Eryn enquired. "Since when are the two of you getting along?"

"Let us say we have decided to enter into a state of mutual tolerance for the greater good," Valrad said carefully.

"Really? The greater good being what exactly?"

"Enabling Vern to make use of his potential and thereby benefiting two countries as a consequence."

Junar exhaled extensively and closed her eyes for a moment. "That means he has decided to let Vern stay, doesn't it?"

"He has, yes," the healer confirmed and seated himself comfortably between the two women, smiling at little Téa who beamed at him from her mother's lap. "Your daughter is developing nicely. I can see that she reacts to her surroundings more consciously and selectively than before." He moved his index finger before her eyes. Little Téa followed it for no longer than a second or two, then lost interest and turned her head towards the sounds of Orrin and Vern approaching.

"That kid always smiles. Is that normal? Isn't she supposed to get in a bad mood every now and then or at least hate the occasional stranger?" Eryn asked.

Valrad shrugged. "It is a pleasant change. There are indeed a few children with a more friendly inclination towards their environment."

"I wonder who she might have that from..."

Junar just lifted an eyebrow. "You'd better be careful, we have yet to see how your son will turn out. Right now he still sleeps a lot, but you just wait."

Vern gasped in surprise when he saw Valrad sitting between the two women.

"Hello. What brings you here?" the boy asked carefully with a sideways glance at his father.

"Your father asked me to come," Valrad explained. "Why not take a seat so we can talk?"

Vern nodded slowly, obviously not really trusting the unusual situation.

Orrin sat down next to his son, then started speaking, his voice sounding earnest.

"I have decided to let you accept Valrad's offer to stay in Takhan and continue your training here." He lifted his hand when Vern's mouth dropped open and his eyes widened in outright astonishment. "But there are a few conditions I would like to apply. I have no intention of letting you roam the city to your heart's content. You are still under age and require supervision. Valrad has agreed to let you move in at the Vel'kim residence during your stay here. He will have an eye on you, check on the progress of both your healing training and whatever artistic ambitions you have. And he will keep me informed of both. In great detail. For the duration of your stay here you will be subject to his requests and rules. If you decide to ignore them, you will be sent back to Anyueel. If you break any of his rules, or the laws in this country, you will be sent back. If you get yourself into any other trouble..."

"I will be sent back?" Vern offered when he had finally found his words.

"This is not a joke, young man, I mean it!" Orrin growled.

The boy shook his head in wonder. "It's really true? I can stay here?" His gaze wandered to Valrad. "And you are going to let me stay with you?"

"Yes," the Head of House Vel'kim confirmed. "And keep an eye on you, just how your father told you."

Eryn smiled at the three men, both glad that Vern had this outstanding opportunity and at the same time sad, as it would mean that he would be all but missing from her life for quite some time. As if his growing up and having an affair was not enough. Now he would even be spending the next few years in another country.

"You'd better come back as soon as you have finished your training here," she warned him. "You are still one of my healers. That is an order."

Vern laughed giddily, causing his little sister to follow suit and clap her hands happily. Then his exited expression turned into a worried frown.

"The Order! Will Lord Tyront agree?"

Eryn shrugged. "I don't see why not. I will write to Lord Tyront and the King and tell them that I have granted you permission to stay here and ask them to confirm that. Even in case they are miffed because I have assumed undue privileges here they will at least be mollified by my asking for their assent afterwards. It should give them a nice, warm feeling of me bowing before their greater authority."

Orrin shook his head slowly. "You really have come a long way, haven't you?"

"I am a fast learner, as people keep telling me. And since taking over House Aren and dealing with Malriel, there has been little choice, anyway." She stilled when she heard a muffled wailing. "If you would excuse me now, my son has obviously just woken. And then I should get myself ready as I am expecting Ram'an. He assists me with a few contracts that will help me spend Malriel's money as expeditiously as possible," she smirked.

"Why did you change your mind?" Vern turned towards his father with a broad smile.

"Let us say that Enric had a thing or two to say to me. He obviously likes to repay his debts in a timely fashion."

The boy laughed. "I knew it paid to have him on my side!"

CHAPTER 9

Political Balance

Enric leaned back at the teahouse, content with life as it was. His son was sleeping against his chest, there was a light breeze that was pleasantly refreshing, and Eryn was seated next to him, absorbed in one of the documents Ram'an had just handed her.

The lawyer had invited them to meet him at one of his teahouses, and Enric was glad that he had.

Eryn was spending too much time locked away in Malriel's study for his taste, planning her orphanage project and taking care of the daily business that being in charge of House Aren brought with it. He remembered that he, too, had spent many hours a day in that very room and wondered if it had bothered Eryn as much back then as it did him now.

He had been back for two weeks now and his days were oddly free of the duties they had been filled with before, probably for the first time in fifteen years.

His most recent responsibilities with regard to House Aren were now Eryn's. He understood why she wanted to hold on to them for a little longer, but couldn't help wishing that she, too, would have time to spend a few leisurely hours a day with him and their son, talking walks with them, sitting at teahouses, strolling through the gardens or visiting friends.

King Folrin had granted both her request to add another two months to their stay and to Vern's temporary relocation. He had added, though, that he was very much looking forward to having them all back.

"How is the extension of your teahouse going on? Will it be ready to supply the orphanage any time soon?" Eryn asked without looking up from the paper in her hands.

"Everything is going well. I am counting on the works winding up in two weeks at the most," the lawyer replied. "You do not look happy with the reconstruction proposal."

She sighed. "This is the best builder available?"

"They are the best builder available for you, yes," he nodded.

That made her look up and frown. "What do you mean, for me? Are they the best or not? Which are you using for your teahouse?"

"I am engaging the services House Roal offers."

"Which you can do because your House is not at enmity with them like Aren. I see," she grimaced. "So they are the best suppliers but I cannot use them. That is quite vexing."

Ram'an smiled sympathetically. "We do take our vendettas seriously here, I am afraid. Though we are a lot more civilised about them these days. We do not attack with magic but with words, and we refrain from burning down buildings and disrupting contracts if we can help it."

"Then I suppose House Roal may consider themselves lucky the offence was committed in such civilised times," she smiled.

Ram'an frowned that. "It was not. You do not know about it?"

"I don't know any particulars, just what Vran'el told me a year ago. They tried to pin a case of fraud on both House Aren and Vel'kim some time back."

The lawyer chuckled. "Well, I suppose you could say some time back. It is not an exact term as such. We are talking about one and a half centuries here."

"What?" she exclaimed and grimaced apologetically when Vedric stirred. Enric shot her a mildly disapproving look and swayed his son gently to calm him again. "So you are truly and earnestly telling me that I cannot hire the best provider for the construction services and have to make do with the second best because of something the current Head's great-grandfather did to Malhora's grandfather? You people are really ridiculously hobbled when it comes to holding on to a grudge!"

"Firstly, I do not see how an Aren in general and then specifically you of all people is fit to accuse others of holding on to grudges. And secondly, I would recommend being very careful in using the term you people like that. At least as long as you are a Head of House. And even after you relinquish the position in a few weeks you still are a member of a House here, which means that you are both by birth and by law one of *us people*."

Enric smiled at that. This was a typical conversation between the two of them. She was angry about something and Ram'an derailed her train of thought with some or other semantic matter that had nothing to do with the actual reason for her displeasure. She wouldn't like that one bit.

"Thank you for that very detailed and yet completely unhelpful explanation," she growled and pushed the proposal back at him. "I am not signing this. Get me another one. From House Roal."

Ram'an swallowed. "You are truly willing to enter into a business relationship with them? You may not be aware of this, but this would be quite a lot more than just a single transaction that is over and done with after the task is accomplished and the bill paid. Closing a contract with House Roal, even if it is only a single one and there will never be another, is a signal that will surprise a lot of people. And make several of them rather nervous, I would think. We currently have a balance of alliances among the Houses, and what you are planning might tip that with unforeseeable consequences."

"That balance, my friend," she replied dryly, "has already been tipped by Legara's actions and even more so by Malriel publicly ending the alliance. I imagine it doesn't matter that she is technically not in charge right now - it still is an official breach. That means House Aren has lost an ally, and even though I might not be able to win another one in the near future, crossing an enemy off the list might be just as useful."

Ram'an sighed. "As you wish, Theá. I will contact them as soon as I am back home."

Eryn nodded and turned to Enric. "Any objections on your side? Anything I failed to consider here before taking such an extreme step?"

He slowly shook his head, surprised that she had asked him. She had very pointedly avoided seeking his advice in these last two weeks, either to prove to herself that she could manage without him, or to him.

"Nothing I can think of, my love. Though Malriel will probably be... a tad out of sorts."

She grinned widely. "That is unfortunate, of course, but a downside I will have to accept." She turned back to Ram'an. "I need their answer soon. Tell them I will pay in advance, however imprudent that may be from a business point of view. But I want to avoid Malriel being the one to approve that invoice at a later time. And they better don't try to take advantage of that or I will come back from Anyueel, kick their bottoms and return back home the next day."

The lawyer nodded. "I dare say they will be eager to avoid that. And it is their first chance to work towards being forgiven, so I would be surprised if they did not use it wisely. Amgil is no fool."

"I wonder why Valrad handled this issue the same way as Malriel did. I wouldn't have thought him to be that resentful," she mused.

"I told you, we take our vendettas seriously, no matter how peaceful and tame they seem nowadays. Though the actions of both Ved'al and your father have bridged that gap between the Houses to a certain degree by fostering and mentoring Sarol the way they did."

"Not an entirely unselfish thing to do, mind you. Pushing an exceptionally gifted healer aside because he had the bad luck to be born to the wrong House would have been stupid."

"I never said Valrad's actions were entirely unselfish. And I wonder that you still seem to hold on to that picture of him your first visit here gave you. Valrad is a good man, I grant you that, but he has for a long time been in a position where mere benevolence towards those around him would not have kept his House in power. And powerful it is, Theá, no matter that they do not generally aspire towards leadership outside the field of healing."

"Yes, thank you very much," she growled. "Learning of his affair with Malriel while she was bound to his brother has given me a pretty good idea that he, too, follows his own interests at times."

"Speaking of that, how are you dealing with their recent reunion? You seem resigned, but not happy about it as such. Not that I expected you to be."

"I can't do anything against it, can I?" she retorted. "It would hardly go down well for me to tell those two crazy kids to keep their hands off each other, would it? As Head of House I have no right to forbid it, as you are well aware."

"Would you if it was within your rights? I cannot help thinking that you yourself would not accept any such interference in your own love life, Theá," Ram'an smiled. "I remember that you were upset when I myself tried it one year ago." He took a sip from his tea before changing the topic. "How is Vern doing? I hear Valrad is working on a teaching schedule for him now that he will stay here with us. I think he could not have found a more advantageous mentor than your father."

"Vern is doing fine. He would move in with Valrad right now if he could, but Orrin wants to spend at least a few more weeks with him before has to leave him behind."

"How about the costs for the education at the clinic? The healer training programme is one of the most pricey courses we have here."

Enric shook his head. "Don't remind me about that topic. We've had lengthy discussions about that in these last few days. Orrin insists on paying for it, and Valrad refuses to let him, as he was the one to offer Vern the choice. That hurt Orrin's pride, of course, as he doesn't want to accept any charity from Valrad, especially as he also refuses to accept any recompense for the cost Vern's stay at his home causes."

Ram'an nodded. "I see. Have you found a solution yet?"

"We have, yes," Eryn told him. "The clinic in Anyueel will cover half of the expenses and Vern will pay for the rest by working at the clinic and handing over his salary to Valrad. He can work nights when there are fewer patients and he can either sleep or use the time for learning if there is nothing much to do." She thought for a moment. "Well, at least that is my plan. I will of course have to clear this with the Head of Healers back home."

Enric laughed quietly. "I cannot imagine Lord Poron having reason to oppose you in that."

She grinned lopsidedly. "Neither can I. But it wouldn't do to take away his authority by forcing him to agree, would it?"

Ram'an cleared his throat. "Erbál has officially accepted his new assignment to go to Kar, by the way."

Eryn nodded. "I know. Vran'el told me. He knows it from Intrea. They will probably announce it at the Senate meeting tomorrow. What of it?"

"You more or less tricked the triarchy into letting you pick the next ambassador to Anyueel, and I was wondering if you have given any thought to who you would like to pick for the position?"

"You are not offering yourself, Arbil, are you?" she laughed. "Apart from the fact that you are tied to your House now, I have to tell you that you were quite a disruptive influence the first time."

He smiled faintly and shook his head. "No, of course not. But there is somebody else in my House who would be interested in going. You have met him a few times, but only briefly. My brother Ram'kel."

Eryn pursed her lips. "I remember that you told me something about him that one evening when you made me have dinner with you at your residence in exchange for the four votes back then. You said he was one of very few magicians who were never caught using magic illicitly as adolescents. That he is the mischievous type, but good at hiding it."

Enric nodded honestly. "Diplomat material if ever I saw it. Why don't you send him over for dinner tonight so that Eryn can have a proper look at him?"

"I will, thank you."

Eryn narrowed her eyes. "You are not doing this because you want to get rid of him, are you? If he turns out to be as unpleasant as Sanaf I shall make you pay for that."

Ram'an smiled thinly. "Dear me, would I ever?"

* * *

Enric accompanied Ram'kel of House Arbil to the Aren main room where Malhora had just placed two large, steaming bowls on the table and Malriel was holding her grandson in her arms.

The three women had so far been getting along with a distant politeness. At least as far as Malriel and Eryn were concerned. Malhora obviously enjoyed having both women close to her – and the entertainment this proximity provided. Living alone at her estate in the countryside for many years had obviously left her with quite a thirst for diversion. And whatever else one might say about having three Aren women under one roof, a lack of stimulation was definitely nothing to lament.

Eryn walked in from the terrace door. She had more or less fled into the garden to keep her distance from her mother until their guest arrived.

"Ram'kel," she smiled and walked towards him to let him kiss her hand. "We have never been introduced officially, I think."

Ram'an's younger brother nodded. "No, unfortunately not. I spend quite a lot of time on the road, travelling from one of our estates to the next to sort matters out there. And when I returned to the city for short periods there were not really any events that would have put us in each other's paths. And I refrained from approaching you for obvious reasons, even though I was very curious about you."

Eryn blinked. "You were?"

"But of course! Apart from meeting the long lost Aren daughter I wanted to lay eyes on this woman who rejected my older brother."

She looked at him for several moments, not sure if there was resentment somewhere boiling under the surface or if he just had a very dry sense of humour. Well, she would find out.

"Which either means that you are unhappy because you wanted to be Head of House Arbil yourself or you are glad because I saved you from just that fate," she said mildly, observing his reaction, disappointed that it was not in the least revealing.

Ram'kel then turned to greet Malhora and Malriel before he followed Enric's invitation to be seated.

"Your warrior friend and his family will not join us tonight?" their visitor asked.

"No. They are dining at the embassy," Eryn explained.

She had wanted a little more privacy than their currently rather extensive household permitted for this. Unfortunately there was no getting rid of Malriel and Malhora. They had insisted that they lived in the place and had no intention of letting themselves be sent off like that. Well, at least they could take care of Vedric while she was talking to Ram'kel.

It was a nuisance, though, that she had to wait until after dinner to broach the subject. Doing it while they were eating would be frowned upon.

"Ram'an tells me that your project is progressing as planned," Ram'kel said conversationally, drying his hands after washing them in the bowl on the table. "I walked by on my way here and I have to say that the building looks a lot more cheerful than it used to. Remarkable what a little paint and minor repairs can accomplish, is it not?"

Eryn nodded and smiled politely, wondering if this was a deliberate choice of topic to make her like him because he showed interest in the orphanage.

She tried to remember the few occasions she had laid eyes on him before. The only one that came to her mind now was the evening not long ago when Ram'an had sent for her because he had found the man who had worked for Sanaf to cause her as much trouble as possible. Ram'kel had been in his brother's study back then, standing guard over the culprit.

"Your brother told me that you currently spend most of your time at the family estates to make sure things are running the way they should," Eryn mentioned, deciding that this should be a suitable topic for a dinner conversation.

"Indeed. I have been doing so for more than a year now, even before my father's death. He thought I was fleeing the city for some solitude and thus did not object. I assume Ram'an told you that our father displayed a very regrettable lack of trust in his sons," he concluded dryly.

"And now everything is going the way it should?" she enquired, determined not to pursue the topic of his father's failure in leading the House. It did not exactly qualify as a neutral conversation topic.

"More or less, yes. I arranged for quite a few changes to be made, which has become a lot easier now that Ram'an is in charge of the House. Let us say that he is a lot more open to taking care of necessary improvements."

"So you welcome the recent developments as regards the matter of leadership in your House?" Malriel asked gently. "You would not have preferred to take over that role yourself?"

"To be perfectly honest, I was a little disappointed at first. Our father always told me to be ready to take over, especially when it became known that Maltheá had been found. And when Ram'an was so very determined to win her for himself I had little doubt that he would succeed eventually and thus give up succeeding our father."

"Only at first?" Malriel then asked.

"Yes. I attended several Senate meetings and they would undoubtedly have been a rather tiresome duty for me in the years to come. And then I was never as fond of dabbling in dreary details as my brother. He does not mind poring over a single paragraph in a contract for hours if need be."

"Ram'an's attention to detail has turned out to be a blessing more often than once, at least for myself," Eryn replied stiffly, annoyed that he seemed to think that diminishing his brother's talents would be acceptable to her. "He has in these last months and especially in the time since I have taken over House Aren been a valuable friend and advisor to me."

She narrowed her eyes slightly when Ram'kel smiled as if amused that she defended his own brother against him.

"I assure you that it was not my intention to disparage him. I merely meant to emphasise that his disposition is certainly more suited to successfully leading a House that requires a lot of attention to detail in its current situation," he placated her. "And I am glad to see that you treasure my brother's friendship the way you do," he added with a glance at her wrist around which the bracelet with his House's crest was fastened.

Eryn smiled noncommittally and continued eating, wondering if he had provoked her intentionally in order to test her reaction. If yes, then she had accommodated him nicely. How annoying. She would be more careful with him from now on.

Enric put aside his empty bowl and rose to take his son so Malriel could eat.

"I will take a walk in the garden with him," he then announced and turned to his companion. "Unless you want me to stay?"

Eryn shook her head, slightly surprised. He was not normally that willing to let her handle matters alone without him being present to help her out of whatever difficulties that might present themselves. "No, I dare say I will manage alone for a while."

"I have no doubt that you will. I was rather wondering if you wanted to," he winked at her and then sauntered off towards the terrace door.

Eryn looked at Ram'kel's empty bowl. "Would you like another helping? Malhora usually cooks more than we can eat without Vern being around."

"No, thank you very much. I have had plenty."

"Then I would ask you to follow me to the study. There we can talk undisturbed," she proposed and rose to walk ahead.

She closed the door behind him little later and motioned for him to sit. She herself opted for standing and leaned against a bookshelf, looking down at him. He did not at all seem perturbed by her position but waited for her to begin talking.

Eryn studied him for several moments, hoping it would make him unsettled. He did not resemble his older brother at all, at least when it came to looks. His voice sounded similar to Ram'an's, though: the same pleasant, deep timbre that tended to inspire trust and confidence.

He had to be about two years younger than herself, she recalled.

Memories of what Ram'an had told her about his brother many months ago returned. That he was the mischievous type who had in his young and wild years managed not to be caught even once when it had come to using magic in socially unacceptable ways.

"Why do you want to go to Anyueel?" she asked without introduction.

If that straightforward approach riled him, it didn't show.

"Because I have developed an interested in your country since Ram'an's return from his visit there. And my curiosity has grown since your own visit last year and Kilan's establishment as ambassador here. I have spent many an evening with him talking about his home. And I have been in frequent contact with Erbál ever since he left for Anyueel with Sanaf."

Well, well, he had certainly come prepared, she mused.

"I trust you are aware of the circumstances that led to Sanaf's dismissal from his position?"

"I am, yes. He has demonstrated a blatant lack of sensitivity when it came to the boundaries of discussing in public what are considered very private topics in your Kingdom."

She nodded slowly and stared into his eyes unblinkingly. "I furthermore assume you are aware of the role I played in this matter?"

"Of course. You were instrumental in having him removed from his position and replaced by Erbál. Your influence made this swift exchange possible."

"Hardly. It just helped to accomplish this more quickly. From what I gathered Erbál was the best available candidate and his family voting against me was the only thing that kept the triarchy from appointing him for the position from the start. Do not attempt to flatter me, Ram'kel," she said calmly with folded arms. "It doesn't usually work. I am deeply suspicious when people compliment me. It makes me wonder what they hope to gain. I am a lot more comfortable with criticism. It tends to be more honest."

He frowned slightly and pursed his lips, thinking for a moment before he replied, "A rather regrettable sentiment, I cannot help but find. A compliment may at times be an attempt to make you more compliant, but then it may just as well be an expression of honest admiration."

"You don't know me well enough to admire me honestly."

"Then I will attempt to change this and earn the privilege," he smiled gallantly.

Too slick, she decided, and wondered why exactly she was so suspicious of that man. "Many people here still consider Anyueel to be a country full of backwards barbarians. Why would you want to go there, anyway?"

"I dare say that people in your country might consider us the barbarians due to what must appear like a lack of restraint when it comes to publicly talking about sexuality. It is a matter of perspective, and I am seeking to broaden mine. Judging a country one has never set a foot in is easy."

"And you are not one to prefer the easy way?" she smiled thinly.

"Not normally, no. It is our House's most prominent trait: being thorough. It is a consequence of breeding a high number of scholars. Our current Head of House fits the traditions nicely."

"And you? Are you a born scholar, too? A collector of knowledge? Is this why you wish to go to Anyueel? To study us?"

"No, I was not tested for scholar but for healer. But as I had been intended as one to take over the House it was not a profession I was encouraged to follow. Unless one is meant to take over a healing House such as Vel'kim, it is not a desired path for a Head of House to follow."

Eryn looked at him with newfound interest. This man had been tested for healer, the result she herself had hoped for in her own case.

"And now you have neither the position you were told you would very likely take over one day, nor the profession for which you seem to be most suited. You are not by any chance trying to get this position as ambassador to make me pay for that, are you?" she asked airily.

Ram'kel chuckled and shook his head. "I am not, you may depend on that. I do remember what happened to the last ambassador to annoy and even cause you harm. And Ram'an would have my head. In addition to the danger of destroying the newly strengthened alliances with Houses Aren and Vel'kim he is also very fond of you personally and would make me pay for causing you any trouble or grief. As I am bound to him with a second level commitment bond this is well within his possibilities."

"This fails to reassure me, to be completely honest," she remarked dryly. "You are telling me that you will behave not because you don't hold any grudges against me but because your brother would make you pay for it. Why would I want to have a man like that in my city? What other qualities do you have despite being related to a man I have come to value and like very much?"

"In your case I would think that the fact that you can easily complain to Ram'an about me should the need arise is an attractive option. Apart from House Vel'kim there is no other Head of House you are that closely connected with and where you can be sure of being taken seriously and thus expect immediate action. My qualities as such are manifold. I have been raised, trained and educated to take over a House one day, just like my brother. This means that I have ample experience when it comes to interacting with influential people both in a professional and also social context. I am a good negotiator, organiser and strategist, am patient, discreet and cooperative, curious about new cultures and people, and I am a safe choice for you thanks to my connection to House Arbil. Apart from sending a Head of House, I am probably the best you can get for this position."

He was confident, she had to give him that. "Yet you are not a trained diplomat such as Erbál," she pointed out.

"Neither was Enric of House Aren when he was sent here. Or Kilan," Ram'kel countered. "Yet they both turned out to be very well suited to the task."

They stared at each other for several moments.

"You are not happy about the thought of my going to Anyueel as ambassador." There was no resentment or annoyance in his tone, it was nothing less than the simple statement of a truth.

Eryn just raised an eyebrow at him.

"You supported Erbál and are fond of him. He managed to gain your trust and friendship, and you have no wish to replace him. You are sad to see him go. You will surely stay in contact with him in his new position, and I know that it would not be a matter of calculation in your case to maintain a useful contact, but a personal consideration. And even though you are friends with my brother now, there might still be unpleasant associations with the House of Arbil."

"I thank you for coming, Ram'kel," she dismissed him, not bothering to deny his accurate analysis. "I will let you know what I decide. I should not take too long."

He stood up immediately, seemingly untroubled by the rather abrupt dismissal, and kissed her hand. "Thank you for seeing me, Eryn. I will be waiting for your message. A good evening to you."

"And to you." She watched him walk out the study and waited for several moments before she strolled out and along the corridor to the main room and then out into the garden, where she found Enric under a tree, his son sleeping on his lap, a book in one hand.

She smiled at the peaceful picture. Enric sitting somewhere and reading a book had become such a familiar sight. She was oddly relieved that Vedric's arrival had not changed that. He was merely an extra element in that picture instead of changing it beyond recognition.

Enric let the book sink when she approached. He didn't ask but waited if she wanted to talk.

"He is not Erbál," she stated glumly.

"No, that he isn't," Enric agreed patiently.

"I have little choice in this matter. Ram'an asked me for a favour, and Ram'kel has not given me any reason to deny it."

"Does this mean you made up your mind but are not too happy about it?"

"I suppose you could say it like that, yes. I normally decide within moments if I like a person or not. But with Ram'kel this hasn't worked. I am not sure about him, and that annoys me. What if I don't like him? Then I have nobody but myself to blame for having him appointed as ambassador."

"He will still owe you something for aiding him in that regard," Enric pointed out.

She wrinkled her nose. "And thus it becomes political again. Granting one favour in order to be able to demand another in return one day."

"The position of ambassador is a very political function, my love. Personal considerations alone may not be the most reliable means to judge whether he is suitable for the position or not."

"I know," she sighed. "But at least he is right in one regard: I can complain to Ram'an if he gets on my nerves."

CHAPTER 10

Vedric's Potential

Eryn strolled next to Ram'an when they left the building that was currently undergoing reconstruction for its new purpose of housing orphaned children. So far almost everything was going according to plan apart from a few minor details Ram'an had been kind enough to take care of expeditiously.

"Ram'kel is looking rather nervous these days. He is still waiting for your reply concerning your decision," Ram'an broached the subject she had been waiting for while walking her back to the Aren residence.

She smiled. "I admit I am keeping him in suspense. He was so very confident several days ago and it does me good to hear that he is nervous."

"I see. So you are teaching my little brother something of a lesson. Am I correct in assuming that you would not be so cruel as to play that game if you intended to deny him the position?" he asked carefully.

"You are correct, yes. Even my tendencies to enjoy other people's discomfort have their limits. Tendencies for which I blame my proud Aren heritage, by the way. Though I admit that in Malriel's case watching her distress never fails to raise my spirits."

Ram'an laughed quietly. "Poor Malriel. Being subordinated to you cannot be easy for her, especially as Malhora is on your side, too. Has she contacted King Folrin yet to try and make him call you back?"

"She has, yes. But she could just as well have saved herself the trouble. He had already granted my request to prolong my stay here when her message arrived." She shrugged. "I told her so but she didn't want to listen."

"You requested two more months, did you not? That means that half of that time is almost over. I admit the thought of seeing you leave here is a decidedly unpleasant one." He took her hand to kiss it. "I will miss you."

She smiled at the gesture and squeezed his fingers affectionately. Back in Anyueel physical gestures like this between friends just didn't happen.

"There will certainly be a lot less entertainment, I imagine. Things here will go back to normal with Malriel in charge of House Aren and back in her function as senator."

"I did not think of your entertainment value, dear. I will miss talking to you."

She sent him a sideways glance. "Well, maybe we will manage to communicate via bird this time. Unless you change your mind again as soon as I am out of sight."

"A low blow, Theá, but not entirely undeserved, I will admit," he grimaced. "What are your plans for today? Can I persuade you to spend another hour with me at a teahouse or do you need to get back and take care of important Aren business?"

"I am afraid I shall have to decline your invitation for now. Enric and I are due at the clinic to have them look at Vedric's magical potential."

"Ah yes, he is old enough for that now. How time flies. It seems like only yesterday with you standing in the middle of the Senate hall, bits of masonry falling down and you in such a mix of rage and shock that you did not even notice that your waters broke."

"I don't appreciate that amused tone of yours. That was not a pretty day for me. And I have not forgotten how you forced that cursed golden belt on me at the clinic."

He sighed theatrically. "It truly is dangerous to anger an Aren woman. They do not only react rather explosively at times but also bear grudges. A worrying combination. Usually it is either one or the other. You warned me that you would take advantage if I ever happened to be helpless in your presence."

"And I meant every word."

"I have no doubt that you did."

They stopped in front of the Aren residence.

"Will you permit me to convey to Ram'kel that he will be the next ambassador to Anyueel or do you wish to do so yourself?" he enquired.

"No, go ahead and tell him. Just add a few dire warnings not to upset me by quoting whatever unpleasant Aren tales you can think of. He may just as well try to get on my good side."

"I will do my best to scare him accordingly. Though I have to warn you that he was never very susceptible to warnings, threats or the like."

She grimaced. "You are telling me that now? How am I to make him do my bidding back home, then? I do try not to resort to blackmail if I can avoid it."

Ram'an grinned. "I can see that the two of you are going to have a lot of fun together in Anyueel. I look forward to reading both your messages."

She rolled her eyes and opened the door. "You just told me that you will miss me and that my entertainment value is not the reason why. The fact that you cannot wait to see me leave here all of a sudden to read about how your brother and I are going to make life as hard as possible for each other makes me doubt your earlier words, my friend."

"It is but a small consolation for being deprived of the privilege of your company so soon, Theá," he winked at her and kissed her cheeks before he turned and walked back the way they had come.

"Eryn?" she heard Enric call from the main room after she had closed the entrance door. "Is that you?"

"Yes," she called back and quickly wiped her face and hands with a moist towel before ascending the stairs. His voice had sounded a little urgent. That probably meant that Vedric was hungry already. She had started to prolong the intervals between feeding him, and so far he had not been too happy about that.

"He is hungry," Enric stated with a look that held mild reproof as if she were the most heartless mother in the world, cruelly withholding nourishment from a starving infant.

"That tends to happen every now and then I am told. Hand him over then," she sighed and took a seat on the cushions next to Junar who was already feeding Téa. The girl had started eating a few days ago and had taken well to fruit pulp. Though she had turned out to be quite a messy eater.

Enric placed her son in her arm after she had opened her shirt and then sat down next to her, draping his arm over the cushions at her back. He joined her as often as he could, enjoying the intimate setting and closeness to her. She wondered if he was still trying to make up for lost time.

"So, today is the big day. Somehow I wonder if this will replace the testing at home," Junar stated. "Have you had a peek? Do you know how strong he will be?"

Eryn shook her head. "No, Ram'an told me how it works in general, but I don't know where exactly to look or what to make of the results. I lack the experience. But I am confident that they will show me today how to go about it."

Junar shook her head and lifted her eyes at her daughter who delighted in sticking her fist into the bowl and then shaking it around to watch were the drops landed.

"I will have to work on making her understand the difference between food and a plaything. Right now she plays with the first and tries to eat the second."

"That's normal," Eryn smiled. "As soon as she is sated she seeks diversion. That is healthy for her mental development. And her gums will soon start showing her emerging first teeth, so sticking things in her mouth is natural at her age. It is in addition a tactile way of discovering her surroundings."

"I know," the seamstress growled. "Knowing all that still doesn't make cleaning up after her any more bearable. Or watching her every single moment for fear she could be sticking something dangerous in her mouth." Then she cleared her throat while wiping her daughter's face and hands with a damp cloth. "Say, when exactly do you plan to return home?"

"In about five weeks. Why? Are you homesick?"

"Well, I admit I am thinking a lot about my sister Gara these days. My daughter will be half a year old when she first lays eyes on her. My sister and her companion are the only family I have left. She writes to me every week and keeps asking me when we are returning."

"You could return home sooner," Eryn proposed mildly. "I sometimes forget that not everybody is as connected to this place as I am. Orrin has done his deed here, he has advised the Senate about defensive measures and has trained the people here sufficiently enough for them to carry on honing their skills without him for a while."

Junar grimaced. "Hardly. I don't think he would appreciate me suggesting it. He is still afraid of you stumbling into some kind of trouble as long as we are here. And then these are the last few weeks he will be able to spend with Vern for quite some time."

Enric nodded. She had a point there. Orrin took it as his voluntary responsibility seriously to watch out for Eryn, no matter if her companion was around or not - or how little Valrad appreciated the competition for that task. He wondered if anybody but himself saw the irony in Valrad taking on that very same duty for Vern during the next few years. They had more or less swapped their children despite not overly liking each other.

"Our son has just fallen asleep. That probably means he is done eating and we can leave for the clinic." He took the boy from her so that she could cover herself again.

"I dare say we will see Valrad at the clinic. I assume he will be interested in seeing how powerful his - or rather Vran'el's - heir will be one day," Eryn sighed. "Let's hope he is not going to be too strong or I will have to fend off even more requests for companionship agreements."

Enric lifted his brow. "Even more? We received some already?"

"Several. There are new ones arriving almost every week. Even for children that have not yet been born or even conceived. I find that disturbing."

He just shrugged. "A cultural matter, my love. And not entirely unexpected considering our son's connections to both Houses and to Anyueel."

"Yes, thank you so much," she shot back testily. "I am aware of that. Yet it doesn't make rejecting them politely and with the utmost care to avoid angering the Houses any more of a pleasure."

He took her hand and pulled her up from the cushions. He understood her sentiments well, of course. The custom of forging companionship agreements had brought her more than her fair share of trouble in the past. Yet he wondered how long it would be possible to avoid that very thing for their son. There was considerable social pressure, after all. Though he hoped Valrad as her Head of House would be smart enough not to push her in this.

*   *   *

"Well, well, your sight is here not entirely unexpected," Eryn greeted her father when they were led to a treatment room. Then she turned to Iklan. "But I wouldn't have thought that an important man like yourself would carry out a mere routine examination such as this."

Iklan chuckled. "I feel I should remind you that your father is quite a lot more important than me, my dear Eryn. And in the case of your son I wonder if it really is going to be no more than routine. I am curious and asked for the chance to have a look at him." He motioned for Enric to place his son on the examination table and then carefully placed his hand on the soft head before closing his eyes.

Eryn watched him carefully and felt slightly queasy when she first saw him frown and then swallow.

"What?" she barked when he withdrew his hand.

But Iklan ignored her and instead turned to Valrad. "Would you be so kind as to have a look as well?"

The older healer studied him for a moment, then nodded and repeated the examination.

He opened his eyes again little later and pursed his lips. "Extraordinary."

"Are you going to talk to me or do I need to shake it out of you?" Eryn threatened when neither of them made to talk to her but both healers just looked down at the baby thoughtfully.

Iklan nodded slowly. "Of course. Eryn, your son is going to be a strong magician. That alone is hardly unexpected. But we are surprised at the degree of power the active area in his brain suggests he will be able to wield one day."

"How strong is he going to be? Stronger than me?" Enric enquired.

"Definitely," Iklan confirmed. "Right now it looks like your son is going to be outside our known scale for measuring magical strength. This would make him the most powerful user of magic in our country – and probably even yours. We will have to extend the referencing system if we want to include him."

Eryn stared at them, then down at the small human on the table in front of her. He was still smaller than others his age due to being born several weeks premature. That helpless, soft bundle was supposed to be the most powerful wielder of magic of his time?

"That would make him the next leader of the Order," Enric next to her whispered. She looked up at him, surprised at the worry in his voice. Considering his own position of power, shouldn't he be pleased about this development? But then he himself had been pushed into his position of authority without his consent and probably wanted to avoid just that for his son.

"We will have to do something about that. At least we have two decades to think of a solution for it. The way it looks now, Vedric and Téa will be forced to take over the Order," he murmured and then squeezed her hand. "At least you have made your objections to granting power in accordance with magical strength known before. That way it won't look as if you are just trying to protect him from being stuck in the Order that deeply."

Eryn nodded slowly and then narrowed her eyes at Iklan. "This revelation makes me question your presence here even more. Did you expect anything like that? Why are you really here?"

The healer rubbed his forehead. "I admit I was wondering about how strong he would turn out after Orrin's daughter. Junar is not aware of any magicians in her bloodline, yet their daughter is uncommonly strong in addition to being the first female magician born to your Kingdom. I was curious to see if there was a tendency to father strong magicians related to the removal of the barrier in the head. And in your case there is also the chance that the mind bond somehow influenced your son's magical potential. Yet this is quite a lot more than I expected." His gaze returned to Vedric, who was looking around with his wide, blue eyes. "We will have to inform the triarchy of that. And I assume your Order and King Folrin will be equally interested in this development."

Enric covered his eyes for a moment. Tyront would not at all be thrilled with that bit of news. But at least he would learn of it now and not in twenty years when he would face a young man at the testing and realise that there was no way he could penetrate the immensely strong shield he presented.

"Those are quite a few theories you have there," Eryn sighed. "So his strength could be a result of the removal of the barrier, the mind bond between his father and me or a combination of those."

Iklan nodded. "Indeed. It would be interesting to look at the children born in Anyueel to parents where the barrier was removed before the conception of the child. I wonder how many more magicians are among them and how strong they are."

She sighed. "I will work this out after my return and we will stay in contact. What is going to happen now?"

"We will have to determine how to extend the scale, for one," Valrad explained. "Currently the highest value is twelve, that achieved by Golir and also Enric. We will have to compare the measurements that determine the difference between the categories and then see where to place Vedric." He looked at his daughter. "This will soon become common knowledge, my girl. News like that cannot be contained long. It also means that we will be receiving even more generous offers for companionship agreements. Vedric has become an even more desirable candidate than before, which is saying something."

Eryn groaned. "Fabulous, just splendid. How nice to see that his market value as breeding stock has risen even further."

* * *

"Whatever were you thinking? How could you do a thing like that? Do you have any idea of the consequences?" Malriel spat at her with arms folded when they entered the Aren main room after returning from the clinic.

Eryn narrowed her eyes at the older woman. "Shut up, Mother. I am in no mood to deal with whatever annoys you right now. I have my own problems."

But Malriel was not to be silenced as easily as that. "Really now? The Head of House Aren has no time to listen to objections when it comes to the thoughtless course of action she has chosen? I wonder why this fails to surprise me!"

Eryn exhaled slowly and closed her eyes. "Alright, out with what is troubling you! Then leave me be."

"You signed a contract with House Roal! Or do you deny doing so?"

"I have no intention of denying it," Eryn snorted. "I decided that being angry at a family for the sins of their ancestors is a stupid course of action, especially as it would have required of me to accept the second-best provider of building services. Is that an Aren-trait, too? Making do with inferior quality so that we can maintain our pride at all costs?"

"You have not been here long enough to appreciate the balance..."

"The balance of power?" Eryn interrupted her. "The sensitive balance that is made up by the alliances and enmities between the Houses and the families connected with them? Spare me that baloney or I will go to Legara right this minute and beg her forgiveness for your behaviour at the Senate meeting, where you declared our alliance with House Finran over."

"Beg her forgiveness for my behaviour?" Malriel hissed. "You would not dare! It would bring ridicule on us all!"

"Then leave me alone with your talk about power balances. Breaking off with House Finran certainly influenced that so-called balance, so making new friends is probably not such a bad idea right now. You can start up a new feud with them as soon as you are back in power. Until then you will have to live with my decision. And now I need some peace." Thus she turned and walked towards the terrace door to treasure a few minutes away from that woman.

"You have no idea of..." Her words were cut off in mid-sentence when Eryn raised a soundproof barrier around Malriel.

Enric sighed and shook his head. "I assume you are aware that the amount of air in there is limited and she will run out of it in a matter of minutes?"

She nodded and watched Malriel's face flushing crimson with rage and indignity, her eyes narrowed.

"Yes, I know. But it seemed a lot less harsh than just knocking her out. I do try to get along with her, you know."

Enric bit his tongue to keep in the remark that this was surely an unusual approach to keeping the peace.

"Is there anything you wish to say at this point?" she asked with a forthrightness that didn't leave him in any doubt that she wouldn't appreciate any criticism at this point.

"No, nothing whatsoever."

"Good. I see we are getting somewhere. I propose you lay down Vedric and when you return you may free her. I will be outside, trying to relax a little. Just make sure she doesn't come after me or I will resort to knocking her out after all."

Enric nodded once and watched her walk briskly out into the garden towards a group of trees to sit in the shadow.

Eryn opened her eyes when she heard the rustling of grass that announced somebody approaching her from the direction of the house. She sighed with relief when she saw that it was Enric, not Malriel.

He had a parcel under one arm.

"Have you freed the Queen of Darkness from her containment?" she asked when he had come close enough to hear her.

"I have, yes. She rushed off, probably to seek shelter with Valrad."

"Good riddance," Eryn murmured and nodded at his load. "What's that? Did a messenger drop that off?"

He shook his head and sank to the ground next to her. "No, it is something I bought in Kar. A gift for you."

"A gift? But you have been back for almost a month now, why give it to me now?"

"I was not sure how you would react to receiving presents from me and was waiting for a suitable occasion."

She couldn't help but smile. "And you think this is one? After finding that my son is going to present real potential for trouble when he is grown and Malriel has annoyed me?"

He shrugged. "I thought you were in need of some cheering up, so yes." He shook his head when she stretched out her arms to take the parcel from him. "Not yet, wait. It is a common practice to increase the perceived value of the gift by elaborating on how difficult it was to obtain."

Eryn chuckled. "Alright, then. Tell me all about it."

"These, you see, are the first items of their kind to be permitted to be brought to the Western Territories or even to any other country from what I gathered. I had to fill in several forms to be first granted the purchase itself and then also permission for the exchange of the required amount of money. Very bureaucratic place, Pirinkar. I was roaming the streets to find something that would qualify as a suitable gift for a woman of your talent and inclinations, and let me tell you that this was not easy. Of course my choice of present was not an uncomplicated one, so I dare say the only reason they permitted me to obtain these items was that they felt bad about Malriel's predicament and intended it as a gesture of goodwill," he concluded.

She nodded solemnly. "I see that you must have put a lot of thought and effort into purchasing these objects. You may rest assured that I will appreciate them accordingly."

"Excellent. That was the idea. Then I may forthwith present you with a little something, which you may safely consider unique in both the Western Territories and Anyueel - just like yourself." He bowed and handed her the parcel.

She accepted it graciously and placed it on her thigh to unwrap the coarse paper and the linen underneath to uncover three books. She frowned and lifted the first one, narrowing her eyes when she tried to decipher the title. Then she looked up at him, wondering if he really thought that giving her a book she couldn't read was such a brilliant idea.

He took the book from her hand and leafed through it until he had found a page with a colourful picture of an insect.

"This is a book on illnesses in Pirinkar, one of them the sleeping sickness that is passed on by a flying insect. The one you learned about a year ago, if you remember. I am told it and many others are described in this book, and also their remedies, though with non-magical means considering their aversion to magic." He reached out for another book. "As the book is obviously not in our language, you will have to acquire that skill first if you want to read it. This here is a book that contains words in their language with their equivalent in ours. And the third one here aims to explain the structure and system of their language."

Eryn stared at the books in silence, her expression inscrutable.

Enric swallowed and waited. Until now the idea of presenting her with these books had seemed inventive and original, but suddenly he couldn't help but wonder if giving her books that she had to spend who knew how much time to learn to access the knowledge they contained hadn't been rather harsh. What if she had no inclination to take that trouble and would instead resent him for expecting her to put that much effort into being able to really use his gift one day?

"The first books ever to be brought here from Pirinkar," he heard her say to herself and felt immensely relieved when he watched a smile forming on her face that grew wider with every second. "I will be the first one to learn their language, the only one to have access to this knowledge…"

A moment later he felt her pull him close and kiss him energetically. He laughed when her enthusiasm tipped him over backwards and she came to lie on top of him, grinning down over him.

"I like your gift, in case you were wondering. Well chosen, warrior man."

"You are very welcome, healer woman. I suppose this alone will not make you agree to join me in a third level bond again, will it?" he asked casually.

"No. But I grant you that it is a valiant effort and will make a note to consider it as a point in your favour when I make my decision at the end of the revision period."

Good. That was exactly what he had been hoping for.

CHAPTER 11

Jolly Good News

Eryn walked next to Orrin in a leisurely pace, each of them with their baby slung across their chest. Junar was meeting somebody from House Feral to talk about an arrangement for shipping fabrics to Anyueel and Enric was visiting Kilan at the embassy. They would all meet at the Vel'kim residence for dinner.

"I am reluctant to return to Anyueel," Orrin confessed. "I never thought that I would be. I was looking forward to returning there until quite recently."

"Because of Vern?" she ventured.

"It is one reason, but not the only one." He looked down at his daughter. "Walking through the streets with Téa is nothing special here, but back home it will certainly make people gossip. In wealthier families neither mothers nor fathers are seen much with their children."

Eryn nodded. Raising children was indeed considered a necessary burden to be passed on to servants if one could afford them. She had never understood that as she herself had been very close to Ved'al. And now that she was a mother herself it was even less thinkable to push the responsibility of raising her son at another person.

"What is more, I must admit that I am not missing the Order as much as I did at the beginning when we came here. I enjoy teaching, but working with the people here has showed me that I infinitely prefer working with adults to teaching children."

Eryn looked at him in surprise. "Do you? Then I wonder what would keep you from doing just that after our return home. I mean, you are the Head of Warriors now, aren't you? Who is to say you have to teach children if you don't want to?"

He smiled without humour. "There is Enric. And Lord Tyront. And you, theoretically. But as you propose that I give up teaching children I fancy you won't oppose me in that."

"Neither will Enric, I am sure. And as for Lord Tyront... I don't see him interfering if you make sure things continue as they always have whether you teach the young nuisances or not. They must have managed somehow while you have been staying here, so this is probably the best point in time to do this."

Orrin nodded thoughtfully. "Yes, you are probably right." He looked at her and her son. "How about yourself? Will you take on a servant to help you with Vedric?"

"That I have no intention of doing. I hope to include Enric as much as his time allows. He has shown promise here, but who knows how quickly that changes when being seen to care for his son would damage his fearsome reputation in public," she grimaced.

The warrior smiled and shook his head. "I don't see much of a problem there. Many people will instead question their own point of view if they see Enric doing this differently. It's the kind of influence he has on people. If he is doing it, it can't be completely wrong."

Eryn frowned doubtfully. "I don't know. This is not my impression. He was criticised in the past."

"There is no avoiding that. The trick is to always have more people behind than against you."

"Wise words from the mighty Lord Orrin," she sighed. "What you call a trick is the real challenge here. I wonder how the Order or rather the Magic Council will react to my insisting on a few concessions from their side so I am able to raise my child myself."

"I wouldn't worry too much about that. As you are the first woman on the Council, you are pretty much the one setting the rules. They have no idea about child rearing, so whatever you tell them they will have to believe. And you have Enric and me on your side. Lord Poron won't oppose you, either."

"That's three votes in addition to mine, but there will be thirteen members in total," she pointed out.

"Then you will have to apply what you have learned about political strategy. Some of the Council Members' companions seek your services when it comes to cosmetic corrections. I imagine that pointing out that you would appreciate their help in that matter would surely induce them to talk to their companions if it helps them to stay in your good favour."

"Orrin!" she exclaimed, truly shocked. "That is blatant manipulation! I wouldn't have expected a suggestion like that from you! How would you like to have Junar used against you like that?"

He shrugged. "If I were the type to fall for a thing like that I wouldn't deserve any better, I think."

"It doesn't exactly feel very honourable," she objected.

"It is simply political strategy, Eryn."

"So the end justifies the means? Is that what you are telling me?"

"No." He stopped and glared at her. "That is not what I said! Don't twist the words from my mouth. Means that cause damage and harm to others but enable you to reach your own goals no matter what cost for others are questionable and dishonourable. But using the resources at your disposal - namely your contacts - to let them know that you would value their help is a different matter entirely. It is almost exactly the way things work in the Senate here in Takhan, as you must have noticed. What is the first thing a senator does when he or she wants a decision in his or her favour?"

"Knock at doors with a good bottle of wine and a list of promises in exchange for a vote - I know," she sighed. She herself had helped her brother do just that once when he had asked her to persuade Ram'an to vote against Enric and his idea of compulsory combat training. She would have to give the idea some thought, she decided. The greatest obstacle here would probably be overcoming her reluctance to approach the irritating women and be pleasant to them.

"How are things between you and Enric going?" he spoke into her thoughts. "I have the impression that you are getting somewhere. He certainly has come a long way."

Eryn smirked. "Has he now? Because he is willing to spend some time with his son and doesn't insist on being in charge for a change?"

Orrin looked resigned and sighed in exasperation. "You truly fail to recognise the significance of this?"

"Enlighten me then, my wise friend. Share your insights with me so that I can become a better person in general and companion in particular, mighty Orrin."

"Silly child," he murmured. "Enric's father, Anwin, raised him to demonstrate superiority with strength in all areas of his life. The Order, as you know, is an organisation that sees magical strength as a justification for wielding power over others. We realised a while ago that this alone is not sufficient for leadership, thus a rigid training programme was established in addition. However, this does not balance a reluctance and disinclination for leadership. Well, at least in most cases. The aptitude tests here have made me realise this on a deeper level. But we managed to turn Enric into a leader, to make him embrace the principles of obedience, strength and power. This you yourself have experienced more often than once. He is used to having orders obeyed without discussion, question or resistance. This was all he knew and thus also applied in his dealings with you. But now he is subordinated to you for a change, and considering where he comes from he is taking this surprisingly well."

Eryn nodded thoughtfully. He was right. She had noticed how Enric had held back in these last few weeks since his return from Pirinkar. He had not criticised her decisions even once nor offered advice unbidden, even though he must surely have had a thing or two to say every now and again. He had accepted her instructions and carried them out and had spent his time doing what he had learned was work for women or servants: taking care of his son.

And interestingly enough, he didn't seem restless or unnerved by his current situation of being for the first time in many years not in the position of leader. He appeared uncommonly relaxed and had accepted whatever decision she had made without objection, be it that she had arranged for their stay to be prolonged for another two months or her choice of revenge on Malriel, who was still his Head of House - not currently, but she would soon resume her position.

Was she not giving him enough credit for all of this? Was this what Orrin was trying to tell her?

"We will see how much of this amazing development will remain once we have returned to Anyueel. I think the Order wants him back to show off his power and glory," she scowled.

Orrin smiled. "Good for you, then, that he has in all this years never given up that rebellious tendency that made him such a tiresome student. A man who doesn't shy back from throttling a King will probably not mind following his personal inclinations to a certain degree if they contribute to your and thus his own happiness."

She nodded, still not entirely convinced. It was one matter to enjoy a carefree state here without responsibility, but this was not a mind-set he could afford back home. But there was little sense in making guesses about that now. She would see how things turned out in only a few weeks' time.

* * *

Valrad opened the door and kissed Eryn on her cheeks before nodding to Orrin and handing them both dampened towels.

"You are the last ones to arrive, we have been waiting for you. Come in."

Eryn exchanged a look with Orrin. That eager energy was an unusual contrast to his generally more serene demeanour.

"It seems being with your mother has returned some youthful energy to him," Orrin whispered when he followed her up the stairs.

"You think so?" she whispered back. "I would rather have counted on the Queen of Darkness slowly but steadily sucking all will to live from his soul."

Valrad turned to her and lifted one disapproving eyebrow at her. "I heard that!"

She shrugged. "Good. It shows that your ears are still fully functional even if your brain currently seems to be suffering from a regrettable state of unsoundness of mind. You might want to see Iklan about that. I am sure he can fix you up in no time and you can then start looking for a nice normal woman."

Her father closed his eyes for a moment, then shot her a warning look before progressing into the main room where Enric, Junar, Vran'el and Malriel were waiting for them.

Enric approached her immediately, kissing her on her mouth and then untying the knot so that he could loosen the sling and take Vedric from her.

"Come, my love. Dinner is ready," he told her and took her hand to lead her to a place next to his.

"How is Kilan doing?" she enquired.

"He is fine, as always, and sends his regards. He told me something interesting today. It seems that Valcredy is expected to arrive here in a matter of days."

Eryn looked at him and frowned, then she remembered the name. "Valcredy? The singer you had an affair with?" She grimaced. "Why?"

"She requested permission to come here once it became clear that there was no longer any immediate danger of war breaking out. She wants to study music here, especially magical music, and has been permitted to do so."

"And they couldn't have allowed her to come here after we have left?"

"This would have been the case if you had not requested permission to prolong our own stay here," he pointed out mildly.

"You do not approve of her coming here?" Vran'el smirked. "Jealous, are you then?"

Eryn shook her head. "Not really. I just don't have very fond memories of her. Enric thought that it would be a fabulous idea for her to teach me dancing, although she used this opportunity to insult and disparage me because she was irritated that Enric had chosen me over her."

The lawyer grimaced. "You had your former lover teaching your companion dancing?"

Enric shrugged. "It was probably not one of my more sensible ideas. But I had not been aware then that she had harboured any hopes about a future with me."

Valrad dished out the food after they had washed their hands and then returned to the kitchen for another small bowl that he handed to Junar.

"Here. This is a more mildly-spiced version for Téa. I assume she has started eating solids now?"

Junar smiled at the thoughtfulness and accepted the bowl. "She has, yes. Though I have to tell you that feeding her is hardly ever a clean business. Your cushions might suffer greatly."

He waved her off. "Do not worry about this, my dear. These cushions survived Eryn's tendency to spit and throw food as a little girl, so your daughter is hardly likely to be more of a strain on them than that was."

Eryn grimaced. "Thank you so much for bringing that up. Should any other embarrassing incidents from my childhood come to your mind, do not hold back sharing them with all and sundry. Really - I don't mind at all. It's not like I will be subject to any teasing or anything later."

"What can I say, dear daughter?" he smiled. "My regrettably unsound mind does at times still seem to be able to come up with anecdotes from a long gone past."

While the others exchanged puzzled glances, Orrin, being the only one who had heard her earlier remark to him, coughed when a mouthful had taken the wrong route.

Eryn didn't reply to that. It had been a worthy repartee, she had to admit.

She noted how Malriel sat close to Valrad, maintaining physical contact with him at all times, be it her leg brushing his or their shoulders touching, not to mention the looks they kept giving each other. Like besotted teenagers, she couldn't help thinking, and managed only with some effort to stop rolling her eyes.

Vran'el collected the empty dishes when all of them were finished eating and took them to the kitchen. When he had returned and sat down again, he nodded at his father once.

Valrad cleared his throat. "I am glad that you have followed our invitation to spend this evening with us. We have news we want to share with you."

Enric's gaze fell on their linked fingers and then wandered to Vran'el, who was watching his sister with what looked suspiciously like dread. He was obviously already aware of the news and did not expect Eryn to take them well.

"Malriel and I are going to join each other in a commitment," he announced.

All eyes were on Valrad for a few moments, then flicked to Eryn, who merely stared at them open-mouthed.

"You are doing what?" she whispered when her voice had resumed cooperating. "You are joking, of course? This is some kind of revenge, is it?" She laughed tensely. "Well done, you! You almost got me there." Her expression grew distraught when nobody joined her. "You can't possibly," she stated, forcing her brain to help her out, to produce logical reasons against this.

Enric cleared his throat and she felt his arm move around her shoulders and press her against him in an attempt to comfort her.

"What Eryn meant," he spoke, "is that you are both Heads of Houses, or rather soon will be, and thus a commitment seems rather problematic in this case."

"Yes, that's it!" she nodded emphatically, grateful for that never-tiring analytical mind of his. "What he said!"

"We are of course aware of this," Valrad explained, "and have found a solution that is beneficial to all involved." He lifted a hand to lay it on his son's shoulder. "I will retire from my position as Head of House Vel'kim and give my heir a chance to take over the function he has been preparing for since he was a little boy."

Eryn felt her throat go tight and raised a hand to her neck. "You are giving up your position for her?" she croaked.

Valrad looked at her and nodded. "I am. Just as I would have done thirty-five years ago. There are a few arrangements to take care of, but I should be ready to hand over the reins to Vran'el in no more than two weeks."

Eryn hastily grabbed a glass from the table, not bothering to check if it was her own and downed the contents greedily.

"Congratulations!" she heard Junar chirp and fought the urge to throttle her friend. Orrin followed suit and so did Enric.

"Wait, wait, wait!" Eryn barked and shot the happy couple a hard look. "I don't approve! Moreover, I forbid it! No commitment. I am Malriel's Head of House, and I do not give my permission, consent, approval or whatever else you require officially. I just won't." She folded her arms and glared at them.

Malriel just lifted an eyebrow. "Now you are the one doing the jesting, Maltheá. Your being my Head of House continues for just a matter of weeks. You are merely able to delay the ceremony but not prevent it. If you are determined to be difficult about this, the only thing you will achieve is angering your father and missing the commitment."

Eryn leaned back, closing her eyes. Of course she couldn't stop them. But she didn't have to watch this lunacy, did she?

"Valrad, can I talk to you alone for a moment?" she then asked with more calm than she felt.

"Of course."

He followed her outside to the garden and far enough to be out of earshot before she whirled around and grabbed his shoulders.

"Don't do this! She is not a good person! She led your brother into doom and might do just that with you!" she implored him, her eyes wide, willing him to understand the truth of her words.

"Eryn," he sighed and took both her hands into his warm ones, pulling them to his lips to kiss them. "I have loved your mother for decades. In a way she has always been mine."

"Valrad," she said, trying to sound as reasonable as possible, "Malriel is no longer that sad-eyed girl trapped in an unhappy relationship, but a woman who devours young men, uses them and casts them aside when she has no further use for them. You can't save her! She has just returned from a country where that very behaviour pattern almost led to her being charged with rape! Doesn't this make you stop to think even a little?" she pleaded.

"A strategy to escape her loneliness, Eryn," he sighed. "And one that caused more harm to herself than to anybody else. Had she been as cruel in her dealings with her lovers as you say, they would hardly have been as willing to allow themselves be taken to bed by her."

"Have you forgotten what she tried to do to me? The accusation of having caused your brother's death?" she whispered. "What you yourself and Vran'el helped to prevent her from accomplishing?"

He sighed with impressive depth. "Desperate measures from a mother who saw no other way, my child. And who am I to judge her?"

"Please, Valrad, there is no need for a step like this. Why can't you just enjoy each other's company without making a commitment? Why give up your position for her? What is she doing that is even remotely comparable to the sacrifice you are making?"

He chuckled and shook his head. "Eryn, my girl, how can this be a sacrifice? Stepping back from this position does not pain me at all when what I shall be getting in return is so much more. Being a Head of House went well for me for a good long time, but it was never more than a duty. It is certainly not to me what it is to your mother: a vocation. Vran'el is willing and more than ready to take over this responsibility, and I know that he will do well, probably a lot better than I have."

"She would then be my mother again, legally speaking," Eryn moaned and covered her face. "I renounced her House to cut that very connection!"

Valrad sighed and pulled her hands away from her face to make her look at him. "She has never stopped being your mother, my girl. Our commitment would not subject you to her command any more than before. Vran'el will be your Head of House just like I am now. Nothing much will change for you."

She glared at him. "Apart from the fact that my companion will be my brother, you mean!"

He chuckled at that. "Well, I never said we were a traditional family, did I? I want you to stop opposing us and I am asking you to officially grant your permission as Head of House for Malriel to join me in a third level commitment bond before your departure. I want you and Enric to be there when we do this. I want to celebrate with you."

She nodded, defeated. "Alright, if there is no reasoning with you and you are still determined to make the Queen of Darkness yours, who am I to put obstacles in your way?"

He gave her an even look. "I would very much appreciate if you could avoid referring to the woman I love like that in my presence from now on."

"Then you should have thought twice before committing to this woman I happen to hate," she shot back.

"Now, now," Valrad sighed, "hate is certainly too strong an expression here. What a pity that you will return to Anyueel so soon. I dare say Iklan would have been able to assist you two with your issues."

"Not funny," Eryn growled. "If you want to help me resolve my issues with her, not committing to her would be a fabulous start."

"I am not discussing this with you, Eryn. My decision is solid and I will not change it to accommodate you. And you have no right to ask me to do just that." His voice had taken one a rather stern tone. "This is my chance for happiness, and I do not intend to let it slip through my fingers again. Now come back inside with me and be civil for one more hour, then you may leave and complain to Enric and your friends to your heart's content." He smiled briefly. "By the way, there is something more that might interest you as it will benefit your clinic in Anyueel."

He waited for her to look up at him again, curious despite herself.

"Yes? What is it?" she enquired suspiciously.

"I will take back the position of Head of the clinic now that I no longer have to lead my House. I was thinking that we might discuss an idea or two I had for healer exchange programmes."

She let him drape an arm around her shoulders and walk her back towards the house.

"That's a bribe," she huffed.

"Indeed," he smiled unperturbed. "But one we both know will work fabulously, not forgetting that you would rather throw it back in my face. A pity that it is just too good a chance to dismiss in order to express your righteous indignation, is it not?"

"Oh, shut up," Eryn murmured, wondering how she was supposed to survive the next hour.

* * *

"I swear to you, this must have been the longest hour in all my life," Eryn sighed and lifted her cup to have it filled by Intrea.

They were sitting on the cushions in the Feral main room, Urban hiding somewhere in the garden, Obal looking for her.

"Why are so unhappy about this? I would think that your parents reuniting like this is not such a bad thing," Intrea shrugged.

"I am worried about Valrad. I mean, you know Malriel. Practically everybody does! And everybody but my own father is smart enough to know that spending more than a few nights with her is not a sensible move."

"Now you are doing her an injustice, Eryn. Malriel has certainly not refrained from joining a man because none have been willing to. And your father is a grown man. Vran tells me he has been in love with her for more than three decades." Intrea sighed and shook her head. "You know that I never liked Malriel particularly, but this is touching. There is no denying it. The thought of those two unhappy people finally being reunited after all these years, him giving up his position of power for her…"

Eryn rolled her eyes. "Stop that right now or I am going to throw up. They are idiots, both of them. She has only ever been in one relationship, and that ended in a disaster. I wonder if she is even aware of the principle of fidelity! And he is a lost fool who never managed to let go of a pretty face and fails to see the damaged character underneath."

"Not a very flattering assessment of your parents, I have to say."

"It wasn't meant to be flattering, but realistic. And from what Valrad has told me giving up his position to Vran'el is not that much of a sacrifice for him anyway as he prefers taking over the clinic instead", Eryn huffed. "So much for that grand gesture."

Intrea leaned back and smirked.

"What are you grinning about?"

"Vran has told me that your father bribed you with an idea of his that includes sending healers to your city and accepting yours in return. That this is how he made you permit the ceremony as Malriel's Head of House and attend it as well. So you may just stop acting so very indignantly, because if you really are worried about your father's wellbeing, accepting a bribe to act against your own conscience does not look too good for you, my dear Eryn."

Eryn narrowed her eyes. "I cannot help but feel that my brother tells you way too much."

The other woman shrugged. "And why would he not? I am his companion, after all. By the way, the story of their return that night has gone around. Funny thing, only last night I have heard the term Aren Welcome."

"It refers to being knocked out without any prior warning?" Eryn sighed.

"So you heard it already?"

"No, that was just an educated guess. I just had to think of the most unimaginative possibility. People are hardly ever creative when it comes to jibes or most others wouldn't understand them," the healer retorted dryly.

"Oh. I was wondering for a moment who might have been brave enough to mention it to you."

"You would have been just now."

Intrea grinned and waved her off. "I have nothing to fear from you. My companion is going to be your Head of House soon. I am quite safe."

Eryn smiled cruelly. "Whatever helps you sleep without fear, dear."

CHAPTER 12

Travellers from Anyueel

Enric knocked at the study door and opened it when he heard her call out an invitation to enter. Eryn was sitting behind the desk, one leg draped across one corner, a displeased expression on her face as she read a sheet of paper.

"Bad news?" he enquired casually.

"Not exactly. But one of my many who-knows-what-degree cousins has sent a proposal for what looks to me like a rather hare-brained idea at first glance. He wants to attempt growing a certain kind of plant that is usually only found in high altitudes on one of the estates. He has some ideas about cooling mechanisms, but I don't understand all of it." She let the paper sink and put it aside. "The bit I do comprehend seems unlikely. But Malhora is a lot better with crops, I will let her have a look at this. I would ask Valrad, but I fancy it would not look too good if I asked another Head of House for advice about internal Aren matters, never mind that he is my father or about to join the Queen of Darkness." Then she smiled at her companion. "But you have not come to listen to me lamenting on the challenges of leading House Aren. What can I do for you?"

Enric took in the picture of her. She wore her role of mistress of the House well, almost like a second skin. In this study she was not his companion or the reluctant Order magician, but she was in charge, in control, showed confidence and a more business-like manner than she normally chose when dealing with him.

He knew that she handled matters pretty much the same way at her clinic back in Anyueel. She behaved differently depending on whether she was in her study, in a teaching room or downstairs treating patients.

He wondered how she would take to the change of no longer being in charge of her own clinic when they returned.

"You look thoughtful. What is it you are seeing right now?" she asked mildly.

"A strong woman. A leader. Somebody who should not be underestimated, somebody to take into consideration. An unpredictable person who never ceases to surprise me. The love of my life," he replied after a moment's thought.

She eyed him suspiciously and folded her arms. "Flattery. This does not bode well. What do you want me to do that I will not be happy about?"

He chuckled and shook his head at her. "Can't a man compliment his formidable companion without arousing suspicion?"

"So there is no unpleasant request or bit of news? Nothing whatsoever?"

He waggled his head and came closer. "Well, if you ask like that... You remember that I told you about Valcredy's impending arrival?"

Eryn sighed. "So she is here? Is that it or are you trying to make me meet her, welcome her into these foreign parts or something of the sort? If so, let me tell you that I would consider this Kilan's duty as ambassador, not mine. And I suspect she is hardly much more eager to meet me than I am to see her."

Enric nodded. "I admit your answer doesn't surprise me. Would you mind if I met her? I am the one she is most familiar with in this country."

She regarded him through narrowed eyes, wishing she had access to his emotions through the mind bond right now. Then she exhaled and shook her head. It was somehow touching that he came to her to ask her permission for this. And after she had misjudged his intentions with Malriel so completely it would surely not hurt to demonstrate a little trust at this stage. He had never even once objected to her meeting Ram'an, after all.

"No, go and see her if you must."

"Thank you. I will wait until you have fed Vedric, then I can take him with me. I will ask her to meet me at a teahouse."

Eryn couldn't help but smile at that. This was a very clear sign that he wanted to avoid any misunderstandings concerning his motivation behind meeting her. It was probably meant as a message to both Eryn and Valcredy. And it was quite effective, too.

"You do that," she nodded, satisfied.

* * *

Ram'an waited for Eryn after the Senate meeting at the top of the stairs outside the hall.

"So it is official now. Your brother is soon going to be your new Head of House. I wonder how he will manage leading his two younger sisters."

She snorted. "I don't require leading by anybody. Especially as I have more than enough of that back home with Lord Tyront and the King. If he falls prey to any delusions of grandeur and thinks he can order me about, he will not be seeing too much of me over here in the years to come."

"Theá, dear," Ram'an chuckled, "he will be in a position to make you come here if it pleases him. You will be bound to him in a second level bond, after all."

She abruptly froze on the stairs and felt somebody bump into her from behind, almost sending her tumbling down. Ram'an quickly grabbed her upper arm and pulled her to his side.

Eryn turned and looked up at face set in a disapproving expression. Tanif, Head of House Landred.

"Forgive me," she apologised.

"Come on, before you cause any real accidents," Ram'an urged her on and preceded her down the remaining stairs.

"I have no intention of taking that bond with Vran'el," Eryn huffed when they had reached the bottom.

"You are aware that swearing an oath of loyalty to your Head of House is common practice here, are you not? Your father skipped the formality of making you do it out of leniency and a wish to avoid angering you any more than necessary. But this is a luxury Vran'el cannot afford as a new Head. He must be seen to take control quickly and without seeming weak or he will find maintaining his father's alliances quite challenging."

"Enric never entered into such a bond with Malriel," she pointed out, folding her arms. "I would think that my living in another country would certainly be considered difficult circumstances. And then there is the fact that I am already under such a bond with the Kingdom. Being bound to two masters like that is more than anybody should ask of me. And I dare say that King Folrin will not be thrilled about such a thing, either."

Ram'an just shrugged. "I am just saying that you might want to prepare yourself for this eventuality. You do not need to convince me, Theá."

She exhaled and nodded. He was right, of course.

"I hear that your sister will be coming here for the ceremony," he went on, changing the topic.

"Yes, and she will bring Rolan with her. It must be pretty serious between the two of them if she wants to introduce him to her family. But then they have been together for more than half a year now, so I suppose it's time to finally present him at home. I know that Valrad and Vran'el are both curious about him."

"So am I, to be honest. Pe'tala was never one to indulge in affairs or show more than a passing interest in a man. I look forward to seeing the man who has snagged her interest."

Eryn smirked. "And I imagine the fact that she has found another man after you so callously rejected her hand does wonders for your conscience and makes you feel less guilty."

"I admit this is not entirely untrue," he conceded. "I hear that Valcredy has come to Takhan."

Eryn frowned. "I wasn't aware that you know her."

"But of course. I took dancing lessons with her. A talented musician. And a very pretty, lively woman."

"You think?" Eryn said lightly. "I suppose she is the kind to catch a man's eye."

Ram'an smiled. "I cannot help but have the impression that you are not very fond of her, Theá."

"I don't know her well enough to give an opinion on her."

"Indeed? That is for most people not a valid reason not to do so anyway."

She rolled her eyes. "If you are so fond of her, you might just as well invite her to a nice cup of tea and exchange fond memories."

He nodded slowly. "I might do just that. I imagine that she would like to see a familiar face in a place so foreign to her. Why do you not join us?"

"I would love to, seriously," she lied, "but unfortunately I need to take care of a thing or two. Malhora wants me to approve an experiment with plants on one of the plantations and I need to get a cost estimate for it. Then there is the matter of trying to avoid the oath to Vran'el in case he really wants me to swear one. You don't happen to have any laws that offer helpful exceptions you recommend I throw at him? Preferably something ancient he doesn't even know about and so is not prepared for?" she asked hopefully.

"I am sorry, dear, but no. The senators would never have approved a law of that sort. Half of them are Heads of Houses and would thus not appreciate a rule like that, neither in the past nor today."

She narrowed her eyes at him. "And then there is also the fact that Vran'el would know exactly who had given me such a tip, wouldn't he? As I am about to leave the country and he is going to be the new Head of House of a family allied with yours, you wouldn't help me even if you could. It would anger him and that you can't afford. Don't even try do deny it!"

He laughed appreciatively. "Ah, Theá, my dear, I see that you are a lot less easy to hoodwink than a few short months ago. Can I placate you with a cup of tea and a bread bun?"

Eryn waved to him when she turned and walked away, throwing over her shoulder, "No, thank you. I am off bread buns. There is still a bit of weight I am trying to trim."

"You might want to ask Orrin to resume your combat training," he called after her, "That would take care of whatever surplus weight you think you have in no time."

Eryn saw several heads turn in their direction at that less than flattering statement and just sent him a devastating look before marching on.

* * *

Eryn stood together with Enric, Vran'el, Intrea, Neval and Obal at the pier and watched the ship with Pe'tala and Rolan on deck drawing nearer the jetty.

"Oh dear, she looks so incredibly pale," Neval whispered and then looked at Eryn. "Anyueel must be a dark and depressing place."

She shrugged. "It will certainly be in about two months. We have spent the summer months away from home to return to winter. Thinking back, this was probably not the most prudent timing, especially considering that we don't have any clothes for Vedric for the cold season."

Intrea held on to her daughter's hand and turned her head to search the jetties around them. "Where is Valrad? I would have expected him to want to welcome his daughter after her long absence."

"He is waiting at home with Malriel," Vran'el explained. "I suspect he wants to give Tala the chance to get rid of some of her frustration before meeting Malriel. And maybe use the time himself to implore Malriel to be civil to her daughter to be."

"Good luck with that," Eryn murmured and watched the slowly approaching ship. "Why does this ship look so different from the one we arrived on?"

"It is one of ours," Enric supplied. "It was finished three months ago and is larger than the ones that were sent from here. It can carry almost twice the load and transport more cargo per trip."

"Ours?" she asked suspiciously. "Ours as in the Kingdom's or as in yours and mine?"

He laughed. "What do you think?"

They watched as ropes were thrown to helpers standing near the jetty's edge. They quickly lashed the ropes to shiny iron bollards and slowly the ship came to a standstill. After some shouts and assorted metallic noises, the gangplank was put in place a few moments later to permit the passengers to leave the vessel.

Pe'tala was the first to disembark. Eryn shook her head at how very foreign her sister looked with her pale complexion and the clothes in Anyueel style.

She grinned broadly while striding towards the group that was expecting her, throwing her arms around her brother and pressing him close when she reached them.

Vran'el squeezed her tightly, pressing a firm kiss onto her forehead after they released each other again. He took both her hands and looked her up and down, shaking his head.

"Tala, my heart, you look so very foreign. Just like Eryn when she first came here. We need to dress you properly and make sure you get enough sun while you are over with us."

Pe'tala merely laughed and turned next to Eryn to pull her into a hug.

"You look fabulous, sister, however little pleasure admitting such a thing gives me. You are tanned and the colours suit you. Are you not a little chubbier than you used to be? But then I suppose one has to grant a new mother that."

"Thank you so much," Eryn growled and eyed her sister's trim waist with a certain envy.

When she had greeted Intrea, Neval and Obal, Pe'tala turned to point to the young man who walked towards them.

"This is Rolan," she said simply.

Vran'el let his gaze wander over the newcomer, his immediate expression not exactly welcoming. Eryn rolled her eyes and stepped towards her former assistant, pulling him into a hug.

"Hello Rolan," she smiled. "It has been a while." She was surprised when he squeezed her back.

"It is a lot quieter since you left," he said. "Not entirely, mind you, with Tala around, but still less turbulent than what we became used to," he stated with a ghost of a smile.

"Is this a roundabout way of telling me that you miss me?" she grinned.

"I wouldn't go that far. You are still my superior and I am trying to maintain a minimum of decorum."

Eryn squeezed his arm. "There is no need for that here, Rolan. To be honest I have to tell you that treating me with professional distance is going to seem really strange here."

She watched Enric and Rolan exchanging a polite bow and rolled her eyes again. It seemed that some people just didn't manage to leave their habits behind. She wondered how Rolan would deal with the matter of avoiding the titles in Enric's and Orrin's case. Not too well, she suspected.

When all present had been introduced to Rolan, Pe'tala turned to Eryn.

"Now tell me what is going on here. I leave the country for a few months and find father is preparing to join the Queen of Darkness? I am still hoping that this was nothing more than a cruel joke to trick me into coming back here."

"Unfortunately not," Eryn sighed. "It really is happening. I have been trying to talk to Valrad, but he just doesn't want to listen to me. He thinks he is in love with her, so I am afraid there is no helping him. I would recommend that you avoid criticising his decision. That way he has at least one daughter he doesn't have to be furious at."

Pe'tala snorted. "You are the golden child, Eryn. He has only just got you to accept him as your father, there is nothing much you can do wrong. He would just be suspicious if I did not try to dissuade him."

"Suit yourself. Just be prepared for it not to have any effect on him. Apart from declaring him insane I see little chance of halting him."

Vran'el shook his head at them. "You are terrible, both of you. Father has spent most of his life alone, and now that he finally has the chance to join the woman he loves, you do not have it in you to be happy for him," he admonished them.

Pe'tala narrowed her eyes at him. "It seems like you, too, have gone a little soft in the head. Is it possible that she has managed to enchant you during your little trip up north to safe her?" Her gaze wandered to Enric. "How about you? Are you at least still able to see that she is a manipulating, dangerous, selfish creature with little regard for others?"

Enric nodded earnestly. "Oh, absolutely. I am determined to reject the notion of her possessing any remotely human qualities at all."

"Idiot", Pe'tala murmured.

Enric pressed his lips together to suppress a smile. That had sounded a lot like her older sister.

"Shall we move on now?" Vran'el suggested. "Not that this jetty is not a very cosy place, but father is waiting for you. He has been talking of little else. And Tala?" He placed a hand on her shoulder. "Try to be civil to Malriel. Promise me."

His younger sister grimaced. "This is a little much to ask, Vran."

"And yet I insist. She is going to be our mother, legally speaking. It will not hurt to be on good or at least civil terms with her. Anything else would hurt father."

Pe'tala rolled her eyes. "I will be civil if she is."

"And you will refrain from addressing her as Queen of Darkness?" he pressed on.

"Yes, yes!" Pe'tala exclaimed and threw up her hands in exasperation. "I will be on my best behaviour, I promise! Now leave me be, alright?" She turned to her sister and linked their arms. "Come, walk with me. Let me tell you how much your countrymen have kept trying my patience. I wrote you that they started calling me Lady, did I not? I swear to you, I still want to kick every single one of them. They just do not understand that I do not like that! They think it is a great honour they are bestowing upon me, a sign of respect! Would it not show a lot more respect if they respected my wish just to be addressed with my name, I ask you?"

Eryn squeezed her sister's hand in sympathy, feeling an odd sense of belonging to this energetic woman who shared so many of her sentiments.

"Is there really no way for us to stop this lunacy?" Pe'tala whispered to her.

She shook her head with a pained expression. "I am afraid not. Valrad is determined to go through with it. Maybe it is better that he lets Vran'el take over the House. He seems to be getting strange with age," she muttered.

Pe'tala snorted. "You just wait. I have an indistinct feeling that Vran will not be the most unproblematic Head, especially at the beginning. I do not mind telling you that I am more than glad that I can leave here again so soon."

"Ram'an thinks he will make me swear the oath," Eryn whispered.

"Of course he will. You may depend on it. He has to build a power base and the two of us are the ones highest up in the House apart from him."

"I don't want to!"

"Neither do I," her sister grimaced. "But there is nothing we can do about it. He can demand it of us and we are bound to follow his request. Where is my nephew, by the way? I was hoping for you to bring him with you so I could have a look at him."

"He is at the Vel'kim residence with his grandfather. I think Valrad took him away as some kind of security to make sure I would return there with you after picking you up from the port."

Pe'tala sniggered. "Then I am afraid that he is not quite as soft in the head as you like to believe. Come on, let us free your son from the grasp of his fearsome grandparents."

* * *

Malriel rose elegantly from her seat on the cushions and smiled at the newcomers, holding her grandson in her arms. She appeared very much like the gracious hostess she clearly wasn't in this house.

Valrad laughed and pulled Pe'tala into his arms and held on to her, burying his face in her hair, closing his eyes and enjoying his daughter's proximity.

Eryn sighed and took over the duty to introduce Rolan. "Rolan, I dare say you will remember Malriel of House Aren from her visit to Anyueel. She is going to be Pe'tala's future mother. The man squeezing her and currently making the impression that he never wants to let go of her again is our father Valrad, Head of House Vel'kim. Well, for another few days. Head of House, I mean. He will continue to be our father even after our brother takes over the House."

"Thank you," Rolan deadpanned. "I figured as much."

He waited patiently until Valrad had released his daughter again before approaching him.

"Valrad, Head of House Vel'kim, I am Rolan," he introduced himself stiffly and held out a hand for the formal greeting Pe'tala had undoubtedly taught him. Yet she seemed to have neglected telling him that the higher ranking person was the one to offer it. Or he was just nervous enough to forget that small detail.

Valrad took the young man in, then accepted the greeting nevertheless. "Welcome to my home, Rolan. I have been looking forward to meeting you. Do have a seat. Neval and Enric will take your luggage to your room."

Eryn noted that he had not sent his own son along, probably so that they could start questioning the man Pe'tala seemed to have a serious interest in. Poor Rolan, she thought and sat down next to him to be at his side and help him brave whatever he would have to face now.

"So, Rolan," Vran'el began, taking a seat opposite him. "Tell us a little about yourself. I hear you are currently in charge of organising the clinic?"

The younger man nodded obediently. "I am, yes. I used to be Eryn's assistant, but she promoted me to the position of Head of Administration several months ago."

"You are a little younger than my sister, are you not?"

"Two years, yes."

"What are your intentions, your plans with Pe'tala?" Vran'el asked on.

Pe'tala rolled her eyes and folded her arms. "Stop that right now! This is not an interrogation. He does not have to justify his intentions to you, only to me. Now back off!"

Intrea worked hard at hiding her grin and Obal slowly moved closer to the new blond man as if careful not to scare him away.

Rolan obviously tried to keep all of them in his field of vision as if afraid that there might be an unprovoked attack from somewhere any moment.

He clearly didn't enjoy his current situation and Eryn couldn't blame him for it.

"Tell me how Lord Poron has settled in so far," she asked, even though she had been informed of that in her correspondence both with him and Pe'tala already. She hoped talking about a familiar topic would help him to relax a little.

"Fine from what I can tell. It took him a while to determine which tasks he had to take care of himself and which ones could be delegated. He is very thorough in everything he does and eager to learn."

Pe'tala nodded. "Unfortunately his days are just as short as everyone else's, so he had to learn to prioritise. I took the liberty of assisting him a little in that. He is still not happy when he has to leave something lying on his desk to finish it the next day, but his companion Aurna has very definite views on the matter. She told him rather plainly that he is not a young man any longer and that she intends to see him occasionally before he dies."

Eryn winced. "Not an especially nuanced statement."

"No, but an effective one. From then on he made sure to return home in a timely manner," Pe'tala grinned. "I like that woman. She is certainly not as prissy as the other Council members' companions."

"I am a Council member's companion," Eryn reminded her mildly.

"I know. And if you try very hard you will one day maybe be as likable as Lord Poron's companion," her younger sister sneered. Then her gaze wandered to Malriel and the child on her arm.

Her bearing became stiff when she asked, "Malriel, I would very much like to hold my nephew if you would oblige."

Malriel nodded and handed over her grandson.

Pe'tala looked down at the infant in her arm and her expression became soft when Vedric's small mouth puckered into a lazy smile.

"He is adorable," she murmured and swallowed when tiny fingers closed around her thumb. She cleared her throat, then looked at

Eryn. "He looks a lot like his father. But I suppose you have heard that quite a few times already."

Eryn smiled without humour. "I have, yes. Thank you so much for pointing it out nevertheless."

Pe'tala nodded at her niece and motioned for her to sit next to her. "Come, Obal. Let me tell you why it is going to pay to be nice to your cousin. He will one day take over the function of Head of House and you might find him a useful friend and ally. Only if you refrain from tantalising him too much as long as he is smaller and weaker than you, that is."

Enric, who had just returned from getting the luggage across to the guest room, shook his head. "That is a very opportunistic point of view to teach a child, Tala."

She shrugged. "Is it? That is an interesting thing to hear you say, Enric, considering that young Order magicians are taught a discipline that is called political strategy." She turned back to her niece. "Where was I? Ah, yes - we were talking about maintaining good contact with the mighty and powerful." She nodded at Enric. "Your uncle from foreign parts is also a good candidate for this. He is very influential and wealthy. With your aunt Eryn and your grandmother to be Malriel you might want to be careful, though. Aren women are known to be a rather dangerous breed."

"Pe'tala, I would ask you to not to lecture my daughter about the personal advantages she might gain from befriending certain people. Intrea and I are trying to raise her to look behind such considerations," her brother admonished her.

Eryn smiled and leaned back. Pe'tala had successfully managed to steer the conversation topic away from her lover. In her opinion little Obal would do well in maintaining close contact with her aunt Tala. There was certainly a lot to be learned from that side.

CHAPTER 13

A New Head

"Everything looks fine," Valrad nodded and removed his hand from Eryn's shoulder. He had offered to carry out the routine examination at his home and save her a visit to the clinic.

"You have helped the natural healing process along a little, though, have you not?" he enquired sternly. "It seems quite a bit too good to be true."

Eryn folded her arms. "So what? Even if I did, you said yourself that everything looks fine in there. And it was not my fault that the belt got removed sooner than planned, was it?"

Pe'tala was leaning against the wall next to the terrace door, grinning broadly. "I heard that Enric removed it from you and earned himself what is now commonly known as the Aren Welcome."

Valrad looked at her in puzzlement. "The what?"

"People use the expression to refer to being knocked out unannounced and probably also undeserved," his younger daughter explained smugly. "People in Anyueel are still rather lost when it comes to grasping the principle of Houses here, but they have taken to calling it an Eryn Welcome instead."

"In Anyueel?" Eryn groaned. "They know about that? Why?"

"Vran wrote about it in one of his letters a few weeks ago, and I told the healers. They must have spread it about," she shrugged.

"And the thought that I would not like that very much did not cross your mind even once?"

Pe'tala pretended to think for a moment, then shrugged. "It did once or twice. But then I had to decide between amusing myself and humouring you. The choice was not a hard one, I must admit. People say I am self-centred. They are right."

"Girls, be nice to each other," Valrad said softly.

"I am doing my best, father. I would not want to be treated to an Aren Welcome myself on my brother's big day, would I?"

"You go on like that and this is exactly where you are headed," Eryn growled. "Where is the new Head of House Vel'kim, by the way?"

"He is at the clinic. This is where quite a large part of our House can be found at the same time. He has taken over my new study for today to have people sent up and swear the oath to him," Valrad explained.

Eryn swallowed. "Have you sworn the oath to him? Do you even intend to?"

Her father smiled. "But of course. I was the very first one to do so. It is a powerful gesture that shows that I truly am stepping back from the position and place all my trust in him."

"So there is no ceremony, no public gathering involved in that?"

"None whatsoever. But then you should remember that there was none when Ram'an took over his House. It is a private internal matter that does not require any curious watchers."

Pe'tala nodded at her sister. "Eryn here is not too thrilled at the prospect of binding herself to Vran'el with magic. It seems your leniency in that has spoiled her a little."

Eryn shot the younger woman a withering glare. "Thank you so much for addressing this here like that, you nuisance! Isn't there anybody else you should delight with your presence? Old friends? Cousins? Colleagues at the clinic?"

"Not at the moment, no. I can focus all my powers of causing irritation on you."

Valrad frowned and took Eryn's hand. "This is not good, my dear. You should not be reluctant to bind yourself to him. He loves you and I know that he will not use this power over you to tease or harm you. Refusing to swear the oath would be a blatant demonstration of distrust, especially as your son is his heir."

She made herself nod and squeezed his fingers reassuringly. "I will talk to him about it all and try not to anger or hurt him, I promise." Time to change the topic. "How were your first few days back in charge of the clinic? How did your predecessor react to being replaced just like that?"

"He took it well enough. He even told me that at times it did seem to him as if I was never really gone from the position. That is of course a gross exaggeration."

Pe'tala rolled her eyes and snorted. "Yes, right."

"Iklan was the first to visit and congratulate me. As you know he is planning to do some work on couples that had their third level commitment dissolved because of the mind bond. I am in favour of it which means he can be sure of my assent to his plans. He was not very subtle in reminding me of that," he sighed. "He is currently somewhat at a loss about which topic to work with first. Mind bonds have been a great area of interest for him for many years, but now that Vedric and Téa have turned out to be so exceptionally strong, he would also love to work in that direction. He is even considering stepping back from his healing work from a while to do research for a few years."

Pe'tala nodded slowly. "Yes, I can understand that well enough. I was myself on the verge of testing the children who had been born this year in Anyueel to satisfy my curiosity after I heard about

Vedric's incredible results. But I am not really in a position to make a request like that as a foreigner. The Magic Council distrusts me as I am not a member of the Order and thus practically loose and uncontrollable, as it were. I feel they only just tolerate me in the city."

Eryn smiled faintly. Yes, the Order had a tendency to distrust those who were not bound by their rules.

"We will take care of this when we are back. I already promised Iklan to let him know what I find out. We are both expecting an increase in children with magical potential, especially girls. And if Téa and Vedric are any indication, we should also be prepared for increased magical strength. Enric thinks we need to be quick and rethink the Order's current way of granting authority, namely in accordance with the degree of strength each member shows."

Valrad nodded appreciatively. "I am all for it. The way it is looking now is that Vedric might otherwise be made to take over the Order one day. As we also expect him to lead House Vel'kim, this would definitely be a conflict of interests."

Eryn didn't comment on that. From her point of view it didn't really matter which leadership role people were trying to force on him once he was old enough. If she had any say in it, neither the Order nor House Vel'kim would choose his path in life for him.

* * *

Enric, Malriel and Vran'el entered the main room of the Vel'kim residence.

"You look exhausted, Vran," Pe'tala commented. "Been having a long first day in office, have you not?"

He nodded and sank down onto the cushions next to Eryn who was breastfeeding her son.

"But it is almost over, and then all that remains for now is visiting a few of the estates to have people give the oath there. I will take care of this in the next few days." He gratefully accepted a glass of water from Enric and then smiled at his younger sisters. "That makes the two of you the only members of House Vel'kim currently in the city who have not yet bound themselves to me."

Enric saw how Eryn's shoulders tensed slightly. He hadn't asked her how she intended to handle the matter with the oath, but it seemed like he was about to find out.

Pe'tala rose from her seat next to Rolan to sit closer to her brother and lifted her hand for him to take. "Then let me go first so my nephew can finish his meal."

Their hands linked so that their palms were touching.

"Vran'el, I herewith accept and welcome you as my Head of House, to whom I owe obedience and support in acting in our House's best interest. I pledge my allegiance to you, brother."

Vran'el smiled and released her hand to pull her close and kiss her forehead.

His gaze then wandered to Eryn, who had handed her son to Enric so that she could readjust her clothes.

"You know, Vran," she said slowly, "we need to talk about this oath. I am afraid this is in my case not quite as easy."

"It is not?" he asked mildly and Enric couldn't help but suspect that he had expected her resistance. "Tala, sweetheart, please be so kind and go to the study to fetch the green box on the desk for me, will you?"

His sister rose wordlessly and did as she was told, returning only little later with the item he had asked for before sitting down again.

"I am listening, Eryn. What objections do you have?"

"I am, as you know, already bound to the Kingdom with a second level commitment. Taking this oath with you would mean binding myself to two countries at the same time. I cannot bow to two masters like that. What if there are conflicting orders? Trying to comply with both bonds would probably tear me apart," she elaborated, keeping her voice calm and reasonable. "I was scolded by King Folrin for joining Enric in a third level commitment, so you may imagine what trouble I would be getting myself into by swearing another second level oath here."

Vran'el nodded. "I can of course understand your concerns about this. Let me put your mind at rest, though." He opened the flat green box on his lap and pulled out two letters.

Enric saw that they were not the rolled up paper slips the birds delivered, but real letters. And they looked official. One of them displayed the Royal seal of King Folrin, the other the Order's official emblem. It seemed that Vran'el had come well prepared. Eryn would not take well to that.

"This here are official authorisations both by the Order and your King that permit you to enter into a binding oath with your new Head of House, as is customary in our country. They both accept that not taking the oath would constitute a transgression of our rules and customs."

Enric felt her distress through the mind bond and saw how her breathing became a little heavier while she was staring at the papers in his hand. He noted that both her hand and her voice appeared deceptively calm when she reached out for the documents.

"Do you mind if I have a closer look at this?"

"By all means," Vran'el replied generously and watched her read them thoroughly. The expression on his face was a little smug, Enric couldn't help but notice. It seemed as if he was looking forward to whatever she might try next.

"They seem to be in order," she admitted reluctantly. "You obviously anticipated my objections and took care of all and any possible obstacles. How very thorough of you." Her voice sounded flat, making it clear that the words were not exactly meant as a compliment but rather a complaint.

Vran'el sighed and took her chin to turn her face towards him. "Eryn, I hope that you know I would never abuse my power over you. I would never attempt to harm you or Vedric in any way. Quite the opposite; accepting that oath from you binds me to you in turn. It is my duty to protect you and act in your own best interest."

She smiled sadly. "I know. It is not that I don't trust you, Vran. I just have certain issues with magical oaths." She paused for a moment and looked at Valrad, then back at her brother. "Your father never made me swear the oath to him."

"I am aware of this, yes. But I am not my father. I have chosen a different path. And I think that you do no longer require any special treatment. You have had time to adapt to being a member of this family with all that entails." He lifted his hand and waited for her to take it.

Eryn's gaze found her companion's.

"Enric?" she asked with a pleading expression as if hoping that he would present her with a miraculous way out of this. "This oath would bind not only me, but - owing to your third level bond that is still active on your side - also yourself. You are a member of another House and might not find this an appropriate course of action."

Enric exhaled slowly. "The decision is yours, my love. I will go along with whatever you decide. Malriel obtained the same permission from Tyront and King Folrin for me. She wants me to swear the oath to her as soon as you have given up your position as Head of House Aren."

Eryn stared at her mother icily. "I would have thought that your influence over him is considerable enough already thanks to your very friendly connection with our King. Why would you have him swear the oath to you?"

"I have every right to ask this of him," Malriel replied, "especially as you are about to give one to Vran'el. I would, in fact, be giving up some of my power over him to your Head of House if I did not bind him to me the same way."

She looked back at Vran'el who was still holding out his hand to her. "I would be delivering Enric into Malriel's hands if I swore that oath to you."

He shook his head and smiled faintly. "Not any more than before, sweetness."

"What happens if I do not take this oath?"

Her brother's gaze became intense. "We would have to take this before the Senate. They would adjudicate on whether your reservations were valid. If they were considered such, you would be able to remain a member of House Vel'kim even without swearing the oath. If not, you would no longer be a member of my House. Though this would not apply to your son. He will continue to be Vel'kim, no matter what."

Enric saw how the others in the room straightened themselves and began exchanging worried glances.

"Though putting this whole matter before the Senate will do my reputation great harm, as you may imagine. If even my own sister, who I took so much trouble to save from falling prey to Ram'an's scheme not so long ago, does not trust me enough to bind herself to me this will make a very bad impression."

She exhaled slowly. That had been a blunt reminder that she owed him a great deal and that refusing him now would be ungrateful and begrudging. She closed her eyes and finally took his hand.

"Then I dare say this is the moment when I step back as Head of House Aren and return the position to Malriel. One Head of House can hardly be subjected to another one, I assume."

"Exactly," Vran'el confirmed.

Eryn looked at the woman next to her father, who was obviously waiting eagerly for her next words.

"Malriel, I herewith return to you your former position of Head of House Aren. I trust that you will honour the arrangements I made and entered in the name and on behalf of your House."

Malriel nodded graciously. "I accept the position gladly and will keep your project alive. Especially as you have so convincingly elaborated on the consequences for House Aren should I not."

Eryn returned her attention to the man next to her. "I don't even know what to say. Is there a particular wording I need to adhere to? Do I repeat Pe'tala's words?" she asked, defeated.

Vran'el's voice sounded infinitely relieved when he answered, "You need to confirm that you accept my position as your Head of House and will henceforth follow my instructions and bow to my judgement."

Eryn took a deep breath and felt the warm magic from his palm seep into hers when she started speaking, "I herewith accept you as my new Head of House. I will follow your instructions and bow to your judgement," she repeated his words.

When the magic stopped flowing, she felt herself be pulled into an embrace.

"Well done, Eryn," he murmured close to her ear. "I appreciate that this was not easy for you and thank you for doing it nevertheless."

She nodded silently and leaned back when he released her. Bloody King Folrin, she cursed inwardly and ground her teeth.

Vran'el then cleared his voice and rose. "Now that this has been taken care of I want to address two more matters." He looked at Pe'tala. "Tala, I have the impression that you are settling in rather well in Anyueel and might even consider staying there for longer. I do not approve of this. You will return to Takhan as soon as your services are, in your professional opinion, no longer required to improve the running of the clinic in Anyueel."

Pe'tala's face became pale. She jumped up from her seat. "You! How dare you! Father! Tell him that this is misuse of his position!"

Valrad grimaced and shook his head. "I am afraid that is not my place anymore, Tala."

"You are aware that I am in a relationship, are you not? Are you genuinely asking me to leave Rolan behind?" she hissed, her face now turning red with anger. "Is having me back here alone and unhappy better than far away and with the man I love?"

Vran'el remained calm. "I am not asking you to leave Rolan behind, Tala. If your attachment to each other is serious enough, he will accompany you to Takhan, and we will find a way to put his talents to good use at the clinic. I have talked to father about this."

"Now you wait a moment!" Now Eryn, too, rose from the cushions, her eyes narrowed. "Rolan is running my clinic, I would not like you trying to lure him away one bit! This does not only affect Pe'tala, but my clinic as well! This is utterly self-centred of you! She is a grown woman and if she wishes to stay in Anyueel, you should do her the courtesy of accepting this!"

"I am not saying that she cannot return there occasionally for a few months at a time, but her main place of residence will be Takhan," Vran'el stated flatly, unimpressed by both sisters' angry glares and postures. "I am quite adamant about this and there will be no discussions. Pe'tala will return to Anyueel with you in two weeks and stay there until your clinic is running to your satisfaction. I would advise you to use this time to find and train a successor for Rolan in case he wishes to accompany her. This is my final word in this."

Pe'tala cursed and raked her fingers through her hair. "You really do this to me only minutes after I swore that damn oath to you? I could kill you right now!"

Vran'el ignored that remark and looked back at the other sister. "And now to you, Eryn."

Her eyes narrowed. "Careful, Vran'el. Don't try any more nonsense with me right now."

"You may remember a conversation I had with you a few months ago. It was about spending half your time in Anyueel and the other half here in Takhan." He smiled thinly. "Back then it was nothing more than an idea I was hoping to interest you in, but today I am in a position to assert more pressure and turn it into reality."

"What? No!" Eryn wailed, causing her son in Enric's arms to start crying. "Are you completely cracked? This is baloney! I have responsibilities in Anyueel! I am going to take a seat in the Magic Council, where Enric happens to be a member as well! And I can't just leave the clinic to its own devices now that you are taking away Pe'tala and even Rolan! What do you think you are doing here?" she snarled.

Enric kept swaying his son, but he reacted sensitively to his mother's agitation and there was no calming him. For Enric this demand was hardly a surprise. As opposed to Eryn, he had not forgotten the conversation Vran'el had had with him about three months ago. And it was to a certain degree a logical decision. He needed to have a hand in raising his heir, prepare him for the duty of taking over the House one day. He himself had been intrigued by the idea back then and it had lost none of its appeal for him so far. It would free him from some of the Order's and the King's influence, after all. And he liked Takhan. But Vran'el might imagine this to be easier than it was. He was not the only one with a claim on Eryn.

He cleared his throat to make himself heard over his son's wailing.

"This could be a bit more difficult than just making Eryn do your bidding, Vran'el. You know that we are not free to accept or refuse your plan just like that," he stated carefully.

Vran'el bent down wordlessly and opened the green box once more to take out another sturdy sheet and hand it to Enric.

Enric pressed Vedric into Valrad's arms and took the document, holding it high enough for Eryn to read it as well.

It was an agreement between the Kingdom of Anyueel, the Order of Magicians and the Houses of Vel'kim and Aren related to their joint claim on Lady Maltheá of House Vel'kim and Lord Enric of House Aren and explained that both sides would be best served by sharing the considerable asset each of them constituted for either country by claiming half of their time apiece.

Eryn stared at the lines, refusing to believe their content. But reading them again and then a third time didn't change their meaning. Finally she looked up and stared at Malriel.

"Of course you had your fingers in that as well," she hissed at her mother. "Luring King Folrin into bed with you obviously turned out to be a well of favours being granted to you, didn't it, you shameless creature?"

Malriel just narrowed her eyes without replying to the snide remark.

Eryn looked back at her brother. "Damn you!" she spat. "I wish I had insisted on not swearing that bloody oath to you! You have managed to make me regret it within minutes! I should have left your House!"

Pe'tala stepped next to her sister, glaring at Vran'el. "Congratulations, Head of House Vel'kim! I hope playing the powerful leader has given you a feeling of deep satisfaction, because you will need to be careful when turning your back over the next two weeks, brother!"

Enric sighed and handed the agreement back to Vran'el. "I suppose that is my cue to start looking for a suitable residence tomorrow. Two weeks is not very long, but then I suppose we can stay at the embassy until we have found something when we next return."

Vran'el shook his head. "That will not be necessary. You and your family will of course stay at the Vel'kim residence whenever you are here in Takhan. Father will move in with Malriel since she is required to live at the Aren residence as family Head. This building is large enough to accommodate all of us easily."

Enric nodded slowly, wondering how brave a man had to be in Vran'el's situation to really insist on spending several months every year under one roof with both of his currently extremely angry sisters. But then they would surely have calmed down by the time they were expected to return to Takhan in a few months.

He watched when both sisters turned on their heel and stomped off towards the stairs and out the entrance door.

"What are they doing now?" Rolan asked, his forehead creased in a troubled frown. "Should we go after them?"

The other three men shook their heads.

"I would not recommend that," Vran'el said, his expression still tense. "Being close to either of them is not what we want right now. Even less to both of them together. Trust me on that, my young friend."

* * *

Intrea blinked in surprise when found herself facing her companion's very obviously fuming sisters who were glaring at her with narrowed eyes and folded arms as soon as she opened the door.

"Did you know anything about that?" Pe'tala barked.

"What?"

"Were you aware of this lunacy he has obviously been planning for quite a while now?" Eryn added with forced patience.

"Who did what?" Intrea cried out in confusion. "Is this about something Vran'el did?"

Pe'tala rolled her eyes and pushed her aside to enter the house and grab two moist towels, throwing one to her sister.

"Of course this is about Vran'el! What did you think?"

"Oh, do come in, will you?" Intrea muttered, starting to get a little unnerved herself.

She walked up the stairs, her two uninvited guests following her.

Enkil, her father and Head of House Feral was just coming in from the terrace and attempted to smile at the newcomers, but his brow merely furrowed at their plainly visible foul moods.

"Ladies," he said carefully. "Is it safe to offer you something to drink or will I be cleaning up shards if I do?"

Pe'tala snorted. "You may. The strongest stuff you have. For me, that is, not for the nursing mother."

Enkil nodded for them to take a seat and went to open a high, artfully decorated cabinet to take out glasses and fill one with a dark brown liquid that clung to the glass and the other with juice of a more cheering yellow colour.

"I take it you had an unpleasant day?" he asked while taking the glasses to them and sitting down in what he probably considered a safe distance. His daughter took a seat close to him, eyeing the two women suspiciously.

"They kept throwing unfriendly questions at me. I think Vran has upset them somehow," she murmured, not taking her eyes of the Vel'kim sisters.

Enkil's eyes widened in mild surprise. "Has he now? On his first day as your new Head of House? I take it he has made his first unpopular decision, then."

Pe'tala snorted and tilted back her head to empty the glass in one large gulp, wincing for a moment at the burning sensation in her throat, then placed it on the low table in front of her.

"You assume correctly, yes," she growled. "The new Head of House Vel'kim has first made us swear loyalty oaths and then informed us that he had decided that I am to return to Takhan as soon as the clinic in Anyueel is running smoothly and that he had agreed with Anyueel to have Eryn spend half of every year here as well." She folded her arms again. "Judging from the documents he presented Eryn with he seems to have been planning this for a while now. I am asking you once again: Did you know about this?"

Intrea shook her head. "I did not, no."

"I find this hard to believe, if you do not mind me saying so. He tells you everything else!"

"Are you calling me a liar, Pe'tala of House Vel'kim?" Intrea hissed back. "He is not stupid! He knows that we are friends and refrains from telling me things you are not supposed to learn about. I asked him for just that as I have no intention of keeping any secrets from you. And if you insult me like this again, I am going to hurt you!"

"Alright, alright," Pe'tala murmured sulkily.

Enkil took a sip from his own glass, then regarded the youngest of the three women with interest. "I take it that you had been intending to continue your stay in Anyueel? Otherwise your brother would not have seen it necessary to order you back, I assume?"

"I wanted to stay there a bit longer, yes. I have taken a liking to the place and they certainly profit from my being there. But that is obviously no longer open to me. And do you know what is even worse?" She threw up her hands. "Rolan! Vran'el just decreed that he is either to come and move here with me or stay back home! I have no idea if we are anywhere near that point in our relationship! He has no right to push us into something like that! Even if we had progressed far enough, asking him to give up an important position to come to a foreign country is certainly not Vran'el's place to say! How dare he!"

Intrea grimaced in sympathy. "I see what you mean. That is certainly unpleasant. How much longer do you think you will be able to stay in Anyueel? Are you the one to judge when the clinic is running smoothly? If so, that is all a matter of interpretation, is it not?"

"I wish it were that simple," she sighed. "He said I was to judge this from a professional point of view. That means that as soon as I am looking for reasons to prolong my stay, the second level commitment will pull me back. I have next to no scope to manoeuvre here. If I had to guess I would say that I will probably need another four or five months."

"That should be enough time for your young man to decide if he wishes to come here with you," Enkil threw in. "You need to understand your brother, Tala. Both his sisters were about to return to another country, maybe to stay there permanently, save for occasional visits. He needs you both here. Little Vedric is currently his only heir, and House Vel'kim needs at least one daughter to keep the direct line intact. And his nephew needs to familiarise himself with his House in the years to come. This is not possible if he grows up in Anyueel the entire time."

"So you are on his side?" Pe'tala snapped. "Really? Is everything alright as long as a Head of House is doing it?"

"No, Tala," Enkil retorted sternly, "but sometimes a Head needs to make unpopular decisions to keep his House going and do what is best. Your father would have called you back to Takhan in time, you may safely rely on that. He might have watched you for another few months and if you had not showed any inclination to return he would have compelled you to do so. Your brother is just less willing to accept uncertainties and told you in advance that you have to prepare yourself to come back home." His gaze wandered to Eryn, who had not spoken a single word since she had sat down and was just sitting there with her arms crossed wearing a displeased expression.

"Eryn. The same goes for you. Valrad would have been forced to do something now that your son has been born, and fairly soon, too. He very probably held back until now for fear of estranging you again after everything that has happened between you, especially as you are known not to be in favour of his and Malriel's commitment. Vran'el has just had the bad fortune of taking over his House at a time that required him to make inconvenient decisions. I very much admire him for taking care of them so speedily, especially as it has cost him the goodwill of both his sisters."

"Be that as it may," Eryn replied coolly, "But he may certainly have taken care of this in a more cooperative and less final manner. It is not as if I will be free to drop everything every six months to rush off to a faraway place without trouble. With myself and Pe'tala gone, my clinic is practically without a fully trained, experienced healer!"

Intrea raised her brow. "But Valrad has sweetened his deal with exchange programmes, has he not? That means that this should not be such a great issue. He is in a position to send you whichever person you request. That he has taken back the clinic here is a stroke of luck for you, there is no denying that."

"That may take care of the healers, but how would you like relocating every few months with your child? There will be no continuity in his education, his training! He will be torn between two places, be separated from his friends on both sides of the sea for months at a time! That is simply cruel," Eryn snapped, unwilling to admit to any mitigating circumstances in the thing.

"Rubbish. Children are very adaptable, and if he grows up in two different places he will learn to see it as something completely normal," Intrea said, trying to dispel her concerns. "He might even end up with twice as many friends and profit from the diversity of impressions he is exposed to."

"Oh yes? Then suppose you pack up Obal and send her along with us, eh? Then we will see how much she benefits from all these great new influences in her life," Eryn shot back craftily and with an edge to her words.

Enkil put an arm around his daughter when she pressed her lips together and simply stared at the other two women.

"I am afraid, my girl, your friends are currently not in the mood to appreciate the positive side effects this arrangement may have in time. What they might need now are not attempts to solve their problems or change their points of view, but a little sympathy. We should try and understand that this is an unpleasant situation for each of them. And I agree that your companion would have done well to seek their cooperation instead of presenting them with facts that have such a great impact on their living circumstances, yet require so little adaptation from his side." He smiled at his guests. "But I have no doubt whatsoever that he will soon start questioning his own approach in this. I am confident that you will make him regret his assertiveness."

The two sisters exchanged a dark look, then smiled at each other with an evil glint in their eyes. Whatever Vran'el's immediate future held, sisterly benevolence would definitely not form any part of it.

* * *

Enric adjusted his son on his arm and walked down the stairs from the terrace to the Vel'kim gardens. Vran'el stood with his back to the House, looking into the distance unseeing, his hands on his back.

The blond magician was standing next to him, quite silent.

"Are you, too, angry at me, my friend?" the new Head of House asked after a while. "I hope you understand why I chose not to tell you about this. I had the impression that you were willing to give this arrangement a try when I first mentioned it to you back then."

"No, I am not angry at you. Not knowing in advance saved me a lot of trouble with Eryn. I understand why you did it, but I can't help but wonder if how you handled this is the best way."

Vran'el exhaled lengthily and let his head sink back, staring up at the sky. "I wanted to leave no doubt about who is in charge now. I will have to convince quite a few people that I need to be taken seriously. Until now I was at my father's side, taking care of matters in the background, providing information, advice and suggestions. Many know me as soft, a little peculiar even, with a strange sense of humour, a love for men and a rather too feminine sense of style and beauty."

"So your sisters were what - test subjects for your new way of dealing with people?"

"I suppose you could call them that, yes. They knew and treated me as a brother, a friend, somebody they could tease and be teased by in return. But not as a man to be obeyed. The way they will treat me in public, especially now at the beginning, will signal to other people how they are to deal with me. Joking with me when others can hear us or teasing me will make me look weak, like a playmate rather than a leader."

Enric nodded slowly. He understood that sentiment well. It was a challenge he himself had been forced to master after his elevation to second in command of the Order after being known to many as a lazy scallywag and troublemaker.

"Still, they respected you as an expert in your field, somebody to consult and listen to when in trouble," Enric pointed out. "I don't think that your new position should stop you from having friends in favour of being respected or even feared, Vran. That is a mistake I myself made for many years. I have only recently started correcting it."

"I had little choice here, Enric. You will all leave here in two weeks and I had to do something quickly, however little they see the value of that now. They will come to terms with this eventually."

The taller man shrugged. "I am not criticising you. You are the one who has to deal with them now. I am fine with this arrangement. It suits me nicely, even though there are a few adaptations I shall need to take care of in the long run. Yet treating your sisters like pieces in a game will take its toll, I can safely promise you that. Eryn is getting better at recognising attempts to play her and has recently discovered the joy of taking effective revenge on those who manage it. And as for Pe'tala... You have put her and Rolan in an unpleasant situation. He has known her for about a year now and needs to decide whether to give up his life and position in Anyueel for her. They might not yet be ready for such a decision."

Vran'el sent him a cool look. "My sister deserves a man who is willing to commit to her completely, not those half-measures they were enjoying in those final months. If he is not willing to stay with her with all that entails, he had better step aside and makes space for somebody who is."

"Fair enough. Though the question might just as well be if your sister is ready for that kind of commitment herself. Speaking of your sisters and commitments, you might have diminished my own chances with Eryn and for renewing our third level commitment considerably today."

Vran'el frowned. "How so? I thought I had rather saved you from trouble by not telling you in advance?"

"I am trying to make her agree to a magical oath, and this is now the third time she regrets entering into one. The first time was the second level bond to the Kingdom, shortly after which she cursed us for stealing the chance to leave the country with Ram'an. Then there was the third level bond with me that brought us the mind bond, and finally you binding her to you only to relocate her to your heart's content. I would have hoped for this to be a positive experience for her for a change."

The Head of House Vel'kim smiled faintly. "Do not tell me I have destroyed your chances for success? Mighty Lord Enric is giving up?"

"Certainly not. I said diminished, not destroyed."

Vran'el nodded tiredly. "Good. It would have pained me to no end if you had not considered her worth the effort any longer. There is one more thing. You need to look for somebody to take over your financial matters here in Takhan for the time of your absence in my stead. It would not look good for House Aren if the Head of another House were to handle them. I can recommend other lawyers to you whose Houses are allied with yours if you wish."

"Thank you, Vran, but this will not be necessary. I already have an idea who to ask."

CHAPTER 14

The Cold Shoulder

Enric got up from the cushions in the Aren main room when he heard the entrance door opening and closing. Vedric was already starting to get slightly restless. It had been about three hours since he had last been fed.

"Hello, boys," Eryn smiled. "I dare say you have both been missing me, though for different reasons." She unfastened her tunic while walking to the cushions to have a seat.

"Well, that is true," Enric confirmed and handed her the baby when she was ready. "Though we both see the value of it when you undress."

She looked a lot less agitated than he would have expected, yet not exactly calm. There was an aura of grim determination about her.

"We need to talk," she murmured while watching her son.

"I think we should, yes."

"Where is Malriel? Has she returned yet?"

He shook his head. "No, she is still with Valrad."

"Good. I would rather be gone from her house before she returns."

"I had a feeling that you wouldn't want to continue staying here now that you are no longer required to as Head of House. Orrin and Junar will accompany us to the embassy, as will Malhora. Kilan is having the guest rooms prepared for us as we speak."

Eryn blinked and looked up at him. "I am torn between marvelling at your consideration and wondering if I have become a lot more predictable than I am comfortable with."

"Then I recommend the first one. And I would not say that you are predictable, only that I have got to know you quite well," he smiled.

"What about Vern?"

"Vern sent me a message that he will be staying with his lady friend until we have left. I assume the idea of moving around so much does not appeal to him very much, considering that he will be going to the Vel'kim residence in two weeks."

"And Malhora really wants to come with us to the embassy? She repeatedly pointed out that this very house used to be her home."

Enric shrugged. "She said she has no wish to stay with Malriel without anybody else being around but rather wants to enjoy the last

155

two weeks with her granddaughter and great-grandchild before we are gone for a long time."

Eryn wondered how Malriel would react when she returned to her house and found it completely empty. Even her mother would be gone, rather staying with them than her own daughter.

She pushed aside the sympathy; it was wasted. Malriel had plotted together with Vran'el how to tie them to this city. The agreement had included both Houses, Vel'kim and Aren.

"How did Kilan react when you told him that he has to take us in once again? I dare say he will be more than glad when we are gone from here."

"He was the perfect host and opened his doors to us. He said that at least he finally has a chance to fill most of the guest rooms for once and put all the surplus space to good use."

She chuckled. "Good, old Kilan. It is certainly not easy to unsettle him. One has to admire a man who stays calm in the face of providing shelter to seven people without warning, two babies among them."

"At least he knows that he will be getting rid of us fairly soon."

"Does he know that we are supposed to return here in six months?"

"I told him that, yes. Though he is a lot more delighted with this development than you might feel is warranted. He likes having us here. Try not to hold it against him if you manage somehow. He is letting us stay at his place, after all."

"I will be on my best behaviour," she promised solemnly. "That means all that remains to be done now is packing our things up, then we can leave this house."

"No. Our things have already been taken across to the embassy. We can just walk out of here."

Eryn stared at him for several moments, then sighed. "Thank you. Thank you so much. I had counted on returning here, feeding Vedric, contacting Kilan and hastily throwing all our belongings into our chests. This is so much better. These are unexpected moments of peace you have just given me. I love you."

Enric leaned his forehead against hers, bathing in the joy her words gave him. "And I love you."

She readjusted her shirt, then got to her feet. "Come on, then. Let's leave the lair before the Queen of Darkness returns." She whistled for Urban who came in from the terrace at a leisurely pace and preceded them down the stairs in anticipation of an evening stroll.

"As lairs go, this has been a nice place, though," Enric pointed out.

"It has," Eryn shrugged and set in motion. "At least before Malriel returned from Pirinkar. It has lost quite a lot of its appeal since then."

* * *

Enric pushed himself up from the seating cushions at the embassy, putting aside his breakfast bowl with the colourful mix of fruits, when a knock came at the door.

"Stay seated, Kilan. I'll take care of this."

"An unusual hour for visitors," the ambassador commented. "I hope nothing untoward has happened."

Eryn grimaced. "That would just fit my theory that bad news always arrives during meals."

"An interrupted meal in itself is bad news anyway," Junar shrugged and tried to coax another spoonful of fruit puree into her daughter's mouth.

Enric's brow shot up when he opened the entrance door and found himself looking at Pe'tala and Rolan, carrying a sizeable wooden chest between them. That looked suspiciously as if they intended to move in here.

"Good morning, Enric," Pe'tala nodded to him. "I fancy we are interrupting breakfast. Sorry for that, but it cannot be helped. Is there a chance of talking to Kilan?"

"Good morning to you, Tala. Rolan. Why don't you come in? Kilan is in the main room."

Rolan bowed without speaking, then entered after Pe'tala.

They carried the chest inside and placed it in a corner where it wouldn't be in the way, then accepted moist towels before following Enric up the stairs.

Rolan bowed to Orrin. "Lord Orrin."

Pe'tala rolled her eyes. "I told you, we do not hold with this title-nonsense and bowing here. It just makes you look stuffy and unnecessarily formal."

Eryn grinned. "Oh, leave him be. We will just Lord him right back, eh, Lord Rolan? In his case it would at least make sense, his being the first one to be granted the title due to accomplishment instead of birth."

"Thank you so much," Orrin growled. "That was a very unflattering assessment of all the other magicians back home, yourself included."

She shrugged. "I don't mind that one bit. I can do well enough without being addressed as Lady."

Pe'tala cleared her throat. "Can you shut up for a moment and take care of that debate on principles later? I need to ask the ambassador something."

Kilan looked up at her and sighed. "First corridor on the right, second door to the right. You will have to make do with a guest room that overlooks the city instead of the inner yard, the others have all been taken."

Enric smiled at Pe'tala's evident relief. "Welcome to our full house. So you decided to flee from your brother's residence?"

"As have you from Malriel's, it seems," she smirked and found a seat, pulling Rolan along with her.

"That was their own doing and serves them right enough," Malhora shrugged, walking in from the court yard with Vedric in her arms.

Pe'tala nodded to the old woman. "Malhora. It is a pleasure to see you. It has been a while. I may introduce Rolan to you. Rolan, this is Malhora of House Aren, Eryn's grandmother and the former leader of her House. She may look harmless enough now that she is holding a child, but do not let that deceive you. There are people who were admonished by her when they were children who still change direction when they see her walking down a street. One or two of them are Heads of Houses, I will have you know."

Malhora smiled thinly. "That is right. Though I have mostly delegated upholding the family reputation to the younger generations nowadays."

Kilan nodded. "Yes, and Eryn seems to be a fast learner in that regard, too. I dimly remember a certain crumbling Senate roof. And I have heard of the so-called Aren Welcome."

Rolan frowned. "I thought it was Eryn Welcome?"

Pe'tala shook her head. "No, your people call it that because they have little understanding of our concept of Houses, but her name just sounds similar enough for this to work nicely."

"What did Vran'el say when you packed your things and left his house?" Eryn enquired, eager to leave the topic of the famous Aren anger issues behind.

"We waited until he was gone. He does not know yet," her sister replied with a stony smile.

"So he may come storming in here later and either demand of you to move back in with him or kick me for granting you shelter?" Kilan grimaced. "You are putting me in a rather awkward situation here, Pe'tala."

She waved him off. "He will certainly not do any such thing. It would look bad for him, as if he had lost control. Right now people will speculate if he was the one to kick me out of his house because I failed to obey his orders."

"In combination with the rest of us abandoning the Aren residence? Hardly," Enric threw in. "But it won't do Vran'el much harm either way. Pe'tala is known to possess a rather adverse nature."

Pe'tala narrowed her eyes at him. "Careful, you foreigner. Aren temper is not the only fearsome one around. But I will refrain from having a go at you in favour of holding your nephew if Malhora would be so kind and give him up for a moment."

"Don't call him that," Enric growled.

"Why not? My father is about to join your mother, which makes you Eryn's brother and thus her child's uncle," she sneered. "I wonder how your Magic Council will react to your being in a commitment with your own sister. They are a little conservative, I seem to recall. But the gossips at least will be delighted."

Enric turned to Kilan. "I have changed my mind. Accepting that woman under your roof would constitute a major diplomatic breach of etiquette. I advise you to kick her out this minute. You may keep Rolan here, though. He is an Order magician, after all."

Pe'tala just laughed and accepted Vedric from Malhora. "Look at your uncle, my boy," she cooed, "He would kick out his poor, shelterless sister just like that. He should rather appreciate my soothing, calming influence around here with you being born to two Aren parents - one by birth and one by choice."

"Soothing influence indeed," Enric muttered and shook his head in exasperation. "If you call him my nephew once more I will do to you what Eryn did to Malriel not long ago: lock you within an airtight barrier."

Pe'tala turned to her sister and released a delighted laugh. "You did that to the Queen of Darkness? When? Tell me all about it!"

Enric rolled his eyes. The threat had obviously not hit its mark. But he had to smile while watching how Pe'tala sat down next to Eryn, both of them rejoicing in an evil deed carried out well.

They were good for each other, he decided, and was glad that Vran'el's arrangement would enable them to spend at least part of every year together in the same city. He hoped that they would in time also accept their brother back among them.

* * *

Enric looked up from his book when a movement from the corner of one eye caught his attention. Pe'tala was strolling towards him across the yard, smiling at the picture of him sitting under a tree, his son sleeping on his outstretched legs and the mountain cat dozing on the grass next to him.

"I bet not many people back at your home know that side of yours," she commented and sat down next to Urban to scratch her head.

"And what side would that be?" he enquired.

"The domestic, caring, fatherly one. I will admit that I, too, was surprised at how much attention you pay to your son. Still am. It is not exactly in accordance with Anyueel values, is it? And then you bullied Eryn around a great deal not too long ago."

"I bullied her around?" he repeated, wondering why this woman took such great delight in provoking him. "So you have come out here to disturb me in my peace and quiet to insult me, Tala?"

She shook her head, looking at him thoughtfully. "No, Enric, for once I do not mean to insult or tease you. But you cannot deny that you have not been too gentle with her in the past. You pushed her into sleeping with you at that Freedom Night, then kissed her after exhausting her in that fight you tricked her into, bullied her into combat training with you, made her accept you as her lover when she was locked in your quarters, more or less forced her to join you..."

"Alright, alright," Enric interrupted her. "Let's say your sister and I had a bumpy start, shall we?"

159

She smiled. "That is putting it rather mildly. I wonder how Eryn would describe it."

He looked up at the sky for a moment, then admitted, "Probably by making use of the word bullying at some point."

"There you go. But I am inclined to forgive you for that as you seem to have turned into the kind of companion a woman and the kind of father a child would wish for."

"Dear me, this is not going to become a compliment at one time, is it?" Enric smiled. "That coming from you would probably overwhelm my honed skills at dealing with unexpected situations."

Pe'tala rolled her eyes. "Shut up, Enric. You certainly do not make it easy for me to be nice to you for a change. I wanted to tell you that I have come to like Eryn. A lot. I care for her not only as a sister, but as a friend. And knowing that you are good for her when I am so very far away gives me comfort. I was sceptical about your tendency to control everything in your own and her life, but lately you seem to have managed to reduce it to a healthier level that allows her to make her own decisions and develop. I was astonished that you left the decision whether to swear the oath to Vran'el to her without trying to influence her in accordance with your own preferences. I made a few enquiries, and it certainly looks like you have been spending the time following your return from Pirinkar looking after your son, enabling Eryn to take care of House Aren and her orphanage here." She smiled. "I would even go so far as to say that you show the qualities of a Vel'kim-father."

"That is high praise indeed," Enric chuckled.

"The highest I can give, Order Lord," she said haughtily.

"You must be aware that I have not been a member of the Order for the past half year."

"I trust you will fit back in famously once you are back."

"And back to insulting me," he sighed. "And you were doing so well just now."

She grinned broadly. "How very interesting that you perceive it as an insult when I tell you that you will fit in with the institution that raised and formed you. Do not tell me that your picture of them has changed that much?"

"Firstly, the insult is based on your opinion of the Order, not mine. And secondly, you know well enough that I did not part from the Order on completely amiable terms."

"Yet they are eager enough to have you back, I can tell you that much even without being a member myself. I cannot tell you how often your names were mentioned in these last three months. They were wondering if and when Malriel would return from up north so that they could claim you back. From what Rolan tells me Lord Tyront did not seem to be too thrilled about the King granting you another two months here instead of calling you back immediately after Malriel's return to Takhan. But then it is the King who controls the second level bond, is he not? So there is little the Order can do about that, apart from addressing very careful and polite requests to him."

"Exactly. Tyront will be even less thrilled when he learns that the King only recently granted me another two weeks extension," Enric smiled.

Pe'tala raised both eyebrows. "You wish to extend your stay here even longer? That does surprise me a little. You really are that reluctant to return to your home?"

He shook his head. "We will not stay here. I want to make a detour on our way back and introduce my family to my sister. Eryn told me some time ago that she would like to meet her, and I am eager to introduce my companion and son to the only family member I am on good terms with. Don't tell Eryn, though. I want to surprise her."

"I will not", Pe'tala promised and nodded to the door to the main room. "There she comes. She looks determined. I have seen her sitting and talking to Malhora, so that is probably going to be interesting."

Eryn nodded to the two of them. "There you are. There is something we need to talk about." She sat down on the grass. "You remember when you kept complaining that I never let you spend any money on me?"

"I do, yes," Enric nodded. "I take it you are about to graciously offer me an opportunity to do just that?"

"I am asking you to spend an indecent amount of gold and time and risk angering a Head of House," she said slowly.

"Go on," he pushed her mildly.

"I want you to build us a house here in Takhan. I talked to Malhora and she told me that you asked her to represent you in all financial and business matters as long as you are gone now that Vran'el cannot do that any longer. She informed me that there is little I can do when it comes to Vran'el ordering me here every year, but that I can at least circumvent his demand of living in his residence."

Pe'tala frowned. "How?"

"Once by building a house. He told us not to buy one, but never said anything about not building one. And then Enric will be the one doing it, not me. He has no power over Enric, thus he is, unlike me, not bound to obey Vran'el's orders. And once the house is finished and Enric moves in, he can hardly force me to live at a different place from my companion, especially as he is still bound to me through a third level bond."

Her sister smiled appreciatively. "I admit I am impressed. Owing to his profession Vran'el is not normally that lax with his wording, and after you used this loophole to your full advantage, I suspect he will be a lot more careful in the future. So you are wriggling yourself out of having to live with him. This does not work for me, more is the pity. I will still be stuck under one roof with him. Any helpful ideas that might aid me, too?"

"That depends on what Enric says. He has not yet agreed to my not exactly humble request."

He pulled her close and kissed her lips. "It will be my pleasure to build you a house, my love. I admit the thought of staying at another man's abode and being subjected to his rules is not a pleasant one."

Eryn exhaled in relief. "You are of course aware that Vran'el will not be happy about this?"

"Neither was I about him decreeing that I am to live at his place. This is to a certain degree a trial of strength. He is currently eager to show the world that he is somebody to be taken seriously, to be respected. Though right now he is a little too assertive for my taste and needs to learn that with his family a more cooperative approach might be more productive than simply ordering them about. As for Pe'tala," he turned to her and smiled, "I think we can do something here. Provided you find living with us half of every year a viable alternative to spending the entire year with your brother?"

She sighed in defeat. "If you are offering me the chance to move in at your future residence, I am afraid that will not be quite as easy. He can easily order me back home. I have no convenient third level bond as an excuse. And I do not plan on entering into one just to escape my bossy brother."

Enric lifted his son when he started to stir and placed him on his chest, stroking his back soothingly. "That is exactly what I am offering you. It would otherwise stand empty half the time. The trouble with orders issued by a Head of House, you see, is that they are supposed to be for the good of the family. This applies especially when they happen to constrain your personal freedom. It may be in the interest of House Vel'kim to have you back in Takhan, but there is little difference if you live at the Vel'kim residence or ours. If he insists, you can take this before the Senate and have them decide on it. And as he himself admitted only yesterday, that would not look good for him, especially when the ones challenging him are his own siblings."

Pe'tala laughed and leaned forward to press a kiss on his cheek and hug him. "I accept your generous offer. How very useful that you are so well-versed in our rules. The time you were in charge of House Aren was obviously not wasted. Have you considered studying the law here, by any chance?"

"I admit I have actually," he replied and smiled at Eryn's surprised expression. "I was tested for scholar, you remember? And it seems that I will be mostly free of my Order duties when we are here. That would certainly be a useful way of using the surplus time on my hands."

His companion sighed. "And again you turn out to be a lot more adaptable than me. While I am plotting how to keep my brother's influence over me to a minimum, you have made long-term plans on how to employ this situation to your best advantage."

"Our best advantage, my love. Vedric is his only heir, and I fancy it won't hurt to be aware of how much influence over him we have to grant Vran'el in the years to come."

Pe'tala beamed at him. "You are an immensely resourceful man, Enric! You do not happen to have any brothers, do you?"

"As a matter of fact, I do," he laughed. "But I seriously doubt that you would find the one in Anyueel appealing, and the one in Takhan you are currently plotting against."

Eryn rubbed her hands and stood again. "I will return to Malhora now. We are going to have a look at the city map and see which of the available locations are as far away as possible from the Aren and Vel'kim residences yet still within easy walking distance of the city centre. Then Malhora can take care of purchasing the land, have House Roal draw plans for a nice house and then send them to us in Anyueel."

"House Roal?" Pe'tala swallowed. "That is a rather blunt provocation for both our Houses, you know. You are aware that they have been at loggerheads for a while, are you not?"

Eryn snorted. "I am indeed. And Ram'an told me that the cause for this lies in a very distant past. One hundred and fifty years, to be more exact. They are the best builders in the city, and I refuse to accept lower quality just to accommodate outdated and completely ridiculous grudges. And I am told that House Vel'kim takes that vendetta a lot less seriously than Aren, as Sarol's acceptance as a healer has shown." With that she turned and rushed off, eager to return to her grandmother.

Pe'tala slowly shook her head and looked after her sister. "She is a bit like a sandstorm, is she not? Wherever she has raged nothing is the way it used to be any longer. Your Order must have their hands full with her. She is certainly not one to bow to traditions and established rules."

"That is an accurate assessment, yes," Enric agreed. "The Order is still getting used to her and will probably be doing so for a while longer yet. But life has certainly become a lot more interesting since she has come to our city."

"Yes," she nodded. "I can believe that without any trouble whatsoever."

* * *

Eryn waited until she saw that every seat in the Senate hall was occupied before she entered. She wanted to join the meeting at the last possible moment without opening up any opportunities for Vran'el or Malriel to seek a few private words with her.

The mood in the large hall was one of collective anticipation and expectation. They had of course seen Malriel taking what used to be her seat, thus it was fairly obvious that she had resumed her position at House Aren. The question for many of the other senators was probably if her daughter had relinquished it voluntarily or not.

Vran'el's gaze rested on her and she made herself nod to him once in a short but obvious greeting. This was meant to demonstrate to the other senators that everything was alright between them, however little that reflected their current state of affection for each other.

He nodded back at her, his intense gaze and the thin smile promising her that there was a thing or two to discuss between the two of them later. Well, not today if she had any say in it.

She had no intention of staying here until the end of the Senate meeting. She was no longer a senator for whichever House and would merely announce that she had returned the responsibility over House Aren to Malriel and then leave again.

And if Vran'el thought that calling at the embassy would help him get in contact with either of his sisters today, he would be sorely disappointed. Pe'tala and she were determined not to be available.

She marched on to the centre of the room and stopped in front of the three triarchs, looking up at them.

"Would you allow me to make a short statement before the Senate before you proceed?"

Torke'na's eyes flickered to Malriel for a short moment, then back at Eryn. There was clearly little doubt as to the nature of her announcement.

"Do go on."

Eryn turned and looked at the senators, waiting for them to settle down and focus their attention on her.

"Senators, I wish to inform you officially that I am no longer in charge of House Aren. I have stepped back and Malriel of House Aren resumed her former position as of yesterday evening. It was my honour to serve the Senate at your side and I take this opportunity to give my farewell to most of you, as I will soon be leaving your country."

Having said that, she turned back to the triarchs, nodded at them and walked towards the double doors through which she had entered.

She exhaled and slowly descended the stairs. This had just been her last official appearance at the Senate. From now on she was free of all and any political burdens connected to any of the Houses.

It came as a relief. There had been quite a few unpleasant occurrences in these halls, many of them during her first visit during the trial Malriel had made her face, others more recently like Valrad officially acknowledging her as his daughter, Enric pushing the responsibility over House Aren at her, the unmasking of Sanaf and the day she had destroyed the roof and later given birth to her son.

But she had to smile when she thought back to a few other occasions that had not been entirely unpleasant. Such as informing Malriel that she had no intention of giving up her role as Head of House back then or facing down Legara of House Finran.

"Maltheá!" she heard a voice behind her and grimaced before schooling her expression into one of polite interest and turning towards Malriel.

"Mother," she smiled coolly. "I would think that leaving your first Senate meeting after being back in power does not make a good impression."

Malriel sighed and shook her head at her daughter. "I wish you would stop using the address like an insult, Theá. Though I am of course aware that this is exactly how it is meant."

When Eryn didn't comment on that but just waited, she continued, "I was not pleased when I returned last night and the House was completely empty. You would have been more than welcome to stay. I would have appreciated spending these last days with all of you."

"What did you expect? After stepping back from my role of Head of House Aren my presence at the official residence is no longer required. I have never pretended to enjoy staying under one roof with you, so I don't see how this could have surprised you much. Especially after your joint efforts with Vran'el to have Enric and me return here like that. I bow to you, Mother," she said coldly. "You did not manage to trap me here for two years the way you had initially planned, but it seems that this now has worked even better for you." She lifted her finger into Malriel's face. "You may have managed to make me return here, but I am warning you: If you attempt any of your nasty tricks in order to get your hands on my son, you are asking for more trouble than you can handle."

"Get my hands on your son, Theá?" Malriel asked mildly, ignoring the finger. "I would never take a child away from his mother. I know well enough how painful that is."

"You made sure to get me pregnant, so I have no doubt that you have further plans in this regard. They very probably do not include taking my son away from me. You would anger your own heir with that, after all. And you owe him quite a bit now after he went after you to bring you back here, don't you? It just wouldn't look good for you to treat him badly, would it? But I suspect that you are trying to have Vedric join your House somehow one day. Be prepared to fight me, though, Mother."

Malriel smiled faintly, her eyes sparkling as if delighted with the challenge. "I would not have expected anything else, Theá. I assume I will still see you at the commitment ceremony?"

"Of course. Not going to that would hurt Valrad and look bad for House Vel'kim."

Eryn shot her a final icy stare, then turned and descended the rest of the stairs without looking back. She felt bile rising inside her throat at the thought of spending several months every year in the same city as this woman.

Damn Vran'el and his idiotic need to prove himself! She would get back at him for that. Dearly so.

CHAPTER 15

The Commitments

Eryn held on to a glass of wine at the Aren residence, trying to remain in the background as well as she could. The main room was already filled with guests, and every single minute somebody new seemed to arrive.

She was in a grumpy mood after the mayhem of preparation at the embassy. Eight people plus two infants had needed to prepare for the commitment ceremony, getting in each other's way, stepping on toes, bumping into each other and fighting to be next in line for the bathrooms.

Junar had asked Orrin the evening before to take the dresses she had made for Eryn and Pe'tala to their rooms, and in the morning it had turned out that he had mixed them up when Pe'tala had complained that the dress was much too loose around her breasts.

Little wonder since the bust measurements were intended for a nursing mother.

When all of them had finally been ready to leave, Malhora scolded the Vel'kim sisters when they had dragged their feet and started looking for reasons to postpone their departure.

Pe'tala stepped next to her, her expression equally dark and grabbed her wine glass to down it in one go.

"Hey! That was mine! Get your own!" Eryn hissed.

"You are not supposed to be drinking alcohol, anyway," her younger sister shrugged. "And I need every drop I can find to get through this some way."

"I can't get drunk, so I don't see why you should be allowed to."

"You are not suddenly finding yourself with a bloody Aren mother, so shut up! This is a very dark day for me."

Eryn snorted. "I found myself with a bloody Aren mother without any warning when I first came here, so spare me your suffering. And after renouncing her House she is officially re-establishing that connection by making my father join her. Tell me again why you are the one needing to be pitied here, will you?"

They both turned with an unnerved expression when Vran'el stepped towards them and grabbed them each by one arm and pulled them with him into the nearest unoccupied guest room before they had a chance to flee.

He closed the door behind him and leaned against it with folded arms, glaring at them.

"I have been trying to get a hold on you for three days now! Every time I went to the embassy you were either not yet back or had just left without informing anybody where you were headed or when to expect you back. This is childish and inconsiderate!" he scolded them. "Pe'tala, your moving out without a word and behind my back is not acceptable, either! If you were not leaving here in only a couple of days, I would have dragged you back home by your ear!"

"Look at the new Head of House, putting his foot down to show off to his disobedient sisters who is in charge. Again," Eryn snapped back angrily.

"Go away, Vran'el," Pe'tala growled at him. "This day is bad enough already without having to deal with you as well."

Her brother regarded her for a moment, then leaned forward to smell her breath. "Have you been drinking?"

"Not really. But I have every intention to," she retorted. "And every reason to," she added as an afterthought.

"You had better practise some restraint here today," her brother warned her. "If you ruin this day for them, this will hurt father and look very bad for our House, do you hear me?"

"But of course, Head of House!" Pe'tala exclaimed in mock veneration. "Everything you decree, Head of House!"

Vran'el pinched the bridge of his nose and closed his eyes for a moment as if to remind himself to hold on to his composure.

"I see there is no talking to you today, Tala. Let me warn you, though, that I will keep an eye on you and intervene if you are on the brink of exposing us all. I have no qualms whatsoever about taking you out if I see fit. Eryn, I trust you to demonstrate that admirable restraint you have proved you are capable of and keep an eye on your younger sister's alcohol consumption."

"Of course, Head of House," Eryn smiled sweetly. "Because taking care of my son would just not be enough to keep me busy."

Vran'el angrily shook his head at both of them, then opened the door to allow them to leave. "I will be visiting you at the embassy tomorrow after breakfast. I expect you to be there or I will forbid you both to leave Takhan until we have sat down and talked about this matter like adults. I leave the choice to you, ladies."

The two women waited for their brother to leave them, then returned to the crowded main room at a slower pace.

"Great. Things are getting better and better," Pe'tala muttered and grabbed another wine glass from a nearby table, taking a few greedy gulps.

Eryn snatched it from her grip when she had emptied about half of it. "Give me that. You stole my first one." She made to tip back her head when determined fingers plucked it from her hand from behind.

"I will take that, thank you so much," Ram'an said tartly and lifted his arm when Eryn turned and made to take it back.

"Go away if you are going to be a nuisance, Arbil," Pe'tala growled at him.

"Your mood is certainly no better than I expected," he smiled wryly.

Eryn's gaze fell on a blond female head of hair several paces from them. It was not Junar's.

"That is Valcredy," Pe'tala pointed out the obvious. "I had dancing lessons with her. What is she doing here? I was not aware that she is acquainted with Malriel or father."

Eryn scowled. "What in the world is she doing here? And there I was thinking this day couldn't become any worse."

Ram'an cleared his throat. "She is my escort. And I would appreciate your being civil to her, Eryn."

Pe'tala had in the meantime obtained another glass of wine and snorted, "You take Enric's former lover to her parents' commitment and expect her to be nice about it? This would be hilarious if it was not so tasteless."

The Head of House Arbil closed his eyes for a moment and breathed out steadily. "I have concluded a business agreement with Valcredy. We will enter into a commitment and she will provide heirs for my House."

"What?" Eryn shouted, making about fifty heads turn toward their direction, eyeing them curiously, among them the woman they were currently talking about.

Ram'an laughed loudly to pretend that her reaction was an amused one and exclaimed, "Yes, is this not amazing?" He took Eryn's elbow and steered her back into the corridor she and Pe'tala had only minutes ago returned from. Pe'tala followed them.

"You must be pulling our legs!" Eryn hissed. "That is Enric's former lover! Not long ago she flew off the handle because she was jealous of me after my commitment to Enric! What are you thinking of? Or rather, why do you fail to do just that?"

"Listen, I told you many weeks ago that I am in need of a companion to provide for the next generation. And I mentioned that I am not currently in a position to take a companion from a House as I can at the moment not afford to compensate them for permitting my children to be members of my House instead of theirs. This is an advantageous solution for both Valcredy and me. She will have the lifestyle she values and can dedicate as much time to studying music as she pleases, and I am in a position to perform my duty as Head of House."

"This is terrible! Why would you enter into a farcical setup like this? I don't want you to buy yourself a woman! You deserve better than that!" she implored him, shocked at this seemingly callous scheme.

"What do you want from me, Eryn?" Ram'an snapped at her, his own patience wearing thin. "I was waiting for you for a very long time, fought for you in vain. What do you propose now? Am I to wait to see if I ever fall in love again? I would very much prefer that myself, believe me! This was honestly not my ideal scenario when I thought about having a family. But I cannot afford to wait any longer." His voice had become bitter. "I am thirty-two years old. I need to do something soon. I regret that my choice of companion is not to your liking, but you cannot push me away in favour of another man and then demand a say in who I chose next. I do not care if she was involved with Enric. I, too, have my past. This is not a romantic relationship. We are exchanging services, nothing more."

Eryn swallowed, staring at him. This outburst was so out of character for him that she was at a loss for words for a few moments. He had even refrained from calling her Theá, a clear sign of his discomfort.

She shook her head. She knew he was right. She really had no grounds to criticise him, none whatsoever.

"I am sorry, Ram'an." She took his hand and squeezed it with a pained expression. "You are right; this is your decision, yours alone. But I would have wanted so much more for you. You deserve more. This sounds so... cold."

He sighed, his anger draining away visibly. "This is similar to what your brother has, Theá. And I have never heard you objecting to his arrangement with Intrea."

She just nodded, thinking of the friendship that connected Vran'el and his companion, unable to imagine anything like that between Ram'an and Valcredy.

"Of course. You are right," she nodded, trying to hide her disappointment.

"Theá," he smiled sadly, "now you have become all stiff and formal. I see that this was not a good time to tell you about this. I should have taken you to a teahouse instead of making this day even more of a trial for you. Come on, let me take you outside to the garden."

She shook her head and slipped her hand from his. "No, please don't. I would rather hide somewhere until the ceremony starts. Just give me that glass back and don't tell anybody where we are."

He eyed first the glass, then her sceptically, before handing it back with reluctance. "I trust that you will not let your frustration let you forget that you are supposed to be nursing a child." His gaze wandered to Pe'tala. "I expect you to keep an eye on her." With that he turned and left them standing in the corridor.

Pe'tala grunted. "Now I am supposed to be looking after you while you have been commissioned to look after me? Come on, let us lock ourselves inside one of the rooms here until that ceremony starts. We can try to cheer each other up. Hey, we could play imagine and pretend that this gathering is some kind of farewell ceremony following Malriel's untimely death!"

Eryn nodded sulkily. "Very well. But only if we can first go through possible causes of death and choose a grisly one."

Pe'tala nodded seriously. "I am insulted that you think I would skip that part."

* * *

Valrad sipped from his glass and let his gaze wander over the guests that kept moving from the main room out into the garden. He nodded towards his son who was in a conversation with one of his companion's brothers.

"Vran looks tired and jaded. It pains me to see him like that. The differences with Tala and Eryn are proving quite a strain on him. I want to do something, yet I know that I cannot. Talking to him would only serve to make him think that I am on his sisters' side, and if I try and make those two see his point of view they will only be angry at me, thinking that I prefer him to them."

Enric nodded, understanding the dilemma well.

"I cannot see the girls. Do you know where they are? They arrived with you, did they not?" the healer enquired, appearing slightly worried.

"Ram'an told me that they have retreated to one of the guest rooms and want to enjoy a little peace before the ceremony." He patted his son's back. "Vedric is getting hungry, so I need to go looking for them anyway. I will return with them both."

Valrad nodded at him gratefully and smiled when Iklan approached him to congratulate him.

It took Enric about five minutes to work out where they were hiding.

He pushed open the seventh door and found them sitting on the floor. They seemed to be in the middle of an agitated discussion. He caught expressions like less painful, quick loss of consciousness and little chance of survival.

They looked up when he pushed open the door wide enough to enter. "That sounds like a rather morbid topic at an occasion like this," he commented.

"That is what you think," Pe'tala murmured and shrugged. "It is certainly aiding in lifting our spirits at least a little."

She took Vedric from Enric so that he could help his companion unbutton the dress at her back before handing the boy to his mother for his feed.

"Ram'an told me about his arrangement with Valcredy," Enric began. "And that you did not take very well to it."

He could see the wariness in her eyes when she looked up at him. "So?"

171

"We will try to stay out of her way today. There are enough people around, and Ram'an told me that they will not be staying too long."

Eryn raised an eyebrow, clearly waiting for more to come. "That's it?"

"That's it."

After a few minutes Eryn turned so that he could help her refasten the dress.

"How much time do we have left until the ceremony starts?" she enquired.

"A couple more minutes."

She nodded and handed him his son. "Good. That leaves me enough time to go to the bathroom. I will meet you two outside."

Pe'tala waited until the door had closed behind Eryn, then narrowed her eyes.

"So. Is there anything you would like to get rid of? Any wise words you wish to impart?"

He looked at her curiously. "Me? Such as?"

She folded her arms. "Such as criticising us for hiding in here, for example. Or a thorough analysis of how Ram'an and Valcredy might not be devoted to each other in love, but nevertheless make an advantageous match for each other. Or how we should try to understand my poor brother's point of view with him being in such a difficult situation right now, how we owe him our support instead of avoiding him for the oh so necessary steps he took to serve our House."

He smiled faintly. "Is that what you would wish to hear?"

"No, but I would have thought that this is what you would want to say. There was not a single attempt at showing us the right path or instructing us what to do. I find that unsettling, to be completely honest. I hardly recognise you, Order Lord. Where is that superiority, that conviction that you have the one and only solution for every single problem?"

"I remember that you commended me on finally letting Eryn make her own decisions only the other day," he remarked mildly.

"I did, yes. But at that time I was focusing more on your unexpected yet remarkable father qualities, especially considering your origins. This just now goes quite a bit further than I had expected. It is not merely holding back but appears to be a change in your personality."

Enric smiled at her perceptiveness. "I tried to push and pressure her into making up with Valrad a few months ago," he explained, remembering that time with dread. "And the result was that she started avoiding and retreating from me just like from everyone else around her. That was terrible. I was truly afraid for her back then. Your father was so worried he forced her to see Iklan for that talking treatment he does. I learned my lesson back then. If she wants to talk about the trouble with Vran'el, she is welcome to do so. If not, then I will not try and make her. Your brother has angered the two of you, he will have to bear the consequences. I would be doing neither him- nor myself a favour in interfering unbidden."

She whistled, clearly impressed. "Where is that arrogant prig who was sent here as ambassador hardly more than a year ago?"

He got to his feet, balanced his son on one arm and reached down to pull her to her feet as well.

"Nowadays I only let him out at those occasions when I see he could be useful. I expect he will become more active again as soon as I am back home and supposed to attend Council meetings."

"This sounds like you are developing additional personalities here. You know that this is something Iklan should have a look at, do you not? We consider this a mental illness here. I am sure you must have read about this somewhere. You do still read everything you manage to get your hands on, I assume?"

"Shut up and get moving, Tala. You wouldn't want to miss witnessing Malriel joining the family and becoming your new mother, would you?"

"Prig," she muttered, but did as she was told.

"Malriel's future daughter," he shot back and grinned when she flinched.

* * *

Eryn stood next to Vern out in the Aren gardens, waiting for the ceremony to begin and listening to the news about the two art academies and how the Senate had decided to make them cooperate on creating the artwork for the Senate roof.

"The old academy was unhappy because they had hoped to be the ones to take care of this alone, but the new academy is thrilled with the opportunity as it is a chance for them to prove themselves," he explained. "And of course it is a major commission that will earn them a fair bit of money. You did the local art world a real favour by collapsing that roof," he added with a grin.

"Glad to hear it," she grinned. "Are there any other buildings with impressive paintings you wish me to damage?"

Vern nodded solemnly. "If you are asking like that... I have always found that the library is in desperate need of a more modern design approach."

"Fair enough. Though I am afraid that we can no longer make House Aren bear the costs for that now that I have no more official connection to them."

The boy grimaced. "And your relationship with House Vel'kim is currently rather tense, I know. Well, then let's postpone any destructive activities on public property for now, shall we?"

"Spoken like a sensible adult," she nodded. "Well done. So, how are the academies going about this project? Are they willing and able to cooperate?"

"It has been a rather stony path to take, but they are now, more or less, yes. Their first approach was presenting a design that divided the dome in half so that each academy could kind of do its own thing. The Senate did not approve, and I cannot blame them," he shrugged. "They argued that they wanted one entire, self-contained, harmonious piece of art instead of a mix of different styles and contents - reflecting conflict within the local art world - in their sacred halls where they try to uphold a spirit of cooperation and mutual respect."

Eryn nodded. "That does make sense. And now they are trying to create something both academies can imagine doing?"

"Exactly. The new academy has asked me to participate in the project, and the great and mighty Elwoi, leader of the old academy and master of what the world is permitted to consider art, is not too thrilled about that. I have no problem working with him, though. We have finished two design proposals for now and will present them to the Senate next week."

"Big times for you, my lad. How are things at the clinic going? You have so far only joined the lessons sporadically when the topic sounded interesting to you. Next week your official training will start where others be telling you what to study."

"Yes, and I am looking forward to that, very much so. Valrad says I can join the second years and probably move on to the third years earlier than usual. According to him I have a sound understanding of the basic principles and have also fairly some advanced knowledge in several areas while at the same time showing some gaps that need to be filled."

"Just make sure to make as many notes as you can and have every book you deem useful copied to take back to Anyueel. By the way, how about your living arrangements? Valrad will no longer live at the Vel'kim residence but move in with Malriel. Will you return here as well or shall you stay with Vran'el?"

"I was offered both options, but I think I will stay at the Vel'kim residence. I don't think I want to stay with a freshly joined couple. Vran'el may not be a healer, but he is still the Head of a healing House with an impressive private medical library I can use without fighting for books with the other healer trainees. Provided Valrad doesn't take all the books with him to his new home, that is."

She shook her head. "I imagine he won't. They are the House's property from what he told me. He will most likely only take his private collection with him. And he still has access to whatever he needs at his place of work."

Enric and Pe'tala came to stand next to them. The latter pinched the boy's cheek.

"You are growing into a man, my young friend. You have got taller, the growth of your facial hair has set in, and I heard about your affair with Alefer."

Vern frowned at her. "That was embarrassing. I am glad that you will be returning to Anyueel in only a few days."

"Do not be grumpy. Rather be glad that you have not chosen to join your family at the embassy. It currently resembles a stable housing too many horses. But that means that you have to put up with me using every other opportunity to tease you a little whenever I see you. Though I wonder..." Her voice trailed off when her eyes wandered to the terrace door.

Eryn's gaze followed hers and she drew in a shocked breath when it fell on Malriel who had stepped outside and approached the sitting arrangement in the back of the garden with a quiet smile.

"What has she done? And why?" Pe'tala whispered.

"Valrad has asked her to put a halt to making herself appear younger from now on," Enric supplied quietly. "He says he doesn't want to be mistaken for her father. It seems she has complied with his request."

"That's what she looks like without the aid of magical cosmetic corrections?" Eryn asked in dismay. "She still looks ten years younger than she is!"

Pe'tala grimaced. "Great. Now I hate her even more."

"She looks fabulous!" Vern whispered, his eyes wide. "I didn't know that looking older could make a woman even more attractive!" He ducked when both women next to him tried to swat the back of his head at the same time. "What? It's true, isn't it?"

"Without doubt," Enric nodded with a smirk, "yet it is not something that is received well by other females. Though it gives me a nice glimpse into what my own future holds." He winked at Eryn, who just sent him a sour look.

They watched her glide past them in her light orange dress. She had avoided painting her face or styling her hair in any particularly artful way, yet her skin looked radiant and her dark hair falling down her back in soft waves gave her an almost mystical glow.

Malhora walked a step behind her daughter, her expression calm but very obviously satisfied. Eryn wondered if she rejoiced in the fact that the connection she had intended to forge between the two Houses with the companionship agreement half a century ago finally was working out, even though not exactly the way it had been planned at the outset.

Valrad's face had broken into such a happy and blissful smile that Eryn hoped for the first time since learning of their involvement, that Malriel could truly be for him what he wished for, however little the chance of it probably was. She was still the Queen of Darkness, all said and done.

Abrak, the triarch who was known to be just a tad more tightly associated with Malriel than was advisable, waited together with Valrad and Vran'el for the two women to join them. He would carry out the ceremony.

The ceremony was very similar to what Eryn's own had been about a year ago. Malhora was the one to give away her daughter, mentioning that a man with firm principles and a calming influence was exactly what was needed for a strong Aren woman. Vran'el said that he was glad that his father had finally found a home for his heart after such a long time while guiding Valrad's hand to Malriel's.

Malriel took his hand between the two of her own and leaned her forehead against his for moment before she started speaking, giving her commitment oath.

"Valrad, our long history together did not commence the traditional way, but with acts of deceit and shame while we were both joined with other people. But I cannot bring myself to regret a single moment of those times when I look at the gift we have bestowed upon each other." Her gaze rested on Eryn for a moment, then wandered to their grandson. "You have back then been a stable influence when I threatened to drown in madness. And even after the things that have happened to tear our Houses apart, you were a friend indeed when I needed one, a voice of reason when I was about to get carried away. I spent so many years fleeing from the loneliness inside me, looking for what I finally found in your arms. You are my reward for every hardship I had to encounter in my life, my safe haven, my home. You gave up your position of Head of House so we could give ourselves completely to each other, saving me from making this sacrifice. I will endeavour to never make you regret that decision." She fell silent and kissed his hand.

There was a trace of moisture at the corner of Valrad's eyes when he tenderly kissed her knuckles.

"Malriel, you have been haunting my dreams since I was little more than a boy, yet my brother was the lucky man to make you his back then. I am glad that I am now in a position to make you mine, to be able to leave my House in good hands and give myself into yours. For so many years I did not dare hope that your regard for me was anywhere close to my own for you, and now your willingness to join me has exceeded even my wildest dreams and boldest hopes. I will be there for you, always behind you when you need to lean on somebody, give you the luxury of not always having to be strong with me when everybody else depends on your strength. The prospect of spending the rest of my life with you has not only taken away my reluctance at getting old, but turned it into an appealing path to walk with you. We have given away decades with each other, and I am determined to treasure every single moment with you from now on."

Eryn swallowed, touched despite her reservations against this connection, and felt Enric's warm hand take hers and lift it to his lips and kiss it. They watched how all five persons on the seating cushions on the grass joined their hands on top of each other to let the magic for the third level commitment bond flow and manifest the connection, just like when the two of them had taken theirs what now seemed like an eternity ago, but had only been last year.

She felt regret at how their own bond, or at least her side of it, had faltered and ended. She loved Enric, there was no doubt about that, yet she was nowhere close to being ready to renew the bond for now.

It had been such an immense hurdle for her to lower her defences enough for her to join him that once, and there was quite some healing necessary for her until she could bring herself to do it again. There were still the echoes, the memories of the pain after he had left for Pirinkar, the nightmares, the anger and fear of being abandoned, the loneliness, the conviction that he had exchanged her for Malriel.

She lifted her glass together with the other guests when the bond was complete.

"I cannot believe that I am now Malriel's daughter," Pe'tala muttered behind her.

"It could be worse," Eryn snorted. "Your companion could be your brother. Hey, we could try to make them adopt Intrea and Rolan, then we could all be joined to our siblings…"

Her sister had to grin at that picture, however reluctantly. "If you put it like that…"

"And apart from a mother you cannot stand you at least have got another adorable brother," Enric supplied.

"Yes, lucky me," Pe'tala snorted. "As if one older brother has not been enough of a strain these last twenty-six years. Only last year I was the younger of two, and now I am the youngest of four. If any more siblings turn up in the future, I insist on their being younger than me for a change."

"You never know," Vern shrugged. "Malriel could theoretically still have children, especially as she is now joined with a magician healer. Maybe she will take care of the issue for providing an heir for her House that way now."

Eryn and Pe'tala both shuddered at the thought.

"That poor child," Eryn murmured, making her sister nod in heartfelt agreement.

"Come, you insensitive creatures," Enric sighed and pushed them both forward. "Time to congratulate our parents. And better make it look convincing. Pretend you are loving and considerate human beings, however great that challenge may be for you."

"Your brother is getting on my nerves already," Pe'tala huffed.

Eryn sent her a dark look. "Shut up and go embrace your mother, you brute."

CHAPTER 16

Parting with Jakhan

Pe'tala winced when the knock at the entrance door of the embassy sounded.

"I would guess this is our honoured Head of House who intends to have a word with us."

Eryn nodded and adjusted her son in her arms. "That is a safe bet, yes. Off you go and let him in, Tala. I am determined to appear unimpressed and relaxed when he enters, a picture of sophisticated grace."

"Yes, good luck with that," the younger woman huffed, but got up to admit their brother.

Eryn sighed, steeling herself for the inevitable conversation with Vran'el. The embassy was all but deserted. Kilan was taking a walk with Rolan, showing him a little more of the city. Orrin, Junar and Téa were roaming the markets for last minute purchases to take home with them.

Malhora had decided to spend the day with her freshly joined daughter as she, too, was about to leave the city and return to her estate in the countryside. Eryn smiled in grim satisfaction at the thought that Sanaf, the former ambassador to Anyueel, would certainly find his working assignment at Malhora's estate becoming more unpleasant after the mistress of the house returned there.

She straightened unconsciously when Pe'tala entered the main room with Vran'el. He looked a trifle pale, but determined when he went towards her to kiss her cheeks.

"Good morning to you, Eryn. I will first talk to Pe'tala, then to you. Kilan was so kind as to let me know that I am welcome to use his study for that purpose. This should not take too long." He motioned for his youngest sister to walk ahead and followed her.

Eryn frowned. She had counted on having this conversation together, but she could certainly see why he would prefer to avoid being outnumbered by the two of them. Why had she not considered that before? She shouldn't have let Pe'tala go first, she mused. She would probably defy Vran'el and then his mood would certainly not too cheerful when he had to talk to his second sister. It should have been the other way round. What use was being the older sister when she was in no position to profit from the privileges that should be part of the package?

She lifted herself gently from the seating cushions, careful not to jar Vedric too much in the process. She certainly did not wish to be found sitting and waiting for him once he was done with Pe'tala. Yet being nowhere to be found was of course not going to look good, either. He had given them an order, after all, and opposing him on petty matters such as this was childish, however satisfying that would be for a short while.

She decided to move around a bit outside and stepped out into the court yard. Compared to other residences she had been to this was small and not so imposing, yet still a lot larger than any of the courts and gardens in the city of Anyueel, save for the garden between two houses Enric and herself owned there.

Wandering idly between the few trees, careful to remain in the shadows as much as possible, she wondered if their own residence here would be finished in time for their return here in six months. She earnestly hoped so. She was weary of staying at other people's residences. She wanted to have a say in shaping her surroundings to a certain degree - the pictures to hang on the walls, which place to position her own bed - small matters like that. They had spent exactly half a year here now, and that was far too long for being anybody's guest.

Enric had said something similar when he pointed out that he was not fond of the idea of spending half of every year at Vran'el's home, being subject to his rules as host. She shared that sentiment with all her heart.

They would be leaving here tomorrow. She tried to decide whether she felt sorry about that or rather glad at returning home and found the question curiously hard to answer.

She would leave Vern behind. That was a definite downside, even though she knew that it was the best thing that could happen to him.

Valrad was another person she would sorely miss. After everything they had gone through in the first few months after her arrival, she found the idea of leaving her father behind a wrenching one.

Getting rid of Malriel was a definite advantage, however.

Kilan, Intrea, Malhora and Ram'an she would definitely sorely miss. It was yet to be determined, though, in what category Vran'el would fall. The way it appeared right now, a certain distance between them would probably be a good idea.

And of course she was looking forward to seeing how things had progressed back home with the clinic and the orphanage. She had received regular reports, but that was hardly comparable to seeing things for herself.

She would see Plia, Vyril and her healers again. Well, Lord Poron's healers now. And also Tyront and King Folrin, which was certainly less of a cause for rejoicing.

Enric and she would have to work out a daily routine with Vedric, what with his returning to the Order and her getting involved in whatever they now expected of her.

She had no idea if she would even be allowed to return to the clinic and work as a healer any longer, now that she was supposed to join the Magic Council and become a pillar of the Order.

"Eryn?" Vran'el's voice behind her interrupted her thoughts. "Can we talk now?"

She nodded and followed him back into the house and to Kilan's study.

Pe'tala offered to take Vedric off her but Eryn shook her head and held on to him. People tended to show a lot more restraint when faced with a woman bearing a child in her arms.

She wondered briefly if using her own child in such a calculated manner painted her as an unscrupulous mother, but pushed the thought aside. If it did, it was surely Malriel's fault somehow.

Vran'el motioned for her to sit and sank down on the chair next to hers, opting against taking Kilan's seat behind the heavy desk.

Eryn approved of this obvious attempt at creating an atmosphere of equality instead of bluntly reminding her who was in charge in his opinion.

"How do you feel?" he asked gently. "Did you get used to the thought of thinking of your parents as an official and true couple yet?"

She shrugged. "I am still in the process of adapting to that, I think. The ceremony was touching, though. Yet it remains to be seen if they can deal with what they have got themselves into with each other." Or rather what Valrad had saddled himself with Malriel, she corrected silently.

"Indeed. But they are both adults, and as long as they appear to be of sound mind we have little choice but to accept their decision," he smiled, looking slightly tired. "Though I expect that you will have your own rather unfavourable opinion of our father's soundness of mind."

She didn't comment on that and waited for him to leave his attempts at lightening the mood behind and get to what he really wanted to talk about.

He stared at his hands for a few moments, then looked back up into her eyes.

"Eryn, I want you to know that I love you. This is not something I say lightly to people, especially as we have not really known each other for that long. Yet you have, from the moment you have entered my life, enriched it in so many ways. I know that learning of ourselves truly being siblings has not been easy for you, but it was for me a source of pure joy. It felt right and just for me from the start, the most natural thing in the world."

"Vran'el, I..." she started but stopped when he lifted his hand for her to let him finish his line of thought.

"Give me another few moments, will you? What I am trying to tell you is that I have come to treasure you in a very short time and that having you angry at me pains me immensely, especially as you are about to leave here. I understand that this place is not only connected with pleasant memories and experiences for you, but you have become a part of it, of my House, of my life. I do not want to be hoping for you to return occasionally for a few weeks and then be gone again, but embrace this as your home, build a life here."

Eryn nodded. "I know that with Vedric being your heir this…"

"Eryn, no," he sighed wearily. "I am trying to tell you that this is not about political considerations, about duties or matters of succession, but about me wanting to share my life with my sisters. With both of them. Your son was an immensely helpful excuse to make your King and your Order agree to grant me a stake in your life. If I had my way, they would be the ones asking me to let you visit them every now and then, not the other way round. And I do not mind telling you that I would be a lot less generous than they were when it comes to allocating your time."

She swallowed. He was being a lot more open than she had expected of him, making himself vulnerable. But that was very likely was meant to have the side effect of softening her and making her react with more consideration than she would have otherwise. It had worked.

"I love you, too," she replied calmly. "And I see why you are doing all this, but your attachment to me does not justify your taking control of my family's life like that. Or of Pe'tala's. Are you even aware what situation you have put Rolan in? Or how Pe'tala should be allowed to make her own choices?"

"I talked about that with Pe'tala. There is no need for you to argue with me on her behalf right now. She gave me a piece of her mind on that already. Not that it helped her much, mind you. My orders stand. As they do with regard to you."

"So you have come here to tell me that you do not want me to be angry at you any more, yet you are not willing to make any concessions whatsoever?" She frowned at him, displeased that he thought a few pretty, airily-crafted words would be enough to console her.

Vran'el closed his eyes for a moment and leaned forward, resting his elbows on his knees while he exhaled. "Eryn, I have come here to justify my decisions to you, not to take them back or even enter into negotiation about them."

She shook her head and stood up smartly. "No, Vran'el, you have not justified yourself, but tried to play me with a few sentimental assurances of your affection for me without showing any understanding whatever that you are aware of what you are actually doing to me. You are forcing me into leaving everything behind each six months to rush off to the very city Malriel lives in. This alone earns you a proper kicking in my book."

"Wait," he instructed and got up from his chair as well. "We are not yet finished."

"I have nothing more to say to you right now," she growled. "I see you tomorrow at the quayside, I dare say. Have a nice day, Head of House Vel'kim." Thus she opened the door and walked out, leaving Vran'el standing in Kilan's study.

* * *

"How did your talk with your brother go?" Malhora enquired when they were sitting together over the dinner Orrin had just served.

"Just do not get me started," Pe'tala growled and took a generous bite.

"Me, neither," Eryn huffed and rolled her eyes.

"It seems that he messed that up pretty badly," the old woman commented dryly. "Yet I advise you to crush him gently."

All eyes rested on Malhora. "What are you looking at me like that for? Of course they need to do something instead of just nodding in acceptance and obey. This is no way for a Head of House to treat his family without trying to find a more amiable solution first. I should know about this, I was leading House Aren long enough. And Vran'el is about to learn as well, and better to have his sisters teach him than anybody else. This way it will remain a private lesson instead of a public defeat and avoid harming his reputation."

"I am glad that his reputation is the main consideration in this whole affair," Eryn said sweetly.

"There is no other way, you are bound to follow his orders," her grandmother shrugged unperturbed. "And I do not mind them at all. It is only right and proper that you will spend half of your time here in Takhan. I have no intention of crossing that wretched sea every time I wish to see you."

"Yes, be on his side, why don't you?" Eryn spat.

"Do not be so daft, girl. I am on my own side, as always. The trick for everybody else is to make it worth my while considering them to be on the same side as me," Malhora sneered and took another bite from her meal. "You cannot countermand his orders regarding returning here. But you can show him that he has gone too far and fight him concerning a few of the details. And that is what you are doing already with your plans to have your own place here instead of moving in with him. Your being angry will in time make him see that he needs to make amends. And when he has reached this desirable state of mind you will be ready with suggestions."

Pe'tala shook her head and gave the old woman a lopsided grin. "Remind me never to get on your bad side."

"I trust that that will not be necessary. People do not normally need that kind of reminder, as you should be well aware. But you may trust me to let you know when you are on the verge of displeasing me."

The younger woman swallowed. "So the scary Aren grandmother is obviously part of the new Aren-family package. How reassuring."

Eryn smiled at Malhora affectionately. "That's alright. Really, she is the one worth having in the family."

"Now, now," the old woman rolled her eyes. "You know that Malriel is not as bad as you are making her appear. She is not any better or worse than your usual influential politician, just a lot more cunning and thus better at what she is doing. I grant you, though, that her skills as a mother will need improvement. Which is hardly something you can hold against her after her only daughter was snatched from her so many years ago."

"Did you just defend Malriel?" Eryn asked incredulously. "That is a first. Orrin, whatever you mixed into our food, I would recommend using it more sparingly from now on. It seems to have a rather scary effect on my grandmother."

"You just wait until your own child opposes you, my girl. Then we can talk again," Malhora smiled with quiet irony.

"In case you expect me to become best friends with her because we finally bond over our grievances with our children, I need to warn you that such a thing is rather unlikely," she snorted.

"Believe what you may. I am just saying that Malriel has been noticeably more civil to me since she met you a year ago."

"You know what?" Eryn shivered. "The thought of one day being good friends with Malriel is a lot scarier than remaining on bad terms with her for the rest of my life."

"I am sure the citizens of this country will appreciate that sentiment," Kilan grinned. "I fancy Malriel uniting with another Aren woman would be a nasty surprise for most of the senators."

Malhora nodded. "Yes, whatever else you may think of my daughter, she is a formidable woman. There is no denying that."

Eryn sighed and swallowed an acid comment. The old woman was obviously proud of her daughter, no matter that Malriel still liked to play her power games with her. She wondered if Malriel would have turned out any differently if she had every now and again been allowed to catch a glimpse of that pride.

* * *

"This is the third time I am saying farewell to you here, even though you have left only twice, do you know?" Intrea grinned and hugged Eryn.

"Thank you so much for that remark," the latter sighed. "I can't help turning my head every few seconds, afraid that a group of guards is about to drag me off to the Senate hall again."

Ram'an waved her off. "There is no need for that anymore, Theá. We are about to get you back here in a few months."

She just sighed and hugged him. Just like most other people who were sorry to see them go, he had not bothered hiding his delight at Vran'el's arrangement.

Iklan had been excited and started considering all the possibilities for cooperation this opened up and had promised to talk to Valrad about this as soon as possible, obviously convinced that he was doing her a great favour.

So far her niece Obal was the only one less than thrilled at the prospect of seeing her regularly from now on, and had shown her dismay openly. It was only the reminder that this would also mean getting Enric back which had cheered her up.

She watched Orrin bidding his goodbyes to the people he had trained in these last months. They kept slapping him on the back and hinting none too subtly that they expected him back soon.

Vern was the next to pull her into an embrace and promise her, slightly tearfully, that he would miss her terribly and couldn't wait for her to return to Takhan. Next came Neval and Kilan.

Malriel and Valrad stood together, hand in hand and waited for their turn. Eryn turned to her father.

"Enjoy the peace and quiet over the next few months, Valrad."

He smiled. "I would rather forego that quiet and deal with the mayhem that having my two daughters here working at my clinic would mean." He took her face between his hands and kissed her forehead before hugging her firmly. "And maybe we can continue working on the matter of your addressing me not with my name when you return."

She nodded. "Sure, let's work on that one day..."

Malriel smiled faintly. "We did not have a lot of time together, Maltheá. But having you here was certainly an adventure, just like last time. I look forward to your presence here; it will certainly make my life a lot more interesting. Though I will probably need the rest of the year to recover from it unless we find a more peaceful way of coexisting one day." Then her mother hugged her carefully. "Take good care of yourself and my grandson, daughter."

"Certainly, Mother," Eryn replied, smirking at the hint of irritation her tone still caused.

Pe'tala was the next to accept her father's best wishes and then faced Malriel.

"Tala, I dare say we will have to get used to each other now that we are family. Goodbye and return soon, my girl."

"Of course," Pe'tala nodded, then added with a cruel smile in almost the exact tone as her sister before her, "Mother."

Eryn stared at both of them for a moment, then started chuckling at Malriel's aghast expression. She saw that even Valrad was having to bite his lip to stop himself from grinning.

Enric looked down at her and shook his head when she wiped a tear from the corner of one eye.

"Are you fit to hold your son for a moment so that I can say goodbye to your parents, or do I need to worry that you might drop him in your current state of merriment?"

She nodded and took Vedric from his arm, winking at Pe'tala, who grinned with a wicked knowing. Both their expressions grew serious and a touch cool when they saw Vran'el waiting for them next to the gangplank at the end of the pier.

They approached him slowly, taking their time.

When they finally were standing before him, he bent forward and kissed first Pe'tala, then Eryn on the forehead.

"I wish we had a little more time to work on our issues. I am not at all pleased at having to let you leave with things between us like this," he said calmly. "We should write to each other and stay in regular contact until you return. Be nice to one another and try not to give the name of Vel'kim any bad connotation," he smiled faintly.

"Goodbye, Vran," Pe'tala said and patted his cheek. "Try not to bring the rest of House Vel'kim to its knees as well while we are gone."

"I do not see you on your knees, but rather walking over me, Tala," he sighed and turned to the other woman. "Eryn, I am sorry that we have to part like this, but I trust that our affection for each other will enable us to deal with this."

She nodded. "Yes, I know. Goodbye, Vran'el. I will see you again in six months."

Both women stepped onto the plank and carefully walked aboard the ship, watching the rest of their party approach while leaning against the railing.

"I remember when we arrived here together and you kicked the Queen of Darkness into the river," Pe'tala recalled with a dreamy smile. "I must admit I was hoping for a similar farewell today."

"Valrad was holding on to her hand, so he would either have been thrown into the water together with her or tried to stop me."

The younger woman shrugged. "What better way to introduce him to the troubles that will from now on be his constant companion?"

"They seem happy," Eryn sighed resignedly, looking at the couple. "I just wonder how much of that will be left when we return here."

"I managed to tame a fearsome Aren woman," Enric's voice said from behind them. "Who is to say he is not capable of accomplishing the same feat?"

Eryn rolled her eyes. "You didn't tame me. You wore me down and exhausted me."

Pe'tala smirked. "And from what I have seen, it currently seems rather like my sister tamed you, Order Lord."

"How about Rolan and you?" her sister enquired. "Who is the one doing the taming there?"

Rolan raised both eyebrows when all eyes were on him. "I would say that I surrendered in the face of overwhelming force."

"That's not the impression I had when I saw you shouting at her at the clinic back home," Eryn laughed.

"I didn't surrender immediately but rather at the final hurdle," he shrugged and put an arm around Pe'tala's shoulders. "This is an interesting city, you know. I look forward to returning here in a few months."

Pe'tala's mouth dropped open in utter astonishment and she stared at him.

"I can't help but notice that they have obviously avoided breaching that particular topic so far," Enric murmured into his companion's ear.

Eryn swallowed and whispered back, "And he has reached a decision as it seems."

They watched in fascination when Pe'tala tried to say something several times, but didn't manage. Then without warning tears were running down her cheeks and she threw her arms around his neck, burying her face against his skin.

"I did not... I mean... I was so afraid to... to... I had no idea..." she stammered.

Rolan smiled and stroked her back, pressing a kiss into her hair.

Orrin and Junar boarded the ship and stopped dead when they beheld the weeping woman.

"What is the matter with her?" the warrior enquired, displaying the expected unease men showed when encountering a crying member of the opposite sex.

Eryn shook her head slightly. "I am not entirely sure, but I think she just discovered traces of human emotions inside her. I would have to conduct additional research to confirm this, of course. It is a rather unlikely theory, after all."

"Idiot," Pe'tala snivelled and used her sleeve to wipe away her tears.

"Rolan just told her that he will return here with her," Enric explained.

Junar smiled, touched at Pe'tala's reaction. "Does that mean that the two of you will be joining each other?"

"Yes, though only after we have returned here. That way her family can celebrate with us," Rolan nodded, smug when Pe'tala's tears started flowing anew and he pulled her with him across to a crate so he could sit down and pull her on his lap to hold her.

"Oh dear, I think he broke her - she is leaking, and not just a bit," Eryn sighed. "I am not really sure, because this is not how it usually goes, but he did just propose, didn't he?"

Enric thought for a while, then nodded hesitantly. "One could probably say so, I suppose. But my impression was that he not only proposed but also accepted it on her behalf as well. An effective approach, I will admit. I wouldn't have thought he had it in him," he added with an undertone of admiration.

Eryn snorted. "And I wouldn't have thought that he would survive it."

CHAPTER 17

Meeting Family

Eryn resisted the urge to fall onto her knees and kiss home soil after getting off the ship in Bonhet. For one, it would have looked rather strange to the onlookers and also she was still trying to avoid any sudden movements that might upset her stomach unduly.

The passage on the ship had been less unpleasant than she remembered from earlier journeys. This was due to the size of the ship, just as Enric had promised. The larger the vessel, the less susceptible it was to pitching on a small swell and thereby triggering nausea.

There had still been some queasiness but not to the degree she had experienced in the past.

Enric was carrying their son as she was still a little unsteady on her feet.

"I hardly recognise this place," she marvelled and looked around, taking in the new buildings, broad streets, carts and general busyness. "It has grown even more since we last passed through here."

"Naturally," Enric shrugged, but also noted the changes with interest and satisfaction. The place was developing well thanks to the increasing exchange of goods with the Western Territories and would go on doing so if everything went according to his plans.

Eryn lifted her brow. "Are you building another jetty here? Why is it so far away from the others?"

He followed her gaze. "That is the first one meant to accommodate larger cargo ships that sit lower in the water thanks to their weight when they are fully loaded. The water is not deep enough for that so close to the shore, so the jetty needs to reach out a little further and even out there the workers need to do some dredging."

"Dredging? Under water?" she asked incredulously, imagining people who were fighting against currents and sea creatures with weights tied to their feet to avoid floating back up. And then there was the matter of breathing.

"Yes. I have employed a few magicians from the Western Territories for that. They more or less blast the ground away. It is a lot less complex and time-consuming than traditional building methods."

She nodded slowly. That did make sense. Yet the thought of having magicians doing actual work here in this country was still a novel one. No matter that they were not from here. For now Enric had little choice but to hire foreign magicians for certain types of tasks such as acting as captains on his ships in order to pass the magical barrier that was still out there. But she hoped the idea would catch on here, too, and local magicians would embrace the concept of making themselves useful and be productive members of society one day not too far away. If there really was an increased number of magically gifted children now, the Order could hardly train all of them as fighters or healers. It would simply cost too much money and make little sense.

Junar stepped next to them, nodding appreciatively. "That place has turned into a real town. That probably means that there is a good chance for a proper meal?"

Enric nodded. "Certainly. I was told that they opened their third tavern here only a month back. We will eat, then you need to be off on the boat that takes you upstream to Anyueel."

Eryn's head snapped to him with a worried expression. "What do you mean by that? You are not planning to accompany us back to the city, then?"

"No, I am not. Though my plans are not limited to myself but also include you and Vedric. We will take a detour."

"A detour? Where? And for what purpose? And why did you fail to mention this to me until now?"

"It was meant to be a surprise. I have requested another two, three weeks to be able to take you to my sister and her family. You said you would like to meet her. Even though that was a while ago I assumed that this hadn't changed." He watched the frown on her forehead smoothing while she considered that new development. "It will be our first journey with no other purpose than pleasure."

A slow smile spread across her face. "That sounds fabulous. Though I would have appreciated more timely information so I could take care of proper clothes. Almost all the clothes I have with me are fine for the Takhan climate, but not for late autumn and early winter here. I will probably not want to venture out of bed the whole time to avoid freezing."

"Your lack of trust in my organisational skills wounds me, my love," he laughed. "I had a chest of clothes sent from our house to my sister's place, so we should be able to get through that one week without major inconvenience."

She nodded with relief, pushing aside both the thought that she wasn't even sure if she would fit into them already and the minor stirring of regret at having her return to what was now her home being delayed. She had been looking forward to returning to her own four walls, to Plia and the clinic.

But of course she was curious about his sister, the only family member he seemed to be close to, and this was very likely the best opportunity to finally make that trip. Returning a little bit later after such an extended stay was certainly a lot easier to organise than having another absence granted any time soon.

"We will eat something now and then be on our way. I ordered a coach for us that will take us all the way. I am going to wake Urban. She can either run along or stay in the coach with us," Enric explained.

"Your sister won't mind your little pet?" Orrin enquired and nodded at the crate currently being unloaded by four men.

"No, I have warned her. And she has always been the braver one of us. Even if she was afraid she would never admit to it."

"She was?" Eryn asked curiously.

"Oh, yes, absolutely. That was a constant matter of embarrassment for an older brother during my childhood, as you may imagine."

Pe'tala joined them and chortled. "Big, strong Enric had a more courageous sister? That is hard to believe. But look at Vran'el; of us siblings he is the only one being uneasy about Urban, irrespective of the fact that he is the oldest. I think it has nothing to do with being younger or older. Men are just less brave in general."

"Thank you for that pearl of wisdom," Orrin rolled his eyes. "How nice to have you accompanying us on the boat."

"Do not be grumpy, Orrin," she smiled. "There is no use denying a basic principle of nature or being angry because of it."

"Is there any chance I can persuade you to take her with you to your sister's place? Please?" he grumbled.

Eryn laughed and shook her head. "None whatsoever. But you could train her in unarmed combat to keep her busy and at the same time bash her to your heart's content."

Pe'tala straightened. "Could we do that?" she asked eagerly, excitement radiating off her.

Orrin blinked at her. "You would want that? Seriously? Voluntarily?" he added with a sideways glance at her sister.

"I have been wanting to learn fighting for a while now, but I did not want to approach the Order. They would probably have called a Council meeting or something to make that decision."

The warrior smiled. "I would be delighted to teach you. We have about two days to kill on that boat, so we may just as well use that time. Try not to fall into the river, though." He turned to Eryn. "I changed my mind. We will allow her to accompany us."

Pe'tala grinned broadly.

"You could have asked Rolan to teach you. He is not a bad fighter himself, at least with a sword," Enric underlined.

She cringed. "Have my lover teach me fighting? That is a decidedly unappealing thought, Order Lord. I like the dynamics in my relationship being a lot more peaceful than what you obviously find appealing."

Eryn nodded. "I am with you on that one."

"Apart from the fact that Orrin has taken over your training you have not even been doing any fighting in about nine months now," her companion pointed out. "I don't really see how that argument applies in our case."

"The Order will make me resume my training at some point, and as we are to leave Anyueel for several months every year they will definitely expect you to train me again when Orrin is not available in Takhan," she emphasised. "Unless you are planning to delegate that task to Kilan, that is."

Enric shrugged. That was a reasonable argument. Then he grinned when he thought of something the ambassador had told him. "I wouldn't ask that of him. It would be too cruel. And then I suppose he has had his share of being delegated unwanted tasks."

She grimaced. "He told you of my attempts to wriggle out of having to write to the King and Tyront, then. And there people say womenfolk are the ones prone to gossiping. You are just as bad."

"You won't hear me contradict you, my love. Interestingly enough it is something men and women are fond of on either side of the sea, so it is obviously nothing cultural but probably a basic human need."

Eryn rolled her eyes. "The basic human need to gossip? Really?"

"Why not? It certainly cements a community together."

"Unless you are the unlucky cause or victim of said gossip," she pointed out.

"Certainly. But then it is only a question of enduring it until something newer happens. Unless you happen to be the source of that, too, that is," he amended.

She snorted. "Right, tell me about it. I sometimes think I was the main provider of topics for gossip in both countries for these last two years."

Orrin nodded. "That is probably a reasonable thing to assume, yes. It's certainly not boring when you are around. Shall we move on and have something to eat or do you wish to continue your discussion about the merits of gossip here?"

Junar sent him a grateful smile and waited patiently for Enric to take the lead. "Your sister keeps calling Enric Order Lord. She is aware that Rolan is one, too, right?"

"Of course I am," Pe'tala rolled her eyes. "But he was made one only recently and Enric has been this pillar of society for many years now."

"Why does this sound like an insult?" Enric sighed. "Considering that first your father and now your brother are influential politicians I find your attitude rather disconcerting."

She laughed at that. "You do? You should not. I know what I am talking about, after all. You may seem mighty and powerful, untouchable, far above the worries of everyday life, but you are not.

You are just as easily thrown off track by small events that make some of us wonder if you have really ever reached the state of adulthood. Vran has kept fighting me for my share of the yellow fruit in the breakfast bowl for what must be two decades now, and my highly esteemed father has obviously fallen prey to premature mental deterioration considering to a degree that he fancies himself in love with the Queen of Darkness."

Eryn nodded solemnly. There was nothing much to add to that last bit.

They followed Enric to a building that looked considerably grander than those around it.

"That is the new tavern?" Junar marvelled.

"A bit more than that," Enric explained. "They also have a number of rooms available, which makes sense considering that more people will be wanting to travel to Takhan in the months to come. They will need a place to stay while waiting for their ship to sail or dock."

"This building doesn't happen to belong to you by any chance, does it?" Eryn asked suspiciously.

"No, as a matter of fact, it does not."

"Do not be greedy, sister," Pe'tala smirked. "Not everything can belong to the two of you. Let other people be in possession of things every now and again, too."

"When exactly can we leave her and be on our way?" Eryn mumbled with a sideways glance at Pe'tala and followed the others through a large door into a spacious room.

The surfaces were shiny, not from being polished through constant use but from what had to be some kind of oil. There was a smell of fresh wood that penetrated the air. It was not unpleasant, but a little more intense than would have been comfortable.

Junar whistled through her teeth. "I bet my sister would like to see that. She has been wanting to modernise her pub for a while now, but after spending most of their savings on apothecaries when she fell ill, that plan has been on hold for these last three years at least. She would love to see that here, though."

"It's a pity Vern is not here. He could have drawn a picture for her," Eryn said and let her gaze wander over the colourfully decorated walls.

It looked like the owner was trying to gently prepare travellers for what expected them on the other side of the sea. Though the execution of the principle of cheerfully coloured decoration was clearly based on stories and not done by somebody who had ever laid eyes on how people in the Western Territories made a room comfortable and pleasant to be in. It had none of the taste and style from the west but was more like a random assortment of whatever cheerful piece of fabric the owner had been able to get his hands on.

She had to grin at the thought that if people from Takhan passed through here for the first time on their way to Anyueel and beheld that assortment, they would probably think it reflected the local

192

customs and get the shock of their life, wondering what strange country they had ventured into. They would definitely not guess that this was supposed to imitate what they were used to from their own homes.

They were led to a table that was surrounded by chairs with real padding which actually looked comfortable.

"How long will you be staying with your sister's family?" Junar asked Enric.

"About ten days," he replied. "If Eryn and my sister don't get along, we will leave earlier."

Eryn cleared her throat. "Are you saying I am not sociable?"

"No, that's not what I am saying. But my sister is, not unlike Pe'tala, a strong, self-confident woman. And you surely remember what a bumpy start the two of you had."

"But that was all her fault!" she protested. "She resented me before she had even laid eyes on me back then!"

Pe'tala sniggered. "Meeting you in person did not change that very much, anyway. But if your sister truly is anything like me she must be a wonderful, intelligent, warm-hearted person with a great sense of humour."

"Without a doubt," Rolan snorted and earned himself what was clearly a kick under the table.

"Shut up," she smirked. "You are crazy about me."

"Yes, crazy is certainly the word that comes to mind, considering that he wants to commit to you. Voluntarily," Eryn grunted. "Have I mentioned that I do not approve as it will cost me my Head of Administration?"

"Have I mentioned that I do not care in the least what professional inconveniences my commitment will cause you?" Pe'tala shot back.

Rolan shook his head at them. "I think having you two of you in Anyueel will turn out to be quite suspenseful. I would have guessed that this would change now that you like each other, but I am less sure about that every day I spend with you."

"It could be worse," Orrin sneered. "Pe'tala could be a member of the Order. The Magic Council would despair with two of them."

Rolan nodded. "Definitely. They are still bearing a grudge against Tala for the way she talked to them when Eryn wanted to stop her combat training."

Enric grinned and shook his head when the two sisters exchanged a look and both started smiling with an evil glint in their eyes at the memory of how Pe'tala had treated them that day. "Just look at them. Malriel's daughters, united in malicious recollection."

Eryn and Pe'tala both shot him a devastating glare before saying in unison, "Oh, shut up, brother."

* * *

Eryn stood on the riverbank, her hand in Enric's, and watched the boat with her friends and family on it sail off towards the city of Anyueel. The mountain cat was a few paces away, rolling lazily in the grass of her homeland, still a little groggy from her long sleep on the ship.

"How is it possible for a ship to go upstream like that?" she wondered and tried to discern if the wind was indeed strong enough to counter the pull of the stream that should have pushed them back towards the sea. But what if the wind abated or came from the wrong direction? Would they have to row back to the city? With magicians on board that would surely not be too much of a problem, they could generate gusts of wind; but with non-magician passengers rowing would require more crew members than would fit on a boat like that.

"They depend on the wind for that," Enric explained. "Right now the wind comes from the side, which is not ideal considering the direction they want to go. But do you see the position of the sails? They are flexible, and right now their position is adapted to catching the wind from the south."

His companion squeezed his hand and chuckled. "Why am I not surprised that you know about that? I suppose there was a book on that topic lying around somewhere?"

He shrugged. "I wouldn't say lying around, but yes, that was certainly my source of information. I thought I should be able to understand a few basics when going into the shipping business. It generally pays to demonstrate that I possess at least basic knowledge whenever I talk to people where I need to avoid being taken advantage of. Usually a small hint suffices. People are considerate enough to automatically assume that I am much better informed than I really am. Just give them a small piece of information and their heads will supply the rest. A very convenient human tendency."

Eryn whistled through her teeth. "So you basically bluff people all the time by making yourself appear a lot more well-educated than you actually are. That kind of damages that picture of you I have."

"That devastates me, my love," he sighed and adjusted his son on his arm. "But let me tell you that I usually aim to close gaps in my knowledge, even if my initial searches for information generally are less thorough. Does this re-establish your trust in my great intellectual prowess?"

She pretended to think for a moment, then smiled. "For now. But you may count on my being a lot more sceptical when you once again appear unusually well-informed about whatever topic that may come up. I will make sure to ask into a lot more detail from now on to look for the limits of that seemingly endless pool of knowledge inside your head."

"I suspect I have just made my life at your side a lot more difficult," he commented.

"Why? You might just as well admit to not being omniscient every now and then. Or is the prospect of not being better and smarter all the time so revolting?"

"No, my love. I am just trying to be the kind of partner to you who stimulates you intellectually," he replied softly and gently pushed behind her ear a strand of hair the wind was playing with. "Especially now that I am on a quest of binding you to me once again."

Ah yes, she thought, that topic again. "I am still bound to you, Enric. I am not at liberty to bind myself to anybody else, and neither do I have a wish to."

"A start, but not enough. That is another human habit, you see? Going without something we have never known is a lot less problematic than experiencing it only to be forced to give it up again."

"Not forced, Enric," she remarked calmly. "It was a decision you made."

"I know. One I am paying for. Dearly so."

"I'll grant you that," she agreed. "But so did I when you left me behind like that, forcing the bond off me. I must tell you honestly that your situation could be a lot worse than it is right now. I find that I am very forgiving in this matter."

He just nodded, knowing well enough that she was right. Who would have blamed her for pushing him away completely, keeping their son out of his reach and refusing to speak to him at all? Not many, even though people in Takhan would have acknowledged the sacrifice he had made to help them. He was lucky, he knew. She had even told him that she loved him since his return, a statement he heard from her so rarely that he had not dared hope for it anytime soon.

"I didn't mean to complain," he said softly and made himself smile. "Come on. The coach is waiting. It is usually little more than a day's journey from here, but we will not be able to travel through the night and will have to rest frequently so you can feed Vedric without the two of you being jostled about."

She nodded and let him guide her towards the coach, making sure that Urban followed them. "Can I ask you something? It has been on my mind for a while but I didn't want to address it while the others were around."

"Of course. What is it?" She could ask him all she wanted as long as they would leave that other topic behind them for now. He regretted bringing it up.

"It's about Ram'an and Valcredy."

Enric stopped and looked down at her with one eyebrow lifted in smug amusement. "Not jealous, are you?"

"What? Why would I be? That's complete nonsense! I rejected him so many times I lost count. Of course I am not jealous."

"What is it that bothers you, then?"

"That her only ambition in life seems to have been snagging herself a mighty magician! I remember well enough how angry and frustrated she was when you and I were joined, how she told me that I was nothing more than an interesting pet for you. Which is ludicrous considering that this was exactly what she wanted to become. And what she has obviously finally been able to achieve."

"And you don't think she deserved a mighty magician for herself?"

"I couldn't care less what she deserves or gets, but I don't think that Ram'an deserves to be stuck with her. He is the ultimate feather in her cap! He is the one who deserves better!"

"Eryn, Ram'an is a Head of House and has to worry about securing his succession. After losing you he pretty much gave up any great hopes of finding love. And he cannot afford to start looking now. This match suits him just as fine. Valcredy will have the lifestyle and status she had been trying to secure for herself for several years now, and Ram'an will have the children his House needs without having to negotiate with another House and pay a price he cannot afford. And as Valcredy is pretty, their children will no doubt be handsome enough."

Eryn groaned and looked up at the sky. "I know! It's just not what I wanted for him!"

Enric sighed and pulled her close to wrap his free arm around her shoulders and kiss her forehead. "You are feeling guilty because you think not getting you made him resort to that callous, desperate measure of accepting Valcredy as his companion." Her sullen expression showed him that he was right. Though he wouldn't have needed it for confirmation, he felt her guilt plainly enough through the mind bond. "Valcredy may not have shown you her best sides, but she is a halfway intelligent woman, attractive and a very talented musician to boot. These are three attributes that make her desirable enough for any man. And they both agreed to grant each other as much freedom as possible. They are both free to have affairs, follow their own inclinations in whatever other areas of their separate lives and just share the responsibility of raising their children together."

Eryn folded her arms. "Really. You know, if that truly is as fabulous as you make it sound you and I might try that as well." She winced when she felt his hand gripping her neck to make her look up at him.

"Our connection and theirs cannot be compared," he explained patiently, but she saw the spark of danger in his eyes at the mere idea of doing just that. She had meant it as no more than a jibe, but he seemed to take it a lot more seriously than that. "Our companionship is no business arrangement, however reluctant you may have been to join me or however wrongly you think I have treated you."

He exhaled slowly, releasing her neck and reminding himself of what their initial topic had been just now. She had wanted to talk about her disapproval of the connection between a man she considered a close friend and a woman she didn't like. And he had let his fear of losing her get the better of him. Again.

She studied him for a few seconds, then shook her head. "I should probably be more careful what I say to you. One would think that having a child together provides for a certain bond even without a third level commitment."

Enric smiled sadly. "If only it were that easy, my love. Bearing our child was forced upon you. And children have served in neither Valrad's nor Malriel's case to keep their companions with them."

Eryn raised both eyebrows and climbed inside the coach as he held the door open for her. "Alright, I admit that I was not exactly joyful when I learned about being pregnant, but I am now. And as regards my luckless parents, I dare say that it was in both cases a blessing that their companions didn't let their children trap them in a loveless relationship." She watched Urban follow her into the coach and then lie down under one of the benches. She really had to be worn out if she voluntarily climbed into a coach instead of first trotting along for a few hours.

When Enric had taken a seat next to her, he gave her a measured look. "This contradicts your own argument as it shows that having a child is no guarantee for staying together," he pointed out.

"Firstly, I was against having children in general but have found that I am quite content with having one with you. I think that this certainly accounts for an above average attachment. And then you still have access to my emotions thanks to your side of the mind bond, so you have even less to fear as you would be the first to notice a change in my regard for you."

He nodded. "Nice, logical arguments, I'll grant you that."

"But none that aid in reducing your fear of my rushing off as long as I have not agreed to re-enter into that blasted third level bond with you?" she asked with a grimace. "How is it possible that a man who was obviously a desirable target for many women for quite a while is so very insecure when it comes to his own companion?" She shook her head in incomprehension and braced her feet against the opposite bench when the coach set in motion.

"That might have something to do with the fact that you were trying to run from me, even after we were joined. It demonstrates clearly that you are not as attached to me as I am to you and thus merits a certain... careful awareness."

Her head snapped to him. He had said that so calmly and without even a trace of anger or resentment, as if it was just another fact of life.

"That is a very harsh thing to say to me," she whispered, hurt.

He looked at her, clearly surprised at her reaction to his words. "This was not meant as reproach, my love. This was how we started - I was in love with you already while you barely tolerated it when I touched you. That gap between our regards for each other has kept shrinking more quickly than I had dared hope, though right now it seems to have stagnated at best. It may even have become a little wider again, I fear. One day we will have reached a stage in our

197

relationship where the gap will not be noticeable anymore. I can wait for that."

"This was not the impression I had before you left for Pirinkar," she stated, looking out the coach window, seeing how the multitude of new buildings of Bonhet passed by. "I felt, for the first time in my life, safe again with another person after my father had died. I had the feeling that I could talk to you. About everything. The mind bond has helped, I will admit. You knew so much even without my sharing it with you consciously. If this was not enough for you I wonder if I can ever give you what you wish for. Or even if you really are that much more attached to me than I to you, as you seem to believe."

She pushed away his hand when his fingers made to turn her chin towards him. She didn't want to look at him right now.

"Eryn, look at me," he implored her. "I want to look into your eyes for what I have to tell you. So I can show you that these are no empty words and that I can see that you understand what I am telling you." He waited for her finally to turn her head hesitantly, and only after she had lifted her gaze up to his did he go on, "The thought of losing you makes me choke. It is like you are the very air that I breathe and my body rebels against the danger of having to do without you. I wasn't even aware that an emotion can have a physical effect like that. They warned me about keeping my end of the commitment bond intact as it would pull me back to you and make me suffer. But it was nothing, it was even sweet agony compared to the thought of having no connection to you at all, of being cut off completely. And even if I had been gone for years, I know that this bond, however painful the effects, would be the only thing which kept me sane. Because a painful link to you was so much more preferable to what would have resembled stopping breathing altogether. I felt you suffering through the bond, yet it was nothing compared to what I would have gone through in your place. This is how I know that there still is a gap."

Eryn swallowed hard and closed her eyes, causing the moisture that had collected under her lids to run down her cheeks. The thought of being loved by another person with such intensity, such self-destructive vigour was almost overwhelming.

"How am I ever to live up to that?" She shook her head and her voice took on a slightly panicky quality. "What if I am not even capable of loving that deeply? What if living alone for such a long time, hiding, never trusting anybody has destroyed something that keeps me from reciprocating to such a degree?"

Enric smiled and pulled her hand to his lips. "You are truly worrying about not being able to love me as much as I love you? And you call me competitive?" He turned serious again. "We have many years ahead of us to find out about all of that. And in these years our regard for each other will undergo changes, will have to face further tests and grow. Challenges like having to raise a teenage boy who is going to be so strong that neither of us will be able to contain him if he misbehaves. Or the strain that moving between cities will mean for the three of us, or whatever trouble being members of different Houses may cause in the future. Yet every test, every struggle means that we will be able to emerge from it a little wiser and stronger than before."

"There will be struggles that might never cease," she said softly. "The King, for example. You took me away from Anyueel to protect me from him. Now we are returning to him, and everything will be as it was."

He smiled broadly, a knowing glint in his eye. "Oh no, my love, believe me when I tell you that the woman I will take back to his city is not the one who left half a year ago. I have no doubt whatsoever that you will stand up to him. Compared to everything you had to go through in Takhan, a King who might try to play us by taking liberties with you is no longer a challenge I feel you cannot handle."

She stared up at him, astonished by the pride, the confidence in her she herself felt far from secure enough to agree with. Yet the idea of disappointing him was impossible. Not after what he had just told her. Was that the power that made people grow when they were loved and loved in return? The dread of failing the one person that mattered, the need to comply with that unrealistic, much too favourable picture the partner had?

If yes, then this was a nasty trick of nature, a political strategy with no equal.

*   *   *

Enric pointed to a collection of wooden buildings with heaps of tree trunks and sawn planks that was visible from the coach window.

"This is the first saw mill my sister and her companion opened several years ago. This was shortly after my rise to power in the Order. I had little other use for my newly increased income and thus sponsored her, rediscovering my joy for doing business."

"You once told me she ran off with a lumberjack," Eryn prompted.

"She did, yes. She was eighteen years old back then. Father had intended her to aid our brother, taking over menial tasks while he took care of the more involved work. You surely remember my father's rather... outdated views on the role of a woman. But Leris was never as meek as our mother, she had her own ideas. Taking orders from her brother was definitely not one of them, especially as she didn't get along with him during their childhood. I was glad that she left our home as soon as she was able. She would have wilted staying there." He stared into the distance. "Just like our mother."

Eryn leaned against the backrest of her bench and studied him thoughtfully. He looked solemn. She wondered if enabling his sister to start her business was a substitute for saving his mother.

How great the contrast to her own family was, she couldn't help but notice. Formidable, powerful Malriel would never have bowed to a man like that. A thought occurred to her. Was that why he liked the Queen of Darkness? Because she was such a stark contrast to his own mother and this impotence that worried him so much? Did he wish for his mother to be just a little bit more like Malriel and free herself from what he considered an unacceptable situation?

"You said this is her first saw mill. How many does she have now?" she asked to distract him from the unpleasant thoughts.

"Five. One of the first business areas I started dabbling in was construction. This complemented her own line of work nicely as she was the one to provide the raw materials for my undertakings. And still does. She is a reliable supplier of high quality building materials," he explained, smiling proudly.

"And her companion? This sounds like your sister is taking care of the business all alone."

"Ardegen. He pretty much lets her do whatever she feels right. Father may not have trained her to take over his business one day, but she has always been a smart one and has picked up quite a bit more than he had intended to show her. When he had made sure that she learned how to merely calculate numbers correctly she had in addition to that taken a look at how to cross-reference expenses and analyse deviations from planned budgets. It meant she was the one with the business background while Ardegen stuck to the more basic areas like hiring and training lumberjacks, checking the quality of their goods and getting the things done that Leris wanted to have carried out."

"A fortunate match for both of them, then," Eryn said lightly, observing him. There had been something in his voice when he had talked about his sister's companion. It was nothing as strong as disdain or disapproval, but there had been a certain lack of warmth.

"Definitely," he agreed without hesitation. "He is nothing like our father, which is a great point in his favour. He acknowledges her superiority in some areas and contributes to the success of their business with his own knowledge."

"But?"

He didn't bother with pretending that he had no idea what she was talking about but was instead pleased that she had got to know him well enough to spot that there was indeed something that bothered him.

"It sounds foolish. I don't have any reason whatsoever not to like him; he is good for my sister and from her letters I can tell that he treats her well and makes her happy. I have met him five or six times over these last fourteen years, and he has always kept his distance to me and treated me with what I can only call detached politeness."

"When did you last see them?"

He thought for a moment, then sighed and shook his head. "More than five years ago. She was pregnant with her first child back then. I haven't even met my niece and my nephew. We have always promised in our letters to each other that we shall meet again soon but somehow something always cropped up to foil any such plan."

"The latest of which was me, I imagine," she smiled.

He laughed and nodded. "That you were. But as troubles go, you were worth every moment."

"I dare say that most of the Order would beg to differ on that point."

"Who cares what the Order says?" he said gently.

"You used to," she said softly, pleased with his reply.

"Yes, I did. Funny how things change, isn't it?"

Yes, indeed, she thought, convinced that Tyront and the Order would not find this new attitude at all amusing but instead rather disturbing.

"How much further do we have to go? It's almost time for Vedric to eat."

"We should be there in less than half an hour. Can you delay it for that long?"

"I think so, yes. Not for much longer, though. He has already started sucking on my fingertips and will soon get frustrated with the lack of nourishment," she explained dryly.

Enric nodded wistfully. "Ah, those carefree and less troublesome days when a woman's breasts were nothing but a source of food..."

She snorted. "Thank you. That did not exactly sound like a compliment for me, you know."

He smiled lazily. "Less troublesome also means less enjoyable, my love. I certainly prefer the changed nature of my... attachment to female breasts."

"Good. Because anything else would have been rather unsettling and I would have signed you up for Iklan's talking treatment next time we are in Takhan."

"So you are less sceptical about his special treatment now?"

"Not necessarily. But if I needed to worry about your competing with your son for my milk, I would take every help I could get, however unusual it might seem."

* * *

Enric smiled at her reassuringly when the coach came to a halt. He found the slight stab of nervousness he could sense through the mind bond endearing.

"Come on, my love. Time for me show off my new family." Saying this, he opened the coach door without waiting for the coachman to do so and climbed out, holding Eryn's hand to help her down without slipping and endangering herself and the precious load on her arm. They had decided to put Urban to sleep for now and awaken her the next morning.

Eryn blinked when a woman sped past her and threw her arms around Enric, squeezing him and laughing happily. She let her gaze wander over the sturdy build and the unusually short, blond hair that didn't even cover her neck. She was wearing a long shirt, thick leather trousers and robust boots that looked worn but well cared for.

After what must have been a minute at least, the woman released him again and held him at arms' length to study him critically.

"Enric, you look good. Strange with that unnaturally brown skin that the sun in those foreign parts has obviously given you, but good still," she grinned and pulled him close once again to kiss him noisily.

Eryn straightened when his sister turned towards her, curious to finally see her face. It was Anwin's face; she resembled her father - probably a lot more than she appreciated. Clear blue eyes, same as Enric's, examined her with unconcealed curiosity for several moments before she nodded.

"You are Eryn, then. The woman who ensnared my brother. Good. I had started worrying that he might end up old and lonely." She reached out shook Eryn's free hand.

Eryn blinked at the brisk greeting, but saw from the humorous glint in these blue eyes that it was meant as a genuine welcome.

"Leris. I am glad I finally have a chance to meet you. Enric has told me about you."

Leris smirked. "Has he now? But not a lot, I'll bet. He was never the sharing kind. Let me have a look at that child of yours." She didn't wait for Eryn's consent but bent forward, expertly snatching the small bundle from its mother's arm. "Look at that! Dark hair like his exotic mother, but the rest of him certainly resembles his father. Well done, brother! Now come, let's get you out of the wind. Ardegen is waiting inside with the children. You can see their noses pressed against the window panes."

Eryn turned and focused her attention on the robust, two-storey building that consisted - as was to be expected - almost entirely of wood. The window next to the heavy entrance door did indeed show two small faces with noses and palms flat against the glass, their eyes big and round.

The door opened as soon as they were close enough and then a man as tall as Enric with shoulders broader than any Eryn had ever seen before stepped aside to let them enter. He looked like he could just wrap his arms around a tree and pull it out of the ground without much effort.

"Enric," he said with a low, reverberating voice and nodded curtly. Then his gaze wandered across to Eryn.

She was shocked when he bowed his head. "My Lady."

My Lady. It sounded completely out of place, not only considering that this was a family meeting, but also because she had not been addressed with that blasted title for however many months. Having it tossed at her like that was a slightly jolting surprise.

Leris sniggered. "She doesn't like the title, Gen. I remember telling you how Enric wrote that in his letters."

Eryn made herself smile. "I would be grateful if you would leave it off, Ardegen. I have indeed always considered it more of a burden than a privilege."

The massive man nodded again in silent acceptance of her wishes. Eryn watched his companion pressing Vedric into his arms and was about to offer taking him back. But Ardegen just took the bundle without hesitation, nestling the baby in the crook of an arm which had the circumference of a medium-sized tree trunk. He did this with such natural gentleness and indisputable skill that she stared at him for a moment.

"Don't worry. He is very good with children, even though he looks like he can handle nothing more breakable than an axe," Enric's sister reassured her and pointed to the two figures that still stood in front of the window, but had turned to stare at the newcomers. "This here," she pointed to a boy who had to be about four years old, "is our son Dorn." Then she nodded to the slightly older girl beside him who had to be about Obal's age. "And our daughter Nera. Children, these are your uncle Enric and your aunt Eryn."

"I am four," the boy announced proudly and grinned shyly at her, ignoring Enric completely.

Eryn smiled back. It was nice to find a child liked her for a change. They normally gravitated to Enric and tried to stay away from her.

"But of course you are."

The girl, on the other hand, took a step back, hiding behind her older brother. Well, that was certainly a lot closer to the kind of reaction she was used to when encountering children. Or was it just with girls? She had not really met many little boys now that she came to think of it.

"Come join us," Leris invited them into the next room, pointing to a table large enough to easily accommodate twelve people. "Take a seat and let me get you something warm to drink. Do you want me to heat the drink for you or will you do it with your magic, Enric?"

"Are you trying to appear polite, Leris?" Enric smiled. "Normally you just place a cup of cold water with herbs in front of me without saying anything."

She shrugged, unabashed. "I was trying to make a good impression on your companion. A feeble attempt thanks to your unflattering if not entirely untrue words."

The boy, Dorn, followed his father and waited for him to sit on one of the chairs at the table to look at the baby.

"What is its name?" he whispered.

"His name is Vedric," Ardegen explained. "This is your cousin."

"Is he a magician?"

"He will be, yes," Enric supplied.

Dorn slowly turned his head, staring at Enric as if reproaching him for his unbidden interference.

Enric leaned closer to Eryn and whispered, "I think he doesn't like me much. That is new."

203

"Girls normally like you," she whispered back and smiled encouragingly at the boy, liking him all the more for not automatically adoring Enric.

"Your hair is different," Dorn stated and approached her carefully.

"Only in looks. It feels the same as yours."

He eyed her curiously, his eyes wandering over her braid as if tempted to make sure of that by touching it. She waited for a few more moments for him to muster the courage, then offered, "You can see for yourself if you don't believe me."

That seemed to have been the permission he had been waiting for and he stepped next to her and gingerly let his fingertips glide over the interwoven strands, then he touched his own hair to compare.

"Do you have a mirror?" Eryn asked him. "I can show you a trick, if you like."

Without replying, Dorn rushed off to return a few moments later with what looked like either his mother's or his sister's hand mirror.

"Mine!" a squeaky, indignant voice from under the table protested.

So much for that. Eryn had not even noticed that the girl had followed them in.

"I told you to ask before you take your sister's things," his father reprimanded him mildly.

The boy ignored both his sister and his father and pushed the mirror into Eryn's hands, his eyes eager with anticipation.

"I don't think I can show you if you just took your sister's things without asking, Dorn," she sighed, feeling that some solidarity among parents was in order.

Dorn grimaced, then bent down to his sister under table, asking irritated, "Can I take your mirror?"

"No!"

The boy straightened again, giving Eryn a look that bespoke unimaginable suffering. "I asked."

"But she said No."

"You never said she had to say Yes!" Dorn pointed out.

"That was implied," she sighed.

"What?" the boy asked in confusion, completely lost with this complicated grown-up talk.

"If you stole my things and only asked me for permission afterwards, I wouldn't give them to you, either," she explained patiently.

The boy's face fell when he realised that this obviously meant that there was no trick in his immediate future. Then his face brightened. "Mother, can I take your mirror?"

Leris placed two large, earthenware mugs with what looked like red wine with herbs swimming in them before them and nodded to her brother to heat them up. "You may, yes. Don't break it, do you hear me? No running down the stairs with it!" She took a seat next to her companion.

"What exactly is this?" Eryn asked carefully. It also smelled like wine. But warm wine?

"This is what we drink on cold days to warm up quickly in these parts. Warm spiced wine. I mixed yours with a little water, so it shouldn't be a problem for your son when you next feed him. Do try it."

Eryn tentatively sipped at her drink. It was not too bad, but nothing she would have chosen for any other purpose than warming up.

Vedric's eyes had finished roaming his surroundings or however much thereof he could perceive and had locked onto Ardegen's face, staring at him for several seconds before breaking into a slow grin. The man's own placid features reacted by transferring his expression into a wide, genuine smile that had Eryn blink. This heavy, quiet, seemingly unflappable man went soft at the smile of a baby. She felt a draw to him all of a sudden, curious about this reserved man that had such a natural and appealing way of dealing with children.

Dorn's noisy arrival with a hand mirror almost identical to the one he had brought before freed her from that strange spell and she motioned for him to look himself in the mirror. Then she touched his hair, applying a weak shield to make it turn brown like her own.

She was quick enough to grab the handle and save the mirror from falling to the floor when his eyes went wide and his fingers limp with astonishment. A moment later he touched his hair, still staring at his mirror image.

Leris whistled appreciatively. "Neat. I didn't know you could do that."

"We couldn't until recently," Enric explained. "This is one of the new things we learned from Eryn's home country." They both watched when Eryn touched her own hair to turn it green and the boy's to change it to blue, making him squeal with delight.

The girl slowly appeared from under the table to see what the commotion was about and her mouth dropped open at the shock of blue hair on her brother's head.

Eryn turned to Ardegen when her son started whimpering. "It's time for his feed now. Is there a place where I can sit down comfortably for a while?"

Ardegen got up without handing her the baby first and indicated for her to follow him. They climbed up a staircase that creaked with every step and Eryn couldn't help but wonder if the first one to go down to the kitchen in the morning would wake the rest of the house that way.

The tall man pushed open one of several doors on the first floor and revealed a cosy guest room with a flood of pillows on the broad bed that could be rearranged into a comfortable prop for feeding Vedric without making her arm go limp after a few minutes.

She thanked him and took her son from his arm, waiting for him to leave the room and close the door behind him before undressing.

As far as meeting various parts of their respective families had gone so far, this was the first occasion that had so far turned out to be unproblematic and amicable. Learning of Malriel had certainly not been a pleasure, and neither had meeting Pe'tala. Nor had bumping into Malhora at the Aren estate been much better. Then there was Enric's father who had turned up unexpectedly at their home in the city, getting himself kicked out by Enric who was seeing him for the first time in seven years.

This right now was definitely preferable to any first-time family encounters they had been through so far. She felt a little overwhelmed by Enric's sister and was not sure how to respond to that brusqueness. Yet her companion had shown her in his quiet competence handling Vedric, even though he was not particularly talkative, that he was approachable. Maybe she would concentrate on him for a start.

CHAPTER 18

Family Dynamics

"How about a stroll around the saw mill today, Enric? I have made a few changes lately and want you to tell me what you think of them," Leris asked, stowing her half-chewed bite of bread in one cheek while talking.

Eryn took a sip of tea from her mug, forcing herself to look at something else. She had grown up among country people and was familiar with less dainty table manners than those she had been surrounded with in these last two years in the city. Aristocrats on both sides of the sea knew what was expected of them. She herself had been raised by a man who had on more than one occasion pointed out the necessity of genteel behaviour as a sign of respect towards her environment. This had in his book included not treating others to the sight of what was going on inside her mouth by not talking while chewing, avoiding any noisy or otherwise distasteful body functions at all costs and behaving in a way that was pleasant to behold. Now that she knew that he himself had been a member of an important family, this was only natural. This was how he himself had been raised. It certainly explained a few of his habits she had always found oddly out of place and exaggerated in a country village where people were usually less concerned with etiquette.

She wondered if Leris had been treated to such lessons as a child. Enric's mother had been raised by an influential and wealthy family in the city and would surely have passed on certain rules of behaviour to her children. Maybe surrounding herself with craftspeople had blunted Leris' manners over the years; or she had discarded them on purpose to distance herself from her upbringing and her parents.

Eryn tried not to be offended at not having been included in the invitation to visit the saw mill. She had never been to one and would have liked to see it. Nonetheless she knew that this was something that concerned only the two siblings. It would be good for them to have some time together after not seeing each other for several years.

She could see that each of them enjoyed the other's company, that Leris kept placing a hand on him briefly during their conversations, and that Enric seemed to hang on every word she said, every anecdote or story she shared with him.

As was to be expected, his niece had discovered her fondness for Enric just as Obal had. Dorn, though, made no secret of his own preference for Eryn. He was currently beaming at her, happily chomping on a hunk of bread. He had begged her for a change of hair colour before he sat down to his breakfast and was currently sporting a bright grey that made him look odd, like a child who had aged prematurely. But he had decided to show solidarity with the sky, and that was exactly the cheerless colour it sported today, with a blanket of clouds that did not permit a glimpse of even the faintest trace of blue.

"I would like that, yes," Enric accepted his sister's invitation, then looked over at Eryn as if only now remembering that abandoning her like that was not a chivalrous thing to do.

She waved him off before he could say something. "Good. Have fun. I will wake Urban and take a walk with her. After sleeping that much in these last few days she could do with some exercise. As could I."

Ardegen was removing his children's dirty dishes from the table and hesitated for a moment before he made a suggestion, "I can show you a nice route to walk if you like. We can send Nera with her mother and Enric, and you and I can take the boys."

Eryn smiled up at him and nodded eagerly, delighted at so unexpectedly finding herself not only saved from unwished for hours of solitude, but also with a convenient opportunity for spending a little time alone with that man so she could attempt to work him out.

"Splendid, that's settled then!" Leris called out, rubbing her hands, obviously equally satisfied with the arrangement that made it possible for her to have her brother to herself for a time.

Eryn caught Enric's curious gaze resting on her and lifted her brow questioningly. He nodded his chin almost imperceptibly towards Ardegen's retreating figure and then looked back at her. Only then did she realise that he had very likely caught her pleasure at having Ardegen offer her his company through the mind bond. Being Enric, he would of course not ignore it when she was so obviously delighted at spending time with another man. He never had in the past, after all. But his posture was relaxed, she noted. Meaning he was clearly not jealous, but probably just surprised at her willingness to spend time with a man he himself had never been able to connect with.

She was fairly sure that the blame for that was Enric's to some degree. Judging from what she had been told, he had not exactly been the social type who took the trouble of establishing and maintaining amiable relationships with people around him in these last one and a half decades. He seemed only recently have taken to socialising, in many cases much to Eryn's chagrin. She would not have minded skipping all those dinner invitations and balls which people kept inviting them to - since they were a couple - in favour of staying at home in peace and harmony instead. Even if it meant being considered hermits by those around them.

"I will clean up the children while you feed Vedric. That should give us enough time for our walk before he gets hungry again", Ardegen proposed, obviously well enough aware of a baby's feeding routine. "We will have cold fare for lunch. I will cook something proper in the evening."

Eryn nodded and emptied her mug, taking it to the sink before walking upstairs to the guest room to wake Vedric for his feed. Leris' companion was very obviously the one taking care of the family and the household from what she had seen. Though she had got used to seeing men doing their share in the kitchen in Takhan, encountering that phenomenon here, where such a domestic inclination was unusual and considered unmanly, was confusing.

Yet she imagined that a man of Ardegen's stature and general appearance did certainly not have to worry about having his masculinity called into question too often. And even if somebody was brave - or rather foolish - enough to challenge him about that, he surely knew how to respond. She imagined that a casual jostle from him would probably cause considerable distress to the unlucky target. Or targets. Or for that matter, crowd.

Vedric was already awake when she entered, gurgling contentedly and giving her a broad, toothless smile when she stepped next to his crib. Her heart warmed immediately and her features relaxed as she smiled back. There was something about his presence that calmed her, just like the world falling into place. She wondered whether it was the sight or the smell of him, or a combination of them. It was probably a built-in feature of nature that ensured that parents didn't abandon their children and thereby reduce their chance of survival to near zero, the healer - or more likely the explorer - in her supplied.

Eryn lifted him up and made sure his wraps were still dry before making herself comfortable to feed him. Luckily, he was a quick and eager suckler. She had seen babies that took a lot more time with their feeds, kept falling asleep several times and more or less only finished shortly before it was already time for the next one.

When she returned downstairs, her son slung across her chest in a sling, Ardegen was preparing his son for their walk. That seemed to be a procedure that required a good deal of patience. Dorn insisted on trying everything himself first, squirming to somehow fold himself into the thick jacket, trying valiantly to wrestle it into submission before giving up and sending his father a pleading look. Ardegen then lifted up the jacket for his son to slip into, guiding the small arms into the sleeves. Then the same game started again with the boots.

"Leris and Enric have already left with Nera," Ardegen told Eryn. "Why don't you go ahead and wake up your cat? It might be better if she has only familiar people around her when she wakes up in a strange place."

She nodded and slipped into another vest, buttoning it over Vedric to only leave his head sticking out before slipping into her own boots, grabbing her cloak and leaving the house.

The wood shed a few paces to the house's left side was unlocked and she pulled open the door, registering that it didn't make the creaking sound she had half-expected of it. When she had lived in the countryside alone in her cottage, she had not made more effort than was absolutely necessary to keep her place inhabitable. Ardegen was obviously a lot more conscientious in that regard. She looked around the spacious storage half-filled with chopped wood, marvelling at how uncharacteristically tidy it was. The floor was swept, the tools he kept out here were neatly arranged on a wall, dangling from sturdy nails.

In the centre stood Urban's wooden crate, the lid loosely placed on top. She pushed it off, revealing the sleeping feline form in the nest of blankets they had made to keep her warm.

Eryn crouched down, touched her cheek and sent a weak impulse that made Urban stir only moments later. The cat drowsily lifted her head, letting her gaze wander over the unfamiliar surroundings. She didn't panic, though. Probably because she was used to waking up in unknown places by now. As long as either Enric or Eryn were present, Urban seemed to assume that everything was fine.

"Come on, my fearsome predator," Eryn murmured affectionately and scratched the cat behind one ear. "Time to get some exercise."

She watched the animal get up on its feet and yawn, displaying an impressive rank of sharp teeth, then stood up as well and opened the door of the shed.

Ardegen was already waiting in front of the door, his son perched on his hip. Probably to wait and see how dangerous the mountain cat really would turn out to be before exposing his son to it.

Dorn stilled when he beheld Urban and his eyes went wide with what looked like panic.

"She is friendly," Eryn assured the boy hurriedly and patted the furry head to demonstrate. She remembered her niece's reaction back in Takhan. Obal had been Dorn's age back then, but unlike a boy growing up in the countryside, she had never been warned to stay clear of dangerous animals. There were not many around in the big city.

Dorn had been taught a much more realistic attitude than Obal when it came to judging the danger of beasts of prey that were faster, stronger and bigger than him.

Urban looked around, lifting her nose up into the air to take in the olfactory information this new place offered. This here with the woods nearby was the closest thing to her natural habitat in quite a while now.

The boy was obviously not convinced and slung both arms around his father's neck, pressing his face against a stubbly cheek.

Ardegen himself appeared unruffled, though clearly on his guard. He watched Urban strolling towards him and slowly lifted a hand for the cat to sniff. Urban did just that, thoroughly, then turned away when her curiosity was satisfied.

"Enric wrote to Leris that you found her in the woods," he then prompted.

Eryn nodded. "I did, yes. I was on an expedition with a group of herb gatherers, and after a storm that felt like the world was about to end, I found her next to her dead mother. My friend Vern forced me into taking her with us."

"Forced you? How?"

"By giving me the choice of either killing her myself or taking care of her."

Ardegen regarded her thoughtfully. "Taking a mountain cat with you to live in the city was quite a big step to take."

"I know. It was not exactly an uncontroversial one," she sighed at the memory of the herb gatherers and guards very pointedly avoiding asking her if she had gone completely and utterly mad. It was not a liberty people tended to take with a magician. "I was lucky Enric accepted the animal like that."

They started walking, Urban falling into step behind them, her eyes still roaming her surroundings.

The lumberjack nodded towards a path through a meadow behind the house that lead up a hill and along a close by forest. Eryn walked next to him, noticing how he adapted his long strides to make keeping up not too much of a strain for her. That was considerate. She wondered how to start a conversation with him. He did not seem like the talkative type, so maybe he wouldn't appreciate any lengthy conversations, but rather prefer a walk in companionable silence. Well, in that case this was not his lucky day. She was determined to find out more about him.

*   *   *

Enric left the sawing room after his sister and they walked a few steps until the noise had subsided enough for them to talk comfortably without shouting.

"Impressive," he admitted and waited for his niece to catch up with them. "This place has grown quite a lot since I was here last time."

"That was more than five years ago, Enric. This clearly shows that you should take time to come here more often," his sister scolded him. "At least you found your way here after your son was born. You certainly didn't choose to visit us after your commitment."

Her brother winced, knowing that the reprimand was well-deserved from where Leris stood. "It is not quite as easy as that. Eryn joined the Order only days after our commitment; then the delegation from the Western Territories arrived shortly after. In the time following this she was busy building up her healing place before we were sent away to Takhan to return their visit. After our return from there, she had to do a lot of catching up as she had not been trained by the Order from childhood as the rest of us have. And then, well... we were sent to Takhan again, this time for half a year. Not much time for family visits."

"No need to justify yourself," she shrugged. "Just make sure not to let another five years pass until we meet again. That's all I'm saying."

"You are aware that you could just as easily have come to the city to see me, aren't you?"

"I have a business to run here, Enric! I can't just saunter off to have a little fun in the city when the mood strikes me," Leris frowned.

"Unlike myself - because I only sit around all day, idle and bored, pretending to be mighty and powerful?"

"That's not what I meant, and you know it! Don't you dare put Anwin's words in my mouth!" His sister looked at him through narrowed eyes, then let her head sink back to stare up at the grey sky above. "Let's not fight, Enric. There is little enough time I have with you. Why don't we agree that we should both try harder to spend more time together? It's only a two-day journey from here to the city, after all. Now, tell me more about that companion of yours. You have not been particularly forthcoming with information in your letters."

"Alright. What do you want to know?"

"Start at the beginning. Why did you join her so quickly? I didn't dare to hope that you would find somebody anymore, and then you join a woman that was being held prisoner by the King, in a matter of days after starting an affair with her? That doesn't seem like you at all. What happened really?"

"The King happened. He pushed me into making her join me quite a lot sooner than I had intended to."

Leris stared at him in dismay. "You forced her to commit to you? Have you gone bonkers?"

Enric rolled his eyes. "Is that what you see when you look at her? A woman who has been forced to join a man she doesn't want?"

His sister pursed her lips while regarding him. "I am not entirely sure what I see when I look at her. What I see when I look at you, though, is a man reluctant to let her out of his sight or even reach. Your eyes follow her whenever she moves, and I could see that you hesitated before accepting my invitation to come here to the sawmill with me. I also see that she is not quite so loath to spend a little time without you. My conclusion is thus that you are more attached to her than she is to you, and I can't help wondering if this isn't a burden for both of you."

Enric's eyes narrowed. His voice was calm but cool when he asked, "What exactly is it you are saying? That I am a love-struck fool wasting my time with a woman who does in your opinion not reciprocate my feelings? Or that I am keeping her hostage, forcing her to stay with me against her will?"

"Neither!" Leris cried out. "I just can't help wondering! There were never many things in life you wanted, but the few that I recall you pursued with relentless stubbornness. Is she one of them?"

He folded his arms, his expression hard. "Stop it. She may not have been happy about joining me in the first place, but things have changed between us since then, very much so. Talk to her if you don't believe me." He scowled down at his sister. "What kind of man do you take me for?"

She glared right back at him. "One who has probably got used to having his every wish fulfilled and every command obeyed over these last years. So, can you assure me that she definitely wants to be with you? What if she decided to leave you and return to her own country or wherever else she would rather be - would you allow her?"

Enric faltered at that question. Of course he wouldn't let her leave just like that. He would do anything in his power to make her stay with him, beg her, fall to his knees, promise her whatever she wanted.

"My relationship is none of your business. I am a grown man and don't have to justify myself to you," he told her coldly. "If you feel you need to make sure that she is staying with me voluntarily, I can only repeat my suggestion to ask her about it yourself."

"I will," she promised him fiercely, "Depend on it! You may be this great and important magician, Enric, but that has never impressed me much. I don't think that you are entitled to any special treatment or privileges because of it."

"I never asked you for either, did I?" Enric shot back.

"No," Leris admitted and released a long breath, calming down visibly, "you never did."

He watched her lift her fingers to press them against the bridge of her nose, a habit he knew he himself had as well. As did their father. He wondered if his sister was aware of that. Probably not, or she would have suppressed the impulse.

"It has been a while since we last had a go at each other like that," he remarked after a few moments of silence.

"Yes. Thirteen years ago. You tried to take me to the city to live with you instead of staying here with Ardegen."

"I was wrong back then."

Leris sent him a suspicious look. "You are only saying that because you hope that I will tell you that this time I am the one who is wrong."

He didn't reply to that, only smiled.

"I won't. Not yet," she insisted, but the heat was gone. "I don't want to fight with you of all people, Enric. But if I have the impression that you are pushing a woman into the same kind of life our own mother has, I can't simply watch and keep my mouth shut."

Enric looked down at her, feeling regret at how deeply their parents' bad example had scarred her. She had spent a lot more time with them than he had himself, as he had been sent off to the city at the age of twelve which meant he had been more or less free of them from then on.

"I have not turned into father, Leris," he promised her. "And Eryn is nothing like mother. She is not the meek kind, let me tell you that. You will see for yourself when you have spent more time with her. She even knocked me out back in Takhan."

He grinned when he saw Leris' delightfully surprised expression.

"Really?"

"Really. Ask her about it, I know she won't mind telling you in colourful detail. Back in Takhan it is known as an Aren Welcome, Aren being the name of the family she was born into."

They walked on, reaching the bank of the river at which the sawmill was situated. The water reflected the bleak grey sky.

"How are you adapting to being a father?" Leris then asked, changing the topic. "I find it hard to think of you in that role."

He lifted an eyebrow, wondering if he had just been insulted. Again. "Well enough, I would say." He thought of Eryn's determination never to have children. "Vedric is a miracle. I am a very lucky man."

They walked on, passing rows of drying lumber.

"I sometimes notice how my own upbringing catches up with me when I deal with my children," Leris said thoughtfully. "I need to remind myself again and again that I can't scold them every time something is not to my liking. Ardegen is much better at this than me. His parents were a lot gentler and more supportive than ours. As a child I swore that I would never become like Anwin, but now I see that I am in constant danger of automatically acting the way he did with us." She shivered. "It scares me. And it makes me wonder if we can ever outgrow our roots, leave them behind. I have Anwin's temper, you know? You are more like mother, the calm and controlled type. I envy you that."

Enric smiled faintly, thinking of the many occasions when Eryn had managed to make him lose that calm. "Don't worry too much about that," he said softly and put an arm around his sister's shoulders. "You may have traces of his temper, but you are not like him. If you were, I would have kept my distance from you."

He looked down when he felt warm fingers close around his other hand. Nera had been utterly silent during the adults' at times rather heated discussion and was clearly relieved at this obvious display of affection that signalled that everything was well between her mother and the tall man.

"Can we go home now?" the girl asked hopefully. "I am hungry."

Leris nodded. "Yes, that we can. We are through here."

"I think Eryn would be interested in seeing this," Enric considered. "Would you mind if I brought her here?"

His sister cast a doubtful glance at him. "Are you sure about that? Women don't generally show an interest in how logs are turned into lumber."

He nodded. "I am. She is very eager when it comes to learning about new things. Unless it's something the Order wants her to learn, that is," he added as an afterthought.

*   *   *

Ardegen opened the entrance door to his house for Eryn and let her enter first. She was glad to get out of the cold and took off her cloak, rubbing her hands and then feeling Vedric's cheeks. They were a little cooler than they were supposed to be, but his hands were warm and he would warm up in no time now that they were back inside again.

Little Dorn struggled out of his jacket and let it drop to the floor, from where his father retrieved it with a sigh and put it on a hook on the wall.

Eryn paused when she heard Enric's voice from the kitchen.

"Eryn, the spy from the Western Territories," she heard him say in a voice he pitched slightly higher than usual. She frowned, but then remembered where she had heard these words before. It was when Anwin had come to their house in Anyueel almost a year ago. Enric was obviously telling his sister about how that visit had gone.

"I hope you just wear these trousers at home?" Eryn heard him continue and had to smile at how well he did the impersonation. Even the tones of disapproval and contempt were there.

She pushed open the kitchen door and gave her companion a withering glare. "Then my son has obviously not learned how to keep a woman under control! That was because he was taken from his family when he is still too young; he didn't learn how things are to be done properly," she spat, and grinned when Leris stared at her for a moment, then burst into laughter.

Enric rose from his chair immediately and pulled Eryn into a gentle embrace, careful not to squeeze Vedric between them. Then he undid the sling around Eryn's chest so he could take the baby from her.

Leris shook her head. "So Anwin was his usual charming self - first he imposed himself on you without any prior warning whatsoever, and then he insulted you in your own house. I would have kicked him out!"

Eryn noted that Enric's sister referred to her father with his name, just like she herself did with Malriel.

"I did, but not right away," her brother explained and sat down again, pulling out the chair next to his for Eryn. "I sent him away only after he told me that he didn't have to listen to me being impertinent and disrespectful again."

Eryn took a seat next to him, frowning when her foot brushed something soft under the table.

"Ow!" an indignant complaint came from somewhere in the vicinity of her legs.

"Come out from under the table, Nera," Leris instructed and rolled her eyes. "It's not polite. Come on! Or there will be no bedtime story for you tonight."

A moment later the girl emerged from under the massive table, her face a sulky grimace. She shot Eryn a devastating look and hurried towards her father, who entered the kitchen with Dorn on his arm.

"What happened?" Ardegen enquired with a troubled expression and lifted his daughter with his other arm.

"She is grumpy because I told her not to sit under the table when we have guests," Leris explained.

Her companion nodded and shrugged. "Your mother is right, Nera. Will you help me prepare something to eat?"

The girl nodded after a moment's thought, then pointed at her brother. "He can't help, he is too little."

"If you say so," her father agreed without mentioning the fact that she was merely a year ahead of her brother.

Eryn's attention returned to Leris when she bent over to take Vedric from Enric's arm onto her own.

"How was your walk, Eryn?" the hostess asked.

"The walk was refreshing," Eryn replied politely. It had also been quite frustrating. She had tried to get Ardegen to talk to her, probing a little here, dropping hints there, but he had either pretended not to notice that she was trying to discover more about him, or her attempts had been too subtle. "I spotted your sawmill from the hill. I was wondering if I could have a look at it while we are here? I have never been to one."

She saw how Enric gave his sister a smug grin.

Leris nodded slowly, regarding the other woman. "Enric said that you might be interested in seeing it. I don't mind telling you that I didn't really believe him. It's not normally an area of interest to our female visitors."

Eryn gave her a measured look. "I see," she said, forcing herself to keep her annoyance at bay. This was the only family member Enric was on amiable terms with, meaning she would show restraint for his sake. "I try not to limit my interests to what is considered suitable for a woman. I wouldn't have expected this to be hard to believe for a woman who runs a successful lumber business herself."

Enric's sister looked at her and replied haughtily, "I try not to apply my own standards when it comes to other people. It hardly ever pays."

"I wonder if you are not rather demanding for yourself the privilege of escaping the prison which being a woman in many cases implies, and are unwilling to grant it to others as well. It makes you less unique, after all," Eryn retorted, lifting her chin. So much for restraint.

Leris stared at her, then her lips twisted into a smirk. "Yes, I can see what you meant, Enric. Clearly not the meek type. It will be my pleasure to show you the mill, Eryn."

Enric took his companion's hand, squeezing it reassuringly. Standing up to his sister had been a good move. It would certainly help to dispel Leris' concerns when it came to their companionship. And of course it would earn Eryn his sister's respect.

"Anwin has been trying hard to get into the timber business lately," Leris addressed her brother. She snorted. "He even made a bid on our sawmill down south."

Enric nodded. "I know. He has attempted to sell wood to me three times so far. Through intermediaries, of course. I am fairly sure he still isn't aware that it's the two of us who are blocking his access to the business. If he were smarter and a lot more patient, he would start with a smaller mill and try and build up the volume little by little."

His sister grimaced. "That's not Anwin's style. All he sees is that somebody is building a lot - and that somebody else but him is making money by providing the building material. I mean, what does he think? He has never been in the lumber business, he has to make himself a name first! Bloody fool, that man."

Eryn stared at both of them, then lifted a hand when Enric was about to reply. "Now, you just wait a moment. What you are saying here is that you are combining your forces to keep your father out of a line of business he wishes to enter into, and that he isn't even aware that you are the ones blocking him?"

Enric chuckled. "You are certainly not about to tell us how heartless that is? Not after you took your own mother's life savings to fund a charitable project with them."

She blinked, then shook her head and said lightly, "No, of course not. I am merely asking."

He looked back at his sister. "My agents tell me that father is currently looking for a site to construct his own sawmill on. He has finally hired somebody to advise him. So far he has only tried to sell the lumber he buys from smaller mills, but it seems he is more ambitious now that it has become common knowledge that the Western Territories are buying our wood."

"Which will not work for him, either, as you are the only one with a shipping permit so far," Eryn cut in, then sighed and shook her head. "That man really has bad luck. Are you planning on telling him anytime soon that his attempts will continue to be futile?"

Leris shrugged. "Why? It gives him something to do, after all. His quest keeps him busy and provides a challenge. We are practically doing him a favour."

"How very noble of you both," Eryn remarked sarcastically and folded her arms. "I hope at least that he is not the type to take his frustration at his continued failings out on his family." She watched the siblings exchanging a tense look. "I see," she commented when none of them spoke. "So you are making life for your brother and your mother a misery, and you don't care about it in the least."

"Listen," Leris growled, "my mother has brought this on herself. Anwin was cheating on her for as long as I can remember, and it is impossible that she never suspected anything. She wants to stay with him, so suffering his ill temper is what she has to deal with. As for our brother - he finally has what he has always wanted as a child: his father's attention. When nobody knew of Enric's magical abilities and he was still meant to take over the business one day, the younger son was considered useless; nothing more than a stand-in. When Enric left, our brother rose in Anwin's esteem and was ultimately considered important, had the attention he had always craved. So I don't see what sympathy he is due here."

Eryn slowly shook her head. That was a sad picture, and Leris herself either didn't want to see it or wasn't able to. She imagined three children - a boy pushed into working with a father he had no respect for, another son ignored and disregarded, and a daughter who had been intended as little more than a servant once she was old enough.

And now that they were all grown, two of them had turned their backs on their brother and their parents.

"Don't look at me like that," Leris said briskly. "Enric told me that your own family situation is anything but harmonious and jolly. You must be aware that relatives can be a burden. So don't waste your pity on me."

Eryn's eyes narrowed. It seemed that female relatives were somewhat of a challenge for her to get along with, no matter whether it was on her side of the family or Enric's.

"Pity? You are right, that would be wasted on you," she said cuttingly and slowly rose from her chair, leaning forward and bracing her flat palms on the table. "I pity that brother of yours who is still stuck with your father, abandoned by his siblings and doubtlessly a lot less contented with life than the two of you. And I pity your mother, who you feel nothing but disdain for just because she has either decided to honour the oath she gave to her companion at no matter what cost, or simply lacks the strength to walk away." Eryn shook her head. "I don't pity you, Leris. Instead I feel the urge to shake some sense into you. You may have been the only one to break free of that family by your own effort, but it hardly gives you the right to look down at those who haven't." She straightened, walked around the table to take her son from Leris. Then she walked out of the kitchen.

Ardegen stepped towards them and placed a large wooden plate with an assortment of cut meat and cheese in front of them, indicating to his daughter where she was supposed to place the bread basket. He looked at his companion and her brother, who both stared at the door through which Eryn had just disappeared.

"She is right, you know," he said simply. "I like her." His thoughtful gaze returned to Enric and stayed there for several moments.

"Interesting. Not the kind of woman I would have expected at your side."

Enric looked at him with a telling expression. "Because a man like me is bound to prefer women who don't talk back or think for themselves?"

"No," Ardegen replied calmly, "because nobody likes to be criticised, and a man in your position surely doesn't have to endure it all too often. Unless he chooses a woman bold enough to challenge him." He then picked his son up from the floor where he was playing with his wooden toys and placed him on a seat next to his mother.

"I like her!" Dorn crowed happily and grabbed a piece of bread to take a hearty bite.

"Of course you do," Enric smiled wryly. "Men tend to like her." He looked at his sister. "It's the women she has generally trouble getting along with. At least in the beginning."

Leris grunted and took a sip from her mug. "Is that the truth, now. I can't imagine why."

*   *   *

Eryn yawned and stretched out in bed. Enric had already opened the curtains and brilliant daylight was streaming in through the window. The sky was a sharp blue for a change, not a cloud in sight.

"How good are the chances for your sister to still show me her sawmill?" she wondered. "Judging from her attitude towards her own family, she is not exactly the forgiving type. I suppose I should have kept my mouth shut yesterday."

Enric shook his head. "Don't worry about that, my love. She may be resentful when it comes to our parents and our brother, but you haven't wronged her in any way. She may not have liked hearing what you had to say, but she is not one to keep her thoughts to herself either, when she has something to say."

Eryn gave him a doubtful look, but didn't contradict him. She would soon enough see for herself if he was right.

"You impressed Ardegen, by the way," he told her.

She blinked. "I did? By giving his companion a piece of my mind? I was trying to make him talk to me during our walk for more than two hours without much success - and being angry at Leris did the trick?" She shook her head. "Well, that probably means that he will give me the tour through the mill in case your sister refuses to."

"Come on, get up and get yourself dressed. You must be feeling hungry after abandoning us just before dinner last night."

Nodding, she swung her legs out of the bed and shivered when her soles touched the chilly wooden floorboards. "I am ravenous. Making grand gestures is a lot less fun when the price is going to bed with an empty belly."

Enric grinned. "Next time just remain seated and stare daggers at her instead of rushing off. Or wait with criticising people until after you have eaten."

"Thank you so much. Your words of wisdom are a constant wellspring of inspiration for me," she chirped and batted her lashes at him. "Is Vedric still asleep?" she then asked, getting up to check for herself. "I suppose the walk out in the cold yesterday was rather exhausting for him."

Her companion stepped next to her and gingerly touched his son's soft cheek, closing his eyes for a few moments before saying, "But at least he hasn't caught a cold or anything."

Eryn raised an eyebrow and shook her head indulgently. "You just performed a medical check on him because he was exposed to a bit of cold air? Without there being any sign that he might be ill? You are not turning into an annoyingly overprotective and overcautious father, are you?" She sniggered. "That would cast me as the fun parent."

Enric didn't comment on that but looked down at the baby. "Do you want to wake him or shall we let him sleep? It's time for his feed."

She shook her head. "Leave him. We may just as well start prolonging the intervals between his meals now. His stomach should be able to deal with more milk at a time and keep him sated for a bit longer." A quick search in the chest Enric had sent here from the city produced a pair of trousers and a shirt.

He watched her dressing and then nodded at the shirt. "That's a bit tight, isn't it?"

"Of course it's tight. I am nursing an infant, so my breasts are bigger than before. These clothes were made before my pregnancy, so it's only natural that they don't fit as well as before. At least the trousers are halfway comfortable even if still a bit tight around the hips."

"I like it when your clothes fit snugly. I think I will ask Junar to be a bit less generous with the fabric from now on."

Eryn flashed him a dark look. "You do that and I will propose the same thing for your trousers. Not that we are going to have any more children, so there is no need to worry about causing any damage through tight fitting down there, but it would still be a lot less comfortable for you."

"Fair enough," Enric sighed. "Point taken. At least the ball gowns will still be slinky."

"Good. I am glad to see that at least one of us will be enjoying himself when I am being made to wear them."

"It's not as though I don't have to pay for the pleasure of seeing you in a tight dress," he countered.

"You have to pay? How? Provided we are not talking about such trivial things as gold here."

"By enduring your bad moods."

"You know, an incredibly simple solution for that comes to mind: Just don't force me to go to balls any more. That would save me from being in a bad mood, and you from needing to endure it."

Enric just sighed and refrained from pointing out that he was not the one making her go there, but the King.

They walked down the stairs and entered the kitchen, walking into an idyllic family scene of the children seated at the breakfast table with their parents.

"Good morning," Leris greeted them and shook her head at her son when he was about to jump up from his seat. "No! You stay where you are and finish your bread, my boy. We don't get up from the table until we are finished eating."

Dorn sank back with a pained look at Eryn, but obviously didn't dare disobey his mother.

"Are you still up for the tour around the sawmill or have you changed your mind about wanting to see it?" Enric's sister asked, her tone and expression challenging.

Eryn bestowed a cool smile upon her. "I haven't changed my mind about that, no. But I thought that you might have."

"I told you I would show you around, and I stand by my promise," Leris stated with slightly narrowed eyes as if warning his brother's companion not to imply anything else.

"A family trait, then," Eryn smiled casually. "It's something Enric is known for as well. I see why doing business with each other has worked out well for each of you."

That seemed to pacify Leris, and her facial features relaxed visibly. "Yes, dependability is a virtue I cannot do without, neither when it comes to myself, nor the people I work with. There are enough pitfalls that are simply part of the daily business. Nature tends to be a tricky enough influence already, I don't need people around who I can't rely on in addition to that."

Eryn didn't contradict. Her own business, healing, was certainly not an area that worked without people being committed to their profession and ready to adhere to rules. She understood the need for reliability well enough.

Ardegen pulled his daughter's plate towards him to slice her bread, but Nera determinedly shook her head and held on to the brim.

"No, I want to do that! I am a big girl!"

"That you may be, but this here is a sharp knife. I don't want you to cut off your finger," her father replied patiently.

"No! I want!" the girl insisted, giving her father a pleading look. "I can do this!"

The lumberjack was clearly torn between aiding his daughter's quest for independence and his reluctance to hand a five-year-old girl a well-honed blade. He finally gave in and sighed.

"As you wish. But first you let me show you how to do this properly." He held the chunk of bread with one hand and demonstrated how to place the knife correctly, how to move it back and forth instead of simply pressing it down. "Make sure to keep your fingers out of the way."

He then handed the knife to Nera, watching like a hawk when she took it gingerly and started sawing the bread inexpertly, but with enthusiasm.

All four adults watched her efforts that left the bread rather in tatters than in neat slices.

The girl looked up from the plate when she was finished, putting down the knife and beaming proudly at her father. "Look!"

"Well done," Ardegen commended her, not mentioning the scatter of breadcrumbs she had made on and around the plate. "Now hand me back the knife."

Without looking down, Nera grabbed the knife. And howled a moment later when her fingers had closed not around the handle, but the blade. Ardegen's face turned pale in an instant, and he made to snatch up his daughter, but Eryn rose and shook her head.

"No. Allow me." She took a look at the clean cut across the inside of four fingers. Ardegen really did keep his knives keen, she couldn't help but thinking. "That's no great tragedy, I can heal this easily."

Nera pulled back her hand and shook her head vehemently. "No, not you! I don't like you! Him!" She pointed the index finger of her unharmed hand at Enric.

Eryn rolled her eyes. "The story of my life. Girls really don't like me, no matter where they are from or how old they are."

Enric obediently stretched out his arms to lift his niece up from her chair and sit her on his lap. "Let me have a look, then."

Leris bent closer curiously when her brother closed his eyes with her daughter's small hand on his long fingers. Ardegen tried not to appear too eager to watch, but there was clearly interest hidden behind that nonchalant gaze of his.

Eryn watched the cuts and how the flow of blood from the wound stopped. Only moments later Enric picked up the blood-stained napkin and wiped Nera's hand, revealing unmarked skin.

Enric's sister whistled through her teeth. "Neat. You wrote to me that you had learned that, but watching it with my own eyes is something else." Then her gaze dropped to her daughter's face and her voice became stern. "I hope that will teach you how to handle a knife properly. We don't just grab sharp items without looking what we are doing. And when somebody offers help, we do not insult that person, but decline politely if we feel we cannot accept it. Have I made myself clear?"

Nera swallowed and avoided looking at Eryn when she nodded contritely. "I'm sorry."

"You should be. Now go and dress yourself. And help your brother."

Ardegen cleared his throat, then looked at Enric. "I thank you for that. I should not have given her the knife. It was thoughtless of me."

Leris shook her head. "Nonsense. We can't protect her from getting injured all her life. Pain sometimes is a part of learning. I can't count how often I cut, burned or scratched myself as a child, and it certainly hasn't done me any harm."

Eryn wondered how this kind of scene would run in a few years when Vedric was old enough to try out things for himself. Would she be the one to worry about every scratch or rather Enric? She had not been a mother long enough to really work out if she was the overprotective or rather the relaxed kind of parent. It seemed there was yet quite a lot she would be learning about herself in the years to come.

"Ardegen will stay here with the children while we are at the sawmill," Leris said and emptied her mug. "Just let me know when you are ready to leave. Enric, will you be coming, too, or will I have some quality time alone with your companion?"

Eryn tried to detect whether there was a trace of reluctance in that question, but wasn't sure. It was hard to tell with that woman. But so far she had been blunt enough, so if she didn't want to be alone with Eryn she would probably have said just that.

"I think I will stay here with Vedric," Enric replied. "Just try not to go for each other's throat."

His sister snorted. "I'd be bound for failure in that case. She has magic."

"Which I am not allowed to use against non-magicians, not even the annoying ones," Eryn pointed out.

"Are you saying I am annoying?"

"Are you implying that I would make use of an unfair advantage?"

"Oh yes," Enric stated wryly, "I will definitely stay here. Having three children around might be the more relaxing option here." He turned to his companion. "Only if you feed our son before you leave, that is."

Eryn sighed. "If you were the only one to suffer from it, I would seriously consider leaving right now after that statement of yours."

"Good to see that you are a better mother than companion, then," Leris chuckled and rose. "Let me know when you are ready to leave. I'll put together a few papers I need to take to the mill in the meantime."

When Leris had left the kitchen, Eryn breathed a heavy sigh. "I am not sure where I stand with her. She either likes me, but doesn't want to show it, or she does not and is rather clumsy at being tactful about it."

"She is undecided," Ardegen told her honestly. "She normally takes her time when it comes to deciding whether to like somebody or not, unwilling to err and then being forced to reassess her judgement. She doesn't like being wrong. Not at all."

Eryn bit into a slice of buttered bread. She certainly knew that character trait from Enric. He, too, was an avid collector of information and knowledge to avoid being wrong. Who she was basically dealing with here was a woman with Pe'tala's blunt and sarcastic forthrightness in combination with Enric's annoying urge to control everything around and his struggles to be in possession of the one and only truth at all times.

Well, at least that would make spending time with her anything but dull.

* * *

Eryn followed the other woman across a wide area that was filled with stacked boards, planks and shorter lengths of wood in what looked like different states of completion. They approached a tall, wooden building that stood elevated on several massive columns of bricks. Underneath the building more wood was piled neatly.

The building was situated directly at the river bank, the large waterwheel attached to one side turning slowly, but with what looked like unstoppable determination. The closer they came, the louder became the ringing ripping sounds of what were unmistakeably saw blades on wood.

Leris turned left instead of climbing the stairs to the entrance and stopped at the riverbank, pointing to an area where what had to be several hundred tree trunks were floating on the water.

"The logs are transported here on the river," she explained. "It is a lot faster and less complicated than having them brought here with horse carts. Unless the river is frozen, that is. But we don't do a lot of work at that time of the year. The trees are felled at several places upstream. Otherwise getting them here would be quite a challenge. Ardegen is in charge of the trees until they are here at the sawmill. He chooses the right spots for the harvest, makes sure the right trees are felled the right way and then overlooks the bucking."

Eryn frowned. "The what? And what are the wrong trees?"

"The bucking. That is what happens after the trees are felled and delimbed."

"Delimbed? Which means that the branches are cut off, I suppose?" It was the only logical explanation she could come up with.

Leris nodded. "Yes. That makes transporting the logs a lot easier. They are then cut into the right length. Every kind of product has different specifications depending on what it is going to be used for, you see. That already starts at the selection of the tree depending on its diameter and length. And also imperfections."

Eryn let her gaze wander over the multitude of logs bobbing in the water. Who would have thought that so many things had to be considered when cutting a tree?

"That means that you should know in advance what you are going to sell, then. So do you produce to order or do you stock certain products that generally sell well?"

"Both," Leris replied, obviously pleased with the interest Eryn showed. "For larger orders we need some prior notice. Supplying

Enric with enough wood to rebuild Bonhet, then raise a new port in Anyueel and finally construct his ships would not have been possible without his informing me in advance. I don't have that many particular kinds of wood in exactly the right quantities lying around. But smaller quantities we usually have in stock." She then pointed to the tree trunks in the water. "When they are here, they need to be scaled. That means they are measured, their quality, volume and species is determined. Sometimes we also sell just the logs as a whole, and then scaling is necessary to determine a price for them."

Eryn's gaze wandered to the ramp that led from the wooden building to her right into the river. "And after that you pull them out of the water and up the ramp to saw them into boards?"

"We haul them up, yes. But first the bark needs to be removed, and then they are sorted by species, size and end use. Only then does the actual sawing start."

"How many men do you need to haul a large trunk out of the water? I suppose they are rather heavy, especially when they are soaked in addition to their usual massive weight?"

Leris smiled proudly. "We don't do that manually here. At least not since we expanded five years ago. The waterwheel not only powers the saws, but also helps us pull up the logs. Any more questions or can we go up?"

Eryn shook her head.

"Good. I suppose I don't have to mention that you are not supposed to touch anything that looks dangerous without me watching you?"

"And yet you mention it nevertheless," Eryn replied sweetly. "And it's not like I couldn't repair whatever damage I take up there. So there is no need to fear your brother's wrath at me returning in slices."

Enric's sister sneered. "I have never in my life feared Enric for whatever reason; not even when we found out about his magic. Which is more than you can claim, for what I know."

Eryn's eyes narrowed. So Enric had told his sister about their bumpy start in quite some detail, as it seemed.

"I didn't fear him," she replied, stretching the truth so far that it would probably snap any moment. "I merely hated him. Big difference."

"That's not what he thinks," Leris retorted, clearly enjoying the conversation and the other woman's discomfort.

"I don't see the point in demolishing his illusions if they give him pleasure," Eryn shrugged, determined not to rise to the provocation.

"Illusions, eh? Funny, he was always the down-to-earth type as far as I remember."

Eryn smiled brightly, showing rather too many teeth. "Incredible how things change, isn't it? Shall we go up to where that whining noise is coming from or do you feel you need to get rid of any other warnings of danger in the form of sharp, pointed, splintery objects in there?"

Leris just smiled knowingly, then turned and climbed the creaking, wooden stairs up to the entrance.

After stepping through the open door after Leris, a wave of noise and sawdust greeted Eryn, and she had to resist the urge to form a magical shield in front of her to avoid breathing in the fine wood particles that floated in the air. It just wouldn't look good.

Five men were busy in the large hall, surprisingly few considering the various areas of movement, the noise level and scale of everything. It seemed that the water-assisted hauling-up of the logs was not the only area where Leris insisted on a modern, efficient approach.

"This is the sawing room," Leris explained, her voice raised to overcome the droning racket of metal teeth biting into wood. "We have several different saws here, as you can see," she went on. "Over here we have a line with multiple parallel blades that can cut an entire log into several cants and planks in one go. That is what we call a head rig. That saves a lot of time compared to working on the same log with a single blade several times."

Eryn stared mesmerised at the up and down movement of nine perpendicular, black, fearsome looking blades that were only little shorter than herself. Their pointed teeth bit a little further into the massive, peeled - or rather debarked, as she had just learned - tree trunk that seemed to move through blades as if pushed by an invisible force.

"How exactly do you power the saw? And how does the trunk move without being pushed?"

Leris moved to what looked like a stem with a spiked end turning and beckoned for Eryn to follow her.

"This here is connected to the waterwheel outside. The water causes the wheel to turn, the wheel turns that bar here, and this then connects with that part here with a rod that converts the circular movement of the wheel into the back and forth motion we need for the saws. In most mills they still work with horses that walk around a pole all day long." She shook her head in disapproval. "Not very practical, if you ask me. Apart from the poor animals that need to be blindfold so they don't panic after a short time, you need a stable to keep them in and people to feed them and clean up after them. I would rather spend that money on people who maintain this mechanism. And the output is a lot better. With a river this size here we can power several saws from the wheel at the same time. So much for your first question." Leris nodded at the large trunk that was moving along bit by bit. "As for the other: The trunk moves because every movement of the saw turns a cogwheel. And that is connected to a movable carrier, which causes the trunk to move steadily into the blades, or rather be forced into them." Leris pointed to another line. "As you can see, we have many different types of saw here. This over here is a resaw. After the wood has been cut by the head rig, we can do more precise work on it, such as breaking it down into multiple flitches or boards. Then boards are edged to trim off irregular edges and the result is four-sided timber that can be trimmed into the right length."

Both women moved on to a narrow cart on which two men were loading long, even beams of the same size and width.

"And now they are ready to be sent wherever they are needed?" Eryn enquired, resisting the urge to touch the wood.

"Almost. What you have here is still green timber. If we transport it like that, it will go mouldy or warp. It first needs to season properly. You saw all the timber that is stacked outside, I dare say. Come with me."

Leris preceded her down a second ramp that lead back out to the large yard that indeed held what had to be thousands of drying pieces of timber. "The wood has been in the water for several days, so it usually takes a while for it to dry properly. That depends on the weather, of course. We cover many of the stacks so the rain doesn't soak them again, but the humidity is also in the air. I am considering the option of dedicated buildings to remove the moisture in the wood more quickly. I have been talking to craftsmen, and one said I could build something like a huge kiln. I am still in the process of calculating the cost of first erecting and then heating a large hall and comparing it to the profits to be had from the increased output. I am almost done with the numbers. Enric said he would have a look at them while he is here."

The two women walked over to one of many stacks of sliced boards that were about their height.

"I assume the bits of wood between the sections are supposed to keep the air circulating," Eryn guessed.

"Exactly. That way they dry evenly into straight boards. Otherwise I would get warped planks that are useful only for firewood. We call that planking the log."

Eryn nodded, looking around at the different length, thickness and width of the boards; in many cases there were also entire tree trunks just sliced and stacked with bits of wood between them, the general shape still largely the one of a tree. So it seemed that some builders also needed products that were closer to the original shape. Probably for decorative purposes, more crude structures or rustic furniture.

"So." Leris folded her arms, her stance broad, reminding Eryn of the stance Orrin liked to adopt. "What do you say to my dusty kingdom?"

"I admit I am impressed. Magicians don't really tend to build mechanical things, from what I have seen in the Order - simply harnessing magic is so much more convenient. And I am no exception there, I am afraid. Seeing things move all alone without magic is an eye-opener."

"Yes, Enric said something like that yesterday. Magicians really are a funny lot. He also told me of that country he was in, that place that doesn't like magic and keeps building mechanical things to make magic unnecessary wherever possible. Pity, you know? I think if magicians started tinkering, the outcome might be useful. They could use their magic for something sensible, for a change. Something ordinary people might profit from."

Eryn raised her brow. "You won't hear me objecting to that."

"Yes, considering your own efforts with the clinic and all that I didn't really think you would." Leris pursed her lips. "Not that it would have kept me from voicing my thoughts, mind you. I have no problem with giving offence."

"You don't say," Eryn chuckled.

Enric's sister let her gaze wander over the woman opposite her. "I wasn't sure what to expect when I learned of you. Enric never showed much inclination towards having his own family, and considering that you were a prisoner when you ended up with each other, I wasn't really expecting too much."

"I assume there is a But about to follow? Or are you trying to tell me that you don't approve of me?"

Leris laughed. "But I was pleasantly surprised. I was half-expecting a meek, cowered creature - no matter that Enric described you as completely different in his letters."

Eryn nodded slowly. "You were afraid he would end up with a woman like your mother?"

The other woman seemed torn between offence and agreement for a moment, then obviously decided in favour of the latter. "You could say that, yes. I would have regretted that. I wanted more for Enric."

"You really are angry at your mother, aren't you? Not that I can't understand the principle as such, mind you. I am not exactly on amiable terms with the woman who gave birth to me, either. But I find being angry at her because of what she did to me more justified than your resenting your mother for what she is doing to herself."

"Really. How remarkable that rejecting your mother is in your eyes so much better than me doing the same thing with mine. It seems my brother is not the only one in your relationship harbouring some kind of illusion."

Eryn nodded once, determined not to get drawn into a fight here, but instead to accept that this was a trigger topic for Leris and stop talking about it.

"We should return now. Our companions are probably worried about us being alone with each other in the midst of sharp tools and massive pieces of wood," Leris proposed. "But you know what, we got to understand each other a little better, didn't we? We now know that our mothers are a topic we should better avoid from now on."

"That's true," Eryn commented. "That should at least make sure we both survive until Enric and I leave again."

*   *   *

Leris leaned back in her chair and took a careful sip from the still slightly over-hot tea.

"And?" Enric asked cautiously. "How did it go? Are you still on speaking terms?"

"It went well enough," his sister shrugged. "She is smart. I like that in a woman."

Enric smiled broadly. That was high praise indeed from his sister.

"You like her, then," Ardegen stated with satisfaction. "Good."

She thought for a moment, then nodded hesitantly. "Yes, I suppose I do. Don't tell her that, though."

They looked up when the door opened and Eryn came in after feeding her son, carrying the boy on her arm. She blinked when she found herself the centre of attention. "What? Don't believe anything she said. I was on my best behaviour."

"That was your best behaviour?" Leris smiled thinly. "Then I certainly don't want to see you impolite."

"No, you don't," Enric confirmed. "There is a good reason for why Lord Tyront keeps punishing her with stable duty."

"He hasn't done that in a while," Eryn contradicted.

"Because we have just spent half a year in another country far away from him. Let's see how much time passes until your next assignment," her companion grinned.

She just sent him a glare and took a seat next to Ardegen.

"I brought my calculations with me if you want to look at them now," Leris said and sent her brother a questioning look.

"The ones for that drying house you mentioned?"

"Yes. I have them in my office. Unless you can't stand parting with your companion for another hour so soon?" she added with a mocking half-smile.

"I part with her reluctantly, as always. I never know what she is up to when she is out of my sight."

"That would have been rather sweet if you hadn't added that second remark," Eryn sighed and shook her head at such blatant lack of chivalry.

"You usually are uncomfortable when I say something sweet in public. I was just aiming to please you, my love. But it seems that is an impossible task."

"Off you go and play with your numbers! I will stay here with Ardegen, enjoying the company of a man with manners," she waved him off.

When both siblings had left and the kitchen door closed behind them, Eryn pulled Enric's half-full mug towards her and emptied it.

"Enric told me that Leris ran off with you as soon as she was of age," she then started without introduction. This time she intended to be a lot less restrained with him. It had not worked last time. She stopped herself from rolling her eyes when he just nodded in confirmation instead of offering any additional information. "And that he helped you start your first business."

Ardegen's jaw muscles tightened visibly at that, and Eryn silently cursed herself for saying just the wrong thing. That way she would not get him to open up. But the damage was already done.

"I am sorry. That seems to be a sore subject for you for some reason. Is that why you don't like Enric?" she ploughed onward, opting for boldness.

He looked at her, obviously at a loss what to make of her. After a few moments he shook his head and exhaled. "You are not at all a shy one, are you?" he asked in defeat.

Eryn grinned lopsidedly. "I have been called many things, but never that. But I really wonder how hard it can be for you to deal with this having a companion like Leris."

"It is not. I am just not used to any other women that blunt. There was a time when I seriously wondered if there even were any."

"Well, yes, there are a few of us. So?"

"It's not that I don't like Enric," Ardegen said slowly, giving in to her curiosity. "I don't know him well enough for that. And no, taking another man's money to make something of myself is not something I am proud of. Though of course I am grateful for his generosity back then."

"You could pay him back," she shrugged. "Then you wouldn't owe him any longer."

"We paid him back the money he gave us. But that doesn't mean that we are even," he insisted, looking not at her but straight ahead with a dark expression.

Eryn eyed him doubtfully. "You know, I am fairly sure that this is not how Enric sees it."

"It is how I see it," he shot back curtly.

"So you don't like him because you think you owe him? Or is owing him a problem because you don't like him for some other reason?" she probed.

"I already told you that..." he started but Eryn interrupted him.

"I know, I know. You don't know him well enough to not like him. I understand. Though I can't help but wonder why you didn't bother getting to know the only family member your companion has a good relationship with."

Ardegen shot her a cool glare. "Nor are you exactly reserved when it comes to prying into other people's businesses," he accused her.

Eryn beheld his narrowed eyes, impressed at the detachment in them when she had only seen them warm and gentle so far. "That would certainly depend on what people we are talking about. Enric's business is clearly mine to take an interest in, and you, Leris and your children are basically a part of my family now."

That last statement seemed to soften him a bit and he sighed. "It was not my place to make any attempts at approaching Enric. He is a magician; and not just any magician, a damned important one, as it happens. And Enric certainly never wished to get to know me better. We did not have a particularly smooth start, as you probably know."

She shook her head. "No, I don't know. Tell me."

"Leris was seventeen years old when I met her. She wanted to run off after only a few weeks, but I told her that we had to at least wait until she came of age. Otherwise we would land ourselves in more trouble than we might be able to handle. And I was not convinced that she would still think that leaving her comfortable if not harmonic parental home to live of the modest income I had, was a good idea. I wanted her to think properly about this instead of rushing into an act of defiance that she might regret for the rest of her life."

Eryn smiled. "It seems to me that you misjudged her a bit in that regard, then."

"I admit that I did. The day after she came of age we left and came here, spending the little money I had on a small room in the village. It didn't take Enric long to find us after he was told about things. He talked to Leris, telling her that she didn't have to throw herself at the first available man just to hurt their father; that there were other ways to accomplish just that, and that he was more than willing to let her live with him in the city in those grand quarters they had given him."

She grimaced. That was certainly not a very flattering offer to make.

"Leris told him that she didn't consider their father important enough for her to throw her life away for him; that she had gone with me because she loved me, and not to hurt Anwin. It was clear that Enric was not too enthusiastic about that, but he accepted it and then sat down with her to discuss with her how he might help her."

Discuss with her, Eryn thought, not with both of them. So Enric had made his sister's companion not only feel that he wasn't good enough for his sister, but had also refused to let him participate in planning his own future. Oh dear. That had indeed not been a good start. And Ardegen had probably not dared saying anything or asserting himself - Enric had just been promoted to power and glory, after all. It certainly explained the reserve, disregarding the fact that thirteen years had passed since then.

"You were joined with Enric by the King himself, from what I heard," Ardegen said into her thoughts.

Eryn respected his wish to change the topic and nodded. "Yes; it was at the very first ball I was compelled to attend," she said vaguely.

"Leris thinks that this commitment was not an entirely voluntary one. She says that though Enric mentioned you in his letters, he never wrote of any plans of that sort to her." He waited for a while, and when she didn't reply, he added, "You are not asking me about such personal things only to refuse talking about private matters yourself now, I hope?"

Eryn nodded reluctantly. He had a point there. "She is right. We were made to join by the King. He forced our hand. He wanted to bind me to Enric and thereby the city and the Order before the delegation from my home country was due."

"Forced into commitment," Ardegen mused and nodded at Vedric, who had fallen asleep against her chest. "Looking at the three of you, I wouldn't have guessed that. You have obviously managed to make the best of it."

"We have, yes," she confirmed, not willing to elaborate on all the obstacles they'd had to overcome to reach what now looked like blissful family harmony.

They both fell quiet.

Eryn was thinking hard on what to say to end the uneasy silence, when Ardegen asked her, "Do you get along with Anwin, their father?"

She grimaced. "Not that I can say, no. I am afraid he was not very taken with me. Not after his objecting to my wearing trousers and calling me a western spy. And you? Have you ever met him?"

"Once, yes. It was a few months before Leris and I left. He told me to take my dirty hands off his daughter and find somebody closer to my own status," he said darkly.

"You know, with Anwin I wonder if not being liked by him isn't the better option anyway," Eryn snorted. "But at least he keeps his distance. My parents have turned out to be a lot more complicated to deal with - especially as I considered them dead until fairly recently. I like to call my mother Queen of Darkness. That may seem a trifle heartless, but it is a term completely and utterly deserved, believe me. Thanks to her adopting Enric, he and I are now not only companions, but also siblings - legally speaking at least. If you want to tease Enric effectively, just refer to Vedric as his nephew."

Ardegen raised his brow in surprise. "They seem to have some quite... interesting customs in the west," he ventured carefully. "Tell me more about why you thought your parents were dead when they are not," he asked, clearly intrigued.

"That is a longer story."

"I have no pressing obligations for now," he smiled and leaned back comfortably to signal her that he was ready to hear it right here and now.

Eryn sighed in defeat and pushed Enric's empty mug towards him. "Alright, then at least get me something to drink first before I dive into a story of crime, escape, a life in hiding, shocking revelations and intrigues."

He blinked in surprise, then rose quickly to do her bidding, clearly eager to learn if she promised too much.

* * *

Enric let his gaze wander, his expression content with the homely setting of himself and his sister sitting around one large table with their families.

Nera was sitting on one of his knees, concentrated on a drawing that showed crude trees and a number of houses in the distance. Her way of drawing stroke him as unusually advanced, but not because her images held any particular artistic appeal the way Vern's work did. Her approach bespoke a natural understanding of structures, distances and angles he might expect of a child at least ten years older. He marvelled at how she already managed to work with perspectives instead of making everything appear the same size as it would be more common for a child her age. He tried to remember if Leris had ever showed any such talent as a girl, but couldn't remember. If so, encouraging her to develop it would have been the last thing on their father's mind. Quite the opposite, in fact - he would have considered it an unwelcome distraction from his own ideas of how she was supposed to make use of her time. Certainly not by doing something that served no other purpose than her own pleasure instead of his business interests.

Eryn was playing with Dorn, entertaining him by letting thin streaks of water flow through the air in complicated patterns. She was using the technique of medical shielding that kept the blood flowing inside the blood vessels when there was an injury. The boy watched with fascination and tried to grasp at what looked like a watery worm making its way through thin air, giggling every time his fingers broke through the weak barrier and touched the water.

Enric saw how Ardegen's eyes rested on Eryn, his expression thoughtful. Eryn had told him the story of her life, and for a man who had been raised in stable and loving surroundings this was proving rather a lot to take in. He was aware of his own companion's problematic relationship with her family, yet this was mostly a thing of the past and did not have quite such a considerable impact on her life as in Eryn's case.

This was their last evening together; the time here had passed quickly.

"Look at our families," Leris next to him murmured, holding her dozing nephew in her arms. "Strange, isn't it? I guess that means that we are all grown up now."

Enric smiled at that. He was thirty-six years old and his sister was not that much younger.

"So you think it's having children that finally let's people grow up?"

"To a certain degree, yes." She shrugged. "It's a change, a shift of priorities away from yourself to another person. Your own wellbeing comes second, and if necessary you would even sacrifice your life to ensure your children's wellbeing."

Enric didn't comment on that. His position in the Order had brought with it the understanding that he would do precisely that - give up his life if there was no other way to protect the King and the

Kingdom. His life had never really been entirely his anyway. But he understood what his sister meant, of course. His role as protector as defined by the Order was a duty, the one towards Eryn and Vedric was so much more. It was a new purpose in life.

"So," Eryn said lightly from her side of the table, "It will be a lot quieter here when we are finally on our way again."

Leris smiled. "A little. But with two young children quiet is not exactly what we are used to by now. I suppose you will be glad to get some distance to anything remotely connected to family - both your own and Enric's - for some time."

Eryn returned the smile. "I wouldn't say that. I have come to like Ardegen and the children."

"Ardegen and the children, eh?" Enric's sister said calmly. She didn't seem to take offence at that statement, probably well aware that it was an attempt to tease her. "I am glad to hear that. At least my boys appear to have taken a liking to you as well. My daughter is obviously less easy to impress."

Eryn nodded solemnly. "As is her mother from what I have seen."

Enric sensed a certain tension between the two women, but nothing that warranted any interference on his part. They were rather open about not being too thrilled with each other, but at least there was something to build on: a mutual respect.

He looked at Ardegen, who was watching the two women as well, his expression cautious. He, too, was assessing the situation. Their gazes locked for a moment, a silent exchange, a shared understanding. It was the closest they had ever come in these last thirteen years.

Leris lifted the sleeping baby and sniffed. "I think his wrappings need changing."

Enric rose to take his son, but she shook her head and instead nodded at her companion. "No, let Ardegen take care of that. He keeps pestering me about another child, and I think this is a nice reminder of what that would entail."

Eryn was about to object, but Ardegen chuckled and got to his feet to pick up Vedric. "As you wish. That won't deter me." And off he went to the washroom where they kept the clean nappies.

Leris sighed deeply. "Damn. There is no changing his mind it seems. Even worse, he is so annoyingly patient - he won't give up. And I can't even argue that I won't have enough time for our business, that I will be tied to the house and children - he takes care of most of that already." She looked at her brother. "How about you? Will you have another one?"

He shook his head. "No. Eryn doesn't want to, and I respect that."

"But you are not happy about it, I can see that. She is the one to make that decision alone, then?"

"I resent being talked about as if I weren't sitting right here," Eryn cut in, her expression stern.

Leris shot her an amused look. "As you wish. Why are you denying my brother another child?"

"That is none of your business," Eryn replied coldly. "I don't have to justify myself to you."

"Her mother slipped her a fertility potion to impregnate her," Enric supplied. "This child is one more than she wanted at the start."

His sister stared at him, then at his companion. "Is that true? Her own mother?"

Eryn shot Enric an angry look, dismayed at having that little detail revealed. It was a private matter she didn't want to share just like that.

"Yes," he confirmed. "Thus I will certainly not pressure her for another child. And I thank you for not doing just that on my account now that you are aware that it is a sensitive topic."

Eryn was glad when Dorn next to her decided that he had been quiet and well-behaved long enough and demanded attention by pulling her sleeve and pointing to his hair.

"Blue!" he crowed and she obliged him gladly, smiling when he jumped up to run to the mirror in the hallway to behold himself in his new glory. It had been nice to meet Enric's sister and her family, but she felt the longing for her own house that she did not have to share with others like here or back in Takhan stir. It was time to return to Anyueel.

CHAPTER 19

Finally Home

Eryn watched Nera and Dorn run next to their coach, waving their small hands in farewell and smiled when she lifted her own arm to wave back at them. Leris and Ardegen were standing in front of their house, his arm around his companion's shoulders while their eyes followed the departing coach.

Enric sank back into the cushions of the coach when his niece and nephew were no longer in sight. "I really enjoyed seeing Leris again after such a long time, but now I can't wait to finally return home."

Home, Eryn thought and couldn't help experiencing a stab of apprehension. She did consider Anyueel her home, yet living there had so far not turned out particularly peaceful. Not that either of their stays in Takhan had been free from trouble - quite the opposite. But home was supposed to be a refuge, a place where one should be able to feel safe. She seriously doubted that being in the same city with the King and the Order would enable her to ever truly feel safe there. And now she was supposed to be raising a child there. Well, part of the time. Unfortunately, Takhan was not exactly a secure haven, either. Not with Malriel back in power and full glory. But at least the Queen of Darkness would be out of their sight for the next six months.

"You look thoughtful", Enric commented and adjusted Vedric against his chest to afford him a better view out of the window. "A fraction displeased."

"Mind bond?" she asked.

He shook his head. "No, your emotions are not strong enough for that. But there is always the good old method of looking at someone and judging their mood from their facial expression."

She smiled. "Ah yes, there was that. I was just thinking about Malriel. And the King and the Order. And what returning to the city will be like. It will be strange without having Vern there. Somehow the idea of his not being there is... disconcerting. It's like the place is incomplete, hollow. And then there is the matter of facing the King again after what happened before we left."

Enric nodded slowly. He understood her well - on both concerns. Vern was her first friend here - he had helped her through her captivity, had turned out to be a kindred spirit, helped her stay sane when the Order forced her to train fighting and used her like a piece in a game. Of course she would miss him. As for the King...

"I am not too eager to meet King Folrin again myself, as you may imagine. But I am fairly confident that there will be no more... unwanted attentions from him. First, the chances of having you before him shackled in gold again, rendered defenceless, are rather slim; and second, he had to make quite a few concessions to make sure we return here again voluntarily. He was without a doubt anything but thrilled by Vran'el's request at having us stay half of every year in Takhan. He very likely assumed that it corresponded with our wishes when he granted it."

She scowled. "That is unfortunate. I suppose there is little chance of his changing his mind about that if I ask him nicely?"

"None whatsoever," Enric confirmed. "It wouldn't look good and make him appear untrustworthy and unreliable. But you may rest assured that this is no permanent arrangement. As soon as Vedric is old enough to choose where he wants to live, we will be expected to spend the majority of our time in Anyueel again."

Eryn rolled her eyes. "We are talking about two whole decades here! That's permanent enough from where I am standing. But for now I suppose getting away from the King regularly might not be such a bad thing - even if it means putting up with Malriel instead. He makes me nervous. I don't like the way he manipulates me and plays with my feelings. I wish I could set him boundaries somehow without getting myself locked up doing so."

Enric studied her for a moment and pursed his lips. "He delights in making you nervous because he knows that you are suspicious and you fear him to a certain degree. Counteracting his attempts at manipulation will not always work, since recognising them is a matter of getting to know him and learning to predict his next move. This is something you will need more experience for. But what you can do is demonstrate to him that you don't fear him any longer." He leaned forward. "You went to the Western Territories, faced all that distress through discovering that Valrad is your father, with Ram'an, took over the leadership of one of the most powerful Houses in Takhan, dealt with the Senate and unmasked Sanaf and his attempts at harming you - and all that while you were carrying a child. I believe that now you have gone through all this the King will find you less susceptible to his little intrigues and schemes."

She exhaled slowly. He sounded so confident that she would be able to handle the King when she had failed more than once in the past.

"I find your faith in me flattering, yet I wonder if your usual ability to judge people aptly has taken a back seat here and let your fondness for me do the evaluation."

Enric laughed softly. "I know that love has a tendency to make people blind to another person's faults. I pride myself on being less prone to falling into that trap. As your superior I am supposed be aware of your shortcomings and cannot afford the luxury of overlooking them. And then there is my personal conviction that true love does not require making the object of one's affections better than they are but instead provides for an attachment that is strong enough to love despite whatever weaknesses may exist."

"Shortcomings and weaknesses, eh?" Eryn smiled in a none too friendly way. "Would you care to elaborate further with this?"

"I'd rather not if you don't mind. But then I suppose you want to have proof that I really do see them," he grimaced. "Well, at least I am safe enough from retribution as long as I am holding your son."

"Sheltering behind an infant? Really? High and mighty Lord Enric has to resort to measures such as this?" she quipped.

Enric shrugged. "Desperate measures, my love."

"Go on, then. Cower behind your son and talk to me about my deficiencies. Educate me. You do enjoy that so much."

"As you wish. Just to make one thing clear: I am talking to you as your mentor and your superior now, not as your companion. In the latter capacity you are without fault."

Eryn stared at him for a moment, then laughed loudly at that outrageous fib. "Duly noted. This is a professional appraisal of my potential to improve myself as an Order magician, not an opportunity to change some of my more annoying or troublesome characteristics when it comes to living with me."

Enric's face was serious when he replied, "I meant what I said. I didn't fall in love with a conscientious Order magician, a dedicated sword fighter or an obedient subordinate and wouldn't want to turn you into anything of that kind. It would simply not be you anymore."

"Very well, I acknowledge that you want me to be who I am when I am with you. Now let me know what Lord Enric, Second in Command of the Order of Magicians does not appreciate in the Order's third."

"There probably will not be a lot that you are not already aware of. If I had to guess I would say that some of it is even deliberate." He paused and cleared his throat, knowing that she would not appreciate hearing many of the things he was about to tell her. The easy way out for him that would spare him her anger would be to omit most of it. But then he had been lecturing her about the necessity of honesty between them for quite a while now and thus owed her just that. "You are in many cases a slave to your impulses which means that you lack self-control. This makes you rather easy to manipulate when it comes to getting yourself into trouble or making decisions without thinking through their implications first. You have major issues with authority in any area that is not related to knowledge or skills you see as worth honing. You apply your own standards when it comes to deciding whether somebody is fit to lead you. They basically focus on proof of expertise superior to your own. Your refusal to accept the formalised way of granting power the institutions around you apply makes you a destructive influence on whatever organised structure you are part of." He watched her brow twitching while the rest of her face remained impassive. "You dedicate your time to one single field", he went on, "in which you feel you have a moral obligation to work out of a feeling of duty to your deceased father instead of spreading your effort more evenly among various different ones and making proper use of that potential inside you instead of limiting it to what you were as a child taught was the most noble discipline of all. You continually and openly defy your superiors and in so doing undermine the credibility of the Order, which after all has granted you this high rank. You keep trying to free yourself of its hold on you and thus demonstrate that you do not share the values you are not only obliged to uphold but do it in a way that makes you a bad role model for all magicians lower in rank than yourself. You express your dismay or dislike openly without considering any diplomatic or economic consequences which means you are not only prone to causing political tensions but also endangering the success of the businesses and lines of work that are somehow connected to you, instead of taking advantage of possible alliances."

Eryn's stare grew darker with every new sentence. Enric halted when she folded her arms and pursed her lips.

She was grinding her teeth. He had not even thought about what to say or how to express himself - all of this had just come out as if it was nothing more than a logical conclusion, a couple of obvious facts. She wondered how much longer he would have gone on if her apparent displeasure had not induced him to shut up.

"I see," Eryn replied coolly. "So, what you are basically telling me is that I am easy prey for whoever wants to use me because I don't have a grip on myself, that I waste my time on healing and that I am a poor role model. I take offence at that. As regards what you consider my lack of compliance with your kind of authority and the refusal to suck up to the rich and important - I don't consider them failures but a show of common sense."

"I had not expected you to embrace this assessment. And your words confirm what I said before - your defiance is deliberate," Enric replied evenly.

She nodded slowly. "I suppose I shouldn't complain or even be surprised at how you regard me. I asked you to put words to it, after all."

Enric shook his head. "No. What you asked me for and what I just gave you was a list of your shortcomings from the Order's point of view to prove to you that my feelings for you haven't turned me blind to them. What I just said didn't reference any of your numerous and very considerable strengths and abilities that make putting up with your weaknesses worth the Order's resources and patience. Would you like me to talk about those next?"

Eryn looked out of the window. "No, thank you. I don't need any compliments to pet my hurt ego."

"You should by now know me well enough to be aware that I don't cater to petty needs like that. When I pay a compliment, you may depend on its being justified as I see it. The kind of woman to be flattered by empty words would not be one who appealed to me - neither as a trustworthy and reliable subordinate, nor as a companion." His voice was calm, though not particularly friendly. "If you are asking your superior to share his views with you, you might want to work on your attitude when being granted your wish."

She turned her head back to him, marvelling at the absurdity of his uttering words like that, playing the grand superior when their son was snoozing peacefully against his chest. She thought back to when she had been in charge of House Aren and thereby his Head of House. He was content enough with letting her run everything in connection with the businesses and her dealings with Orrin and Vern in her capacity as their superior without interfering. It seemed that placid attitude had made way for his Order persona again. What a pity.

"I don't think you are entitled to reclaiming your position as my superior quite yet, unless I am very much mistaken," she said lightly. "As far as I am aware you are at present not a member of the Order. But it is reassuring that you find returning to the mind-set so very unproblematic."

Enric sighed and his expression softened. The superior was gone for now. "You do remember why I told you these things, don't you? I paid you a compliment which you refused to accept on account of, in your opinion, my being biased in your favour. I just proved to you that this is not the case, and now you are offended because I was more convincing than you expected."

Eryn blinked and then nodded slowly. He was right. "I am sorry." She rubbed her face. "I think the prospect of returning to the Order and the King has put me on edge. And you slipping back into that role so effortlessly as if we had not just been gone for half a year unnerves me. I liked how it was towards the end before we left Takhan - when I led House Aren and we took care of Vedric together. If it wasn't for having Malriel under the same roof, I could imagine a life like that. Not being at the Order's beck and call, having a role of authority that actually grants me a say in how I lead those under my care..." She stopped and frowned, wondering when living in the Western Territories and not returning to Anyueel had turned into such an appealing prospect.

"I know. I enjoyed being free of any other responsibility than taking care of my businesses, even if it was only for a short while. And you did a good job at the top in House Aren. Your style of leading is more suited to a House than the Order. Which is little wonder, considering that you were raised by a man who had in turn been brought up to substitute for his older brother and lead the family whenever the need arose. Ved'al surely did not plan to turn you into a capable Head of House, but then pushing away the influence of our own education is probably nigh impossible." He thought of his sister and how she kept fighting her own impulses sometimes to treat her children the way Anwin had treated her.

Eryn looked at him in surprise. "Did you just say that I am a good leader despite my many disadvantageous character traits?"

"Disadvantageous from the Order's point of view, my love, but not so much when looked at from a different angle. I told you that my appraisal was merely from an Order magician's point of view, not a universally valid picture of you. In contrast to your position in the Order, being in top position at House Aren appealed to you. And you did well enough, moreover. Better than I did. Just as my style of leadership is more suited to the Order than to an extended family, with you it is the other way round. If I had any say in it, I would free you from the burden of your rank, provide you with all the books we were able to get our hands on and let you do whatever struck your fancy, confident that the outcome would not fail to impress."

She searched his eyes, trying to be sure that he was not teasing her. His blue eyes looked at her, their expression serious. "That... is quite unexpected," she said feebly.

"Is it now?" he asked mildly. "I wonder why. I see that being in the Order doesn't make you happy, and your happiness is instrumental to my own. I see that there is a lot you can do and that you are confined to an institution and a place that don't have the means to aid you in unfolding that potential. This was one reason why I agreed so readily to Vran'el's plans to have us return to Takhan regularly. It frees you at least for a time from the limitation which being in the Order implies. I am convinced that being in the same city as Malriel is a small price to pay for that."

Eryn closed her eyes for a moment. "Again doing what's best for me without including me in the decision?"

"The decision wasn't mine, as you will surely remember. I am not particularly happy with how your brother treated you, how he just took the liberty of changing our lives at the drop of a hat, without talking to us first. However, that the decision was not made the way I would have preferred it to does not mean that it not a good one as such. And it certainly does not mean that we won't teach Vran'el a lesson, one that I hope will keep him from trying anything like that again."

"You keep surprising me," she murmured. "In good and bad ways." Good as in showing this unexpected understanding in what directions her skills and inclinations ran, and bad as in forcing the commitment bond off her to run off to a strange country, leaving her alone only weeks before the birth of his son.

"I will work on tipping the balance in favour of the good surprises," he smiled, glad that the tense discussion was over.

* * *

Enric affectionately squeezed her shoulder as the coach came to a halt in front of the city gates. There was a short exchange between the coachman and one of the guards, then the vehicle set in motion once again.

Eryn's eyelids opened slowly and she grimaced at the twinge in her back. The bench did not exactly afford a comfortable sleeping position. Her gaze fell to the window and the urban view. She sat up straight.

"We are back, are we?" There was relief in her voice.

"That we are, yes," Enric confirmed, then frowned when the coach stopped in front of the Palace instead of taking them to their house as he had instructed. A moment later the door was opened by the coachman, who was wearing an apologetic scowl.

"His Majesty wishes to see you right away," he explained and stepped aside to let Enric exit first.

Eryn accepted her companion's hand as she climbed out of the coach and then stretched. "He could at least have deigned to offer us a meal, a wash and a change of clothes," she muttered in dismay.

"I dare say he wants to see with his own eyes that we truly are back," Enric commented and looked down when the small figure strapped to his chest began to stir. "I hope he keeps this brief or Vedric will make this a very noisy audience. It's almost time for his next feed."

Eryn followed reluctantly when she felt the tug on her hand. Her eyes took in the familiar dark grey stone of the Palace, the tall gates with the usual two guards on duty beside them, the polished floor, the soaring columns. A flash of memory from long ago caught her by surprise and made her gulp, reminding her of the day when she was here in this very spot for the first time. Two magicians flanked her at that time, escorting her to an interrogation room that had to be somewhere to her left along the first corridor. It had also been the day she had first met Enric, when he had sent her to the floor with a single, strong bolt of magic.

They walked on, following the main passage straight ahead that led to the throne room.

"I hope there won't be too many people with him," she sighed. "That would simply prolong the visit."

"No, I shouldn't think so. Otherwise he would have let us return home first to make ourselves presentable. It's not in his interest to expose us to scrutiny like that."

They turned the last corner that brought them into view of the double doors of the throne room, the guards on either side quickly opening them as soon as they spotted the anticipated visitors.

Enric's eyes took in the three people on the dais. The King stood straight with his hands behind his back, a faint, contented smile on his lips while he watched them walking towards him. Then there was the familiar sight of his advisor Marrin to one side and two steps behind. The third person present was a man in his mid-fifties, his blond hair streaked with grey, broad-shouldered and looking impressive in his dark red robes. Tyront.

They stopped in front of the dais and both bowed to the King, Enric with one hand on his son's head to keep it from tilting as he moved.

It was silent for several long moments after they had straightened again. The King looked at them, taking his time, safe in the knowledge that nobody would speak before he did.

"It's good to have you back again. Lady Eryn," he finally said, then looked at her companion. "And... Enric."

Eryn blinked in surprise, then remembered that Enric was currently not a member of the Order and was therefore not entitled to be addressed as Lord. Still, hearing the King say his name just like that, unadorned by the title, was strangely absurd. She watched as the King set in motion, slowly descending the few steps until he stood before her, his scrutinising gaze wandering over her, making her feel tense and apprehensive as if she had never been gone.

She straightened. But she had been gone, and it had not been a time free of strain or challenge. She remembered Enric's confidence when he had told her that he had little doubt that she would be able to deal with the King after everything she had been through in Takhan.

When the King unclasped the hands behind his back and stretched them forward to take hers, doubtlessly to kiss them, she took a breath and decided to play it bold. Taking his hands, she resisted his movement to pull them to his lips but instead took a step towards him and kissed him first on the left cheek, then on the right.

The room seemed to freeze. Nobody moved. Marrin's eyebrows were raised in surprise and Tyront's forehead showed a hint of a worried frown. Enric, though, seemed unruffled; his expression showed nothing more than interest, not a hint of alarm or worry.

King Folrin looked down at her, the flicker of surprise in his eyes, however faint and brief, still recognisable if one was looking, or as in Eryn's case, hoping for it. She allowed herself a small smile, watching how his own lips curved in response in appreciation of a demonstration performed well. He was still holding on to her hands and squeezed them for a moment before releasing them.

Then the monarch turned his head and nodded to the Order's leader, who then smiled and stepped forward, putting both hands on Enric's shoulder and looking at him for a moment as if to judge the wisdom of showing any sign of affection in this setting, then obviously disregarding whatever considerations were holding him back. He pulled the younger man towards him into an embrace, careful not to squeeze the infant between them.

"Welcome back, my boy," Tyront murmured with feeling.

Enric worked hard to keep the surprise from showing in his features while he took a moment to recover from this unexpected show of affection from a man who had admittedly been his mentor and friend for more than a decade now, but was still his superior. And then there were those remnants of tension between them from eight months ago.

Tyront let go of Enric and then stepped towards Eryn, who gave him a lopsided smile, curious if she, too, would be treated to a show of fondness. He looked down at her, smiled and lifted both his hands to cup her face and kiss her forehead.

"You managed not to provoke a war. Good. I am so proud," her superior nodded in mock appreciation.

Eryn laughed quietly. "What can I say? I aim to please."

Tyront turned back to Enric and studied him for a moment before he said, slowly and deliberately, "There is a small matter I would very much like to deal with right here."

Enric raised his brow, then smiled lazily. "It doesn't happen to have anything to do with a certain oath you wish me to give? Why do I have the feeling that there is little chance for me to be released from this room before that small matter is taken care of?"

The older man's gaze became more intense. "Because you are an exceptionally smart man, my friend. Are you telling me that you would wish to be released from here before giving the oath? That you have no intention of returning to the Order?"

Eryn sensed the tension - despite Tyront's efforts to appear relaxed. There was a long pause, and a look at her companion's face told her that Enric was enjoying himself. She decided to bring things to a head. She needed a bath and a hearty meal.

Rolling her eyes, she growled, "If you refuse to swear the bloody oath, I will cause you to suffer. Badly. If I need to attend those dull Council meetings, then you have to, as well. Don't make me shackle you in gold and be persuasive."

There was a flash of mischief in his eyes, which probably meant that he was about to say something she wouldn't like to make her pay for unduly shortening his pleasure of bothering Tyront.

"Please don't hold back on my account, my love. I remember how much pleasure putting me in gold gives you," he grinned unabashedly, enjoying the annoyance and embarrassment that flushed her cheeks red.

She forced herself to remain calm and covered her eyes with her hand for a moment before she said slowly, "Would you just get on with it? I really, really want to go home. Our son needs to be fed and I have no intention of doing it here."

Enric gave an exaggerated sigh and turned to Tyront. "It seems I don't have much choice in this. Back into the Order it is, then."

Tyront's relief was evident from the less rigid set of his jaw and shoulders. "Then let's not keep your family waiting."

He waited while Enric untied the sling across his chest to pass the baby to Eryn, who was already reaching out for their son, when the King's voice next to her said, "Allow me."

Eryn slowly let her arms sink and stepped aside reluctantly. There was little else she could do. Yet she could somehow not imagine him holding a small infant. Did he even know how to go about it? Was he aware that the head needed supporting?

She watched Enric hand their son over to King Folrin with an unperturbed expression. It seemed that he didn't share her concerns. To her surprise, the King seemed neither awkward nor clumsy with Vedric, but placed him in his arm in a way that allowed him to study the small face with the dark blue eyes that would very likely turn brown in the months to come.

"Not nervous, Lady Eryn, are you?" the King smiled without looking at her. "I solemnly promise to return your son to you unharmed."

She didn't reply, but observed how he studied Vedric with a thoughtful expression.

"He clearly resembles his father in appearance. And his magical potential seems to be so immense that it cannot even be compared without revising the scale. I will follow his development with interest. As will the Order and no doubt your parents in Takhan."

Eryn didn't reply but looked up when Enric and Tyront joined their palms in a strong grip. A few moments later her companion's calm voice rose.

"I swear to the people of this Kingdom, here in these halls before the King, that I will protect them against any and all threats with my life." Enric stopped after the first sentence and waited, staring into Tyront's eyes, which had widened. This was not the traditional oath with which magicians bound themselves to the Order - this was the one Eryn had sworn back then, the one they had changed so that she would not have to magically bind herself to the King personally. The silence stretched on and Tyront closed his eyes for a few moments, the two men's hands still in a tight clasp.

"Your Majesty?" the Order's leader asked quietly without taking his eyes off Enric.

Another pause before the monarch said calmly, though with clenched teeth, "Proceed."

Eryn forced herself to release her breath slowly even though it wanted to escape her lungs in a rush. That had been quite a stunt to pull. He had not mentioned that little surprise to her with one single word. It had been a daring move, one that not only demonstrated his wish to be bound to the King less tightly, but also tested the extent of their eagerness to have him back in the Order. And obviously they were very eager.

"I will not leave this place or you," Enric proceeded, "without orders or the intention of returning. I will bring honour upon the Kingdom by serving the King and the Order in all that is right. I will obey my superiors in good faith and without deceit. I will, according to the statutes of the Order of Magicians, hone my skills in fighting to be ready to use them in your defence at all times."

Eryn cast a sideways glance at the King beside her. He was swaying the child to and fro on his arm absentmindedly while regarding Enric with slightly narrowed eyes that were the only visible sign of his displeasure. He turned his head to her and gave her a smile. It had an edge.

"Lady Eryn. Do me an honour and have lunch with me tomorrow. In my quarters."

She nodded once. "The honour is mine, Your Majesty," she replied without missing a beat. A look at Enric told her plainly enough that he was aware that this was the punishment for his unauthorised change of the oath.

Marrin turned to a small table behind him and took from it a dark blue bundle of fabric to hand to Tyront.

"With this, Lord Enric," the Order's leader spoke, his tone formal and slightly annoyed, "I welcome you back into the Order and return to you with immediate effect the authority that comes with the rank of Second-in-Command. I look forward to seeing you in my quarters tomorrow at noon for an informal lunch." His voice promised that it would not be a purely joyous occasion for Enric.

* * *

Eryn was holding herself back with some effort until the door to their house clicked shut behind them. She had imagined returning here after their long absence, her enjoyment of all familiar items big and small, the moment of bringing her son to what now comprised one of two homes for the years ahead. But now that the time had come she was not in the mood to enjoy and appreciate it calmly, but rather felt the urge to smack the man next to her properly.

"Have you gone completely bonkers?" she sighed and shook her head. "What came over you when you pulled a thing like that off? What would you have done if the King had not let you go through with it?" She patted Vedric's back. He had been fidgeting about on their way back, probably a mix of rising hunger and the air of annoyance his mother radiated. "What can you possibly gain from irritating Tyront and the King? Is this supposed to be some kind of revenge for what happened before we went to Takhan? Are you planning on being a nuisance from now on just to show them that they must treat you with respect if they want you to play nicely with the other magicians? Have you considered what kind of role that pushes me into? I will be caught between you and them! And I can't believe that I am the one lecturing you about defying the Order and the King!"

Enric looked at her and fought hard to keep himself from laughing out loud. She wouldn't take that well.

Her eyes narrowed. "If you dare letting out that laugh I see in your eyes, I will hurt you. I mean it!"

"There was not much risk of them not granting me your version of the oath," he reasoned. "I, too, would have preferred talking it through with them first, but I had not expected them to drag us before the King minutes after passing the city gates and getting me back into the Order right then and there. That shows that they rather desperately wanted me back within and bound, so they would not have denied me this concession. And it was not even done publicly, so it is little more than a reminder for them that I have still not forgiven them completely and am to be treated with care."

"Your little demonstration got me a lovely invitation to take a meal with him in his darned quarters!"

He grimaced at that. "Yes, he certainly retaliates quickly. But he would have summoned you alone anyway sooner or later, though very probably not to his quarters. That is the part that is meant to vex me. And it does - even though I know it makes little difference where he is alone with you. He doubtlessly missed his little exchanges with you and wants to talk over the things that happened in Takhan with you. You have your magic at your disposal and can shield yourself if necessary. Not that I think it will be necessary, mind you. He has nothing to gain but a lot to lose if he gets too close to you again."

Eryn handed the baby to his father while she unfastened her tunic and took a seat on a settee. Enric placed his son back in her arm when she was seated comfortably and had stuffed a cushion under her arm so it didn't have to bear the full weight of the pawing, hungry bundle that started sucking greedily as soon as his lips had fastened on the food source.

"It's strange to be back here now," she said and let her gaze roam around the parlour, which was looking strangely austere as if it had not been used in a while. Plia had obviously not spent a lot of time in the place. "I have no idea how to go on from here. I will return to a clinic that is no longer mine. I have to take orders from Lord Poron now. And I don't even know how much time there is left for healing with my new Council duties and raising a child." She looked at Enric. "We still haven't decided anything about Vedric and how to divide our time. I have no intention of letting my child be raised by a nursemaid the way the other rich people here do it. Yet as we are both supposed attend the Council meetings at the same time, we need somebody at least for a few hours every now and then. I suppose I could ask Lord Poron to let me do night duty. That would leave my days free for Vedric and the Council." She sighed heavily. "Sleeping is overrated, anyway."

Enric looked at her doubtfully. "Is that advisable? It wouldn't help if you collapsed after a few months."

"I won't work at the clinic as much as I did before, and with night duty there is still a good chance that I can catch a few hours of sleep provided there aren't too many emergencies needing my attention. I will probably ask Junar to mind Vedric during the Council meetings or wherever else we are supposed to be turning up together. I expect if she knows in advance she can plan accordingly herself." Then her face lit up. "You know, that schedule certainly doesn't leave a lot of space for attending social dinners and balls. Especially as Junar is likely to be invited to them as well."

He shook his head and chuckled. "You found the silver lining. Now delightful. I hate to destroy your vision of years without having social evening duties, but I am afraid that having a child will be no valid excuse for staying away from them completely. We may take turns with Junar and Orrin so the ones who are at home take care of the children while the other couple goes out to dinner."

Eryn rolled her eyes. "So the one person I depend on to stay sane at these occasions will not be there? Just fabulous."

"There is still Vyril," Enric pointed out.

"Yes, that's true," she admitted. "But with Junar I can quietly abuse the other guests without being afraid that she is shocked at my lack of decorum. Don't get me wrong; I like Vyril very much. But she is a lady - and joined with Tyront. She might not take kindly to my views on the rich and mighty, being one herself."

"As are you."

"But I don't like it. And I didn't really choose my place at your side, did I?"

Enric leaned forward, his elbows resting on his knees. He waited until she looked at him, then asked carefully, "That is true, you didn't choose to join me. Would you do so now? Of your own accord?"

She frowned. "I don't understand the question. I fairly much reinforced our connection by joining in a third level bond with you back then, didn't I?"

"Reinforcing something that is already in place is not the same as making that first step," Enric insisted. "Let's assume the King had not forced my hand to make you join me. Would you have chosen it voluntarily at some point?"

Oh dear. What a question. She opened her mouth to tell him what she knew he very much wanted to hear, but stopped and thought for a moment.

"Probably not," she admitted reluctantly. There was none of the pain or frustration she had expected when she looked at him. "You are taking this better than I would have thought."

He smiled faintly. "I know that you love me. It took you long enough to realise, and the mind bond is a convenient means of confirming this. It means I assume that the problem is not me as such, but rather my position."

She nodded and changed Vedric to the other breast. "You are right. If I were not joined to you, I wouldn't be a member of the Order, either. I would be content enough with being your lover. No tiresome social duties, no troubles with the King and Tyront, no Council meetings..."

Enric leaned back again and shook his head in amusement. "I think you fail to consider a few facts in that idealised alternative reality of yours. First, had you not been joined to me and bound to the Order,

Ram'an would very likely have taken you with him when he came here as ambassador. Second, the Order would not just have given up on making you join them regardless of whether you were bound to me or not. And third, I would have pursued you relentlessly until you had agreed to bind yourself to me."

Eryn shrugged. "Ram'an would surely not have taken me without my consent. And the Order might have continued pestering me to give in, but with that nice new skill of changing my hair colour they wouldn't have managed to keep me here much longer. I would have accomplished my escape away from the city sooner or later."

"True enough. Meaning you would have left me behind," he said quietly.

She swallowed hard. There was not much sense in lying to him. "I might have. But I would have missed you."

He nodded. "You would have, yes. And I would have gone after you to bring you back. And succeeded. You are good in the woods, so it would probably have taken me a while. But gold can buy good trackers, so I wouldn't have needed to depend on only my own skills. Would being the King's prisoner for who knows how long really have been the lesser evil compared to being in the Order and enduring social duties?"

"Why do you begrudge me my little illusion of how nice everything would have been without the King's forcing us to join each other?" she grumbled.

"I don't want to come second to any notions of how things could have turned out better." His voice was serious. "I want you to look at me and think that this here, the three of us, is the best possible outcome there could have been - no matter how unpleasant some of the steps on our way here were."

Eryn nodded slowly and looked down at the baby boy who had placed one hand on her breast as if to clutch it securely in case she decided to move it away before he was finished. Her son who looked so very much like his father. It was not quite as stunning as her own resemblance to Malriel, but still plainly recognisable. Then she looked up at Enric, who was studying her, waiting patiently for her to comment on his statement. His expression was calm and serene. She knew he would accept it if she was not yet convinced that this truly was the option that made her happier than any of the possible alternatives. He would just continue to try and change her mind in the months or even years to come.

"You are a stubborn one," she smiled.

"I prefer the term persistent." He leaned over to take his son who had stopped suckling and was about to fall asleep.

Eryn watched the scene of the tall man handling this fragile human being with such natural ease. The memory of her ever having been shocked and dismayed at the news of her pregnancy was now so absurd, so unreal that it seemed like a mere figment of her imagination. Enric had been thrilled from the start, so much that she had suspected him of having tricked her into having his child. Wrongly so. He wouldn't have done anything as underhand as that to her and in hindsight she was ashamed of having accused him. The King had been right back then - such a course of action would have been against everything Enric represented. This was so far beneath him that she wondered how he could have forgiven her so easily for assuming it back then.

"You are," she said softly.

He looked up from his son, his look inquisitive.

"You are the best possible outcome there could have been for me. And I fancy I would have realised this at one point no matter how things would have progressed without the King's interference back then."

The smile grew slowly on his lips. "Join me in a third level bond, Eryn. Please."

She hesitated for only a moment before she nodded and simply said, "Very well."

His eyes bulged and he blinked, unsure if he had truly just heard her agree.

"I seem to have managed to surprise unflappable Lord Enric of mighty House Aren," she laughed, delighted at his reaction.

He exhaled loudly and shook his head. "I admit you have. I would have bet anything that you would let me stew for another few months to put me through it. I stand corrected."

She leaned forward. "If you were not bound to any demands the King and the Order have, if you were free to do whatever you wanted, what would you do now?"

"Right now?" He laughed shakily. "I would call for a coach, pack you and Vedric along and get us back to Takhan to have the third level bond renewed."

"I had a feeling that you would. Which means, I assume, that waiting six months until we can finally do just that is probably not going to be easy for you."

He stared at her for a moment, then chortled. "Incredible. But I have to say that I prefer six months of waiting for the ceremony to the uncertainty of whether it will ever take place. I like it when you are devious. Preferably with other people, though. I liked how you greeted the King. I think this was probably the third time since he assumed the throne that I have seen him show any sign of surprise. Well done, my love."

"That was your fault."

"Indeed? How was that?"

"You had these expectations, you were so convinced that I would be able to handle him that I somehow didn't dare to disappoint you."

Enric raised one eyebrow. "Look at that. But then you have already proved that challenging you is a sure way of getting you to excel."

"Like keeping me prisoner and pushing me until I happen to stumble across an airtight barrier?"

"Exactly like that, yes. And with a son who will very likely prove to be magically stronger than either of us when he reaches Plia's age, a little inventiveness will serve us well."

Eryn grimaced. "Soothing prospects. Speaking of Plia - she doesn't know that we are back already. I will send a messenger to the clinic and let her know that we will expect her home in time for dinner."

Enric waved her towards the stairs. "I will take care of that. You go upstairs and take a bath."

"Thank you. That is most considerate of you."

"You just agreed to renew the bond with me. Right now I am in the mood to grant you pretty much anything in my power."

She thought for a moment, then sighed and rose. "Splendid. Not a single outrageous demand comes to mind right now, of course. And when I finally manage to come up with something, you will no longer be in this blissfully happy mood to grant it."

He shook his head in mock sympathy. "Life is full of great misfortunes."

* * *

Eryn opened the door to the yard to let Urban out and blinked at the sight. When they had left here several months ago, there had been little more than first tentative saplings and grass that covered a few patches of earth here and there. Now the entire area was blanketed with grey-green grass that had doubtlessly been a lot more lush only a few weeks ago, the trees had gained height and there were even traces of moss around the rocks and tree trunks they had brought here for Urban to climb and lie on.

The mountain cat trotted out, still slightly drowsy after just having woken from her magically-induced sleep. She stopped, lifting her nose up into the air to take in the smells and then moved towards the wall at one end of the garden, following the outline to inspect the borders of her territory, reclaiming it by leaving scent marks with her cheek and her urine.

Plia stepped behind her, Vedric in her arms. They had just finished their first meal together after all these months, and the girl had been carrying the baby around since then, refusing to put him down even after he fell asleep.

"Do you like it?" Plia asked. "I tried a few things - different types of soil, mixtures of nutrients to promote growth and a few plants I thought might survive Urban's attentions. It doesn't look particularly impressive right now; the plants began to become dormant for the winter a while ago." She nodded to a patch overgrown with high stems that would carry small green leaves and an abundance of tiny, purple blossoms as soon as it got warmer again in spring. For now only a few dried stems were all that was left. These were the same flowers Valrad had in his garden at the Vel'kim residence, the ones that sent Urban into a state of ecstatic bliss after smelling them. Valrad had sent a few seeds over some time ago.

The cat's survey of the grounds had not yet led her across the new addition, but in this state the plants would trigger hardly any reaction.

Eryn nodded. "I do like it, very much so. I always thought I was good with plants, but I only know how to work with them once they are cut. You have a deeper understanding that extends to their requirements for growing and thriving. I am impressed."

"It gives me pleasure. I find handling plants calming, and I like to watch them grow, to see if what I am doing works."

"I imagine that plant house of yours on the clinic roof must be quite a sight by now, though I suppose that it houses only the most resistant plants at the moment," Eryn smiled and shivered. She had yet to get used to the temperatures here again. Early winter in the Kingdom was quite the contrast to the dry heat in the Western Territories.

"You should have seen it in autumn, it was beautiful," Plia smiled with a faraway expression as if seeing herself in the middle of her plants. "Now only the perennial herbs are left, and they don't look so impressive right now. I can't wait for spring to come. Every time a blade of green penetrates the layer of soil, I want to dance and sing." She blushed. "That sounds crazy."

Eryn turned to her and shook her head. "No, it doesn't. It sounds like you are dedicated to what you are doing, and everybody who looks at your laboratory in the clinic or your domain on the roof can see that you have an amazing talent, that you have found your calling."

The girl smiled at that and made calming noises when the baby in her arms whimpered softly against her shoulder.

"I am sorry that Vern didn't come back," Plia said, a sad undertone in her voice. "I don't have many friends, and he never treated me like many others did and still do at times - as if I didn't count because I am an orphan without powerful connections or money."

Eryn narrowed her eyes. "Who treats you like that?" She would show them what showing disregard to her ward entailed and aid them - gently, of course - in altering that unhealthy attitude to a more... acceptable one.

"Please don't worry, I can handle it. Really I can. And every time one of the healers, no matter which one, witnesses any impolite or unfriendly behaviour towards me, they stand up for me."

A wave of pride at her healers surged through her, warming her from within. Well, not her healers any more, but Lord Poron's. She pushed the thought aside and returned to what Plia had initially said about Vern.

"I miss him, too. I keep telling myself that this is a fabulous chance for him and I know that he deserves it, but a selfish little part inside me keeps nagging." She shook her head at herself. "Which is completely ridiculous as I will be spending six months of each year with him no matter where lives for now."

Plia stared at her, taken aback. "What?"

Eryn winced and remembered too late that Plia was not yet aware of this arrangement Vran'el had insisted on. What she had just said was not the gentlest approach to introducing her to that fact.

"My new Head of House has seen fit that I split my time equally between Anyueel and Takhan. That means that we will change between the two countries every six months."

The girl's face fell. "For how long?"

"I don't know. But at least until Vedric is grown up. Vran'el wants to make sure that his heir has regular contact with his House. And there is the sentimental reason of his wanting his sisters close to him. That's why he ordered Pe'tala back to Takhan as soon as things here at the clinic are running smoothly enough for her to leave."

"Everybody is leaving - you, Vern, Pe'tala..." Plia whispered, her face masked with distress.

"Not everybody, little flower," Eryn said soothingly, for the first time in many months calling her by that pet name again, the name her father had used for herself when she was little more than a toddler. She had stopped using it for Plia once they had started working together, but right now she felt like addressing her with a tender term that conveyed her fondness. "I will always return here, and same as in these last months we will be in regular contact, we will write to each other. Junar will be here, I will ask her to keep an eye on you as long as I am gone. And you can visit me in Takhan if you like."

Plia made herself smile and nodded, clearly putting on a brave face for Eryn's benefit.

Eryn sighed and brushed aside a strand of blond hair that had fallen across the girl's eyes. "Come on, let's go back inside. I'm freezing and it's time to feed and bathe Vedric before laying him down."

"Can I help? With the bathing, I mean."

"Sure," Eryn smiled, touched by this readiness to accept the little boy as an addition to her life as if it was the most natural thing in the world. That was quite a feat for a girl who never had a role model for such a thing.

CHAPTER 20

Back to Work

Enric squared his shoulders before knocking at his superior's door, waiting in the Palace corridor for a servant to permit access. Although soon enough he recognised the sound of the determined strides that crossed the room and was thus not surprised when Tyront himself opened it, nodded at him and stepped aside to let him enter. The older man raised an eyebrow when his gaze fell on the infant slung across Enric's chest.

"I read reports that you were hardly ever seen without your son after your return from Pirinkar. Is this a habit you intend to hold on to here in Anyueel as well? If so, then this is something we need to discuss. I can't have you bringing a child to the Council meetings."

Enric smiled thinly. "I have no intention of taking him to the meetings. But Eryn and I have decided against hiring a nursemaid, so there might be several occasions where one or other of us will have him whenever this is possible." And today the presence of a baby three months old would, he hoped, induce Tyront to keep his countenance in case he felt like getting rid of his frustration. The matter with the oath couldn't have gone down well, and there was little doubt that the purpose of this lunch invitation was meant as an opportunity to talk about just that in private.

"Our lunch trays have just arrived. Do I need to order something for your son?" Tyront enquired.

Enric shook his head. "No, thank you, that won't be necessary. He will stick to his mother's milk for another few weeks. I have read that his intestinal system is not yet ready for other food."

The Order's leader nodded briefly. "I see that you approach non-work-related matters with the same thoroughness I have come to appreciate when working with you on Order issues. Come on, let's eat before we talk. You are doubtless aware why I wanted to see you today even though I am aware that there is quite a lot of catching up for you to do."

The younger man didn't bother to comment. It had not really been a question.

Both men sat down at the table, removing the metal covers from various dishes on the trays. Enric inhaled the warm aromas of the food before him - the blend of herbs that were used here at the Palace regularly - the familiar dish he had eaten so many times when he had still been living at the Palace in his old quarters before moving out and to his own abode with Eryn and the mountain cat.

"So, how has coming home been for you so far?" Tyront asked airily.

"A relief," Enric replied, glad that he would at least be able to enjoy his meal before the thrashing out of what surely awaited him afterwards began. "Our own house, more privacy... Eryn is glad to have Plia back and she was brimming with excitement at the thought of going to the clinic."

"I wonder how well she will adapt to the changes that have happened over these last months," the older man said carefully. "Pe'tala, Lord Poron and Ro..." - he sighed and reminded himself of the unusual name, shaking his head at the thought - "...Lord Rolan were not exactly idle during your absence. I am still having trouble using the title in his case - even though I was one in favour of granting it."

"Eryn and I were rather surprised to learn about that. Pleasantly surprised, but still surprised. May I ask who suggested it?"

"Lord Poron. He approached me with that idea and made sure I supported him before he presented it to the Magic Council. Most of them were against it, but the King expressed his appreciation for Rolan and his efforts at the clinic."

Enric smiled. "What a nice coincidence that he happened to be present at this particular Council meeting, then."

Tyront snorted. "Yes, quite. Coincidence. I never was a great believer in that concept, and when it comes to the King I have taken to disregarding its existence completely."

"A sensible approach," Enric nodded and looked down when Vedric started to kick, fixing his gaze on the fork in his father's hand. He took a teaspoon from the tray and placed it in the small hand, watching the fingers close tightly around it. Both men watched the end of the cutlery disappearing into the tiny mouth. When the kicking didn't cease, Enric untied the sling around his chest and held the baby in one arm while he draped the cloth on the carpeted floor with the other before placing his son on it.

"I can see that you seem to have adapted reasonably well to your new role," Tyront commented and looked down at the infant, studying the happy face that smiled broadly and stared at the spoon in fascination. "He really does look like you. Apart from the hair, that is."

"We will have to see how well we do here in Anyueel. Back in Takhan we were able to dispose of our time more freely than here. For now Eryn needs to make sure to be around to feed him every few hours, and as soon as he has started eating solid food she will have to resume her combat training and make it necessary to consider this, too, in our schedules."

The older magician took another bite and chewed it thoughtfully, then said, "Eryn wants to resume healing, I assume?"

"You assume correctly. She is aware that there is only limited time available for this, but she wants to keep in touch with both the profession and the clinic. She is considering taking over mostly night duty and no doubt discussed this with Lord Poron in the morning."

"Which leaves you with the baby at home. I hope for your sake that he grants you at least a few hours of sleep. We depend on your having a clear head," Tyront said casually, but there was an unmistakable warning embedded. Enric chose not to comment on that. It was not as if he had any great influence on his son's sleeping habits. And Eryn was determined not to hire a nursemaid. That didn't leave much room for delegating the task of caring for Vedric.

When Tyront's plate was empty, he leaned back and waited patiently for his guest to finish. When Enric, too, had put down his cutlery and leaned back, the Order's leader smiled faintly. "Your return yesterday caused quite some amazement, though I must say that I wouldn't have expected this combination. I would have counted on Eryn being the one to cause trouble, but she did extraordinarily well. Greeting the King in that manner showed nerve and sent a clear signal that she is no longer afraid of him. I wondered how much of this was real, but then again she never was a particularly convincing liar. I imagine you are not too happy about her taking her lunch in his quarters right now, but then you are aware that this is meant as a punishment for you."

Enric nodded wordlessly, waiting for his superior to go on.

"You, too, sent a very clear message yesterday, namely that you have still not forgiven the King for kissing Eryn back then. This was almost a year ago. You came dangerously close to overstepping a boundary by choosing Eryn's oath instead of our standard one. You managed to get through with it, but barely." Tyront's voice was calm, relaxed. He had never really been the resentful type but tended to vent his anger quickly and then return to more level thinking. There were only very few occasions when he had not managed to contain his anger long enough for this explosion to be in public. The more recent ones had all been in connection with Eryn, such as shouting at her in front of a room full of magicians and the King when she had almost got herself killed by dropping the shield at her testing when she was brought to the city. That one, Enric knew, was still nagging at him.

"I had no doubt that it would work," Enric said placidly. "It was obvious that you were eager to admit me back into the Order. You didn't even grant us an hour to go home and make ourselves presentable before dragging us to the throne room."

"There is only so much more indulgence you may expect from the King," Tyront warned him. "I myself couldn't care less which oath you chose to swear - I want you in the Order and bound with magic, no matter if to the King or the Kingdom. But I wonder at your decision to provoke the King like that. If you keep on making him look like a fool, he will retaliate - as well you know. If you are lucky, taking your companion to his quarters will satisfy him for now." The older man narrowed his eyes and studied his second in command for a few moments. "I have been given to understand that your third level commitment bond is no longer in place."

Enric raised both eyebrows in mock surprise. "Have you now. I wonder why that is of interest to the Order. I would have thought this to be a private matter."

"I could tell you about being worried about the Order's stability as there seems to be some discord between my two highest ranking magicians. Or you just tell me about it, considering me a friend who is concerned about your happiness."

That last bit made refusing difficult. He could tell Tyront to mind his own business, assuring him that whatever happened between Eryn and him would not affect the Order, but refusing to acknowledge a friendly overture was another issue entirely. Tyront was obviously testing the ground, determined to find out how large the chasm between them still was. Enric pondered this question for a moment, then decided that he didn't mind talking about it. Definite proof of progress.

"Half of it is still in place - my half. I can still receive her emotions if they are strong enough, but she no longer feels mine. She refused to have the bond re-established after my return from Pirinkar."

His superior's voice was soft when he said, "So she was not in favour of your travelling to Kar to get her mother out of trouble."

"No. She thought I was leaving her to run after Malriel. She somehow got it into her head that I was in love with her mother. But I am happy to announce that Eryn has agreed to re-enter into the third level bond with me as soon as we are back in Takhan six months from now. She considers making me wait for the ceremony impatiently an apt torture."

Tyront laughed quietly at that. "And? Does it work? Are you that impatient? You still have access to her emotions, after all. There is not much that changes for you."

"It works alright. I have even considered inviting a few magicians from Takhan here and have the bond re-established, but who knows what else she would think of if she had the feeling that I am not suffering sufficiently."

"A valid consideration." Tyront's face then turned serious again, his brow furrowing slightly. "I am not at all impressed with that ill-fated scheme Eryn's brother and the King have agreed on. I am meant to do without both of you every six months. I was astonished King Folrin permitted it. I see that you might be willing to put up with it, even enjoy the prospect of returning to the relative freedom which being away from the Order and the King allows you. But Eryn... there is this profound dislike for her mother that makes me doubt that she is enthusiastic about spending half of every year in the same place as

257

Malriel. From what I heard about how Eryn used her mother's savings to found an orphanage and refused to give up her position as Head of House Aren for another two months after Malriel's return, I can see that the relationship between the two of them is still tense. How did she take to Valrad committing to Malriel?"

"None too well," Enric shrugged. "Though after the first blow of learning that Valrad was her father and the next one that the two were still in love with each other, it was more a matter of being angry that Malriel has managed to undermine what Eryn took such great pains to accomplish: severing at least the legal connection between them. With joining her father, Malriel officially returns to her status as Eryn's mother." He permitted himself a small smile. "Vran'el was fairly composed about this whole matter, is even happy for his father, but Pe'tala has never been a great friend of Malriel. She and Eryn were none too subtle about their sentiments."

Tyront nodded slowly. "Yes, I can imagine that well enough. In the past neither of them exercised undue restraint when it came to expressing their feelings," he commented flatly. "About Vran'el... he has chosen a rather assertive course of action after taking over his father's position as Head of House Vel'kim. My reports gave me the impression of a rather agreeable, gentle and intelligent man. Either he wants to demonstrate strength by showing that he doesn't shy away from ordering his two unruly sisters around and is successful in making them comply with his wishes, or he has discovered a liking for power and has let himself be changed by it very quickly. What is your opinion on that? You are rather close to him from what I gathered. Will he turn out to be a problem?"

Enric bent down to pick up his son who seemed to be tired with his spoon and had started complaining in sounds which were a precursor to wailing. He calmed down immediately after being placed on his father's lap.

"My impression was that he is a little overwhelmed by the new situation. Sure, he has been preparing to take over the House for more than two decades, but the development with Malriel and his father was rather more rapid than anybody would have expected. He is, as you said, struggling to show strength. But then Valrad was on the brink of ordering Pe'tala back to Takhan himself. He was more lenient with Eryn. He didn't make her swear the second level bond when she joined his House and wouldn't have attempted to make her return to Takhan so regularly and for such extended periods of time, but he is clearly in favour of the idea and I suspect that he is glad that Vran'el is so determined about keeping the family together."

Tyront grunted. "He is causing us quite a lot of trouble with his desire to have his sisters with him. Don't get me wrong, I understand him well enough." He nodded at Vedric. "The heir to his position was meant to be raised in Anyueel, which is a problem for him. And Pe'tala has been living with a local man for several months now and was rather open in considering staying for a while longer. There was a definite risk for her to be attached to... Lord Rolan enough to relocate here for good. But now instead he will leave with her and be gone after he has turned out to be useful beyond expectation. We even made him a Lord! And as if this wasn't enough, Eryn's father offers Vern a chance to stay in Takhan as well. This family is causing me sleepless nights - and of them, Eryn is currently the least of my troubles!"

While Tyront's dismay was understandable, Enric himself had little reason to be unhappy with the current development. Losing Rolan was unfortunate, but he would still be here for several months and could thus train his successor properly before he left. Vern would return in a few years with knowledge that would benefit the clinic and thereby the Order and the Kingdom as a whole considerably. As for Pe'tala, she had been here longer than anyone had counted on initially thanks to falling in love with Rolan, and her efforts had doubtlessly moved along the process of turning the clinic into a smoothly running organisation. All in all, things had turned out reasonably well for all the people involved. Even if doing without his second and third in command for six months at a time every year was an unfavourable development for Tyront, the Order would somehow manage to survive. They had surely been doing well enough in these last months. Enric knew that these frequent absences would cost him his influence and power in the Magic Council, but his importance in Takhan would rise and counterbalance that well enough. He would be one of very few people with very good political and business connections on both sides of the sea. That meant that his reach when it came to information was even further than the King's and Tyront's. And information was at times a currency more powerful than gold - especially as it could easily be converted into the precious metal if one knew how to use it to one's advantage.

"You could have forbidden Rolan to move to Takhan. Still could," Enric smiled, knowing well enough that such a course of action was not something his superior would pursue.

Tyront gave him a withering look. "And have Pe'tala curse me, Vran'el of House Vel'kim angry at me for denying his sister her happiness, risk Rolan fleeing the country and having Eryn against me in the Council? Thank you so much for that suggestion. If I thought that you were serious I would have to ask myself if you have either lost your common sense over there in the Western Territories or if you continued harbouring resentment to a degree I need to worry about."

"Compared with a degree of resentment you don't have to worry about?"

Tyront leaned forward, his gaze intent, his smile thin. "You are a smart one, Enric, and always have been - no matter how hard it was to convince you to act accordingly. You know well enough that there is only so much you can gain by not letting the King and me forget that you are the wronged party. What is more, I am convinced that you are aware that you have fairly much reached the limit of any concessions we both are willing to make in order to accommodate you. So no, I don't worry about your resentment any longer. You used your situation to your best advantage, and I respect and even admire it. Yet I couldn't help but notice that you brought your son to a meeting you knew I had scheduled to let you know how little value I attach to that little ruse with the oath yesterday. You could have opted to counter me with self-righteous stoicism, but you decided to bring an infant to encourage me to hold back. That shows that you think that this course of action no longer works and that you need to resort to tricks."

Enric laughed, not bothering to deny a single word. "So far it has worked beautifully, hasn't it?"

Tyront grinned back. "I don't know. Maybe I am just glad you are back, my boy. So, how did you manage to snatch your son away from Eryn so she wasn't able to take him to her lunch with the King?"

"Bribery, of course. Threats don't work, she just considers them a challenge. I promised her two weeks without social evening duties."

"I see. Well, at least there are a few things that still haven't changed. Seeing the two of you with reversed roles - you defiant, she cunning - did unhinge my view of the world. And now hand me that child. You did bring him along to pacify me, after all."

* * *

Enric looked up in relief when the entrance door opened and Eryn walked into the parlour. He had been pacing up and down with Vedric, trying to soothe him even though such an endeavour was doomed to fail when the source of discontent was hunger.

"Good. I was about to come looking for you. Your son is starving," Enric called out to drown the high-pitched wail originating from the boy in his arms.

Eryn rolled her eyes, pushing aside a stab of guilt. "Waiting a few minutes longer won't cause him to starve. And it's not like I compelled you to take him with you to Tyront." She quickly pulled the shirt over her head. The crying had made her breasts release a few drops of milk and she took a seat, lifting her hands to take her son from her companion.

"How did your lunch with the King go?" Enric enquired and took a seat on the settee next to her, watching Vedric's lips greedily close around his mother's nipple.

"It was rather pleasant, which was surprising. He turned it into a test in political strategy, which was not at all surprising. I indulged him, of course. You know me - complaisant to a fault."

He nodded seriously. "Oh, quite. I have heard you repeatedly described as such. Your most striking character trait. What did he ask you about?"

"Whatever came to his mind. About your motives for going to Pirinkar, Sanaf's attempts at inflicting harm on us and how I failed to use my brain to work it out much sooner, the consequences of my parents' commitment, Vran'el's new position, Vedric's role in this whole bundle of confusion and so on. He complimented me on how I took revenge on Malriel and made sure I had a say in choosing the new ambassador to Anyueel. Though he hinted that he would have appreciated my consulting him in this matter before making a decision on my own here."

"Does this mean he doesn't agree with your choice?"

"No, he says he is fine with Ram'kel of House Arbil. He just would have preferred for me to remember that I was still bound to Anyueel and thereby to him and include him in my political considerations. The interval of my reports and my attempt to have Kilan write to him in my stead did not sit well with him, either."

Enric grinned lopsidedly. "Tyront said something similar. He also would have preferred receiving reports more frequently."

Eryn grimaced in pain when small jaws pinched at her nipple none too gently. "Gentle, my lad. No need to chew on anything yet. As soon as his teeth are fit for use, I'll wean him off my milk or I'll have to heal myself every time he is done eating. Where were we?"

"Infrequent reports to the people you are answerable to," Enric supplied helpfully.

"Well, lucky for them I am back now and they can pester me so much more effectively in person instead of with bird-messages."

"Believe it or not, but Tyront is happy to have you back. I think he secretly looks forward to watching how you do at the Council meetings. He has received reports about your doings in the Senate in Takhan and is impressed."

She snorted. "I caused the senators quite some trouble - and I am not even counting the damage to their roof."

"You were causing the Order enough trouble already even without being on the Council, so they might delude themselves into thinking that this is a handy way of keeping you under control. And Tyront and the King both know that there must be changes in the Order or our son will take over as soon as he is old enough for the testing - provided we retain that custom, despite having since learned how to determine magical potential only a few weeks after birth. Having you contribute to these changes means that you won't resist them. You and I will have quite some influence in that matter - especially as many Council members will count on us insisting on keeping things as they are."

Eryn smiled. "Because we want to see Vedric having full glory and power, presiding over the Order as the most powerful magician of his era?"

"Exactly," Enric nodded, his expression serious.

"Sure. Because being subordinated to my own son is such a fabulous prospect. And it's not as if he wasn't destined to move to

Takhan one day to take over House Vel'kim - provided Malriel doesn't manage to trick or lure him into House Aren somehow."

"That is a possibility we need to take into consideration. As long as Vedric is the only child born to House Vel'kim, Vran'el won't give him up - no matter what Malriel offers him. We are lucky that using underhand tactics is out of the question for her since she would have Valrad against her. He would not take well to having his son coerced by his companion, nor to leaving his House without any successor. That, however, will change as soon as we either have another child..."

"Which we won't," Eryn cut in briskly, her tone brooding.

"...or," he went on as if she hadn't spoken, "Pe'tala provides a child."

"I would rather have him take over House Vel'kim if there is no way of avoiding his being a Head of House one day."

"I know. Avoiding it altogether won't be a choice we will have, I'm convinced of that. At the moment two Houses are keen on having Vedric as heir. The trouble is that the chance of Pe'tala never having children are rather slim, especially as she is about to commit to a man. As soon as she is pregnant, you can depend on Malriel doing everything in her power to get her hands on her grandchild and secure him as her heir."

Eryn lifted the baby up when he had switched from suckling to playing with her nipple and handed him to his father. She slipped her shirt back over her head. "I can't tell you how sick this whole mess makes me! Being compelled to join the Magic Council here is bad enough, but in the Western Territories this whole political game is happening inside families. There is no separation from one's private life like here - trusting family is a foolish thing to do. Both Vran'el and Malriel have demonstrated that to me in a way I am not about to forget in a hurry," she growled.

"Family and politics are interwoven to a large degree in the Western Territories, that is true. But both your brother and your mother love you, no matter how much they need to consider keeping their Houses prosperous and in power."

Eryn shot him a hard look. "Malriel doesn't love me. She sees me as an obstacle to be overcome and she delights in every victory over me."

Enric regarded her patiently, feeling through the mind bond the turmoil which talking about Malriel fomented inside her. "Convincing yourself that she doesn't love you is the easy way out. It makes you feel less guilty and troubled about not loving her the way convention dictates you should. She does love you, a lot. But you have seen enough of House Aren to know that this is how they handle family matters. This is the price for their power, for producing formidable leaders - they don't get along with their mothers and instead seek counsel and warmth with their grandparents who are not in charge of moulding them into fearless politicians and can thus afford to show affection. But you are right, she likes to challenge and defeat you -

just as you enjoy winning over her. This doesn't show disregard for you but demonstrates that she considers you an opponent worth fighting. She is proud of you, immensely so. And she doesn't have to be afraid of being outwitted by you in public - you are Aren, after all. Your accomplishments, even if they consist in defeating her, reflect favourably on Malriel."

Eryn stared at him. "What you described is an incredibly twisted way of using one's own family. I don't approve and I don't want to have any share in it."

He shrugged and lifted his son to change the nappy that had started to give off a familiar odour. "I know. And yet there is no way for you to escape. Regular six-month breaks is all you can expect. Be content with that; it could be worse. And I have a feeling that after serving in the Council for half a year you will be glad enough to escape from Anyueel."

She swallowed, watching him walk upstairs with their son on his arm. Cheerful prospects indeed. She gained her feet and followed him up to the washroom. Leaning against the door frame, she observed Enric's practised moves in undressing the baby and then cleaning him with a wet cloth. It was a sight that would shock his colleagues here no end: the mighty sword fighter handling his son with such ease, completely disregarding that what he was doing was a task for either women or, in more prosperous families, for servants.

"How was your morning at the clinic?" Enric asked into her thoughts.

"Surprising. Interesting. Strange."

He looked up at the hint of sadness in her voice. "Why that?"

She lifted her arms and let them fall again, at a loss for words. "It's nothing. Just…"

"Just what?"

"Forget it. I feel stupid when I say it like that."

Enric finished tying the new, clean nappy on his son and lifted him onto his hip before stepping towards his companion, brushing a strand of hair behind her ear with his index finger. "Why don't you let me be the judge of that, my love?"

Eryn sighed. "It's not the same place I left behind eight and a half months ago. Don't get me wrong - I really like what Pe'tala, Rolan and Lord Poron have done, they have improved a lot - be it the arrangement of the treatment rooms, the teaching schedules or the shift rotation. Everything looks marvellous. But different. I somehow expected to return to the same place we left, but Anyueel, too, has become different from before. At least the clinic has. And Erbál will soon be leaving here, too, and I will have to get used to a new ambassador."

"One you yourself picked," Enric pointed out.

"True enough. But I would have preferred not exchanging him at all," she said sulkily, aware that she was moaning about. "I will get used to it. It was just a little unexpected for me to feel like a stranger here. Will I experience that every time we go from one country to the other?"

He smiled sympathetically. "Maybe. There will be changes in the six months we are gone - on both sides of the sea. We will never really be able to return to the same place we left. But we will be better prepared for such a thing next time. And I suppose keeping in close contact with the country we are not currently staying in will help us keep track of what's going on and reduce any element of surprise when we go there next time."

"I wonder if Orrin and Junar are experiencing this the same way I am."

"You can ask Orrin tomorrow after the Council meeting."

Eryn grimaced. "Tomorrow, eh? I suppose we can consider ourselves lucky that they gave us at least one day to settle back in."

"Try to understand them. We were gone for a long time and there are things they want to learn and others that need to be discussed. The revelation that Vedric is very likely going to be the strongest magician in both the Kingdom and the Western Territories in a few years is not something to be brushed aside. Or the knowledge that we don't have to wait until a magician is fully grown to determine their strength. Then they will want to address the concern of how to handle our frequent absences in the future. We will continue to be members of the Order and the Magic Council despite staying in Takhan. That means they will have to include us in their decisions somehow by first providing us with classified information in a safe way. Then there is Rolan leaving..."

Eryn lifted her hand for him to stop and sighed in defeat. "Alright, I can see that they have every right to be impatient and eager to talk to us. You made your point."

"Good. I wouldn't want you to go there tomorrow and be irritated or unnerved at your first meeting as a member of the Council."

"Will I be sitting next to you?"

"I don't think so. I expect Tyront will place you further away, where he can keep an eye on you more easily without bending forward."

"How sweet. That probably means I will end up on the other end of the table directly opposite him."

Enric shrugged. "We will find out tomorrow. Tell me, did you ask Lord Poron about night duty?"

"I did, yes. He thinks it's a good idea but is worried that without a nursemaid I will overexert myself sooner or later."

"I sentiment I share, as you know."

Eryn shook her head. "There is no need for that. The Council meetings are not quite so frequent from what I remember, and I will just make sure not to work the night before. That way I should be well rested - provided your son lets us sleep. I was planning on visiting Junar and Orrin tonight and asking Junar if she would mind Vedric while we are at the meeting."

"I will accompany you. Strangely enough, I have begun to miss them since we separated in Bonhet."

She raised an eyebrow at him. "Lord Enric has truly made friends, then. Shocking!"

He nodded. "Quite. So you see - the people here will probably find adapting to us quite as challenging."

"Is that meant to comfort me?"

"It is. It's a shared burden, and suffering alone is always harder than spreading it evenly."

"Aren't you a wellspring of wisdom today. I am almost sorry I have to leave you to return to the clinic and learn about all that has been done there in my absence." She bent forward to kiss first her son and then Enric. "Play nice, boys. No wild parties while I am gone."

* * *

Enric smiled down at his companion and squeezed her hand. They were the last ones to enter the Council hall, all other members were already inside. As was the King. Of course he would not miss the first meeting after their return - especially as there was a chance that it would be entertaining with Eryn as a new member of the Council.

Tyront had asked them to make an entrance, so they had arrived a few minutes later and waited until they were sure that everyone was seated.

"Are you ready, my love?" he asked gently and pushed open the doors when she nodded and lifted her chin. They strolled into the room, their fingers intertwined. Twelve pairs of eyes rested on them, some were happy to see them, others looked worried or dismayed and a few went for impassive. The table was now surrounded by thirteen chairs instead of twelve, two of them unoccupied. Enric's old place on Tyront's right side was free, and another one on the opposite side right next to Orrin.

Enric saw a faint smile playing around the corners of her mouth. She was clearly pleased with the arrangement. They stopped in front of Eryn's chair and her companion and superior pulled it out for her to sit before he rounded the table and sat next to the Order's leader.

Tyront cleared his throat and then raised his voice. "It is my pleasure to welcome Lord Enric and Lady Eryn back from the Western Territories. Lord Enric has been, as you were informed, re-established in the Order and Lady Eryn becomes a permanent member of the Magic Council as of today. As you are aware, there are matters of importance to discuss, recent developments that must result in changes unless we wish to face utter chaos at some point. But let us first hear about the occurrences in Takhan. I shall invite Lord Enric to give us a brief summary about his and Lady Eryn's stay in Takhan."

Enric nodded once in confirmation, then addressed the room as a whole, turning slightly in his chair to include King Folrin, seated on his throne to the right, in the audience. He quickly considered what to leave out of his report, then started, "On the day of our arrival in Takhan we were introduced to a fact that was hitherto unknown to us. That is that Valrad of House Vel'kim, whom we had considered to be Lady Eryn's paternal uncle at that time, was in reality her natural father." He saw several nods among the assembled magicians. That was obviously common knowledge already. "After Malriel's departure for Pirinkar I took over the lead of House Aren. Lady Eryn managed to pass the last missing exam to obtain the certificate that qualified her as a healer with full recognition in Takhan, and then worked at the clinic in this capacity. Sanaf, the former ambassador to Anyueel, plotted certain actions with the intention of harming Lady Eryn as he was angry at her for robbing him of his role as ambassador. Ram'an of House Arbil, who you surely remember from his stay here, assisted in apprehending Sanaf in my absence. The Senate in Takhan received a message from Pirinkar that informed us that Malriel had been taken prisoner and accused of a crime. I left with Vran'el of House Vel'kim - Lady Eryn's older brother - to take care of this development and returned a few weeks later to Takhan with the freed Malriel. We needed some days of negotiation to secure her release. Two months after our return from Pirinkar we attended the commitment ceremony of Lady Eryn's parents and then left for Anyueel. We were granted two more weeks of absence to visit my sister and her family, and finally - here we are."

Lord Woldarn's snort interrupted the subsequent silence. "A somewhat... abridged account of what happened, was it not?"

Enric saw Eryn narrow her eyes at him and raised his own brow as if surprised by the statement. "What makes you say that, Lord Woldarn?" Let's see how much you really know, he thought.

"Well, for one the dissolution of your third level commitment bond was omitted completely, as was the fact that Lady Eryn had caused the Senate roof to collapse on the day your son was born. And then I recall the fact of an orphanage being established with what amounted to Malriel of House Aren's life savings."

"Family matters, all three of them," Enric replied placidly. "I don't see how they are of interest to the Order. And you are obviously aware of these facts anyway."

"We are," Lord Seagon cut in, his upper lip curled in dissatisfaction, "yet your reluctance to provide a complete report gives rise to suspicions what else you may find prudent to hide at this point."

Enric suppressed a sigh. The first challenge after his return. He would have to remind the Council that provoking him was not a smart move. Leaning forward, he braced his palms on the heavy table as if to push himself into a standing position any moment. "Are you implying, Lord Seagon, that I am somehow untrustworthy? Are you accusing me of withholding information to the Order's disadvantage?" He narrowed his blue eyes and fixed them on the other man with a glacial stare.

"I said nothing of that sort," the Lord huffed. "But the fact remains that you have divided your loyalty between the Order and the House you let yourself be adopted into. Both yourself and Lady Eryn are the next in line for a leading position in Takhan. In the case of your companion your son will assume that place as soon as he becomes of age, yet in your case the matter is considerably more problematic. You are not only to succeed Lord Tyront if necessary, but Malriel of House Aren might decide to retire and pass on her responsibilities in the course of the next few years. Where will we stand with you, then, Lord Enric of House Aren?"

Enric maintained his inexpressive mask, thinking how to go about dealing with this. This was a sore point - one that several other Council members considered a problem as well. So he had to be careful how to reply to it as otherwise he might alienate more than one colleague. Their willingness to cooperate was now more important than ever if they wanted to deal effectively with the changes that the future would bring. He needed to dispel the concerns in general and still make a point in reigning in Lord Seagon as an individual.

"But then you could always offer Malriel of House Aren your son as an heir in exchange for not calling you to Takhan again when she feels she needs your assistance," Lord Seagon went on with a determined sneer.

Eryn's sharp voice cut through the hall, snapping like a whip when she spat, "You'd better mind what comes out of your mouth if you wish to retain its use!"

"This is not quite the tone we are accustomed to here. We don't simply hurl insults or threats around when meeting in these halls, and neither do we collapse roofs when something does not suit our liking," Lord Seagon said patronisingly. "It seems you have quite some adapting to do as it stands, Lady Eryn."

"You lost all and any right to be treated with respect or even politeness when you proposed treating my son as a commodity to ensure the succession in the Order," Eryn replied coldly.

Enric looked at her, feeling through the mind bond the fury she was experiencing and the effort it cost her to appear calm and collected while expressing controlled disapproval. She was doing well, he thought - setting boundaries in a manner that demonstrated that she was not to be taken lightly because she was the youngest member of the Council, more yet a woman, though keeping her temper in check to avoid losing her credibility.

Orrin next to her had folded his arms and glared at Lord Seagon through half-closed lids. He, too, was anything but thrilled with the suggestion. The other magicians were waiting in tense silence, watching Eryn and Lord Seagon in turn, worried and at the same time eager to see what would happen next.

Enric cast a quick glance to Tyront to see if he intended to intervene, but his superior just lifted an eyebrow at him, thus signalling to him that he expected Enric to take care of this situation himself. Which made sense, Enric thought and sighed deep within. He had to regain the respect he was owed.

"What a very... inspired input, Lord Seagon," Enric raised his voice, letting a hint of sarcasm resonate in it. "Yet as far as I am aware, history suggests that neither the Order nor the Kingdom have taken to selling their citizens. I would thank you for not attempting to establish this practise with my son. I share his mother's lack of enthusiasm at this prospect."

There was no sniggering or other audible sign of amusement, but a few eyes had a gleeful glint in them and every other mouth looked rather more tense than usual from the effort of not grinning.

"As for the other matter you addressed," Enric went on, "my divided loyalty, as you chose to refer to it - let me assure you that Malriel of House Aren, who is only a few years younger than Lord Tyront and does to my knowledge not intend to retire from her position any time soon, is very well aware that her claim to me comes second to the Order's. His Majesty approved my adoption into House Aren back then, so if you wish to dispute the wisdom of this decision, I would refer you to the very man who made it, as I am hardly in a position to speak for him - especially if he is so conveniently present today."

Lord Seagon's face had gone pale, his lips squeezed together into a thin line, and he very pointedly avoided looking at the throne, whose occupant was following the discussion with interest.

Enric let the older man stew for another few moments, pretending to give him an opportunity to address the matter to the King, then decided that it was time to return to business.

"There are several important points for us to discuss that will influence the Order long-term. These discussions will very likely take several months until we reach agreement. Such points include Lady Eryn's and my regular six-month absences from Anyueel, the fact that my son is going be stronger than myself - and also Lord Tyront for that matter - before he is fully grown, Lord Orrin's magically gifted and also very strong daughter, and the implications of this for our traditional method of granting power. In addition to this we are, thanks to knowledge obtained in Takhan, now in a position to determine the presence and strength of magical potential in children when they are only a few weeks old. We need to decide if and in what context we wish to make use of this skill."

He nodded to Orrin when the Head of Warriors raised his index finger. "Yes, Lord Orrin?"

"There is another point I wish to add to your list. Since my return here two weeks ago I have frequently been approached and asked about the game we introduced in Takhan. In my capacity as Head of Warriors I wish to invite the Council to consider this as a competitive and effective approach to teaching magical combat."

Tyront lifted his head, signalling that he was taking back the chair. "Duly noted, Lord Orrin. It seems that Lady Eryn's idea has been well-received on both sides of the sea."

Several heads turned to Eryn, who merely arched her brow as if challenging them to voice disbelief at her being able to come up with a useful idea. None dared.

*　*　*

Eryn marched across the Palace square towards the warriors' quarters to pick up her son from Junar, who had been minding him. Enric and Orrin were not far behind her. Her strides were long and spoke of impatience.

"So, how did you like your first Council meeting?" Orrin asked lightly. "Was it what you expected?"

She shot him a dark look over her shoulder. "It was a waste of my time and a strain on my nerves. It was worse than I had expected. I mean, these are all grown men! Why these useless discussions about nullities, underhand insults and derisive remarks that just cost time as they give rise to squabbling? How many hours of my life did the Council just steal that I could have used otherwise?"

"Two and a half," Enric supplied helpfully.

"No more than that?" she grimaced. "It felt like four at the very least!"

"It could have been worse," Orrin shrugged and opened the door for her to enter first when they reached the building. "At least Lord Seagon kept his mouth shut after Enric told him to question the King when he had a problem."

"That was a small blessing at least," Eryn grumbled. "Seriously, what was he thinking when he made that remark about Vedric and Malriel?"

"Lord Seagon's thoughts are not a realm which into which I would wish to venture in the near future," Enric said softly. "But at least he made himself useful by offering himself as a target for both of us to assert ourselves. It would have been unavoidable in the long run, and now it's taken care of."

She frowned in confusion. "I see why I needed to demonstrate my unwillingness to be treated like that, but why would you have to assert yourself? Don't tell me your fearsome reputation appears not to have survived a few months being away from here?"

"Memories are a tricky thing," her companion explained while they climbed the stairs. "Impressions lose their intensity unless there is constant affirmation. And this affirmation has been missing for these last six months. I will probably have to set one or two more examples to remind them why they used to be more careful around me."

"And I suppose knocking one or two of them out is not something you'd consider...?"

"Not until they attack first or provoke you enough for you to get away with it," Orrin smiled. "But I like the simplicity of the idea."

They arrived at their destination and the warrior trainer opened the door to his parlour, preceding his superiors into his quarters. Junar was sitting on a chair with her daughter on her lap, both of them with pale green mush smeared across their faces, clothes and hands. The table in front of them was equally messy and held a small bowl with remnants of a meal along with a spoon.

"Oh my," Enric swallowed. "This looks like a war zone."

"I am so glad you are here!" sighed Junar, as she almost wept with relief.

"Looks like you were having a party here," Orrin smiled and lifted his daughter, carefully holding her at arm's length to avoid having his clothes decorated in the same manner.

Junar rose quickly to fetch a wet towel and remove the worst of the mess from both the child and herself. "We are still getting used to taking our meals with a spoon."

At that moment a high-pitched wail came from the direction of what used to be the guest room but had now been converted into a nursery.

"Ah yes, it seems somebody has just awoken right on time," Eryn smiled and turned to pick up her son from Téa's crib. "How long did he sleep?" she asked when she returned with Vedric happily gurgling in her arms.

"For about ten minutes. And another five before that. Don't ask me how often we have played that little game. He falls asleep on the sofa, I pick him up to put him in Téa's bed, he wakes up a few minutes later and cries, I bring him to the parlour again - and we start the whole procedure again."

Eryn swallowed. "That sounds like you had a very... entertaining time. I suppose we had better work out a new arrangement for when the three of us need to be at the Council meeting." Damn. That was inconvenient.

"When is the next one scheduled?" Junar asked, exhausted.

"In three weeks," Orrin supplied.

His companion closed her eyes for a moment and sighed. "That might just be enough time for me to recover enough to want to give it another try."

"You don't have to do this," Enric said softly. "We can ask Plia to look after Vedric for a few hours."

The seamstress shook her head. "The girl already works too much. She'll just add on another few hours to her day when everybody else has left. No, I will manage. I just need to find a rhythm that works with two kids."

Eryn bit her lip. Plia's working routine was something Lord Poron had mentioned yesterday at the clinic as well. He was considering starting somebody to assist the girl, and had asked Rolan to check if he could squeeze the extra expense into their budget somehow.

"How did the meeting go?" Junar then asked and looked at Eryn. "You look tense. So probably not too well."

"It was tiresome and irritating. I didn't believe Enric when he said that after six months I would be glad to get away from the Council for a while - I do now. I wouldn't mind getting rid of them a lot sooner. Tomorrow, for example."

"That bad?"

"At least from my point of view. Orrin and Enric seem to be used to that foolish drama, I just find it an unnecessary drain on my time and patience."

"So there was no useful output whatsoever?" Junar grimaced.

"It wasn't quite that bad," Orrin smiled. "Despite minor quarrels and power games we managed to agree on a thing or two. Eryn and Pe'tala will spend the next three weeks collecting information by testing those children born in the city in the last six months for magical potential. Eryn is meant to present the findings at the next meeting. I was commissioned to draw up a plan for starting up the game here in the city including a complete set of rules and a recommendation for a designated area to be closed off."

Eryn noted that he left a few other matters unmentioned that were not meant to be shared outside the Council, like the first catastrophic attempts at discussing the traditional way of granting power in the Order, namely in accordance with the magical strength a magician was born with. Or that Eryn was to be included in a lot more everyday administrative matters that concerned the Order than she would have wished. As the division into the two areas of warrior training and healing didn't include her, she was, together with Enric and Tyront, one of three people to be directly responsible for both. As if being dragged to these tedious meetings every two or three weeks wasn't already enough of a strain.

Enric held his son while Eryn disrobed enough to grant Vedric access to his food supply. They had returned just in time for his meal. He handed the baby back, kissed his companion and then took his leave. It was Eryn's turn to mind him, Enric was expected in Tyront's study. They were now starting to put their new daily routine with the Order and Vedric to the test.

* * *

"I am sceptical," Pe'tala frowned and leaned back in her chair at her study at the clinic. "This works fine at home in Takhan, but people here are not used to sharing the tasks raising a child involves - and neither are they used to showing consideration for the needs of people who attempt it. You and Enric have several occasions where you both need to be present at the same time. This will not work without employing somebody to assist you. What does the rest of the Order have to say about that?"

Eryn rolled her eyes. "They haven't said anything, at least not to our faces. They gossip behind our back and mostly agree that we have lost our minds completely, and that this is what happens when being exposed to foreign influences for too long."

"Not entirely unexpected, is it? Most of the Council members are spineless, and the rest are not high enough in rank to criticise you just like that. You have been back hardly more than a week and I see that you are tired. This is not good. You should refrain from working at the clinic for now, at least until Vedric is old enough not to depend on you for breastfeeding any longer."

Eryn looked patiently at her younger sister. "Tala, I'm not willing to spend my time between raising a child and pandering to the Order's whims. I need something for myself, something that enables me to interact with adults and gives me a feeling of accomplishment - I need to know that what I do means something. My first Council meeting showed me fairly clearly that being involved in the Order more will not give me that feeling. Healing, be it ever so occasionally, is what I need to stay in a good frame of mind and in contact with the discipline as such and my colleagues. I was gone for more than eight months - I can't afford to stay away from the clinic any longer or I will become an outsider. I already feel like I don't belong here anymore after all the things that have changed."

Pe'tala sighed and rested her cheek on her fist. "I know this is hard for you. Both reconciling your family with both your professions and getting used to everything we changed around here. But I trust you are in the meantime at peace with Lord Poron being in charge of the clinic, are you not? Even if the Order had given the position to you before, they would have taken it away from you now with Vran'el rearranging your life the way he has."

"Yes, I'm fine with that. Lord Poron is the best choice I could have wished for, after all. From the reports I read in my new capacity of being responsible for both disciplines I can see that he is doing pretty well. He is in contact with Valrad to arrange for the exchange programme between the clinics. I look forward to seeing how that turns out."

The younger sister raised her brow. "Still referring to him with his name, sister? I remember his parting remark about that."

Eryn rolled her eyes. "He isn't here, so why should I bother? I've known him for about one and a half years now, half of that time thinking he was my uncle. I think my calling him father in public and referring to him as such with other people around should be enough for now."

"He wants you to mean it, though, Eryn. He will not give up until you stop considering it an act of protecting his reputation and really seeing him as your parent."

"Leave me be, will you?" Eryn groaned. "I have six months before I have to deal with that again. There are several issues I need to get through, and Valrad and his hurt pride are not among them presently."

"That is what you think. You write to him frequently, do you not? If you keep addressing him with his name instead of father - the title he is due from his point of view - he might decide to use his position of head of his clinic to... gently persuade you to change your attitude by making his cooperation dependant on your accommodating him."

Eryn's expression clearly displayed her dismay. "He would sink as low as that?"

"I wonder at your questioning his methods after he took it upon himself to supervise you after you received your insignia. You really should know better than to cling still to this amiable facade he uses to cover the iron determination lying underneath."

Pe'tala was right, she thought. And Enric himself had pointed out more than once that Valrad would hardly have managed successfully to lead a powerful House such as Vel'kim without asserting himself regularly.

"I will think of something for my messages to him. Maybe I can just forego addressing him at all for now. I was raised in this barbaric country here, after all. It's just one of the things I was never properly taught - how to write a message..."

The younger woman waggled her head for a moment, considering that idea. "He might let you get away with that. Do not deceive yourself into thinking that he will not see right through it, though. He is not slow to catch on, you know. But let us use the last half hour before your night duty starts to talk about how to go about determining the magical strength of those children born around here recently."

Eryn straightened. Good, that topic was definitely more to her liking than that last unresolved issue with Valrad. "I think we should set a few dates and inform the children's parents that they are expected to come here to the clinic. That is far more efficient than our running across the city from door to door. Rolan surely has the birth lists somewhere and can send out the messages."

"I agree. I will instruct the other healers on how to go about performing this examination. Or do I need the Order's permission for that?"

Eryn shrugged. "Consider that suggestion approved. If the Council complains, I will take the heat. I would rather apologise than ask for their permission. They are such a sluggish, uncooperative lot."

"That is the price you have to pay for your importance, sister," Pe'tala grinned.

"Thank you so much. Remind me not to come to you if I need comfort and sympathy," Eryn snorted.

"Come on, it cannot be that bad, can it? You have Enric and Orrin to back you. Then there is Lord Poron, and Lord Tyront is also mostly on your side. And I doubt that all the other eight Council members are against you on principle."

"That maybe not, but they are sceptical, annoyingly traditional, and resistant to change and progress. Trust me - Senate meetings in Takhan are a walk along Kingsway by comparison. By the way, from what I heard your own dealings with Lord Tyront were not exactly always amiable, either."

Pe'tala shrugged. "What can I say? He does have a certain propensity for ordering people around, and I happen to be outside his immediate area of influence and do not shy back from reminding him of this from time to time." She sneered. "I can tell you in all honesty that he will not be sorry to see me leave here in a few months. I wonder if he made my being called back to Takhan a condition for agreeing to letting you and Enric spend half your time there."

Eryn laughed. "You mean he bought himself six months of peace each year by getting rid of both of us for that time? I seriously doubt that. He has come to like me - especially considering that I am no longer in a position to oppose him with impunity."

"That may be the case - yet there is always the chance that the irritation I cause him will exceed his newfound fondness for you." With that she got up. "I will leave now for today. Do you want me to drop by your house to see if Enric needs any help with my nephew?"

"That's really sweet of you, but I'm confident that he will manage without help for a few hours. He will come by later so I can feed Vedric before they retire. And his mood is currently not so great, so you might want to stay clear of him for the moment."

"It is not? Why is that? What have you done now?"

Deciding not to comment on the insinuation that she was to blame for it, Eryn explained, "A letter from his father was delivered today around noon. It seems news of my importance and noble birth have finally reached Anwin in that little town he lives in, and he has decided that I am no longer to be considered a western spy, but a worthy addition to his family. He congratulated Enric on choosing such a useful woman for himself that has not only such formidable connections to the high circles of might and power in Takhan, but will without a doubt increase his own standing in Anyueel as a consequence. He concluded with an invitation, mentioning that Enric's mother has expressed a wish to meet me and her grandson. Enric was - and probably still is - furious about the supposition that he chose me for nothing other than my political worth. It was what Anwin would have done according to him, and he doesn't want his own deeds to be associated with his father's motives."

Pe'tala whistled through her teeth. "It seems that he, too, has some reconciling to do with his family. Will he accept the invitation?"

"I don't know. I am trying to convince him to take me and Vedric there, even if only for a day or two. I think it would do him good to see his mother again. They write to each other once or twice a year, but haven't met for about ten years from what I know."

"Good luck with your attempts at making him go, then. Do you need anything before I leave? I think I showed you everything you need." Her eyes stared at the floor unseeingly while she was going through the most important points. "The resting room with the bed, the box for the money you collect, the night treatment room with all the medications and instruments you will likely need, the file where you need to write down patient information and the treatment you carried out... I could stay here for two or three hours, you know, just in case there..."

"Off you go!" Eryn interrupted her and waved her off. "I'll manage, don't worry. Go home. Now. And make Plia leave as well if you want to help me."

Pe'tala nodded once, then grabbed her cloak from the hook on the wall. "As you wish. I will see you tomorrow morning, then."

* * *

Enric yawned loudly and looked up from his report when Vedric in the crib next to his desk stirred. He had taken to sleeping mostly during the day - in return for being kept wide awake and active at night. Little Téa in contrast started sleeping through the night a while ago, affording her busy parents a few hours of peace and quiet to regain their strength.

A moment later he heard the entrance door opening and shutting and the rustling of clothes that suggested that Eryn was wrestling her robes off and hanging them on the hook in the niche next to the door. Little later she appeared in the door frame to his study, her cheeks red from the cold air outside.

"Hello, boys," she smiled and came closer to kiss Enric and then turn to the crib and the happily gurgling infant. Lifting him up, she took a seat on the small sofa to the left side of the large desk.

"And?" Enric asked, glad for the interruption. The figures had started dancing in front of his eyes; a sure sign that he was in need of a break. "Did everything work out as planned? Did you have a load of babies and toddlers at the clinic today?"

"Yes, they did turn up alright. It's amazing how eager people are to obey when a message bears the Order's seal."

"As well they should. We are a fearsome lot."

Eryn snorted derisively. "Fearsome lot indeed. When did you last have a chance to demonstrate your fearsomeness - not counting the training grounds where you just play around a little to stay in shape? But then I suppose one could consider the Council a formidable force - their most lethal manoeuvre is boring their opponents to death."

"You need to stop talking about them like that. You are a member now, and so am I. You ought to demonstrate a little more respect here."

"I'll work on it," she shrugged, her tone making it clear that it was an empty promise to shut him up.

He shook his head at her, wondering when she would stop referring to the Order in a way that indicated that she herself was not a part of it. "So, how did the examination turn out? And surprises so far?"

Eryn smiled broadly and leaned back, pushing her plait out of Vedric's reach just before he could grab it. He had recently discovered that it made a fabulous plaything and caused quite a funny reaction in the form of grimaces and exclamations of pain when it was pulled the right way.

"We tested the daughters of two magicians today - one of them has the gift. She will be quite strong, too. Not as strong as Téa, but not too far behind, either. And of the other forty children of non-magicians we had a look at, four girls and three boys turned out to be magicians as well. With women back in the game, there will be a significant increase in magicians over the years to come."

Enric leaned back in his chair and nodded thoughtfully. "Indeed. And that's only in the city. We have not even started to remove the barriers in the heads of all the people in the countryside. How much longer will it take for you and Tala to test all children that have been born here in the last year?"

"Another two days. Do I need to send word to Tyront already or can it wait until we are through with all children?"

"I suggest you inform him of what you know now. He will consider it a gesture of goodwill - especially considering your usual approach to reporting to him."

She shrugged. "It's not as if his spies don't tell him what's going on even without me providing him with information. All this is just his way of making sure that I don't forget who is higher up."

Enric hid his smile and nodded seriously. "Which is absolutely superfluous in your case as you would never ever forget that and are known to act accordingly."

"I never asked him to take upon himself the burden of leading me - you lot wanted me in the Order and refuse to let me leave it again," she shot back and decided that she didn't want to pursue that topic any longer. Instead she pointed to an envelope on his desk that looked suspiciously foreign. "What's that? Mail from the west?"

He nodded, not objecting to her change of direction. He had wanted to tell her about that anyway. "Yes. Malhora has sent us information about three possible plots of land that are available for purchase and that she determined as appropriate for us." He picked up a folded map of Takhan and spread it on the surface of his desk, covering his paperwork underneath.

Eryn stood, placing Vedric on her hip. She looked at the three red marks indicating the locations her grandmother had singled out.

"This one here is not suitable. Too close to the Aren residence," she stated with determination.

Enric chuckled. "Why don't we have look at what Malhora has to say about the land plots before just picking one at random? There are minor matters to consider - such as size, price, location and suitability for construction." He reached over for the information sheets Malhora had attached. "Let's see. The first one, which you excluded on principle, has the largest piece of land. Good price, good location; on a slight slope, but not so much as to make the construction of a building difficult. Then we have the second one over here," he said, indicating another mark more towards the west of the city. "Quite a bit smaller, still a good location; the price is slightly higher."

"The price is higher despite the fact that it's so much smaller?" Eryn frowned.

"That's because of the location. It's closer to the city centre, not far from the cultural hub of the city and yet not in the centre of activity. It's a quiet place that's not too remote."

"And the third one?"

"The one further south... closer to the docks and therefore in the less prosperous part of the city. This one is the most inexpensive plot of land of the three. A bit larger than the second one, still within easy walking distance to the city centre."

Eryn grimaced. "I don't really have to ask which one you favour, do I?"

He shrugged. "Your choice, my love."

"So if I chose the cheapest one closer to the docks and further away from both the Vel'kim and Aren residences, you would be absolutely fine with it? You would make no attempts whatever to persuade me to overlook the minor disadvantage of the proximity to the Aren premises in order to have a large garden in a more fancy part of the city?"

Enric grinned broadly. "Is that what you want? The phrasing of that question somehow indicates that you yourself think that the first piece of land would be the best choice, but are unwilling to admit it."

"You know, I don't need a particularly posh part of the city to live in," she sighed. "I am absolutely fine with a less wealthy neighbourhood. I'm not really willing to pay more just to be closer to the other residences."

"The one in the south is also the furthest one from the clinic," he pointed out casually.

"Is there one Malhora prefers? Any recommendations from her?"

"She thinks the first one is a real bargain."

Eryn rolled her eyes. "That is probably because of the proximity to the Aren residence. She just wants to have us nearby when she comes to the city and stays at Malriel's place."

Enric raised his brow. "What makes you think she will stay there and not at our place? She gets along with you a lot better than with her daughter. What's more she will probably want to spend as much time as possible with her great-grandson whenever she has a chance. So I would think that the distance to the Aren residence is not necessarily a consideration for Malhora."

"So you think we should choose the first one, the largest plot?"

"I think it is the most advantageous option. There is good infrastructure around, the price is right, it's only a ten-minute walk to the clinic... which is an advantage not only for you, but also for Pe'tala and Rolan who will both live with us and work at the clinic, too."

Eryn exhaled and tilted her head back, defeated. "Very well, then we'd better make the rational decision and take it."

Enric nodded. "I bow to your decision. Well done," he said quickly before she could change her mind. He had reached that same conclusion already and was glad she gave in so quickly. "I'll despatch a bird to Malhora tonight and ask her to purchase it under my name. Unfortunately our gold is still in the Vel'kim vaults, and her going to Vran'el to ask him for the money would make it impossible to keep our little scheme to circumvent his order a secret. He wouldn't rest before he knew what I needed such a large amount for. But then he was the one to tell me that he as a Head of House can no longer handle my financial and legal matters in the Western Territories, so I will just ask him to deliver all our gold into Malhora's custody." He folded the map again and pulled a blank sheet of paper out of a drawer to note down his thoughts. "The next thing will be to have the residence planned. I would say we leave the general outline to a local contractor and just make such changes as we see fit. I have read a little about the architecture in these parts, though not nearly enough to know about the right sort of ventilation with the correct number, size and positions of openings and whatever other considerations one should deal with in such a climate."

"I want House Roal to take care of that. I was satisfied with their work on the orphanage," Eryn pointed out.

Enric frowned and pursed his lips while considering that. "I know that they are the best choice from a business point of view, yet both our Houses are at loggerheads with them. You were pushing it already when you entered into a contract with them with the orphanage, but you had the authority of your position as Head of House Aren behind you back then. In this case we would both be going against the wishes of our current Heads. That might be going a bit too far."

Eryn's smile was grim when she remarked, "By purchasing land and having our own residence built we are already going against the Head of House Vel'kim. And House Aren is in a business relationship with them already thanks to the agreement I entered into with House Roal, whether they like it or not."

"As you wish," he sighed, resigned to the trouble they were both about to get themselves into, and resumed writing on his sheet. "Malhora might need to ask somebody from another House to arrange for the construction, though. It wouldn't look good if a member of House Aren is seen to be talking to House Roal. I will suggest that she ask Ram'an for assistance in this matter. We can rely on him to keep this to himself. And once Vran'el hears of the whole thing, Ram'an can always duck behind his obligation to confidentiality when it comes to his clients."

Eryn watched him scribble a few lines, waiting for him to put aside the pen before saying, "Why don't you take care of this tomorrow? You look tired. You should go to bed early."

Enric nodded and rubbed his face. "I probably should, yes. I had better make use of the few nights you are not on night duty due to your current day assignment with the examinations. I dimly remember that Téa was not as active during the nights when she was Vedric's age."

His companion nodded. "No, she wasn't. But then I suppose that's only fair. Junar's pregnancy was a lot more trying than what I went through, so I suppose being able to sleep through the nights almost from the beginning is her compensation for that." She nudged him on. "Go on, catch up on some sleep. I'll feed your son and then maybe take a walk with him and Urban to clear my head after having the entire day with wailing children." She lifted her mouth for him to kiss before he left his study and went upstairs. Eryn looked after him, feeling a twinge of guilt at seeing him so exhausted. She had wanted to address the subject of visiting his parents again tonight, but he was in no shape for discussion and needed to rest. Tomorrow would be better. If she managed to persuade him somehow, he could at least not claim later that he had been too weak to resist and insinuate that she had used this to her advantage.

* * *

Eryn grinned broadly when she and Orrin left the Council hall after the meeting was over. As Council meetings went, this one had been a lot less tiresome than the last one. There was progress, however much resistance they had to overcome. Eryn had delivered her report about the results of testing infants recently born in the city, and the Council members had been shocked about the extent of the magical potential they would need to deal with in a few years. Removing that tiny shield in people's brains had obviously had considerable impact on the level of magic that was passed on to the newest generation of magicians.

Now, at least, everyone was aware that they soon had to change the manner of granting power, or the Order's fate would lie in the hands of a couple of young adults in a mere two decades. Vedric was, so far, still the one showing the most significant level of magical potential, but several others came very close to Enric's strength. Unless things started changing, that would make for a very interesting time in the Order when the new magicians were old enough to take over.

Eryn had refrained from pointing out how much she welcomed the current development, though she could see that her sentiments were certainly not lost on most of her colleagues in the Council. Having stronger magicians and more of them meant not only that the Order had to rethink its long-established structures, but also that magical abilities alone would no longer be a guarantee to being considered special; it would become a secondary skill that required more effort than just being lucky enough to be born with the gift.

After her own report, Orrin had presented a detailed plan to his colleagues of how games similar to the ones carried out in Takhan could be organised here. Eryn was surprised at how smoothly that topic was handled - hardly any resistance at all. A few of the Council members had even mentioned with suspicious casualness that they were willing to aid Orrin's endeavours at establishing this new way of assessing combat skills by agreeing to participate themselves. Only to aid in lending the event more credibility, of course, and not out of any ordinary motive such as feeling the urge to be playful or anything...

Eryn couldn't help but snigger at the memory of the attempts at concealing their eagerness to join the game. Orrin's reaction had been appropriate. Nodding earnestly, he had thanked his colleagues for their sacrifice without having a single muscle in his cheek twitch and reveal his amusement, thereby enabling the men to sign up for the game without losing any face. Having to admit that despite their advanced age, the idea of sneaking through the night-time streets of Anyueel hunting their fellow magicians excited them, would hardly have enabled them to maintain any pretence to dignity. But their willingness to participate in the game, whatever disguises they required to admit themselves to doing so, did not only stop them from trying to choke off the game from happening, but would also signal to other magicians that joining it was acceptable.

"Nicely done, old man," she murmured to Orrin low enough for only him to hear. "Keeping a straight face almost finished me off."

"Which was plain enough to see for those who know you at least a little," the warrior mumbled under his breath.

Eryn knew he was right. Tyront had sent her a warning glance across the table, Enric's lips had twitched once in recognition of her amusement, and Lord Poron's eyes had glinted with a spark of humour as well when looking at her.

"What can I say? I am an honest person who prefers to communicate sentiments openly instead of hiding my true feelings behind a mask of deception," she smiled.

"Hardly," Tyront's voice behind her contradicted. She resisted the impulse to turn around and kept walking. She didn't like people being able to sneak up close enough to listen to her without her noticing it. "You are just a terrible liar."

"Shouldn't you be glad about that?" Eryn retorted lightly. "Imagine I managed to lie to you more effectively - that would certainly make your life even tougher."

"How about not lying to me at all?" her superior growled, but there was no real weight in his question.

"I'll give that option some consideration," she promised and glanced over her shoulder to wink at him.

Enric turned up at her side. "What option?" he enquired.

"Not lying to Tyront," she explained.

"Ah, that one," her companion nodded as if they had already been discussing that topic at length on several occasions.

"Lady Eryn," another voice behind her called out. Lord Poron. She stopped and turned to him, the three men around her following suit. "That information on the increased number and strength of magically gifted children had made me think," he offered.

Enric noted how the other magicians who had left the Council hall after them stopped as well, unable to move on without pushing aside the group that was blocking the way and that, inconveniently enough, consisted of the five highest ranking magicians in the Order.

"My love, I think we should continue this conversation elsewhere or at least step aside to let others pass," he murmured in Eryn's ear. "We are causing some congestion, and nobody really dare to squeeze past or push us aside."

She looked at the men shuffling around, some of them pretending that they were not at all being inconvenienced by the impromptu meeting in the corridor, others shooting them annoyed glances. She stood to one side and watched Orrin, Lord Poron and Enric do the same. Tyront remained where he was. The great leader could obviously not be bothered to make room for his underlings, Eryn thought with wry amusement.

When only the five of them were left alone in the corridor, she turned back to Lord Poron. "You were saying?"

The septuagenarian magician looked thoughtful. "I couldn't help but wonder about something I read in Lord Enric's report after you returned from Takhan from your first visit. The Houses in the Western Territories established the custom of forging companionship agreements for children about three hundred years ago."

Eryn frowned. "They did? I thought they have been using their offspring to connect their Houses longer than that."

Enric next to her shook his head. "Not quite that emphatically. Before the war they merely joined their children when they were grown up without promising them to other families at such an early age."

Tyront cleared his throat. "So you think this change had something to do with the war between our countries?"

Lord Poron pursed his lips. "It would be quite a considerable coincidence, wouldn't you agree? Especially considering our recent discovery of the effect which removing the shield in the head has."

Enric nodded slowly, seeing were his older colleague was going. He turned to his companion. "Do you remember what you said when we had Ram'an over for dinner that one evening?"

She thought for a moment. "The one when he told us about the war? No, what did I say?"

"You were dismayed at how Ram'an told you about your origins - about your being the progeny of two powerful magical bloodlines.

Later that evening you said that this sounded like a breeding programme to you."

Eryn smiled. "That was probably a little strong."

Lord Poron slowly shook his head. "I wonder if that was not some unconscious insight very close to the truth. The Ambassador mentioned that our magically gifted women were taken to Takhan after the war. We assumed that it was merely to stop our ancestors from producing strong magicians, but what if the purpose was at the same time to enable people in the Western Territories to have powerful offspring by mixing their bloodlines with ours?"

Tyront let his gaze wander along the ceiling, thinking. "It would make sense," he said slowly. "Judging from the considerable increase in magical strength in our children since the removal of the barrier, our ancestors were likely somewhat stronger than we are nowadays. The Ambassador said that the Western Territories barely won the war, and even that through luck instead of superiority. They could have come up with the idea of joining magically gifted offspring so as to create new generations with increased strength in case they had to brave another attack from our side of the sea."

Eryn's brow furrowed. "Nothing I read or heard during our stay in Takhan would suggest that. The companionship agreements are merely used to cement the alliances between the Houses, even though magically gifted children are in greater demand than those without that potential."

"I suspect that they themselves are probably not aware anymore why the companionship agreements were established like that after the war," Enric mused. "I think that the knowledge of our magician's considerable strength faded into obscurity over the centuries. That would explain why Ram'an thought that the barrier caused the strength in individual magicians here in Anyueel to rise as a counterbalance to their reduced numbers. He was wrong. The barrier kept our numbers down and reduced our strength." He looked at Orrin. "If what we see in Téa and Vedric is what we may expect in future magicians regarding strength, I see why our former enemies must have been terrified and eager to even the odds in case of another war. Vedric is going to be stronger than any other magician that we know of both here in the Kingdom and the Western Territories, after all."

Orrin grimaced. "Then you'd better make sure to teach that boy that protecting those weaker than him is a lot more rewarding than subduing us. I'm too old to be enslaved." Then he added as an afterthought, "And don't even think of making me train that boy sword fighting. If he turns out anything like either of his parents, he would finally drive me insane."

Eryn patted him on his back and said lightly, "No worries, Orrin. As we are forced to switch countries every six months, it makes more sense for Enric to train him, anyway."

The warrior's face broke into a happy grin. "Justice at last."

Enric raised an eyebrow at him. "Vedric might turn out to be a well-behaved and quiet child for all we know."

Tyront and Lord Poron both chuckled, and even Eryn looked doubtful.

"Sure," Orrin chortled. "You just go on believing that."

* * *

Eryn took a deep breath and steeled herself to broach the topic she had been pushing ahead of her for several days now. It was time to address it again. She shifted Vedric on her hip. Taking him with her to what would probably turn into a confrontation with his father was playing unfairly, she knew. But the child had a calming effect both on Enric and herself, so that might prove the advantage she needed. Well, calming was maybe not exactly the right term here; rather that the presence of an infant made them each show more restraint than they might otherwise.

She knocked at the door to his study and entered before he had a chance to invite her in. He looked up at them and a slow smile spread across his face; one Eryn was positive wouldn't remain there for long as soon as he heard what she had come to talk about.

"My two favourite people," Enric said softly and rose from his chair to take his son from her and sit on the sofa to one side of his desk, patting the spot beside him for Eryn to join him.

"Yes," she smiled. "It's amazing what an impact a family can have on a man's happiness, isn't it? Speaking of family," she ventured and knew that it was a clumsy start as soon as the words had left her mouth. Enric's expression darkened when he realised what she wanted to discuss.

"No," he just said, deceptively softly.

"I received another letter from your father," she went on as if he hadn't spoken at all. "He has invited us to visit your family. He would really like to see his grandson. And there was another letter from your mother as well. You know, she seems really nice - at least from what I can tell from a single sheet of paper. I would very much like to meet her. She would love to see Vedric too. As well as you. It has been a while since…"

"Yes," Enric interrupted her, keeping his voice calm to avoid startling his son, "more than a decade. It was in her power to come here and see me. She is aware well enough what has kept me from visiting my parents' place in all these years."

His parents' place, she thought; not his home.

"From what I gleaned she is very conscious of your father's wishes, and seeks to avoid disharmony," Eryn said, very carefully.

He closed his eyes and exhaled. "That was an unusually tactful way of phrasing it. Let's refrain from blandishing the facts and face the cold truth: Avoiding her companion's wrath was more important to her than seeing me or Leris. Never once did she visit either of us."

Eryn watched him, her heart bleeding for the pain he felt. Even without the mind bond she could see it plainly enough in the tenseness of his jaw muscles, hear it in the detachment his voice had, something that hardly masked the sorrow underneath. But letting him continue ignoring his family in this way would not help him. Neither would showing him sympathy; he would just brush it aside. She needed to challenge him. Maybe even trick him so that he could permit himself to undertake that trip without giving in to his father, but instead to his companion.

* * *

Enric unrolled the large sheets of paper on Eryn's desk.

"This is the proposal for the ground floor. As you can see, this is the typical outline for a Takhan residence. The entrance area in the front, behind it the storage rooms and the stairway to the main room." He removed the first sheet and revealed plans for the first floor. "The large, open main room in the centre, from which four corridors branch out in all directions. Each corridor contains five rooms."

Eryn looked at the drawings with a sceptical expression. "I know that grandeur is a must for a Takhan house when it comes to space and all that, but we don't really have to adhere to that custom, you know. They will forgive us if we are a little more modest with our abode. It is not the main residence of a House, after all. When I asked you for our own place in Takhan, I didn't really have a full-blown mansion in mind, but something a bit more restrained."

"Restraint is not our friend here, my love. If we moved into a regular city house without extensive premises, this would give rise to speculations that might harm House Aren and Vel'kim. People would wonder if there were any problems between us and our Heads of Houses since we chose to live in a confined space rather than stay in their spacious residences. And we have a second family with us. Tala and Rolan will need an entire corridor for themselves. A bedroom, a study for either of them, bedrooms for prospective children..."

"Which would still leave three corridors with fifteen rooms for the three of us," she pointed out. "That is a good deal more than we need, than we could even use if we really made an effort. One study for me, another one for you, a bedroom for us both, another one for Vedric, two or three guest rooms for whenever Orrin and Junar visit," she listed with the aid of her fingers. "That makes seven rooms at the most. We can easily do with three corridors."

"Malhora will be staying with us occasionally. And there might be occasions when your sister has guests as well."

"That will hardly occur at the same time."

"It might on occasion. It doesn't hurt to be prepared."

She eyed him suspiciously. "I suspect that you have fallen prey to the splendour of Takhan lifestyle after spending half a year in one of the residences there. That means that no argument I can come up with will make you reconsider."

Enric shrugged. "I admit that I enjoyed the copious gardens there immensely. And rambling stretches of greenery with only a small house located somewhere at the edge of the plot would just not do."

She sighed, knowing that she had lost. "And this really is worth the additional expense of building a residence that is at least twice as large as it really needs to be? If you don't know what to do with all your money, I can suggest two orphanages which wouldn't mind taking off your hands that load of gold you seem to consider a burden needing to be spent."

"Look at it like this, my love: We will spend half of every year under the same roof as your sister and Rolan. I imagine that the two or even three of you will squabble every now and then, and then it will be very useful for you to be able to avoid each other for a while."

"That is complete nonsense," she growled. "As long as we are sharing the same main room and kitchen, there will be no avoiding them. That is not an argument that holds. And why is there another staircase on the first floor? Don't tell me there is a second floor?"

"No, this one here leads up to the roof." Enric lifted the sheet to reveal a third one underneath. "There we have a terrace, similar to the one at the Vel'kim residence. Considering the plot's location on a hill, this should afford us a very nice view over the city, especially in the evenings." He rounded the desk and pulled her against him. "We could devote one of the many surplus rooms to a library," he said seductively. "Two even, if you wish. A general one and an extra, medical library. With comfortable seating arrangements for reading in either."

She chuckled despite herself. "Are you trying to bribe me into indulging you by agreeing to all that unnecessary expense?"

"Without a doubt," he admitted openly. "If this doesn't make you give in, I have run out of ideas."

"Build your fancy residence, then," Eryn sighed. "And I graciously accept the two libraries, thank you very much. And I am delegating the task of justifying our plans before my Head of House as soon as he gets to hear of them."

"Which can only be a matter of weeks now," Enric added darkly, not looking forward to dealing with Vran'el's wrath upon hearing that his sister had chosen to ignore his orders of staying at the Vel'kim residence when in Takhan. "When a new residence is being constructed, there is no way of keeping secret who is paying for it."

"Well, at least he will get to hear of it while we are still here in Anyueel. He will surely have calmed down again until we have to face him."

He grimaced. "Which will be when he learns that his other sister has decided to defy him as well by moving in with us. I wouldn't count on this encounter being too harmonious, my love."

"We could send Tala ahead. He has been her brother for a lot longer than mine. I suppose she knows how to handle him."

"That is a very unsisterly thing to do," he grinned.

"Well, maybe when it comes to your sister, but with Pe'tala different rules apply. We are talking about the woman whose first remark upon meeting me was an insult. And even that was not addressed to me directly, but delivered by way of talking about me as if I weren't even present. As if she were sizing a mare up at a horse market."

"And you call me resentful?"

"I am not exactly carrying a grudge against her any more, but she is my little sister and I am trying to teach her respect for her elders."

Enric rolled his eyes. "You are trying to construct a reason why letting her take all the heat from your brother would not make you a terrible sibling. Let me tell you that you are failing miserably here."

They both looked up when they heard a high-pitched wailing from the upper floor.

"Your turn," Eryn told him. "I am supposed to be leaving for work now anyway. Have a nice night with your son." She kissed him on the cheek. "I'll see you two tomorrow morning."

* * *

Erbál shook his head at Eryn while sitting in her study at the clinic.

"You do not expect Vran'el is going to take this well, do you? He will be furious. It will make him look bad if both of his sisters oppose him like that so soon after he took over the House."

She shrugged. "He has nobody but himself to blame for that. If he hadn't decided to start issuing unpopular orders mere minutes after making us swear the oath to him, we would have been more accommodating. And he certainly did not waste any time at all to consider how it looks when I am being made to return to Takhan every year or how it would disrupt my own and my family's lives. Our building our own house there instead of moving in with him is a minor act of rebellion compared to what he would have to face if he really had to live under one roof with Pe'tala and me, I can promise you that."

Erbál chuckled. "That I can believe without any trouble whatsoever. Tell me about how well you have managed to re-adapt to life here in Anyueel since your return."

Eryn looked slightly pained. "I am still in the process of finding a routine with Vedric, the Magic Council and the clinic."

"I have heard that you mostly work nights at the moment. And that Lord Enric seems to be looking rather tired lately. Tending to his son at night is obviously proving a rather demanding task."

"It is, yes. My son is starting to grow teeth unusually early, and they are troubling him, mostly at night for some reason. Healing away the pain doesn't work as the source, namely his growing teeth, is still active. He will have to get through this just like any other child without a healer as a parent." She leaned back in her chair and took a sip from her drink. "This is the last time we will sit together before you leave for Takhan and then Pirinkar. I assume my son's teething progress is not exactly what you would wish to talk about."

Erbál inclined his head. "I will admit there is another matter I wanted to address before I leave here tomorrow. One that may or may not turn into a serious problem at one point. But it generally pays not to ignore certain signs that point in a direction that could cause trouble if not addressed in time." He leaned forward and looked at her insistently. "The mood within the Order has noticeably changed since you left here all these months ago. The flow of information between our countries has increased drastically, and not only about matters of trade or state. People hear about the lifestyle, the rules, the system on the other side of the sea, and quite a number of your fellow magicians here have become aware of a country where users of magic have a lot more freedom in almost every aspect of their lives, be it their choice of profession or place to live."

Eryn blinked at the unexpected revelation. "What exactly are you telling me, Erbál? That the Order is about to face a rebellion amongst its members?"

The ambassador shook his head. "This is not what I am saying. I am merely pointing out to you that I have received information that hints at the chance of discontent, which might be building underneath the proper and disciplined surface of the Order. It may be a fleeting sentiment, one that will disperse again once the fascination of the novelty of Takhan life has faded. But then it may not and instead erupt into a violent outburst, which is probably something to fear in an institution that consists of magicians trained in combat."

She swallowed and took a few moments to think about his words. "Do you know if the Magic Council is aware of this, or at least Lord Tyront?"

Erbál grimaced. "The Magic Council as such is not what I would call an open-minded group of people who welcome new development or are sensitive to indicators of imminent change or danger. Lord Tyront may be a little more willing to adapt, yet at heart he still is a traditionalist, especially when Lord Enric is, as over these last months, not around to remind him that progress has its merits at times."

"I don't think my chances of making them aware of that possible danger are so good. I have a few friends in the Council, but the majority still considers me a disruptive element to their traditions and values. Many of them think magical healing is an abomination that the Order should avoid having anything to do with, that should be banished from the Kingdom just like it was done several hundred years ago."

"Addressing the Council directly is certainly not the most advisable way to go about this for you, I agree. But then you are close to several of the more influential members such as your companion and

Lord Orrin. Considering how well-informed King Folrin tends to be, I would be surprised if he was not at least partially aware of what is going on. And then there is the chance that I am wrong, mind you," he conceded. "I may just be being overcautious, a tendency that comes with my position. I would just advise you to keep your eyes open and be prepared. This is all I am saying." He rose. "And now I think it is time for me to leave as your shift must be starting soon. I hope to see you tomorrow before I leave, my dear Eryn."

Eryn nodded. "Thank you, I will heed your warning. I will be there when you get on that coach to leave us after spending hardly any time here in Anyueel."

He laughed. "You are at least partly to blame for my being sent to the great big unknown, unless I am very much mistaken. You initiated the vote on the matter in the Senate in Takhan."

"They would have sent you anyway. I just wanted to make sure I had a say who they sent here as your successor. We wouldn't want another Sanaf coming here."

Erbál looked at her thoughtfully. "And you picked Ram'kel of House Arbil. An interesting choice."

She frowned. "You don't think it was a wise one?"

"That is not what I am saying. Though you may want to keep in mind that he is very different from his brother. More confrontational. Ram'an's and my own more moderate temper compliment your own heated one rather well, but Ram'kel is less... obliging at times. Be careful when you challenge him. He will likely try to outwit you just to see if he can. He is also unusually smart. Not smart enough to always avoid trouble, but certainly smart enough to get himself out of it unscathed."

Eryn sighed and got to her feet as well. It seemed she would get a lot more than she had bargained for by agreeing to have Ram'kel sent here. It remained to be seen whether doing Ram'an a favour would be worth whatever trouble his brother might cause her.

CHAPTER 21

A Country Visit

Eryn opened the lid of the wooden box and curiously pushed aside the wood shavings that protected the contents while Enric was scowling over her shoulder.

"This is such a transparent attempt at manipulation," he growled. "I can't believe that you are falling for it. This man has never in his life given away something without expecting more back." He had been in a bad mood ever since he had discovered that his father was the sender of the package.

Eryn didn't comment on that and simply lifted one of several dusty bottles from the box, inspecting the label thoroughly.

"This is the expensive stuff," she then commented with delight and caused Enric to roll his eyes.

"Everything in our cellars and in our bar is the expensive stuff. I make the expensive stuff in my own vineyards! How can you be excited about that gift?"

"It's a sign that he is accepting me into his family."

"I don't accept him into my family! Why does this fail to make a difference with you? Should somebody having had such bad experiences with her own mother be that insensitive when it comes to an issue like that?"

Eryn regarded him analytically. "Should the man who has let himself be adopted by the said mother really be throwing the stones here?"

Enric grimaced. "Alright, I had that one coming." He pointed at another bottle in the crate. "Look at that. This one is one of mine even!"

"Shut up, you! He writes that he selected wines of the finest quality in the Kingdom he could find, and that yours are among them is a compliment. If you weren't so very careful to hide your success from your father, he would have known about that and refrained from gifting us with the wine we make," she scolded him, getting tired of his attitude. This was one of the rare occasions when both of them were at home, awake, and Vedric was asleep. And he was ruining it with his grumpy attitude towards his father.

"This is nothing less than a bribe," Enric tried again. "He discovered that you are high-born and important and now wants to suck up to you."

"Of course he does. And it certainly has nothing to do with my being your companion or his grandson's mother. Because he has no regard whatsoever for you. It must be because he hopes to gain something."

"He called you a western spy when he was here! He knew well enough that you were my companion already back then."

"Try to look at this from his point of view: he finds out that his son has joined a woman without telling him, then he comes here to meet me only to find himself face to face with an woman who is clearly not from here. We both know that he found that hard to deal with as he is not the most open-minded person, but neither are you yourself right now."

"Don't compare me with my father," he said slowly and deliberately, his arms folded, his eyes sparkling with anger.

"You know what? Why don't we just change the topic now? I am tired; it was a rather long night at the clinic."

"You should send the wine back," he insisted, completely ignoring her words.

"I won't!" she spat back, her patience wearing thin. "You know what I am rather thinking right now? Asking the Order to grant me a short leave of absence so I can visit your father and thank him for his generous gift in person."

"You wouldn't!" Enric narrowed his eyes.

"Watch me!"

He quickly grabbed her wrist when she turned to stalk away. "Now you wait here a moment! This is not a good topic to demonstrate your usual defiance!"

"Defiance? Defiance?" She threw up her hands, freeing herself from his grip. "This is a discussion with my companion, not my superior! How can my having a different opinion be defiance here?"

"Eryn," he tried again, "he is manipulative. Don't fall for it."

"I'm not considering a visit to accommodate him as much as myself. I want to meet your mother, and she wants to meet me and her grandson. And whatever your problems with your father are, punishing her for it is beneath you."

"Don't make me look petty!"

"I don't have to," she said with a saccharine smile. "You are doing a rather good job on your own here."

"Why are you so stubborn?" he groaned.

"Why did you fail to realise this until now? I've never really hidden that fact, have I?" she commented dryly.

He took a deep breath. "Eryn. I don't want to visit my father."

"Fine," she shrugged. "Then don't come. I will go alone with Vedric."

"You are truly proposing I let you travel alone? Every time I take my eyes off you something happens to you! The last time I left you alone for a few days you made the Senate roof in Takhan crumble in!"

Eryn glared at him. "Says the man who almost fried the apothecaries after they attacked me. You talk to me about losing control? Honestly? Look," she said in her most reasonable tone, "there are exactly two options available to you: either you accompany us or you stay here. It's as simple as that." With this she sent him one last measured look and turned to leave the room.

"I forbid it!" he called after her, saying the words more to vent his frustration than counting on them to change anything.

"Oh, come on now! Don't be ridiculous," she snorted without looking back and continued on her way to the bedroom to finally catch up on the sleep after a long night of work and an almost equally exhausting morning.

* * *

Eryn watched Erbál's coach disappear through the city gate, feeling a little downcast. Enric next to her held his son on one arm with the other wrapped around her shoulders.

"I will miss him," she sighed. "I hope he likes it in Kar. At least not being a magician won't be a disadvantage for him over there."

"It certainly is a great chance for him to prove himself," Enric added.

"That doesn't make watching him leave any easier. Finally there was someone I could talk to about things, a devious, sly sort who was on my side for a change, and now he is gone."

He raised his brow at that. "There is always me to talk to, you know. I, too, have been described as devious and sly at times."

"Yes, but I can hardly ask you to help me against yourself when I there is something I want to achieve, can I? I dare say even your willingness to help me has its limits." She smiled thinly. "Or do you wish to advise me how to get you to visit your family with me? I'd be most exceedingly obliged to you for any helpful suggestions here."

Enric didn't comment on that but turned her around to return back home.

"Did you talk to Tyront about what Erbál said?" she asked, guiding the topic away from the matter that kept causing such friction between them.

"I mentioned it, yes. He is aware of a certain dissatisfaction, especially among the younger magicians, but doesn't really consider it a major issue at the moment. He is confident that a few of the changes that will happen in the Order in the time to come should take care of at least a part thereof."

"So he sees no grounds for imminent action?"

"No, apparently not."

"But he realises that our continued contact with the Western Territories will very likely increase that discontent even further? It is one thing to not know anything apart from the rigid structures one is subjected to when living in an isolated country, and then finding out about how magicians elsewhere are allowed to do so much more."

"He does, yes. And he sees the need for improvement as well as I do, yet radical changes would cost him the Council's cooperation. Moderation is the trick here," he explained.

They walked on in silence for a while, Vedric drooling on his father's shoulders in his sleep.

"I suppose it can't be easy for the others to see how some of us have the chance to escape the Order's rules for a time by going to Takhan," she pondered. "I have been testing the waters for having healers sent to the countryside to work there instead of only in the city, but every time I hint at it, it is dismissed with a derogatory comment or a wave of a hand. Not that there is a realistic chance for that as long as the healers' quota isn't increased, mind you. But then this might just be the reason to have more healers anyway." She rubbed her temples. "Sometimes it feels like fighting against a massive stone wall with my bare hands or trying to make the wind change its direction by talking it into submission. The Council's narrow-mindedness is just as elemental as any force of nature."

Enric kissed her on the temple. "You have changed so much here in a very short time, my love. I have no doubt whatsoever that the Council will in time succumb to your efforts. And then you do have a few allies as well. Lord Seagon or Lord Woldarn will probably never be on your side, but there is always Orrin, Lord Poron, Tyront and me. If you manage to keep a civil tone with Tyront, that is."

"I have been doing well enough since our return, haven't I?"

"Yes, but we have only been back for a few weeks, and so far there have been no occasions for the two of you to butt heads. Not yet."

She opened the door when they reached their house to let Enric enter with the peacefully sleeping bundle against his shoulder, and noticed the letter on a tray next to the niche for their cloaks. She lifted it and read her name written in an elegant female hand.

Enric furrowed his brow. "That's my mother's handwriting. Why is she writing to you?"

Eryn shrugged and opened the message, letting her eyes dart along the lines.

"She writes that your niece is ill and that she is worried about her coughing so much."

His eyes narrowed. "You are not trying to tell me that this makes it necessary for you to travel there to heal her as your noble disposition makes it impossible for you to act any other way? You surely don't think I am gullible enough to fall for something like that, do you?"

She pursed her lips. "Of course not. I should definitely stay here and let it be known that my noble disposition, as you like to call it, doesn't induce me to aid my companion's family when they are in need of medical care. I am sure that will do wonders for my reputation."

"That is nonsense, and you know it," he retorted, fighting for calm. "How would anybody ever learn of this? I seriously doubt that my mother would spread the tidings of your heartless decision to leave her family alone in their hour of dire need."

"Yes, I agree. Your mother surely wouldn't. But you yourself told me that we both have spies on our heels reporting whatever we do or don't do to whoever pays them." She reached out to take her son from Enric when he started to stir, disturbed by his father's agitation.

"So you are truly determined to do this? Whatever my own wishes concerning this?"

She sent him a frosty look. "I told you before, the choice is yours. You either stay here or you come with us. I can't force you to accompany us, and neither would I wish to do so. You are a grown man and can make your own decision about this. And I will thank you very much for granting me that same freedom. If you will excuse me now, I need to feed and bathe Vedric. I intend to pay Tyront a short visit before I start work so I can ask him for permission to leave here for a few days and find out whether my oath requires that I apply to the King as well." Thus she climbed the stairs, a faint smile on her lips.

* * *

"I was counting on your covering my back in this," Enric complained to his superior.

Tyront gave him a doubtful look. "Don't expect me to fight your battles, my dear boy. I have no sensible reason to deny her time off to visit her companion's family. She told me that she is asking only for herself, not for you as you don't want to go. I assume you won't want to have her travel alone with the child, will you? She has a tendency to land herself in trouble when unsupervised."

Enric closed his eyes and let his chin drop to his chest. "Of course not. Her safety is a lot more important than avoiding Anwin."

"That's what I thought. I thereby officially grant you permission to leave the city for five days. At least your mother will be happy to see you again. Eryn told me she wants to leave at the beginning of next week. That suits me well. It means that you will be back in time for the games. The both of you should be seen to participate, especially since Eryn was the one who initially came up with the idea."

Enric just grunted discontentedly, imagining her smug expression at having him accompany her against his wishes.

"Don't be disgruntled, Enric. Even the best among us have to give in to a higher power at times." He looked his second in command over. "You look tired. That child of yours keeps you busy. The two of you might want to reconsider the matter of hiring a nursemaid." He lifted his hands when Enric was about to object. "I know that Eryn is dead against it to avoid being anything like other rich women in the city, but this is not exactly a practical attitude when you can hardly keep your eyes open anymore."

"If you know that Eryn is the one who is against it, why are you trying to convince me?" Enric asked, stifling a yawn.

"Because I cannot interfere with domestic matters as her superior."

"But that is obviously not a problem in my case, is it?"

"I am talking to you as your friend here, not as your superior." He raised both eyebrows. "At least I assume we have returned to this status after our disagreement before your departure for Takhan?"

Enric smiled tiredly. "Are you asking me if we are friends again? I find that incredibly touching. Yes, old man, all is well again between us."

Tyront rolled his eyes. "I am really glad for your mature attitude. How is that house you are building in foreign parts coming along? Will I be able to reside in style in case I decide to visit you there in a few months?"

"That you would be in any case. There is always the ambassadorial residence to provide you with shelter. The ambassador is a member of the Order, after all. We have only recently informed our builder that we approve of the plans, though Eryn would have preferred reducing the size by half. They should start laying the foundations soon."

"Does the Head of House Vel'kim know about his sister's defiance?" Tyront grinned broadly. "How pleasant to see that I'm not the only one having to deal with it."

Enric shook his head. "Not yet. Or at least he has not yet contacted us. I expect that to happen soon enough. As soon as a building project of that magnitude takes on a recognisable shape, there is no keeping the client's identity a secret any longer. There is always somebody with access to the right information who knows somebody's aunt, second cousin or former lover. It will soon be public knowledge that I am having a residence built."

"Well, at least Malriel won't object to it. As the residence will officially belong to you, it will fall to House Aren after your death and so add to her House's wealth."

"Theoretically. I intend to leave it to Vedric specifically and thus it would fall to House Vel'kim - provided Malriel isn't able to coerce Vran'el into giving up the heir to his House and therefore his future property to House Aren."

"Which would be a realistic option," Tyront mused, "as soon as Pe'tala has children. And considering that Rolan is about to relocate to another country for her and intends to join her, that is a reasonable possibility."

Enric rubbed his face. "Yes, I know. It's a pity Vran'el's daughter is not available to take her father's place one day. So he has to make sure one of his sisters' children will succeed him."

"Do you have any preference about which House you want your son to be the Head of one day? It doesn't really look like he has much of a choice whether or not he wants to follow that path with both sides of the family eager to have him."

"None whatsoever. Both Houses are respected and successful. I know that Eryn's preference is House Vel'kim, of course. Though she would much rather have him free of that burden than be forced to take over either House if he doesn't want to. How about Rolan? Will you retain him in the Order once he has moved to Takhan? Or will you set him free with your blessing?"

Tyront shook his emphatically. "Dear me, I couldn't possibly release him from the Order. Imagine the precedent this would set. Every magician who feels that the Order's rules restrain their personal freedom too much would relocate to Takhan just to be rid of us. No, Rolan will remain a member of the Order and act in our best interest in his new location."

Enric nodded slowly and wondered, if Tyront noticed what picture of the Order his own words had just painted. They made the institution sound like a prison. He thought back to his conversation with Eryn. She had always felt locked in, restrained in her ambitions, and now it seemed that she was no longer alone with that sentiment. He felt the urge to do something, to address that particular matter once again, but when he had mentioned it last time, Tyront's attitude had been rather carefree; he didn't really see any imminent danger. Enric hoped he was right.

*　*　*

Eryn looked out the coach window and smiled with relief. The village had just come into view and the prospect of getting out of the cramped coach and stretching her limbs cheered her no end. Enric, however, had become gloomier with every passing hour. He was so very obviously dreading their arrival that Eryn had given up her attempts at cheering him up a while ago and just let him brood.

They had left Urban at home, deciding that the trip was too short to put her through the strain of travelling for three out of the five days. She still seemed to have been suffering the change of climate and had kept a lot to her yard lately, even spending the rather cold nights out there perched under tree trunks.

Enric reached out for her hand without warning, startling her. "I make you an offer," he said urgently. "We can turn around right now, and I will make sure the King agrees to letting you skip the next ball."

Her brow shot up in genuine surprise. She whistled through her teeth. "My, my, you really are desperate, aren't you? And you were thinking of making me this offer only now? After we spent more than a day and a half on the road and have virtually reached our destination?"

"I don't care," Enric insisted. "Just consider it a nice family outing with the two most important men in your life. Think about it."

Eryn shook her head. "No, my dear. This offer is an insult. We are talking about two days with your family in exchange for one evening in the throne room. Definitely not."

"The next two balls," he amended quickly. "I can make that happen. All you have to do is to tell the coachman to turn around."

Again she answered in the negative. "No, we are doing this, no matter how many balls you offer to let me skip. I wrote to your mother, so your family is expecting us. How would it look if we simply decided not to turn up, I ask you?"

"I couldn't care less what it would look like," he growled in defeat.

"Come on, act like the grown lad the Kingdom knows you are and face the scary people you are related with. I have never before encountered such shrinking from obligation with you!"

"This has nothing to do with shrinking from obligation. I am not afraid of seeing them - I just don't want to."

She pinched his cheek, earning a dark look from him. "You will just have to get these two days behind you somehow. Consider this one chance for personal growth, for demonstrating that restraint you were so eager to teach me."

He sighed heavily. "I can't believe that the woman who locked her own mother in an airtight barrier to shut her up is telling me to be civil to my family. Am I the only one seeing some contradiction here?"

She waved him off. "This is something completely different. Those were exceptional circumstances. And then we are still talking about Malriel here. You yourself admitted that Malriel is more terrifying as a parent than Anwin."

"I was letting you win. You were having a tough day, and I pitied you," he replied morosely.

Eryn shook her head at him and leaned forward to the opposite bench to check if Vedric was still asleep in his makeshift cradle that was secured against the inner wall of the coach. "There is no use talking to you. I will wake your son now so that I can feed him before we arrive. It's bad enough if one of you is in a rotten mood."

* * *

Eryn took a deep breath before opening the coach door. They had finally arrived.

Two men and two women stood in front of the door. One of the men she recognised as Anwin, and the woman in her mid-fifties with the greying hair in a tight bun and her hands anxiously kneading her apron had to be his mother. She was the only one of the four to hurry towards the coach after it had stopped, halting in front of her son, obviously at a loss what to do. Enric's sour mood was not as such plainly visible on his expressionless face, but the tension was still palpable.

"Enric," the woman said quietly, her voice tight as if this one word caused her pain, her arms half raised as if unsure whether an embrace would be acceptable to him or not.

Eryn heard her companion sigh and then say, "Mother. It is good to see you."

Then he took her hands in his and slowly pulled her against him until her head rested against his shoulder. Eryn watched his mother melt against him, her lower lip quivering slightly, a tear forming at the corner of her eye before silently rolling down her cheek and then her throat to be soaked up by the fabric of her collar.

They stood like this for several long moments, locked in an embrace that was completely motionless yet strangely intense to behold. The other three figures watched from several paces away, not moving a muscle.

Enric's mother then released him again with evident reluctance and surreptitiously drew her sleeve across her face to remove the wet trace. She closed her eyes for a moment and smiled when Enric bent down to kiss her forehead in a gesture that seemed tender yet at the same time tense. Then she turned and her face softened when her gaze fell on Eryn and the child on her arm.

"Eryn," she said, her voice reverberating with feelings she couldn't or wouldn't put words to, her eyes alight with joy. She turned away from Enric without letting go of his hand and stepped towards the younger woman, letting her gaze eagerly roam the face in front of her as if she had waited to be able to do so for a long time. "I am Gerit. I can't tell you how happy I am to meet you. She gripped the one hand Eryn wasn't using to hold her son and squeezed it tightly. "And this must be Vedric. May I hold him? Or is he afraid of..." She paused as if the word she was about to utter was stuck in her throat. "...strangers?"

Eryn smiled and handed her son to his grandmother. The baby boy scrutinised the new face before him with wide eyes before breaking into a wide grin, whereupon he poked two fingers into his mouth to chew on them.

Anwin waited for them to come closer, making no move to approach them. When Enric stood before him, he nodded once. "Son. You certainly took your time. Your absence caused your mother grief."

Eryn reached out for her companion's hand, giving it a warning squeeze. Enric was wearing his mask of detachment.

"Anwin," he just said, then turned his head to the other two people standing not far away. "Noren," he greeted the man who had to be his brother, without any particular warmth. Eryn remembered that he was three years younger than Enric and had two children.

"I assume this is your companion?" he added after a while with a nod at the woman in her early thirties when his brother didn't move but just stared at him with an expression Eryn wasn't sure of how to interpret. Dread? Anxiety? Reproach? A mixture of all three?

The woman gave Noren a shove with her elbow and a displeased look before raising her chin at the newcomers. "I am, yes. My name is Werna." Her expression clearly conveyed that she was not thrilled about their arrival and Eryn noted that she didn't bother with any insincere assurances that it was her pleasure to meet them. So far Enric's mother had been the only one to express genuine joy at seeing them. Or any kind of joy. She let her gaze wander over the couple. Noren's features resembled his father's, and so did his tall if slightly bulky stature. She imagined that this was what Enric would look like if he didn't adhere to the training the Order insisted on and let himself go a bit. But then the idea of Enric indulging himself without remorse was so absurd that she pushed the thought aside immediately.

Werna, on the other hand, looked prim and almost bony, a contrast to her companion, as if she was eager to compensate his culinary sins. Her hair was wound into a bun even tighter than Gerit's, and there was not a single stray strand of hair that was permitted to escape.

Eryn looked up at the house they all stood in front of, taking in the well-made structure that spoke of able craftsmanship. Everything looked well-maintained and she bet that there was not a single creaking door in the entire building. She had little doubt that Werna would be the one to run the house, not Gerit. Enric's mother somehow seemed to lack the hardness that going against Werna surely required. Eryn imagined that a fight for dominance between those two women couldn't be a long one.

Anwin opened the door and stepped aside hesitantly, as if reluctant to grant his oldest son admission to his house. Eryn couldn't help sensing some foreboding. She had hardly ever in her life felt as unwelcome anywhere as here at this very moment. The thought of whether accepting Enric's bribe wouldn't have been the smarter course of action flickered through her mind, but she pushed it aside with determination when she looked back at Gerit, who appeared so blissful in holding her grandchild and indulged the little boy while he played with the pendant on her necklace.

* * *

Eryn sat quietly at the table in the somewhat crowded dining room. Around her an array of expensive looking chests and cupboards was arranged, displaying crystal vases with and without flowers, small marble statues and other fragile looking items of decoration. There had been a visible effort at arranging the many objects appealingly, but the sheer multitude made it impossible to avoid an impression of overload, however they were placed. It was like an attempt to demonstrate wealth by exhibiting as many costly possessions as possible.

The mood around the table was little more relaxed than several minutes before in front of the house, the only one of them who seemed at last somewhat content was Enric's mother with her grandson on her lap.

Werna was in the meantime serving lunch. That alone was a clear sign of who was in charge of the household. Eryn accepted the bowl of soup with a polite smile which Werna acknowledged but didn't return. When all of them were seated and had started to eat, Noren cleared his throat.

"So, brother," he started. "It has been some time since you last graced us with a visit. I assume we have to thank your new companion for that... honour."

Eryn made herself smile. "I admit I suggested the visit. Enric knows my family, so I thought it was time for me to meet his. I heard that you have two children?"

Noren frowned for a brief moment, clearly not too happy that the conversation deviated from where he had wanted it to go. But he replied nevertheless. "Yes. Gorem is eleven years old, and his sister Temina is eight."

She nodded, refraining from asking why the children were not taking their lunch with them. "I heard your daughter is a bit ill. I can have a look at her later. I am a healer."

Werna let her spoon drop into her bowl with an audible clink. Her expression was disapproving. "This will not be necessary. It is just a little cough. She will get over it soon even without any fancy treatments."

Gerit on the other side of the table next to Enric looked worried. "Werna, she has been coughing for days now, and then there is the fever. She doesn't eat enough and tosses and turns at night. Don't you think that..."

"No," the younger woman cut in sharply. "And this is my last word in this matter. She is my child and I won't have anybody tell me how to raise her."

Eryn saw how the muscles in Enric's jaw tensed. She cast a look at Anwin, who either didn't notice or care that his companion was being treated with so little respect by his son's mate in his own house.

"It wouldn't be any effort, really," Eryn tried again. "I should say I am a little on edge if I know that an ill person is around and I am not in a position to help," she said with a disarming smile.

Werna's glare could have melted stone. "I have no intention of spending money on something that will soon be over."

Eryn felt how the smile started to hurt her cheeks. "I wouldn't charge you anything for it. It would be my pleasure. If you don't feel comfortable to have her healed with magic, I could at least check if it is anything serious and mix you a herbal cure."

"I said no," the other woman said brusquely. "I will thank you for respecting that and staying away from my children. We have been doing well enough here without your fancy magic and grand city ways."

Eryn felt how the little hairs on her arms stood on end. That woman truly put her own pride and resentment before her daughter's well-being. She breathed in and out once to keep the acid remark that fought to get out from between her lips inside. After all, there was nothing she could do here. She couldn't treat a patent who didn't welcome her attentions. And when it came to minors, their parents or other legal guardians were the ones to make that decision. But that didn't mean she had to like it.

"Of course," she said stiffly and resumed eating, starting to look forward to leaving here again in two days.

Anwin pushed his empty bowl away from him and leaned on his elbows, focusing on Eryn opposite him. "How did you like the wine?"

Ignoring Enric's unnerved glance at his father for claiming thanks for his gift, she smiled again, trying to put some warmth into her reply. "It was a very generous present, thank you very much. I have not yet been able to taste any of it as I am abstaining from drinking alcohol as long as I am nursing Vedric, but I look forward to sampling the wine when he has switched to solids completely."

"A little wine every now and then doesn't do any harm to a child," Werna interjected unbidden.

Eryn decided to ignore her instead of pointing out to her that she preferred basing her decisions on her medical expertise instead of the views of a narrow-minded, stubborn woman whose medical insights about her own daughter's illness amounted to nothing more than that it will soon be over.

Werna got up to collect the empty bowls once everyone had finished their soup and replaced them with large, fragile looking ceramic plates. She went several times to the kitchen to bring serving bowls with different kinds of vegetables, sauces and finally a silver platter with a huge chunk of meat which Eryn couldn't identify.

"Help yourself," Anwin offered generously and nodded towards Eryn. She swallowed and accepted the dubious honour of being the first to load her plate with food while everybody watched her. When she had taken a few spoonfuls from the different bowls and leaned back again, all faces but Enric's regarded her with surprise.

"Is there something wrong with my roast pig?" Werna enquired with an annoyed undertone.

Eryn sighed deep within. Ah yes, there was the matter of her diet. Somehow she had the feeling that they would not be very understanding. But there was no way out, she had to tell them.

"I stopped eating meat a while ago." She watched as Enric, too, ignored the meat and just heaped vegetables on his plate. She wanted to be angry at him for provoking his family by pretending that he had adopted her lifestyle as well, but right now she rather decided to interpret it as a sign of support.

"Stopped eating meat?" Noren frowned in incomprehension. "What for?"

"For various reasons," Eryn replied evasively and hoped that her tone would convey that she had no wish to discuss that topic and even less to justify her motives to anybody.

"That is unnatural," stated Werna with conviction. "It can't be healthy."

Enric slowly lifted his cool gaze to her and studied her for a few moments before asking, "And you would be in a position to judge that, would you? May I ask if you have received any particular training to determine which nutrition the human organism requires to remain in good health?"

His brother's companion narrowed her eyes. "I don't need any special fancy training for this, common sense serves me well enough."

"I see. So the argument that a trained healer with the ability to check her body with magic to check for any signs of deficiency at any time would certainly be qualified to determine whether her lifestyle is healthy or not fails to impress you, I assume?"

The others all let their eyes dart between the two of them, waiting in tense silence to see if this would somehow escalate.

"Let me tell you what doesn't impress me, Lord Enric: people from the big city coming here to tell me in fancy words why they are so much better than me and why my food is unhealthy."

Enric smiled thinly. "I never maintained anything of that sort. Quite the opposite; you were the one to tell my companion that you considered her choice of nourishment unhealthy. I see that things have changed quite a bit since I grew up here. In my time insulting guests was frowned upon in this house. It was considered bad manners."

"Werna," Anwin said sharply, and the one word made her ground her teeth and look down at her plate in sullen silence, her posture making it clear how little she appreciated having been called to order in front of an audience.

Without another word, everybody resumed eating, the scrape of cutlery on plates the only noise.

Eryn made sure to keep her gaze fixed on her food, thinking that this had to be the most oppressive meal she had ever taken. Not even the dinner after learning that Valrad was her father when she had insulted him came close to this here. But the interactions so far had given her a fairly clear picture of the hierarchy in this family. Anwin seemed to be on top, closely followed by Werna. Noren had to come next somewhere, though he was nowhere close to his companion. And then, pretty much at the bottom of the pecking order was Gerit, relegated to watching her house being run by the woman chosen by a man she herself had raised.

Eryn imagined Malriel in this house and felt reluctant relief at the thought that her mother would never endure anybody pushing her aside or around. She started to understand why Enric felt a certain pull towards the Head of House Aren. He probably wished that his own mother would have at least a tiny fraction of that strength instead of suffering in silence and with her gaze averted.

"So, brother, how is the magician business going? A lot of meetings to attend and paper to push around?" Noren ventured after a long while.

"I congratulate you on your insights into my daily routine," Enric replied good-naturedly. "But fortunately my Order duties will be limited to six months every year from now on as we will spend the rest of the time in the Western Territories."

"What?" Gerit whispered, her eyes wide. Her arms held on a little tighter to Vedric, as if the thought of having him taken away to another country for such a long time and with such regularity stressed her.

Eryn wondered why. Did she expect to see her grandson more often now after the visit? Did she hope that Enric would be coming here regularly with his family? She doubted that very much; not after this kind of welcome by the other three family members.

"My brother insists on our spending some time there as Vedric is the heir to his position and needs to learn how to lead a House from his early years onward," Eryn explained, feeling that this, too, was not the best topic to follow.

Noren's gaze rested on his nephew who had fallen asleep with his head nestled against Gerit's neck.

"How nice," he commented with a hint of disdain. "So the little prince is already intended for his place amongst wealth and glory."

Eryn swallowed when Enric's head came up with a jerk and his cold blue eyes fixed on his brother. Noren swallowed and involuntarily leaned back slightly before straightening his shoulders and meeting his older brother's gaze as if he was telling himself that he was grown up now and there was no more need for fear any longer. Eryn dimly remembered that Enric's magical abilities had been discovered when he had shot a bolt at his younger brother when they were children. Maybe things like that tended to stick in the mind. It certainly couldn't have been a pleasant experience for Noren.

"Your idea of a position of leadership always was limited, Noren," Enric said evenly. "In your mind it is nothing more than leaning back in a comfortable chair and pointing your finger at things you want people to take care of and making sure your various whims are being catered to. You have no concept of being responsible for others, making sacrifices, making unpopular decisions nobody will thank you for, even when they finally turn out to be the right ones. You may believe me that I would not wish for my son to be pushed into such a position without having much say in it. I would prefer for him to choose whatever makes him happy. That is true luxury, not having your path predestined because you happened to have been born to the wrong parents."

"So being a strong magician seems to be quite the burden for you," Anwin said, and smiled nastily. "I suppose your mother and I should apologise for passing the ability on to you, then?"

Enric returned the insincere smile. "There is nothing to apologise for you, Anwin. Mother is the one with the noble magician ancestors, after all."

Eryn saw a blood vessel at Anwin's temple pulsate dangerously and decided to intervene before matters got out of hand.

"Enric," she said carefully, reaching out for his hand. Before she could say any more, Gerit's quiet voice spoke up.

"Is this really necessary? Do you have to provoke him in this way after he comes here for the first time in fifteen years? Can't you just pretend to get along for two days? Is that too much to ask?"

Noren flashed her a look of being insulted. "Of course. The prodigal son has returned and must be protected at all costs. Why not pretend if it makes his stay here any more bearable, no matter how the rest of us feel?"

Enric smiled sardonically. "Don't worry about that. Right now I don't see any danger of encountering any particularly bearable aspects in our stay here."

Eryn sighed when Gerit rose without a word and left the room with the infant on her arm, her half-finished meal remaining on the table.

"Well, that was charming," she said, her smile slightly edgy. "Enric, dear, why don't we check on Vedric and then take a nice long walk together?"

*　*　*

Enric walked between Eryn and his mother, his son slung across his chest, climbing the low hill behind his parents' house. His mother had immediately wanted to join them on their walk, eager to spend a little time alone with her guests without any tense exchanges with the rest of the family. He didn't mind that, not at all. His mother was the only one who seemed truly happy to have him here, so he felt no regret whatsoever leaving Anwin, Noren and Werna behind. But that also meant that the talking-to Eryn was about to give him would not be quite as private as he would have preferred. Yet there was no avoiding it, he had no doubt about that. Her posture was determined and her usually full lips were pressed together into a thin line. She very likely only waited for them to be out of earshot of the house before giving him an earful.

And indeed, when the path took a bend, she glared across at him. "What do you have to say for yourself? Lecturing others on the many downsides of your position and at the same time failing to display the restraint that should go with it is quite a feat for Lord Enric with the legendary iron control!"

"I did exercise quite some control, I'll have you know," he retorted with a smile. Getting out of the house into the fresh air had lifted his spirits. "Otherwise I would have banged their heads together. You are not telling me that you would have preferred it if I hadn't intervened when first my companion and then my son were the target of their snide remarks?"

Gerit took his arm and leaned her cheek against his shoulder, closing her eyes for a moment. "Of course not, Enric. I understand why you had to speak up. You know how they are. They don't mean it that way."

He sighed. "Mother, I wish you would stop defending them. They meant every word. As did I." His gaze wandered to his companion. "I knew this wouldn't be a harmonious visit. I tried to warn you, but you didn't want to listen. Are you happy now? Depend on this - it won't get any better."

Eryn gave him a cool smile. "My primary objective in coming here was to meet your mother. That hasn't changed. I knew that I would have to endure Anwin, and I will manage to survive your brother and his endearing companion just the same." The last bit was pressed out from between clenched teeth.

Enric looked at her and smirked. "You might want to let it out, my love. You'll feel better afterwards."

She growled, "Let what out? Anwin is intimidated by his own son and attempts to overcompensate by being rude. Noren is jealous because you were always the more important son, first the great heir, and now the great magician. I feel nothing but pity for either of them. Their problems are rooted in their lack of self-confidence when it comes to dealing with you. And Werna..." Her nostril twitched. "She is right. It is her decision about how to raise her children. And if she sees fit to let her daughter suffer unnecessarily even though she could have a healer take care of her ailments within a few minutes, free of charge, then I have to respect this. Well, accept. Tolerate. Deal with somehow."

They walked on in silence for a while before Enric suggested, "Hit her over the head with a stick until she sees reason?"

Eryn groaned. "If only I could! What kind of mother puts her own pride before her daughter's well-being, I ask you? Even Leris was willing to let me heal her daughter even though she didn't like me!"

Gerit stilled, her eyes fixed on the ground. "You saw Leris?"

Enric noted how the mood changed. His mother's grip on his arm had become stronger. Though there was no other sign of her agitation, he felt it clearly.

"We did, yes. We went to visit her a few weeks ago after our return from the Western Territories. She is doing well for herself. She and her companion Ardegen own a thriving business and have two healthy, lively children. A boy and a girl."

He had to swallow at the expression of pain, of longing on his mother's face when listening to the account of how her youngest child was faring.

"So she is happy?" whispered Gerit.

"Oh, definitely," Eryn chuckled, obviously trying to lighten the mood. "She has a companion who lets her be bossy, a successful business that challenges her and an older brother she can squabble with. What else does a girl need to be content?"

Gerit managed a weak smile at that. "She always was an energetic one, my little Leris. So that man of hers, Ardegen, he treats her well? He doesn't mind that she is not always someone to be quiet?"

"Ardegen is a jewel of a man," Eryn stated with a conviction that made Enric raise his brow. "He is confident enough to realise what his own strengths are. And fortunately for him his stature is intimidating enough to allow him to concentrate on raising his children without any... disrespectful feedback from people around him."

That took Gerit a few moments to process. "He is raising their children?"

Eryn nodded as if this were the most natural thing in the world. "Mostly, yes. She has a very good head for business, from what I could glean, and he certainly seemed glad enough to take care of the aspects of their business that fell within his area of expertise in addition to keeping the family running. But then I don't see why not. Enric himself is very good with Vedric, so I have no scruples whatsoever leaving him alone with his son while I work nights at the clinic."

His mother blinked a few times, clearly finding it hard to imagine two impressively built men voluntarily taking care of small infants. She stopped and held on to both her son's hands to keep him from moving on. "Enric," she whispered insistently, her eyes searching for something in his face, "are you happy? Truly? Is this what you want?"

He smiled across at her, lifting one of her hands to his lips before replying softly, "Yes, mother, I am. This is more than I ever dared hope for."

She blinked several times to keep her tears at bay, then nodded. "Good. I am happy. For you and for Leris. It seems that leaving here was the right thing to do for both of you."

Enric was about to ask if staying behind had been such a bad thing for his brother Noren, but held the question back. He didn't want to spend the little time he had with his mother talking about what was to him fairly obvious anyway.

They passed a group of trees, and Gerit stopped again to look up at her son pleadingly. "Ten years is a long time for a mother without seeing her son, Enric. Too long, much too long. I hope you will never need to find out yourself how painful that is, my boy."

Enric remained silent, not pointing out that she could have visited him in the city at any time.

"Let's not wait that long before we meet again. Promise me," she insisted, her tone urgent. "I want to see my grandson growing up. I can't bear the thought that I wouldn't even be able to recognise him one day should I pass him on the street by chance... Just like with Leris' children."

He sighed heavily. "Mother. You are always welcome to come to the city and see me. But you must understand that coming here regularly is not something I would wish to burden Eryn and Vedric with. You saw how it was like just now. This is not the idea of family I want to introduce my son to. I want him to consider his relatives as people who enrich his life, who he can count on. Not people like them," he grimaced with a nod back the way they had come. "His own uncle has shown him nothing but a disdain born of jealousy, and I don't even want to mention his charming aunt Werna. Or his grandfather - who barely spared him a glance." He leaned his forehead against Gerit's. "I feel the urge to protect my little family from them, mother. Please try to understand."

Gerit took a step back, breaking the contact. "So I will not have a share in either of your lives? Is that what you are telling me?"

"No, mother. What I am telling you is that I would very much like you to be in our lives, but if this depends on our travelling here again in the near future, then I am afraid it won't be possible."

"I see," she whispered and remained standing there for several moments with her eyes closed, as if to collect herself. "If you will excuse me now..." she then said and turned back towards the house, hurrying away.

Enric lifted his face towards the bright grey sky, the frustration evident.

"I warned you that this would be disagreeable. We have been here for hardly more than two hours, and every single one of them is wishing me away."

Eryn rubbed her face. "It was necessary to go through with this. For your mother. Moreover, she doesn't wish you away; she is just hurt that the only person treating her in a halfway civil manner is about to vanish from her life again never to return while she is stuck here in this dreadful place."

He wrung his hands. "She is stuck here out of her own choice! I wrote to her time and again that she doesn't have to stay with Anwin if she wishes otherwise, that I would make sure to provide for her. But she chose to stay. I can't do anything more than present to her a way out, I can't force her to make use of it!"

"And neither should you if you could. As she is the one to bear the consequences of whatever decision she makes, the choice must her hers alone. And if the prospect of spending the rest of her life with Anwin is the lesser evil compared to living alone, then you need to respect that."

Enric rolled his eyes. "The way you respected Valrad's choice when he decided to make Malriel his companion?"

"I did eventually, didn't I?" Eryn growled. "And don't stray from the topic. This is just the same self-righteous indignation your sister showed when talking about your mother. You are both in happy relationships, so how dare you look down on somebody who has not been as lucky in hers?"

306

"I don't believe in luck," he stated indulgently. "Luck is nothing more than the failure to understand causal relations."

She folded her arms. "Is that the truth, now? So you are telling me what exactly? That our relationship turned out the way it did because you in your infinite wisdom and your knowledge of coherences planned it like this? That the merit for doing so is yours?"

"Well, I would maybe not put it quite like that, but I like to think that..."

She didn't wait for him to finish but turned on her heel and walked off, muttering, "Idiot!"

Enric exhaled slowly and shook his head, marvelling at the fact that this day had turned out even worse than he had imagined. He wouldn't have thought it possible.

Determined not to return to the mayhem and nastiness of his parents' house as yet, he continued on his way, raising a watertight shield over his head to keep himself and Vedric dry when the first drops of rain began to fall.

* * *

Eryn grimaced after she entered what used to be Enric's old room. Another family meal over, and it had not proven any more enjoyable than the first. There was less conversation this time, but the silence had not been of the companionable kind, but the tense, uncomfortable edginess where people either didn't have to tell each other anything or they just didn't feel like wasting their breath.

Enric followed her in, giving the heavy, slightly warped door a push that didn't quite close it, but left it slightly ajar. He let himself fall onto his old bed and patted the spot next to him. They had left Vedric with his grandmother. She seemed to be determined to spend every possible minute with him in the little time before they left again.

"You are the first girl I have ever brought to my room. This is quite an honour, you know."

She followed his invitation and sank down next to him, smiling. "You were twelve years old when you left here to join the Order. If you had starting bringing home girls before then, I would have been impressed a year ago, but now, being a mother myself, I would be shocked."

"Analysing the facts around a statement is a sure way to kill the romance, my love," he replied and looked around at his old toys and books on sturdy shelves. Eryn followed his gaze.

"Your mother fairly much left the room the way it was since you left, didn't she?"

"Yes. It would have been more sensible to clean it out and give it to one of Noren's children instead. But then the house is large enough for this not to be a necessity. Still." He sighed. "It's a strange feeling - coming back to a room from the past where every detail is still the same as back then. It makes me slightly uneasy. I remember sitting on the windowsill over there, dreading the sight of the coach that would bring Anwin back from one of his many journeys. The general mood in the house was a lot more relaxed and worry-free when he was abroad. Noren didn't fight for his approval, Leris didn't make it a point to hide from him, and I didn't have to sit down with him to go through the books and listen to his lectures about how my attitude then would never let me amount to much."

She bit her lip. "That sounds cosy. But then you went away, Leris ran off, and I suppose Noren doesn't have to compete for his father's attention with anybody any longer. So everyone is..." Happy seemed to be the wrong word here. "Satisfied," she concluded.

Enric shrugged. "I don't know about that. Looking at Noren, I can't help but feeling that he hasn't changed much. I suppose being close to Anwin all that time hasn't left much room for development. He is still jealous of me. He has been fighting for Anwin's attention, and later approval, all his life, while I - who never sought either but would rather have kept my distance - had my share of that when I turned out to be a magician. When it was decided that Noren would work with father to take over the business one distant day, that certainly made my brother more important than before, but still not enough to compete with my newly found glory. Anwin was the one to seek my attention, visited me in the city, tried to impress on me that we were family. Not for unselfish, fatherly reasons, mind you - he just wanted to use me for his own purposes. A magician in the family could be exploited for business purposes, after all." His voice sounded resentful.

Eryn looked around the room once again. It clearly showed that Enric's family had already been anything but poor when he was a child. The toys were of good quality, not crudely carved, and there were quite a number of them. She remembered her own little sleeping area with the small desk in the cottage she had shared with her father. Well, uncle, she should probably say now. Treban. Though that had not been his real name. Ved'al, then. There had not been many things that had no purpose other than to provide amusement. There was always paper and pens in different colours available. She copied the drawings in her... in Ved'al's medical books and hung them on the walls. The memory of her crude sketches of the human body scattered unevenly across the wall made her smile. Then there were books where she pressed herbs, little flasks where she had mixed flowers and herbs with oil to use them for decoration. Had she been raised by Malriel, her nursery would undoubtedly have looked a lot different.

"What are you thinking about, my love? You look a bit sad," he enquired softly.

"I was just thinking of how very different your and my childhood were. We were certainly less well off than your family, although I enjoyed working with my father so much more than you did with yours. When did you start accompanying him on his trips?"

"When I was ten years old. These were probably the two most trying years in my life. Not even catching up on all the knowledge and training after being assessed for second-strongest in the Order was that unpleasant. Suddenly the occasions before when he had been gone leaving us children alone with mother seemed like pure bliss in retrospect."

"It was that bad?" she asked sympathetically, taking his hand in hers.

"It was dreadful, especially after I discovered that he had been cheating on mother. I remember the particular evening well. I had just turned eleven. We were up north to negotiate for the supply of wool and were staying at an inn." His eyes had this far-away expression, as if the pictures were right in front of his eyes. "I had found a mistake in one of the contract clauses and went to Anwin's room to let him know. I walked in without knocking and found him in bed with the innkeeper's companion, her legs slung around his backside, her arms braced against the headboard of the bed while he laid, groaning, on top of her." His lips curled in disgust. "I stood there for a few moments, frozen in shock, then turned around, closed the door and returned to my room to hide under the blankets, trying in vain to get these pictures out of my head. I haven't managed to do it to this day."

"What did Anwin say?"

"Nothing at first. He didn't even run after me, not willing to interrupt his activities for such a trifle. I well remember the expression on his face when I barged into his room - it was more annoyed than shocked. As if my finding him in bed with another woman was nothing more than a nuisance, an unwelcome interruption for him while for me it was an experience that strangled the last bit of regard I had for him, the last morsel of dutiful love that was still left alive in me. The next morning we had breakfast and I tried to avoid looking at him as best I could. Neither of us said anything about the night before. From this time on I became more sensitive to his frequent straying. I noticed noises coming from his room, surreptitious glances before he entered another room that was not his. It was only several weeks later that I lost my temper and told him that I didn't want to come with him on his trips anymore, that I found his conduct despicable. He just glared at me and told me not to be so childish. He explained that this was a natural thing to do, that a man had needs that one woman was hardly ever able to satisfy, that I would understand this well enough once I took a companion." He squeezed her hand and managed a brittle smile. "He was wrong. I understand it even less now that I have you."

They both froze when they heard a noise from the corridor outside the room - behind the door that had not been closed fully. It sounded like a mix of a gasp and a sob.

Enric was the first to jump up and race to the door to yank it open. He paled when he found Gerit standing there, Vedric on her arm, silent tears running down her cheeks, her eyes wide, her lower lip quivering.

"Mother!" Enric whispered and cursed himself for his carelessness. Back in Anyueel he took precautions when having confidential conversations, such as soundproof barriers or choosing remote places, and here he hadn't even made sure the door was properly closed. It was a good thing that stupidity was not painful, or he would be twitching on the floor, in agony.

Gerit shook her head without saying a word, pushed the baby into her son's hands and turned around to run down the stairs.

Enric cursed and passed Vedric onto Eryn before running after her.

* * *

Enric sighed with profound relief when he heard the coach that would take them back to the city arriving. That meant that their stay here was coming to an end in only a few more minutes. He was sitting at the dining table with Eryn, who held Vedric on her lap, with Anwin leaning against a wall at the far end of the room. Nobody spoke. He didn't know where Noren and his companion were - and couldn't have cared less about it. But neither did he know where his mother was, and that bothered him greatly. Since she had fled from the house yesterday evening after overhearing his tale of her companion's continued infidelity, nobody had seen anything of her. And apart from him and Eryn, nobody really seemed to be worried about that. Did she make disappearing without giving a reason a habit so that the others here were used to it, or was it simply that nobody cared? He wasn't sure which option angered him more when proven correct.

The urge to be gone from here and leave Anwin and Noren behind him battled with the wish to stay at least long enough to locate his mother and ensure everything was alright with her. Though that term certainly was a tricky one, wasn't it? How could a woman who had just found out that her companion of several decades kept having casual sex with other women be alright? Again he cursed himself for his lack of caution when telling Eryn about this.

Eryn got to her feet and nodded to Anwin. "Our coach is here. Please tell Gerit that we said goodbye." There was nothing more to say at this point and she turned towards the door. Anwin had plummeted even further in her esteem since Enric's story yesterday. She was glad to be leaving here and swore to herself that she would never again drag Enric or Vedric to the house for another visit unless either of them expressed an urgent wish for it.

She had to think of Malriel and Valrad. Both her parents had cheated on their respective companions back when she was conceived. Gerit seemed to be the only one of their parents who had never gone astray and remained faithful to the man she had chosen to spend her life with. That was a sorry ratio indeed.

She hoped it was not a propensity to be passed on to the next generation, or the prospect for her and Enric's relationship was not exactly a cheerful one.

Anwin nodded once and didn't bother accompanying them outside.

Enric released a sigh of genuine relief once the coach set in motion. "That was a nightmare." And it was probably not yet over for his mother, he thought.

Eryn didn't look especially happy, either. "We really wreaked havoc yesterday evening. How is it possible that we could do so much damage in one single day?" She looked at him, her expression deeply concerned. "Do you think Gerit is going to handle the shock? She wouldn't do anything... rash, would she?"

He shook his head. "No, she wouldn't. She was always the controlled, prudent type who never lost her countenance in the face of trouble. I cannot recall ever hearing her raise her voice in anger at Anwin. And I don't need to tell you that there were more than sufficient opportunities for that."

Vedric slowly drifted off, swayed to sleep by the motion of the coach rocking. The fact that he had been active during the night might have helped as well.

Eryn looked out the window, thoughtful. "How is any woman supposed to react when she hears of a thing like that? How would I react? I suppose I would first wreck the house and then take off somewhere. I wouldn't keep it inside and suffer in silence."

Enric smiled without humour. "I wouldn't have pegged you for that type. Malhora blew up a wine cellar after finding her companion in bed with another woman, after all. But then I wouldn't do anything like that."

She raised one eyebrow at him. "That is very romantic, thinking that our affection will always be what it is now and all that. Even so, there might come a time one day when you are no longer as attached to me as you are now. Or you fall in love with another woman. It happens."

"That is possible, though highly unlikely. Yet even if that was the case, I would not cheat on you but leave you before engaging in anything that meant a breach of our oaths to each other. And I would expect you to do the same. If you ever put me in a position to find out that you had an affair or spent even a single night with another man while you are mine, I will kill him."

Eryn nodded. "I know." Then she chuckled. "But at least I know what to do in case I want to get rid of somebody and don't want to spend money on an assassin."

"Hilarious," Enric deadpanned, then returned to the topic of his mother. "I wish she hadn't run off like that, I wish I could have scooped her up and taken her with us to the city, away from that depressing place back there. Did you see how Werna treats her? As if she were little more than a servant? Even in her own house? I could kick Noren and Anwin for doing nothing to stop that. And now her life will be even more unbearable after discovering about Anwin and his infidelity. She didn't leave him after he grew distant and cold towards her all these years ago, so it would surprise me if this is enough for her to finally leave everything here. If she just packed her things and went away, I would even be glad that she had found out about it."

She sighed, wishing she could ease his pain somehow. But that was beyond magical healing. "She is a grown woman; she has to make her own choices, however little they may appeal to you."

He nodded curtly, his jaw muscles tightened like hawsers.

CHAPTER 22

Parenting for Beginners

Eryn opened the door to their house, glad to be back home and out of that coach. She was immensely grateful that the visit to Enric's family and the travelling in connection with it were over and she had a relaxing, quiet evening at home with her two boys ahead of her. She tried to avoid thinking back. There were just too many unpleasant events like how things were with Gerit, the fact that Werna had made sure that her children remained out of sight as long as their uncle and aunt from the city were there, and Anwin's aloofness to both his son and Eryn, even though he was the one who had repeatedly invited them over.

She turned when she heard Enric muttering to himself, "Oh dear." He was holding an envelope in his hand and lifted it with a grimace. "Mail from Takhan. Real mail. It seems that Vran'el has quite a bit more to say than would fit inside a bird tube..."

"No, please not now," Eryn groaned. "Can't we burn it and pretend it never arrived? I don't want to deal with this tonight. I'm in dire need of a cheery and cosy evening. Vran'el's reaction to discovering our little project doesn't fit the bill."

"It won't get any better if we ignore it. Even if we don't open it right now, we will still end up thinking about it. Come on, let's get this over with. It might not be as bad as we imagine." He held the letter out to her. "Here."

She snorted and took a step back, lifting both hands in front of her. "I am not going to open that. You do it. You are the one who can't wait to see what he writes."

"It's addressed to you."

"But you wanted to get the opening it behind us!"

"My other hand is full," he countered, nodding at Vedric on his arm.

"I'd be happy to relieve you from that load," she huffed and stepped towards him, her hands lifted towards her son.

"That's fine, rather take the letter. The boy is so much heavier, after all, and I am trying to be a gentleman here."

They both turned their heads when Plia came down the stairs, shaking her head at them. "So my two favourite magicians are back again. I could hear your bickering from my room." She came closer, and reached out for the envelope. "Give me that."

Enric chuckled and handed her the letter. "There you go, oh gallant one."

Plia's mouth twitched once before she ripped the envelope open and pulled out two sheets of paper. She started reading and looked worried after a few moments. "Uh, he really is rather displeased with you. He writes that your building a residence is a blatant demonstration of disloyalty and disobedience. And that he would have made you sign a legal document had he known that you would circumvent his instructions in such a way. Furthermore, he says that he probably shouldn't have expected anything different from an Aren woman, that you can obviously not be trusted any further than your mother."

Eryn threw up her hands. "Oh, come on! That was a low blow!"

Plia read on in silence for a few moments before nodding at Enric. "And he says you are not much better, that not being born into that damned House certainly hasn't prevented you from adapting to their ways within a very short time. He has made it known to society that he approved the project beforehand to avoid looking like a total dolt who has no control over what is happening in his House. That also includes his taking over all legal matters in connection with your residence from Ram'an as a demonstration that he is eager to assist his beloved sister in making her wish for her own place come true and to show the world that you are all one big, happy family with no tension between you whatsoever."

Enric whistled. "He does sound a fraction out of sorts with us, yes. Fortunately, he still has a few months to calm down before we meet him once again."

Eryn looked at the two sheets. "That's all? The letter seems rather longer."

The girl shrugged. "There are quite a few unflattering terms for both of you that I left off for now. I concentrated on the gist."

Enric took the letter from her hands and skimmed over it, looking for the entertaining passages. "Scheming minx," he murmured. "Very flattering." And a few moments later, "back-stabbing, insidious son of a jackal. That refers to me, obviously. Oh, that's rich, coming from a lawyer of all people." He read on. "And you are... wait, that I have to quote, that's almost poetic - a treacherous snake I nourished at my trusting, unsuspecting bosom only to have you turn on me and sink your poisonous fangs into my defenceless posterior. Look at that, he gets really creative when he feels upset with us. He is on a roll here. Let's provoke him more often, the result is hilarious." He laughed. "Here is another good one: You - Malriel's heartless progeny - are apparently determined to use your dark gift of invoking unspeakable misery to undo your only brother without a care in the world for his humble efforts to act in your best interest and ensure your happiness."

Eryn narrowed her eyes. "How very charming that you are so amused about the unflattering terms he uses to describe your companion who you claim to be so very protective of."

"He is your brother, my love. My trying to stop him from insulting you is like going against a law of nature."

She just shook her head at him and Plia, who giggled, finding this all immensely amusing.

"Any closing insults you wish to impart before I go upstairs to bath Vedric?"

Enric took another moment to let his eyes dart along the lines, then nodded. "Yes, there is another choice one that is aimed at both of us. He writes that he must have been of unsound mind when deciding that trusting a couple consisting of one Aren by birth and another one by adoption, and that he will have himself tested by Iklan at the earliest opportunity to avoid any more such wild misjudgements in the future."

"Fabulous," Eryn growled. "And that man is now officially in charge of having our house constructed? We had better check the entire building for booby traps before we move in."

He waved her off. "No, he wouldn't endanger Vedric."

"Then probably just our bedroom?"

Enric thought for a moment, then nodded. "Yes, that might be advisable. I don't think he might do anything that would truly harm us, but I bet it wouldn't be beyond him to use some of the herbs your father plants in the Vel'kim gardens to cause us some discomfort by way of itching bedsteads or door handles."

Eryn lifted Vedric onto her hip and sighed. "That's your uncle, my boy. And you are supposed to succeed him one day. I seriously dread the things you will learn from that nutjob."

*　*　*

Pe'tala, sitting in her chair in her study at the clinic, raised and then lowered her brow several times while reading the letter her brother had sent to her sister.

"I like it where he calls you a treacherous snake. He does have quite a way with words, does he not?"

"You just wait until he finds out that you are going to move in with us. Lucky you, you won't have to wait for a letter, you'll have the whole fun face-to-face with him," Eryn growled. "Then it will be my turn to laugh."

"I am hardly surprised," the younger woman said without much enthusiasm. "At least I have a pretty clear idea about the degree of support I will have from your side when the time comes."

"I've had my share of being cut down to size under the pretext of brotherly solicitude. And, you know, at least you won't harbour any misconceptions. Dashed expectations are such an unpleasant thing to deal with, after all."

Pe'tala shook her head. "A little sisterly consolation might have been a nice touch nevertheless. Yet as Vran writes, I am dealing with - wait, let me get this right - here it is: Malriel's heartless progeny."

"Oh, shut up. I assume that he will come up with a few equally flattering terms for you soon enough. And quoting them in return will tickle me no end," Eryn snorted. "So, you need to excuse me now. I am due at the Council hall in a few minutes. Why can't they have those meetings in the afternoon, I ask you? Going there directly after a night shift does not exactly do wonders for my ability to stay awake and appear halfway attentive. A few hours of sleep would certainly help. Not that being at home with Vedric is much more restful for Enric, mind you."

"You are both insane. You should hire a nursemaid," Pe'tala stated with conviction. "Or stop dabbling in so many different areas at once as long as my nephew is so small. Why do you not take a break from the clinic for a year as getting out of the Council is not something you can effect?"

Eryn rolled her eyes. "Not you, too! I don't want to pay a stranger to raise my son for me. I know it's common practice here, but I don't approve of it."

"I am not suggesting you delegate raising him entirely, just for a few hours every day or second day. Why are you so damn stubborn with regard to this? When did Enric last get a proper night's sleep? This is not only about you, he is suffering from your obstinate refusal to be sensible as well. A child is not just another element that needs to fit into an established routine, you need to adapt to its needs without destroying yourself in the process."

"We have changed our routines a lot, I'll have you know. I have stopped working during the days, have relinquished teaching the trainees to you and..."

"Eryn," Pe'tala tried again. "You have not reduced your hours at the clinic, just shifted the time of day you are there. And Enric works during the day instead of catching up on lost sleep. None of this is healthy. And while you may be able to catch a few hours of sleep at night here at the clinic every now and then, Enric does not look like he is able to be as lucky."

Eryn sent her a stern look. "I have no intention of giving up working at the clinic - it keeps me in contact with adult people and I have worked too hard to make all this here possible just to step back like that. And it's only for a few more months. Vedric will sooner or later start sleeping through the nights, then everything will be easier. Why don't we continue that talk when you have children yourself?"

"Sure, oh wise and knowledgeable one," Pe'tala called after her when she stepped out into the corridor. "A few months of motherhood definitely taught you the way of the world and how to triumph over common sense when it is applied by those who have not yet reproduced!"

Eryn let the door slam closed behind her, battling the urge to throw back another insulting remark in favour of arriving at the Palace in time for the Council meeting. Being responsible was no fun at all.

* * *

Eryn listened to Orrin presenting the rules and particulars of the game, which would take place in only a few days. About half the Council had signed up for it, among them Tyront, Enric, herself, and of course Orrin. Surprisingly enough Lord Seagon, the old sourpuss, would be participating as well. Eryn hoped he would be on the other team so she would have a shot at taking him out.

Exactly as in Takhan, Enric would take over the first team while Orrin would lead the other one.

The meeting had been going on for almost an hour now. Firstly, Lord Poron had presented his plans for searching for a replacement for Rolan, as he would be gone in a few months, then Tyront had informed them that Ram'kel was due to arrive in about ten days to take over the position of ambassador to Anyueel, and then the results of this year's testing sessions were discussed and so on and so forth.

She had her head propped against one fist, trying to appear interested and alert while her head became heavier with every passing minute. She was wondering idly how much longer this would be going on today and if she could convince Tyront to hold meetings a little later in the day from now on, when suddenly the entire room fell silent and made her perk up. She frowned and followed the direction of where every single gaze was pointed: at Enric, who had leaned back in his uncomfortable chair, his head lolled slightly to one side, his eyes closed, his chest rising and sinking in a slow, deep rhythm.

Eryn swallowed, shocked. He had fallen asleep, right in the middle of the Council meeting - and everyone was aware of it. She was too far away to give him a surreptitious nudge or anything of that sort to wake him. Well, at least he wasn't snoring, one part of her brain added with a streak of gallows humour.

Tyront lifted his hand to place it on Enric's shoulder. The contact jerked the younger man awake and there was a minute moment of horror when he realised what he had let happen before his features composed themselves into a contemplative expression with a swiftness that made Eryn blink.

"It appears as if I lost my focus for a moment there. My most sincere apologies for that, esteemed colleagues. It will not happen again," Enric offered with a smoothness that made the fact that he had just been caught napping in a Council meeting appear almost surreal.

Lord Woldarn was opening his mouth, judging from his frown and displeased look to air a critical remark, but Tyront cut in quickly, "I suggest we continue with what Lord Orrin was telling us and then conclude this meeting for today."

Orrin nodded once, then wrapped up his contribution in a matter of minutes, clearly speeding things up.

When all magicians around the table arose, Tyront cleared his throat and nodded at Eryn. "A minute of your time, if you can spare it." Then he turned to Enric. "And you go home and lie down. This is an order."

He didn't wait for Enric to acknowledge the command, but got up to step next to Eryn while they were waiting for all others to leave the hall.

Once the door had closed with its customary loud boom, leaving them alone in the room that suddenly seemed eerily large and empty, Tyront leaned against the table, folding his arms and looking down at Eryn who had remained seated.

She waited for her superior to speak, but he didn't and just stood there, watching her with a strangely contented expression, though clearly waiting for something.

When he still hadn't uttered anything after more than a minute, she started kneading her fingers, then burst out, "I know there is some need for change, and it's more urgent than I would have suspected."

Tyront pursed his lips and just kept looking at her.

Eryn cursed herself for her inability to keep her mouth shut. She should have played it cool: sitting there, staring right back at him, show him that she had no problem whatsoever with just waiting for him to break the uncomfortable, mind-numbing, oddly penetrating silence. But she was so very obviously no match for him in this little game that anger at herself was nothing more than a waste of her energy.

"You think this is my fault, don't you? That my decision not to hire a nursemaid is the reason why he is so exhausted that he can't even keep his eyes open any longer and dozes off in the middle of a bloody Council meeting."

He raised his brow at her, yet remained silent. She wanted to grab the front of his robes and shake something out of him. A single word, a grunt, a derisive chuckle, anything.

"I know what everybody thinks of my way of raising our son," she went on, again filling the quiet with words despite her better judgement. "And yes, it is a great strain on Enric." She exchanged another long stare with Tyront, then threw her hands up into the air in frustration before exclaiming in defeat, "Alright, you win! I'll think of something! Give me two days to find a solution I can live with."

Now Tyront smiled and finally spoke. "That's what I wanted to hear. That's my girl!"

She grimaced in disgust at the term and shot him an annoyed look. "Anything to earn your approval, My Lord."

He clucked his tongue. "You were doing so well just now. Don't spoil it. And now get out of here and start thinking about that solution you promised me. Off you go."

She swallowed an acid remark, bowed and left, wondering why his sober mirth provoked her so much more than any sternness could have. And how was it possible that she had done what he wanted even though he hadn't uttered a single word? Never until now had she realised what an oppressive and powerful tool directed silence could be.

*   *   *

Eryn was walking with Vedric up and down in the parlour, trying to tune out his constant whimpering. Urban had already fled back out into the yard, as far away from the continuous noise as possible.

She had raised a soundproof barrier along one wall and the ceiling to reduce the noise level enough for Enric to catch up on much needed sleep. Vedric was restless and whiney, repeatedly dropping asleep against her shoulder only to be wide awake again as soon as she attempted to lay him down or even take a seat with him on her arm. Walking up and down seemed the only way to reduce his discontentment to a level that was at least bearable for her ears for a longer period. Without the benefit of magically aided strength her arms would probably have fallen numb and dropped the child at some point in the course of the more than one and half hours she had been at this now.

The temptation of sending him to sleep with just a very tiny dose of magic was so great that resisting it was almost physically painful. It was a dangerous path to follow. If it was done once then there would be even less hesitation doing so again. And again. It was a practice that was condemned vigorously, and rightly so. If a child showed discontent for whatever reason, it was always the expression of an unfulfilled need. And sedating a helpless human and robbing him of his limited opportunities to communicate with his surroundings was an abominable course of action. Furthermore, it would hamper his progress in developing both mentally and physically. It was an immensely wrong thing to do. And yet...

The more exhausted she was, the sterner she had to be with herself not to fall into that trap. Once again. The last time she had used her healing magic for selfish reasons had cost her dearly. Not ever again. She released a long sigh and kept on pacing and swaying Vedric, hoping against hope that he would drift off for more than a few minutes so that she could at least sit down with him.

She had taken the night off. Enric needed to sleep, and she needed time to think. She wondered if she would be able to find a solution that would not force her to go against her conviction to trust a stranger with her son. But then there was little choice unless she didn't want to stop working at the clinic, was there? How about taking Vedric with her during the nights? No, that was absurd. There were nights where this wouldn't be a problem, but others were so very busy that she wouldn't have any time at all for him. Apart from the cruelty of ignoring her crying son beside her, the patients would surely also not be too thrilled at having to endure the constant wailing in addition to their own ailments, which were serious enough to make them attend the clinic in the dead of night.

Asking Junar to take Vedric more often was out of the question, as well. Though Téa was a model child concerning sleeping through the night and being content with being close to either of her parents when awake, Vedric was a lot more demanding. Being in his line of sight was not enough to keep him quiet. He wanted to be carried around constantly and demanded attention to a degree he simply couldn't get when there was another infant around but only one adult. If Eryn had considered having another child anytime soon before, she would have changed that plan now at the very latest.

Eryn stopped in her tracks. Had there been a knocking at the entrance door? She was pretty much deaf to the world around her right now. She hadn't had a chance to lie down since her night shift and the subsequent Council meeting, and her brain was getting more and more sluggish. Even identifying sounds was an effort, especially with the alternating levels of Vedric's crying.

She was considering whether to check if there truly was a visitor or if the sound had been a figment of her imagination, when it came again, a little more loudly this time.

Opening the door, she froze at the sight and blinked a few times to make sure her brain wasn't taking revenge on her for depriving it of the sleep it needed by providing hallucinations.

"Gerit?" she asked, determined to have her ears back up the evidence her eyes kept trying to convince her of.

"Yes," Enric's mother said quietly, her cheeks more hollow than they were only a few days before, her eyes slightly puffy as if she had spent some time crying recently. Which was very likely exactly what had happened.

It took Eryn another few moments to overcome her initial shock and remember that stepping aside and letting her visitor enter instead of leaving her standing outside in the frosty darkness of the street would be a splendid idea.

She tried to make her brain come up with an appropriate question, but the ones that wanted out needed to be avoided, they would have sounded abrupt and unwelcoming; such as What are you doing here? or Does that mean you have left Anwin?

But there was an unchallenging question she could ask. "What would you like to drink?"

Gerit seemed slightly taken aback at the question, but recovered quickly, put down the bag she had slung over her shoulder, took off her cloak and then reached out to take her grandson from Eryn. "Something warm would be lovely, if it isn't too much bother."

Eryn felt a quick stab of guilt at the relief when she handed over her son to the other woman. Freedom had many faces, and one of them was being able to be released from the dependence of another human being, even if only for a few short minutes. She wondered briefly it that made her a bad mother, then decided to deal with those thoughts when she felt rested. In case such a state of mind and body was something that was meant to be part of her not too distant future. She clumsily fished two mugs out of a cupboard, added a few spoonfuls of powder and mixed it with cool water that she then heated with a touch of magic.

"You look dreadful," Gerit said seriously when Eryn handed her a mug.

Eryn replied without thinking, "So do you." Then she closed her eyes for a moment and was about to apologise.

But Gerit only nodded. "I imagine I do. But then my exhaustion is emotional, yours is physical. Overcoming mine will take months, maybe even years. Yours can be solved in a day with just a little sleep."

"Enric is asleep upstairs," Eryn explained, not exactly sure why this was supposed to be important right now. Maybe as a justification why he wasn't here to welcome his mother who he had been worried about since their departure after the mess they had made?

"Good. Then you should join him there once you have finished your drink," Gerit instructed her with a faint smile.

"Vedric's room still has a proper bed in it," Eryn ventured, wondering sluggishly if that would be perceived as the invitation to stay she had meant it as.

"I am glad to hear it. I am sure I will be most comfortable in it. Drink up, girl. And be mindful of the steps, be sure not to stumble. I assume Vedric has already been fed?"

Eryn nodded groggily.

"Excellent. Now up you go, my dear. My grandson and I will be fine. He will distract me from my worries and give me the chance to be useful again after quite a long time."

* * *

Enric woke slowly from what had to have been at least twenty hours of sleep judging from the late morning light that spilled in through the window. He lay there a moment longer with eyes half-open and took stock. Not the way Eryn did with a pulse of magic through her body that would report to her whatever needed mending inside her. He just tried to work out what his general condition was at this very moment. Well rested, for one. That was a state he had not been in for several weeks now. He tried to remember when he had last slept more than two unbroken hours and decided that it must have been back in Takhan.

Funny, how he had never been thinking much about sleep. It was just something one did when the mind and body got tired and signalled that they wanted to shut down for a while. Now it had evolved in importance and turned into a luxury.

He turned his head and raised both eyebrows in surprise when he spotted Eryn next to him, prone, her pillow caught in a death grip between her forearm and her face. She was snoring quietly, an unusual occurrence. He remembered that she had not been able to go to bed after her night shift yesterday and also not after the meeting as Tyront had ordered him to lie down. That meant she had been forced to stay up all day. He had felt bad about that before collapsing on the bed.

Rising carefully to avoid waking her, he dressed quietly and then moved to the washroom, regarding his reflection with a critical eye. The usual bags under his eyes where still visible but not as pronounced as they tended to be lately. He closed his eyes for a moment, and when he opened them again, the dark shadows were gone. He rubbed his hand over his short beard and turned his face this way and that, wondering if it needed trimming. He tried to remember when he had last done it and failed to come up with an answer. Somehow these routine tasks had merged into an oddly indistinguishable blob lately.

When he re-emerged from the washroom a little later - scrubbed, trimmed and smelling clean - he stepped towards Vedric's room, opening the door as silently as he could manage. He frowned. The little bed against one wall was empty. How tired had Eryn been yesterday? Was it even possible to misplace a wailing child? He listened for any tell-tale sounds of an abandoned infant, but there was nothing.

He wondered if she had left the boy with Junar. Probably.

Trotting down the stairs he lifted his nose and breathed in the smell of food. The servants had obviously prepared breakfast.

He froze in mid-step when he followed the scent into the dining room, staring in utter disbelief at the woman who was sitting there on a chair, her grandson on her lap, feeding him morsels of soft bread and what looked like some mash of grain or fruit.

"Mother?" He wasn't still asleep and dreaming, was he?

"Enric," Gerit said and smiled. "A good morning to you. I arrived yesterday evening, and Eryn was so kind as to invite me to stay." She seemed a little unsure now. "I hope this doesn't upset you. You offered it to me in the past, so I thought..."

Enric had recovered enough to approach her and bend down to kiss her forehead. "Don't be ridiculous, mother. You are more than welcome here, always." He smiled and shook his head. "And not just because you seem to be the reason why Eryn and I were both able to lie down for a couple of hours at the same time. You know that you don't have to earn the right to stay here by tending to Vedric, I hope?"

Gerit lifted her chin. "I know. You were never one to charge others for your generosity. And this is why doing it is even more of a pleasure for me." She wiped Vedric's face with a damp cloth to remove the smears from his breakfast. "He is an energetic one. You were not like that, you were the quietly mischievous kind where I only started worrying when I couldn't hear you anymore. Your son must be turning out more like his mother, then. I haven't known her for long, mind you, but we hear stories."

He grinned lopsidedly. "Yes, it certainly seems like that. He will certainly keep us on our toes in the years to come." He sat down next to her, heaping food on his plate, marvelling at the strangeness of sitting at a breakfast table in the big city with his mother, who he had never in all these years been able to convince to visit him. He wanted to ask her about the significance of this particular visit, if it meant that she had finally decided to leave her companion or if she had taken some time away from her home to consider her next steps. Enric hoped for the first, very much so, yet couldn't bring himself to phrase it as a question. She might misunderstand it in such a way that he was asking her to divine when he might get rid of her again. And nothing was further from the truth.

He wasn't sure how to approach the topic. Gerit had always been one to keep her grievances to herself instead of sharing them with somebody. Her companion had certainly never been one to encourage her to do so, and she would never have burdened her children with any of her distress. She had been the one to listen to others instead.

He heard how a door upstairs closed. That had to be Eryn. Plia was usually already busy at the clinic at this time of day. And sure enough, little later his companion appeared in the door frame, fully clothed, obscuring her yawn with the back of her hand before sauntering into the room, kissing Enric on the top of his head and then moving on towards Gerit to release her from her grandson.

"Good morning."

Gerit held on to Vedric when Eryn tried to lift him. "Why don't you leave him with me a bit longer, my dear? Better eat something first."

Eryn shrugged and did just that. She was not about to argue with a woman who willingly granted her a few undisturbed moments to take care of basic human needs such as sleeping and eating. She pushed a few pieces of fried vegetable from the platter onto her plate, then hesitated before looking at Gerit.

"We are sorry for what happened when we visited you. That was certainly not the best way to repay your hospitality. Is there anything we can do?"

Enric's mother pursed her lips and leaned back, handing her grandson a spoon to occupy him with something blunt. "Are you now. We may start with the understanding of hospitality," she started softly. "The way Anwin, Noren and his companion treated you had certainly very little to do with the concept. The way I was raised, it includes somewhat more than providing food and shelter. As for the other..." Her gaze wandered to her son. "I grieve for the kind of experiences you made when on the road with your father. It would have been my duty to protect you from things like that." Her voice turned slightly bitter. "But how could I - it would have required opening my eyes to my own situation first, helping myself before thinking of helping others."

"Mother, you don't..." Enric started but halted when his mother lifted her hand to stop him.

"No, please let me finish. It will do me good to get it all out after all these years." She returned to what she had been talking about. "I wanted to bring Vedric to you that evening when I heard you talking. I was raised in the belief that eavesdropping is a despicable thing to do, but after hearing the first few words I couldn't help myself. In these last few days I have kept asking myself whether I was always aware of his infidelity deep inside me, if I just didn't want to see it or if I really was that blind. I don't know which is worse. I spent that one night at an inn in town and returned only after you had left." She glanced at Enric. "I was so ashamed, I couldn't bear facing you. You would never do a thing like that to your companion, I know." Her eyes wandered to Eryn. "And you would never stand for it, would you? You are strong. Just like my Leris. I was so happy when you told me that she has found a gentle man who lets her be herself. Anwin was wrong to reject him just because he was a lumberjack. And then there is Werna. She and I never really got along too well, I have to admit, but I always admired her bravery, her unwillingness to accept anything less than she felt she was due. At least that's what I thought." Gerit shook her head at a memory. "When I returned to the house, I was furious. I have never been one to share with the world what was going on inside me. I wasn't raised that way. It was considered inadvisable and unladylike. But that day..." She smiled faintly. "That day I made the decision to not hold back any longer. I wrecked the living room, then moved on to the kitchen to break everything that wouldn't withstand being thrown to the floor before I finally went upstairs to cut Anwin's clothes to pieces and stab the pillows with a knife."

Eryn stared at her, impressed that this serene woman had made a decision to wreak havoc instead of just losing control. Now she had a very clear idea where Enric had his control from. Enric seemed equally surprised, but found his words quickly.

"And Anwin just watched you without interfering or trying to stop you?" he asked.

Gerit lifted her chin. "He tried to, once. But then I jabbed him hard in the stomach with a broomstick. Nothing life-threatening, he merely doubled over and fought for air for a few moments, but then he made the very wise decision to stay out of my way until I was done. Noren was utterly shocked and stood there and stared while Werna kept wailing and pulling out her hair." She swallowed once. "The only thing I regret was scaring the children, though I suspect that after a while they might have been more fascinated by the spectacle than afraid. But the worst thing," she continued with an expression of disgust, "was to come yet. When I had exhausted myself and all but collapsed on the ruined bed upstairs, Werna came in and started lecturing me.

She told me that I had acted in a most disgraceful manner, that I was to pull myself together and stop acting like the highborn lady I obviously still thought I was. That I needed to be mindful of our reputation, of not giving rise to any unpleasant rumours that would reflect badly on all of us." Her lips were pressed together into a thin line. "Can you believe that? After learning a thing like that about my companion, she lectured me on preserving appearances! And then she told me something that almost made the blood in my veins freeze from shock. She stated in the most matter-of-fact way you may imagine that this was just the way men were, that Noren, too, had been bedding other women for many years now and that she as a dutiful companion would never in her wildest dreams have acted as childishly as I was doing. That almost broke my heart, you know. Not Werna's twisted ideas what a companion's duties are, but that Anwin's atrocious behaviour has impressed on Noren that this was the natural way to act when in a companionship, when having a family. He has thus not only brought misery to his own family, but made sure to spread it to the next generation as well." She lowered her gaze. "Looking back, it certainly was a blessing that you and Leris went away as soon as you could - no matter how much it hurt me to lose you both. It might have been what saved your own chances for happiness."

Enric rubbed his face. Well, Eryn had certainly managed to get his mother to talk. "Would I be right in assuming that you have no intention of returning back to Anwin?"

Gerit lifted her chin proudly, and Eryn could see what might have induced Werna to make that remark about the high-born lady. There were definitely still traces of that left in her bearing, no matter how much time she had spent in the countryside away from her origins.

"You would be, yes."

"Good, I approve. Very much, in fact. That means we will look for a house for you not too far away from here within easy walking distance. Until then you will stay here. Vedric can sleep in our room until we have found something suitable."

Eryn cleared her throat. "Hold your horses, Order lord. Not everybody who happens to spend more than a minute in that city is bound to follow your commands, you know. What if your mother has no intention of staying in the city? Or if she would rather stay here at our house? Or if she would rather live in a different part of the city? You can't just run around and pick houses you like for people to live in!"

Enric smiled. "It worked well enough with you, if you remember."

She rolled her eyes in exasperation. "Because anything would have been preferable to the Palace for me! But that doesn't mean you should turn this into a habit."

He gave in and turned to his mother. "Forgive me, mother. I will of course take your wishes into consideration here. What is it that you want to do now?"

Gerit absent-mindedly pushed a fork out of Vedric's reach when he attempted to grab it. "I was considering staying in the city. Though I do not have the means to buy a house here." She shook her head when her son made to speak. "I know that you would be more than willing to pay for it, but this is not how I intend to spend the rest of my life - depending on your charity."

Eryn snorted at that. "You know, I am on his side in this case. His money provides shelter for about two hundred orphans in this city, so I would say that letting him take care of a place for you is not too much of an imposition. It also helps him - he doesn't have to worry about you that way. And it's not like that will be a drain on his funds, let me tell you that much. He is filthy rich - on both sides of the sea."

"It won't be a drain on our funds," Enric corrected her with only a hint of reproach. "And we are filthy rich."

"Whatever you say, darling." She leaned over and patted his head, pulling her hand back quickly when he swatted at it.

Eryn then turned towards Gerit. "Though I would advise that you and I take care of selecting a house for yourself. Enric might otherwise set you up with a residence where you would get lost three times just on your way from the parlour to the nearest washroom." She continued at Enric's irritated look, "May I remind you of the house we are building in Takhan? The one that is easily large enough to house five or six families instead of only two?"

He sighed in defeat. "As you wish. But I trust you will at least let me determine the quality of the places you consider suitable?"

"Certainly. I wouldn't want to exclude you completely from this," Eryn granted him generously and finally attacked the vegetables on her plate, not minding in the least that they had gone cold in the meantime. "By the way, I promised Tyront I would think of something to make sure that you don't fall asleep during Council meetings anymore because taking care of that lively son of yours exhausts you so much."

Both of them turned towards Gerit, when she rose from her chair and smiled. "I think I can be of service here. So finding a place near your house would be advisable, after all. If you would excuse us now, I have the distinct feeling that my grandson needs cleaning up."

Enric watched his mother leave the room and climb the stairs to the upper floor before turning to his companion. "I know you are dead set against a nursemaid, but I hope having my mother aid us is an acceptable alternative for you? It is maybe not advisable to trust her taste in men, but she certainly knows how to raise children."

Eryn laughed. "Are you kidding me? This is perfect! We won't ask her to tend him every day, but if she can help us two or three times a week - this would be fabulous. And I wouldn't have to admit to the world out there that I was wrong by hiring a nursemaid. See? That is the ideal solution for all of us!"

He shook his head at her and sipped at his drink. "Of course. If your pride doesn't have to take a dent, everything is fine, isn't it?"

"You said it!" she agreed cheerfully and gobbled down another spoonful of fried vegetables. "I like it when there are unexpected beneficial things happening for a change."

CHAPTER 23

Fun and Games

"So, how are things going with your mother and your companion living under the same roof?" Tyront enquired.

"Well enough, luckily. Mother is glad for the distraction Vedric provides, and Eryn and I appreciate that we can work and now occasionally even sleep in peace," Enric explained.

"Tell me again why having Gerit mind your son is so much more acceptable for Eryn than hiring a nursemaid, will you?"

"She says it's a difference whether somebody looks after him because they are paid to do so or is genuinely concerned with his wellbeing. She doesn't want Vedric to be in somebody's custody who considers him little more than a duty."

Tyront shook his head. "And she has managed to get help without being seen to give in to the pressure of hiring a nursemaid. Especially after your little nap at the Council meeting."

The younger man smiled. "She mentioned something like that, yes."

"If you keep collecting people to live at your house, you will soon have to start working on making inhabitable that second floor you keep for nothing more than storage right now."

"My mother living with us is just a temporary solution. I don't think it is advisable for a man to live in the same house with one or both of his parents after a certain age. Eryn will soon start viewing houses with her."

The Order's leader nodded. "She intends to stay in the city, then. No intentions to return to her companion, it seems."

Enric shook his head, his expression cold. "No, and I can't tell you how glad I am about this. I had given up on the chance of her ever leaving him, but it appears that the degree of suffering has finally reached a level where staying with him would have been worse than leaving him. Considering how things have turned out so far, I no longer feel bad about her overhearing me when I told Eryn about Anwin's infidelity. It obviously gave her the push she needed."

"And Eryn will be the one to look for a house with her? How come you are not doing that yourself?"

"As our residence in Takhan is going to be quite a bit more spacious than she approves of, she is afraid that I will settle my mother with a monstrosity of a house where she will continuously get lost. So she insists on doing this in my place. And I don't really mind, it is a good occasion for her to get to know my mother better. Eryn does generally not do too well with female relations, at least at the beginning, so this will do them both good. They will start their search after the game."

Tyront leaned back in his chair. "That sounds like things are turning out well enough. Speaking of the game, I was surprised to find Eryn on the list of Orrin's team. I thought that maybe after being on different sides in Takhan you would for a change wish to fight together. There are no considerations of being seen to be on the right side here in Anyueel for either of you, after all."

Enric smiled and shook his head. "I think she enjoys opposing me every now and then, and the playing field is a place where she can do so without fearing retribution. And our powers will be on the same level for a little while - that is a chance she won't have again so soon. She took me out with Ram'an in the first game. I suspect she will try it again this time."

"Is she aware that it is going to be quite a bit harder here?"

"Not yet. But I am very much looking forward to introducing her to that little snippet. Orrin has paired her up with Pe'tala."

Tyront grinned. "Is she aware of the significance of this?"

"No. Not yet. Battle strategy was one of her least favourite subjects. But I suppose she will have a look or two at a few of the books afterwards to avoid being used like this in the future. Which is probably exactly what Orrin is aiming at, the sly old dog."

"You are paired with Rolan, so it seems like Pe'tala and him have no objections to fighting on different sides, either. The attitude in your companion's family is quite an interesting one."

Enric chuckled at the memory of the first game. "You can say that again. Everybody thinks Aren are the belligerent ones, but Vel'kim certainly has a streak of that as well. People are fooled by the fact that most of them train to be healers and think it makes them more compassionate in all aspects of their lives. Back in Takhan Eryn paired up with her brother, and I with his companion. We even had a short encounter in the streets. I fear the day Eryn and Malriel participate in the same game. But at least with the manacles their powers wouldn't amount to enough to lay waste to their surroundings. Even so."

Tyront grimaced. "Then let's make sure to try this first in Takhan and not here, shall we? They are used to Aren women reducing structures to rubble over there."

"That they are, yes. But they are even more wary of Malriel, because unlike her mother and her daughter, she has so far refrained from doing anything of that sort. It's like people are waiting for her to get it out of her system. The fact that she has held back so much despite the unpleasant things that happened to her in the last two years, such as finding her daughter only to have her renounce her family and then after Malriel's return from Kar refuse to give up her position as Head of House and spend Malriel's life savings for a charity project... And still no crumbling walls or falling roofs."

"So people are afraid of having it all erupt at once? What do you think? Is that a real danger?"

"I wouldn't think so, no. But I suspect that Malriel secretly enjoys the sentiment. Malhora told Eryn once that collapsing the odd building without injuring anyone was a handy way of reminding people to think twice before messing with an Aren. So it is a strategy that runs in the family. Her grandmother was enormously pleased when Eryn collapsed the Senate roof. That it really was loss of control and no calculation that induced her to do it makes obviously little difference."

Tyront exhaled. "What a family. And you are right in the middle. After getting to know Pe'tala a little I wonder which House I would want your son to take after. With our luck he will be a nice mix of the worst from each side of his mother's family."

"You know what I like about you?" Enric asked with a grin. "That you always stay positive."

*　*　*

Eryn leaned back in her chair in the treatment room and took a sip from her hot beverage. She had already reheated it three times because she always forgot to drink until it had become cold again. Only a few more minutes and her shift would be over and she could return home to a warm, soft, spacious bed. The expression on her face became dreamy at the mere thought.

The night had not been particularly busy; there had just been enough patients spread across the night to prevent her from getting any sleep at all. And being awake all the time without continuous activity was tedious and thus almost as exhausting - if a lot less satisfying - as actual work.

She was about to get up when there was a knock at the door. Rotten timing. She had hoped that it would be quiet enough for the last few minutes that any incoming patients could then be taken over by the day shift. No such luck, as it seemed.

"Come in," she called, trying to keep the irritation from her voice.

Her eyes bulged when the door opened and Ram'kel of House Arbil stepped inside, a bright smile on his face. He was dressed suitably for this season - a warm tunic in dark red and black trousers, sturdy dark leather boots and a cape that looked as if it could brave the local winters. He had chosen a style that reminded people of his origins, but was a lot less bold and colourful than what his countrymen usually liked to wear. Ram'kel clearly was adapting rapidly.

His tan face was surrounded by dark, almost black hair that was much shorter than she remembered. His features, so unlike his older brother's yet appealing, suggested rogue much rather than ambassador. What had she been thinking when asking for him to be made ambassador, she wondered.

"What are you doing here? You are not supposed to be here yet, but to be arriving in two days!" The words escaped her mouth before she could reign in her tongue. So much for greeting a diplomat adequately.

"Lady Maltheá of House Vel'kim, it is my pleasure to see you again," he replied slickly, wrapping all the elements she found trying at the best of times into one greeting that made the tiny hairs at the back of her neck rise: addressing her with Lady, calling her by the name her mother had given her and reminding her that she was a member of Vran'el's House when she currently wanted to throttle him for his insensitivity. They were certainly off to a good start, she thought grimly. But then her own welcoming had not exactly been warm, either.

"Careful, Ambassador," she warned him with a smile that really wasn't one. "Provoking an Aren woman is not said to be good for the health - especially when she hasn't slept all night long."

"How lovely to see that motherhood has given you that shine, that tender radiance of gentleness I have heard people mention," he remarked, unperturbed.

Eryn sighed, too tired for these games right now. "What are you doing here, Ram'kel?"

"Here in the city when you would have expected me only in two days or here in your treatment room where I am currently keeping you from your doubtlessly well-earned sleep?"

This man was playing with fire, and judging from the glint in his brown eyes that were pretty much the only thing that reminded her of Ram'an, he was perfectly aware of it.

She reminded herself to be polite and calm. She had picked him, after all. It wouldn't do to give him a proper kicking under these circumstances. And the King wouldn't like it. He tended to be polite with her in a way that made her feel like a scolded child afterwards when he didn't like something.

"Why don't you start with the first? When did you arrive? And why so early?" She made an effort to make the words sound less like an accusation and instead more like a politely directed enquiry.

"I arrived late last night. I heard that you were about to stage your first game here and wanted to observe how it goes. It is going to be quite an event, I understand. I briefly considered asking Lord Orrin to let me join in, but then I do not think I would stand much of a chance against the training your colleagues have received here over the course of many years. Another reason for my earlier than planned departure from Takhan was the ongoing evaluation of the triarchy. It is always a rather tense time, especially for the senators. And I happened to live with one, as you know. I do not know if you are familiar with our law in this regard? Our triarchs are chosen for a given period of time, namely five years, and then a thorough check of their past actions and decisions is carried out. If their performance and conduct are beyond reproach, they are granted another term."

Eryn remembered that. Ram'an had told her about that when he had been here as ambassador back then. They had joked together that they should probably refrain from suggesting a similar system to King Folrin. "Alright, I understand. And what is it I can do for you on this bright if rather chilly morning?"

"As you were instrumental in getting me this position I felt that I should not wait for you to hear of my arrival from anybody but myself. And then there was this unquenchable desire to lay eyes on you again, to bask in your beauty and have your benevolence shine over me." He stepped closer, took her hand and pressed a kiss onto her knuckles, lingering longer than was polite.

Eryn rolled her eyes and pulled away her hand. "You are so full of it. Go and strain somebody else's nerves, will you? And if you dare talk to me like that in public, I will kick you where it hurts most. Publicly. And that is the gentle option, mind you. Enric wouldn't be as kind."

Ram'kel leaned against her desk and grinned widely, obviously enjoying himself immensely. "I would never be so undiplomatic as that, my dear Lady Maltheá."

"Call me that again and you will get that kick right now," she growled.

"Ah, but you see, it would appear disloyal towards House Aren to address you with the name Ved'al chose to hide you from them for so long. You would surely not want to put me in such a predicament, would you?" he purred.

"Surely not! How could I ever?" Eryn exclaimed in pretended horror. Then she rose. "Not that I don't appreciate it immensely that you came all the way to the clinic to get on my nerves after a night shift, but I really need my bed right now or I will lack the restraint not to inflict pain on you, after all."

He nodded in seriousness. "I do commend you on your restraint and will of course no longer be the obstacle that keeps you from a good day's sleep. Can I induce you to have lunch with me instead?"

"No. Go away."

"Dinner, then. I will pick you up. I know that you are not working tonight as you wish to be fit for the game tomorrow."

"No!" she repeated with emphasis.

Ram'kel bowed with a broad grin. "I shall see you later, then. I trust you still do not eat meat?" he said as if she had not just refused his invitation outright.

Eryn closed her eyes and counted to ten, relieved, when she heard the door close and the new ambassador was gone.

She knew he presented no danger to her. His flirting was blunt and meant to provoke her, but wasn't serious. Ram'an had never played around like that; when he had touched her or paid her a compliment, it had been sincere and he had meant it. Ram'kel made it into a game to irritate her, but she doubted that he really wanted to make her his enemy but just to amuse himself.

Eryn exhaled slowly. She would have to teach him a lesson. The trouble was, though, that his diplomatic immunity couldn't be broached in the process. Damn that.

* * *

Eryn closed the door behind her and stepped out into the cold evening air. She had woken up only an hour ago and would much rather have preferred to stay at home, especially as Plia had left the clinic early tonight for a change. Gerit and the girl were tending to Vedric while Enric was in the other building cooking dinner - something that had taken his mother by surprise. She had so far not been in contact with the few western idiosyncrasies they had decided to adopt into their daily life.

But a nice, cosy dinner at home was not at all likely tonight. Had it only been for Ram'kel's invitation, then she wouldn't have bothered. Not at all. His impertinent invitation despite her obvious displeasure was nothing she felt compelled to accept. But the note the King had sent her changed things rather.

He wrote that the ambassador had mentioned his invitation to him and that he was not sure whether Eryn would accept it as she had seemed rather exhausted in the morning after a night of work. And that the King himself had assured the diplomat that he had no doubts whatsoever that it would be her pleasure to spend the evening with him. Furthermore, there had been a none too subtle warning about not making him look like a liar by not turning up.

She had been so angry that she had made the note go up in a brief burst of flames that left nothing more than a few flakes of ash and curls of smoke floating through the air after a few seconds. Enric had watched her from the door to her study and just commented that this looked like she would be accepting the ambassador's invitation after all.

So Ram'kel had truly bothered the King with a trifle like that to make sure she would join him for dinner. He wouldn't have met him for that reason alone, of course, but mentioned it casually, probably just before he was about to leave the throne room where the King had doubtlessly received him. This was a game of power, and Ram'kel certainly knew which players to get on his side. The thought of whether replacing Sanaf against that one had been such a smart move popped up briefly, but evaporated again a moment later. A man who had, in addition to his complete incompetence, proven not to shy back from endangering two pregnant women and who had attempted to disrupt the long-standing alliances between three Houses was nobody she wanted close to herself or her family. But that didn't mean that Ram'kel was the best alternative. Erbál had been perfect - a man she could trust well enough simply because he liked her and felt that he owed her because she had recommended him for the position of ambassador. Somebody who wanted to be her ally, who didn't delight in challenging her. She knew that Ram'kel had no such notions of a debt owed. She had done his brother a favour, not him. She wondered what exactly his agenda was. Did he just delight in provoking her or was he getting back at her for either breaking his brother's heart by refusing him or costing himself the position of Head of House?

She asked herself again exactly what had made her promote this man's appointment as ambassador. Probably guilt for breaking his brother's heart... Well, at least she had no one to blame but herself. Maybe she needed to accept this as self-inflicted penance, as atonement - even though she knew in her head that nothing of that sort was necessary. She hadn't done anything wrong. Still... The fact that she had come to like Ram'an a lot made her heart disagree.

The Palace had come into view and she gripped the bottle of wine harder in her hand. Enric had insisted she bring a little present for her host, a bottle of the wine Enric made that fetched such a good price in Takhan and so was acceptable as a token of appreciation. Yes, exactly. Appreciation. She indulged in a little daydream where she imagined bopping Ram'kel over the head with it. What would be the harm of it? He knew how to heal himself, after all. And if she made sure nobody was there to witness it... Maybe she could pretend to stumble and mask a well-aimed stroke that way?

She stopped in front of the two guards at the Palace gate and asked them if Ambassador Ram'kel had been put in Ambassador Erbál's former quarters. She nodded her thanks when she received an affirmative answer and proceeded into the Palace, up the stairs on the right side and along several corridors.

When she reached his quarters and raised her hand to knock, the door swung open before her fist had a chance to connect with the wood. She managed to draw back before she hit his shoulder.

"Eagerly expecting me, were you?" she said with a smile that was more a baring of teeth than any expression of joy.

"I admit that I was a little unsure whether you would show up tonight," Ram'kel nodded and stepped aside to invite her in with a flourish.

"Really? That surprises me a little. You managed to make the King intervene on your behalf, after all," she said frostily.

He shrugged and closed the door behind her. "You have a certain reputation of being, er... easily roused to anger. Considering your reputation and your origins that might include Royal orders just as well as not."

Eryn decided not to reply to that and instead took a good look around. The parlour still looked the way Erbál had left it. Either Ram'kel had decided to follow his predecessor's example of adapting his living circumstances to those of his host country or he had not yet found the time to rearrange his quarters to his wishes. He had arrived less than a day ago, after all.

"I would very much like to have prepared a dish myself but, alas, the residents of the Palace are not meant to be inconvenienced by taking care of their own sustenance which is why the quarters are not equipped with a kitchen. But of course you know that from your own stay here, do you not? I hear that Enric... or rather Lord Enric, as I should now be referring to him, has taken a liking to cooking and is putting what your brother taught him in Takhan to good use as a result."

Eryn ignored his attempt at small talk and pushed the bottle into his hands with one hand while the other undid her cloak to then carelessly drop it on a sofa.

"Here. Enric insisted I follow your little custom of bringing a gift when invited to a meal."

"And you would rather not have done so yourself?" Ram'kel enquired with a knowing smile.

"I would rather have given you a proper whacking with that bottle, yes," she growled and folded her arms. "What game are you playing here, Ram'kel? Why do you antagonise me in this way after just arriving here? This is a dumb course to follow, and I know that you are smart enough to be aware of it. Enric will watch this a while and may even find it amusing to see how I will react to your provocations, but after some time he will become angry, and that is something you don't want, honestly. Aren temper may in your home country something that people have decided to fear, but Enric represents a different kind of dangerous. He is influential, and not only here in this city or even Kingdom, but in Takhan as well. He does not normally give in to outbursts of anger, but wields his influence in a calculated and thoughtful way that is likely to make you suffer longer than a mere loss of temper from my side would."

The new Ambassador seemed to find this not, as she had hoped, disturbing, but instead laughed and took her hand and kissed it in the fashion of his native greeting. "I am aware of all of this, Malthea, rest assured. But I have no wish to turn you into an enemy, believe me. Quite the opposite."

She pulled her hand back and raised one eyebrow. "Then you have not got off to a good start. Tell me what your intentions are, please. Peace and harmony between the two of us certainly doesn't seem to be on your list of priorities."

"Take a seat, will you? You are still nursing, I assume, so I will not offer you wine. Perhaps berry juice should be acceptable." He stepped towards a cabinet without waiting for her reply and poured them two tall glasses that he then brought to the sofa she had sat down on. "I am aware that you are not happy about my being here, even though you were the one to approve my appointment. The sad thing for you is that I am neither Ram'an nor Erbál. You are fond of them both, as they are of you. I am only here because my brother asked this of you.

But there is one point in my favour: I am not Sanaf. Should I ever humiliate you publicly, you may at least rest assured that it was not accidental."

Eryn stared at him, not sure what exactly she was supposed to think of that statement. "And this is meant to reassure me? You think malevolence is preferable to incompetence?"

Ram'kel leaned back in his commodious chair, his posture relaxed and natural as if he didn't come from a country where a comfortable seating arrangement consisted of large cushions on the floor. "Malevolence? No, my dear, I bear you no ill will - none whatsoever. This was supposed to be a joke, but I see that your opinion of me is not favourable enough to credit me with a sense of humour. Not yet, at least. What I am trying to tell you is that even though I am not the quietly dignified and honourable kind such as my brother and Erbál, meaning I may not match the ideal for an ambassador those two might have given you, I might still prove a useful contact for you."

She eyed him coolly. "That stunt with making the King send me to have dinner with you rather makes you someone I'd better be wary of. Did you think it would induce me to consider you trustworthy?"

"That was meant to prove to you my ability to accomplish matters expeditiously. In addition to dignified and honourable there is one more thing I am not: patient. I do not intend to spend weeks or even months trying to win your respect by waiting for a chance to be useful to you. Why would I want to make my life more difficult and waste my time? Aren women respect strength, and even though you were not raised by your mother, you certainly display that particular trait."

Eryn nodded slowly. "I see. An interesting strategy. And one with quite a downside if you don't mind me pointing it out to you: you are aware of how Aren women are known to react to challenges generally, aren't you?"

"Such as collapsing a building here and there?" He smiled in a relaxed manner. "I have little fear that a harmless exploit such as my making you accept a dinner invitation despite your inclinations to the contrary would enrage you enough to make the Palace collapse on top of me. Last time it took a combination of Legara's misguided loyalty towards that idiot Sanaf in combination with your going into labour to make you that angry, so I feel safe enough for now. They finished the repair works on the Senate roof, by the way. Your young friend Vern was invited to do a good part of the repainting. It looks very impressive. People even say that you might have done the city a favour by collapsing that roof and paying for the new artwork. Apart from the historians, of course. They only value things that date back beyond their lifetime, so it will take a while until this bunch comes to appreciate the improvement. Just give them another hundred years, then they will come around."

Eryn needed a moment to adapt to the rapid switch of topic. How had he managed to start with her anger at being tricked and after less than a minute end up talking about historians and their sentimental attachment to all things ancient?

"Look," she said and lifted a hand to make him stop in his deliberations. "If you want to get on with me, don't manipulate or trick me, is that clear? You have proven to me that you are somebody to be taken serious, that you deserve my respect because you are determined and smart. If you think you can amuse yourself by manipulating me while you are here, I will pay you back for it. Threefold."

"Oh my, have we progressed to threats so soon? And that on an empty stomach," Ram'kel sighed and stood to indicate the dinner table, on which two sizeable place settings were already prepared with their plates still covered to keep the food warm. "Let me feed you, my dear. It will make you more amiable."

She shook her head at him, but got up. "You really are a piece of work, you know. I just told you to be very careful how you treat me and yet you continue mocking me. You don't happen to have an urgent death wish or similar?" she concluded dryly.

"Oh no, nothing of the sort. And even if it were the case, there are less cruel ways to die than provoking a mighty Aren. Though probably not many that are quicker."

"What would you brother say of your behaviour towards me?"

Ram'kel grinned. "He would disapprove, of course. And start with lengthy lectures on the centuries-old alliance with Houses Aren and Vel'kim. And how my behaviour does not only reflect upon myself, but on my House and, in my current position, on my entire country."

Eryn sneered. "It seems to me that you could really benefit from a lecture like that. Why don't I send a jolly little message to Ram'an and tell him how you have impressed me with your diplomatic manners since your arrival here?"

He seemed completely unperturbed when he waived her off. "You will do no such thing, I am almost certain of that. It would mean admitting defeat if you go to my brother to keep me in check, would it not? And not only to me, but to Ram'an as well. He would no doubt feel flattered if you come running to him to protect you from his insolent younger brother, but I seriously doubt that this would satisfy you in the long run. You would not want others to fight your battles for you. Or even worse - to win them."

He had a point there. Or two. "Taking your chances with me instead of your brother might not be the lesser evil here, Ambassador. You might remember that I had Sanaf sent back to Takhan in disgrace. What would keep me from doing the very same thing with you if I wished it?"

"Me, for one. I will not make getting rid of me quite so easy. I will be competent, appropriate and charming. That means that I will soon make useful connections with influential people here. People who will be sorry to see me go back to Takhan. I will not embarrass myself or anybody else or share secrets carelessly. You will find coming up with a reason to have me removed from my position very tough."

"Tough, but probably not impossible. I remember something your brother told me about you a while ago." And Erbál more recently, but he didn't need to know that. "He said that you were one of very few adolescents who never got caught and punished by that special court you have to discipline those using magic inappropriately and irresponsibly. And that he was absolutely sure that you were too smart to be caught, yet not smart enough never to have done anything punishable. If I had to make a guess I would think that this trait has not vanished over the years but instead grown as you were never taught your limits as a boy the way most others were." She leaned forward, encouraged by the narrowing of his eyes. "So I trust that I would find something if I only looked very thoroughly."

Ram'kel looked at her thoughtfully for a long minute, then one corner of his mouth curled up into an appreciative half-smile. "I bow to your powers of observation and deduction, my dear Eryn. I know for certain you do not wish to hear this, but your exterior is definitely not the only thing where you resemble your mother most strikingly. Let me assure you that I mean this as a compliment. I am an ardent admirer of Malriel of House Aren. May I now invite you do sit with me and enjoy the dinner your Palace kitchen allows me to offer you with so little effort from my side?"

Eryn decided not to comment on the remark on Malriel. She knew he was serious - he really had meant it as a compliment, so a miffed reaction from her would only amuse him. She took a seat on the chair he put in place for her and wondered if they had just very politely declared war on each other.

* * *

Enric's gaze wandered along the crowd on the Palace square and lingered for a moment on Eryn across from him on the other side. She had already stepped to the side where Orrin's team was gathered. Vedric, his colourful clothes a stark contract to her dark grey ones, was perched on her hip, chewing happily on the end of her braid, while his mother was listening to the introductory words her team leader was speaking for the benefit of the players and onlookers.

She was flanked by Pe'tala and Gerit, the latter ready to take her grandson with her as soon as the signal announced that his parents would go into battle against each other.

Tyront stood next to Enric with folded arms and murmured, "Why couldn't I be paired up with you again?"

"Because nobody would dare shoot a bolt at us two together," Enric explained patiently. "Our dear colleagues are wary enough when it comes to one of us, but the mere thought of both of us in one team would send them scampering."

"Which would have been a formidable advantage in a game where we are supposed to keep the enemy away from the Palace," Tyront gave back quietly.

Enric knew that this was no serious discussion. Tyront knew as well as he did that making use of unfair advantages would reflect badly on each of them. He was just masking his agitation with grumpiness.

"The day we have to resort to things like that against our own magicians is a sad one indeed," Enric grinned. "But there is no need to be nervous, old man. You will do well enough. You are an experienced strategist and will prove to the world that neither old age nor manacles serve to render you anything less than an imposing opponent. They will be composing odes to praise your prowess in battle, sing them in front of the fire..."

"Oh, do me a favour and button up," growled Tyront.

They both looked back to Orrin when he instructed the magicians to take their sides as per the lists that were pinned to the Palace doors. The defenders led by Lord Enric would have their coordination meeting here in a room at the Palace while the attackers under Lord Orrin would follow him to the southern gates where they would prepare and coordinate their efforts.

When a group of eighteen magicians surrounded him and Tyront, Enric cleared his throat and called out. "Lord Orrin? I wish you the best of luck. May the better man win."

Orrin gave him a lazy grin. "I fully intend to."

"Confident, I'll give you that. How about another wager? The losers prepare a repast for the winners, just like last time?"

"Suits me fine. We'll have it Takhan style at your place. Floor cushions and all that," the warrior nodded and then added generously, "I'll even look after your son while you do the cooking."

"Or I after your daughter in case you are the host," Enric amended.

"Certainly," chuckled Orrin and made it very clear how very unlikely he considered that turn of events.

Eryn handed Vedric over to Gerit and kissed him on the nose before she joined the others, who followed Orrin across the city. When she entered the room they had been assigned, her gaze fell on the manacles on a table at one side. Unlike in Takhan, there were no water pouches prepared this time. The temperatures were quite different here after all, especially as snow would likely be falling in just a few weeks from now. And the time allocated for the game was a lot shorter, too. This was both a product of having a much smaller play arena available and the challenging magicians who had been trained to be fighters from childhood on.

Orrin cleared his throat when all his players had entered and motioned for them to gather around him. "So, I trust you all had a look at the set of rules that was given to you when you signed up. What colours signify what state of a shield?"

"Green for a fully intact one, blue when one hit is taken and red when the shield is at its weakest," Pe'tala volunteered.

"What happens when an opponent's manacles turn black?"

"We let him pass unimportuned so he can reach the nearest exit from the play arena," another obedient voice replied.

Orrin nodded once and then asked on. "What about the citizens who have chosen not to leave their houses for the duration of the game? Which will be most of them, as they want to witness what we are doing here."

"We try to hit them as infrequently as possible while they are leaning out of their windows to watch how we chase each other," Eryn grinned.

The Head of Warriors sent her an unnerved glance. "Wrong. We should strive not to hit them at all. Should a healer even be saying things like that?"

Pe'tala shrugged. "She is a belligerent Aren. That overrides the compassionate part. And I do not really understand why people think that healers are this peaceful, harmless lot just because we tend to make injury and illness good. It does not mean that we are unable to deal it out just as well as any of you."

A few doubtful looks were cast her way at the words peaceful and harmless as if these were terms none of the assembled would have associated with her or her belligerent Aren sister next to her despite their being healers.

Orrin explained the objective of the game again - namely entering the Palace through the gate, repeated the most important strategic considerations when encountering enemy teams, such as attacking the weaker targets with red or blue shields first and engaging in lengthy battles only when there was an advantage to be had - other than enjoying oneself, obviously. Then he set out his battle plan, which consisted in sending two teams as decoy along Kingsway to draw the defenders' attention and subsequent fire while two pairs would approach from the south. The remaining teams would head up north and move around the Palace, keeping in the shadow of its walls only finally to spring an ambush from the west and take the gate.

Eryn noticed that other than in Takhan, he didn't caution anyone to stay out of Enric's way. Unlike there, here they had all been taught the same things as the mighty second in command. No more advantage for the powerful leaders in this game, neither in training, nor in strength. She imagined that this would make Enric and Tyront their colleagues' favourite target. What other opportunities were there to go against those two without having to fear retribution, after all? And wouldn't that be something to boast about afterwards?

Putting on the manacles and testing their restraint on the wearers' magic was a matter taking little more than five minutes. The magicians here were obviously familiar with the procedure. It was probably something they had frequently been told to do during their training.

Orrin assigned the pairs, sending Eryn and Pe'tala as one of the two teams that would approach via Kingsway.

"We shall have to cross the entire city," Eryn sighed in dismay when they assembled outside the southern gate. "Whose idea exactly was this starting point?"

"Don't complain," her team leader told her. "It's not as if you couldn't enhance your speed with a little magic."

Pe'tala rubbed her hands. "So, how much longer until the signa…" She broke off when a low rumble started that quickly grew to the monotone, deep drone of a large horn. "Yes," she grinned, "that one exactly. Come on, sister. Let us conquer that foreign place here."

The ten teams took off together and followed the road for a while until about half of them split off to the left to move towards the western bridge, the one closest to the Palace. Eryn and Pe'tala let themselves fall back a little.

"Should we really take the bridge?" Pe'tala asked. "I mean, Orrin said that they would be expecting us there. Why not go through the water instead? With a little extra strength in our arms tackling the current should not be a problem. And we can dry ourselves easily after we reach the other side."

Eryn considered her words. "I don't know. If somebody spotted us while we were in the water, we would be defenceless should they attack us. Or they could await us on the shore, hiding somewhere, and then attack us as we came out. I rather think we should cross the bridge with the others. I doubt whether Enric has sent half his force to guard that one bridge. That means we should be the larger force and have an advantage through that. If we keep up, that is."

They increased their speed and caught up with the others just as they reached the bridge.

Eryn let her gaze wander over the opposite shore in the dawn, looking for figures lurking in the shadows. But either there were none or they were well enough hidden not to be spotted so readily.

Lebern, one of the healers, took cover behind the broad stone parapet. "There should be no more than two teams on the other side, which means that we very probably outnumber them. The downside is, though, that the bridge is narrow enough for them to keep us busy for a while even if their numbers are smaller. We have next to no protection. But the chances are good that they won't risk attacking us if it requires giving up their own cover between the buildings. That means they would have to wait until we have crossed more than half of the bridge before we are within their striking range."

Another magician, one of Lord Seagon's treasurers, Eryn remembered dimly, nodded. "True. We should proceed cautiously and slowly to the middle of the bridge, then put on a spurt forward and jump over the sides of the bridge as soon as there is dry ground beneath. That will remove us from their immediate line of sight and we can then use the trees along the bank as cover and fan out."

341

When all others had nodded their agreement, they set off at a deliberate and cautious pace, their eyes roaming the buildings ahead. As soon as they had reached the middle of the bridge, Lebern hissed, "Go!" and the group darted forwards and then one after the other jumped over the parapet.

Eryn saw the streaks of bright blue strikes racing towards them first, but they just hit the bridge seconds after she and the other magicians had safely crouched under the thick wooden planks.

"Did anybody see where they are hiding?" a magician asked.

"One is on the left side," panted Pe'tala. "Between the second and third house where that little bush is."

"Another two are waiting, dead ahead between the two streets before us," Lebern added.

"Shall we take them out or just get away from here?" the young treasurer from before asked.

"Take them out," one of those Council members, whose name would forever elude Eryn's memory, said. "We don't want them at our back even should we manage to get past them."

"The only direction we can go without being caught between them is east," another magician pondered. "I would suggest that four of us run to the trees to the right - that should cover us from the attackers ahead. And from there we move on to the buildings while those who stay here under the bridge keep those on the left side busy."

"Sounds good to me," Pe'tala nodded and added eagerly, "I'll stay here and shoot bolts! You boys go and play targets." That earned her a few raised brows. "What? You were trained to sacrifice yourselves for your country, I was not."

"No," Lebern corrected her, "we were trained to make sure the others sacrifice themselves for their country. Important difference. Very well, I'll go." His teammate and another pair joined them and they took a few deep breaths and then surged forward with magically aided speed.

Eryn shot two bolts in quick succession when she spotted two dark figures where Pe'tala had indicated they had a hiding place. They hastily withdrew after releasing their bolts at the runners.

"Go and check if the others have reached the buildings yet," Eryn instructed her sister.

"They have, yes," Pe'tala informed her from the other side of the bridge. "Lebern was hit once, but the rest has made it unscathed. We do not need to cover them any longer. What will we do now? We cannot go after them as there is nobody to cover us."

The Council member shook his head. "We will stay here and wait until they have taken out the pair in front of us and then distracted those to our left enough for us to join them - provided they don't do the smart thing and retreat back towards the Palace as soon as their colleagues are under attack."

"They might help them," Eryn pointed out.

The older man chuckled. "Not if they were properly trained. If they join their colleagues, the odds would merely even out and the four of us here could move on. They will try to keep us pinned down here and when they see that this is too dangerous for them, they will leave. If you cannot contain a larger number of opponents without any immediate danger to yourself, retreat and regroup. Basic battle strategy. I thought you were tested on this subject, Lady Eryn."

Eryn blushed, glad that it was dark enough already for this not to be obvious. "I was, but it is one thing to read about this kind of thing and how it was done a few hundred years ago and another to be in a street skirmish and applying it to that very situation while being under attack!"

"This ability to keep a cool head in situations like that is what qualifies the Order's leaders," he added somewhat reproachfully.

Eryn swallowed the remark that she had never even once asked to be made one of the Order's leaders, quite the opposite - being stronger than most others made them push her into it. But this was neither the time nor the place to discuss the basic underlying principles of the Order's hierarchy.

"Alright, then let's wait," she pressed out instead and tried to spot what was going on ahead of them without leaning forward so much as to expose herself to any hostile bolts.

Several minutes later they heard fire to their left. That meant their colleagues had managed to either take out or put the others to flight. They ran to duck behind the nearby trees on their left side, and when no attacks came, dashed on to the spot where the other enemy team had been hiding. They skidded to an abrupt halt when they saw bolts flying across an intersecting alley in front of them and pressed against the house walls.

The Council member inched closer to the corner and cast a quick look around it before he sighed. "They got away in time."

Lebern and the other three who had left before joined them again and informed them that they had indeed taken out the first team and that from what they could see, the path to Kingsway should be free now. He himself would move on to the west and then provide a diversion from the south as planned.

The teams nodded to each other and then split up without a word. Eryn and Pe'tala decided against the larger main road to their right and instead remained in the alley that headed up north towards Kingsway.

"This place is a nuisance," Eryn complained in a whisper. "In Takhan there is not so much open space between the houses. Here an attack can come from basically anywhere."

They reached the end of the alley where it opened into Kingsway.

"Do we really want to turn left here into this wide, open street?" Pe'tala asked doubtfully. "We would be mostly unprotected." Pe'tala indicated with her chin an alley which by and large ran parallel to

Kingsway. "We could creep between the houses and approach the Palace square more stealthily that way."

Eryn shook her head. "We are not supposed to be stealthy, remember? We are one of two diversions. They need to see us in order to be diverted."

"Why do I feel like I am being sacrificed?" the younger woman said suspiciously.

Eryn lead forward to take a quick peek around the corner. "Looks empty. Come on."

They both stared at each other after several bolts hit them at once from different directions and left their manacles black in an instant.

"What was that?" breathed Pe'tala perplexed.

Eryn exhaled. "That means that we were removed from the game mere minutes after setting off on our own. That is so embarrassing."

Pe'tala grimaced. "Damn. I cannot even see where they are hiding!" Then she sighed in defeat. "Then let us be off. Where is the nearest exit to the playing field?"

"At the central square somewhere next to the money lenders' building, I think. There should also be a pub somewhere where we can have a drink and wait until the game is over."

"This was no fun. Was it also like this in Takhan?" Pe'tala asked sulkily and kicked a stone ahead of her while they were walking along the deserted Kingsway in the dark.

"No, not at all. I just realised that I truly underestimated the extent of the training which magicians here get. Did you see how they were running and shooting at the same time? I am glad if I hit something while standing still!"

Pe'tala narrowed her eyes. "Funny thing that Orrin put the two of us in the same team. Would it not have made more sense to pair each of us with a more experienced fighter? It would have prolonged our survival considerably, I would think."

Eryn stopped and looked at her. "You are right," she said slowly. "He wanted to get rid of us quickly."

"Probably to make you see what an inadequate fighter and therefore player you are," her sister mused. "And maybe even to motivate you into putting more effort into improving your skills. You are the inventor of the game, after all. It looks a little strange if you are the worst player at it ever, does it not?"

Eryn sent her a withering look. "I'll get back to him for that. Darn! And it worked, too."

*　*　*

Enric listened to the faraway commotion to his left. Orrin had sent a good part of this troops to the north and west, but the question was if they were to be the diversion or the actual attack force that was meant to be taking the Palace gate. There was another battle going on behind the warrior's quarters, but without knowing how many were involved there, it was hard to tell which ones were to be simply kept in check and which ones to wipe out. He decided to remain at the Palace square for another few minutes in case the attackers from the south managed to gain ground. He had divided his forces evenly, and if this one part here managed to stand against their opponents, he could leave them and join the others who were currently fighting up north somewhere near the clinic.

He knew for sure that four people were out of the game from Orrin's side. Eryn and Pe'tala he himself had helped take out, and two more had been reported to him. That left sixteen more against eighteen on his side.

He watched as one of the magicians that were fighting down south came running back towards him.

"Lord Enric, there were four people. We managed to take three out, one ran. We lost one man in the process," he reported.

Enric nodded. One in exchange for three. This was quite an advantageous proportion. That meant the two teams from the south had indeed been the diversion, and the true attack would come from the north of the Palace.

"Rolan? Come. Let's go up north to where the action is."

His teammate grinned broadly and followed him when he set off to enter Kingsway. When they were about to turn left, they both looked up into the dark night sky that was suddenly illuminated by a bright bolt that split into several smaller ones with a loud crack. This was the emergency signal to stop the game. Enric started running in the general direction where the signal must have originated from, Rolan close behind him. Soon after a series of smaller bolts was shot up straight into the air to indicate the location where something must have happened.

He briefly thanked his lucky stars that Eryn was out of the game already and whatever was going on couldn't mean that he had to worry about her. He sent a little more magic into his muscles and felt the restraint the manacles placed on his powers.

When they turned the next corner, there was a half caved-in house wall and a large heap of stones and brickwork on the street.

Lebern and several others, among them Orrin and Lord Woldarn, were kneeling on the street and frantically digging in the stones.

"Here," barked Orrin and Enric saw that he had uncovered a hand that now stuck out from under the rubble.

Lebern jumped up and ran there, gripping the hand and closing his eyes for a moment. When he opened them again, they were wide with panic in a face so white it stood out in the dark. "Eryn... I need Eryn here! I can't do this alone... it's too much! He will die!" he panted and started shaking while he kept holding on to the lifeless hand in his.

Enric turned to Rolan. "Run and get Eryn and Tala. They will have exited the field at the central square. Make haste." When the younger man had raced off without another word, he turned to the opposing team leader and knelt next to him to help remove the stones from the figure that was buried underneath. "Who is this?"

Orrin's lips were little more than a thin line when he answered, "Lord Tyront."

Enric's heart turned cold.

* * *

Eryn stared sullenly into the half-full glass in front of her, pondering her inglorious and above all speedy defeat. She hoped Enric would win this one, just so she could march up to Orrin and tell him that this was what happened when he squandered his resources like that. She dreamed a little, imagining that he would nod with a serious expression and admit to his mistake, asking her for her forgiveness, begging her to let him make it up to her somehow...

She looked up in annoyance when Pe'tala's fingers dug painfully into her forearm and was about to ask what her problem was and if a girl couldn't indulge herself a bit with a few completely and utterly unrealistic daydreams, when her eyes fell on Rolan, who stood panting in the door to the pub, his hair standing on end, his face dusty and white, his eyes wide with a mix of panic and relief.

Both sisters jumped up from their bench at once and headed towards him.

"An accident," he wheezed, "Come!"

Eryn followed Rolan who looked like he was about to collapse any moment. The manacles had cut his powers and he must have pushed everything he had left into his muscles to carry him faster. She wondered what might have happened.

When they turned the next corner, she saw a crowd of people surrounding a heap of bricks and stones and Lebern, who kneeled on the cobblestones and clutched the motionless hand that belonged to an equally lifeless body that was grey with dust and debris except for the numerous cuts that oozed blood. The healer's eyes were squeezed shut and he gently rocked to and fro as if he was keeping himself calm with considerable effort.

Pe'tala and Eryn both squeezed extra magic into their muscles and dashed past Rolan to skid to a halt and fall to their knees in front of the recumbent figure, which looked as if it had until recently been buried under some considerable mass of stones and earth. Eryn gulped as she realised who it was.

"His heart wants to stop..." Lebern whispered without opening his eyes, his face a grimace of pain. "I am forcing it to go on... His lungs, too..."

"Keep the heart going," instructed Pe'tala with a look at Eryn, "I will survey the damage and start mending it. Lebern, go to the clinic and prepare a room for Lord Tyront there. Wait until we come. Enric, come here and shield the head wounds so they stop bleeding."

Eryn closed her eyes and needed a few moments to find that place of peace and quiet inside her. It was harder when the patient was seriously injured, and even more so if it was somebody she knew. But she was a professional and knew how to do this. This was no more than a patient who needed help, nothing else mattered now. There was no space for panic at seeing a man she had come to like die in the street or for thoughts of what might happen if he truly didn't make it and Enric had to take over the Order.

She sensed another figure kneel next to her. Enric. His mere proximity calmed her immediately. Her gratitude swelled for the peace he gave her, and she immediately found it less of a strain concentrating on the slow and steady rhythm that she needed to force on Tyront's heart. She was even able to relax enough to examine the heart while she maintained its beat. There were contusions that had caused severe damage to parts of the heart muscle, so it was not strong enough to obey the impulses to beat any longer without external help. She was tempted to continue her survey, but held back. Pe'tala was taking care of this.

"Done," she heard Enric's calm voice next to her. It was more clipped than usual, a sure sign that he, too, was finding it hard to keep the placid mask in place.

Eryn returned her attention to the ruptured tissue in and around the heart. The heart sac leaked blood, which was not supposed to exit that way. Parts of the heart muscle were ripped and she kept up the shield Lebern had raised to keep the blood within it. This must have been very close. Without a healer being so near at hand, Tyront wouldn't have survived this, she was absolutely sure. She kept feeding a constant impulse to the heart so it wouldn't stop its work. The rhythm needed to be steady but not too fast or the blood would be pumped too quickly and cause him to bleed from his numerous wounds even more heavily.

She started sending small energy impulses to the damaged muscles fibres to induce them to mend themselves, careful not to use up more magic than she could spare for ensuring the uninterrupted rhythm.

Suddenly she felt energy surge through her in a mighty wave. Somebody must have removed the manacles. She waited until the flow had ebbed and it was no longer like riding on masses of water after a dam had broken, but a steady stream. She redirected the magic to several areas in the heart at once, speeding up the repair process. Parts of the valves in the hearts were simply ripped away and she made them regain their shapes slowly, elongated them until they met and were again able to steer the distribution of blood in the chambers. When the aorta directly above was no longer torn, she sent a last exploratory impulse through his heart and then stopped her assistance to see if the heart would beat on its own again. It did.

Without any externally visible change in her posture or breathing, she let her attention wander to the lungs. She only caught a quick glimpse of torn tissue before she retreated again. Pe'tala was taking care of it already. The stomach was intact, as were was the rest of his intestines. It seemed that the chest and head had been the main areas of damage. His liver was undamaged as well, so she moved on to the head. She kept Enric's shield in place while she cleaned the first of two large wounds. The skull was fractured in three places, so she started there before closing the wounds. It might be there was fluid build-up that needed to drain to avoid pressure on his brain.

Eryn opened her eyes and found herself surrounded by what had to be at least two hundred people. Where had they come from all of a sudden? By looking at how much healing she had already done, she determined that quite some time must have passed. She looked to her left and saw Pe'tala kneeling next to her with open eyes and one hand on Tyront's chest so as to monitor the activity in his body while her colleague was healing.

"He will live," Pe'tala announced loudly and the crowd around them seemed to release a collective sigh of relief. She looked as exhausted as Eryn felt.

"Take him to the clinic," Eryn said to no-one in particular and was not surprised when Enric and Orrin were the ones to bend down to gingerly lift him up. With the aid of a little magic either of them could have carried him alone, but they opted for extra cautiousness and tried to keep him as still as possible.

Rolan stepped next to the two women and slung an arm around each of their waists to make sure they stayed upright when they set in motion to follow the two men and their load.

Enric cast a look over his shoulder. "A pity that Vern isn't around to draw a picture of this. With these two women in your arms at the same time, you would have become a hero in Takhan overnight."

Rolan smiled tiredly. "I am going to make Tala my companion and end up with Eryn in my family. By choice. That should make me hero enough."

It seemed to take an eternity to reach the clinic, even though it was right at the end of that very street, hardly more than five minutes under normal circumstances.

Lebern opened the door before they could push it open themselves. He was still pale and looked miserable.

"He'll make it," Eryn assured him and patted him on the shoulder in passing. The healer leaned against the wall and closed his eyes while the rest of them proceeded to the room they kept for the rare occasions when a patient had to stay overnight. Lebern had prepared one of the two beds.

Orrin and Enric took a look at the clean white sheets and then at their dusty, still bloodstained load.

"We better clean him first," suggested Eryn. "We have a washroom here next to the changing room. Come on."

Rolan strengthened his grip around her waist for a moment as she attempted to walk ahead. "I think you'd better let me do this. You might be this professional medic with no qualms about nakedness in a healing context, but he is still your superior and won't appreciate hearing that you were the one to wash him. He would probably ask himself for the rest of his life if you are imagining him naked again whenever he scolds you."

Eryn shot him a look from narrowed eyes. "Why do you say that? Is that what you are doing? You saw me naked once when I tried to make you change with us for you healer training, after all."

Enric's brow rose at that, and the look he cast Rolan was not a friendly one. "Did he now."

Rolan swallowed. "I have never thought of you that way! I swear! And all the other healers saw her naked, too, so why am I the problem now?"

Enric waited for him to walk ahead to the changing room before he followed with Orrin and their load. "Because the others are all healers. Professional medics, as you just termed them. You are not."

"I am so glad we have no greater problems than my having seen your companion naked at this very moment," they heard the administrative Head of the clinic mutter under his breath. "Such as an unconscious Order leader who barely has survived his severe injuries or something of the sort."

Eryn took a seat on the second bed in the room while Pe'tala plopped down on a nearby chair. Lebern hesitantly came inside and stepped before Eryn, his head bowed and his gaze on the floor.

"I am sorry, Eryn," he all but whispered. "I failed you. I didn't stay calm. I was overwhelmed and felt helpless... If you two hadn't turned up, Lord Tyront would be dead by now. I wasn't able to start repairing the damage, even though I should have been..."

Eryn sighed and pressed the palms of both hands into her eyes. "Sit."

Lebern cast his eyes around for a place to sit and finally stepped towards the bed when Eryn patted the spot next to her.

"Lebern," she said softly, and took his hand to squeeze it. "You are an idiot. And I say this with all the love and respect I can muster right now."

"Dear me," murmured Pe'tala, "you certainly do have a way with people. I, at least, am only harsh with my patients. I usually treat my colleagues well - you never know when you might need their help. Like taking over a shift or healing an otherwise lethal injury. Little things like that."

Eryn ignored her. "How would you assess the damage Lord Tyront took?"

Lebern closed his eyes to recall the picture his senses had shown him out on the street. "The lungs were damaged, but not as badly as the heart was."

"What were you doing when we arrived?"

"I was shielding the heart so the blood wouldn't be pressed into the thoracic cavity, and I kept feeding it impulses so it wouldn't stop beating."

"Why did you do this?" Pe'tala cut in.

The man looked at her, confused at being asked a question where the answer was that obvious. "To prevent him from dying."

Eryn nodded. "Exactly. You kept a man alive, who would have been dead after mere minutes, until help arrived."

Lebern got up again and went a few steps while raking his hands through his hair. "I shouldn't have depended on help arriving! What if there hadn't been any help around which arrived in sufficient time? What if this had happened somewhere out in the woods? He would be dead now! I wouldn't have been able to save him! What healer can't save his patient unless his colleagues turn up to push him away and take care of the things he is too incompetent to take on?"

Pe'tala sighed and closed her eyes while sinking deeper into her chair. "I'll take it back, sister. You were right: he is an idiot."

Eryn suppressed a groan. She was too exhausted to deal with this right now, but it had to be done. She couldn't send her colleague away like this. Who knew what he would do?

"Listen carefully because I am too tired to repeat myself. You saved his life. Without you, we wouldn't have been there in time. We didn't push you aside because you failed, but because you looked exhausted - because you did your part well enough so that there was still something left for us to take care of. Had I been in your place there is a good chance that he would have died on me as well because there is some damage where one healer is simply not enough, and sometimes even two won't suffice. I have been a healer a lot longer than you, and even I've had patients die on me on occasion. And being overwhelmed is only human - and in your case you still managed to do your job. He'll live - thanks to you. So now go and get us all something hot to drink. And an extra set of sheets for the second bed. I have no intention of staying awake all night."

Lebern stood there motionless, his brow furrowed and his gaze thoughtful. After more than a minute he looked up. "I would like to stay here with him tonight if you don't mind."

Eryn was about to send him home to get some sleep and recover from the strain when Pe'tala said without opening her eyes, "Very well. We will certainly not battle you for the privilege to guard that grumpy leader of yours. If he wakes, make sure he drinks something. If not, we will feed him in the morning."

Only when she saw Lebern's relieved expression did she realise why sending him away would have been a mistake: he would have considered it some proof of distrust, as if him failing once caused her to get rid of him so he couldn't bungle anything else. Pe'tala had probably dealt with this kind of problem before considering that she used to work in a large place filled with healers. She had done the right thing.

"Who is on night duty tonight?" Eryn asked.

"Onil. I sent him back to have a sleep after he helped me prepare the bed."

"Alright. I'll write him a note to send for a proper breakfast for you and Lord Tyront tomorrow. Try to get some sleep. I'll show you a little trick how you can make sure you hear it in case your patient stops breathing."

Lebern raised both brows. "How?"

"You just make sure he snores. You can do that by laying him on his back and then let his mucosa swell a bit. If that doesn't get him to snore, I don't know what will. You'll wake if it's too quiet."

Enric and Orrin returned with Tyront between them. They had dressed him in a clean purple set of the healers' working clothes. Rolan trailed behind with the filthy, ripped and bloodstained mess his latest attire had become.

"Lebern will take care of Lord Tyront tonight," Eryn announced and got up from the bed. "That means we can return home for now."

"You do that," Orrin nodded. "I'll stay outside in the waiting area."

"What?" Pe'tala asked, perplexed. "Why would you do that?"

Enric frowned and waited for the answer that didn't come. So it was probably something he couldn't talk about in front of an audience. Something in connection with the incident that had almost cost Tyront his life. "Do you need me here?" he just asked instead of insisting on an answer. "I could stay."

Orrin shook his head. "No. Take Eryn home. I will see you tomorrow."

CHAPTER 24

Revelations

Eryn fastened the sling with Vedric across her chest and slung it over her shoulder.

"Are you sure you don't want me to mind him while you visit Lord Tyront?" Gerit asked worriedly. "I am here, after all."

"No, that's fine," Enric assured his mother. "It will be a pleasant little walk for the three of us. We haven't had much time for those lately. Since Tyront likes the boy I hope that seeing him will brighten him up a bit."

"Alright then, that means that I might as well accept Inad's invitation."

Eryn's head jerked up. "Inad? She invited you?"

Gerit nodded, clearly surprised by Eryn's reaction. "She did, yes. She is the only one from my family who has never stopped writing to me in all these years since I left the city."

"The only one from your family?" Eryn asked weakly and swallowed. "You are related to Inad?" she added unnecessarily.

"She is my cousin, yes."

Her gaze wandered to Enric whose expression was resigned. He knew well enough that the walk to the clinic would not be a particularly relaxed one for him.

They all turned when there was a knock at the door. Enric opened it and took the note the Palace messenger handed him with a bow.

Eryn sighed. "It's a rainy morning, it's cold and I am in a bad mood. The only thing to make this day even more enjoyable would be a message from the King."

Enric turned the envelope around and showed her the Royal seal before he ripped it open and began to read, "Lord Enric, I hope this finds you in good health on this grey and dull morning. Look at him, all cheerful and obliging today", he commented and then continued,

"Please oblige me by informing me at your earliest convenience concerning the incident that almost caused Lord Tyront to lose his life on the streets yesterday evening. Be sure also to illuminate me regarding the magician who is currently being held in my dungeons on Lord Orrin's orders. I very much look forward to seeing you in my study. I trust that you are up to the task of acting as the Order's leader for as long as Lord Tyront remains bedridden."

"At your earliest convenience," Eryn mused. "I would say we should first go to the clinic as we had planned. There is not much you could tell him right now without first talking to Orrin. And considering that he had somebody incarcerated, he seems to be just the man to shed some light on what happened."

Enric nodded. "Yes. Let's take care of this then, acting Number Two of the Order."

She grimaced. "Delightful. Let's not call me that, please?"

They left the house and as soon as the door was closed behind them, Eryn narrowed her eyes at him. "How come that in all that time you never mentioned that you are related to Inad? How in the world could you have forgotten to mention that little tidbit?"

"I had the distinct feeling that you wouldn't appreciate it. And it's not like it was a connection of great importance considering that I had no deliberate contact with any of my mother's relatives after they decided she was dead to them because she ran off with a lowly merchant."

"Until now, when your mother is back in the city!"

"Yes, so it would seem. But I had no idea that mother and Inad had stayed in contact all that time. I am truly amazed that Inad left that unmentioned. I would have thought her to be the kind of person who would make use of the opportunity to boast of her family connection to me."

Eryn groaned. "Inad of all people! Your mother's cousin... That makes her your... what? Second cousin or something?"

"First cousin, once removed."

"Removed from what?"

"No, that's what you call it."

"That's a stupid term."

"It indicates that Inad and I are not the same generation. It's like saying minus one. Vedric is thus Inad's first cousin, twice removed."

She shivered. "The thought alone that my son is connected to that woman by blood..."

"It will change nothing for you or Vedric."

"We'll see about that. Any other scary relatives here in the city you should mention? No matter how many times removed? Lord Seagon maybe? That would just make my day."

"No, none that I'm aware of. But I never really had access to the family tree from that side, so I can't make any promises."

353

"Right. I suppose I'll have to leave it at that. Or interview your mother on one occasion. Now, what was that with a magician in the dungeon?"

"I don't know anything more than you do."

"This doesn't happen to have anything to do with why Orrin insisted on spending the night at the clinic, does it?"

Enric nodded. "I am sure it does."

"Why didn't you ask him about it yesterday before we left?"

"Because Orrin didn't want to share it yesterday with all these people around. He is a very capable man and I trusted him to do what was necessary. Plus I wanted to get you home quickly; you could barely stand on your own two feet."

They turned right into the street that led to the clinic. "Yes, that was the most exhausting healing I have undertaken in quite a while. I am glad Pe'tala was there or I don't know if I would have managed. I could only tend to either his heart or his lungs first, and both were in rather bad shape."

"Good thing then, that both of you were there to save him," he said grimly. "I am really interested in what Orrin will tell us. If he had somebody locked up he must think that it was no accident."

Eryn stopped. "You think somebody attacked Tyront deliberately?"

"I think that is what Orrin will tell us, yes."

They walked on in silence, each lost in their own thoughts. Eryn's brow was creased in worry while she absentmindedly caressed her son's back. Why would any magician attack the Order's leader to injure or even kill him? Or had Tyront been a victim simply in the wrong place at the wrong time? Had it even truly been a deliberate act instead of an accident? Maybe Orrin was just being overly cautious.

They reached the clinic and entered. The waiting area was busy with patients who were waiting for treatment. Eryn and Enric passed a healer, who bowed to them and then called the name of his next patient.

Enric knocked and pushed open the door before anybody had a chance to invite them in or instruct them to remain outside.

"I am not eating this!" they heard Tyront's gruff voice complaining. "You can feed that to Enric's son, he will appreciate food that requires no teeth. Take this away, it looks revolting!"

Lebern sighed heavily and tried once again to push the bowl with the brown puree towards his superior. "My Lord, this is exactly the kind of sustenance your body requires in order to recover from the healing it received last night. If you would just..."

Eryn rolled her eyes. "What's going on here? The mighty man refusing to eat his nourishing morning mash?"

She saw Orrin leaning against one wall and observing the scene with quiet amusement, his arms folded. He might seem at ease, but she could detect that he was not relaxed.

Tyront sent her a glare. "This is what you feed grown men here? I wonder how any of your patients ever walk out here on their own two feet!"

"You ungrateful old..."

"Eryn!" Enric warned her.

"...ahem... man. This man here saved your life, so the least you could do is to eat the damn food he gives you! If he wanted you dead he wouldn't try to kill you with food. He just would have left you to die on your own under that heap of bricks yesterday."

Tyront blinked and looked at Lebern. "You truly saved my life?"

The healer swallowed awkwardly. "Well, I merely kept you alive until Lady Eryn and Lady Pe'tala arrived to do the real saving."

"Which makes you one of three healers he may now thank for being able to enrich our lives with his antics," Eryn said and stepped closer to take the bowl out of his hands and hold it out to Tyront. "You eat this right now or I will apply to a higher authority."

Tyront sneered. "I would very much like to be present when you ask the King to order me to eat my breakfast."

Eryn grinned darkly. "The King? Don't be ridiculous. I'll tell Vyril. She will come down on you like a ton of bricks. Well, like another ton of bricks. Your choice, mighty leader."

Her superior gave her a sour look and grabbed the bowl. His face contorted when he ate the first spoonful. "Unbelievable! It tastes even more repugnant than it smells and looks!"

"It's good for you. It will replenish the resources we used for healing you. A lot of it came from your bones and muscles, so you need to eat what we tell you to or it will take you a lot longer to regain your strength. If you are a good Lord, you should be up and about in a matter of days," Eryn smiled.

Tyront swallowed another repellent bite and frowned. "Days? I thought your healing was more immediate."

"The healing is immediate enough or you would not be in any shape to antagonise me right now. The materials we used we had to take from somewhere else inside your body where they were not essential for your survival. Which means your bones and muscles are not as sturdy as they were before the process. That's why you need to eat this food. It is highly concentrated protein your body will use to rebuild what we depleted," she explained. "As a result you will also need to stay in bed for a few days. Your muscles are too weak to keep you upright, and any extra strain might cause your bones to fracture. Any further questions?"

He didn't answer and just continued eating with a sullen expression.

"Fabulous." She turned to her colleague. "Lebern, thank you very much for staying here tonight. Go home now and get some sleep."

Lebern bowed. "Alright. Lord Tyront. Lord Enric. Lord Orrin," he said in the proper order of rank before he left.

"Where is Vyril?" Enric asked and looked around. "I would have expected her to be hovering somewhere nearby."

"I pestered her into going home and at least getting dressed properly and eating something. She came here in the early hours wearing her nightgown and slippers."

Eryn looked down when Vedric started to whimper. Maybe she should have left him at home with Gerit after all. They were about to have a serious discussion here and a wailing child would not provide for a clear frame of mind. But then she already seemed to give him to other people to mind so very often.

"He is teething, it's nothing severe," she explained when Tyront sent her a worried gaze.

"Couldn't you just heal his pain away?" he asked.

"I could, yes. But I'd have to do it every few minutes. And it is frowned upon - for good reason. Cosseting the body like this by protecting it from every ache and pain does not exactly serve to make it strong and endurable. He will only become overly sensitive to pain if he doesn't learn how to deal with it. We will just have to deal with the background noise while Orrin is telling us in the name of all that is good and decent what is going on here." She beamed the warrior a pointed look. "Talk, warrior. We got a message from the King where he wanted to know why there is a magician locked up in his dungeons."

Orrin nodded and pushed away from the wall to join the circle around Lord Tyront's bed.

"The basic facts are that Lord Tyront was buried under parts of a house wall that was repeatedly being shot at until it gave in. One shot with the manacles on wouldn't have sufficed. This is why I am convinced that it was a deliberate act. I don't know if Lord Tyront was the intended target or if there was the intent to kill behind it, but it certainly was more than a mere accident. The culprit was a member of Enric's team. His name is Darnet. A young magician who is training to become a warrior trainer himself. I made sure to have him locked away for questioning while you were healing Lord Tyront yesterday."

"We need to do this before the Council and the King," Enric insisted. "An open attack like this on the Order's leader is unprecedented."

"Yes," Orrin threw in, "because until now we never before shackled our strongest magicians and sent them running through the streets in this way. If somebody wanted a stronger magician dead or harmed, this is the best opportunity I can imagine. The strikes themselves are too weak to kill, but they can still do damage if one knows what to aim at. Like an unstable wall, for example."

"Darnet," Tyront said thoughtfully. "I remember that name. He kept applying for a position as a trainee healer even after we refused him repeatedly. Might this be an act of retribution? Though choosing me as the target for revenge instead of Lord Poron is quite a choice to make."

"Or me," Eryn added. "One of the three votes for or against a trainee is mine, after all."

"You are not an advisable target," Orrin shook his head. "Enric is known to be immensely protective of you. By now it is an open secret that he almost obliterated the apothecaries after you were attacked back then."

"But killing Lord Tyront, even if he had managed to do so without being caught, wouldn't have induced Lord Poron and I to accept him for a position as healer. He must either have thought for whatever reason that Lord Tyront was to blame for the rejections or he was so blinded by rage that he simply took a convenient opportunity to hurt him when it presented itself during the game."

"All that I hope we will find out when we question him," Orrin stated and then looked at Enric. "I assume you will take over the Order for now. Will you do the questioning yourself?"

Enric nodded. "Yes to both. Tyront, do you want to be present at this Council meeting? If so, we will wait another two days until you can at least walk upright again. I would advise against your doing the questioning, though. As the intended victim you might wish to take on the role of the observer. We wouldn't want anybody to claim that you conducted that investigation with anything less than the required diligence because you were so eager to see Darnet punished."

Tyront nodded. "So be it. I will be nothing more than an observer. Eryn, will I be able to appear as a robust if somewhat damaged leader instead of an old man who can barely keep himself upright in two days' time?"

She nodded solemnly. "I have little doubt about that. Provided you eat your pureed food."

* * *

Enric approached his house and raised a weak shield to protect himself and Vedric from the rain. He was returning from the Palace where he and Eryn had just deposited Tyront in his companion's tender care. The baby's quiet whimpering had at one point turned into an outright wailing, so Enric had decided to take his son home while Eryn stayed a little longer to instruct Vyril on how to have his food prepared and how much exercise he was allowed.

Enric saw a faintly familiar female figure walking several paces ahead of him. It took him a while to identify her from that angle, mostly because this was not a place he would have expected to see her. She looked around at the houses as if looking for something. When she heard the sound of footsteps and the noises of a discontented child, she turned and an expression of relief was visible, but only briefly. Enric attributed this to the fact that she was certainly not happy to see him as such, but he could at least show her the way to her destination which, judging from the part of the city she was wandering around, was very likely his own house.

"Werna," Enric said and stepped close enough so that she was protected from the rain that had already darkened the upper half of her brown cloak and damply plastered part of her hair to her face. "That is unexpected. I assume it is my house you are looking for?"

His brother's companion nodded stiffly, clearly not too comfortable in his close proximity.

"Very well, then follow me. I am on my way there." He walked ahead, fighting the urge to ask whether his brother or Anwin were also in the city or if she had come here all alone. It was not hard to guess why she was here. Doubtlessly to try and persuade his mother to return home with her. Anwin could obviously not be bothered to make the journey and attempt it himself. She had only a small bag with her, so she did obviously not intend to stay long. That was fine for him; he doubted that the mood in his home would be a very relaxed one as long as Werna was here.

They walked on in silence and reached the house only a few minutes later. When he had let her enter first and dispersed the shield over his head, he held out his hand to take her cloak and had to wait for a few moments until she relinquished it with obvious reluctance, as if she was afraid never to get it back.

"Why don't you take a seat while I prepare you a warm drink?" he offered and nodded toward the sofas in the parlour.

He saw how her eyes widened at the sight of the splendour around her and she hesitated before she approached one of the settees and primly smoothed her skirt after sitting down. So far she hadn't uttered a single word and he was beginning to get somewhat annoyed with her. It was one thing not to like him, but coming to his house and not even obeying the basic rules of politeness was another entirely. At least he had Vedric to tend to which meant that he would not be standing around awkwardly without anything to keep himself busy. He set the herbal drink down in front of her and then unfastened the sling around his chest. He opened a drawer and took out a box of dry wafers they kept there for Vedric. He cooled one piece with magic so it would soothe his gums a little and pressed it into the pudgy hand, which immediately grabbed it and moved it towards his mouth.

Werna watched him warily as if fearing an attack from him any moment. He wondered what Anwin and Noren had told her about him. He imagined that there were few less intimidating sights than a man handling his baby boy, and yet she was nervous as if afraid of him. He wished Eryn was here. Werna hadn't appeared to like her any better than him when they had visited his parents' house, but she would most probably consider another woman less of a threat.

"Am I correct in assuming that you are here to talk to my mother?" he ventured.

Werna nodded without looking at him.

"I am afraid she is still out, so you are welcome to wait for her. Will you need accommodation for the night?"

"No," she spoke for the first time, quickly as if the mere thought of spending a night under the same roof with the likes of him was unbearable.

Enric briefly considered enquiring about her companion and Anwin just so he would say something, anything, but decided against it. He couldn't care less how either of them was doing. And asking her about her children when she had not long ago made sure to hide them from their aunt and uncle during their visit was not a useful line either.

He thought back to when they had visited his sister Leris and her family. There had been tension between him and Ardegen, too, but this was more a remnant from old times than a matter of personal dislike. He and Ardegen might not yet have progressed to actually liking each other, but at least there was mutual respect. There was nothing of that sort with Werna. She made it plain enough that she disliked and feared him, and the most amiable reaction he could come up with was indifference.

He considered whether or not to send a messenger to fetch his mother from Inad's place, but decided against it. He wanted his mother to enjoy reviving the contacts she had left behind so many years ago, and then he had no wish to oblige Werna with her stiff bearing in any way. He kept walking up and down the parlour with a leisurely pace while he swung Vedric gently and found that he started to enjoy his visitor's discomfort. He tried to feel bad about it, but then he considered the reason why she had very likely travelled here: to instruct Gerit to return to a disrespectful and unhappy family instead of finally starting to live her own life here in the city away from her cheating companion.

Enric wondered briefly if retreating to his study and leaving Werna here in the parlour to herself was a way out of the awkwardness. It was not as if she enjoyed his company, after all. And instead of tormenting her with his presence he could do her a favour and free her from it. What is more he could try to get a little work done if Vedric allowed him. But his mother wouldn't agree with that, he knew. It was utterly impolite and not how she had taught him to treat guests - however unwelcome they might be. He smiled to himself. Funny, it had been a long time since that particular consideration had had any impact on his actions. He wished once again that Eryn was here and he could share that thought with her. She would have found it amusing and maybe even joked that she hoped that Vedric, too, would one day judge all his actions on the basis of what his mother would think of them.

The door opened after what he knew had not been more than half an hour but had felt like two hours at least. Oppressive silence had that tendency to stretch time until it almost seemed to stand still.

Gerit entered with a happy smile on her face and opened her mouth for what doubtlessly would have been a cheery greeting until her gaze fell on Werna. Her eyes widened and her hand flew to her throat. The two women stared at each other for some silent moments before Werna slowly rose and cleared her throat.

"I have come to take you home, Gerit. It is time. You had your little tantrum, and now it is time to behave like an adult again and return to your duties," the younger woman said coldly.

Enric watched the transformation in his mother with glee. It happened slowly, little by little. First her chin rose a fraction, then her shoulders straightened and after she had unconsciously broadened her stance she finally folded her arms before she said with a voice curiously stripped of emotion, "Then I am afraid that you have undertaken this journey in vain, my dear. I have no intention of returning in the near future. And I would advise you all not to wait for me to change my mind. It might prove to be a rather frustrating endeavour."

Werna pressed her lips together and then cast a quick glance at Enric. "A little privacy would be appreciated."

He just smiled and shook his head, not in the least perturbed about denying her this wish. There was no way he would leave his mother alone right now. "I fear that would be little use. I can listen through walls." That was complete nonsense, but she didn't know that. He could merely make walls translucent for a short while and let light pass through them, but not sound.

Werna stared at him for several long moments before she seemed to decide that he no longer existed and turned back to her companion's mother to take care of the task she had come to accomplish.

"Gerit, you are behaving like a stubborn child. We all saw that you were angry. Now you had the attention you felt you were due, so you can come back and stop causing us all so much worry."

Gerit looked directly at Werna. "You think I did this to get attention? That I am playing some game here? I have given almost four decades of my life to this man only to discover that he didn't even consider me worth the trouble of being faithful after everything I gave up for him! I hurt, Werna, I hurt a lot. And your attention is the last thing on my mind right now. I would, in fact, rather avoid your attention altogether so I won't have to deal with your misguided attempts at getting me back there. Leave me in peace! I gave him four decades, he will have to be content with that. I won't give that man another day of my life." Her voice had remained quiet, though not with placidity but with barely contained anger.

Werna laughed in a mocking way. "You think you are the only one whose companion seeks diversion every now and again? Noren has been doing that for several years now, and you don't see me running around and crying because I am not the only woman in his life! He is a man, and that is how men are. I can't believe that you truly are that naive! Did you have your head up in the clouds while the rest of us were struggling in the real world? Is that how things go in that fancy rich city world you grew up in?"

Enric felt how the muscle in his cheek hardened, but he remained quiet. As long as his mother was standing her ground, he wouldn't interfere. He would grant her a shot at winning her own battles and bask in the satisfaction afterwards.

"Your words just show me that I failed. And spectacularly, too. My oldest son was traumatised by his father's infidelity, my daughter ran off because he treated her like a servant, and my second son has adapted to this flawed understanding of morale by making it his own paradigm," she murmured as if to herself. Then she looked up at Werna. "You just accept this? Have you no self-respect? Is that what you want your children to turn into - a boy who thinks treating his companion like that is completely normal and a girl who lets herself be treated this way one day because she never learned that she is entitled to her share of happiness in her relationship?"

At that moment the door handle moved and somebody tried to push open the door in front of which Gerit was still standing.

"Hello?" Eryn's voice called from outside. "Is there a chance you'll let me in or have I been barred from the house for some reason?"

Gerit quickly moved aside and opened the door for her.

Eryn stepped inside without looking up and rubbed her hands together. "I hate the winter. Did I mention that? We should time our stays in Takhan differently so that we go there when it's cold here and return in spring." Only then she looked up first into Gerit's pale face and then across the room where the other woman stood. "Werna! What are you doing here?"

"She is trying to make me return with her," Enric's mother pressed out.

Eryn frowned. "I don't think I approve."

Werna huffed and folded her arms. "Of course you wouldn't. It's a cheap way of having somebody around to take care of your son so you can continue to be mighty and powerful instead of staying home with your child like a proper mother would do."

"Like I took care of your children while you were playing the dutiful companion and taking over my own house?" Gerit hissed, her voice shaking with the effort.

"Are you saying I am not a proper mother?" Eryn growled. "Because not doing it your way is doing it the wrong way?"

"I don't care how you do anything! You can play the helpful healer all day long for all I care, but looking around that grand house of yours I would think that you can at least afford a nursemaid and needn't resort to stealing women away from their families to raise your son for free!" Werna spat back.

Eryn raised her index finger and pointed it at the visitor that had now definitely turned into an intruder. "You be very careful how you talk to me in my own house or I will show you the door!"

Enric felt rage through the mind bond and swallowed hard. There was more he needed a moment to identify. There was guilt for some reason, and pain.

Werna looked back to Gerit and her voice took on a pleading undertone. "Is this really what you want to do? Just run away and leave us all behind? What about your grandchildren? They love you and will miss you!"

That one hit the mark, Enric could see, and waited expectantly if it was an argument powerful enough to make his mother relent.

Gerit looked away and closed her eyes. Her voice sounded tired when she spoke, "I have spent most of my life raising children, first my own and then yours. Your children have you, Werna. And if they so wish and you permit it, they may stay in contact with me, visit me even here in the city. But I will not return to this house that has meant little more than humiliation for me in these last years. Decades even, now that I learned about Anwin and how long he has been straying. Go away, Werna. Rather think about your own situation and whether you truly want to let this go on like that."

Thus she stepped aside and opened the door. "Farewell. Give my regards to my grandchildren if you will. And tell Anwin that I expect him to sign the papers for the dissolution of our commitment."

"You are really doing this? How about what people will say? You will bring shame to the whole family! It will affect us all! How can you be so indifferent?" Werna exclaimed, her cheeks now spotted red with agitation.

"I was not the one to bring shame to the family, my girl. You do some thinking on the way back and then put the blame where it belongs. The only thing I admit to being guilty of is having kept my eyes closed for that long. And I am too old to let what people might say behind my back dictate how I lead my life. That, too, you might consider when you are next confronted with the decision whether to please yourself or everybody else."

They watched the woman slowly bend down to pick up her bag and then walk towards the open door and the cold air that was blown in as if in a trance, as if she couldn't believe that she had failed.

Gerit briefly touched her arm as she passed. "And the gesture of Anwin not coming himself but sending you was not lost on me, either. That alone is an insult. I deserve better than that. I would not have returned with him had he come himself, but an apology would have been the very least he could have given. Off you go now. Be careful on your journey back."

Enric exhaled and stepped towards both women to hug one after the other, as Vedric still occupied one arm and thus prevented him from pulling both of them close at once.

"Well done, ladies."

Eryn smiled tiredly and stretched out her arms to take the baby. "I think you are due to see the King. I would rather go sooner than later unless you are hoping for another cheery invitation letter with comments on the weather."

"Alright. I'll be off then. This shouldn't take too long, there is not a lot that I can tell the King before the interrogation takes place at the

Council meeting in two days." He whistled for Urban when he opened the door again. The King would probably not be too happy about having her in his study, but he needed something to cheer him up, and the King's face when he entered with the mountain cat would accomplish that beautifully.

Gerit released a long breath and then reached out to take her grandson. "I think the two of us will now go and take a nice warm bath," she cooed and wandered off towards the stairs.

Eryn looked after them with a pained expression Enric's mother couldn't see. And again her son was taken care of by somebody else than her. This felt wrong, but she didn't have it in her to deny Gerit the distraction she obviously needed right now.

*　*　*

Eryn walked beside her companion and tried one last time to dissuade him from accompanying her.

"Look, he summoned me alone, he doesn't want you there. You just go back home and play with your paperwork. Or go and visit Tyront and tell him not to make Vyril's life a nightmare by being a difficult patient."

Enric shook his head. "He knows well enough that I am not inclined to let you near him alone since he overstepped that one boundary around a year ago."

"You are aware what this looks like, aren't you? As if I were a little girl who needs to be accompanied by her big, strong protector because she can't take care of herself even though she has quite formidable powers at her disposal and is trained in fighting!"

"I am not going to accompany you inside the study; I'll just wait outside."

"Which makes next to no difference as he will know for sure that you are there. He will think we are afraid of him. Is that the impression you want to give?" she asked, hoping to provoke his ego enough to return home just to prove her wrong.

He didn't rise to the challenge but kept on walking next to her towards the Palace. "No, he knows well enough that I'm not afraid of him. The message my presence will present is that I don't trust him."

"And that is better? How wise is it to spell that out for him so very unmistakably? It might annoy him and he could make you pay for it."

He shook his head with absolute certainty. "He won't. It'll amuse him. And gratify him, too, because it shows him that I don't consider him harmless or any less of a danger just because he is not a magician."

"You think he'll take it as a compliment?" she snorted doubtfully. "If you want to make him happy that way, why not just walk in there, point a finger at him and say Your Majesty, you are a damned dangerous bastard!"

Enric laughed. "It's a little blunt. You need to be more diplomatic with a man who can have your head taken off with one command. But I'll keep it in mind in case subtleties fail to impress him."

"So, how will this work? You wait outside and have nice drink with Marrin while I try to keep my emotions under control because if you sense the slightest sign of distress through the mind bond you will otherwise come storming in and save the damsel?"

"I'll keep my impulses to storm the study under control," he promised. "If you need me you just shout my name, alright?"

"And unless I do that you will remain outside?" she asked as they passed the Palace gates.

"Definitely. The decision whether or not to be rescued is yours entirely. I'll not have it said that I'm a barbarian who isn't modern enough to let the damsel in distress first try to save herself before she calls in reinforcements," he grinned.

Eryn sighed. "That's very modern of you."

"I agree. Travelling to foreign places has certainly broadened my horizons."

Enric led the way through the maze of corridors until they reached their destination. Marrin answered the knock a moment later and called them in, obviously not in the least surprised to see Eryn not alone but in the presence of her companion.

"Lady Eryn, His Majesty is expecting you, go right in. Lord Enric, will you take a drink while you are waiting?"

Eryn pulled the door to the King's study open and stepped inside without hearing Enric's answer to the offer.

The King was sitting behind his desk, leaning back in his chair and nodding to her after she had bowed to him. "Take a seat, Lady Eryn."

She did and watched him for any sign that would allow her to gauge his mood. He didn't exactly appear sombre, but there was no trace of his usual amusement when she was in his presence.

"I trust Lord Tyront is well and on the road to recovery?" he asked lightly.

That was nothing more than small talk - that she knew for certain. The King knew probably better than herself how Tyront was doing. Well, maybe not better as in more detailed, but his information was surely more recent as it had been several hours ago that she had visited Tyront. Was the King stalling for time? That seemed untypical.

"He is slowly regaining his strength, yes," she answered obediently and wondered why he had called her here. To commission her with an unpleasant task? To give her bad news? She had a feeling that it was not to play one of his little games this time.

The King steepled his fingers and regarded her. "I know that your interest in all things political is marginal at best, but I trust that you are aware of how the evaluation of the triarchy works?"

She shrugged. "I know the basic principle, yes. They are elected for a period of five years and then the Senate evaluates how well they did. If their performance was satisfactory, they get to stay, if not, they are exchanged."

"Crude, but to the point, yes. Do you also know that such an evaluation has taken place just now in these last few days?"

Eryn nodded. Ram'kel had mentioned it as one of the two reasons why he had left his home early. One was that he wanted to watch the first game here, the second that he wanted to escape the hustle and bustle around the evaluation.

"It should already have been carried out several months ago, but the Senate wanted to see how the situation with Pirinkar would develop. And now that the situation is less tense and they have even been able to establish a more or less permanent ambassador there, it has been possible for them to take care of this overdue task," King Folrin explained. He paused and started drumming his fingers on his desk. His clipped, clean fingernails made a quiet tapping sound on the polished wood surface. "I received a message from Takhan only this morning. The process has come to an end and the result is final if not yet official."

Eryn raised her brow. The result was not yet officially announced in Takhan but he already knew of it? This man really had talent when it came to collecting information.

"Golir was kind enough to send me word of the outcome. We agreed to stay in contact, him and I," he said as if in answer to her thoughts. "To my great satisfaction Golir was confirmed in his position in the Triarchy, as was his colleague Torke'na. Their conduct has apparently been beyond reproach as their leadership was approved for another five years within moments, as it seemed. The third member, however, Abrak, was less fortunate in this regard. He will no longer serve his country in this function and was replaced by another senator."

She smiled faintly. "I suppose that won't please Malriel too much. He was known to be very... sensitive to her causes." Why exactly was he telling her this? He himself had pointed out of how little interest such things were to her only two minutes ago. He seemed to consider this a matter of importance, or he wouldn't have sent for her to talk about it. Why wasn't he telling this to Tyront or Enric? They would both be very interested in learning of this while she merely waited politely but without real curiosity for him to go on.

"Indeed, Abrak's obvious preference for Malriel's concerns was the main reason for his recall."

Eryn chuckled. "Then I suppose his replacement will be less eager to cater to Malriel's whims if he or she wants to hang on to that position when the next evaluation is due."

The King pursed his lips and slowly shook his head. "No, I can say with absolute certainty that you are wrong in your assumptions."

She laughed. "I doubt that the Senate selected another one of her special friends for the position, especially if Abrak's blatant favouritism cost him the seat on the Triarchy. Unless they elected

Malriel herself, I don't think that House Aren will benefit that much..."
She stopped when she noticed how the King's gaze had become more
intent and was focussed on her eyes as if willing her to finally
understand what he was trying to impart to her.

"Yes," he said softly when her mouth dropped open in an
unladylike manner and she stared at him.

"No," she whispered and started shaking her head.

"Yes," he repeated.

"They didn't," she contradicted weakly. "Please tell me those
insane fools didn't make that woman a triarch."

"I am afraid I cannot oblige you in this. It is true. Malriel of House
Aren will, in no more than two days, start her first term as triarch of
the Western Territories."

Eryn closed her eyes for a moment to consider what this truly
meant for her. She would have to return for six months out of every
year to a country that was ruled by that sly minx. As if Malriel didn't
already have more than enough influence on her life in her current
capacity as Enric's Head of House and now her father's companion. In
the future, whenever Malriel had anything she wanted to take before
the Senate that was to Eryn's disadvantage, she would find
overcoming resistance among the senators a lot less troublesome.
Malriel was now even in a position to influence the process of making
laws. That was massively more power than this woman should
possess.

"This is bad," she murmured while staring at the carpet and seeing
only a blur before her eyes.

"I agree that it might in time cause... frictions, yes. Though Malriel
will find in Golir a colleague who does not hesitate to reign her in
when he sees fit. And Golir has taken a liking to Lord Enric and
yourself, so I am fairly confident that he would not just watch the two
of you struggle to fight her ever-so-tight grip on you, but intervene
when necessary. And let us not forget that Malriel knows how to hold
on to power. She would surely not endanger the position she just
gained by misusing it to serve her own needs too brazenly."

Eryn swallowed. The picture of having Malriel on that pedestal next
to Torke'na and Golir made her throat go dry. The King pushed his
half-filled cup towards her and she gripped it gratefully and downed
the bitter brew within in one greedy draught.

"Take a moment to think," the King told her, "then we will talk."

Think? How was she supposed to think when utter panic
threatened to overwhelm her? She forced herself to breathe deeply.
She needed to calm down or Enric might truly barge in here despite
his promise only to come to her rescue when she asked for it. The
King was right, she had to keep control and think calmly. He was
good with these matters, so she needed to learn as much as possible
from him - and he seemed more than willing to aid her in the
endeavour. Her thoughts kept returning to the question why anybody

would do that to her, so she decided to rephrase it a little and put it out in the open.

"Why would they choose Malriel for that position? If Abrak was known to be aiding House Aren, they must be aware that Malriel herself is hardly less likely to do just that." She was relieved that her voice did not at all sound whiny as she had feared, but instead simply grumpy.

"A Triarch who is seen to follow another's lead is seen as little more than a puppet on a string, while the one working the strings is the powerful one. It means they might just as well appoint Malriel - at least in her case it is expected that she will favour her own House to a certain reasonable degree. Another factor against Abrak was that he supported Malriel when she tried to convince the Senate and Triarchy to contact us to send an Order magician as an official delegate to consult in matters of defence and combat. The Senate was afraid of the threat from the north on the one hand, but on the other they still didn't trust us enough to ask for a grand favour like that and risk rejection."

"Would you have rejected them?" Eryn asked.

"It would have been a difficult decision to make. I could have sent them an Order magician, but had war truly broken out between the Western Territories and Pirinkar, we would have been involved - whether we wanted that or not. Aiding one side means standing against the other. That would not have been advisable after barely getting in contact with our new friends. It is more of a commitment than I would have felt comfortable with. I am glad enough that the Senate didn't support Malriel's motion back then. Abrak did, though, and it meant that he was willing to go begging to me. They are a proud people, as are we. They didn't want to go begging to somebody they didn't trust enough to be willing to help them, especially considering that our countries' last encounter was not a peaceful one."

"Why would they hold supporting Malriel in this against Abrak, but nobody seems to have a problem about Malriel bringing it up in the first place? That seems a bit hypocritical to me, if you ask me."

"Malriel had a different relationship with the Order at that time. Let us not forget that her long-lost daughter was already a high-ranking member of the Order and her own newly adopted heir was even higher up and a trained warrior and strategist. Malriel was merely asking to involve her own family while Abrak was proposing approaching another country. And then Malriel managed to solve that very dilemma by getting Lord Enric and Lord Orrin to the Western Territories in an unofficial capacity. She had done nothing more than invite her heir to take over her House for the duration of her absence and graciously extended that invitation to his good friend Lord Orrin and his family. No grovelling whatsoever was required on the Senate's side - and they still got two masters in the field where their own expertise is practically non-existent. A feat even Malriel's enemies had to acknowledge as impressive. And it made a lot of people wonder if her primary objective in adopting Lord Enric had been not so much a desperate attempt to hold on to you somehow, but was a show of hitherto unexpected foresight. Another point in her favour."

Eryn nodded slowly in understanding. In this light Malriel's actions seemed impressive indeed. She pondered whether to pose the next question, as it was one that would reveal more about herself than she cared to. Yet the King would answer her honestly without attempting to spare her feelings, she knew. And it wasn't as if he didn't already know more about her than she was comfortable with.

"What do you think? Was my companion's adoption a move that bespoke providence beyond compare?" She tried to make the question sound light and casual, but the King wasn't fooled.

"No, Lady Eryn, that is not what I think. In my opinion it was as much a desperate step to ensure that her House does not end up without an heir as it was an even more desperate attempt to keep you bound to her in whatever capacity."

Eryn was grateful that he had not been patronising in answering that particular question. It made her feel less vulnerable and foolish for asking. She scolded herself for even wanting to know the answer and for being relieved that he thought that there had been more on Malriel's side than cold calculation.

"And then," the King continued, "there were of course Malriel's heroic efforts in Pirinkar. They, too, aided her standing in her country considerably."

She grimaced. "Despite the little incident where her affinity for barely grown-up lovers got her into more trouble than she could handle on her own and thus almost got herself killed, had Enric not hurried to her rescue?"

"That didn't change much, no. Malriel could have freed herself from her predicament with the aid of magic at any time but avoided doing so to avert war. That is how a true politician should act in order to serve her country."

Eryn snorted. "We don't know if she truly would have sacrificed herself had they found her guilty. She might have waited for the verdict and then run off in case they sentenced her to death."

King Folrin smiled broadly. "That is the beauty of it; people just assumed that she would have bowed to such a judgement as her actions seemed to point in that direction. Noble, self-sacrificing Malriel..."

"She wouldn't have done that. Ever," she said with absolute certainty. "She would have bolted. I know it."

"That we will never know, will we? But be that as it may, it was another step towards gaining her seat in the Triarchy."

"She didn't even return with any signed agreements which actually prevented a war! Additionally, she herself had to be rescued!"

The King smiled indulgently. "She may not have brought peace, but she brought a realistic chance of the same, which was more than they had before. Despite her predicament, she managed to make them agree to accept an ambassador within their city. And as for her rescue… it was a member of her own House that came to get her out, so it was basically a family matter. The more now that she has joined your father. It means Vran'el is family as well. Not at this precise time, but after the commitment. And looking back, matters tend to blur a little. Now Vran'el of House Vel'kim is her son, legally speaking, precisely like Lord Enric. She was saved by her two devoted sons while her daughter and her mother were taking care of House Aren. This is one family that put quite an effort into preserving the country's safety. What better way to repay Malriel for all her hardships than to present her with the highest rank there is in the Western Territories?"

Eryn sighed and closed her eyes. "And I bet she even made them think she was doing them a favour by accepting it."

"A woman that shows nothing but true proficiency in all that she sets about."

She narrowed her eyes at the slightly dreamy expression in his. "Apart from the fact that it is my mother you made the suggestive remark about just now, I feel I have to remind you that she is now joined to another man. Who happens to be my father."

King Folrin grinned broadly. "Dear Lady Eryn, so indignant. How delightful that you seem to come to terms with accepting each of them as your parent."

She flinched slightly. That was still a sore topic. She had no qualms about referring to them as her parents when it served her aims but still didn't want to have the term given back to her as fact. Time to steer the course of the conversation. "Does the Order know about that fabulous bit of news yet?"

"No, you are the first one to hear. Would you care for a little wager, Lady Eryn? I will bet that if we called in Lord Enric from the room next door and told him about Malriel's promotion to the ultimate ranks of power, he would show hardly any surprise."

Eryn laughed. "No, I'd never accept that bet. Of course he wouldn't show surprise. He is exceedingly good at hiding it."

"This is not what I meant, and I suspect you know that very well. I am saying that he very likely was expecting something of that kind."

"Which you couldn't prove. His complete lack of surprise could either mean that he simply hides it too well or that he expected it. There is no way of telling the difference."

He leaned back in his chair and looked at the ceiling. "Maybe, maybe. So, if I managed to prove to you beyond a doubt that Lord Enric would not be thrown off track by the news - what would you be willing to bet?"

She swallowed. He really wanted to bet on this? Then she was probably well-advised to avoid just that. He would surely use that opportunity to make her do something she would under different circumstances never agree to.

"I would rather not..." she started carefully but stopped when he interrupted her.

"If I turn out to be mistaken, I am willing to present to the Magic Council with a Royal recommendation that all magicians within the Order have to acquire basic healing skills - not only the children and adolescents who are currently being taught it as a part of their training. This would apply to every single magician and," he paused for effect, "consequently also to every single member of the Magic Council."

Eryn stared at him and bit her lip. Oh dear, that was a powerful incentive... "You could never get them to agree to that, no matter if Royal recommendation or not," she said hoarsely.

The King laughed. "I am sorely disappointed in your lack of trust in my abilities to be persuasive. In arguing that the incident at the game has shown us that the ability to heal magically can be a decisive intervention between life and death, and that not having more magicians with the ability to heal had almost cost them their leader's life, they can hardly object without appearing indifferent to Lord Tyront."

That was devious and manipulative. And it might just work. She knew she was being baited, but the incentive was too good to be pushed aside like that. If every Council member had a first-hand impression of what it truly meant to heal, she was convinced that there would be more common ground between her and each of them in the future. They would understand a little more of what she was doing instead of simply rejecting what they didn't know and as a result distrusted or feared. She didn't share the King's confidence in Enric's powers of guessing a thing like Malriel's becoming a triarch. He would surely have warned her about something like that.

"What would you want in return, in case I lost that bet?" she finally asked.

"I was thinking of the privilege of being appointed your son's guardian," he replied immediately and smiled at her. "It is an old custom that is hardly practised anymore nowadays. Very much to my chagrin, I have to admit. There are some remote areas in the country that still appoint a guardian for a child occasionally, but in the cities it has become almost an extinct tradition."

Eryn frowned. "I have heard that term mentioned a time or two but I'm not entirely sure what it entails."

"It is an old function that was often taken over by an older family member or friend of the family to take upon him or her a part of the responsibility of the child's education and development. Furthermore, it is one of the guardian's duties to take in the child in the tragic case both parents meet untimely death."

Her eyes narrowed. "You are not trying to get your hands on my son by killing me and Enric off, are you?"

The King lifted both eyebrows. "Dear me, what would I as a non-magician do with a child with unparalleled magical powers at his disposal? No, spare me. Rather than your grisly scenario, this arrangement would induce me to strive to keep the two of you alive, honestly," he concluded dryly. "Think again."

She suppressed a sigh. It seemed he was turning this into another lesson in political strategy. "You want to increase your hold on Vedric, since he is bound to Takhan somewhat tightly with his being the designated heir of my brother's House. But I don't really see how this guardian thing could stand up against Vran'el's claim. Or what exactly it is you are trying to accomplish here - keep him from moving to Takhan once the time comes?"

"This guardian thing, as you so eloquently put it, will be a lot more than a casual verbal arrangement. It is connected to old laws that are still as valid now as they were more than one hundred years ago, when this custom was still widespread."

Eryn exhaled. This sounded dangerous, hugely so. "Why would I agree to enter a wager like that? Why would I grant you such a hold over my son when it might turn out to be an immense burden upon him when he is older?"

"Because, Lady Eryn," he replied calmly, "there are worse fates for a young boy than having a King as his mentor. And I do not intend to hold him back when it is time for him to choose his path in life. I merely want to be in a position to connect him to this place, as your brother will doubtlessly attempt the same in Takhan. I cannot lose, Lady Eryn. Either he stays here and will no doubt be a powerful, high-ranking member of the Order and with that a potential ally for me, or he will go to Takhan to take over a hardly less influential position and then turn out to be a valuable contact for me there." He leaned forward. "Moreover, your son would benefit from this arrangement as well. When he is old enough to finish his training in the Order, his skills in political strategy would be honed beyond what anybody would expect from a young man of no more than twenty-one years of age. I can promise you that. This is a situation where both parties benefit, dear Lady."

She shook her head slightly. "Enric would not be happy about this."

The King smiled thinly. "How suitable, then, that his reaction is the one to determine the outcome of this little bet. Provided you accept it? A Royal recommendation set against your son's guardianship. And I win if I manage to make Lord Enric reveal in a manner credible to you that he is not surprised by the news about Malriel."

Eryn knew she shouldn't accept. This was a political manoeuvre, as he had admitted openly and without hesitation. There was no saying what the consequences of such arrangement were if she lost this bet. But the chance to increase the acceptance of the practice of healing in the Order and the opportunities this might open up in the future... But no. Vedric came first. His wellbeing was her main concern. She wouldn't deliver him to the King just like that.

"I swear to you that I would never act against your son's interest," King Folrin smiled in that way that implied that he knew exactly what she was thinking. "You might not be inclined to believe my goodwill in this, but perhaps another argument will convince you. A guardianship is a matter that is made public, and a King who is seen to have broken that promise of protection and mentoring he gave to a child will suffer considerable damage."

She shouldn't do it, she knew she shouldn't. It was a foolhardy thing to bet against him, no matter how attractive the reward was. Or how little he made the danger of losing sound. She would reject his little challenge, show him that he couldn't play her like that.

"Very well, I accept," she heard herself saying. Damn!

King Folrin smiled broadly and got to his feet. He strode to the door to Marrin's study and opened it. "Lord Enric, please be good enough to join us for a brief moment, will you?"

Eryn saw Enric gingerly put down his cup and stand up to follow the command.

"Your Majesty," the tall magician said and bowed after the monarch had closed the door behind him.

"If I tell you that the evaluation of the triarchy was concluded the day before yesterday, and that two out of three candidates will remain in office while one is replaced - which thoughts would come to your mind? Both with regard to the replaced triarch and their likely successor," King Folrin said without introduction.

Eryn watched her companion closely. If the question had taken him by surprise, he didn't show it. He adopted a comfortable broad stance with his hands on his back and let his gaze wander over the ceiling for several long moments before he answered, "If I had to guess, I would suggest that Abrak is the most likely candidate to be replaced. I know for a fact that many senators resented his open support of Malriel of House Aren - even those who were allied with House Aren themselves. It was considered a breach of etiquette."

"Go on," the King prompted him.

"As for his replacement... There are a few options. One would be House Roal. The younger son has made the construction business thrive and has proven to be a level-headed senator. The fact that Eryn has entered into a business contract with them after one-hundred and fifty years of enmity between Houses Roal and Aren has strengthened their standing even further. Another possibility would be House Landred, though their association with Legara of House Finran might cast something of a bad light on them after how she handled the matter with Sanaf. The most obvious choice, however..."

"Yes?" the King encouraged him with a predatory smile.

Enric cast a quick glance at Eryn before he continued, "...would probably be Malriel of House Aren."

King Folrin laughed happily and clapped his hands three times. "Excellent, Lord Enric. I commend you on your very accurate assessment of the situation."

"Enric, you bloody idiot," breathed Eryn and covered her eyes with one hand.

He frowned at being so unexpectedly addressed with such an unflattering term right in front of the King, who appeared suspiciously cheery.

"I take it I was right? The evaluation is over and Malriel is the new third triarch?" Enric asked her.

"You are right, yes. Congratulations. Maybe you should try to share such insights with me in the future. Doing so would not have caused me just to have lost a rather important bet," she growled.

"What bet?" he asked, slightly troubled. "What makes you think entering into bets with His Majesty is a particularly wise move?"

She ignored the last part and just responded to the first. "Vedric has just obtained himself a fancy new guardian."

Enric's head snapped to the King, who had in the meantime taken a seat in his chair and followed the exchange with obvious pleasure.

"A guardian?" He paled slightly. "With all that entails?"

"Indeed," the King replied happily.

Enric turned back to Eryn with a stern look. "You and I should have a little talk. Your Majesty, may I be so bold as to request our dismissal?"

"By all means. I wouldn't want to keep the two of you from what clearly is going to be a very important discussion. A good day to you. I will see you again tomorrow at the Council meeting."

He smiled broadly while he watched them leaving his study at a brisk pace. He really liked that woman; she never disappointed him.

* * *

They left the Palace, Enric's hand around her wrist, urging her on. Eryn sent a little magic into her legs so they could keep up with his long limbs.

He pulled open the door to their house and more or less dragged her after him to his study without even giving her the chance to take off her cloak. He closed the door and leaned against it.

"Why?" he asked with an accusing look. "Why would you do a thing like that? Why did it not occur to you that he is not to be trusted? Have his dealings with us in the past not been enough evidence to convince you? Whatever were you thinking?"

Eryn unfastened her cloak and threw it over his small sofa on her right. "I'll tell you exactly what I was thinking: I was thinking that he offered me something I was convinced was a great chance for the healers and the Order! And do you want to know what else I thought? I thought that there was little chance that he would win that bet because I was sure that you would have come to me with any such suspicions instead of keeping them from me - especially as you are the one to always insist that there shouldn't be secrets between us!"

"Had I known that you would use my son as a stake in a bet with the King I would have told you the first opportunity I had!" he barked back.

"I didn't lose him to the King. I just got him enrolled onto some extra tutoring in political strategy from an early age on. He will survive that and even benefit from it. Being tutored by the King should at least cause Vedric to develop a feeling for when he is being used."

"Splendid. Then let's just hope that works out better than in your case! You just fell into that trap as blindly as a new-born child! How is this possible? We keep teaching you all these things and you do a silly thing like that without thinking!" he scolded her.

Eryn put her hands on her hips. "You think that stuff you teach me has helped me even once? You think that reading one dusty, old book after the other is a sensible way to teach somebody? The only remotely useful things I learned in political strategy is what the King taught me!"

Enric balled his hands into fists. "Is that so? I am immensely relieved to see that you and he seem are such solid friends now that you even entrust your son into his care! I won't trust this man with anybody who is dear to me after what he pulled to make us go to Takhan!"

"Had you not let me walk into that study to learn of the distressing news that you seem to have suspected all along, I might have been a lot less angry and upset! A clear head would have helped me to deal with the situation properly!"

He narrowed his eyes. "So now this mess you got our son into is my fault? Because I chose not to burden you unnecessarily with things that might never even have come to pass?"

"Ah yes, back to your protecting helpless little me from the cruel world around me! Your decision to keep your mouth shut contributed to this snarl up, whether you want to admit it or not!"

"How very convenient," he shot back. "You get pulled into something and then put the blame on somebody else! A very grown up strategy! Let's make sure to teach our son that very thing as soon as he is old enough - it will make his life so much easier!"

Eryn stared at him and hissed, "Are you saying that I am irresponsible and immature and as a result unfit to raise a child?"

He threw his hands up into the air. "I don't need to say it! Your actions speak more clearly than I could ever manage it with mere words!"

She managed to shield her brain before the mind bond could reveal to him the full impact his words had on her. They were like a punch in her midriff and a dizzying blow to the head all at once. He considered her unfit to raise his son, a bad role model, a person unwilling or unable to take responsibility for her own actions.

The knock at the door behind Enric almost made her gasp with relief. She needed to get out of here. Away from him and these angry words he had just hurled at her. Never, since they had been together, had he said anything even remotely as painful to her.

Gerit's voice called from outside, "Could the two of you tone it down a little? Vedric has just fallen asleep."

Enric breathed once deeply and then opened the door, his voice calm when he addressed his mother. "I'm sorry, mother. Thank you. We will be more mindful."

Eryn walked past him, forcing herself to proceed with a moderate speed when she would have preferred to run and get some distance between herself and him as quickly as possible. She swiftly moved her hand away when Enric tried to grab it.

"What are you doing? We need to talk about this!" he insisted.

She shook her head and walked on to the niche with the cloaks, only now remembering that hers was still in Enric's study on the settee. "We will. But not now. I need a break."

She hastily grabbed Gerit's cloak and slipped out the door into the wet street. She would return to the Palace and check on Tyront. There at least he wouldn't come looking for her.

*   *   *

Enric strode into the Council hall and his eyes immediately searched the room for Eryn. He found her in conversation with Orrin and Lord Poron next to the great oval table.

When she had left the house yesterday evening, he wanted to go after her but his mother held him back. She had explained to him that Eryn looked like she needed some time to herself to collect her thoughts and that she herself would have appreciated that very luxury of being allowed to draw back every now and then. But Anwin had interpreted every such attempt as weakness and followed her to deliver the killer blow that would make it absolutely clear that he was the one winning the argument.

Then she had pointed out that Enric looked rather too agitated to follow her in order to have a sensible conversation right now. She advised him to give them both a chance to cool off before tackling whatever the issue there was between them.

Enric had followed her advice, but very reluctantly so. Letting Eryn run off like that didn't feel right. But his mother's words made him think. Was he like Anwin in this regard? Couldn't he stand it if an argument was not won immediately, implying he had to push until it was resolved to his satisfaction instead?

Eryn had returned rather late from wherever she had been and then asked him not to broach that subject before they went to bed. He had granted her that wish and decided to talk it over the next morning before they left for the Council meeting, but when he had opened his eyes in the morning she had already gone. And not only from the bed, but also the house.

The Council members stood around in small groups. There was a certain tension, an air of anticipation at the interrogation that was about to follow.

He turned when all eyes in the room focussed on the door. Tyront was walking in, leaning heavily on a finely-carved, wooden walking stick at every step. Vyril walked next to him, careful not to touch him, but clearly prepared to lend him support should he show any sign of unsteadiness. Enric wondered briefly what she would do if Tyront really did fall, as she was hardly strong enough to keep him upright on her own. But now that they had reached the Council hall this was no longer a problem. Every single magician in that room, no matter how old or frail in appearance, could easily lift Tyront in his arms as if he were no more than a girl of five years.

He pulled out a chair for Tyront when he had finally reached the table. The older man carefully lowered himself into it and sighed with relief.

"You never appreciate how long those corridors are unless you have to walk through them in a state like mine," he chuckled and looked around. "It seems we are almost complete."

At that moment another figure drew the glances in the room. King Folrin had arrived and entered the room with his advisor. He stopped briefly as the room bowed as one and then proceeded to the throne to one side.

Enric sighed and took his seat just like his colleagues around him. He had hoped to have a few moments with Eryn before the meeting started, but there was to be no such luck. He would corner her afterwards. Enough of this chasing endlessly.

"A good morning to all of you," he started, feeling strange in chairing this meeting despite Tyront's presence. "This meeting today was called with the purpose of cross-examining Darnet, the magician we have kept locked up for these last two days as there are reasons to believe that he attacked Lord Tyront with the intent to hurt or kill. There is another matter I wish to address, a piece of information the Council is doubtlessly interested in. We received word that the Triarchy in the Western Territories has changed its composition slightly. Two out of three members, Golir and Torke'na, will stay on and continue their work while the third, Abrak, has been exchanged for Malriel of House Aren."

He saw the Council members exchange looks with each other and look at him and Eryn.

"That surely ratchets up your own importance another notch," Lord Poron joked. "Not that you would need such a thing, mind you."

Enric smiled faintly and didn't comment on that. He would rather have done without that additional importance that Malriel's increased influence would bestow upon him.

"The Order will send her a message in which I will congratulate her on her promotion on behalf of the Council," he went on. "And now let's move on to the incident at the game. Lord Orrin, would you convey to us what you witnessed that made you lock up Darnet?"

Orrin nodded. "Of course."

"Will you agree to a truth block?"

The warrior nodded again. "Certainly."

He and Enric both got to their feet and approached each other until they met halfway. Orrin pushed back his sleeve and offered his bare forearm which Enric gripped tightly before releasing a low-level stream of magic.

"Describe to us what happened to injure Lord Tyront during the game."

"I was approaching the Palace from the east, together with nine others of my team. We were about to reach the Palace when we met six members of Lord Enric's team who were barring the way. Among them were Lord Tyront and young Darnet, both members of the defender's team. We engaged in a skirmish that lasted several minutes. I watched several bolts being thrown from one alley to my right at a house wall to an alley on my left side. Judging from the position of the shooter I knew it couldn't be one of my people, and neither was the target. They were both too far ahead for this. I was wondering if there was some kind of mutiny going on our opponent's team at that time. All of a sudden the house wall gave way under the repeated strikes and buried somebody underneath. I remember I was worried that the entire house would collapse, but luckily it remained upright. At that time I was not aware that Lord Tyront was the person under the bricks and masonry."

"So you believe that it was a deliberate attack aimed at Lord Tyront?" Enric asked.

"I believe that the attack was deliberate, yes. The bolts were aimed at the wall until it finally gave way. A few stray strikes wouldn't have managed that. The enchantment on the manacles makes sure that doing real damage is quite an accomplishment during the game, both to people and to objects. Whether or not Lord Tyront was the intended target or merely a random one I cannot say."

"How did you know it was Darnet who shot the bolts? Did you have a clear view when it happened?"

"No, I did not. But afterwards he was the only magician to emerge from that particular alley. This led me to assume that he was the shooter. After we had freed Lord Tyront from the rubble and Lady Eryn and Lady Pe'tala were healing him, I approached Darnet and asked him whether or not he had been the one to collapse the wall. He admitted it without any attempt at concealing his involvement and I even had the impression that he was proud of his deed. Thus I changed the enchantment on the shackles he was already wearing to null his powers entirely and had him brought to the dungeons."

Enric nodded and turned back to the Council and the King. "Lord Orrin speaks what he believes to be the truth. Are there any more questions you wish to ask him at this point?"

When several heads shook but nobody spoke up, Enric removed his hand again. "Thank you, Lord Orrin. We will now proceed with the interrogation of Darnet."

He motioned for the guards on each side of the high double doors to have the alleged culprit brought in. Darnet was marched in a few moments later, seeming small and insignificant between the two guards who escorted him. He didn't look rumpled or dishevelled, so he had obviously been allowed to wash and change his clothes before facing the Council.

Enric looked at the young magician. He looked nothing like what he would have imagined a man who dared attacking the Order's leader. He was in his mid-twenties, a bit on the short side, his curly hair bound in a tight knot at the nape of his neck. His eyes wandered nervously along the magicians at the table before him and stopped when they had reached Eryn. Enric didn't like the smile that then appeared on his pale lips one bit.

"Darnet," he raised his voice again. "I assume you are aware why you are here? And why you were made to spend the last two days in the dungeons?"

"Yes, My Lord," the man answered in a voice which, considering his current predicament, sounded strangely free from nervousness or fear.

"You will now be questioned by the Council under the influence of a truth block," he explained and kept looking for any sign of discomfort. In vain.

"Yes, My Lord," was all the reply he got.

Enric took the young man's wrist and pushed up the sleeve of his brown robe to grip his forearm as he had done with Orrin before. "Darnet, did you cause the wall in Lord Tyront's back to collapse with your bolts at the evening of the game?"

"I did, My Lord," he answered without hesitation.

"Did you do it intentionally? Was this a deliberate act with the aim of causing harm?"

"Yes, My Lord."

The hall had fallen utterly silent. There had not even been a feeble attempt at concealment or lying, as accused persons generally were prone to try.

"Was Lord Tyront the intended victim?"

"He was, yes," Darnet answered unperturbed.

"What was the objective behind this attack on Lord Tyront?" Enric asked on, wondering why this felt so completely absurd. The man appeared as if sitting in a nice parlour and having small talk instead of admitting to a severe crime.

"To kill him, of course."

Several gasps could be heard from the table. The attack itself had suggested as much, so the revelation couldn't be that much of a shock. But the casual way it was admitted was.

"You wished to kill Lord Tyront?" Enric repeated, amazed at how willing Darnet was to confess all this. And how little it seemed to bother him.

"I did, yes."

"For what reason?"

"To have the Order led by you, My Lord."

Enric blinked, not sure if that was meant as a compliment and he was supposed to be flattered now. "What did you hope to gain from a change of leadership from Lord Tyront to me?"

"A more modern approach to all things magical." Darnet's eyes had begun to shine. "An increase in efforts to promote healing beyond the borders of the city, more freedom for members of the Order to return to their families in the countryside. The chance to profit from a more liberal approach as they do in the Western Territories, where magicians are not bound so tightly."

Worthy causes that he knew Eryn supported as well, he thought. Yet his ideas of attempting to achieve them were not acceptable in any society, not at all.

"I see," he said to put a stop to the murmuring among the Council members that had ensued. "Are you the only one in the Order who wishes to make this happen? The changes in the Order you just mentioned?"

"No, My Lord. There are several of us who think this way."

Oh dear, Enric thought and hoped fervently that he didn't have a mutiny on his hands that would make it necessary to throw half the Order into the dungeons. He dreaded the answer to his next question.

"Were any of them involved in or informed about that attempt on Lord Tyront's life?"

"Only one other person was informed and instructed me accordingly."

The reply was a relief. So this was a matter of two overzealous idiots and not as wide-spread as he had feared. "You acted on orders received?"

"I did, yes."

"Who gave you those orders?"

Darnet smiled and his gaze returned to the table and to one particular Council member. "Lady Eryn."

CHAPTER 25

A Shocking Accusation

Eryn gaped at the man who smiled beatifically at her. She was supposed to have done what? He was lying! Despite the truth block! How was this possible?

She felt how her stomach clenched at the thought what this meant. They would believe him because he had spoken under the influence of a truth block. They all now truly thought that she had arranged for Tyront's assassination!

Enric's face was a mask of bewilderment as he, just like everybody else, stared at her. He very carefully removed his hand from Darnet's arm and took a step back before he said deliberately, "I herewith delegate the control over this investigation to Lord Poron. As my companion is now accused of a crime, I would no longer be impartial and my proving her innocent would give rise to doubt. Does the Council agree with this course of action?"

All hands except for Eryn's rose to confirm this decision.

Enric nodded once and then said, "I suggest that we next ask Lady Eryn about her involvement in this matter with a truth block and then send her away as she is now a party in this investigation. Then we may proceed with interrogating Darnet."

Eryn's vision swam. He truly had proposed that just now. He, who should know that she would never resort to killing after she had endured her father's death under such dire circumstances and had wholeheartedly objected to the apothecaries' execution even after they had attempted to kill her, should know better. His betrayal hurt and almost made her double over. She braced herself with her palms on the table in front of her to avoid just that. Breathe! she commanded herself and felt her vision clear after a few moments. Her heart still pounded in her ears and she felt chilled and alone.

How could he think her capable of a thing like that? Did he know her so little? But then he had given her to understand clearly enough what he thought about her yesterday evening, hadn't he? That she was irresponsible. This here would just prove to him that he had been right all along.

"Who will carry out the interrogation of Lady Eryn?" Lord Seagon called out. "You yourself are clearly not suitable and neither is Lord

Tyront, as he is the intended victim. Every other magician here is too weak to attempt applying a truth block to Lady Eryn without her wearing manacles."

Orrin nodded towards Darnet. "Then I would suggest we use the manacles our suspect here is currently wearing and use them on Lady Eryn. That means our choice of interrogators is no longer limited to only two men."

"I propose that Lord Seagon should apply the truth block," the King suggested gravely.

Eryn's gaze returned to the young man, who was still standing in front of the table, his unsettling smile never ceasing. He straightened a little when her attention was on him. "I apologise for revealing all this, but the truth block left me no other choice. Fear not, My Lady, this is but a minor setback. This is not over! Others will continue where we left off, I know it!"

She just shook her head, completely lost in the absurdity of his claims. But he had told the truth! Was she slowly going insane? Had she truly planned to assassinate Tyront and merely suppressed the memory? Either this or this man was either convinced of some falsehood or had learned how to withstand a truth block. She didn't know which option she would prefer.

She looked up when a man stood next to her and spoke her name. Lord Seagon. He was holding Darnet's manacles in his hand. She hadn't even noticed that somebody had taken them off the young man.

"Lady Eryn? If you would get up and hold out your hands, we may get this unsavoury business behind us."

She rose slowly and had to hold on to the backrest of her chair for a moment to steady herself. When she trusted her feet enough to keep her upright, she stepped away from the table and held out her hands to Lord Seagon, who fastened the manacles around her wrists and then took her hand in his. Her own powers disappeared completely from one moment to the next and instead she felt the warmth that passed from the Lord's warm, dry hand into her own clammy one. The sensation was almost pleasant if one didn't consider what it did. If the older man felt any pleasure to have her in this situation - her, the disruptive influence on the Order's values and traditions and the reason why his nephew had been publicly humiliated at that one ball - he concealed it well. His face showed nothing but serious consideration and tension.

"Lady Eryn. Did you instruct Darnet over there to kill, harm or merely attack Lord Tyront in any way?"

"No," she whispered and shook her head slightly.

"Did you instruct any other person to cause harm to Lord Tyront at this or any other time?"

"No," she said again.

"How is it possible then, that he was able to make this assertion under the influence of a truth block?"

"I don't know. I really do not. It shouldn't be possible."

"Were you aware of any attempt at harming Lord Tyront even if not ordering it done yourself?" he continued his questions.

"No."

"What would you have done had you been aware of such a thing?"

"I would have warned him and Enric."

"Do you wish to see Lord Tyront removed from his position as the leader of the Order of Magicians?"

"No."

"Why not? It would put your own companion in charge and enable him to promote those ideals Darnet mentioned and that you are known to share, after all."

She swallowed. The answer to that question would not be received very favourably, she knew. But the truth block didn't allow for any diplomatic omissions or rephrasing to conceal anything. "I don't want Enric in charge of the Order because it would chain us down here in Anyueel. It would be like a prison. There is more freedom for us in Takhan, more options to develop my skills, more openness, more tolerance when it comes to a person's talents and inclinations. I want to be free to go back there regularly, spend time with my family and enable my son to benefit from that wealth of knowledge and opportunities over there. This wouldn't be possible with Enric leading the Order."

Lord Seagon stared at her and said after several moments, "A convincing argument that you wouldn't want Lord Tyront removed from his position, though hardly one to convince us of your attachment to the Kingdom of Anyueel. It states very clearly where your loyalties lie, Lady Eryn. And your general opinion of the Order is also no secret."

She shot him an irate look. "My loyalties?" she hissed and made to pull her hand from his grip, but he held on to it, the warm magic still flowing through his fingers into her skin. Oh, what did it matter? What she was about to tell him was nothing but the truth, so the truth block wouldn't hold her back. "You know nothing of my loyalties! This city here is my home just as much as Takhan is, and my attachment and my connections to my birthplace are the very reason why I am in a position to develop my skills and increase my knowledge in order to serve the people here better! I have little love for some of the stupid regulations in the Order, in that you are absolutely right! But as long as you all provide the legitimation to let me do what I feel is useful and needed and helps to improve people's lives here, I am willing to put up with your absurd rules, your demands, your limitations, your quotas on healers, your bureaucracy..." She stopped when she felt a tear running down her cheek and lifted her other hand to wipe it away, but of course they had all seen it. So she was crying in front of the entire Magic Council and the King while she was being accused of a heinous crime.

Lord Seagon nodded slowly and stopped the flow of magic. "She speaks what she thinks is the truth," he announced. "Are there any other questions you wish to address to Lady Eryn at this time?" When nobody spoke up he removed the shackles from around her wrists and said more quietly, "You convinced me, my dear, but the fact remains that either you or Darnet seem to be able to overcome a truth block. I hope this will soon be resolved in your favour, My Lady."

Eryn stared at him, speechless. This was the very first time ever that he had spoken a word in support of her.

"I will take Lady Eryn away now and leave you to carry on according to Lord Poron's discretion," Enric announced and stepped towards Eryn to take her hand and pull her against him to wrap an arm around her shaking shoulders and lead her away out the double doors, away from all that lunacy that had just begun to unfold.

* * *

Enric didn't intend to wait until they were at home, he needed to talk to her now. He pushed open the doors to another meeting room at the other end of the corridor and pulled her inside with him.

"You thought I did it!" she cried out and freed herself from his grip. "You really thought I had tried to kill him! You told them to interrogate me like a criminal - with a truth block! You should have known better!" She tried to swallow the sob, but it burst out nevertheless. "You should know better! You should be the only one who knows better, even if the whole world was doubting me!"

He stepped closer again and gripped her shoulders before she could draw back. "I knew you didn't do anything of that sort, that's why I needed that truth read to show all the others as well. If the King hadn't suggested Lord Seagon as the one to carry it out, I would have made that very same proposal. A man who is known to have opposed you on every occasion lends your testimony additional credibility." His hands moved from her shoulders upwards to cup her face. "I knew that you were not involved in this as sure as I know that I am not. I knew that even before feeling your shock at the accusation through the mind bond. Having you questioned presented no risk whatsoever." He made sure she looked in his eyes before he said the next words, "Had I believed anything else, I would have done whatever I could to make sure they didn't subject you to a truth block."

It took a few moments before the full impact of his words sank in. "You would have protected me if I had been guilty?" she whispered, her eyes wide with incredulity. "If I were a criminal?"

"Yes. I would have taken you and Vedric away from here. There is no way I'd have let them take you from me." He leaned his forehead against hers and closed his eyes.

"It would then have been just another one of my deeds for which I wouldn't take responsibility, eh?" she whispered with bitter sarcasm.

"I never meant it like..."

She pulled his hands away from her face. "No. You were right. There is always something I seem to mess up so badly that somebody else has to fix it or pay for it. It seems to have been like that almost all my life, if I look back. First my father's death as a result of my breaking Krion's arm; then letting Vern teach me magical fighting, for which he alone was punished; my attempt to go to Takhan that first time when Malriel almost managed to keep me there; and finally yesterday when I fell for the King's bait in a wager for which Vedric might one day have to pay. There is little doubt as to why you think I am unfit to raise your son, why you think of me as irresponsible and immature."

Enric exhaled deeply and leaned against a column to his right while he rubbed his face. This was the worst possible way he could imagine having his unthinking, harsh words thrown back at him. They seemed to have hit her so hard that she even assumed that he lost his faith in her completely and would have thought her capable of a deed like plotting Tyront's death. Just another irresponsible deed...

He wished he had managed to clear all that before this new catastrophe happened upon them. Dealing with this accusation while this other issue still stood between them was even harder now. They had to deal with this here and now, there was no way around it. They needed to be strong right now, be able to trust each other fully, lean on each other for strength. He pushed himself off the column and went to the square table in the centre of the room.

"Sit with me, if you will," he invited her formally and pulled out a chair for her.

She stared at him for a few long seconds before to his great relief she accepted his invitation and came to sit. He took a seat not across from her, which would indicate that they were on opposite sides in this, but alongside on her left.

When she had taken a seat with folded arms and without looking at him, he started speaking. "What I said yesterday was wrong. And now that I see that you are not just angry for my thoughtlessness but also seem to think that my words were justified, I am horrified. I was tense yesterday. First the matter of Tyront almost dying and my being forced to wait idly for the Council meeting finally to do something here; then that conflict with Werna, followed by the revelation that Malriel was even more powerful than we would ever wish her to be; and finally the King who chose that moment to spring another one of his games on you. And when you said that my holding back my suspicions about Malriel being an eligible candidate for a position as triarch was to blame, I didn't want to face the fact that I might have contributed anything to that horror. I didn't want to see that my keeping my thoughts to myself had not protected you as I had intended, but aided in making you an easy target. I was angry at myself and didn't want you to put your finger on the problem." He resisted the urge to take her hand in his. She would probably snatch it away. "You are neither irresponsible, nor immature. You are the most responsible person I have ever met, because you take on responsibility for everything you stumble across, be they orphans here or starving children in Takhan, people who can't afford medical treatment in an entire Kingdom or those close to you when they are in need of help." He smiled faintly at a memory. "Such as a certain warrior who was accused of having used magic against a non-magician and found himself faced with an order to lift his hand against the only female member in the Order." He saw her swallow and held out his hand for her to take, leaving the decision if she could already stand his touch to her. She looked at it for a second, then lifted her own to it. He pulled her fingers to his lips and pressed them against her cool skin for a moment. "You are impulsive, creative, incredibly smart, passionate about everything you take on, honest to the point of bluntness, and you care about others more than yourself. You are all that I am not and more. Having you raise our son with me is a privilege I wouldn't give up for anything in the world."

Eryn closed her eyes. "Thank you. That helps, so very much. The reason why your words hurt me so much was that I couldn't help but feel that they were not entirely unjustified. People keep telling me how wrong I am in the way I am going about raising our son. There are those who think I should dedicate all my time to him alone, and the others that keep telling me to hire a nursemaid and have somebody else take care of him, appropriate to my status. I keep trying to find a middle way here, and it doesn't work out the way I hoped. I constantly feel like I am neglecting my son, and every time he is troublesome for hours and I am relieved when he finally falls asleep, I feel bad because I think I should instead be grateful for every waking moment I have with him. I am at the same time selfishly grateful that your mother's decision to leave Anwin and move to the city came at such a convenient time for us, though I feel sad then every time she takes Vedric to bathe him or put him to bed because I should be the one doing it. I remember when we were first in Takhan and Valrad told me about the time when I was little and my father kept taking me with him whenever he met with somebody because he was worried that Malriel wouldn't make me feel as loved as I was." She shook her head. "And look at us now. We are little more than enemies with a fragile détente in existence between us. What if I am the same kind of mother? What if my own ambitions cause harm that can't be undone in relations between Vedric and me in the long run? What if our relationship with each other turns into that same jumble of emotions Malriel and I have?"

Enric blinked. It seemed as if she had been dealing with issues here that made the recent accusations almost pale in comparison. What he had taken to be no more than exhaustion had in fact been quite a bit more than mere lack of sleep and time to relax.

He made himself smile even though he would rather have wanted to kick himself for his insensitivity. "Ah, those self-proclaimed experts on child-rearing. A few of them also approached me - very carefully, of course. Almost all of them had either no children of their own - such as Tyront or even Lord Poron - or had the responsibility for their children delegated to servants and nursemaids, as with almost every other member of the Council. Has Orrin ever approached you with any well-meant if unwelcome advice as to how he thinks we should raise our child?"

Eryn thought for a moment, then shook her head. "No, never."

"I didn't think so. Do you see the significance here? He is virtually the only one of this whole bunch who actually knows what he would be talking about, having raised one child on his own and having his second with a woman whose ambitions reach higher than just being a nice ornament on his arm and in his parlour. He knows that ensuring his companion's happiness by not asking her to be nothing other than a mother is worth more than reducing her to this one role. And he is a man who wouldn't deny Junar what he himself wouldn't wish to give up. Orrin is as much a warrior as his companion is a seamstress and successful business woman. I would like to think that I am that kind of man as well. If you decided to give up healing or whatever you decided to pursue to spend all your time with Vedric instead, I would consider this a great failure on my part."

He could see the surprise on her face as she thought about his words.

"You were raised by a mother who dedicated all her time to you and your siblings. I bet you never had cause to doubt her affection and dedication," she said as if she wasn't yet ready to accept this easy way out of her doubts and self-flagellation.

"No, that is true. But it was apparent to me from when I was very young and later that she wasn't a happy woman. She always attempted to hide her grief, but a child feels if a smile is genuine or has this constant, underlying gloom of an attempt to conceal misery. Looking back, I would have wished for her every now and again to be more than merely our mother and Anwin's silently suffering companion, but to grant herself some time to be just herself. And if you look at my mother and her own relationship with her children, then sacrificing so many years to nothing other than our upbringing certainly didn't pay well for either her or us. Leris ran off at the first opportunity that presented itself to her, Noren is a bitter man who cheats on his companion because he learned from Anwin that this is the way of the world, and I have stayed away from my parents' house as much as I could for almost two and a half decades now. I would think that this should show us both clearly enough that it is not the amount of time you spend with your child that counts, but how well you use it." He intertwined her fingers with hers. "Apart from your unwarranted feelings of guilt, are you happy with how your life is right now?"

"Apart from being the prime suspect in an investigation right now you mean?" she joked weakly.

"Yes, my love, apart from that," he smiled, noting how the tension between them had all but vanished.

"Mostly, yes."

"What is missing for making you completely happy?" he asked.

She sighed and stared at the table. "Healing is important, I love it and feel that I am doing something valuable."

"But it is not quite as fulfilling as it used to be when you were the only one doing it or when you were still building this place up, before it started running smoothly enough without you there to direct everything?"

Eryn looked up at him and frowned. "Yes. How did you guess that?"

He smiled. "Remember your test results of that aptitude test in Takhan? The result was not healer, but explorer. As long as healing was a journey to increase knowledge, to learn new things, constantly to push your limits, it catered to the explorer inside you. But currently you are doing nothing more than routine work. You don't even have to handle those challenges the organisation of a clinic brings with it, as this is now Lord Poron's realm. No matter how many hours you dedicate to healing, you miss the difficulties, the problems that need solving that exceed your current skills. Your hands are busy, yet your brain is under-stimulated."

She closed her eyes and leaned back. "Yes. You are right. So I am not even using the time away from my son to do what really makes me happy. That is not only sad, it's pitiful."

"No, it's neither. The realisation is a chance for you to change it. Why not reduce your hours at the clinic to half of what you are doing now and spend that time differently? How about those books I brought back from Pirinkar - why not make a serious attempt at deciphering that language of theirs and work out how they treat that sleeping illness?" The expression of longing in her eyes made him grin. "My ever restless lady. I suggest you talk to Lord Poron about that. And to your father. I bet there is at least one healer specialised in illnesses in his clinic who would be thrilled to cooperate with you."

She nodded slowly. "I will do that. Thank you, so very much. For everything you said. I love you."

He got up from his chair and pulled her into an embrace. "That is completely justified. I am quite a catch", he quipped and then lowered his head to kiss her. "I love you, too. Come on, then. Let's have lunch and then see Tyront. I want to make sure he knows where not to lay the blame for his near demise."

* * *

Enric knocked at the door to Tyront's quarters and waited patiently until what he recognised as Vyril's footsteps came close enough to permit entry.

"Enric, Eryn, come in," she said and stepped aside. "Tyront said you would very likely turn up soon. Go on, they are in his study."

"They?" Eryn asked. She didn't really feel like facing too many people right now. Stepping before the man who she allegedly had tried to have killed was likely to prove trying enough.

"Yes, Lord Poron is present, and so is Lord Orrin and your sister."

"Pe'tala?" Eryn frowned. "What is she doing here?"

"I cannot tell you this, dear, you will have to go in and find out for yourself," Vyril replied and nodded towards the study door.

Enric pulled her on with him and rapped at the door, receiving permission to enter only a moment later.

Lord Poron had taken a seat on a chair at the table in front of the window, while Pe'tala had made herself comfortable on a sofa. Orrin was the only one who had opted for standing. He was leaning against a bookshelf with folded arms. Tyront, as ever, presided behind his desk. Luckily the study was large enough not to feel crowded with six people in it.

"So, how did the second part of the interrogation of our young assassin go?" Enric asked without bothering with a greeting.

Orrin sighed and shook his head. "Strange. And unsettling. He doesn't seem to see anything wrong with his actions. He appears to be deeply awed by Eryn and imagines for some reason that she told him to get Lord Tyront out of the way. We asked him about details, which is usually the part where liars struggle. But not him. Which should not surprise me, I suppose, considering that he somehow circumvented the truth block. He came up with minutia of his meetings with her - which words she used to instruct him, the clothes she wore, what advice she gave him about remaining undetected and so on."

"How did the Council react?" Enric wanted to know.

"Confused. They have two conflicting statements, both given under a seemingly manipulation-proof spell. They currently basically believe whatever they wish. Though Eryn seems to have impressed Lord Seagon a great deal today. He did not try to assert the idea of Eryn being innocent as such, but neither did he join with those who expressed considerable doubts about that. There were a few rather ridiculous discussions that don't bear repeating, but so far the Council is content to wait for more evidence before calling for action. As is the King," Orrin answered Enric's next question before he could voice it. "Though we all know that he wants Eryn to be proved innocent, even if he cannot be incautious enough to say it out loud like that. It would appear as though it were undue favouritism and his reputation would suffer from that, even if she turns out to be innocent in the end."

"Even if she turns out to be innocent?" Pe'tala cried out. "Of course she is innocent!" She turned to Tyront. "And I hope for your own sake that you are aware of it. I mean, consider the facts here, will you?" Pointing a finger at Eryn she said, "That woman over there is a bloody Aren, and they not only do their own killing when they consider it necessary instead of using hired help, they also make sure everyone knows it and henceforth stays out of the way to avoid a similar fate."

"Thanks a lot," Eryn growled and rolled her eyes, "that definitely serves to convey the impression of my being innocent. Do me a favour, will you? Don't help me!"

Pe'tala ignored her and went on despite Tyront's polite attempt to interrupt her. "Furthermore, she played a key role in saving your life after you were buried under that wall. I do not know for sure if even my considerable, and above average, capabilities as a healer would have enabled me to have done it alone. And you may or may not believe this, but I would not have been able to tell if anything was amiss if she had assessed that your heart was simply too damaged to go on. She could have let you die there without raising any suspicions, which she did not - that in itself must show you that she is not..."

"I know she didn't try to kill me!" Tyront barked and finally made her pause. "And now shut up or I will personally remove you from my study just to have some peace! I don't need you to try and convince me of something I am perfectly aware of."

Eryn closed her eyes for a moment. He knew she wasn't after his blood, even though the evidence was nowhere close to being unequivocal.

"Why is Pe'tala here?" she then asked.

Lord Poron answered her. "I told her about what happened at the Council meeting and she made a suggestion I consider worth pursuing. Pe'tala?"

She raised an eyebrow and looked at Tyront, who rolled his eyes and growled, "You have my permission to speak. Unless you happen to try my patience again."

"I think that man is crazy," she said simply.

"Crazy as in insane and not as in evil, I assume?" Enric asked. "Is that even a medical term? It seems a little derogatory to me."

Pe'tala rolled her eyes. "Yes, I know. And healers especially should not speak in a disrespectful manner of those of unsound mind. But we are talking about a man who is trying to incriminate my own sister, so I kindly ask you be lenient with me, will you?"

He frowned. "Even if you were able to find proof of his insanity, the evidence wouldn't be accepted if it came from you. People would doubt that you are trustworthy since they would assume that you would do anything to clear your sister, even resorting to false testimony or manipulated evidence. They won't let you anywhere near Darnet."

"Exactly. And unfortunately neither Lord Poron nor any of the other healers are anywhere close to being advanced enough to detect sights of such an illness. I thus propose for Lord Poron to contact his colleague at the clinic in Takhan, a certain Valrad of House Vel'kim, I have been informed," she added with a grim smile, "and ask him whether he would consent to having one of his most esteemed healers sent here in order to provide the evidence that will certainly help clear his daughter from the suspicion of having tried to murder her superior."

Eryn grimaced. "You want to inform him of everything we have on our hands here? Is that really necessary?"

"Yes," Tyront cut in. "It is. He would get to hear of it soon enough anyway. Too many people know of it already to keep this a secret. Tomorrow by this time the entire city will know, and one day - or within a bird's flight, if you like - later all of Takhan will be aware of it. Lord Poron will contact your father, while I will ask the King to contact the Triarchy to request them officially to send this healer to Anyueel." He looked to Pe'tala. "What's his name? You wanted somebody particular, didn't you?"

She nodded. "Iklan. That is who we want."

"Iklan?" Eryn asked, feeling a rush of affection at the mention of the man who had helped her deal with her issues with accepting Valrad as being her father only a few months ago.

"Yes, he is the best, and father will not hesitate to despatch him," her sister assured her and then grinned lopsidedly. "You see? At times it is some use to have family in high places. With your mother in the Triarchy and your father in charge of the clinic there is little to no chance that this request will be denied - even in the unlikely case that Iklan should refuse to come. They would simply knock him out, put him in a crate and have him shipped here before he knew what had hit him. And will it not be an agreeable task for Malriel and Valrad to undertake this joint effort at getting their illegitimate lovechild out of yet another fix? It will strengthen their relationship."

"So glad to be of use to them," Eryn growled.

"How will you proceed with Darnet now?" Enric enquired of Lord Poron. "As Eryn is now a suspect as well it might seem strange to incarcerate him while Eryn goes free."

Lord Poron shook his head. "No, I wouldn't think so. Darnet is involved in all this, there is no doubt about that. He is guilty of attacking Lord Tyront and has admitted this himself in addition to Lord Orrin's testimony. The question in his case is merely if he was in this alone or acted as somebody else's minion, as he is convinced. These are the facts even those who are inclined to believe Lady Eryn guilty acknowledge. Against Lady Eryn there is no other evidence than his word under truth block against hers. I will, however, send a pair of guards with her whenever she leaves your house so as to avoid the impression of any undue privileges here."

Tyront nodded. "I agree." He looked at Eryn. "And in addition to this I have to bar you from all Council meetings for the duration of these proceedings. You are for now suspended from your duty to serve the Council."

Pe'tala laughed loudly when Eryn couldn't suppress a grin. "Now you really have dealt her a heavy blow! If this is how you rewar... ah... punish suspects that allegedly tried to kill you, you might want to watch yourself very carefully from now on as you might just have given her an incentive for a few timely and friendly assassination attempts in the future whenever your meetings are becoming too tiresome."

Tyront sighed heavily and shook his head. "And I am to have another healer from Takhan here soon. I can hardly wait," he said gravely. "Is there a chance that this one is not related to either of you, not even remotely, and might turn out to be a pleasant fellow for a change?"

Pe'tala pretended to think about that. "Well, Eryn and my sharing a few drops of blood with him is more likely than not when considering the frequent interconnections between the Houses in Takhan. And no matter how trying you may find me at times, My Lord, I am sure you will miss me dreadfully once I am gone from here in a few months."

He snorted. "Yes. With you and your sister in Takhan the peace and quiet here will undoubtedly be unbearable."

*   *   *

Enric entered her study while she was sitting at her desk, bent over a few sheets of paper, reading. Vedric was sleeping in his cradle next to her, probably exhausted from yet another restless night.

Eryn looked up when he entered, a worried expression on her face. "Can you believe that? He describes his made-up meetings with me in such detail that I am starting to doubt my own sanity here." She pointed to one sheet. "Here he even describes what colour the ribbon on my braid was! Or that I smelled of..." she consulted the sheet again, "...dried herbs and a whiff of sweet flowers."

"Yes, I've read the report. I am a little disconcerted that he made up intimate details like your smell. It seems he imagined getting quite close to you. I hope we are not dealing with some kind of infatuation here." He stepped closer and let several small metal bird-cylinders drop on her desk. "Messages from Takhan."

Eryn grimaced. "Oh dear. Word certainly has spread fast if not only Valrad knows of it." She picked up a tube and identified the little crest embossed on the tiny screw-cap. "Arbil." Then she picked up the others. "Vel'kim, another Vel'kim, Aren, a third Vel'kim, Feral and Aren again." She picked up one tube. "I'll start with Ram'an. I assume that it will be friendlier than anything that bears the Aren crest," she commented dryly and removed the slim slip of paper and smoothed it out. She smiled. "He assures me that he knows that I would never resort to a thing like that and that he wishes he had enough knowledge of the Kingdom's laws to rush here to my aid himself. He is confident that this absurd case will be resolved in my favour and asks me to keep him updated." She took the next one. "Malhora. She calls me a walking catastrophe and asks whether any of these people here know me well enough to work out that Aren and underhand attempts to murder don't sit well together. If we kill, we advertise it.

That's pretty much what Pe'tala said. I find it a little disconcerting that my grandmother seems to think of this as some kind of virtue." She took the three Vel'kim tubes aside and opened them all. "Valrad is worried but promises to send Iklan as quickly as possible. The Triarchy has agreed to it. He says he would come himself if he didn't know that Iklan is the better man for this task and that he as my father would not be very credible when giving testimony in my defence. Then Vran'el says that he is confident that this nonsense will be cleared up soon enough and that he advises me to have Iklan look not only at my accuser's mental health, but also at my own to prove to the Council that only one of us is mad. Charming," she snorted but saw that he was right. One of the Council members would very likely have demanded it anyway. It would look better if she offered it voluntarily. "This one is from Vern. He says that there is obviously no keeping me out of trouble and that it pains him that he is so far away and can't be at my side to get through this together with me." She smiled sadly. "That's really sweet." Then she unrolled the Feral message. "Intrea. She is outraged on my behalf and wishes she could come here herself to tell them what senselessness all this is, that the surest proof that this wasn't my doing is obviously that Tyront is still alive." Eryn snorted. "Funny, how people primarily assume that I am innocent not because they think I would never do a thing like that but because it was carried out sloppily and that I would have done it myself and owned up to it."

Enric nodded at the last tube with the Aren crest when she didn't reach for it. "Come on, my love. I doubt that your mother would send you unkind words in a situation like now."

She sighed and freed the last message from its metal prison. "Malriel confirms what Valrad wrote, that Iklan will be sent here as soon as possible. She is confident that this will all be cleared up quickly enough but warns me that the problem behind this attempt at Tyront's life is what I need to deal with afterwards. That it is upon me to catalyse the changes that I have started in that society of ours." She frowned. "So she thinks this is my fault after all even if I didn't arrange for this wall to collapse on top of Tyront?"

Enric shook his head. "No. That's not what she is telling you. Remember what Erbál told you? That he has reason to believe that there is a rising dissatisfaction among the magicians here? I think the attempt on Tyront's life was the first eruption of it and that we need to act if we want to avoid further ones of such magnitude. Darnet may have been the only one to plan and carry out this attack, but both he and Erbál said that there were more magicians who started to think when our contact with the Western Territories opened their eyes to a society where magicians are neither bound by an institution such as the Order nor forced to live in the city instead of wherever it pleased them. And then there is the choice of profession that is so natural to your people but is here limited to warrior or some function connected to keeping the system alive - and more recently healer.

You made that contact between the countries possible, so Malriel says that you need to take a lead in making sure the changes this causes here go in the right direction. And she is right. I think that you are the best person to take a leading role here as well - however little that will please Tyront and the Council."

Eryn swallowed. "I am expected to lead you all into a new era of... what? Increased freedom for magicians?"

He chuckled. "Don't tell me you don't feel up to that. So far the trouble has been rather keeping you from tearing down the Order as a whole. I would think that merely promoting changes would even mean toning down your efforts somewhat."

She shot him a look. "Hilarious."

Then they both looked to the door when Gerit appeared. "Eryn, my dear, are you ready?"

Enric looked from one woman to the other. "Ready for what?"

His companion rose and gently lifted the baby boy up, careful not to wake him while she fitted him into the sling. "We have an appointment to have a look at a house for your mother. Lord Woldarn is selling some property and we are meeting his steward today so he can show us around." She frowned. "Do we have a steward or agent or someone? I mean, we seem to own quite a lot of property, don't we?"

He nodded. "We have a few people to handle things for us, yes. But their responsibility has always been only for the one property they are stationed at. The rest I take care of myself. I don't like to depend on any of them too much."

"Any advice you would like to impart to us before we leave?" Eryn asked.

"Only one: make sure whatever house you pick is not too small. It wouldn't look good if I settled my mother into anywhere too cramped."

Gerit shook her head. "I don't like the idea of spending more of your money than totally necessary only to pander to what other people expect."

Eryn snorted. "That has been an ongoing discussion between us for, what, two years? Frugality is certainly not your son's forte, and then for no more sensible reasons than what others think."

Enric leaned to her to kiss her forehead. "At least that's what I tell you to hide the fact that I am a man who loves living in luxury."

"Not only that. You try to impose it on others as well."

"A cruel fate you will have to come to terms with, my love. And now off you go to see what Lord Woldarn has to show you." He briefly thought about offering to mind Vedric in the meantime, but thought better of it when he remembered the conversation they'd had only recently. She needed the time with her son to know she wasn't neglecting him.

* * *

Pe'tala leaned back in Junar's parlour, balancing her nephew on her knee. Little Téa sat on the carpet and chewed happily on a wooden toy under her mother's watchful gaze.

"So, sister, how did your viewing of that house go? Is Enric's mother about to move out soon and return Vedric's room to him?"

Eryn gave her a stern look. "We are not doing this to get rid of her."

"Of course not. Yet if you keep inviting people to stay with you, you have now effectively run out of bedrooms. Or do you intend finally doing some work on that second floor that is little more than random storage space right now?"

"Says the woman who will move into our house in Takhan when it's finished."

Junar sighed. "Stop this bickering, the two of you. Now, back to that question. Was the house suitable or not?"

Eryn swayed her head a little. "I liked it, and so did Gerit. The size is a nice compromise between what Gerit herself thinks she needs and what Enric thinks she must have so he doesn't look like a miser. It's bright, airy, comfortably furnished, more than enough space for whatever visitors she might invite..."

"But?" Pe'tala enquired.

"But Enric says the price is too high. Can you believe that? First he forces us to spend more than we think is necessary, and then he complains about the price!"

Junar shook her head. "This is not about the price but what he gets in exchange for it. If I pay several gold pieces for a bale of cloth, I certainly won't accept second quality. And as a businessman he cannot afford to be seen to be paying more than the market warrants. Especially as the owner is his colleague in the Council. It would mean that Enric would be deferring to Lord Woldarn. Not good at all, considering Enric's higher rank."

"Well, if you look at it like that..." Eryn relented. "Though it's a pity. I mean, what are the chances that the very first house we looked at would fit so perfectly? Now we have to continue with our search and we will doubtlessly compare every other place to this first one."

Pe'tala nodded seriously. "Meaning you will never find one that meets your requirements. Maybe you really should convert that second floor of yours into some proper living space. You will be gone half of every year anyway, so the house would be empty but for Plia. Why not keep Gerit?"

"Keep Gerit," Eryn murmured and rolled her eyes. "She is not a stray cat we found somewhere. She wants her own home, and I understand her well enough. Firstly, not everybody is comfortable with a mountain cat living under the same roof. And secondly, she would always be something like a guest in somebody else's house instead of being free to do what she wants. Furthermore, Enric says that he is too old to live with his mother."

"I do not see the problem here. At home we sometimes live with our parents for decades, especially the leading families of the Houses," Pe'tala frowned.

"That's because your residences are vast enough so that you can keep out of each other's ways for days if you wish to. That is not exactly the kind of housing policy we practice here," Junar smiled. "Though I admit that having a larger family around when there is a small child certainly has its merits. I certainly appreciated having Malhora around at the Aren residence."

Pe'tala nodded. "Yes, it certainly does. Though I will confess that living alone for at least half of every year will be quite pleasant. It will take away the pressure of having to work again so soon once I have children."

Both mothers stared at her perplexed.

"What was that?" Eryn asked confused. "You want to stay at home and do nothing but tend your child and give up your work for who knows how long? And not having any relatives around who would mind your children is a convenient means of avoiding working? Why does that not fit with the picture I have of you in any way whatever?"

Her younger sister glared at her. "Just because you and Junar delight in showing the other rich women here that you are too active and ambitious to be content with something as simple as raising a child does not mean that this is how every woman would want to handle such an event in their life. I would very much like to be there for my baby as much as I can. And I do not intend to be ashamed for what you two doubtlessly consider an old-fashioned and trite approach to raising a child. I look at you, Eryn - too proud or stubborn or whatever to hire a nursemaid despite continuing your work. I see how you struggle, how pale and exhausted both you and Enric became before Gerit showed up. I do not have to justify myself for not wanting such a thing!"

Eryn blinked in amazement. "Of course not. It just surprises me a little, especially as women in your country are encouraged to work again soon after having a child."

"Encouraged, yes. Pressured? No. Look at Intrea. She is happy enough raising our niece and has been for a few years now. Every time she feels the need for some adult interaction or wants to do some painting or drawing, she has her father or Vran'el take care of her daughter. But she wants that to be an occasional thing, not regular. And as for me... Open your eyes, Eryn. My mother ran off when I was a little girl, and I have been missing her ever since. This is not something I would ever want my own child to experience. I want my children to know that I am there whenever they need me." She looked at her older sister. "I was a little envious when you first came to Takhan, I will admit. You disembarked from that ship and suddenly found yourself reunited with your mother. And your father, even though you were not aware of it at that time."

Eryn grimaced. "Yes, and a harmonious reunion it was indeed..."

"This does not matter. Even having Malriel as a mother is better than having no mother at all." Her voice turned bitter. "I would even prefer for her to be dead instead of knowing that she is out there somewhere in the wilds of the desert and quite happy with having abandoned me and my brother. Malriel at least cares for you, even if her way of showing it is not the most admirable one. But that's Aren for you."

Junar and Eryn exchanged a look at this unexpected revelation. Pe'tala didn't normally volunteer such personal insights into her feelings.

Eryn cleared her throat, determined to get over this gloomy mood in the room. "Would you like to hear something funny? Funny for you, that is; I wasn't particularly happy at that moment. Gerit scolded me for speaking ill of Inad."

The seamstress raised her brow. "Did she now?"

"She did. I asked her how she liked her occasional meetings with Inad since they had only been writing to each other for around four decades. You will remember that they are cousins, of course?"

Junar nodded.

"I pointed out that I found Inad infinitely tiresome and considered her a shallow creature with too much time on her hands and too little purpose in her life. I said that I was surprised how they seem to get along so well with each other. Gerit didn't take very kindly to this evaluation of mine. She was very correct and calm when she had me know in that same controlled and superior tone that Enric likes to adopt that I am of course entitled to my personal opinions on other people but that she herself has developed a deep fondness for Inad over these years. Inad was the only person in her family to keep in contact with Gerit, despite the reprimands that earned her. And then she had me know that she would appreciate it if I kept my unflattering views about Inad to myself in her presence, since she would be equally unwilling to tolerate anybody speaking ill of me if she was anywhere around."

Pe'tala grinned. "That surely put you in your place, did it not?"

"Quite. I am feeling torn now. Am I supposed to like Inad now because she was the only family member who had it in her not to damn Gerit for going away with somebody so decidedly lower in status than herself? Now I feel bad for not liking her, for finding her bothersome."

"You can't decide whether to like somebody or not, it is something that comes from within you," Junar pointed out. "But what you may decide is to respect her for the kind of friend she was to Enric's mother all these years. It is possible to respect somebody without particularly liking them. And she is basically part of your family now, so that alone should induce you to make the effort."

Eryn snorted. "That motivation certainly does not work in my case. I don't even like my own mother, so the family bonus is a feeble argument with me."

Pe'tala smiled faintly. "You like Malriel well enough, sister. You are just too stubborn to allow yourself to acknowledge it."

"Oh, spare me," she growled.

"What? I thought we were dealing with our mother issues here, and as I opened up already, it was now your turn. My mistake," she grinned, obviously not at all sorry at having brought it up.

Eryn sighed and rose. "So much for that adult interaction I thought I needed. Maybe you just don't fit the picture when it comes to adult. Give me my kid back, will you? I need to take him home to Enric before my appointment with Lord Poron."

"You might just as well leave him with me for a bit so he can have some quality time with his favourite aunt."

"You don't know if you are his favourite aunt," Eryn pointed out mercilessly. "He has three more."

"Nonsense. Of course I am his favourite aunt," Pe'tala huffed indignantly. "You go and see Lord Poron. I will teach my nephew a few creative swear words in the meantime."

"That is no use whatsoever, he isn't talking yet."

"I know that. But hearing them repeatedly will enable him to remember them when he starts."

Eryn folded her arms and frowned. "You just made me question the wisdom of letting you move in with us in Takhan."

"Complete rot," Pe'tala waved her off without looking at her. "Go."

When Eryn stood her ground, Junar sighed and promised, "I'll keep an eye on her. Go see Lord Poron."

Eryn nodded slowly and took her cloak. She couldn't shake off the feeling that she left Junar to babysit three people.

*   *   *

Enric came down the stairs after his mother, holding his son on his arm. The breakfast table had already been set and Eryn was sitting in front of a place mat. She seemed to be more or less patiently waiting for them while talking to Plia next to her. So she had managed to leave the clinic on time after her night shift, enabling them to have breakfast together. Which was good. But that also meant they had to hurry and sit down because Eryn tended to become rather grumpy when she was hungry.

He found this homely scene with his companion, his mother, his son and Plia at the same table appealing. There weren't too many occasions where it worked out like this. Plia tended to stay late and have dinner at the clinic, as did Eryn before her night shifts. Then Eryn often came home from the clinic too late to have breakfast at home, and lunch was always a matter of chance of whether either of them was at the Palace, at the clinic or wherever else. But that would change now that she had talked to Lord Poron about reducing her shifts not only to three out of ten days, but also moving her working time from night to day again, now that Gerit was available to take care of Vedric. Enric approved of this, very much so. He was sick and tired of sleeping alone in their huge bed. Well, sleeping... finding himself alone in it every time he had to get up and carry his son around when he woke up. Still. He wanted her beside him at night. It had been hard enough to get her to accept sleeping in one bed with him back then, yet their sleeping in the same bed but at different times was not at all what he'd had in mind.

Eryn smiled when she spotted them and rubbed her hands. "Excellent! I really am starving!"

Which was a complete exaggeration, Enric knew. Had she been anywhere close to starving, her mood wouldn't have been that cheerful. He kissed her on the forehead and let her take their son from his arm and sit him on her lap before she opened the coverings on her tray. She had taken to eating more mashed and pureed food in the mornings so Vedric could have a few spoonfuls as well. She still nursed him and intended to go on doing so for another two months, but a few weeks ago he had already started taking some solids and seemed to enjoy the new diversity in his diet. The act itself was a distinctly messy business and getting dressed had become a matter of strategic consideration. Changing into a clean set of clothes before feeding Vedric a few bites was a mistake Enric had made only once. Eryn had even agreed to have a few extra sets of clothes made for herself as she kept running out of clean ones regularly these days.

Gerit took a seat at the chair she had chosen as her regular place at the table and bit her lip when she found the manila envelope next to her tray.

"What's that?" Enric enquired. "Were you expecting anything in particular?"

His mother exhaled and nodded. "I was, actually. I sent your father the papers for the dissolution of our commitment, and I was hoping against hope that he had sent me back the signed documents. I suppose I had better open it after breakfast."

Eryn grimaced. "Is that wise? You will just keep staring at it and wonder whether he signed them or not. Go on, get it behind you."

Gerit stared a few moments longer at the envelope and then gave in and picked it up to tear open the long side. She pulled out a single sheet of paper. A handful of neatly cut strips that had without doubt originally been the papers Gerit needed for the dissolution tumbled out.

Plia swallowed. "Oh no, that's bad news, isn't it? What happens now? Can you still dissolve the commitment somehow?"

Gerit shook her head, her lips pressed together into a tight line.

Enric was the one to explain the problem to her. "In order to dissolve a commitment, both parties need to agree by signing these papers. If one of them wishes to do so without the other party's consent, there must be proof of a breach of trust or mistreatment. A breach of trust we have, proof thereof we have not. My testimony would not count for much; the incidents I witnessed took place more than twenty years ago, and Anwin could claim that my memory can hardly be trusted after all this time and that I was still a child and had misinterpreted what I had seen and added a little of my imagination."

"Is it so important to dissolve it? Can't she just stay in the city without that dissolution?"

He shook his head. "Not for long. If there is an unsanctioned absence of one partner in a commitment without a dissolution, the companion left behind may after two months claim that the commitment has been abandoned without justification. That is punishable with either a prison sentence or an amount of money to be paid. And then of course she would have to return to him unless she wishes to be penalised again."

Plia stared at him. "Really? That's terrible! I wonder why people would ever enter into a commitment willingly if getting out of it turns out to be that troublesome!"

Eryn silently agreed. Had she not been coerced into the commitment with Enric, she doubted that he would have managed to make her agree to it particularly soon. She further doubted that Enric would make a dissolution easy for her should she one day decide that she could no longer stay with him - something she fervently hoped would never come to pass. Despite the minor and major catastrophes that kept befalling them at regular intervals Enric had for the first time after her fath... Ved'al's death given her the feeling that she belonged. And not just to a place, but to him. Even though she was initially angry at her brother's order to return to Takhan so often and for such extended periods of time, it didn't really matter where she lived as long as Enric was there as well. Home was no longer a place, it was a man. One who currently looked anything but happy with the paleness which the note Anwin had sent put on his mother's face.

"What does that pathetic maggot write?" he asked coldly.

Gerit didn't look up from the paper when she spoke, "That there is no way that he will ever agree to a dissolution as long as he lives. That he will not bear the shame of being left like that. He told everyone that I went to the city to help you with our grandchild and that I will be back soon. He promises to have me brought back to him if I don't return within the two months." She let the letter sink to the table and closed her eyes. "I can't go back to him. I would rather spend time in prison every two months."

"You won't have to go back," Enric promised. "And neither will you have to go to prison. I'll pay the fine gladly - every two months if need be."

His mother looked up when he stepped next to her and lifted a hand up to his cheek, gently stroking over the stubble that Eryn knew was just long enough not to poke, with three days' growth.

"That is very kind of you, my boy. Yet I am a grown woman and there is a limit to how much care and assistance I can accept from my son. I want to serve that sentence. It means that I have made a decision I know I am able and ready to pay the price for. It is a price I shall pay willingly." Her eyes narrowed. "Two weeks in prison every now and again is nothing compared to the thirty-eight years before. At least I will have my peace and quiet."

Eryn saw how Enric fought with himself, appalled by the thought of watching how she would willingly go to prison instead of letting him take care of her, yet hesitant at denying her the chance to stand up for herself with her head held high.

"Maybe we can discuss this again when the time comes," he said evasively when he couldn't bring himself to voice his agreement to such a scheme. "Let's see if he really resorts to such measures," he added, pushing aside the thought that Anwin would definitely go through with it. His pride was more important than respecting the fact that his companion simply couldn't bear living with him any longer.

Gerit obviously was thinking the same, as she just gave him a weak indulgent smile and squeezed his hand.

CHAPTER 26

Backup from Jakhan

Enric found her in their bedroom, Vedric asleep and appearing even tinier on the huge bed, Eryn prone and absorbed in a thick, archaic looking book.

"What are you reading?" he enquired as he crouched next to her and glanced at the pages she had currently open. "Is that a book on law? I am shocked. That's not one of ours, is it? Don't tell me you smuggled it out of the library?"

She grinned. "Smuggling wasn't necessary. The new librarian is not as strict as Lord Poron used to be when it comes to holding the books there. And thanks to my being such an important person he was very eager to oblige me here. That's one advantage about people not getting to know me when I was still a prisoner: they only see the mighty lady magician. The tales of the fearsome Aren temper people delight in spreading do their bit as well, I would think. I imagine Pe'tala is amusing herself by circulating them, if you ask me."

"Alright, that explains why it was possible for you to take that book away from the library, but not why you picked it as reading material. Considering your aversion to rules and regulations I would have thought that you would rather set fire to a book filled with them and dance around it."

"Don't forget being naked and under the full moon," Eryn quipped. "I remember that Lord Poron once showed me a few books on healing that were written by either a lunatic or somebody who just likes to mess with people. I think it was something about bathing in the river under a full moon in order to heal something broken or something of the like."

"Are you deliberately avoiding answering my question or are you just distracted?"

She grimaced. "Alright, I admit I am a bit reluctant to answer it. I'm currently doing some research on the legal background on guardianships. Learning about the particulars of whatever vexations that a lost bet with the King might cause Vedric in the years to come seemed advisable."

"Spoken like a loving and caring mother," he nodded seriously.

She glanced at him and pursed her lips. "There is something else you want to say. I can see it in your eyes. Probably something along the lines of me at least being loving and caring, as I am clearly not a cautious or smart mother who wouldn't have entered into such a bet in the first place."

Enric, full of innocence when facing such opprobrious accusations, raised his brow. "Dear me, would I ever?"

"Yes, you would. And now go away and let me finish the last few pages on that fascinating chapter as long as I can still manage to keep my eyes open," she said, trying to drive him off.

"Not easily done, I'm afraid. I came here with a purpose. You are expected at the harbour, and soon."

She looked up in confusion. "At the harbour? What for? The only..." Her voice trailed off when her eyes widened. "Don't tell me Iklan is here already? That's impossible!"

He smiled widely. "Not with your parents, my love. They more or less sent him off a day after they received Lord Poron's and the King's request." He picked up Vedric, waking him in the process. "Hurry. We are to meet Lord Poron, Pe'tala, Ram'kel and Marrin there."

Eryn left the book lying on the bed and jumped up with renewed vigour. "I bet Lord Poron is beside himself with joy at the prospect of having such a venerated healer here for a time. Iklan's being here to get me out of trouble is probably only an added side benefit for him."

"Nonsense. He is in charge of the investigation and will certainly not keep Iklan from doing his work by assailing him with constant questions about healing. He used to be second in command for quite a while, and that requires discipline and the ability to prioritise. Honestly, I should know." He fixed the sling around his chest to secure his son against him. "We should have another two hours before he gets hungry again. I suppose we'll manage to be back by then. If not, we'll stop by at Pe'tala's place and have her feed him. She at least can change her clothes afterwards then and there."

Eryn quickly braided her hair in front of the mirror and rummaged in her little wooden box with the ribbons. She had a long time ago given up her attempts at keeping them tidy and so it took her a minute to free a dark red ribbon that matched her tunic from the tangled snakes' nest inside. When she had finally managed to accomplish that feat, she had to redo half the braid that had unravelled.

"Alright, off we go!" she called out and clapped her hands three times as if she had been the one who was waiting for Enric and not the other way round.

They stepped outside into the grey streets and Eryn grinned lopsidedly when the first tiny snowflakes of the season silently floated down only to melt immediately upon touching the cobblestones. "That will be quite a surprise for Iklan. His very first time experiencing snow."

Enric intertwined his fingers with hers and pulled her onward. "Anything to increase the adventure factor for our guest."

They walked on and then turned right into the next larger street down south, passing the clinic a little later and then crossing Kingsway before they went over the bridge directly next to the docks.

"Hurry," she murmured when she spotted the small ship that had just arrived and was tied up so that the passengers could safely disembark. They approached just as the gangplank was being put in place and stopped next to the others who were awaiting the healer's arrival.

Ram'kel nodded his head. "Lady Malthéa. Lord Enric," he smiled with a glint of mischief in his eyes when he looked at her.

Eryn ground her teeth slightly. So he was obviously determined to call her that in public. This man really was an irritation. And Marrin right next to him looked so suspiciously bland that he had to be hiding a grin. Such an utter lack of expression was always suspicious.

"Careful, Ram'kel," Pe'tala warned him. "You are begging for trouble here. That is rather brave considering that you are far away from home and more or less on your own here."

The women waved when Iklan was leaving the ship and Eryn frowned when she saw there was a second foreign looking man behind him. "Who is... No! I don't believe it!" she cried out. "Is it really him?"

Pe'tala chuckled lowly. "Indeed. In all his arrogant glory. And he did not even bother to send word of his impending arrival, doubtlessly sure of his being welcomed like the gift to humankind he thinks he is."

The two men stopped in front of them and bowed as they had obviously been instructed to when facing magicians in the Kingdom. Eryn laughed at the absurd sight and stepped forward to take Iklan's hands and squeeze them. "Thank you so much for undertaking the journey here at such short notice. I sincerely hope they didn't pressure you too hard."

The healer laughed. "Pressure me? I would never have exchanged words with your father again had he sent anyone else here!"

While Iklan was being introduced to Lord Poron, Eryn turned to the other new arrival and grinned broadly before pulling him into a firm hug. "Sarol! Is this really possible? You! In my city!"

Sarol of House Roal rolled his eyes and said with his usual impatience about the world in general and people in particular, "Will somebody free me from that foolish woman and tell her that we are in public and she is not supposed to fraternise with an opponent of her House with such obvious mindlessness?"

Eryn shook her head at him and released him again when he didn't reciprocate her embrace. "I'm really glad that the other healers here have endured Pe'tala for more than a year already, so your charming self will merely startle them instead of making them run off in all directions."

Sarol ignored her and exchanged a nod with Pe'tala and then Ram'kel before graciously allowing himself to be introduced to Marrin and Lord Poron, who seemed to have lost control over his broad grin at so unexpectedly facing two healers of such exalted standing owing to their accomplishments.

"We have arranged for coaches to take us all to the Palace where you will reside for the duration of your stay," Marrin announced after they had exchanged their greetings. "You are doubtless exhausted from your long journey and will appreciate getting out of the cold."

Iklan smiled gratefully while Sarol gave the overcast sky a diffident look. "Frozen water falling from the sky. What a curious place."

They boarded the two coaches Marrin had arranged for, both bearing the Royal crest which would ensure that all other carts, wagons and people on horses or on foot would make space for them to pass at once and enable them to reach their destination without let or hindrance.

Lord Poron and Marrin rode with their visitors while Eryn, Enric, Pe'tala and Ram'kel followed in the second vehicle. When all of them had stepped inside the Palace and the heavy doors were closed to change their surroundings from frigid to merely cool, Iklan sighed with relief.

"Now come here," Sarol instructed Pe'tala who obediently approached him to let herself be hugged.

Eryn shook her head incredulously. "What about fraternising with the enemy? You are aware that she is a member of the same House as me, aren't you?"

Sarol squeezed Pe'tala a moment longer, then let go of her again when he answered, "I distinctly remember that I pointed out that I had a problem with open fraternising, not with the concept as such. And now stop complaining and greet me properly. You may embrace me now."

She stared at him and folded her arms. "Who says I even want to anymore?" It sounded childish, even to her ears. But if there was a man in this world who understood about pride, it was him.

"Of course you want to. You are overjoyed that I have come and are grumpy because I am right. Now that we have this out in the open there is no reason for you to make a fuss. I am sure the people around you are used to your being in the wrong." He lifted his arms and waited for her to step into them.

Eryn stared at him for a few more moments, then sighed and shook her head. "You really are a piece of work, Sarol. You don't encounter much opposition at home, do you?"

"At times. I just do not let it slow me down. And now come here before my arms drop off. As you are surely aware I do not possess magic to infuse my muscles with extra strength."

Enric behind her gave her a gentle push and she stepped forward and was enveloped by his arms. He smelled of wood and leather, odours he must have picked up on the journey here.

He released her again after a surprisingly long hug and then patted her shoulder, making her roll her eyes at the condescending gesture. But this was Sarol she was dealing with. Arguing was just no use here. Human emotions were to him something he analysed and explained with such cold precision that the object of his observation felt all but naked. Yet also he seemed to lack the understanding for those emotions, which exceeded the mere intellectual approach he was so good at. That made it all the more painful when he was right. Which he tended to be more often than people appreciated.

"Now you may guide us to our accommodation. Ram'an told me that the quarters you provide are rather spacious and there is usually more than one bedroom. It means Iklan and I will share our quarters."

"We will?" Iklan asked more from amusement than surprise.

"Of course," his colleague confirmed.

"And I have no objections at all with regard to that?"

Sarol looked at him with a patient expression as if explaining the obvious was a burden he knew superior intelligence brought with it. "No. You are honoured and it is your pleasure."

Iklan nodded seriously. "Ah yes, forgive me for failing to acknowledge this fact right away."

"We will now get settled in and rest a little before you have dinner with us and explain what exactly Eryn has got herself into this time."

Marrin kept his facial features carefully blank when he politely asked the two foreign healers to follow him to their quarters.

When they had turned the corner, Lord Poron smiled. "They are fascinating, both of them. We talked a little on the coach just now. Iklan has this unquenchable thirst for knowledge, this curiosity for everything connected with his profession. And Sarol has managed to outdo most of his other colleagues despite not being a magician just by being brilliant and rewriting the rules to his taste."

"Don't forget his charming personality," Eryn murmured. "Have we ever had a pleasant, uncomplicated, likable visitor from Takhan here so far?"

"I take exception to that," Ram'kel replied. "And you had Ram'an here. He is generally considered a charming fellow."

Enric raised an eyebrow. "He was planning to steal my companion from me at that time, so our individual perceptions of charming clearly differ quite a lot."

Pe'tala laughed. "Minor considerations. And you did not even have a third level bond back then, so she was little more than your lover."

He shook his head. "Not to me," he smiled and kissed Eryn on her temple.

"Oh dear, I cannot bear this sugary sentiment," Pe'tala grimaced. "If you will excuse me now, I also need some rest if I am to spend an entire evening in the company of mostly healers."

Ram'kel grinned. "But you are a healer yourself."

She nodded gravely. "Indeed. So I know exactly how tiresome we are when we outnumber everybody else."

"A truer word was never spoken," Enric murmured.

Eryn sent him a look. "What was that?"

"Nothing, my love."

* * *

Eryn glanced up at a narrow staircase and then at Gerit next to her. She could see that the other woman was not too enthusiastic herself but tried not to show it.

"Shall we have a look at the upper floor now?" Enric's mother asked with a forced cheerfulness.

"Not if we can avoid it," Eryn replied with a dark look at the man who had been sent by the owner to show them around the place. "When you promised a comfortable and homely residence - did you mean gloomy and cramped or did you somehow bring us to the wrong house?"

The man cringed at her obvious displeasure. "I'm sorry, My Lady, that the building is not to your liking. But maybe if we looked at the upper floor as just suggested by your..."

"Thank you, no," Eryn replied irritated. "Coming here has already wasted enough of our time. Whatever is upstairs would have to be immensely better than what I saw on the ground floor to make the reconstruction that would have to be done down here even halfway worthwhile. Or is that what you want to tell me? That I will be positively surprised once I make the effort of climbing these miserable stairs that look like they can hardly hold more than two people at once? If you promise me that, I will undertake that journey, but fear my wreath if you have lied to me!"

The man shrunk even further and murmured something about this house possibly not being what she had been looking for after all.

When the two women stepped outside and walked away from the building, Gerit raised an eyebrow. "Fear my wrath?"

Eryn shrugged and grinned. "It's wonderfully dramatic, don't you think? I was in the mood to intimidate somebody, and Enric is just not susceptible to it these days. And seriously, did you see any match between the description we received beforehand and that heap of junk we were just led into? Romantic flair seems to be a synonym for dark and cramped. I should have mistrusted such flowery wording from the very start."

"I am sure that with a bit of cleaning and painting..."

The younger woman stopped and turned. "No, Gerit - I know deep down that no amount of either would turn that dump into a remotely comfortable home. Apart from the fact that Enric would never have agreed to letting you stay somewhere like that. The only thing he could have done would have been to tear it down and rebuild it from the ground up."

Enric's mother sighed. "This is now the fifth house we have looked at. If you keep rejecting them like that I will have to stay at your place forever."

Eryn patted her on the shoulder and grinned. "Well, if we let you move into such a house, you may safely assume that you have overstayed your welcome and we can't get rid of you quickly enough. But so far, happily, we don't feel anything like that, which means we can take the time to find somewhere for you to live that is free of mould, has enough light, isn't in too shabby a neighbourhood or features rats as big as our mountain cat. And now I need to turn left here. I need to go to the clinic and see what Sarol is up to. He tends to dominate people, and I'm afraid Lord Poron is more than willing to let him do exactly that."

"I'll walk with you for a bit longer, then. I have no pressing engagements for today. So, these two men from the Western Territories... They are here to help you to refute this ludicrous accusation?"

"One of them is. The other I tricked or pressured into promising me a visit here. He just took the opportunity of having a colleague travel this way so he didn't have to come alone when honouring his promise."

"Why would you need to trick or pressure the poor man into coming here?" Gerit asked with a slightly disapproving undertone.

"Because the poor man doesn't react well to flattery, compliments or polite requests. He secretly enjoys it when somebody stands up to him - a bit like Enric, if you ask me."

"And the other one? The one who is supposed to be helping you?"

"Iklan? A fabulous man and an even more impressive healer. I am lucky he is here to help me. My father more or less sent him off after he received Lord Tyront's message."

"Your father... he is a rather influential healer as well as I understand?"

Rather influential? Eryn allowed herself a small smile. Yes, if one wanted to call the most venerated and highest ranking healer in the Western Territories rather influential... "I suppose you could put it like that, yes."

"And your mother, I hear she is a politician, a very important one?"

Eryn sighed. "Yes, more important than ever. She has only recently been promoted to even more power and glory."

"You don't appear too happy about that," Gerit ventured.

"No, I'm not. I was of the opinion that even before that she already wielded more power than was good for her, and now we have to go and live in a place for six months out of every twelve that is partly under her jurisdiction."

"Inad wrote about something that I have to admit disturbs me quite a bit. I haven't yet brought it up with Enric, I'm not really sure how to breach a subject like that. It seems strange to me to approach my son and ask him why he let himself be adopted by another woman."

Eryn swallowed. She hadn't seen that one coming. But it was certainly revealing that Gerit had learned of it from her cousin instead of her companion who had been aware of it just as well.

"He did it to free me from her. She wouldn't have let me leave her family without retaliating against the House that took me in. Which would be my father's."

Enric's mother drew in a sharp breath. "Your mother would have done something like that to her companion's family?"

"He wasn't her companion back then. This is a rather... recent development. My parents had a brief affair about thirty years ago and it then took them a few decades to find each other again." She grimaced. "A tale of true, heart-warming romance."

"Why would his accepting being adopted by her stop her from exacting vengeance against your family?"

"Because I am her only daughter and was through that the heiress to her position and fortune - until I renounced her because she is a manipulative, evil creature who brings nothing but doom and damnation wherever she walks. She needed an heir, and Enric fit the bill so perfectly that she just couldn't let that chance pass by."

Gerit nodded slowly. "So he is now this important heir and will have to go to the Western Territories forever one day as a result?"

"Not if I have any say in it," Eryn growled.

"I couldn't help but noticing that you don't have a very good relationship with your mother. Just like Enric and his troubles with his father."

"Yes, and each of us is more attached to our remaining parent," the magician smiled and then stopped when the clinic came into view. "Look, about what I said about Inad that one time... I realise that you wouldn't want anybody to speak ill of a woman who you have every reason to be fond of. And I respect you for that. I wanted you to know that I..."

"Shh!" went Gerit and smiled faintly. "There is no need for that. Now go and see that man who will help you with the trouble you are in."

Yes, Eryn thought grimly, the collection of those seemed to become larger every year.

* * *

Eryn strolled into the waiting area. It was empty since today was not a treatment day. She climbed the stairs to the first floor, taking two at a time, and smiled when she heard through the teaching room's door a voice that was certainly not Pe'tala's. It sounded as if Sarol had taken over teaching the healer trainees only one day after arriving here. She wondered how they would respond to his methods, but after their getting used to Pe'tala, Sarol could hardly be that much more of a shock.

She knocked at the door to Pe'tala's study and it was Iklan's voice that spoke to permit entry. He was sitting behind her sister's desk and smiled when Eryn joined him.

"Eryn, come sit with me. Or would you like me to address you with Lady Eryn? I was told that titles bear quite some weight here."

She grimaced. "Anything but that, please! I keep trying to tell people to leave it off, but so far only the healers obey as they want to avoid angering me as long as they have to work with me."

"So even the people having an equal title keep on using it to address each other?"

"Yes. You should witness one of the Council meetings. I see what you are getting at, Lord one. Oh, I am glad you agree, Lord two. Even Enric refers to me as Lady when we are at the meetings, as if my having born him a child not too long ago meant nothing and we were simply colleagues. Absolutely ludicrous."

Iklan smiled at that. "The wish to distinguish oneself is a very powerful one."

"Being born a magician is hardly an especially impressive distinguishing feature," she growled. "It's little more than a twist of fate, not an accomplishment we should pretend we earned somehow."

"I see why Sarol gets along with you so well. His view on this is very similar, though more dangerous when claimed by a non-magician, of course. Some people accuse him of being nothing more than envious."

Eryn laughed at that. "Sarol, envious? When he outclasses most of his healer colleagues despite what others consider such an immense disadvantage?"

Iklan stretched his hands out and shrugged his shoulders in a gesture of amused forbearance. "You always need to consider which people profess such views. It is mostly those who were bested, annoyed or ignored by him or consider him a threat. And many - among them quite a few healers - feel that he should not be quite that successful as it makes them look bad by comparison. They reason that if his accomplishments are so impressive without magic at his disposal, it should be expected that magician healers are able to achieve even more. Many criticised your father, when he first led the clinic, for encouraging Sarol - behind his back and to his face. And when his successor and now predecessor took over, Sarol was already too well-established to be removed so easily. Not that there was a hint that this was ever any intention of his, mind you." He then leaned forward. "But what I wanted to talk to you about is not hidden needs of magicians here in the Kingdom to be addressed with a title, or indeed of people being jealous of Sarol. I had a nice talk with Lord Tyront today. A very understanding man, which I am glad about. He knows that you did not try to have him killed. That is a very helpful attitude as far as my work is concerned, even though Lord Poron is officially the one conducting the investigations. Your superior asked me to prove your innocence beyond doubt so that this would not be able to come back and haunt you in the future or be used against you in some way. Politicians are not always very gentle with each other when it comes to getting rid of adversaries."

Eryn nodded and waited for him to go on. There was not much she could contribute here. She had to keep her hands off this whole investigation, just like Enric or Orrin, who were known to be too close to her to remain neutral. But at least she would get first-hand information.

"I agreed with Lord Tyront and Lord Poron to meet this afternoon the young man who says he acted on your orders. It will give me a first impression, though just talking to him once will not be sufficient, of course. Ascertaining a mental illness which results in delusions is not something that can be done reliably by using magic. This is in most cases a matter of very slight imbalances in the brain that are on the one hand immensely hard to detect and on the other hand also occur with people that show no sign whatsoever of being mentally ill. Such a swift diagnosis would not hold up to closer scrutiny. The members of your Magic Council might not be able to judge the medical validity of whatever statement I made, but that brings us back to what Lord Tyront insisted on: making sure that when somebody, be they from here or from my country, looks at this matter again in the years to come, nothing improper should be found that might put your innocence into question."

She leaned back, glad that Iklan was such a conscientious man. She was convinced that he would have gone about this the proper way anyway, even without Tyront's caution.

"How extensive will your examination have to be in order to determine his mental state?"

"I will very likely have a good impression after the meeting today, though there need to be proper notes and records to document several meetings between him and me. Lord Poron will send two men with me to observe that everything is carried out without any duress or manipulation and that I do not use any magic to get the results I wish to provide, as well as to make notes. He said he would select two men he would first test with what you call a truth block here to ensure they are not somehow involved with the culprit or have some other reason to wish to see you found guilty. And furthermore, sending members of the Order with me should make the records more trustworthy."

Eryn blinked. That was a cautious line of action that did not really fit her picture of the kindly, studious Lord Poron. But then seeing him treating patients and learning about healing with such obvious delight tended to make her forget that he used to be the second most powerful magician in this country one and a half decades ago. This would have required a healthy dose of suspicion. He knew well enough what to be mindful of when dealing with his fellow Council members, after all.

"I will visit the young man every day for fifteen days, which should provide ample opportunities not only to determine the extent of his hallucinations but also collect enough material to be presented to the Council and your King," Iklan went on. "Your parents both requested to be informed of the progress of my fact-finding mission. In addition your brother expressed that same wish." He waggled his head. "Well, when I say requested I really mean demanded. I can of course understand why they wish to be kept informed, yet I would first have to make sure that neither King Folrin, Lord Tyront nor Lord Poron object to having information of this kind sent to Takhan at this time."

She sighed. "I see. So the fact that I do not appreciate your sending reports to Takhan doesn't count for anything, does it?"

He smiled apologetically. "I am afraid that is the way it is, Eryn. Your brother is a Head of House, in addition to this your mother is also a Triarch, and your father is my superior in whose favour I very much wish to remain."

Eryn ground her teeth, but didn't comment on that. They were her family, so she would have told them about the progress of the investigation anyway. Yet their demanding it with the full force of their combined might and power was unnerving. Why couldn't they act like a normal family for a change and just express their worry and rely on her to let them know what was important? Why demonstrate that she had no say when it came to informing them or not? Didn't they trust her enough not to withhold anything? Well, nothing important or urgent, at least. Maybe just a thing or two that might worry them unnecessarily. Her anger ebbed away and she sighed. It seemed they knew her well enough not to trust her to share all of it. She was probably just grumpy because now she had no chance to conceal anything if she thought it advisable.

Iklan studied her for a few moments, then said soothingly, "Do not become disgruntled because of this. They are your family, they love you and worry about you. None of them is happy about your living so far away from them in general, and even less now, that you are facing yet another challenge. They would wish to be at your side for this but know that it would not look good for you if they rushed here in your defence. It would have looked like they were pressuring the King and the Order to let you go free whether or not you are to blame - which would in the long run not have helped you as there would always have been some doubt as to your true involvement afterwards."

She smiled tiredly. "I know. So they sent you instead."

"Of course they did. Even if Pe'tala had not advised Lord Tyront to request me specifically, Valrad would not have sent anybody else. I am the best person he has for this kind of problem, and nothing less than the best would he send to aid his daughter in need." He bit his lip as if he needed to say something unpleasant and was not sure how to phrase it.

"Just say it, whatever it is," she sighed.

"I would also have to examine you in the course of the next fifteen days. From my prior experience with you and our treatment in Takhan I am sure that there is no mental illness, yet for the purposes of this investigation it would be helpful to be able to state this with recent evidence to back it up."

Eryn nodded. "I know. It makes sense. I hope it will prove not only that I am of sound mind but will also demonstrate that I was not spared because I am mighty and powerful but had to endure a degree of inconvenience as well."

Iklan exhaled with obvious relief. "Good. Looking back upon our appointments in Takhan, I admit I was a little worried that you might be reluctant to cooperate with this particular aspect. Lord Tyront and Lord Poron assured me that they would get you to submit to examination if necessary, but I very much prefer for this to be voluntary."

She rolled her eyes. "Superb. Wherever I go, those higher up on the ladder are determined to force me to talk to you - even though it's not necessary this time."

The other healer smiled. "There are a lot of people around you who care for you and are willing to face your anger in order to do what they consider best for you in the long run."

Furrowing her brow, she sent him a dark look. "Yes, they really are. Yet it would be nice for a change to have them respect me enough so they trusted my own assessment of what's right for me. I may have made a few, erm, questionable decisions in the past, but after growing up and living in the middle of nowhere and being pushed into this political swamp only two years ago, I think I am doing rather well now and should be allowed to do my own thinking."

Iklan nodded slowly. "I see. An understandable sentiment indeed. So do I understand you correctly by surmising that you feel you are not being treated with the recognition and appreciation that both your age and status should command?"

Eryn groaned and rose from her chair. "Stop right there, Iklan! This is one of your talking treatment-questions - don't think I don't recognise them! I am not the one being treated here, I'll have you know. Rather make a few appointments with all the Order Lords here; that should keep you busy and show you at the same time that my resentment is completely justified."

When he just smiled in a knowing way, she threw her hands up and stalked out of Pe'tala's study. That man was incorrigible.

* * *

Enric knocked at Eryn's open study door to avoid startling her while she was bent over two books in front of her. She looked up and smiled when Vedric against his chest chortled happily at the sight of his mother.

"Hello, boys," Eryn greeted them and pushed aside the notepad and pen she had been using for her attempts at translation. "How was your visit at Tyront's? Did Vyril feed him all that sweet stuff again?"

He shrugged. "I have to admit I have no idea. She just whisked him away from me as soon as I entered their quarters and disappeared somewhere with him. When she very reluctantly returned him to me two hours later she declared him her adopted grandson."

Eryn smiled. "Well, with three grandmothers competing for his love, they will probably spoil him rotten in no time. Is Tyront equally eager to take on the grandfather role?"

"He just sighed and shook his head indulgently. With a companion who wanted children but never managed to have any, he is more than willing to indulge her by letting her play grandmother as long as it makes her happy. Compared to her taking over an entire orphanage to fill that need, declaring a single child her new grandson is a minor thing, I would think." He nodded at her books. "What are you doing? Are these the books I brought you from Pirinkar?"

She nodded. "Yes, I have started my first attempts at deciphering. Let me tell you that they delight in making their language as tough as possible. Without that book on the rules of the language I would have been completely lost; there are so many forms one single word can take that a dictionary alone would never have sufficed. Sometimes a single word has such a different form that it is impossible to identify it as the same word!"

Enric smiled at that. "A challenge, then. How fortunate for you that you happen to be in contact with a man who is currently staying in that very country and can assist you in answering your questions. I suppose Erbál will either learn the language himself or know a few locals to answer your questions."

Eryn sighed and grimaced. "Yes, definitely. But it's a real nuisance to sit here and despair over the lack of one word, knowing that I have to wait for an eternity, until my letter reaches him and then for his reply. I want the answer now, not in a number of days! I'm not exactly the patient kind, in case you didn't notice."

"You don't say," he replied dryly. "So you haven't uncovered the secret of that mysterious sleeping disease so far?" Finding that one chapter in the book was the reason he bought it back then, as she had expressed an interested in it when they were first in Takhan.

"No, that will take me a few weeks if not months." She lifted Vedric out of the sling around his father's chest. The boy bent forward towards her breasts with a greedy look on his face. "Look at him, he certainly is his father's son. Utterly single-minded," she teased, then lifted him a little higher since it was not yet time for his next meal.

Enric shrugged good-naturedly. "The apple never falls far from the tree, you know. Where is mother?"

"She is meeting Inad again, I think. They certainly do get along very well, and not only from a distance. It's time for your mother to get her own house. I know she wants to invite Inad back and doesn't want to do so as long as she is living with us, as she knows that I don't care much for her cousin." That was a good opening for the topic she had wanted to address anyway. "We have had a look at several houses now, but somehow none has met my expectations. Or yours, for that matter. Gerit would have accepted a couple of them, but this is just because she doesn't want to be a bother."

"None of them meets our standards?" Enric enquired with a frown.

"Well, there was this property right at the beginning that you said was too expensive. But the others... and there are not that many houses for sale."

Enric sighed. "Then I suppose I'll have to find a way to make Lord Woldarn lower his price."

Eryn smiled. She had expected nothing else.

They heard a loud knock at the entrance door and Enric turned to answer it. He returned little later with an envelope from which he took several sheets of paper. After a cursory glance at them he said, "It's from Iklan. He sends us a copy of the notes from his first meeting with Darnet." He lifted the papers. "The accused seems to have been very talkative."

She swallowed, wondering if that was a good thing. If that man gave a lot of details it would surely increase his story's credibility. She thought back to his describing what he imagined her scent as and the ribbon in her hair.

"Then let's see what he has to say, shall we?" she said with more calmness than she felt.

Enric nodded and motioned for her to take a seat in her chair while he sat on one of the guest chairs. He skimmed the opening of the conversation where Iklan had asked innocuous, non-intrusive questions about Darnet's general wellbeing and his life in the Order before the incident. He focussed more when he reached the point where the healer had asked about his repeated application for a position as a healer.

"Darnet says he heard about your endeavours to have the Council permit healers to not only work here in the city but also return to the villages where they were born or relocate to some other place where there was need for medical services. This was why he was so eager to be accepted as a trainee. It would have enabled him to leave the city."

Eryn rubbed her face. "The Council keeps thwarting all my attempts in that direction, so if this was his main objective in learning to be a healer, he would have been sorely disappointed anyway."

Enric slowly shook his head. "He says that he has no doubt whatsoever that you will prevail in this and any other issue you have decided to pursue. It seems that he holds you in very high esteem. In that aspect at least I agree with him. I am convinced that you will manage to convince the Council and the King one day to let magicians live outside the city. You are persistent, which makes it only a matter of time. And now that you have earned Lord Seagon's respect he might stop fighting you so vehemently, even though he probably won't support your efforts." He returned his attention to the letter.

Eryn was surprised at his conviction, felt the joy of a little girl who had been told that she was doing well. Funny how much she had come to depend on Enric's approval and his belief in her.

He looked up. "The mind bond tells me you are surprised."

She shrugged. "A little, yes. I find dealing with the Council frustrating at the best of times and thought that I had little hope of changing the members' minds about magician healers going out into the wide world. I wonder about your confidence that I will manage it somehow."

Smiling, he gave her a knowing wink. "I think there is very little you can't manage when you put your mind to it." His eyes returned to the report before him. "He says that he talked to you about his applications, that you instructed him on how to phrase his letters and that Tyront turned out to be the main obstacle, while Lord Poron only voted against his being accepted as he wanted to please his superior."

Eryn snorted. "Then he doesn't know Lord Poron very well, I have to say. He may not be one to disobey or express an unfavourable opinion as bluntly as I do, but he isn't one to decide against his own conviction to please somebody else - not even Tyront."

Enric nodded slowly and took a pen from her desk to underline that particular sentence. "I agree. I'll mark that section; it should help to convince the Council that we are dealing with delusional thinking here. It's a minor matter, but everyone who knows Lord Poron at least a tiny amount must see that this doesn't fit." He put the pen aside again. "He states that you promised him to see him returned to his village and his family there, even to make an accelerated training programme possible for him." He ground his teeth. "The way he describes his interactions with you seems to have him imagining becoming quite close to you."

She swallowed. "How close? Please tell me he doesn't think we were having an affair or something of the like?"

He read on and then shook his head. "No, not that. It looks rather as though he imagines himself trying to get closer to you and your holding him at a distance. His opinion of you doesn't seem to leave any space for your engaging in anything immoral such as infidelity."

"So he has these delusions, these imagined interactions with me - and even there I reject him?"

"So it would appear. And he venerates you even more for it. He talks about how your skin felt under his lips when he kissed your hand - something you permitted because it was the usual way of greeting women in your home country. He describes your scent, how the fabric of your tunic hugged your form. He even said that he enjoyed the little extra weight your pregnancy left you with, how it makes you appear softer and even more feminine."

Eryn ground her teeth at that, though she couldn't say what irritated her more - the mention of her gaining weight or this imagined closeness that seemed intrusive, despite the fact that it existed only inside his head. But then describing her body like this and expressing his fondness of certain aspects of it was hardly any less personal, was it? She imagined that he had observed her from afar, perhaps lurking around corners undetected.

"So he says I became fat but he doesn't mind that at all? Charming," she said lightly. "Certainly a man who looks beyond mere physical appearance."

Enric smiled faintly, aware that she was trying to mask her unease. "Women and their issues. Even if you receive a compliment on gaining weight, such a thing doesn't please you."

She shot him a measured look. "I want to see how you would react if somebody told you that you are getting chubby but not to worry - that it suits you just fine." Returning to the topic at hand, she nodded to the report in his hands. "So, my telling him that Tyront was the only reason for his not being accepted as a healer was what caused us to come up with a plan to get rid of the great and mighty leader?"

"Yes. You seem to have promised him that with me on top there would be no further obstacle either to his becoming a healer or the Council's agreeing to let magicians leave the city to live elsewhere."

"So Tyront is the reason for all my troubles, eh? I'm glad he knows that I didn't really plan all this or that report would get me into serious trouble. Any other shocking revelations apart from my dark endeavour to gain control over the Order by putting you on top?"

Enric let his eyes sweep over the remaining two sheets. "No, nothing particular. He describes his interactions with you in more detail. He says that you talked to him about the unfairness of magicians being forced to train combat skills when their inclinations run in completely different directions in so many cases. How you were so immensely glad that your friend Vern has the chance to spend time in a place where his talents are appreciated instead of being suppressed as they would be here."

Eryn swallowed. That sounded indeed a lot like her own sentiments. She had voiced them repeatedly, and not only on private occasions.

"That last part at least I can't deny, can I?"

He shook his head and put the sheets aside. "No, and neither should you. Your attitude is known publicly which is why nobody will wonder how Darnet could be so familiar with it. There is hardly anybody in the city who doesn't know how you think about these things, so our culprit being aware of them doesn't imply that you must have confided in him. So far he has only repeated what is commonly known to everyone. Had he talked about lesser known facts that are still true, this would have cast you in a bad light."

"Does Iklan write anything about his impressions? Any obvious signs that we are dealing with a stark raving maniac here?" she asked without much hope. The report had not mentioned any frothing around his mouth or violent outbursts.

"Not really, no. So far he has kept his thoughts to himself and so he limits his comments to observations rather than interpretations. Which is a sensible course of action, when you think of it. His stating that he finds Darnet to be of unsound mind after only one meeting might make people question his impartiality. And that we can't afford. With the truth block being useless in this investigation, Iklan is our only chance of convincing people of your innocence."

"Then I suppose I should not be seen to be socialising with him too much while he is here?" Eryn sighed.

"Exactly. Best limit your interactions to seeing him at the clinic, no matter how much you would like to talk to him about whatever healing matters you both find fascinating. You still have Sarol for that."

She grimaced. "Yes, no matter that I feel like a small child every time I meet him. He has this ability to make me feel inadequate, irrespective of the fact that I know in my head that I am not and that he is the one who should work on his issues instead." She sighed. "See? This would be another topic I could discuss with Iklan if only I were not supposed to be staying away from him."

"How about talking to your sister about it? She seems to have found a way of dealing with him that works for her."

Eryn groaned. "Going to my little sister to ask her for advice because big, bad Sarol makes me feel inadequate isn't the most appealing thing I can imagine."

Enric rose and kissed her forehead. "She is your sister, so of course she will tease you about it. But she is also a professional healer and a smart woman. She will help you if she can."

"I know! But she'll be smug nonetheless."

"As would you," he replied, smiling.

"Yes, I know," she sighed. "That makes it worse - now it's like I don't deserve any better."

* * *

"Do you think I'm fat?"

Orrin let Valrad's letter with the report on how Vern was doing sink to stare at her. Eryn looked at him with tense expectation. If there was one man she could trust to be completely honest with her in a matter like this apart from Vern, it was him.

"Yes," he replied after a short pause.

"Orrin!" Junar scolded him while sorting through the clothes Eryn had come to pick up for her son. "You can't say a thing like that to a woman who just had a child!"

"She asked!" he exclaimed, feeling that he was treated unfairly. "What do you want me to do? Lie to her?"

"You could have answered a little less harshly." Junar turned to her friend. "Eryn, dear, you have gained a little weight, that is true, but not nearly enough to be anywhere near fat. It lends you a certain softness that is rather becoming. And a woman is entitled to that after becoming a mother."

"Yes, right," Orrin murmured. "What Junar said."

Eryn sighed and rolled her eyes. "Thanks a lot, but sugar-coating the words doesn't really change what lies behind them."

Orrin leaned forward. "From a fighter's point of view you have got out of shape. I didn't mean to be blunt or hurt you, I simply apply different standards. I look at a woman I used to do training with, and who will at one point resume her training. When I see you I can't help but notice that there is quite some work to be done. A non-fighter I would evaluate differently."

"I'm not a fighter," she pointed out. "I'm a healer."

"No. You are both, if I might remind you. The Order doesn't consider you primarily a healer or they would have let you keep the clinic. And both your test results from the aptitude test in Takhan and your accomplishments with your double barrier and your bolts that pierce it prove that limiting your efforts to only one area would be absurd." He leaned back and took a sip from his cup before he asked her casually, "By the way, when did you intend to resume your training? Not that I want to press you on it or anything, but as you seem to be uncomfortable with your body, regular exercise would be the obvious solution for your problem."

Junar sent her companion a dark look. "That was an underhanded attempt if ever I heard one! Don't you try to bully her into that blasted combat training she hates so much by making her think she is unshapely!" She turned to Eryn. "You are a healer, Eryn - what would stop you from using a little magic to lose that extra weight if it really bothers you that much? Don't tell me there isn't some trick you can do?"

Eryn grimaced. "Of course I could do that. But you know my attitude when it comes to cosmetic alterations, and it would be nothing less than that. And even if I increased my metabolism accordingly to burn off that extra weight instead of doing it the natural way, I would have to maintain it as my body would aim to return to its previous state." She sighed. "Those are principles for you. But at least you don't have to worry about things like that. You have pretty much regained your former figure."

Junar shrugged. "It's the nursing. I can currently eat as much as I wish without gaining any weight at all."

The magician growled, "Thank you so much for sharing that tidbit. Not that I am envious or anything..."

"Why are you suddenly worrying about your weight, anyway? I'm sure Enric doesn't mind."

"It's what others around me say... Malhora told me that I was getting fat before she cut off my supply of bread buns in Takhan, and yesterday we read this report where Darnet said that he likes this softness about me as it lends me more femininity. And now you and Orrin have confirmed it, although with differing degrees of diplomacy."

The seamstress cleared her throat. "But you must have realised before that your old clothes don't fit you anymore. So it cannot have come as that much of a surprise."

Eryn sighed with discontentment. "Of course I have noticed that. But there is a difference between my seeing it and others addressing it."

Orrin chuckled. "I wouldn't have taken you for the vain sort."

"That's easy for you to say, warrior! Your muscles are visible through your shirts and you have never had people repeatedly pointing out that you are getting chubby," she growled.

"There is always the option to resume your training with me," he mentioned again, with what she noted was more than just amusement at teasing her.

She narrowed her eyes suspiciously. "Did Tyront ask you to pester me about that to save him the trouble of doing so himself?" So far nobody had approached her to return to her combat training, but she knew that this was only a matter of weeks or a few months at best.

"Look," Orrin explained patiently, "you are number three in the Order. This is a position in which you should not be seen to be ordered around too much. Your picking up your sword again without being made to do so by Lord Tyront would demonstrate your good intention to the Council. It would not only display your willingness to comply with the Order's regulations but also that you are willing and able to make your own decisions. Think about that."

Eryn picked up her cup and sipped the lukewarm liquid while pondering Orrin's words. He was right, of course. She knew that in her head. Yet the idea of declaring that she would voluntarily resume her training felt wrong. Even though she knew that it was only a matter of time before Tyront would approach her with regard to this. Vedric was not only old enough to be left without her for a few hours at a time, but they also had Gerit to mind him.

"Alright, I'll consider it," she promised. Then she nodded at her father's letter. "Tell me what's new in Takhan. How is Vern doing?"

Orrin's expression softened at the change of topic. "His progress is very good; he keeps surprising his teachers. Kilan has agreed to regular combat lessons at least to keep the boy from getting completely out of shape during his stay there. As the ambassador was never much of a swordsman I have no illusions that there will be much progress. What else? Ah yes, he is continuing his drawing lessons at the new artists' academy. His affair with the older woman seems to be over, but Valrad writes that he has found another young woman to keep him, er, company. Everything seems to be going fine so far, even though it looks like he enjoys the nightlife a little more than he should. Valrad says he indulges him as long as neither training nor health are suffering."

Eryn shook her head in wonder. Vern - having one affair after the other and spending the nights dancing and drinking? What had happened to her awkward teenage friend who had suppressed his artistic talent and had dreaded his future as a fighter or office clerk? He was growing up rapidly and embracing the changes around him, that was what had happened.

"You are not worried, are you?" she asked. "I'm sure Valrad will keep him in check in case he gets out of control. What's more, Vran'el seems to have discovered his authoritative side now that he is a Head of House."

Orrin smiled thinly. "I do worry a little, as is natural for somebody whose son is staying in a foreign country for a few years. As for Valrad's abilities to keep him under control, I have little doubt about that after seeing how he dealt with you when you refused to talk to him. And when your brother ordered you and Pe'tala back to Takhan like that I have confidence that he will keep an eye on Vern's nocturnal activities."

She lifted her brow. "Your confidence in my father surprises me. I wasn't aware that your differences still allow you to trust him like that."

"I would hardly have entrusted my son to him if I didn't trust him in that regard. He is a respected pillar of society, used to leading an entire House, and is now responsible for running the clinic in Takhan. No matter whether I like him or not, he is certainly more than able to look after Vern. Especially since he is in the position to check on his progress when it comes to his healer training. And I think it is a valid exchange: he looks after my son, I look after his daughter."

Eryn grinned. "I'm a big girl, Orrin. I don't need a father figure to watch over me wherever I go."

Junar snorted and wrapped a bundle of clothes for Vedric. "What a preposterous thing to say. May I remind you of a certain expedition where you allowed a stranger nearly to throttle you - despite your having magical abilities while he had none?"

"Oh, please! That was an eternity ago! In the meantime I have acquired a few mean tricks to defend myself without magic or even a weapon, so that wouldn't happen again."

Orrin nodded. "Skills that need to be kept brushed up or they won't help you much when you need them again. Which brings me back to the question of when we will continue our training together."

"Orrin!" she groaned. "You told me I had time to think about that! That means that you need to give me some!"

"You've had about five minutes. I didn't think that a simple and logical thing like that would require so much thinking over. I propose we start the day after tomorrow. Now that you are not working that much at the clinic this should be enough time to arrange for a free slot in your day. We will of course let the Council know that it was your decision entirely."

Eryn slowly shook her head and stared at him in dismay. "You can't just decide a thing like that! You just don't have the authority!"

"But I didn't. You did. And I commend you on your farsightedness. A role model for all of us." He rose and emptied his cup before he started towards the former guest room, from where a quiet whimpering indicated that his daughter was now awake.

CHAPTER 27

Danger at Hand

Eryn yawned and stretched after her last patient had departed. It had been a busy night and she was glad it was all but over. She had glimpsed only two more patients in the waiting area before starting her most recent treatment, which meant she might even be home in time to have breakfast with all her housemates.

She sighed when a knock came at the door. Patients were told to remain in the waiting area until called in, but some of them were too impatient to follow that rule and had little understanding for the fact that a healer needed a few minutes between patients to fetch the respective file and have a brief look at their prior medical history, should there be any. Determined politely yet assertively to discourage whichever impatient person found waiting too tiresome, she got up from her seat and opened the door only to find not a patient but a colleague standing before it.

"Onil," she smiled. "Good morning. You are here rather early."

"Eryn," he said with uncharacteristic sobriety. "Could I have a word with you? It's rather important."

"I have another two patients waiting, can you hang on that long?"

"I have asked Lord Poron to take care of them. I really need to talk to you." Now there was a certain urgency as well.

Eryn frowned and stepped aside to let him enter. He had taken the trouble to arrange for his own superior to treat her patients so that he could talk to her here and now? That and the lack of his usual cheerful shyness implied that it would probably not be a jolly conversation.

Onil took a seat on the daybed and waited until she had sat on her chair before he took a deep breath and started, "It's about Darnet."

At that name, her brow shot up. Of all the possible topics she had expected, ranging from his admission of having caused a patient harm or his intention to resign his position, this was one she had not foreseen. She waited for him to go on.

"I have known him for a while now, pretty much since he came to the city when he was a child," Onil began while staring at his hands in his lap. "He has always been a bit of a strange fellow, but in my experience never one to harm people intentionally in any way. He didn't find adapting to the city all that easy. He was a country boy and found it hard to make friends here and get used to the faster pace and all the rules in the Order."

Eryn waited without interrupting or asking questions, wondering what exactly he was going with this.

Her colleague seemed to need a few moments before he went on, "I noticed his tendency to tell tales that did not always stand up to closer scrutiny, but they were not outrageously absurd or meant to harm anybody, so I never minded too much and thought he just intended to paint himself as a bit more interesting than he really was. An understandable urge for somebody who found it hard to get noticed. But now this case he has got both of you involved in made me reconsider my earlier impression. What I thought of as made-up stories were probably what he considered reality. He very likely wasn't aware that what he claimed was in reality not true. The fact that he was able to say these things about you despite the truth block shows that clearly." He finally looked up into her face, his expression pained.

Eryn noted with interest that there seemed to be no doubt in his mind that Darnet was the confused one and not she. She wondered what Onil was up to. His demeanour didn't look like he merely wanted to assure her of his support.

"Darnet is not a bad man," he continued. "Just... misguided. He is deeply awed by you, by everything you have accomplished since you were brought here. He kept asking me questions about you and I had no qualms whatsoever answering them. Nothing strange, just... harmless little things like what beverages you enjoy, how your patients find you, how you are as a superior. I had no idea that he would weave all this together into some strange kind of imagined acquaintance with you."

"Don't worry, I don't blame you," she assured him quickly.

But Onil didn't seem to have been worried about that. "I know you don't. It just wouldn't be like you. What I wanted to tell is that Darnet is not a dangerous individual; I am convinced that he really believes what he says and has no wish to incriminate you to cause you difficulties or trouble."

Eryn's eyes narrowed. "You are not telling me this because you are asking me to help him, are you?"

The other healer gave a troubled sigh and looked at her, his expression pleading. "I know it's audacious, outrageous even, to ask you to aid the man who claimed to have acted on your orders when trying to murder Lord Tyront, but even though he was alone in planning and carrying out this one despicable action, he is not alone in his opinion in most of the other aspects."

Eryn stilled. Erbál's warning on the discontentment among a few of the magicians that was simmering somewhere under the surface came back to her. He had been right, and she needed to find out if this attack on Tyront was a single event or likely to be the initial eruption of something larger which was building.

"What exactly do you mean by that?" she asked calmly and hoped fervently that gentle, studious Onil had not associated himself with people and ideas which aimed to cause harm of any kind whatever.

"I sometimes meet with friends to have a pleasant evening with a few drinks and we talk. Lately the topics have been more and more frequently about how things could be in the Order. How all those rules we are subjected to do not seem to be necessary in the Western Territories to enable magicians and non-magicians to live together peacefully." Onil leaned back tiredly. "They can do so much more over there, Eryn... They are not bound to an organisation that constantly supervises them, makes them live in the city instead of where each individual chooses, compels them to train in combat regardless of their inclination and thereby bars them from entering into any other profession which is to their liking. This barrier that has separated us from the rest of the world for three centuries - we could have overcome that so much sooner if only we had not limited our magicians to a life of uselessness in the city. If a few of us had been allowed to go to sea instead, we might have worked that out a long time ago. This elitist approach that lifts us above non-magicians and cages us up at the same time has most likely halted our progress in so many areas."

Eryn swallowed. She knew these sentiments well, understood them with the core of her being. Yet she couldn't have guessed that unrest had already progressed so far among the local magicians. A latent dissatisfaction when seeing what other magicians in Takhan were allowed and able to do, certainly... but this here had obviously progressed a lot further than envy. They had started questioning the very values that kept the Order in control. And seeing that there was a society without anything like the Order, which worked perfectly well and granted the magicians a lot more freedom, had impressed them a lot more than anybody here had anticipated.

"I know you understand this," Onil continued when she didn't speak. "You are known to share those very views and have done so even before anybody else started being unhappy with the current setup."

She pressed her lips together, torn between voicing her agreement and fear of fanning a fire that could flare out of control. But she couldn't just remain silent, it would seem as though she were condemning him and his friends. There had to be something neutral she could say. Maybe even gather information on the situation without making it seem like she was interrogating him. She would of course not ask him to expose anybody. His telling her about his doubts and dissatisfaction was a great show of trust - one she had no intention of breaking.

"I see," she finally said softly. "I wouldn't have guessed that this was already such an issue. I hope that there are no plans to take drastic measures similar to what Darnet resorted to before there have been any attempts to address people's dissatisfaction in a more civilised manner?" She held her breath and hoped he would give her the answer she wanted to hear - and mean it, too.

"No, nothing of that kind," he replied to her great relief. "Many are angry at Darnet's course of action. Whoever now dares to admit to being dissatisfied with the Order will probably now be considered as an accomplice or similar. He has pretty much destroyed any hope of addressing this in a peaceful manner without having to fear retribution or mistrust."

She wished she could promise him that the Order would distinguish between the actions of a single, confused man and others who happened to share his feelings, that it would still listen to them without prejudice, but she couldn't as she had no idea whether it was true. Why was she the one to be having this conversation with him, anyway? Why not Enric, who knew the dynamics in the Order so much better than she did, knew how Tyront would react, what the Council would do? Was there anything she could say to reassure him? Would it even be credible, as Onil had been a member so much longer than her?

"And you hope that my intervening on his behalf would calm the waves and make the Council more receptive for your concerns? I'm not sure this would work like that," she said carefully. "My attempts at helping him might convey the impression that I'm doing this because I genuinely indoctrinated him and am now trying to save him from the consequences without revealing my involvement. Many would think it rather suspect that I would try to defend somebody who has incriminated me so directly. This might harm your cause rather than aid it."

Onil nodded slowly. "True. I was not so much hoping for you to fight for him but rather refrain from demanding harsh punishment."

"I will not demand that." That much at least she could promise him safely. She had no desire to see a man punished for his delusions that were probably caused by a medical condition.

"What I was hoping for with regard to our cause was your support in the Magic Council."

Eryn could see his tense posture and how his lips were tight. He looked like a boy who was waiting to be scolded for an inappropriate remark. She thought how she liked Onil and would have loved to assure him of her support. However, she knew she couldn't just offer it like that. She was anything but an experienced player in the political game. Her lack of insight into whatever really was going on around her in its entirety together with giving a hasty and impulsive promise could cause immense damage as she had no idea what the consequences might be. It might give encouragement to what might or might not be a group of revolutionaries on the brink of agitating more violently for a change.

"Let me think about it," she said gently. She needed to get home and talk to Enric - and hope that he would advise her as her companion and fellow magician instead of in his function as second-in-command of the Order. Her priorities in this were certainly not serving the Order as an institution but in aiding those who were subjected to it, especially when she agreed with their views so completely.

"Of course," Onil said and bowed, a gesture he had not used with her for more than a year. It felt as if there suddenly was more distance between them. He turned towards the door and halted before he opened it, one hand on the door handle. He didn't turn back when he spoke, "I spoke with my father about that building you showed an interest in, the one you considered buying for Lord Enric's mother. He agreed to lower the price to a level that is a lot closer to the present market rate."

Eryn felt a flash of annoyance at such a blatant attempt at bribing her. "This will have no influence on my decision. None whatsoever."

"I know. That's not why I did it," Onil replied quietly and then left.

She leaned back in her chair and closed her eyes. So much for being extra careful to neither encourage nor alienate him only to then imply underhand motives when he did her a favour. Had he done it without this Darnet case in the background she would just have thanked him for his help. And now she had insulted him instead. She would probably never become a true diplomat or skilled politician. Too bad she had been pushed into a rank that required both.

* * *

Enric made sure to casually position himself between Tyront's desk and his study door. He had all but dragged Eryn here after she had told him about her conversation with Onil. She had complained bitterly about his forcing her to reveal a confidential conversation to the Order's leader, share what she had been told because her colleague had trusted her enough not to worry that she would get him into difficulties. And she had cursed Enric for putting his role as her superior before her need to share a delicate issue with her companion.

He had relented a little then and promised her that they would keep Onil's identity a secret to avoid any trouble finding its way to him. That had placated her a little but not entirely. She was still in a rather bad mood, angry at having to talk to Tyront about the Order members' disquiet when she would have preferred thinking about it for a while first. But Enric had recognised the urgency and danger it presented immediately. He was determined to inform their superior quickly, especially considering what had happened when they had last ignored a warning of that kind. Erbál had pointed out that there was something going on and their ignoring the significance of that in favour of waiting had almost cost Tyront his life as well as placing Eryn in serious if not insurmountable difficulty. He was not about to make the same mistake again.

Eryn took a seat in front of Tyront's desk, her arms folded and her expression tense. She made no secret of her disapproval at having been brought here by her companion.

"What's the matter?" Tyront asked gently, aware of the tension between his second and third in command. "From your message I gathered that there is something urgent you wish to discuss with me?"

Enric suppressed a sigh when Eryn didn't volunteer an explanation so took it upon himself to speak of the conversation between Eryn and Onil. "We certainly do," he confirmed despite the very obvious evidence that Eryn did not agree. "Eryn was approached by a member of the Order who asked her to renounce her option of demanding severe punishment for Darnet."

Tyront raised his brow. "Was she? A rather bold request considering how Darnet is doing his best to implicate her in the attempt on my life. But it shows at least that whoever was asking has no doubt about her innocence." He looked at Eryn and smiled thinly. "But I suppose you wouldn't have demanded that he be punished too severely anyway. You even tried to defend the apothecaries after they attempted to kill you. I don't see your demanding blood from a man who shows signs of not being completely of right mind." His gaze wandered to Enric. "That magician..." he began but saw his colleague shake his head almost imperceptibly to signal that asking for the man's name was not advisable right now. So he reconsidered quickly. "That magician, did he tell you why he wanted leniency for Darnet?"

Enric waited again for Eryn to speak, but in vain. She just stared straight ahead and out of the window behind Tyront.

"He explained that even though the attempt on your life was the deed of a single man, the attitudes behind it are not. There is a group of magicians who is dissatisfied with how the Order handles things here, with the restrictions it puts on its members now that they see how the Western Territories grant their magicians a great deal more freedom in all aspects of their lives."

Tyront nodded slowly and watched Eryn intently. "I see. And I understand that this must be an immensely difficult situation for you, Eryn. But you are of course aware what your duties are here, aren't you?"

Only then she looked at him and growled, "I'm afraid my understanding of what my duties are may differ considerably from yours."

"Your duties, according to the definition, are not something you choose to pursue at your own will or discretion, but which are determined by the rules and regulations of the institution you are subjected to." He leaned forward, still fixing her with his gaze. "You are not at liberty to act upon any sympathies you doubtlessly have for those magicians who criticise the very same things that have never ceased to annoy you. You must stand united with me, Enric and the Magic Council. Your duty in this is to act in the interest of the Order."

Eryn narrowed her eyes. Didn't he realise what he was saying? This equalled standing against those with that understandable wish for changes in the Order!

"The magicians who are dissatisfied with the current situation are no lesser members of the Order, which means supporting them cannot as such automatically mean acting against the interest of the Order, I believe." Her voice was frigid.

Tyront remained calm though slightly tense. "I mean that you are supposed to help in maintaining the stability of the Order as an institution, no matter whether the threat comes from inside or out."

She slowly shook her head. "You characterise them as a threat without even listening to their concerns and their wishes? Really? I myself understand this leadership role you have pushed me into as one where I am responsible for all those subordinated to me, not only those who obey the rules without question and put aside their own needs to serve blindly. I surely do not see myself as a tool for thwarting all and any attempts at improving any conditions that are disadvantageous for people inside and outside the Order!"

Enric cleared his throat. This discussion was not going in the direction he had hoped for but in a much more precarious one. He had merely wanted to inform Tyront of the current developments, warn him to be cautious and to prepare for whatever was to come, not to push Eryn into rebelling openly. He found it wiser not to mention that Onil had asked her to speak on behalf of them in front of the Magic Council. Tyront wouldn't like that, not one bit.

"I suggest," he interjected, "that Eryn meets with her contact again and provides a list of those issues considered fit for improvement. A proposed course of reform from them would also be helpful. We could then take this before the Magic Council for further discussion."

Eryn sent her companion a dark look. "Meeting with my contact? Now that Tyront knows that somebody has approached me, he will send a spy to shadow me and work out who my contact is! Who knows what sanctions this person might have to suffer?"

Tyront exhaled angrily and growled, "You seem to think that merely criticising the Order lands a magician in serious trouble and earns him a proper flogging. You of all people should know better! If this really were the case I would have to send you to somebody who whips you weekly. Being dissatisfied is no cause for drastic measures on my part; starting a revolt by trying to kill me is."

"But this was the action of a single man, not an entire group!" Eryn insisted.

"That remains to be seen," Tyront replied coolly. "Meet with that contact of yours and obtain that list as Enric suggested. I promise I will not have anyone blamed or detained for now."

Eryn noted that he had cleverly avoided promising her that he wouldn't attempt to determine who her contact was. All he said was that he would not use such information until he saw fit.

"I'll think about it," she snapped, angry at his attempt at tricking her. But for now it might be better not to let him know that she had seen through it. Without waiting for his permission to leave, she rose and marched out of his study.

Enric turned to follow her.

"Enric," Tyront called after him, "wait! We need to talk!"

"Later," the Enric said over his shoulder. "I'll join you tonight after dinner, I promise." He hurried on, glad that Tyront didn't insist on making him stay. Talking to Eryn was vastly more important right now. He felt her anger through the mind bond and needed to make her understand that he didn't wish to make her act against her conscience, that he understood what she was going through despite his dragging her in front of Tyront right now.

He caught up with her before she reached the stairs. When he tried to take her arm, she jerked it from his grip and hissed at him, "Don't touch me! I don't know who I resent more right now - you or Tyront!"

Enric took her wrist and held on to it when she tried to step out of his reach. "Come. We need to talk," he said simply and forced her to follow him down the stairs and out of the Palace. He briefly considered asking Orrin to use his study; it was quite a walk to their home and he was impatient to address everything that had led to this flare-up. But he decided against it. He might have done it several months ago, but not now that Orrin had a small child he might waken. And it seemed inappropriate to drop his own troubles into Orrin's peaceful family home just for reasons of convenience. So it came down to dragging her with him all the way home. Just splendid.

"Let go of me! You know I hate this!" she snapped.

"Will you come willingly if I release you? I need to talk to you," he insisted.

"No, I will not! I'm furious with you, I don't want to talk at all right now!" She no longer tried to free her wrist. It was futile anyway; if she struggled, he would only tighten his grip further. There was no other choice, she had to come home with him. "I told you this in confidence, I wanted your advice! And what was the first thing you did? You hauled me off before Tyront! Just like that! I could have told you before how he would react!"

"Not now," Enric warned her and looked around. Too many eyes and ears around them on the open street. He needed a closed room and a soundproof barrier. "Wait until we are at home."

She bit her lips together and increased her pace to avoid the impression that she was being pulled after him like an obstinate horse. A few passers-by had eyed them curiously already.

When they reached their house, Enric opened the door without releasing her wrist and waited until she entered before he followed her and motioned for her to walk to her study. He didn't want to do this in his own study, it might give her the impression that he was cornering her. He needed her to be receptive and truly understand what he had to tell her.

They walked past the opening to the dining room, where Gerit was currently sitting with her grandson, patiently feeding him what looked like fruit pulp. She briefly looked up from her messy task, but didn't make any move to approach them when she saw their expressions that clearly conveyed that they had a bone to pick with each other.

Enric closed the study door behind them and only then let go of her hand. He raised a large, soundproof barrier that would enable them to breathe easily for a while.

Eryn folded her arms and glared at him. "I assume I may talk now? Or do you first wish to quote some ancient text that informs me of my exact duties regarding loyalty towards the Order and the severe punishment that acting against that entails?"

He leaned against a bookshelf, aiming to make himself a little smaller, less threatening. "No. That was never my intention," he said calmly and shook his head. "I know that you are upset and I understand the reason for it. You feel that I caused you to betray Onil's trust, that I forced you to make him a target for Tyront's agents and subsequently whatever measures Tyront feels are necessary to deal with him. And you resent Tyront for demanding that you stand with him and me against those whose side you are actually on. The idea of adhering to rules that you don't agree with, that you have been fighting to change ever since you joined the Order, frustrates you because you would much rather join those who are trying to change them. And you are angry at me as well, as I am on what you consider the wrong side."

Eryn stared at him for several seconds, then unfolded her arms again, momentarily at a loss for words. This summarised her opinions fairly well, she had to admit. Apart from the fact that he had effectively taken the wind out of her sails with this, she was surprised at his insight and what might be termed a certain degree of understanding.

"You and Tyront are making me act against my convictions," she said, endeavouring to sound equally placid. She didn't want to be the hysterical one while he appeared rational and in control. "I knew I would one day have to face this kind of situation - that my ideals and those of the Order would sooner or later be up against a situation that caused them to clash. I just wasn't prepared for it to occur quite so soon." She rubbed her face. "This would have been so much easier without a child that might have to face the consequences of his parents being on opposite sides," she sighed, feeling how the anger morphed into sadness.

Enric pushed himself away from the bookshelf, moving forward to cup her cheeks in his hands before she could take a step back. "I'm on your side, my love. Always." His voice was little more than a whisper, but the determination in it was no less intense.

She closed her eyes and sighed. "No, you are not. You are on Tyront's side, on the side of those who impose undesired restraint on those who have no way to change it should the Council not permit it. And they won't."

"Eryn." She opened her eyes again at the sternness he managed to instil into that one word. "The Order ceased to be the most important thing in my life some time ago. Tyront and I had quite different reasons for wanting you in the Order. He saw a powerful magician - the strategic advantage - that your abilities and knowledge would bring, as well as a useful connection to another country." His thumbs brushed over her cheekbones. "My reasons were of a more selfish variety. Firstly, I wanted you bound here so nobody could take you away from me ever again. And secondly I saw the potential your strong beliefs and your determination to follow them had to change the Order for the better. I don't wish you to act in a way that would betray your convictions, I just want to make sure whatever your endeavour has a good chance of success without getting you into trouble while amounting to nothing." He smiled at the wary interest in her eyes and the mix of relief and hope he felt through their bond. "We make a powerful couple, you and I. And I'm not talking about our magic. You are somebody with the energy and the ideas to change things for the better, somebody to inspire people and make them trust you. I am a strategist, a planner, a politician. Together we can make changes possible, but we need to do it right. No antagonising the Council members through lack of diplomacy or bluntness, no suggestion of measures that might be considered too drastic even to be discussed. No revolution that might leave the Order or even the city in ruins. We need small but incremental steps that will not overwhelm the traditionalists in the Council and make the discontented magicians see how there is development, which although not as quick as they would wish, still heads in the right direction."

She exhaled and felt the tension that had kept her muscles rigid draining away slowly. She leaned forward slightly and touched her forehead to his. "I don't know how I'm supposed to do this," she whispered.

He smiled and lifted her chin to kiss her. "That we will work out. Together."

* * *

Eryn didn't like the way he was grinning, as she approached Orrin for what was to be her first combat lesson after a number of months. It made her doubt the astuteness of letting him bully her into this. He was standing at the centre of the arena, his stance the one he liked to adopt when he was relaxed - or whatever counted as relaxed in his case: feet broadly apart, arms folded.

"There you are," he said pleasantly. "I was wondering if I needed to get you."

"Of course I am here. I agreed to do this, didn't I?" she growled and noticed that he was wearing leather armour. So it would be sword fighting today, not unarmed combat. Her spirits sank even lower. Of course it had been too much to hope that he would start with the less hated discipline without weapons. But then sword fighting was a compulsory skill to be trained under the regulations of the Order while unarmed combat was not. Being a man who took his duties seriously, Orrin would of course set priorities in accordance with the rules.

Eryn sighed in exasperation and went over to the wall against which two swords and her old training armour were leaning. Good thing the clasps at the sides were adjustable or she wouldn't have been able to don it without a lot of squeezing and subsequent limits on her agility. Not that her moves would impress the onlooker when it came to agility. The break since her last training lesson had undoubtedly been too long, by far.

She took more time than she would have needed to put on the leather armour despite knowing that straining Orrin's patience was something he would probably make her pay for later. There was just so much reluctance within her at doing this again. But then determining the point in time to resume her training herself instead of having the Order force it on her was worth it. Orrin was right. This way she was in control and not the Order. Control was important.

Tyront had been pleased no end at her demonstration of responsibility and willingness to bow to the rules of her own accord. He had made sure the Council knew that she was the one to take the initiative. Enric had approved of this, saying that it showed their colleagues that she was not somebody to be pushed around easily but was willing and able to make her own decisions. Which was as such not entirely true. She had merely picked the time. Had she any say in it she would have chosen not to resume the training at all.

"Will you be done fairly soon now or do I need to give you a hand?" Orrin's amused voice came from behind her. "Other people forge a sword in the time it takes you to pick one up."

"That I'd like to see," she snorted and finally took the weapon to pull it out of its scabbard. She weighed it in her hand for a moment, getting used to the feeling of the steel handle wrapped in leather again.

Orrin bent down to retrieve his own slightly longer sword before he let it dance through the air a few times to loosen his wrist.

"Whenever you are ready," he called to her.

Eryn nodded and joined him.

"We will start slow and easy with basic moves to warm up. Nothing too fancy or sudden. I first want to see how much is still there after our break. If you had been training for several years before it, this would not be that much of a problem. But stopping for several months before it had become second nature to you was not ideal."

"Why don't you write a brisk little letter of complaint to Malriel? She was the one to slip me that potion, after all. Had she not decided that she wanted a grandchild quite that desperately, I would never have stopped the training. Just so you know who to put the blame on."

"Shut up and parry," Orrin instructed her and aimed a first thrust at her shoulder. "This shouldn't be too hard without the shackles on."

He was wrong. It didn't take her long to notice that she had lost so much of her skill that she was no match for Orrin despite his being magically weaker than her. She was displeased at how much of what he had taught her was gone and remembered that she had been able to defeat him thanks to her magical strength only a year ago. It would very likely take quite some time to return to that level of skill, let alone to hone it beyond her previous level.

Her trainer seemed to have reached a similar conclusion, she could see it on his face. Not even when she was properly warmed up did she manage to hold him off for long.

Several minutes later she raised her hand to make him pause. "Wait! Give me a break so I can at least heal away the pain, will you?"

He shook his head. "No. The pain is supposed to remind you why blocking and dodging my strikes would be a fabulous idea."

Eryn ground her teeth and readied herself when he lifted his sword once again.

After little more than half an hour she was completely out of breath and wondered how she had ever managed to survive several hours at one stretch.

"Pathetic," Orrin commented without mercy.

She sent him a glare. "Now I see why they made you give up teaching children. Your style of motivation is not the most amiable one."

"They didn't make me give it up. I was the one to decide that I would concentrate on training adults." He gave her a broad smile. "You being the only exception."

"Are you calling me a child?" she growled.

"You have dropped back to the skill level of a third-year trainee, so I would think that this is not too far-fetched."

"I hate you," she murmured and heard him laugh at that. How agreeable that at least one of them was having fun.

"If you think you hate me now, wait until I'm done with you for today," he sneered and lifted his weapon anew.

* * *

Eryn hurried through the Palace corridors and slid to a halt in front of the high doors to the throne room. When the liveried guards were about to open them for her, she lifted a hand to stop them.

"Wait," she panted, "give me a moment and let me catch my breath first, will you?"

She saw how they exchanged a quick, slightly amused glance with each other and then let their hands sink again before they very pointedly avoided looking at her while she was bracing her hands on her knees to work on returning to a more relaxed breathing rate. After several seconds she straightened again and tried to smooth a few wisps of hair that had escaped her braid back with her hands, before she took a last breath, wiped the tiny beads of sweat from her forehead with one sleeve of her robe and nodded to the guards to admit her to the throne room.

King Folrin was sitting on his throne with what looked like a rather more impatient expression than she was used to seeing. Well, it was his own fault that she was late, she decided, and lifted her chin defiantly while marching towards him. She had been in the middle of bathing Vedric when she received a message that he wanted to see her in half an hour. That was immensely inconsiderate. Enric had been out somewhere, Gerit as well and Plia hardly every returned from the clinic before nightfall. Finishing Vedric's bath, fetching Gerit from Inad's place and finally dressing into something that had no residual patches of vegetable pulp or soap on it had taken more time than the monarch had seen fit to grant her.

"Your Majesty," she said when she stopped before the dais and bowed, noting that he was alone without even Marrin at his side.

"You are late," he remarked unnecessarily with a tone that conveyed his dissatisfaction quite clearly.

"Yes," she replied coolly. "I am."

The King looked at her and waited for a few moments before he leaned forward. "There is no apology or explanation you wish to offer me for this?"

Apology? She forced her face into a blank expression. It wouldn't do to let him see her anger. Relax, she commanded herself, wishing that the order alone would suffice to make her body comply. She needed to keep her temper, however much of a strain that was right now. She returned to what had worked fairly well in the past: breathing slowly, deeply and evenly, including not only her chest but her abdomen. Reducing the rate of the intake of air reduced the level of oxygen in the blood and the muscles. This would as a consequence reduce tension in her muscles as there would not be so much restless energy stored in them - no matter that punching the King would be a much more satisfying way to get rid of that energy. How dare he treat her like that, like one of his many useless magicians who felt honoured at the rare occasion when they were noticed by him personally instead of the hard-working mother and healer she was? She could easily forgo the pleasure of being his favourite diversion whenever he was bored!

Eryn noticed how her breathing was becoming faster again and pushed these thoughts away with determination. They didn't exactly aid in calming her nerves. She couldn't afford to lose her temper with that one, she reminded herself. It never ended well when she did. She wasn't sure if he was again trying to provoke her on purpose now, but it was better not to take that risk.

But apologising to him for his own lack of considerateness was not something she could bring herself to do at this moment. She would rather bite off her own tongue.

"No, Your Majesty, I do not wish to apologise," she said in a neutral voice and waited for his reaction. As there were no witnesses to her disrespectful behaviour there was a good chance that he would desist from punishing or even threatening her.

King Folrin watched her, though she couldn't say if he was intrigued or amused.

"What were you doing when my summons arrived?" he then enquired thoughtfully.

"Bathing my son," she replied calmly.

He smiled and nodded slowly. "Ah yes, one of the few occasions when you have time for those small chores instead of Lord Enric's mother, who seems to have taken over many of them. But then you have reduced the number or hours you work at the clinic considerably, have you not? This affords you more time for your son." He leaned back again, obviously inclined to forgive her lack of willingness to apologise. "How are those translation efforts of yours progressing? Have you started to uncover the secrets of their language?"

With effort, Eryn stopped herself from grinding her teeth. Apart from Enric and Gerit she had not told anyone about that last bit. Not that she was particularly surprised by his being as well-informed as ever. Yet she couldn't help but wonder where all his information came from. Was he paying one of their servants to report to him? Or was there somebody regularly breaking into their house to look around and tell his master what things were lying around on her desk? Neither option was at all reassuring.

"I find it quite a pleasant challenge," she said noncommittally, unwilling to volunteer more than absolutely necessary. She wouldn't want to make his spies redundant, would she...

"I am sure you do. And fortunately you have Ambassador Erbál to assist you in your efforts. It certainly does pay to have friends in useful places, doesn't it?"

"That's not why I befriended him - to benefit from whatever use he might one day have for me," Eryn remarked equably.

The King sighed. "Of course not. It would be very much unlike you. If power and a high position ever are a consideration of yours they serve rather to make you reject people instead of seeking their goodwill. That is why diplomacy will for you never be more than a mere discipline instead of an attitude."

Eryn didn't contradict him. He was right, after all. And he didn't need her confirmation to know it. She waited for him to move on to whatever had induced him to call her to him.

"I'm pleased that you have decided to resume your combat training," he went on conversationally. "No, forgive me, that is not quite accurate, is it? Let me rephrase that: I approve of your decision to bring the date for when to resume it under your control. I assume that Lord Orrin had something to do with that, but that is not for the Council to know."

She fought the impulse to roll her eyes. It seemed to her that he was in a mood to impress her with his abilities to collect information and draw logical conclusions. Was she supposed to pat him on his head for it? Feign surprise or admiration? Dealing with him would probably be so much easier if she could bring herself to cater to his vanity every now and then. But the thought alone made her feel unclean. It just wasn't like her.

"Thank you so much. You surely know how vital I consider your approval," she deadpanned. Not at all, she added silently. She watched the smile spread on his lips at the guarded insult. Then she realised that this was exactly what he had been aiming for - that her annoyance was better praise for his prowess than any insincere or even sincere compliments would have been. Well, she thought wearily, at least she had satisfied him without denying her true nature.

"The reason why I wanted to see you, Lady Eryn," he began, finally coming to the point now that he had achieved what he wanted, "is the matter of the role you are to play in the current unplanned developments within the Order."

"I have already had a conversation with Lord Tyront, when he reminded me of my duties in this from the Order's point of view," she replied with a sour expression.

The King nodded. "I know."

Of course he did. Whenever did he not?

He got up from the throne and stepped down from the dais, standing next to her before he lifted his arm for her to take. "Walk with me, my Lady."

She hesitantly took his arm, remembering the last time he had invited her to walk with him. It had been before her herb gathering expedition when he had tested her in political strategy.

"I am of course aware how little you care for the Order's point of view. Or mine, come to that. Accepting you into the Order and binding you to the Kingdom with magic have not served to turn you into a devoted adherent of our principles but rather make you even more determined to hold on to your own values. I find that remarkable, to be honest. Comfort and wealth have not managed to weaken your resolve. This is something I respect with all my heart. Unfortunately, it sometimes confuses onlookers and counteracts my own and the Order's efforts. Were you a mere citizen of the Kingdom, your disapproval would hardly hold the potential to harm our plans. But your position of power requires of you to stand with the institutions that grant it to you."

Eryn stared straight ahead when she said, "And unquestioningly follow the commands I receive without doubting those who issue them. Like a good soldier."

They had reached the door to the gallery and stopped so King Folrin could open it for them to step through.

"No. This is not what you are expected to do, and I suspect that you are aware of it, that this is mere frustration making you say it in such a way. You are supposed to follow your commands in public and question them in a less open manner in private conversation with the one who gave them to you. Lord Tyront is a no-nonsense man who even welcomes constructive criticism when it is offered in a respectful fashion."

"And yet you called me here to tell me that I am to stand with the Order in a matter were my fellow magicians are fighting for what I was known for demanding ever since I joined the Order. You are telling me to push my own convictions aside to help maintain the stability of an outdated institution that now even seems to have lost the only purpose it has followed for such a long time: to serve the needs and wishes of its members as several of them are no longer satisfied with exchanging their freedom for a halfway comfortable life."

To her dismay, King Folrin chuckled. "Spoken like the revolutionary which the Order and myself shall need to keep from rising."

"I have no intention of gathering a group of magicians around me to lead them into battle against our oppressors," she snorted.

He stopped and waited until she turned to him. His expression was now serious. "You speak of this as if it were a joke, an outrageous idea. But in all honesty, it is not. There is a realistic chance of something coming of this, and the case with Darnet and his attack on Lord Tyront - which he thinks he carried out with your support and even under your orders - shows that clearly enough. They even approached you to speak on their behalf in the Council. They would be more than willing to accept you as their leader: a powerful figure, incorruptible, smart, fierce in her convictions, somebody the city looks up to thanks to your efforts with the clinic and the orphanage, the former prisoner who healed strangers on the streets and managed to climb as high as third in command of the Order. You are a shining beacon of a decent person rising, an icon of virtue, a symbol of a mighty magician fighting for those who are neither rich nor privileged."

Eryn stared at him. That sounded completely ridiculous, as if a lovesick teenager had composed an exuberant poem to praise the lady of his heart. Certainly nothing she would expect to have come from this sober, calculating man's lips.

He sighed impatiently. "This is not an attempt at flattery, Lady Eryn. It is the result of careful observation of the population, of reports received. If I wished to please you, adulation would certainly not be my weapon of choice. Think!" he commanded. "Consider what you know about the Order's past, of the healers long gone."

She thought back to the day she had first met Lord Poron in the library. Vern had taken her to him so she could ask him about the things she was interested in, since the old librarian with his vast repository of knowledge was her best chance at finding at least partial answers. He had told her about the fights between healers and warriors several hundred years back, of local battles and the out and out war they had turned into. A war that had cost many lives, both of magicians and innocent non-magicians who became random casualties. A war that had caused warriors to instinctively distrust healers even to the present day.

She finally managed to look at herself from the Order's point of view - a dangerous stranger they had accepted among them despite her reluctance to join them, a woman who had only bound herself to the Order because the King had managed to trick her into a commitment, and even then it had been necessary for them to allow a number of concessions such as letting her establish healing services under the guard and protection of the Order. Since then her services had expanded and the contact to the Western Territories had not only strengthened the healers' right to exist but also brought forward new thoughts and ideas that were about to become dangerous and once again threaten to destabilise the Kingdom. When they looked at her they saw a woman who might cause history to repeat itself.

She swallowed and shook her head. "I wouldn't lead people into battle to sacrifice them to my ideals."

"I know," the King said soothingly and smiled when she looked at him. "You are one to fight for others, but are appalled at the thought of others fighting for you - or even for themselves."

Eryn raised an eyebrow. "I'm certainly not self-sacrificing to quite that extent. I wonder where you get this image of my being so very unselfish from."

"Unselfish? You?" King Folrin laughed and shook his head. "No, that you are certainly not. Your kind of selfishness just has a very different outlet that is easily confused with something else. Not having others fight for you shows you that you are strong and independent, that you can do anything on your own, that you can take on whatever you have to face. I imagine that dealing with all this manipulation since you left your little village must have been incredibly frustrating for you as you simply lacked the experience, the skills to counter it and became reduced to the role of a mere victim as a result."

She glared at him. "You are saying my willingness to help others is nothing more than an urge to prove to myself that I am stronger and better than others?"

"That is maybe a bit of a bleak way of painting it, but in essence I would agree, yes. Fortunately for us all, your father's upbringing channelled this into a profession and an attitude that serves to aid those around you instead of subduing, enslaving or otherwise harming them," he added dryly. "But that very character trait, that urge to lend help to those weaker and less influential than you is what I wish to appeal to now to make you understand why the Order needs you to stand by it. They need to see that you are not about to start another war between those who stand with the healers and the freedom of choice they fight for and those who stand with the warriors to preserve the old structures. There is tension in the Order, and you have the potential to either keep it at bay or make it erupt into something I am sure all of us wish to avoid."

Eryn frowned. "I see what you are getting at. Of course I would not wish to cause people to fight each other and die, but this tension you mentioned is not just about to disappear just because we are able to keep it down. This is like a wound that is only healed superficially, without taking care of the damage underneath, which continues to fester under a seemingly intact surface."

"Precisely," he agreed immediately. "And this is why not encouraging a discontented group of magicians to rise is certainly not where your responsibility ends. You need to promote changes in the Order that will make sure that this ancient institution safely arrives in this new era which you, with all your knowledge and family connections, have triggered. You just cannot be seen to do it by representing those few who are dissatisfied, but for the benefit of the entire population - both in and outside the Order. Which brings me to something I wish to discuss with you. It is the reason why these changes need to be guided, why random concessions of freedom might cause more harm than good if handled carelessly."

She waited for him to go on, swallowing the remark that she could certainly see why he would consider too much freedom for his subjects harmful.

"One of the areas of discontent among magicians is the limitation concerning their choice of professions. Even though you have made a whole new occupation possible for magicians to choose, it still is limited to a rather small number of people, as you yourself know better than anybody else. Imagine if magicians were free to pick whatever line of work they found appealing - what would be the consequences for those craftspeople without magic at their disposal?"

Eryn took a minute to consider his question. She had an idea of what he might be getting at. "You mean that they would be at a disadvantage as the same skill in combination with magic would cause them to lose their customers to magicians who offered the same products or services?"

"Exactly. The population at large may not admire magicians particularly but they respect them nevertheless. Small wonder - they have been taught to do so for who knows how many centuries. It is a form of collective memory that makes non-magicians consider magicians a little more valuable than others."

"I don't agree with that perception," she said grumpily. "I certainly don't consider magical abilities an apt way to judge a person's value."

"Of course you don't," the King placated her. "I never said you did, I just wished to make you aware of the way those around you do. So we established that non-magicians might suffer considerable disadvantages when having to compete with magicians in their line of work. I am not only the Monarch to magicians here, Lady Eryn; I also need to consider ways to avoid the loss of income to thousands of craftspeople through that happening."

She sighed and rubbed her face. "So you are saying magicians can't ever be allowed to enter into any professions that may cause non-magicians to lose their incomes?"

"No, this is not what I am saying, Lady Eryn," the King explained patiently. "I am merely trying to make you see that rash action would have consequences that might be reduced in impact or altogether avoided by careful planning. Your efforts to include non-magicians in the healing profession are a splendid start here. I support this plan with all my heart - and the Crown's funds once your current trainees have progressed far enough to be able to teach others."

Eryn blinked. She had to admit that he was right. And his supporting her plans for non-magician healers was a pleasant enough surprise.

"A potential for trouble, however," he continued, "would in this instance be the fact that non-magician healers would be allowed to live outside the city while magicians of the same profession would still be bound to the city. As this is another issue causing a number of magicians to be angry at the Order, your efforts might serve to make it a focal point that could spark an uprising. So you see why changes need to be made carefully, why planning ahead is essential?"

She nodded slowly. "Yes. This basically means that we would first have to find a way to grant permission to magicians to live outside the capital city before we start training non-magician healers."

"Correct. And thus I hope, my dear Lady Eryn, that this insight will now help you to be a little less frustrated when your efforts at including non-magicians in your trainings do not progress as you would wish at present. It should help you understand that it would make a lot more sense first to concentrate your efforts on the matter of granting magicians the right of choice when it comes to their place of residence. First build a proper foundation before you erect a complex structure. This is not about making changes that have immediate, visible effects but doing things the right way in the right order to ensure long-term stability."

Eryn noted how her throat tightened as first signs of panic clawed their way to the surface. "Do I understand you are placing this enormous burden on my shoulders? Avoiding a war among magicians and more or less reshaping society?"

"Not on your shoulders alone, my dear Lady. But there certainly is a part of the load for you to shoulder, I will not deny it." His gaze became intent. "This is a task for which you will need allies. And I invite you to consider seriously how useful an ally the King can be to you."

She narrowed her eyes. "You are using me!"

"But of course. And I expect of you to use me in return if it serves what we have established to be our joint objectives."

They had reached the end of the gallery. Eryn couldn't even recall having walked all the way, she had been too engrossed in their conversation. She pondered his words. An ally. He had always been more of a dangerous adversary, somebody to be wary of, to distrust, who always seemed to be at least two steps ahead of her. Would working with him be any different? Would he be a reliable fellow campaigner she could trust not to play any games with her?

She looked up when he took both her hands in his and leaned down to her to kiss her on first the left and then the right cheek, obviously enjoying himself.

No, she decided with a strange feeling of relief, the change would clearly not be quite that remarkable and she would not have to feel bad about trusting him about as far as she could throw him. Without using magic, that is.

*　*　*

When he was called in, Enric entered what had become Iklan's study at the clinic for the duration of his stay in Anyueel.

"A good day to you," he greeted the healer who got up from his chair with the good-natured smile that gave away nothing of the sharp intellect behind it. He was quite the contrast to Sarol who was a genius in his own right as well and treated this fact as a universal truth and expected others to act in accordance with it. Iklan didn't insist on being treated with reverence or veneration just because he happened to be exceptionally good at what he did. Enric wasn't even sure whether the healer was aware of the status his accomplishments had earned him. Either that or he didn't really care about it as long as he was granted the opportunity to work in his field of interest and pursue research to his heart's content. Research such as investigating the intricacies behind mind bonds.

"Enric, do take a seat, will you? I am not as well equipped here as in my own study at home, so I am afraid offering you a beverage would involve taking a trip downstairs to the kitchen."

Enric waved him off. "Don't bother yourself, Iklan. I'm quite familiar with the building, so I know where to find something in case the need to quench my thirst arises."

"But of course." The healer sat down again and stifled a yawn. "You must excuse me, I am still in the process of getting used to staying awake all day long without my customary nap around noon. Unfortunately my body still refuses to fall asleep earlier in the evening, so I am basically mixing your custom of not sleeping during the day with my own culture's routine of staying up late."

"Which undoubtedly results in sleep deprivation," Enric smiled understandingly. "Believe me, I know the problem well. I experienced sleeping during the day as quite a challenge in Takhan at first as I wasn't used to it, and when I would have gone to bed in the evening, I was expected to stay up late and be sociable almost every day."

Iklan laughed. "I am glad to hear that I am not the only one who finds adapting to this a challenge. Sarol does not mind at all and never looks tired. But then he has always kept odd hours at home as well. And he is not quite as concerned with showing consideration for your customs or causing offence. When he is tired, he has no qualms about seeking out the nearest level, halfway comfortable-looking surface and taking a nap. Socially speaking this does not exactly make a good impression, but from a medical point of view it is a smart thing to do."

"But then Sarol is known for his attitude. I imagine that is a great advantage for him in situations like that," Enric nodded.

The healer sighed. "Definitely, that is true. The right to be inconsiderate must first be earned by being brave enough to ignore conventional behaviour and risk people's adverse opinions. Sarol has managed to get his colleagues so accustomed to it that they do not even notice it these days and would even be quite shocked at his displaying unexpected modesty or kindness. I am afraid I never was that brash, so I have to deal with this inner urge to comply with the rules." He swallowed once. "Oh dear, now I have presented my colleague in a very unfavourable light, have I not? Let me assure you that I feel nothing but respect for him, mixed with maybe a little envy. He is a great healer and researcher, all the more considering that he never accepted his being born without magic in any way a restraint upon him. And his accomplishments clearly show that it is not the lack of magic that limits a person, but other people. Even though we do of course know that Sarol's seemingly offensive behaviour stems not from a wish to insult those around him but rather of a lack of understanding for obeying rules he does not consider sensible."

Enric chuckled. "I see. And your need to defend him against whatever bad impression your earlier words might have left with me is another one of these things Sarol would consider unnecessary?"

"True enough. He would very likely just shrug and be the first one to admit that my words were nothing but the truth. They would not even offend him and he would just scoff at me for my guilty conscience of talking of a highly esteemed colleague that way. Is it not fascinating, how very different we all are on the inside?"

The blond magician nodded and hid a smile. From one second to the next his conversation partner had moved from feeling guilty to expressing his joy in the mechanics of the human mind. He remembered that Eryn, too, had a tendency to swing from anger or frustration to reluctant fascination when a topic intrigued her. The very first time he had experienced it was after she had tried to flee from the city, while she was still being held prisoner. He had pushed her into talking about the Freedom night, and while she had been careful not let him get close to her - either physically or with his words - she had not been able to fight her interest in the concept of magical music when he had mentioned it to her.

He suspected that Iklan, too, had probably scored for explorer in the aptitude test House Arbil offered.

"When you asked me to see you today, Enric, I could not help thinking that you most likely wished to talk about how things are progressing with Darnet. Am I correct in assuming so?"

Enric nodded. "Yes, that is indeed why I wanted to see you."

The healer sighed and leaned back in his chair. "I am afraid I cannot tell you anything more than what you have undoubtedly already read in my reports. I assume Lord Poron or Lord Tyront show them to you? You do of course know that I cannot send one to you as you are expected not to interfere with the investigation as a result of being the accused's companion? But this surely does not stop you from obtaining them from somewhere, I imagine."

"I usually read Lord Tyront's copies, yes", he confirmed.

"I can of course understand that you would like to have an estimate on the final result of my examination sooner rather than later, considering your very personal interest in the outcome, but I hope you appreciate that after only half the allocated examination time I might do more harm than good in offering any premature opinion. If it became known, this would undermine my credibility and thereby weaken the value of my expert opinion that is intended to serve as evidence. It might seem as though I already have a conclusion in mind and was aiming just to confirm it. My methods and insights might then be called into question - especially as I was sent by a man who is very eager to see his daughter exonerated from the charges brought against her."

Enric smiled faintly at that. This was obviously a man who had either been instructed to be very cautious by either Malriel or Valrad, or had learned from his own experience how mere formalisms could sometimes thwart all efforts to prove the truth and in the end help to allow the law to triumph over justice. But Enric himself was not exactly a beginner in this field, either.

"Of course. I would never carelessly risk anything like that simply to satisfy my curiosity. I would, however, be happy if you can agree to answer a few of my questions with the due care your professional integrity warrants. I am, as you pointed out, not involved in the investigation as such in any official capacity, but naturally enough I am in my role as second-in-command of the Order interested in its progress, since one of my subordinates is concerned. Lord Tyront shares that interest, of course, and will subsequently be informed of our conversation."

He could see how Iklan nodded slowly and smiled at that. He seemed relieved that the Order's leader was aware of this meeting.

"Very well, Enric. Please ask your questions, then."

"Have you in the course of the past examinations of Darnet gained an impression that there is a chance of his not being of sound mind?"

The healer thought for a moment, then took a deep breath and spoke as if he was weighing every single word before allowing it to pass his lips. "Judging from my professional experience I can say that there are patterns in both his behaviour and his perception that would suggest that such a chance does certainly exist. I would, however, not venture to assess at this point if this will form into a certainty, remain a suspicion or turn out to be false by the end of my examination."

Enric nodded, feeling how relief flooded through him. Iklan's extreme guardedness was a little trying because he was so very eager not to let himself be pinned down to anything, so he took pains to be as vague as he could. Yet it was this very cautiousness which made him the right person for the job.

"Then I may assume from this, should your examination progress in the same fashion as it has to now, that the result suggests that Darnet is assuredly the victim of obsessive ideas?"

The healer thought again before answering. "In theory I can agree that would be the case. Yet..."

Enric interrupted him. "Yet there is no saying in what direction the rest of the examination will go and thus such estimates would at the current time be nothing more than speculation based on an imagined development."

Iklan smiled. "I commend you on your way of asking questions. I would imagine that is this very attention to detail is what made my fellow countrymen and women groan when talking of trade negotiations with you during your first visit to Takhan when you were still an ambassador. Did I manage to ease your mind at least a little despite being so guarded in my answers?"

The Order magician nodded and took the hint that the healer wished to stop talking about the subject for now. "That you did, definitely. And I thank you very much for it. I realise that this is not an easy situation for you. I appreciate it all the more that you shared what you could with me." He stood up. "Now I'll leave you to whatever I interrupted."

Enric took his leave and smiled to himself as he was descending the stairs to the clinic's ground floor, passing the waiting room, still half filled with patients who were waiting for treatment despite the advanced hour. And now he would visit Lord Woldarn, who had unexpectedly invited him to discuss the matter of the building he wanted to sell.

*　*　*

Eryn looked up when she heard the entrance door close and a little later Urban trotted into her study to flop down right in front of her desk. After the time it took him to unfasten his cloak and hang it on the hook in the niche Enric followed the cat and smiled when he found his companion poring over her stack of books from Pirinkar.

It was already dark outside and the light from her lamp cast a cone of light on her desk that left anything higher than her forehead obscure.

"Good evening, my love," he greeted her and came closer to kiss her on the mouth. "It's eerily quiet in this house. Where is everyone?"

She leaned back and adjusted the aperture on her lamp so that the light was less intense but illuminated more of the room when he sat down on the corner of her desk closest to her.

"Vedric is asleep upstairs, your mother is seeing Junar for a few new dresses and Plia is visiting a friend, for a change."

Enric lifted both eyebrows, surprised. "She is not at work? She is actually seeing people? Like a normal girl her age? How ever did that happen?"

"It's one of the girls she met during her employment in the Palace kitchen."

"What's that girl's name?" he asked casually.

Eryn had to grin. "Don't tell me you intend to collect information on her and then decide if you consider her good company for Plia? Stop that, Order lord! She is fourteen years old and has had to fend for herself all her life. She won't appreciate any meddling now, no matter how important you are or that she happens to live with you. Rather tell me how your meeting with Iklan went and why you returned that late. Iklan was tight-lipped when I tried to get an opinion on Darnet out of him, so I would be surprised if you managed to keep him talking for that long."

Enric didn't comment on the issue with Plia's friend. She was right, after all. He really couldn't tell the girl who she was allowed to meet or not. That had not in the past even worked with his companion, so he imagined that Plia would be even less inclined to take his recommendations into consideration.

"You are right, I didn't need much time with Iklan. The conversation with him was like walking on broken glass."

"Painful and bloody?"

"Careful and ponderous. He is incredibly guarded, which I of course approve of, but which nevertheless gave me the feeling that I was talking to a lawyer who didn't even dare to admit that the sky was blue. But I was satisfied enough. Right now he thinks that Darnet truly is of unsound mind, which is exactly the result we needed. I should have asked him about you as well. So that he doesn't shock us all on the day of the hearing by declaring the both of you of unsound mind... Ow!" He rubbed his thigh where she had slapped him. She had used a little magic for that hit, not enough to really hurt him, but he felt the stinging.

"Very funny. So, how did not telling you more than there was a faint chance of Darnet's being insane take that long?"

"It didn't. I had another appointment afterwards. Imagine that: Lord Woldarn sent me a message and invited me to talk about the house you and my mother liked so much. We talked for a while, had a glass of wine and finally he agreed to lower the price. Not as much as I would have wished, but he offered to have the restoration work done at his expense, which rather balances things."

Eryn blinked. "So, what exactly does that mean? That you have bought the house?"

He nodded. "Precisely that. We agreed on the terms of the contract and he will have it drawn up within the next days and send it to me for approval. I wonder what made him reconsider. He didn't offer any explanation for his change of heart."

She sighed. "I can tell you, but you won't like it."

Enric's posture didn't change, but his expression became sharper. "Out with it, then."

"His son, Onil, told me that he had a word with his father about the price after he asked me to speak on his and his friends' behalf on the Council. It seems he was true to his word."

He exhaled slowly. "Oh dear. That's not good. I wish you had told me about this a little earlier."

"I would have - had you informed me that you were meeting Lord Woldarn!"

"I wanted to surprise you," he sighed. "Is that just my impression or are there always unpleasant consequences when we don't share every scrap of information?"

"It certainly seems like it. Well, there is one thing to be gained from this, then: no more surprises. What are we to do now? Did you already bind yourself with your word?"

Enric nodded. "I did. If the contract clauses match my notes, I am bound to sign it."

Eryn frowned. "That's unfortunate. Now it appears as if we accepted Onil's sweetener in exchange for support on the Council. I told him that this would not influence my willingness to help them, but your accepting it might say something else. I suppose I will have to talk to him and sort things out."

"How well did you get on with him before? Is talking to his father with regard to the house something he might have done anyway under different circumstances in order to do you a favour?"

She nodded. "I would think so. Does it matter? If this becomes public for whatever reason, it would still show a questionable intention. Do you think Lord Woldarn knows about this?"

Enric shook his head. "Surely not. If Onil had his father's support, he wouldn't have approached you, I think. And Lord Woldarn is a traditionalist. He is not one to fight openly, but still backs up colleagues who are in favour of maintaining the current state of affairs."

"So Lord Woldarn himself would never claim that you accepted a bribe from him to make us support these revolutionary new ideas. It would destroy his credibility. I would think that this considerably reduces the chances of it getting out in the open." She raked her hair. "This is so frustrating! We are buying a house for a reasonable price - even though it was overpriced before - and now have to fear exposure for accepting sweeteners despite not having done so!"

"Politics, my love," he smiled and took her hands from her head to pull her up from the chair and towards him. "Nothing we can't handle. And even if there were any accusations of that kind from Onil or one of his friends, public opinion is in your favour, as well as the King's. I would be very surprised if anything of that sort finds fertile ground here. Don't worry." He pressed his lips to her temple and inhaled her scent, closing his eyes as it increased his heartbeat, relishing his body's reaction caused by nothing more than her closeness.

She giggled when his teeth nibbled lightly on her earlobe. "You know that this makes my skin tingle."

He stopped to check her forearm and grinned with satisfaction when her hairs indeed stood on end. "I certainly do." He lifted her chin to kiss her lips and open them, when her arms encircled his neck. She was warm and soft in his arms, pressing against him while her taste shut down his senses with the need to keep her close and take all that she was willing to offer.

He pulled back slightly when he felt her stiffen in his arms and only moments later he heard the high-pitched wailing from upstairs.

"I swear to you, he does this on purpose," Enric groaned and forced himself to remove his hands from her. "Probably to make sure there are no younger siblings to join him and force him to share everything."

Eryn grinned at his desperate expression. "Then I suppose I'll have a nice, long talk with your son to inform him that the chances for another baby are immensely slim. Maybe he'll be more considerate from then on?"

He just sent her a sour look, none too happy about her mirth in light of his frustration. "Go and tend to that inconsiderate son of yours."

"Now he is my son?"

"Of course. As long as he is inconsiderate. When he is sweet again and people tell me how much he resembles me, I'll just claim him back."

CHAPTER 28

The Council Decides

Eryn blinked twice as she approached the training circle and saw Orrin and Pe'tala standing to one side, talking in a relaxed manner. She scowled when she saw that her sister was wearing leather armour. Oh no, not this. It meant that when Pe'tala mentioned so many months ago that she intended to learn swordplay it had not just been a remark to provoke her father, but a genuine intention. And now it looked as though Orrin had decided to have them train together for the brief interlude before they returned to Takhan.

"Good morning," she said and forced herself to smile. "You brought me something I can hit hard. Good."

Pe'tala looked her over, obviously unimpressed. "If you can, sister. I wonder if that flabbiness your pregnancy has left you with has not slowed you down too much to accomplish that."

Eryn ground her teeth. "Does your father know you are actually going through with this?"

"Our father," the younger woman corrected her with unexpected gentleness. "It is time for you to adapt to this fact finally. And yes, he knows that I was planning on doing it. Though he is not as such in the know that I have truly started learning it."

"Well, baby sister," she sneered and rejoiced at how Vran'el's term of endearment made her flinch, "then I suppose I'll accidentally mention it to him in my next letter."

"Sure, you go on and do that. It will be a nice distraction from his other daughter who is accused of an attempted murder. But then I suppose that is what a man needs to be prepared for when fathering an Aren woman."

Eryn growled and picked up the two swords that were leaning against the stone wall. She infused her arm with magic and hurled one of them at Pe'tala. Her sister ducked instinctively, but Orrin snatched it out of the air and handed it over.

"Careful, Eryn. Or we will need to revisit the rules on how to treat a weapon. Throwing one at people you don't intend to dismember is not considered courteous."

"Who says I don't intend to dismember her? And the scabbard was still on, so the worst outcome would have been a bruise she would have healed away in less than a minute!" Eryn defended herself.

Orrin rolled his eyes and then turned to the other woman. "And your reaction to an item being thrown to you was not exactly impressive, either. Without the scabbard, jumping aside would have been acceptable, even though a magician might prefer to have raised a shield instead. But this sword was no danger to you, meaning that ducking instead of catching it was unnecessary."

Eryn sneered at the reprimand and called out, "Not that I don't appreciate the chance to give her a good whacking, but I almost feel bad about hitting her considering that she had no training."

Her trainer raised one eyebrow. "Your own skills have withered somewhat thanks to your break, so I don't think that the gap between the two of you will prove that great."

She decided not to react to that remark and instead focussed on her younger sister, who was pulling the sword out of its scabbard. Orrin really gave her a sharp-edged weapon when he had insisted on using wooden sticks with Eryn herself at the beginning? Well, she would just have to make sure to nick Pe'tala where it would merely cause pain but could be healed again easily.

The first slow strike she aimed at the younger woman's shoulder revealed a detail that made her frown. Pe'tala blocked it effortlessly and with a stance that revealed that this was clearly not her first training session.

"You have taken combat lessons!" Eryn exclaimed accusingly.

Pe'tala grinned broadly. "You noticed! I am most flattered. Are you becoming a little nervous now that it seems I will not be quite so defenceless a target as you expected?"

Eryn smiled back. "Did Rolan ever tell you about the combat instruction he and I had together?"

The younger woman's expression grew darker. "Yes, he mentioned a few of your unfair tricks with which you gained an advantage despite your inferior skills. He did not know you back then, but rest assured that such dishonourable conduct in an Aren will hardly surprise me much."

Orrin followed their verbal exchange with amusement. What a pity that Pe'tala's stay here would soon come to an end. Not only did he like her, but she also managed to provoke Eryn enough so she gladly picked up her sword. He would suggest to Enric to make sure they trained together in Takhan. The wish to beat her younger sister might be just the incentive needed to let her progress quickly.

"I want to hear more steel clanging and less jabbering!" he called out and smiled when that earned him two hostile stares. Whoever laboured under the misapprehension that women were the more pacific sex had clearly never handed them a bladed weapon.

* * *

450

Eryn, looking flustered and agitated, entered her companion's study when she saw that he was alone.

"Pe'tala has been taking combat lessons for these last two months!" she exclaimed and shook her head as if she were trying to displace that outrageous snippet of information.

Enric put his pen aside and leaned back. He kept his expression cautiously blank. Too blank, as Eryn's narrowing eyes told him. "Did she really?"

"You knew about this!" she cried out with obvious irritation. "How about sharing information now and then? We just had that discussion why withholding things from each other is not a good idea, and you are still doing it!"

He made sure his voice didn't sound like he was lecturing her, even though he was about to do exactly that.

"That means that we need to share secrets that concern us and that we are entitled to share. It certainly does not mean that I can circulate private information that is not mine to spread."

"I see." She folded her arms and looked at him, clearly not convinced by his argument. "Yet this concern for other people's secrets does obviously not keep you from obtaining that information in the first place, no matter if it is any of your business or not."

He shrugged. "No, it doesn't. And without going through all available information first I could hardly tell what of it is my business and what isn't."

She exhaled slowly. "You are seriously telling me that your spying on people indiscriminately is fine, but my wanting to know something such as my own sister's combat training is undue abuse of her right to keep her matters private? You are a piece of work, you know that?"

"Look, the substance of it is this: Every person is responsible for what information can be collected about them. If I manage to gather intelligence of facts somebody would rather keep private, that is their own fault as the information was clearly not guarded well enough. My responsibility starts as soon as the information is in my hands. That means that I need to decide whether passing parts of it on or making use of it myself is justified. In Pe'tala's case there was no justification to betray her wish for confidentiality, since no harm was likely to be caused by it."

"Lord Enric, the guardian of secrets," she snorted. "What makes you think that your assuming that sublime role is even remotely adequate? Who granted you the right to preside over people like that? Surely not the Order, because you also spy on people outside our illustrious institution, as Pe'tala's example shows quite clearly."

"Whoever hires agents, my love, simply assumes that role. It more or less means that anybody with enough money to procure information that way is in a position to decide what is to be done with it. You could just as easily also hire your own agents and then take action as you see fit. Which is just the way things are in the big city.

451

We guard our own secrets as well as we can and do our best to work out other people's. But this is not new for you, you were already aware of it."

She sighed. "You are right, I was aware of it. But I suppose I was surprised that you still keep such things as that, things that have no political or similar impact, hidden from me. It feels as if you don't think you can trust me even with my own sister's secrets, that your knowing about them is so much more secure than letting me in on such knowledge as well."

Enric rose from his chair and stepped towards her to take her hands. "This is not about trust, my love. Information is a business matter for me, just like goods I obtain. If there is no need to act upon or forward it, I don't. Otherwise I would be nothing more than a rumour monger, which is not something I can afford to become notorious for. If you want to have this information for no other reason than being immune to surprises you might want to hire your own agents because I'm not about to share information with you just to satisfy your curiosity. It would be irresponsible. It would be like asking you about privileged information on your patients."

"The targets of your efforts to seek information are nothing like my patients!" she protested vehemently. "Patients share the information willingly and only to the degree they are comfortable with. You collect whatever you manage to scrape together. That is something completely different!"

He nodded. "It is, you are right. Yet considering that I have so much more information at my disposal which has in addition mostly been collected without people's consent, it certainly is even more important to handle it with caution."

"There is no discussing this with you," she growled. "You are being a slippery politician again. That forked tongue of yours must be a great advantage when facing somebody like me who is straightforward and says what is on her mind instead of first bending it until even spying on people sounds like a justified and completely respectable pastime."

He smiled at that. "I admit it is. Can I divert you from your irritation with me by showing you what your grandmother sent us?"

She sighed and pinched the bridge of her nose to release the tension building behind her forehead. He didn't deserve to get off the hook that easily, but she was tired of this discussion. She wouldn't win it, and both of them knew it. He probably considered himself a gracious winner by offering her an easy way out of it now that she had voiced her frustration.

"Something in connection with our fancy new residence, I assume?" The resignation was plain in her voice.

"It is. She reports that the foundation is finished now and that she is pleased with the progress. This time she even held back from complaining that we are using House Roal to do the construction. She has either accepted that there is a contract with them whether she likes it or not, or she is truly satisfied with their work."

"Knowing Malhora it probably took a bit of both to make her stop complaining. Any trouble from the Queen of Darkness because we dared disregard her century-old enmity with House Roal? Or from Vran'el because we got around his order to move in with him and have our own place built?"

"No, nothing I know of. Malriel is seemingly content enough with the fact that we will return to Takhan regularly, so having House Roal connected to her heir in a business arrangement is assuredly a small price to pay for it. She is doubtlessly pleased that we'll have our own house instead of staying at the Vel'kim residence. It ties us to the city more tightly. And as regards Vran'el... I bet he is too busy with his new duties to be plotting revenge for now. Which doesn't mean that he won't make us pay for it sometime later, mind you."

Eryn frowned at his expression. She had the distinct feeling that there was something unpleasant he was not too eager to tell her but knew he couldn't avoid. She waited and watched how he let his gaze wander along the ceiling as if looking for inspiration for phrasing his news as agreeably as possible.

"There is something else," he said finally.

"Yes, I can see that. Out with it, then."

Enric sighed. "Valcredy is pregnant."

She swallowed hard and forced a smile onto her lips. It didn't look particularly joyful. "I see. Well, that is not exactly unexpected, is it? It was the reason for their union, after all - to provide an heir for House Arbil. Well done to the two of them. They certainly got down to business quickly. Very expeditious of them. I admire their conscientiousness. Really." The pitch of her voice was too high and her attempt at appearing happy for them failed to impress.

He exhaled and slowly shook his head. "I know that you are not happy and would have wished for him to find a different arrangement for himself, one that would appear less calculating and business-like to you. Yet I can't help that tiny spark of jealousy when I see your reaction."

Eryn let her head fall back and closed her eyes. She wanted to tell him that what he said was complete and utter nonsense, but she could understand him to a certain degree. Ram'an had pursued her relentlessly to win her for himself, had even resorted to shifty legal tricks to try and bind her to his House. And then she had willingly let herself be kissed by him when her brother had sent her to him to secure his vote against Enric in the Senate. It couldn't be easy for her companion that Ram'an and she had somehow ended up being friends despite everything that had happened between them. Enric had been more than understanding and even generous towards her former suitor, and the least she could do now was to respect his involuntary response to her reaction of learning that Ram'an was about to have a child with Enric's former lover.

"I'm sorry," she said wearily. "I swear to you, there is no feeling of regret or resentment because I am not the one carrying his child. I just wanted more for him than that. I feel responsible for leaving him in an emotional state that made him take such a step. And now that they are having a child together, it seems so... final. It's as if I was until now still hoping that he would correct this mistake."

Enric nodded slowly. "I understand. But he is a grown man and the least you can do is to treat him like one and respect his decision, even if you cannot approve of it. Entering into a commitment that was admittedly not a matter of the heart but rather one of political considerations was for him the lesser evil compared to leaving the matter of succession in his House unclear."

She sighed extensively. "I know all that! It doesn't make things easier for me. But I promise I will be civil and supportive. I will send him a jolly note to congratulate him."

"You will get used to this," he promised tenderly and stepped next to her to take and squeeze her hand. "And Valcredy is not all that bad. You got off on the wrong foot, I grant you that, but she is not a bad person. Who knows, maybe she and Ram'an will in time even come to appreciate each other's company."

Eryn lifted her brow. "You are not seriously attempting to make me think well of the woman you used to sleep with before me, are you?"

He smiled lazily. "You assured me in the past that you are not the jealous type, and yet I can't help suspecting just that."

She gave him a nonchalant smile, expertly hiding her embarrassment at his accurate guess. "You are seriously mistaken on that account, Lordling. Your praising your discarded bed-partner doesn't bother me in the least."

His grin grew even wider as he tapped his index finger against his forehead. "Really? Funny, then this mind bond must be defective, because this is exactly what I'm receiving from you right now."

Her lips mouthed silent curses while blood rushed to her head and made her cheeks burn. Stupid, darn, treacherous mind bond!

"If you'd excuse me now, there is work I need to take care of before Gerit returns with Vedric," she said with as much dignity as she could muster, ignoring his pleased and amused expression as she strode out of his study.

* * *

Eryn lay on her back, staring unseeingly into the darkness of her bedroom and listening to Enric's regular breathing right next to her. It was not so deep as to suggest that he was fast asleep, yet regular enough to make it hard to tell if he was still awake or not. He didn't normally snore, so the absence of any such noises was no hint of whether he had already drifted off or not.

She had difficulty falling asleep, as her thoughts kept returning to the news of Ram'an and Valcredy and the child they were expecting.

Trying to feel happy for his sake hadn't worked so far. If only it had been any other woman but that particular one. She vividly remembered that first time they had met for the dancing lessons Enric had scheduled, the insults that woman had spat at her because she had obviously not been able to accept that her former rich and influential magician lover had chosen another mate not only for his bed but also for a companion.

Eryn tried not to think of the fact that this woman knew what it felt like to be touched by Enric's sometimes tender and at other times demanding - though without exception always skilled - hands. And now she had laid claim to Ram'an. Eryn considered Ram'an hers, she pondered, though in a way that was completely different from the way Enric belonged to her. It was just like Vran'el was hers, or how Vern was. Seeing one of them connected with somebody she didn't approve of was nerve-racking.

She thought back to the kiss she had shared with Ram'an in a weak moment after she realised that losing his affection would pain her a lot - despite the anger at him she had felt back then. Acquiescing to kissing him while another man's child was growing in her womb had been like grasping a lifeline; it had been a price she had at that moment been willing to pay to avoid his affection for her ceasing - no matter how much she regretted it afterwards when she laid eyes on Enric a short while later. This kiss had been proof to her that he still cared for her, and at that time it had not been important to her in what way. She had been lost and feeling alone, far away from home, not long after hearing that Valrad was her father not only by adoption but also in the usual direct meaning of the word.

Eryn sighed silently. Was she still trying to justify or rather excuse her behaviour to herself? Enric had never even once mentioned it since the day Ram'an had so unexpectedly shared that information with him.

"Are you still awake?" she said quietly and hoped that she received an answer. If she couldn't talk about this, this might keep her awake for a while yet.

"Yes, I am. You are thinking rather loudly, my love."

"You are telling me I'm somehow keeping you awake because my thoughts are too loud?" She tried to decide if he was teasing her, but his voice had sounded serious. And she was contemplating rather weighty matters right now, after all. "Does it have something to do with the mind bond?" She was absolutely sure that she had not been breathing any more loudly than usual or been releasing any pained sighs.

"No," he replied and sounded rather amused, "it's rather that a certain kind of nervous energy radiates off you. As if something caused you unrest and you would rather be pacing the room instead of lying here while brooding over it. What is on your mind?"

Eryn swallowed and forced herself to voice her thoughts. "Back then, when I let Ram'an kiss me..." Why did she phrase it like that?

Did she hope that merely not objecting to the deed was so much less condemnable than actively participating?

"Yes?" Enric encouraged her gently.

"You attributed it to my being pregnant and feeling neglected and to my fear of otherwise losing his friendship. Did you really see it as nothing more than that or do you secretly resent me for it?"

"I don't resent you for it, I promise. He used your vulnerable state of mind to manipulate you, and I don't blame you because you fell for it. Our mind bond showed me clearly what you were feeling for me, so I knew that there was no romantic interest in him involved from your side. I was angry at Ram'an, immensely so." His voice held a hint of tension that disappeared at his next words. "But he came to me afterwards and tried not to use it to pry you away from me, but to try and urge me into realising that something had to be done about that state of mind you were trapped in, that unhappiness you were wrapping around you. Why did you bring it up? I never had the impression that this matter stood between the two - or, well, three - of us."

She frowned in the darkness. "It's about Valcredy. I can't bring myself to stop thinking ill of her, and I really want to. It would make things so much easier. But as soon as I manage to convince myself that Ram'an is a grown man and has every right to make good or bad choices, I remember that you used to go to bed with her - then all my good intentions to deal with this like a sensible adult are gone from one moment to the next. So it's not only that I see him trapped with that... person, I constantly envision her lying in that very bed with you amongst crumpled sheets, exhausted after a night of passion with a happy glow of satisfaction on her face and a beatific smile on those absurdly full lips of hers."

Enric laughed quietly and caught her fist after she had hit him with a lucky punch in his general direction and was about to do so again. "I love it! What was that about your not being the jealous type?" he teased her in a voice dripping with glee.

"Bastard," she growled and yanked her fist out of his grip.

He fumbled in the darkness until he had a good grip on her and pulled her closer so he could envelop her in his arms. "Now, now, there is no need to be grumpy because I enjoy it that the thought of me with another woman makes you angry. And let me reassure you that I never had sex with her in that very bed. We either spent a few hours at her quarters or in my guest room - where she then usually spent the night without me."

Eryn rolled her eyes in the dark. "The guest room where I stayed? Great, this gets better and better. Now we didn't just share a man, but also a bedroom!"

"You never shared me with anyone, my love. Sharing would imply that I had you both at the same time. I had stopped meeting her almost a year before I first took you to bed at the Freedom Night. So even without your turning up I wouldn't have been seeing her. You

are the only woman on my mind, you have been for two years now."
He kissed her forehead. "So even though I understand your
discomfort at seeing her joined with your good friend, you will have to
come to terms with that and be civil to her when we are back in
Takhan - for Ram'an's sake as well as for our own. Otherwise people
might think that you were jealous of her because you like her
companion more than you should."

"Yes, I know," she mumbled against his shoulder. "If only she
weren't so damn pretty!"

"Where she is merely pretty, my love, you are stunning and
absolutely breath-taking by comparison," Enric said without missing a
beat.

"You are only saying that to pacify me," she accused him sullenly.

She felt his chest expand and inflate with his deep sigh. "You
know, right now I really wish you had that mind bond in place,
because it would convey to you that I meant every word. I can't wait
to have it replaced, in a little more than three months. But if you truly
doubt my honesty I will in the meantime offer you something equally
reliable - a truth block. I will repeat every single word under the
influence of one if it helps dispelling your anxieties."

Eryn shook her head. The temptation to accept his offer was there
ever so briefly, but of course she couldn't. "No, thank you," she
replied curtly, "I'm not quite that desperate. Yet. Talk to me again
after I have bumped into her in Takhan for the first time."

* * *

Enric surveyed the Council hall where most of the participants in
the forthcoming meeting had gathered already. The King had yet to
arrive, as had Tyront and Iklan. He watched Eryn standing together
with Orrin and Lord Poron and talking quietly not too far away.

Iklan had concluded his assessment of Darnet's mental state only
two days ago and had drawn up a final report in record time with the
aid of the notes he had made in the course of the last two weeks.
Enric had made sure to read it before the meeting today and had
found the document to be carefully phrased yet explicitly stating that
the man who had tried to kill Tyront was in the healer's opinion
definitely not of sound mind. But this conclusion was not based on
rock-hard evidence as Enric would have preferred, but rather on a
number of hints that pointed strongly in that direction. A good lawyer
with basic understanding of healing, who was determined to cause
Eryn trouble, would probably be able to contest Iklan's report and
thereby also his statement. Fortunately, none of the assembled
Council members who would wish to see their only female member
discredited qualified as that. Several of them had a sound legal
understanding owing to their being business people like Enric himself,
yet apart from Lord Poron none of them were adept when came to the

discipline of healing. And Lord Poron had certainly no interest whatsoever in siding with Eryn's opponents.

Eryn, too, appeared fairly relaxed. They had talked about the likely outcome of this hearing today and that there might be attempts at challenging Iklan's findings, though hardly any that would be carried out well enough to convince the Council and the King that she was involved in the attempt on Tyront's life.

Enric was not expecting any trouble, not if Eryn kept her temper in check as there surely would be efforts from some of their colleagues to induce her to lose it. She was known well enough for that inclination, and the fact that word of the legendary Aren temper had found its way to Anyueel would make provoking her an even more promising line of attack. That, too, they had discussed last night. He had impressed on her to stay relaxed and remain unperturbed, even though inside she might be about to erupt with fury, at whatever they might throw at her. If she just kept on breathing evenly she would pass as someone unruffled, as this had in the past almost always worked to help her keep her calm.

The hall went quiet when the guards at the doors loudly announced King Folrin, who entered with Marrin trailing behind him. The magicians bowed as one and then went to their seats at the oval table. The monarch's arrival signalled that they would now be getting down to business. Eryn didn't join them but stood to one side. She was not yet cleared of the charges which meant she was still banished from the Council. Not that this was much of a strain on her. Quite the opposite - not being required to join their tiresome meetings had been the only enjoyable side-effect from this case against her lately.

When she straightened again from her bow, she saw the King's gaze resting on her, his expression considerate. She frowned and wondered at it. Her thoughts started racing. Was he worried for some reason? Did he know something she and Enric were not aware of? Was he planning something? With him there was no telling what he was up to, what his preferred outcome of this final hearing was. He had proved more than once that his interests came first - no matter the inconveniences or troubles he caused others. Was it possible that her not being cleared today would somehow aid him? If yes, would he be bold enough to pursue that course of action and risk angering Malriel, now that she was a triarch? Making such a powerful enemy wouldn't be a good move, and if there was one thing to be said about the King, it was that he was certainly no fool.

She reminded herself to appear placid and unperturbed. The men in this room were without exception savvy politicians who would recognise any sign of worry which belied weakness.

Tyront raised his voice as soon as the rustling and bustling around him had died down. "Your Majesty, honoured colleagues, today we will conclude the case that has caused such a stir within the Order. We are all aware of the facts as they were presented to us, of each involved party's assertions. There is no doubt that Darnet is the guilty party, nor has he tried to make it appear so. Yet there is still the question of whether his accusations against Lady Eryn are of any substance or not. As you are all aware, Iklan, a highly qualified and esteemed healer whose conduct and abilities are beyond reproach, has been spending the time since his arrival assessing Darnet's mental state. He has only recently concluded his survey and has obliged us by most expeditiously preparing his report, as he is of course aware of how pressing the resolution of this case is for us. Let us commence therefore and bring it to an end." He nodded to the two guards who then opened the double doors once again to admit Iklan, who had been asked to wait in the corridor until he was summoned.

Iklan walked in and let his gaze wander across the assembled magicians, bowing when his eyes came to rest on the King. Enric noted with satisfaction that the healer gave no sign that would reveal any particular partiality towards either himself or Eryn that might afterwards be construed as some kind of bias in their favour.

Tyront nodded to Lord Poron, who was officially in charge of the investigation and selected to ask the first questions.

Lord Poron nodded to his colleague from across the sea and then began, "Iklan, let me once again tell you how much we value your efforts and above all your willingness to travel such a long way to aid us with this challenge we have faced. I would ask you to inform us about the insights you have gained regarding Darnet. As I am the only healer in the Magic Council and my own knowledge of the area of mental illnesses is rudimentary at best, I would kindly ask you to consider this and phrase your explanations in a way that enables us all to follow them. Please keep your statement rather more general at the beginning; we will ask if we require more detailed information."

Iklan nodded once and then started to relate his findings. "My first impression of Darnet was one of a balanced young man who merely had an understanding of morality that did not match his society's. He was aware that he had carried out a punishable act, yet he had reasons to justify it before himself. He considers himself a pioneer acting on behalf of the greater good and enjoys his role of the valiant martyr who will be punished by the system he has decided to act against, since he is sure that his like-minded colleagues will hold him in high esteem for it. This meant he appeared less confused or out of touch with reality at the beginning of my examination but instead rather misguided. Misguided is generally considered a state of mind where reality is not assessed in a way that is acceptable for a person's surroundings. Depending on the situation and the degree of deviation from what is considered the norm, this may at times prove inconvenient, annoying or even dangerous, yet is not as such considered an illness. The illness starts where the perception of reality as such deviates - and we are not talking about how it is interpreted. This is actually about what the brain thinks has been delivered to it through all sensory organs."

One of the Council members, Lord Seagon, lifted a finger to indicate that he wanted to ask a question. "All sensory organs? So you are telling us that these wrong perceptions can include a broad range of different areas, such as pictures or even touch?"

The healer nodded. "Indeed, My Lord. Pictures, sounds, touch, even smell and taste - sensations that are usually delivered through all our sensory organs. As you may imagine, such a complex false input can indeed call memories and impressions into being that appear so tangible that the mind has no way of distinguishing whether they are merely being imagined or real. This, I strongly believe, is what Darnet is suffering from. He believes his interactions with Lady Eryn to be reality, he remembers them most vividly with details that would easily convince a casual listener that he must actually have experienced them. He described gestures that I know to be authentic as I myself have seen Lady Eryn using them. He was able to recall precise details about items of personal adornment, such as hair ribbons like the one she is wearing today."

Eryn swallowed self-consciously as all gazes wandered towards her and the braid over her shoulder to look at the dark green ribbon that matched her tunic.

"He used elements that he has encountered before," continued Iklan, "and his brain seemingly merges and twists them into something new, into a figment of his imagination, if you want. In my conversations with him I sometimes experienced him to be in a state of disconnection from reality, where he talked about things I knew beforehand or found out later had never happened in such a manner. And in several cases there was a very clear inconsistency of different components of his personality. His thoughts, emotions and behaviour did not always... connect. He knows that killing is wrong, that it is a despicable thing unless there is no other way to ensure one's own survival, yet his attack on Lord Tyront does not seem to bother him in the least. He does not consider it wrong in any way as for him it is an action sanctioned and encouraged by Lady Eryn, whom he believed asked him to do it."

"So you would classify Darnet's state clearly and unmistakably as a mental illness?" Lord Aldon asked.

Eryn looked at the Council member. There had never been much interaction between herself and this man; he didn't speak up very often during the Council meetings, he mostly did so just to agree with or criticise some or other statement or idea. Looking at him tended to remind her of that one evening when she had played her teary little game with Malriel at the dinner that he had hosted. This must also have been the evening where Malriel had slipped her the fertility potion with the glass of red wine they had shared. Her gaze returned to Iklan, and even without looking at his thoughtful expression she would have known that he was about to admit that a mental illness was hardly ever a matter of clarity. For anything else he was much too careful.

"I am very cautious, My Lord, when it comes to terms such as clearly and unmistakable in connection with an area as varied and often hard to grasp as the state of the human mind. There is strong evidence that supports my assessment, both with anatomical and behavioural clues, yet I do not think so highly of myself as an individual, as one who is prone to mistakes just like any other human being, nor of the level of expertise myself and my colleagues have so far been able to reach in this discipline, to guarantee you a flawless diagnosis."

Eryn refrained from rolling her eyes with effort. Humility was by many considered a virtue, but she felt that Iklan was carrying his self-depreciating modesty a little far right now. Especially as this would not serve her own case at this moment. She would have preferred an expert who was fiercely protective of his findings and challenged everybody who dared to doubt them, making non-healers think twice before voicing anything that might be considered criticism. Right now she would have preferred somebody like Sarol. He managed to make people feel ill-advised and inadequate just for disagreeing with him. That was not a particularly pleasant character trait when dealing with him, but in situations such as this one it was invaluable if one happened to be on the same side as he was.

"Would you be so kind as to elaborate on the anatomical evidence you found to support your assessment?" Lord Poron asked.

"Of course. In case of a mental disorder there is often a physical change of the brain in the form of brain tissue which is reduced in certain areas. Also the structures where the fluid is produced, in which the brain is encased, are enlarged. We do not yet know if this change is the cause of the illness or merely a consequence thereof, but we strongly suspect a connection between deviations in behaviour and the reduction of brain tissue."

Eryn had expected the next question and heard without surprise that it was indeed asked by one of the traditionalists of the Council - Lord Woldarn. These men jumped on anything that wasn't delivered with absolute certainty.

"You said that there is often a physical change - I assume this means that such a change is not always evident when you examine a patient suffering from such a mental illness?"

"No", admitted Iklan, "you are correct. There are cases where such reduction of brain tissue in an evidently ill person cannot be found. At least not to the degree that was outside the average amount."

No, no, no! Eryn wailed silently. Why did that man have to volunteer a tidbit like this? She saw a quick flicker of annoyance on Enric's face before he returned to his usual bland expression.

Lord Woldarn leaned forward, clearly intrigued. "The average amount? Am I to assume that this symptom, which you mentioned occasionally but not always occurring when a person is mentally ill, also turns up when an individual is completely healthy?"

The healer nodded slowly. "Yes, you could put it in such a way. Though I have to point out that the data we have collected in Takhan strongly supports the assertion that there is a correlation between reduced brain tissue in certain areas and behavioural changes," he once again explained. "But this uncertainty you have just pointed out is the reason why a mere examination of the brain with exploratory magic to determine the degree of brain tissue reduction in itself is not considered a reliable way of providing a diagnosis. Nobody in Takhan would take such an assessment seriously. This is why observation of behaviour and assessment and classification of thoughts and emotions are indispensable."

"And his behaviour, thoughts and emotions suggest to you that he suffers from a mental illness," Lord Poron said encouragingly.

"I am certain they do."

"How is it that nobody else had noticed anything abnormal about Darnet's behaviour?" Lord Woldarn enquired.

"I would not think that nobody noticed anything. It is just that as long as there was no escalation such as the attempt on Lord Tyront's life, his friends, family or colleagues might have perceived him as little other than somewhat strange or eccentric in his behaviour. They would not know how to determine if certain behaviour or statements were to be considered proof of a disturbed mind or merely showed some less likable character traits. What is more, mental illness is not a steady progression but characterised by phases of different intensity that occur with varying intervals. Negative experiences and a certain proneness to strong emotional reactions cause symptoms - such as in Darnet's case delusions and hallucinations - to appear more frequently. You may like to compare this to volcanoes with their dormant and acute phases."

There were some moments of confusion where the Council members exchanged frowns and looked questioningly at each other and then Iklan. Then Enric's calm voice explained, "He is talking about mountains that spit fire and ashes from time to time, causing considerable damage when erupting depending on their size and location, but appearing completely harmless and inert most of the time."

Eryn smiled faintly. Of course he would know about that. No doubt he had stumbled across a book on the topic somewhere in the Aren or Vel'kim library. She had long ago given up on tracking the things he kept reading so indiscriminately.

Iklan looked at him helplessly. "I take it you do not have any volcanoes here. So this was clearly not a particularly helpful analogy."

Enric waved him off. "Don't worry, I think we get the similarity. So you are saying that there might have been something in Darnet's recent past that triggered his illness into an acute phase that let him erupt, as it were?"

Eryn noted that he phrased his question in a way that conveyed very clearly that he didn't share his colleagues' doubts whether Darnet truly was suffering from a mental illness.

"This is what my conversations with the patient have led me to believe. And this is also supported by my expertise and prior experience of similar conditions. The trigger may in this case have been his frequent interactions with like-minded people who are dissatisfied with the current situation in the Order. In his mind he saw himself almost as their leader, someone who promised them that they need no longer worry, that he was about to bring about that change they were all wishing for, that he would take measures to lead them into a new era. One in which you, Lord Enric, would preside over the Order and shape it in accordance with Lady Eryn's beliefs and values."

Eryn pressed her lips together and forced herself not to let out what some mischievous force was trying to make her say aloud: that this should be proof enough that she wasn't involved in this - had she planned anything like that, she would aim at dissolving the Order entirely instead of trying to reshape this antiquated institution.

She saw how furtive glances were being cast in her direction and looked at the seated Council members, elevated thanks to her standing position. She didn't avert her eyes; she had nothing to hide. Apart from her contempt for their occasional foolishness, that is.

Orrin cleared his throat and spoke for the first time, "About these - what did you call them? Hallucinations?"

Iklan nodded. "Yes. A hallucination is generally considered a perception occurring without external stimulation yet which is experienced as very real and can involve all senses. They are often connected with, though not to be confused with, delusions, which are firmly held beliefs that a person maintains in spite of evidence to the contrary," the healer explained helpfully.

"Thank you," Orrin said dryly, making it clear that this was quite a lot more information than he had expected, that a simple Yes would have sufficed. "You said that these hallucinations are triggered by what you called acute phases. As the question here for us still is whether or not his meetings with Lady Eryn were imagined or not, it might be illuminating to know if there were any other hallucinations."

Enric kept the corners of his mouth passive when they wanted to curve up in response to the rush of triumph he felt through the mind bond. Eryn was more than half pleased with Orrin's question, as Iklan would now explain what he had already written in his report that they had made sure to read before the meeting.

"There were definitely a few things Darnet said that I decided to have a closer look at, that turned out upon closer inspection to have been a result of his dysfunctional perception. The matter with his being the leader of a group of revolutionaries, for example. There is a group of dissatisfied magicians, as I mentioned before, but after repeatedly talking to one of them, it became very clear that Darnet was nowhere close to being anything like a leader. He always appeared to them rather more sombre and withdrawn - certainly not the type to take charge and singlehandedly change the system and make it better. And considering that Darnet saw himself being commanded by Lady Eryn, you see that there is again this discrepancy between his own thoughts and his imagined perception. It is as if his personality is falling apart and his thoughts lack a consistent pattern to link them."

"You talked to one of the people he met more than once?" Lord Woldarn perked up. "Who?"

Eryn swallowed hard. This was not good, not at all. Onil had been the one who had agreed to do it, and this was the worst possible setting for his father to find out about it from.

Iklan looked at the Council member and shook his head with an apologetic expression. "I am afraid I cannot disclose this information, as absolute confidentiality was a condition for this conversation."

"I can tell you, but I doubt that the knowledge will make you happy," Lord Aldon spoke up. "It was your own son, Onil, who talked to our foreign guest and shared those helpful little insights with him."

Eryn closed her eyes in utter disbelief at how things had looked so good only a moment ago only to go so badly a little later. When she opened them again, she saw that Lord Woldarn had gone completely pale and was staring at his colleague.

"This is not true!" he whispered, but he looked as if his brain was currently furnishing him with all those little clues that might have pointed in that direction, but which only became obvious if one took a step back and looked at all of them at once instead of one after the other.

"It is true," Lord Aldon replied mercilessly. "I was given a transcript of that conversation, and also of another one between your son and Lady Eryn where he asks her for assistance to speak on behalf of himself and his friends on the Council."

Damned, bloody stupid spies! Eryn fumed silently. They were everywhere! How had that one managed to eavesdrop - they had been on the first floor and surely somebody would have noticed a stranger pressing his ear against the door out in the corridor. It was like living in a glass box! How she hated these juvenile games, this hidden hunt for information that could be used as a weapon at the right moment!

She caught Enric's warning look and exhaled slowly. The mind bond had given her away once more.

The Council hall had become eerily silent while the magicians considered the importance of what they had just heard. She glanced at the King, but he was the epitome of calmness and serenity, as always. The perpetual question of whether he had known about this before or was simply an exceptional actor to hide his surprise that well arose once more. She thought back to how he looked at her when he had arrived here and wondered if he had indeed been aware of these facts and had worried about the trouble they might cause if they were brought up. Did he look slightly reconciled or was that just her imagination?

Eryn leaned against a column at her back, not caring any longer if the formal and sophisticated impression she was supposed to be making suffered from this or not. Many of those in the room doubtlessly now thought that she had been plotting something against the Order, even if not necessarily Tyront's death. Funny how the initial objective of determining whether Darnet was mentally ill seemed to have faded into the background somehow.

Lord Poron seemed to have arrived at the same conclusion, because as a loud murmuring suddenly erupted, he arose and clapped his hands three times, enhancing the sound until it rolled through the hall like thunder that was reflected off the walls and the high domed ceiling to be thrown back at them and increase the unnerving effect.

"My Lords," he then said when the noise of both the murmuring and his claps had died down, "let us not forget why we are here today. Our task for this day is to determine whether Lady Eryn had a part in the assassination attempt on Lord Tyront. This is what we need to decide. I see why Lady Eryn's meeting a man of a group that many of us may consider an underground resistance within the Order may cast her in a bad light, yet let me assure you that I also possess a transcript of the conversation between Lady Eryn and Onil that Lord Aldon referred to." The old man smiled briefly at Eryn's disbelieving expression, before he continued, "And I am more than willing to let you have a look at it, even to compare it to Lord Aldon's version, if he cares to release his copy. You will see that Onil's very natural request for help from a like-minded Council member was not met with particular enthusiasm, which will doubtlessly surprise a few of you as you prefer to consider Lady Eryn as a trap that might spring any moment and cause the Order to crumble into nothingness. I myself do not share that belief in her powers of potentially causing havoc and destruction, but that is just a personal note from a man who has had the privilege to work with Lady Eryn for some time now." And whose assessment should as a result weigh more than the words of men who have merely known her from Council meetings and a few social evening occasions, he very pointedly didn't add. He sat down again and picked up a few sheets of paper in front of him, pretending to peruse them for a moment, before he said, "If there are any more questions you wish to ask Iklan with regard to Darnet's condition, then please do so now."

Silence. When nobody had spoken for more than a minute, Lord Poron nodded. "Excellent. I take it that you now possess all the information you consider necessary for making your informed decision. I am aware that the results of Iklan's assessment might not quite seem as unequivocal as you would wish, but consider that Iklan is a very attentive man who doesn't carelessly profess facts he is unable to back up with proof. And furthermore, please take into consideration that the nature of this case makes proving the medical evidence more difficult than the diagnosis of something such as a broken bone. As a healer I can tell you that the very same thing does not always appear the same when two different patients are concerned. This has nothing to do with any shortcomings as regards the expert, nor does it make his assessment any less credible when the conclusion has been reached with care and can be backed up with ample experience as is clearly the case here." He allowed himself a thin smile. "Our new friends in the Western Territories wouldn't have risked embarrassing themselves by sending anyone but the best person they had for this task."

A surge of warm gratitude at these words almost made Eryn's knees buckle and she straightened them with determination to avoid exactly that. Lord Poron, who had his own spies following her to use the information gathered as a shield against what others had collected to cause her trouble; who used his influence in the Council and his knowledge of how to handle his colleagues to aid her. He was the right choice for the position of Head of her clinic. The thought arrived slowly and slipped into place with a finality like the last cobblestone completing a new street. She had known before that he was an able man, but there had always been the feeling that she herself could have handled the responsibility a little better. That feeling was suddenly gone, and with it the resentment that she had not been allowed to take over the clinic. It was in good hands with Lord Poron, and so were all those who worked for and with him. He wouldn't just stand and observe when one of his healers was in trouble, but step in. This was why he had treated Onil's asking her for help in the Council as the most natural and logical thing in the world, why he backed Iklan up and made it clear that doubting the foreign healer meant also disrespecting Lord Poron's good opinion of him, which equalled a challenge. And she, Eryn, was one of his healers, one of those he looked after, regardless of the fact that in the Order structure she outranked him.

"Let us bring this case to its conclusion, then," Lord Poron instructed. "Show of hands if you determine Lady Eryn sufficiently cleared so that she may return into our midst."

She exhaled audibly with relief and then smiled wearily when out of twelve hands ten were raised, only Lords Aldon and Woldarn kept theirs down. Lord Aldon remained with his arms folded and staring sullenly at the table in front of him. Lord Woldarn glared at Eryn as if he was blaming her for the trouble his son was in.

Eryn felt how worry pushed aside her sense of relief, worry about what Onil would have to face later - especially as Lord Woldarn now had a very clear idea why his son had persuaded him to lower the asking price for the house he sold Enric.

* * *

Enric fought the impulse to lean back in his chair and breathe a deep sigh of relief. It wouldn't do to show his colleagues or the King that he had been rather apprehensive towards the end of the hearing when the matter of Onil had been brought up by Lord Aldon. Ideally the Council members would all have voted in Eryn's favour to clear her of any doubt whatsoever, but he knew that these were fanciful hopes. There were not many occasions where the Council had decided unanimously, and considering that many still were wary of Eryn and the changes she had brought so far - as well as those his colleagues suspected or even feared she might bring about in the future - ten out of twelve votes to exonerate her from the accusations was still a clear sign that the majority considered her innocent. He seriously wondered if old Lord Aldon genuinely believed her to be involved in the attempt at Tyront's life or whether he simply wanted to blemish her reputation. And a blemish it would be - she had, after all, not been cleared beyond any doubt or the vote would have been unanimous. At least that's what the public would hear.

In case of Lord Woldarn, who was not usually one Enric would expect to side with a minority, it was fairly obvious what must have been the reason for this blatant display of disfavour. He was known to be a family man, which was in his case both an endearing quality and a curse. Being related to him meant that he was blind to his family members' faults to a degree that at times even appeared preposterous. And now his only son had been accused not only of being a member of what more suspicious people would now dramatically refer to as the resistance, but also seeking help to influence the Council of which Lord Woldarn himself was a member. Enric wasn't completely sure whether or not the Lord believed that Onil truly was to blame for such actions, but one thing was beyond dispute - no matter if he thought his son capable of such a thing or considered him a cog in another party's evil plan to discredit him, Eryn was in his eyes the one at fault for it. That much was evident from the way Lord Woldarn glared at her with lips pressed into a thin line.

He rose with the other magicians when Tyront repeated what the majority of the Council members had agreed on and congratulated Eryn, who nodded gracefully in acceptance of his words.

Enric smiled faintly. He could feel the relief through their bond, but there was also a very faint hint of irritation. Probably at the thought of from having to join the Council meetings again now, if he was any judge.

His eyes came to rest on Lord Seagon, who moved slowly as if to give his colleagues time to leave the Council hall. His casual stroll brought him closer to Eryn. It appeared as if he wanted to have a word with her.

Eryn accepted Orrin's hearty slap on the back, but gritted her teeth. It was kind of him not to discriminate against her on account of her being the only woman in the Order and treating her as if she could take just as much as his male colleagues, but at times she really wished he would make allowances for her being less sturdy physically. Receiving what was to him a friendly tap felt like what she imagined being struck by a small horse had to be.

From the corner of her eye she saw another figure moving towards her and turned her head to look at Lord Seagon, who met her gaze and stopped with his hands linked before him.

Enric approached behind him, his expression blank, but not unreadable to her. He wanted to make sure there wouldn't be any nastiness between them and was determined to be assertive to prevent such a thing.

"Orrin, why don't you go ahead and tell Junar about the outcome of the case? She must be worried. Come and have dinner with us at our house tonight, will you?"

The warrior cast a sceptical glance at Lord Seagon, but visibly relaxed when he spotted Enric not far off. Then he nodded and turned to leave.

When the hall was empty but for the three of them, Eryn approached Lord Seagon. She couldn't read his expression very well; it seemed to her as if he was conflicted about something. Maybe he already regretted voting in her favour despite his better judgement of what he probably considered a flawed character? She decided not to thank him for it and risk a harsh reply.

She stopped a few paces away from him and watched how Enric came to a halt as well. He simply leaned against the oval table, looking unconcerned as if he just happened to find himself there and had decided to use this very pleasant ambiance for his own enjoyment. If Lord Seagon noticed him, he either didn't dare object to his superior's presence or actually didn't mind.

The Lord took another few steps towards her and halted as soon as he was within a comfortable distance that would enable them to converse without raising their voices yet maintain separation.

"I never was a great supporter of the idea of admitting you to the Order," he started with words that were not friendly as such but mitigated by the calm tone they were delivered in.

You don't say, she thought sarcastically, I would never have guessed. She saw a similar thought reflected on Enric's face. He even rolled his eyes. It was a good thing Lord Seagon was standing with his back to him.

Eryn didn't comment on that, but waited. There was clearly more to come.

"I admit that I was surprised at your answers when I asked you those questions under the influence of the truth block that day. They seemed out of line with the picture I had of you." He narrowed his eyes. "I don't like to be wrong about the way I judge people. It makes me question my own ability to assess a person's character. I normally pride myself on being rather accurate in that regard. Which is to say your answers made me think. The result of my deliberations was that my assessment of you is mainly based on a single incident: your behaviour at the ball where your companion ended up breaking my nephew's nose."

That wasn't new or unexpected for Eryn, either. She worked hard at keeping her mouth shut. There were two ways of exercising power in a conversation. One was to be the one asking the questions and thus determining the course, and the other was to be the one to say nothing at all and let the other person struggle to fill an uncomfortable silence.

Lord Seagon looked at her, probably waiting for her to start justifying herself. She wouldn't do him the favour. Defending herself would do nothing more than give him the impression that she thought she had done something wrong. She returned his gaze steadily and raised her brow only a little, as if patiently waiting for him to finally come to the point.

There was just a hint of a frown visible between his eyebrows when he asked after several moments, "Why did you dye your hair that evening?"

Eryn tilted her head slightly. "Why do you think I did?"

"I had my suspicions. But they do no longer fit my impressions."

"These suspicions... they do not happen to be along the lines of my attempting to make my companion jealous by luring some unfortunate man, who just so happened to be your nephew, into a dance with me and subsequently encouraging him to take more liberties with me than was discreet? And that I cared little about whatever consequences this poor man would have to endure when angering Enric?"

She saw Enric smile to himself. Back then she had accused him of making people think that very thing about her when he had punched her dancing partner in the face after he had been a little too free with his... physical attentions.

Lord Seagon hesitated briefly, then nodded. "Yes, exactly that. But as I said, these assumptions no longer conform to the picture your answers to my questions provided about you." His tone became gentler. "I would be very interested in that answer, Lady Eryn. Why did you change your hair colour and make yourself unrecognisable to most people around you?"

Eryn smiled tiredly. "I'm not sure if my answer will give you a more favourable impression of me than the one you had before. I didn't do it to make Enric jealous, but for a more harmless reason: I was tired from being asked to dance time and again and decided to hide rather than reject invitations to dance. I was not so much devious than selfish, which is probably not much of an improvement. I was new in that role of important Order magician and had no idea who the people around me were and who I would inadvertently insult by rejecting a dance, so I thought that being blonde for a little while would save me some amount of trouble."

The Lord pondered her words with pursed lips. "Quite a misconception, I can't help but observe. But probably an understandable one considering your rural upbringing," he granted her graciously.

Eryn just looked at him blandly to let him know that she didn't appreciate being patronised in this way. She didn't need his permission for being thoughtless; it wasn't as if she wasn't the one to pay the price for it every time she misjudged a situation and chose the wrong approach.

Lord Seagon cleared his throat before asking, "Why did Lord Enric see fit to lay hands on my nephew in such a manner? He didn't object to your dancing with other men."

Eryn cast a quick look at her companion to see if he wanted to answer that question himself, but he just flashed her an encouraging little smile, obviously content with watching her handling this conversation so well on her own. Perfectly charming.

"Because I'm afraid your nephew disregarded any gentlemanly behaviour and took more liberties than I was willing to grant. Lord Enric intervened in a rather more violent manner than I would have wished. Unfortunately he did so before I could simply walk away from my dance partner. I was hesitant to do so as it would have caused him embarrassment to be seen being discarded in such a way. I regret that this dithering on my side caused him even greater embarrassment in the end. The fact that Ambassador Ram'an was close enough to witness this incident was another convenient consideration for my companion."

Lord Seagon raised both eyebrows and for the first time turned his head to look at Enric for a few moments. It was an appraising look, one that also conveyed respect for a point well made.

Eryn sighed deep inside. Politicians. You punched my nephew in the face? Well, as long as you had a good reason for it that I can relate to, there are no hurt feelings whatsoever, what, old chap?

"I see," the older man finally said and turned back to her. "I thank you for enlightening me with regard to this incident." He gave a short bow first to her, then to Enric before he turned to leave. At the double doors he stopped and turned back to look at her. "I'm glad the case between you and Darnet was resolved in such a satisfactory manner. I will not be sorry to see you again at the next Council meeting." With that he stepped outside into the corridors and closed the door behind him.

Enric pushed himself away from the table and strolled towards her. "Well, well, well, look at that," he said smugly. "There's another one you managed to win over, Lady Eryn."

She sighed and rubbed her face. "Yes, and it took me only what, two years? And in exchange for Lord Seagon's no longer hating me, I now have Lord Woldarn against me, because he probably thinks that I have corrupted his son somehow."

He pulled her closer to put his arm around her shoulders and guide her towards the exit. "True, but Lord Seagon's dislike and mistrust was based on false information that could be rectified, while in Lord Woldarn's case we are talking about a fondness for his family that causes short-sightedness and a failure to think clearly. That is not something you can set right. I would rather have the ignorant instead of the smart against me - so exchanging Lord Woldarn's goodwill against Lord Seagon's was definitely a step up."

Eryn chuckled and shook her head. "What a heartless thing to say. How am I to learn to respect the Council members when you tell me that you consider them stupid?"

Enric waved dismissively. "I don't generally consider them stupid, only some of them on certain occasions. And when Lord Woldarn's family is involved, you may be sure that there is no talking to him sensibly. This is just something to be prepared for when dealing with him in a case such as this."

She grimaced. "This is like dealing with a bunch of adolescents. Aren't those high and mighty people supposed to be more mature and think before they act or pass judgement? What environment is this to raise our son in, I ask you?"

Enric sighed. "You know, with Tyront as a substitute grandfather, the King as his guardian and Vran'el grooming him to be his successor while Malriel keeps looking for a way to get him into House Aren, a few bickering aristocrats seem harmless in comparison."

Eryn swallowed. When he put it like that, it really did sound intimidating. That boy would probably one day either go crazy or outsmart them all.

They reached the doors and stepped outside into the corridor, whereupon Tyront lifted his head as they emerged. So he had been waiting for them for some reason. She couldn't help but notice that the two guards seemed somewhat less tense now that they were no longer alone with the Order's imposing leader. She could empathise with them about that - she remembered how uneasy she had felt before and quite a while after joining the Order whenever she had been in the same room with him without Enric's being around.

They walked on silently, following the corridor until they were out of both sight and earshot of the guards. The magicians had in the meantime all left the vicinity, so they were the only ones around.

"I assume Lord Seagon wanted to tell you that he graciously forgives you his nephew's broken nose? You seem to have impressed him enough to induce him to vote in your favour even," Tyront asked conversationally.

Eryn smiled. So it was curiosity that had made him decide to stay and wait for them. How nice to see that even high and mighty people like him gave in to small weaknesses such as that sometimes.

"Well, he decided to consider me redeemed when I told him that my intentions at that ball back then were not to drive Enric mad but to hide and avoid being asked to dance."

Tyront nodded. "That fits. He may be a traditionalist and fight against new ideas that endanger what he is used to, but he adapts in the end if the changes turn out to be justified and workable. And so far having you in the Order has worked as well as we could have wished for."

She lifted an eyebrow at the unexpected compliment. "Has it now? Despite my frequent stable cleaning assignments?"

Her superior chuckled. "I admit that there might initially have been a few... adaptive difficulties. But it has been a while now since such corrective measures were necessary."

"Yes, I suppose the fact that you lot sent me to another country for months at a time may have helped to reduce the occasions for friction as well," she commented. "Who knows whether the Council would otherwise have voted in my favour today."

Tyront pressed his lips together. "I would have preferred to have a unanimous vote, yet that was probably a bit much to hope for. Your innocence may not have been proofed beyond a doubt with two members standing against you, but at least to a degree that allows you to return to the Council and hold on to your rank uncontested. A narrow result in your favour would have been far more damaging, so I suppose we should be grateful that it ended the way it did."

Eryn thought back to the meeting several minutes ago and shook her head. "I was more than a little surprised at Lord Poron, though I suppose I shouldn't have been - considering that he has been holding a high rank for what must be a very long time. Yet he has always been so friendly and seemed so bookish and harmless in his dealings with me, so innocent in his curiosity for the field of healing, so sweet in his happiness when he discovered a new and fascinating aspect of an illness. Seeing him today showed me that I'm certainly not born for that political swamp, neither the one here nor in Takhan, as I underestimated him so considerably that I'm wondering if I had my eyes closed all this time. I mean, he set spies on me even while I saw him as little more than a harmless old man!"

Both men laughed at that. Tyront was the one to remark, "What did you expect? Lord Poron has been around longer than most others in the Council, he was an experienced politician before I was even tested. He had been third in command for twenty years before my predecessor died resulting in my ascent to the top after holding Enric's current position for only a few years. He has seen plenty in these last five decades, and even King Folrin's father was careful not to put him off if it could be avoided. After Enric's rise to the position as my second, Lord Poron mostly withdrew from the power games both within and outside the Council, but not enough to be unable to return at some time and be a formidable opponent when he considers it necessary, as you witnessed today. Taking over the library didn't mean that he only guarded old knowledge, he was and also still is an avid collector of more current information - with the aid of spies, if need be."

Eryn nodded slowly. "Then I had better be sure to always keep him on my side."

Enric squeezed her hand. "I don't see him siding against you in the future. He was very open about supporting you today, which might have induced one or two of the more sceptical Council members to reconsider voting against you. Several of them were taught by him many years ago. And there is something about having to face a former teacher that reminds us of the children we once were."

She grinned. "Is that what you feel when dealing with Orrin?"

He wagged his head. "I admit it was something I was still fighting until you came along. From then on my interactions with him increased in frequency quite a lot, which led to my getting to know him better in a different capacity. This enabled me to leave this old hate-love relationship we'd had for quite a while behind me."

"That means I helped you grow up?" she laughed.

"I wouldn't go quite that far," he replied and glanced at Tyront, who followed the conversation with evident amusement. "When do you plan to call for the next Council meeting? We need to decide what is to be done with Darnet. Whether his medical condition allows for him to be given the same punishment as a sane person who had committed the same act. And if not, what else can be done. Are we to treat him or lock him up?"

The Order's leader nodded, his expression now serious. "Yes, that is something to be taken care of, and soon. I first want to talk to Iklan and hear what he has to say on that, ask him how they handle such things in the Western Territories. The concept of identifying a mental illness quite so accurately is new to us and we have yet to reach a decision on how to deal with the consequences. Iklan informed me that he wishes to leave soon after this whole case with Eryn has been brought to an end one way or another, so I will ask him to meet me today or tomorrow. As soon as I have the information I need, I'll call for a meeting. It might be necessary to contact the Senate in Takhan as well, so I can't tell you if it will take place in two days or only in one week at the moment."

Enric nodded. "Is there anything we can do in the meantime?"

Tyront sighed. "Yes, I want you to think about the situation with Onil. For all the Council - and no doubt soon enough everyone else - knows, he might be the leader of a group of people bent on rebellion. No matter whether this is the case, this is bound to cause some trouble. Eryn, I want you to warn him to avoid being both out in public or at home on his own for the next few weeks. And he should avoid joining any gatherings of whatever nature right now. After today he will have quite a number of spies tailing him and watching his every move, so he had better avoid doing anything that might appear suspicious in any way. You might encourage him to move back in with his parents for the time being. Irrespective of whether Lord Woldarn considers his son the victim of slander and thereby innocent, or thinks he might actually be involved in something, he will need his son where he can keep an eye on him. This is surely not the most pleasant thing Onil can imagine right now, but it's in his own interest not to make himself an easy target. One never knows who else thinks they can keep the Order safe by killing off a magician they consider a threat."

Eryn swallowed. "I'll make a detour on my way home and talk to him at the clinic. I'm fairly sure that he is on duty today." Worry made her increase her pace slightly. She had expected the relief over her acquittal to last longer than this. It somehow felt as if the trouble had not ended today, but was only about to start.

CHAPTER 29

Taking Heart

Eryn dressed the gurgling baby lying on the carpet in the parlour with practised moves. He had only recently started sleeping through the whole night, and even though he still woke a lot earlier in the morning than Eryn would have preferred, she certainly wanted that over getting up during the night. He expressed a squeal of delight when she handed him a wooden cooking spoon and his fingers closed around it. Just like most things these days, one end was moved towards his mouth to be examined with lips and tongue while Eryn pulled the small pants over his nappy. They had just finished breakfast, and with every passing day Vedric became more eager to participate actively in the process instead of just watching others doing the fun part without him.

Junar had advised her to switch to more solid food now for that very purpose, just as she had done with little Téa a few months ago. They could already use their gums to masticate certain types of food, such as soft fruits, vegetables and bread, and the main benefit for the one doing the feeding or rather assisting the infant to feed themselves was that the mess was less tedious to clean up. Eryn at times now even managed to get through a meal without having to change her own clothes afterwards.

She smiled when Vedric kicked around wildly while waving his spoon through the air. In her eyes he was gorgeous, and she wondered if others saw it, too, or if this was a mother-child fascination. Certainly, there were the usual compliments, but hardly anybody would tell a parent that they thought their child was ugly or simply average at best. For her he was the most beautiful little boy in the world, and the explorer in her wondered if the reason for this was that all these hormones in her body had made her soft in the head or that Vedric resembled his father so much. He had definitely inherited her brown eyes and, judging from the dark fuzz on his head, also her hair colour, though his features were still those of the man she had come to love more than she had ever thought possible.

"Enric?" she called out and waited until he appeared from his study. "I'm about to leave for work. Can you take your son now?"

He nodded and walked closer, squatting in front of the boy on the carpet and tickling his belly, which elicited a contented chortle from the baby.

"Tyront sent a message, by the way. The next Council meeting will take place tomorrow."

She grimaced. "So soon? That is rather short notice," she said reproachfully.

"I know. But he has received word from Takhan and doesn't want to keep Iklan and Sarol waiting any longer than necessary. They are eager to return home. As they are each an expert in their field, they are both sorely missed by both their patients and colleagues. Are you at the clinic tomorrow as well? You don't normally work two subsequent days there."

"No, not usually, but Onil needs a day off tomorrow. He agreed to moving back in with his parents for the moment and will take care of this tomorrow."

Enric nodded. "A sensible decision. How is he doing?"

Eryn shrugged. "As good as can be expected under the circumstances. He didn't really want to talk about what happened between him and his father, but he did not appear as much traumatised as resigned the last time I saw him." She shook her head. "Those damned spies! If it were up to me, I would prohibit them from the Kingdom altogether. They just cause too much trouble."

He shook his head and picked up his son, narrowly avoiding the spoon that was wielded dangerously close to his temple. "The spies are not the problem, my love. It's those who send them after you. And as a magician you have more ways to avoid being overheard. This should teach you to be more careful and raise a shield when you want a conversation to be private. You have been terribly neglectful in this regard considering that you are aware that fairly much everyone who is important and can afford to pay them uses agents."

She flashed him a resentful look. It was always the same with him. When she just wanted to vent her frustration and complain about something, he ended up telling her how this was basically her own fault for not taking countermeasures. Sometimes it would be a change just to have a sympathetic listener who nodded at whatever she said. But that was not like him, was it? His position required him to find solutions to problems, and fast. People didn't come to the formidable Lord Enric to pour out their heart to him. He wasn't used to anything like that and just reacted the way that was now the most natural one for him: listening, analysing and finally presenting his solution for the issue.

Eryn kissed both of them goodbye and was quickly on her way to the clinic. It was probably time to have an evening with Junar. She was sympathetic, as long as her own views didn't happen to oppose Eryn's. And maybe she would even invite Pe'tala to join them. Her sister, too, was somebody who appreciated the chance to complain thoroughly when something didn't go her way and granted others the same privilege. She smiled at the thought. They would just send Orrin and Enric off with their children and enjoy a grown-up evening without any unnecessary analytical male input.

The clinic doors were still closed, yet a number of patients had already gathered in front of them out on the chilly street. They bowed their heads when they recognised her and stepped aside to make way for her.

Lebern opened the door at her knock and pointed his thumb upstairs. "There is a man waiting for you in Pe'tala's study."

She stopped. "What man?"

He shrugged. "I don't know. Blond hair, solid build..."

Eryn snorted. "Very funny. Blond hair excludes precisely three men in this country right now."

"He looks familiar, I might have seen him somewhere before, but I'm not sure," her colleague told her. "As Lord Poron is already in and Pe'tala doesn't work today, I sent him to her study to wait for you."

"Very well, I'll get myself a drink and then see him. That means that you'll have to handle the patients alone for now."

Lebern waved her on. "No problem, it doesn't look quite as crowded outside today. I'll somehow manage without you for a time."

She nodded and went to the small kitchen to stir a spoonful of herbal powder in with a cup of magically-heated water before proceeding upstairs and to Pe'tala's study. When Lord Poron had taken over her position as well as her study, Rolan had tried to make her chose another one for herself, but she had declined. It was meant as little more than a status symbol, and she was not a great friend of those. Without the responsibility of leading the healing services or taking care of any other areas related to administration, it didn't make sense for her to have her own room here. None of the other regular healers had, and she was nothing more than that right now. Even less, considering that she had not only reduced her working hours that much, but also spent half of every year away from the clinic in another country, at another clinic.

She decided against knocking. This was her building, after all, and whoever wanted to see her without even bothering to make an appointment with her was not entitled to such courtesy.

After pushing open the door and laying eyes on the man in front of the window, she almost let fall her cup, barely managing to hold on to the handle. He stood with his back to her, but she recognised him right away. It was the same stance he at times adopted when she was summoned to the throne room.

King Folrin turned slowly and looked her over in her working clothes. She saw why Lebern had failed to recognise him despite his having seen him occasionally in the past at balls and other official occasions such as banquets, executions and the like. Eryn herself had seem him dressed like this only once before - when he had made her fight him in one of the Palace courtyards the day he had kissed her. The memory made her uneasy.

Lebern was right, he was well built - something his normal, considerably more ornate attire managed to conceal effectively. His broad shoulders narrowed to a slim waist, both accentuated by the simple and tightly fitting clothes. The hair he usually wore bound in a ponytail hung open over his shoulders, curling into blond ringlets at the tips.

She swallowed and wondered how she was supposed to treat him now. Bow? He clearly didn't want to be recognised and would thus probably not want any spies to know that he was here. As Lord Aldon and Lord Poron both had made her realise, they were everywhere.

The King smiled briefly at her surprised expression and then motioned with his index finger. He painted into the air something that looked like a half circle, rolling his eyes when she didn't immediately comprehend what he wanted her to do. He pointed first to his ears, then repeated the half circle.

Only then she realised what he was asking of her and raised a soundproof barrier around them, making it large enough to not only provide enough air for a while but also to allow them some space for moving around without having to get too close to each other.

"Your Majesty," she then said and put her cup down on the desk. She had decided against bowing. He had come to her place incognito, so he would have to deal with not being treated with the usual reverence his official surroundings entitled him to.

"Lady Eryn," he replied and rounded the table to then lean against its edge instead of taking a seat on one of the three chairs. Fabulous - that meant that she, too, would have to remain standing. Or would she? By coming here like that he kind of agreed to a less formal setting, didn't he? She decided to put that to the test and went to a chair next to him to take a seat.

He followed her moves and didn't show any irritation whatsoever with her casual conduct.

"What can I do for you on this dull and rainy morning?" she asked lightly, slightly worried that he had taken the trouble of coming here instead of summoning her as usual. Did that mean whatever he wanted was so urgent that it couldn't even bear the delay that sending a messenger to her and waiting for her to come to him meant? Or was he just after making her nervous now that she had finally managed to become more relaxed in his presence?

His demeanour seemed unhurried, he was at ease, so it was probably the second.

"I was thinking that it might be advisable to have a small talk with you, my dear Lady, after what happened at the Council meeting a few days ago," he replied.

Eryn leaned back. Ah yes, so he probably wanted to favour her with another of his little lessons in political strategy. She thought for a moment and then decided that this was actually not such a bad thing.

There was this underlying tension, this feeling of foreboding she felt and that she could not put a finger on, as if disaster was about to befall them. He was a smart man with ample knowledge about virtually everything that was going on in the city and probably even most of what was happening in the Kingdom at large. If he was willing to share, she could only benefit from it.

"I share Lord Tyront's assessment of the Council's decision: even though you were acquitted, a unanimous decision would have been more desirable in this particular instance. Of course it could have ended up a lot worse. The chance of the majority's considering you guilty were rather small, with four of them so unequivocally on your side, so that never really was a realistic likelihood. Yet two of them distrusting you so significantly was not a good development. They should have cleared you beyond any doubt. This will not only leave you with a slight stigma against your name, but also cause some tension in the Council in the years to come, you can mark my words."

She nodded slowly and took a sip from her cup before saying, "And this will not be a good thing, considering that the Council needs to demonstrate unity in the face of the challenges that we might have to face soon."

King Folrin smiled. "Quite so. Unity is strength, and with several magicians resenting the way the Order limits their freedom, strength is of utmost importance. Discord is weakness, not only because most things that happen in the Council become known to outsiders sooner or later and as a result this is a matter of how it is perceived from the outside. Another area of concern is that this weakness may keep the Council from making much needed decisions. Politics, as I am sure I don't have to remind you, is a complicated game of balance. Some of the Council members who voted in your favour need to find ways to demonstrate to their allies Lord Aldon and Lord Woldarn that they are still in league with them, they need to make up for having been on the other side. There are business interests involved as well in the background. This means that whatever you or those known to stand with you will try to accomplish in the Council is likely to meet with quite some resistance in the near future."

Eryn closed her eyes for a moment. She didn't want this to be true, but the chances of his being wrong were rather slim.

"The trouble is," he went on, "that I need the Order to return to its former stability which will require changes. Changes I need you to suggest and promote. Unfortunately, I can't be seen to be supporting you too openly or too frequently, no matter how much I would like to do just that. This would cause me to antagonise several of the Council members, even more than I do with some of them already."

She stared at the ceiling for a moment. "So no Royal recommendations to support any of my motions. That's what you are telling me before I am able to think of requesting just that from you."

He nodded and there was genuine regret in his voice when he replied, "Yes, this is exactly what I'm telling you. And I'm both angry and sorry that these injudicious games stand in the way of progress that should benefit us all."

She looked up into his face, surprised at the uncharacteristic frustration in his words. He had always seemed to enjoy his intrigues and underhand manoeuvres, outsmarting the other players in what he liked to consider a game. But now he looked tired and grim, an expression she had never before seen on his face. It both worried her and made him appear more human to her.

She stilled when he pushed away from the desk and crouched down in front of her chair, his blue-grey eyes determined. "I need you finally to start applying what you have been taught since you joined the Order. I need you to employ political strategies to reach your goals. I know you can do it, that it is simply your reluctance that is holding you back. Your dealings with Malriel showed clearly that you are a formidable opponent if only your motivation is great enough. I need you to find the motivation to either win over, entice, threaten or otherwise make the Council members cooperate with you. And whatever non-official support you may require for this I am more than willing, eager even, to provide." He took her hand and pressed his lips to her knuckles before he got to his feet again. "I am counting on you here."

With that he turned and walked out, and a moment later she was alone in the study, wondering if this had truly just happened or whether she had also acquired herself an elaborate set of hallucinations that gave her a feeling of being more important than she truly was.

She got up quickly and stepped towards the window that overlooked the street in front of the building. A little later the King emerged from the door and walked out, with not a single head turning in his direction nor any finger pointing at the Monarch walking through the city in plain clothes.

* * *

Enric bent forward on the blanket on the parlour floor to retrieve his son's stuffed animal, the one his aunt Pe'tala had given him and that he had just flung aside unintentionally judging from his unhappy expression, one that generally preceded a loud wail. He pressed the toy sporting one dripping wet ear - that usually landed in Vedric's mouth as the size and form were just perfect for that - back into the baby boy's hands and sighed with relief. He had managed to avoid the outbreak of ear-splitting misery in the nick of time.

When he was about to lean back again and reach for his book, the door opened and Eryn walked in, looking tired but glad to be home after a long day of work. It had been dark outside for a while now, so it seemed that the cold season helped ensure that the healers were not out of work anytime soon.

Enric watched how she unfastened her cloak and hung it. Underneath she was still wearing her working clothes, he noted with satisfaction. He wouldn't have wanted to revisit the subject of her changing into or out of them with her male colleagues around now that she had given up her study at the clinic which had afforded her the privacy Enric insisted she needed.

He lifted his face for her as she bent down to kiss his mouth, before she plopped down on the blanket next to them and reached for her son, lifting him into her arms. Vedric's eyes widened and he started kicking and waiving his hands in felicitous excitement at the sight of his mother.

"Good evening, boys," Eryn cooed. "How did your day without me go? Any major catastrophes while I was gone?" she said, seemingly addressing the boy.

"Nothing whatever," Enric replied and wondered if he should let her relax for a bit before asking her about her day. He decided against it and instead gave in to his curiosity. "What did the King want from you?"

Eryn's brow shot up in astonishment, then her eyes narrowed. "How can you possibly know about that? He came in plain clothes, and I'm sure nobody recognised him. I even watched how he went along the street as if he were nobody of great importance and people just passed him by! You said you don't have me watched - so explain yourself!"

"I don't have you watched. But I've been having the King watched ever since he got too close to you while I was away. It's true, he has this uncanny ability more or less to shed his Royal identity and walk the city without being recognised - despite the fact that his face is on every single gold piece. My agents are prepared for this, however. He does it frequently, so they know who to be on the lookout for."

She closed her eyes for a moment before she slowly said, "You genuinely and in actual fact set spies on the King? What makes you think that's such a bright idea? He is incredibly sharp, there is a good chance he already knows it!"

Enric smiled. "But of course he does. And that's just as well. Sometimes the knowledge that we are being watched helps us to remember what kind of behaviour is expected of us. Or rather which one isn't. If he really doesn't want to be followed, he just shakes the agents off. Which he hasn't done today, so he had no objections to my knowing that he went to see you. It seems, though, that you raised a soundproof barrier this time. This is, of course, commendable as it shows that you are starting to see the merits of caution. Yet it is hugely inconvenient for me, as I now had to wait for you to come home and tell me about it and I furthermore need to trust you to tell me all there was to tell." He watched her for a moment and then ventured, "But on second thoughts it might not have been your idea to raise the barrier. The King is definitely a lot more careful in this regard, whereas you are not." He didn't need her to confirm it, he saw that he was right when he observed her grumpy expression.

"He wanted to tell me that I need to prepare myself for being opposed in the Council, in even greater numbers than before, since some of the magicians who voted in my favour will want to cosy up to Lord Aldon and Lord Woldarn again," she explained without deigning to comment on his guess with the barrier. "He furthermore implored me to finally deploy my underutilised skills of manipulation, issuing threats and scheming in order to make the Council do what I want, or rather what the King thinks needs to be done."

Enric's expression was serious when he nodded. "He is becoming jumpy. The situation is developing, and the Council is too slow to react to it. He is already seeing the Order disintegrate, which is not something he can afford to happen. He has been on the throne for about five years, and right now it looks like the history books may one day refer to him as the King under whose reign the Order fell apart after centuries of stability."

"You think this is about vanity?" Eryn asked and furrowed her brow. This somehow didn't fit her picture of him.

"No, certainly not to a major degree, though it might be somewhere in there as well. If the Order truly split up, fell apart or otherwise turned into something different than one central organisation governing magicians, this would cost him a lot of influence. The leader of the Order together with the Council take over the task of keeping the magicians under control - something he as a non-magician would otherwise hardly be able to accomplish very easily. This is why the King needs to maintain good connections with the Order's leaders without leaving the population in any doubt as to who is ultimately in charge. This, for Royal rulers over these last centuries, has always been a question of preserving a sensitive balance between granting us power and making sure we don't become too influential for our own good and certainly their good as well."

She absentmindedly picked up the stuffed brown bear to put it back Vedric's flailing hand. "Why does he approach me with this? Why not come to you or Tyront? He surely knows that you are both aware that things need to change. You are experienced politicians, and the Council members at least respect you even if not all of them are on your side. Why me? If given the choice, I would leave the Order without even thinking about it."

Her companion smiled at that. "Firstly, because he trusts you more than either me or Tyront exactly because of that fact - you are not an experienced politician. And secondly he counts on the fact that your being stuck in the Order presents a greater motivation for you to transform it into something different, something you would actually want to be a part of."

"That's reassuring," she snorted. "Now I'm not only his toy, but also his tool."

"You are nobody's toy, my love," Enric said seriously. "And you are only as much a tool as you agree to be, as much as it suits you. He wants you to make changes you would have promoted anyway, so you are not acting against your own conscience here. Don't let the fact that he wants you to do it make you consider it a bad idea as such. I agree that you are probably the person most likely to succeed. You are brave enough to try and are not worried about preserving traditions you were all your life told were important and needed to be upheld. Every single one of the Council members was brought up with that belief and even I sometimes struggle with it despite the fact that I'm at least fifteen years younger than each of them."

"I don't even know where to start! If I suggested that the Order grants its members more freedom when it comes to choosing where they want to live or what profession to pursue, most of the Council members would either laugh at me or kick me out of the hall!"

"Well, then, I suggest you paint them a picture of what the alternative would be in the long run. I remember that you tried that once before already when you suggested establishing Heads for the disciplines of healing and warrior skills."

She groaned at the memory. They had agreed to that proposal eventually, but only after her second attempt. The first one had earned her stable duty. Once more. And then they had made Lord Poron Head of Healers instead of her, and Vern had needed to sedate her to stop her from going to pieces right in front of the Council and the King.

"Yes, I remember very well how great that worked back then..."

Enric shrugged. "You were off to a good start until you inadvertently started insulting our colleagues and also me, strictly speaking. That was quite a while ago, and I'm confident that you won't make the same mistakes again. Then with Tyront, Orrin, Lord Poron and me you already have four votes in your favour, five if we count yours. That means only two more are missing for whatever you want to make happen. Lord Seagon has only recently discovered that you are not quite as unscrupulous as he thought, and he likes me because I'm cunning. Him you will be able to convince with facts. And then there is another target I would suggest concentrating on: Lord Remdel, Inad's companion. Despite your contempt for her, Inad likes you. She is furthermore known to be the more dominant force in that companionship, so she is a fairly reliable conduit for making Lord Remdel compliant."

Eryn looked at him and then flinched when she felt a hearty tug at her braid when Vedric discarded his stuffed bear in favour of playing with her hair.

"I don't know... Using Inad like that seems wrong. I mean, imagine others doing that too! What kind of decisions would we have in the Council then?"

He chuckled and shook his head at her. "My love, everybody else is doing it. That's the reason why we have certain kinds of decisions in the Council that mainly aim to preserve things the way they are."

"I don't like the Order," she said sullenly.

Enric grinned. "I know. And now it's on you to change it. The Kingdom depends on you. Don't let us down."

She gave him a sour look. "No pressure, eh?"

*   *   *

Enric closed the door behind them and then nodded at his companion. "You may express your frustration now."

Eryn flung her cloak to the floor angrily and then threw her hands up. "What is wrong with them, I ask you? Why are they being so immensely stupid? Why don't they see the consequences of their stubborn refusal to change one thing, anything! I just want to grab their necks and repeatedly thump their heads against that stone table in the Council hall until they see reason!"

Gerit came down the stairs and raised her brow at the harsh words. Enric saw how his mother tightened her grip on her grandson, clearly not willing to hand him over to his very agitated mother right now.

"I take it your meeting wasn't particularly satisfying?" the older woman ventured, carefully stepping over the mountain cat that was lazily sprawled on the carpet.

"You could certainly say that. If you wanted to understate it grossly," Eryn growled. "I mean, after all the accusations that were flung around just recently they still don't really grasp that something needs to change quickly! Oh, they say they do - but those are just hollow words to hide the fact that they are ignorant, old-fashioned, tight-assed..." She stopped when Gerit very pointedly cleared her throat and looked at the infant on her hip. "They think everything worked out well enough just because Tyront survived the attack. They don't see that this was nothing more than sheer, blind luck and that we might not be as fortunate next time. I'm so angry, I could..." She searched for some inspiration as to how to vent her ire.

"Angry enough to pick up a sword?" Enric asked and picked her cloak up from the floor to put it away tidily together with his own.

"Yes," she replied without even having to think about it.

"Good. Then I'll see you outside in the yard in five minutes. You get the armour, I get the swords."

They faced each other little later, both sporting a drawn weapon their hand. Enric decided to get as much as he could out of this occasion. It was not often that she agreed to fight him. And even though her skills that had merely been average at the best of times were now after the break due to her pregnancy even less impressive, she was at least strong enough to parry and block his more powerful blows without dropping out right away. So this little exercise right now would serve two purposes: for him to have a little fun and for her to get rid of that exasperation and tension. A win-win situation, basically.

"He was right again," Eryn growled before attacking. "I hate it when he is right. Which he almost always is."

"We are talking about the King, I assume?" Enric ventured and sidestepped her move easily. It was carried out with considerably more energy than focus.

"Who else? He told me that they would try to mend fences with Lord Aldon and Lord Woldarn. I mean, why even vote against them if they don't want to risk disgruntling their allies? Why can't they just stand up for themselves and say: I did what I considered just and right, and I don't have to vindicate myself to anyone!"

Enric didn't reply. It had not really been a question, anyway. He quickly parried a few vicious strikes and then waited for her to go on.

"The issue about increasing the healers' quota so we are finally able to send them out to where they are really needed instead of just keeping them stabled here in the city is another dead end! Honestly, many of them want to leave here! Several of the applications for healer trainee positions have stated that explicitly. They want to go back home from where they were sent as children as soon as their magic was discovered. They want to serve their community, return to their families and are willing to give up the comfort of the city to provide help where it is needed! They want a chance to be more than fighters waiting for a war to come. They are frustrated because they see how things could different, better - yet nobody acts upon those frustrations!"

"Not true, my love. You are acting," he remarked and drove her a few steps backwards.

She carefully stepped over a log and kept blocking. "No, I want to act, but I keep running into walls! Walls made entirely of sour-faced Council members! I'm back among you after being cleared - and what for? Just so they can put me in my place!" She aimed a kick at his knee, but he swiftly caught her foot and held on to it, making her hop on one leg and struggle for balance. When he let go again, she jumped onto a medium-sized rock and realised too late, that this was not a smart move. An elevated position was never an advantage in a sword fight.

Enric sighed. "Bad move. I could cut off your legs if you are too slow and you don't have enough reach to threaten me seriously from up there. Come down again. Don't try anything too fancy, stick to what you know."

She followed his advice and returned to the ground, growling, "Sticking to what you know - that only works if you know enough to achieve something."

He lifted his sword and channelled enough energy into his arm to send her weapon flying out of her grip and through the air.

"Listen," he implored her when he had her undivided attention, "you know enough to do things right. You keep trying to break through walls instead of dismantling them."

She moaned and let her head sink back, staring at the dark blue afternoon sky. "Dismantling the wall? What exactly are you telling me through that? To use spies and collect incriminating information to coerce the Council members that are against me? You know I wouldn't ever consider that!"

Enric shook his head. "No, I know that you wouldn't. Leaving your aversion to collecting and using helpful information aside, there is another approach that would better fit your character. Just take the time and sit down to think about what it really is they want, what truly keeps them from agreeing to what you suggest."

"Stupidity?" she spat.

"Eryn, now stop being stubborn and think!" he scolded her, feeling how he became more impatient. "What is it that makes people reject change in general?"

She felt how his mood had shifted and decided to accommodate him. This was unusual for him, he was the more placid and balanced one of them, so this had to be important.

"Satisfaction with how things are," she suggested.

"Yes. And change might...?"

"Take away from them what they don't want to lose," Eryn replied like a well-behaved pupil. "But they are on the verge of losing..." She stopped when he lifted a finger to silence her.

"Yes, take away what they don't want to lose. Focus on that, Eryn. Think about what they don't want to lose."

"Influence, power, money, importance, status..." she listed without hesitation.

"Exactly. Our predecessors did well enough for themselves by following rules and preserving traditions that have suddenly become insufficient. These new developments are considered a threat, and people don't always react sensibly to threats. Several in the Council decided to simply ignore what is happening in the hope that it will go away again. The alternative would be to do something that might be wrong and cost them what they are so eager to cling on to."

Eryn breathed out heavily and shook her head. "How am I supposed to overcome this immense reluctance? I keep presenting them with ideas, and they don't even listen to me."

"This reluctance is based on fear, and that is what you need to consider when trying to get through to them. Throwing facts against fear doesn't work, just as using emotions against hard evidence would be equally ineffective. They are emotional about it? Then meet them on the same level!"

She frowned in incomprehension. "Such as with what? Start bawling and wailing because I'm fuming and frustrated because of their ignoring me?"

He closed his eyes for a moment, wondering if she was being obtuse on purpose. Maybe she was not yet in a state of mind to grasp fully what he was trying to impress upon her, maybe there was still too much tension remaining. "This is not about your emotions, but about theirs. Fear is a powerful motivation, and there is more than one way to make use of it. You can either help them overcome it somehow so that they are more willing and also finally able to listen to you, or redirect and fuel it further - whatever you feel you can better work with." He turned to go and pick up her sword from where it had landed. "Let's go back inside. There is something I would like to show you."

Enric held the door open for her to enter first and then placed the swords on top of a high cupboard so nobody could injure themselves accidentally before he was able to store them away properly later. Then he led her to his study, where he closed first the door and then the curtains.

She watched how he squatted down and lifted a floorboard next to his desk that looked exactly like every other one in the room, to remove what turned out to be a small brass key from beneath it. Then he went to the other end of the room where the bar was and again bent down to lift another unremarkable wooden board. There was a lid with a hole into which he inserted the key and turned it. This time the compartment under was a lot larger and he pulled out a box that contained a number of neatly labelled files. She followed him to his desk and looked down, trying to decipher the small cards tucked into the leather folders. One said Lord Remdel, another one Lord Poron, a third one Lord Orrin... She looked up sharply.

"This is the information your spies have collected on every single one of the Council members?"

He nodded. "Not only my spies, but also what I myself have found out and what my business partners have reported to me over the years." Then he pressed the key into her hand with a serious expression. "Put them back when you are done." Thus he turned and walked out of his study, closing the door behind him and leaving her alone with several years' worth of confidential and doubtlessly very personal information on those who had caused her so much trouble.

Eryn swallowed hard and thought back to the conversation about spies and information they'd had not long ago. How he had talked to her about the need to guard and responsibly use what he learned of those he had observed. Yet now he had put all this at her disposal at the drop of a hat.

She stared down at the box, unsure what to do. She knew with absolute certainty that there were people out there who would kill for the content of these files. Enric was not one for half-measures; when he started looking for information on a person, he would gather whatever there was to be found. So this here would not be any casual collection of random tidbits, but probably more about the Council members and their families than they themselves might be aware of.

There was even one about Tyront, she noted with rising discomfort. He had mentioned that he spied on his superior, but having the file here right in front of her, where she just had to reach out and pull it out...

Eryn let herself fall onto the settee several paces away from his desk and simply stared at the box. Enric had just handed her an immensely powerful tool. These files very likely contained more than one instance of information she could use to intimidate the Council members with. She could force them into cooperating with her by threatening to disclose to the world their darkest and most well-kept secrets. The thought was both intoxicating and repellent.

What was more, it would very likely be effective. She would be able to reach her goals, form the Order into something new, something better than before. She could turn it into an organisation where most if not all members were happy and could thrive, develop, travel... Even Tyront would have to be careful if he sided against her - there was bound to be some explosive material on him in there somewhere. Nobody rose to power and remained that powerful without doing a few proscribed or immoral things every now and then.

This box was treasure, nothing less. Her fingers itched to touch it, but she found that she couldn't move. Forcing people to do her bidding... that was not her! She abhorred the practice of spying on people and would certainly not sink so low as to resort to that or use the information obtained by them. It had been incredibly tempting for a long, seemingly endless moment, but she realised there was absolutely no way she could bring herself to blackmail people.

And what kind of achievement would it be, anyway? If the Council didn't work on this together with her but had everything forced on them, they would only be waiting for her to trip up one day herself and take advantage of every weakness they spotted. It would turn into an underhand war, the kind some of them seemed to engage in already. She wanted no part of it. She wanted whatever changes for the better that happened to be ones which outlasted her because they were based on consent and cooperation instead of intimidating force.

She couldn't tell how long she had been sitting there, unmoving, with the brass key still held in her hand, when there was a knock at the door and Enric entered. He took in the way she was sitting, how the box still stood there exactly as he had placed it on his desk before he had left.

"I can't do it," Eryn whispered without looking at him. "I'm sorry, I know you wanted to help me, but I just can't. It feels wrong. This is not how I want to do this. You probably won't understand this and I don't know how to expl..."

He bent down and interrupted her by pressing his lips on hers for several seconds to silence her.

"I know," he then said with a smile and sat down next to her. "It would have surprised me to no end if you had actually gone through the files."

488

She blinked and shook her head. "What?"

"We may not always be aware or sure of what we really want to do or to be, but sometimes the best way to start finding out is to determine or even just remember what we don't want."

Eryn closed her eyes and smiled weakly. "So you just educated me?"

"Let's not phrase it like that. It implies that I'm superior to you. Shall we instead say that I guided you through a problem?"

"Those are just words, Enric. They don't change the facts. You are my superior."

He shook his head. "Not in this house. Here we are equals."

She smiled faintly. "Are we really? You still like to be in charge, though, also in our relationship."

"Certainly I do. But I also enjoy you not always permitting me." He took the key from her hand and got up to restore the precious box to its hiding place. Leaving it out in the open like that meant inviting trouble.

"Thank you," she said quietly when he returned to her. Squeezing his hand she then continued, "I have to confess something: I was tempted to look at the files. There was this moment when I imagined reaching all that I was striving for, rebuilding the Order in a way I think would benefit everyone. I'm maybe not quite as devoted to my principles as I thought."

Enric shook his head. "No, my love, you are wrong. Being tempted doesn't mean that you aren't dedicated or true to your principles, it merely means that you are human. And the real accomplishment is not avoiding temptation, but resisting it."

Eryn buried her face in his neck and inhaled his scent, enjoying the sensation of his warm skin on her forehead and cheek. "And you resist using whatever knowledge is in there day after day."

"To a certain degree. Though I employ it if I see fit, just in a more refined way than many others might. And I try not to resort to ruthlessly using information if there are other ways that don't earn me more enemies or enrage my existing ones. There was a lesson or two I had to learn in the past in that regard. So, any epiphanies concerning dealing with the Council while you were staring at my secret files?"

"There is something I would like to try, definitely. I want to scare them into working with me." She lifted her head from his neck and he saw her expression was determined. "They are afraid of losing their power and status? Then I will paint them a picture of what will befall them once our son takes over the Order together with a bunch of the new, more powerful magicians."

Enric laughed loudly and pulled her close again to kiss her temple. "That's my girl. And I bet the fact that House Aren is known to collapse buildings is not going to impair your daunting performance one bit."

*   *   *

Pe'tala opened her door and admitted Eryn and Junar into her quarters. As she was the only one without a baby around, it had been decided that her quarters were the most suitable location for a little get-together. Rolan had wisely decided to spend the night at a friend's place.

The hostess took the two bottles from Eryn's hands and eyed them critically. "That is the good stuff, I hope? I am a highborn member of a Takhan House, you know, I am not used to cheap plonk."

Her sister shrugged. "I'm not sure what exactly I brought, but it's something Enric pressed into my hands. I can't promise you that it tastes good or won't give you a headache, but what I can safely assure you of is that it can't have been cheap."

Pe'tala nodded, satisfied with that explanation. She had been Enric's guest before, and he, too, was not one to accept anything he considered sub-standard. Then she nodded at the bottle Junar was carrying. "Your companion is also wealthy. So you had better have something agreeably costly as well."

Junar sighed and handed over her gift. "Has anybody ever told you that you are a snob?"

Pe'tala nodded. "Repeatedly. Yet I fail to see why this is supposed to insult me. The term merely states that I am used to good quality and not content with anything less than that."

"It is also meant to point out that you feel superior because of your privileged upbringing and treat others as if they are less worthy than you," Eryn supplied helpfully.

Her sister frowned for a moment, then shook her head. "Nonsense. I'm nothing like that."

"You just introduced yourself as a highborn member of a House, so your assertion is open to debate," Junar retorted. "And considering that I'm the only one of us here who was not only born into more modest surroundings but also without magic, I know a snob when I see one. I have to endure them every time Orrin and I go to one of these terrible dinners." She turned to Eryn. "I haven't seen you at any of those charming occasions since our return to Anyueel, by the way. Enric is far too lenient with you."

Eryn laughed at that. "You are just envious because you have to go and I don't for now. Enric is still more than pleased with me for voluntarily resuming my combat training with that tormentor of a companion of yours. And I'm important and mighty and need to convince the Magic Council to implement a few changes I deem necessary."

The other two women rolled their eyes at that. Pe'tala nodded towards a group of sofas and went to fetch glasses. "Which bottle shall we open first?"

"Mine needs to be cool," Junar called after her, "so I suggest we put it on the windowsill for an hour or two and start with Eryn's wine."

Eryn smugly grabbed the bottle and applied a little magic to pull energy and thereby warmth from the liquid inside. A thin layer of frosty rime was covering the sleek glass bottle a few moments later as she handed it back to her friend.

The seamstress sighed. "Ah yes, I forgot. Mighty magicians and all that. Well, then we might just as well start with this here."

Eryn nodded. "Sure. It looks expensive enough, so I dare say my spoilt baby sister won't object."

"Do not call me that," the hostess growled and placed three glasses on the table in front of them.

"What? Baby sister or spoilt?"

"Neither. And especially not in combination."

"Vran'el calls you baby sister," Eryn pointed out.

"And I do not appreciate it any more in his case, but I have to appease him when I return in three months since he is my Head of House."

Junar tried to remove the cork from the bottle, then gave up and handed it to Eryn, who pulled it out without any apparent effort before handing both items back.

"Have you told your brother yet that you don't intend to move back in with him but intend to stay at Eryn's new house?" Junar asked while pouring the clear, dark amber liquid into the glasses.

Pe'tala shook her head. "No, though I am seriously considering getting it behind me rather sooner than later. I originally wanted to tell him when I am back in Takhan, but it might be advisable to send him a bird message before that. That would give him a little time to get used to the thought and calm himself down before my arrival."

"And also to work out some legal reason to make you move back in with him again," Eryn pointed out.

Her younger sister shook her head. "He is sure to try that anyway; he would only begin a little earlier. And I have another lawyer who I can consult and ask for something to use in my defence. Ram'an is still in my debt for dumping me, so he will be more than happy to aid me in this little concern provided I promise to keep his name out of it."

Junar and Eryn nodded appreciatively at that demonstration of rational thinking. Not every woman would resort to making her former companion-to-be feel guilty to get her way. But then doing just that would demonstrate to him that Pe'tala was no longer concerned by what was in the past, that she was over it.

"How did that Council meeting today go?" Junar asked. "Orrin wasn't back from his training when I left, so I had no chance to ask him. There wasn't any decision on what will become of Darnet, was there?"

Eryn nodded, swallowing her anger at the meeting in general and focussing on the only practical thing that they had managed to decide on. "Yes, he is to be sent to Takhan. Iklan agreed to treat him, and the Triarchy granted it as well. It seems there is a place dedicated to treating the mentally ill and unstable. And as we don't really have the expertise here to do it ourselves, this is a very convenient solution for us. Nobody really felt comfortable with the idea of locking up a man who has lost touch with reality."

Pe'tala sneered. "How agreeable. You send your insane criminals to Takhan. Maybe we can return the favour and send a few of our regular wrongdoers to you? We could start with Sanaf. I bet he would eagerly take this chance to escape your grandmother's iron fist."

Junar sniggered at that comment and took a sip from her glass before asking, "When are they due to leave, then? Orrin told me that your two colleagues would be returning to Takhan rather sooner than later. And I can understand that very well - they come from a hot country and now have to face the winter here."

"They will leave in two days." Eryn looked around and found two plates with finger food on a chest of drawers. She pointed at it and looked at her sister. "May I? I'm rather hungry, and I should probably eat something before drinking."

Pe'tala nodded. "Sure, help yourself. I forgot to put that on the table. There is more in the guest room when this here is empty." When Eryn had returned with the two plates and placed them so all of them had access to at least one, the hostess asked, "How about the game? Considering how your first one ended I assume the Council might be rather dubious when it comes to permitting another one."

Junar was the one to answer this time. "Orrin said that this is indeed something of a sore topic at the moment, yet as Lord Tyront is in favour of having another one, they can't really object."

Eryn nibbled at a tiny, round piece of bread with some kind of spicy, dark red spread on it. "I'm not so sure if having another one would be such a great idea right now. Darnet might no longer pose a threat, but that doesn't mean that there isn't any more trouble ahead potentially."

The seamstress nodded. "That's what Orrin said. He really wants to make the game a permanent fixture, but doesn't think that this is the right time. Too much tension around, he says."

"Yes, I see that this is a point to be considered," Pe'tala agreed. "In Takhan, however, people are eager to have another game, and soon. Father writes that people keep pestering Kilan to train them in magical fighting."

Eryn laughed at that. She knew from Enric that Kilan was an average fighter at best and would probably not be too comfortable when finding himself in a situation where he had to teach to others what he himself was not overly skilled in. Yet being trained in the Order for so many years surely would enable him to show them at least a few things. Poor ambassador, she thought. He would have to teach them if he didn't want to offend them.

"Father thinks that there will probably be another game after your and Enric's return to Takhan," Pe'tala continued and then nodded at

Junar. "And people keep asking when Orrin will return. Your companion really impressed them; they want him back."

The seamstress smiled. "Orrin knows about that, of course. And he has been giving that topic some thought. He thinks of going to Takhan twice a year to stay for several days and see what Vern is up to, and if he uses the time there to train the locals, there is a good chance that the Order will grant it."

Eryn frowned. "He didn't tell me anything about this!"

Junar flashed her a look of irony. "Imagine that, he dared talking to his companion first. You are aware that I am the most important woman in his life, of course? It might have been you for a short while, but that is over now."

"No offence," Eryn assured her quickly, "I was just surprised, that's all. It would make sense to coordinate those visits with ours, after all. Unless you want to be in Takhan without us, that is."

Junar exhaled. "Sorry, I didn't mean to snarl at you like that. It's just that Téa has been a bit ill these last two days and hasn't been sleeping too well. Which means that I haven't got very much rest, either."

"Why didn't you send for me or Tala? We could have taken care of that."

"I would have if it had gone on any longer, but she is fine again now. How did your family in Takan react to the news that you had not been shackled in gold and thrown into a dark, mouldy dungeon but been discharged instead?"

"Relieved," Eryn smiled. "At least that's what they all wrote. I got up one morning and found a heap of bird messages on my desk, each of them congratulating me and telling me that they had expected nothing less. Vern wrote that it was not much of a surprise to him that I had somehow managed to get myself into trouble yet again - which I find completely unfair as this had occurred through no fault of my own."

"Speaking of Vern," her younger sister asked, "how is he fitting in? Being a visitor to a city and actually living there is quite a difference, as I can attest to. How did he adapt to the training schedules? How are things at the art academies going?"

Eryn rolled her eyes. "How about you writing to him yourself and asking him about all of that?"

"Why would I? You and Junar surely know all about it, so do not be obstructive, just share!"

Junar drained the rest of her glass, then leaned back. "I'll oblige you, then. Because you so generously provided a venue for this grown-up evening tonight. And you even dislodged Rolan."

Pe'tala grinned. "I did not have to dislodge him. He heard that you were coming and fled. Now tell me about Vern."

"He is taking lectures and training sessions with different classes," Junar began, "as his training here in Anyueel with Eryn left him with advanced knowledge in several areas while also with gaps in other areas. He works nights at the Clinic twice a week to pay for his training, though he earns so much with his paintings that he doesn't need to. Though Orrin and I are both glad he keeps working - it should keep him grounded and show him what working for a living means. He still teaches drawing at the New Art Academy and he writes that he finds living with Vran'el uncomplicated."

"And he has been having one affair after the other," Eryn added with a sigh.

Junar's head snapped towards her. "He has what? But that one women he was with..."

"That one is over and done with for him. Ram'an and Vran'el both wrote to me that he goes out frequently and is invited to a number of private social evenings, where he makes new acquaintances easily thanks to his rather exotic appearance, his status as a rising star of the art world and the fact that he more or less started a revolution off that caused artists there to split. He is still a sensation."

Junar just sat there gaping, which was fairly similar to how Eryn had reacted when she first read about it.

Pe'tala whistled through her teeth and then nodded appreciatively. "Who would have thought he had it in him?"

The seamstress frowned. "Oh dear. And I have to tell Orrin about this. He won't be thrilled to learn that his son regularly sleeps with women he hardly knows."

The hostess shrugged. "Why would you tell Orrin about it? It's basically none of his business."

"Neither is it any of ours," Eryn remarked, refilled her glass and while she was at it topped up the two others as well.

"True," her sister agreed. "But we are gossiping, and that requires prying into other people's private concerns."

Junar drowned her glass in one and let her head loll back. "Sorry, ladies - but we need to talk about something different. The sex life of my companion's teenage son is not an appropriate topic for me. That's just uncomfortable."

Pe'tala looked at her sister. "Father keeps asking me about my plans for the commitment ceremony. He wants to start arranging things so that we can have it right after we arrive in Takhan. It will, of course, be at the Vel'kim residence, as is traditional."

Eryn shrugged. "That sounds like you already have the most important aspects covered: when and where. What else does he need? Just let him go crazy - it's the first commitment he is able arrange, mine was more or less a last-minute thing arranged by Ram'an."

"I already told him to do whatever he wants. I do not really care that much about the food or the decorations. He knows which people to invite and I will ask Junar to take care of the clothes." Pe'tala waited for Junar to nod in agreement and then went on, "The question is rather whether you and Enric would like to have a joint ceremony together with us. You are still up for re-establishing your side of the third level bond, are you not?"

"I certainly am," Eryn replied, "but I don't really want to make this into something big. I mean, we already had our ceremony, and I would really like to keep this private. I'm wondering how great the chances of keeping Malriel away from it are..."

Pe'tala started laughing. "Practically non-existent! Her only daughter and her heir remake their bond - she would not accept being excluded from such an event. And there is the fact that she is now even more powerful than ever before thanks to being a triarch. If she does not agree, it will not even take place."

"Fabulous," Eryn sighed. "So it will take place with the Queen of Darkness. Once again."

"You would have had to exclude father as well, because he would not betray his companion like that and conceal it from her."

"Yes, I understand," the older sister growled, "Valrad has to be more careful with this companion than his last - her family is known for collapsing buildings, after all."

"Father," Pe'tala said reproachfully.

"What?"

"Father, not Valrad. You had better get used to calling him that."

"He is not even here to object!" Eryn complained.

Junar chuckled at them. "When I listen to your bickering I can't help but feel that you two are catching up on the childhood you never had together."

"We are about to spend half of every year under the same roof in Takhan," Pe'tala replied, "that will give us quite enough chance for catching up. How is that going, by the way? Knowing Malhora, that residence is probably half finished already."

"When she last wrote, they had just completed laying the foundations," Eryn informed her. "I think she mentioned that they were ahead of schedule, which is hardly unexpected. I would also be trying to finish whatever work she supervises as quickly as possible to get her off my back."

Pe'tala leaned back and seemed to be performing some or other calculation in her head. Then she nodded with a slow smile spreading across her lips. "The chances that we can move in directly after arriving in Takhan are indeed very good. House Roal hires magicians for some of their construction sites, and judging from the progress they have made so far, this is clearly the case at yours. This is very good news." She leaned forward to grab her glass from the table. "By the way, Rolan has today finally decided on a candidate to train for his replacement."

Junar chuckled. "It's about time! How long has he been rejecting applications now? For two months?"

"Yes," Eryn confirmed. "Lord Poron was starting to become a little nervous about that. I'm glad to hear that they agreed on somebody now. Do you know who it is?"

"I do indeed. I will tell you as soon as you have put your glass down."

Eryn narrowed her eyes, but did as she was told. "So?"

"It is Loft."

"Very funny, haha," Eryn sighed. "Really now, who is it?"

Pe'tala grimaced. "I swear to you, it is Loft. The short bald man who was your King's advisor."

Junar swallowed. "Oh, dear. He was never very fond of Eryn. How come Rolan and Lord Poron picked him, of all people?"

"He is an experienced organiser, good with paperwork, has the right contacts and his work for the present King and his father before him taught him to take care of things quickly and not to pause before they were completed," the younger healer told them.

"Loft," Eryn moaned. "This is terrible!"

Pe'tala looked at Junar and then nodded at the mostly empty bottle on the table between them. "Why do you not pour her out the rest of that while I go and get another bottle? She looks like she needs it."

CHAPTER 30

Matters Heat up

Enric heard the knock at the entrance door and looked down at his son. He was in the middle of changing his nappy and Vedric seemed to enjoy the greater flexibility an unclothed lower body afforded him. He grabbed one of his feet and almost managed to push it into his mouth, where most things he managed to lay his hands on ended up lately.

What had before been a tapping sounded again, only that it had evolved into more of a hammering now. Where were the servants when he needed them? Ah yes, in the building across the yard where he had decided to locate those rooms that were required for doing the laundry, cooking, storing cleaning supplies and so on.

"I'll be there in a moment," he called out and hoped that the visitor would hear him. Then he hurried to wrap his son in lengths of clean towelling and dress him before setting the boy on his hip and walking to the door. He pulled it open and blinked at the unexpected sight.

"You? I must be fast asleep and dreaming."

"Enric, you dolt, let me in, will you? That stuff falling down on me is sleet, in case you hadn't noticed. I'm freezing and tired, so get out of the way," his sister grumbled and pushed him aside to enter.

"Sure, why don't you come in?" he smiled when she dropped her bag on the floor and handed him her cloak. Then his expression became serious. "Not that I'm not excited about your visit, but considering that it's the first one ever, I can't help but think that something major must have happened. The fact that you chose this season and have turned up without your family confirms my impression that it is not your eagerness to return my visit that brings you here."

Leris wordlessly bent down to open her bag and pull out a folded piece of paper from a side pocket and handed it to him. She motioned for him to pass her her nephew so that he could unfold and read what looked to him like a letter on slightly damp paper.

While his sister was having a leisurely walk through his parlour with Vedric on her arm and taking a look at how her rich brother in the city lived, Enric let his eyes wander over the lines he recognised almost immediately as their father's handwriting. He pressed his lips

497

together at the overt anger that emanated from the words, the helpless frustration he vented with unkind words and promises that she would regret standing against him.

He read it a second time before letting the letter sink in his hands.

Leris turned to him and narrowed her eyes at him. "You didn't tell me that she left him. Or that she is here in the city with you. Would it have been so bloody hard to pick up a damn pen and send word?"

Enric sighed. "If mother had wanted you to know, she would have written to you herself. It was not my place to do it. Don't blame me that you were not told about this; you were the one who resented her too much all these years to maintain any contact with her."

His sister stared at him for a long moment, her expression grim, then she placed her nephew on the soft blanket on the floor and rubbed her face.

"I know," she then whispered. "I was so angry at her for not freeing herself from that cage he put her into, and now that she finally has, I wouldn't even have got word of it if it hadn't been for Anwin's outraged letter. I feel terrible. He writes that he will show us what daring to stand against him and blocking his attempts to get into the lumber business will earn me, that mother will pay the price for it! He really wants to send his companion of more than thirty years to prison in order to take revenge on me! Can he do that?" She stepped close to her brother, taking his hands in hers, her look pleading. "You can avert that, can't you? You will use your contacts and make the clerks dissolve the commitment, right? I can't have that on my conscience - I can't let her go to prison!"

Enric squeezed her still cold hands. "Firstly, the reason why he wants her locked up is not you. He would have done that anyway - he sent her back the dissolution papers shredded into strips. This is just him using is initial plan to make you feel guilty while he is at it because he is boiling with indignation. And secondly, I have tried it - there is no dissolving the commitment without his consent, I can't do anything. I would pay the fine gladly to keep mother out of prison, but she won't let me. She is stubborn and considers it some kind of proof to herself that she is willing to pay the price for leaving him."

"But she would have to return anew every few months! This cannot just be taken care of within two weeks! Not returning to him means that she would commit the same crime again and again and would be penalised for it regularly!" Leris cried out desperately.

Enric nodded silently. It pained him to see her so put out and helpless in her anger; he felt very much the same. At least he had told her that she was not the one responsible for this. Anwin had chosen his target well - if he had heard that Leris was involved in keeping him from establishing himself in that particular line of business he had been trying to get into for some time now, he had to be aware that his older son was the driving force behind it. Yet he had decided to write to his daughter, as he surely knew that threatening Enric was not a promising path to follow.

He had little doubt as to who must have slipped him that little detail - several if not all of the Council members must have found out about his business dealings, and currently there were two of them who were not particularly happy with himself and especially not with Eryn.

Anwin knew now what Enric had been so careful to keep from him all these years - that he was not just a well-paid figurehead because he happened to inherit his grandfather's magical abilities, but a successful business man with far-reaching contacts that now even went beyond the borders of the Kingdom.

That must have been a nasty shock for his old man, he mused. Not only discovering that he had underestimated his own flesh and blood so enormously, but also that both his children, who had turned their backs on him, had united to create a successful business together that even enabled them to make sure that his own attempts in a similar area were fruitless. He was even furious enough to admit openly to having been abandoned by his companion just so he could send her to prison to inflict pain on his own children. A reckless egomaniac!

The entrance door opened and Gerit stepped inside, rubbing her cold hands together.

"Dear me, I think it is about time to get out the warm cloak..." she started and then froze at the sight of the woman standing in front of her son, holding on to his hands.

Leris, too, went completely still.

Both women stared at each other for several seconds, until Enric went towards his mother to gently push her forward so that he was able to close the door behind her. There was an infant in the room, and she was letting the warmth out.

He waited a bit longer, looking from mother to daughter and when neither moved, each remaining motionless as if they had both turned to stone, he cleared his throat.

"Mother, Leris is sorry about everything and proud of your courageous step in leaving Anwin. Leris, mother is overjoyed to see you again after all this time and is glad you came to your senses."

Tears welled up in his sister's eyes and she nodded emphatically. "Yes! Yes - what he said."

Gerit closed her eyes for a long moment, and when she opened them again, she had tears brimming in them as well. Speaking didn't seem to work right now, her mouth was open, but no words came out. So she expressed her feelings by just opening her arms in a wide, welcoming gesture and sobbed when her daughter, a woman she hadn't seen in almost fifteen years, ran towards her and slung her arms around her to bury her face in her shoulder.

Enric watched them, touched by their emotional reunion and relieved that their apparent love for each other and the fact that they had evidently missed each other so much was not marred by any resentment for now. There might be words between them later, but for now they were both still overwhelmed in each other's presence.

He decided to give them a little time with each other and cleared his throat. "Can I leave Vedric with the two of you for a while? There is something I need to check on."

When each had released the other again, but still held on to each other's hands and nodded at him, he took his cloak from the hook in the cubby hole and left his home. He would use the time to check up on the progress on his mother's future abode.

*   *   *

As the letters swam before her eyes, Eryn pushed away the books, both the dictionary and the one on Pirinkar illnesses. The progress today had not exactly been overwhelming. She kept wasting time with looking up the things she'd already worked out at some other time, checking words she knew she had come across before a few times and that should have been there, ready for recall.

But her thoughts kept running off the track. They returned to Leris' arrival and her reunion with her mother. All it had taken for the two women to reunite was Gerit leaving her companion... It was a good thing Gerit was not the resentful type and forgave her daughter for discarding her like an old piece of clothing and for considering her weak and pathetic. Eryn wondered if this was a character trait particular to Enric's mother or if there was a higher tendency towards forgiveness in mothers in general when it came to their children. Well, she would find out as soon as Vedric was old enough to cause trouble.

She wondered who would be the strict parent and who the lenient one. Or which role she would prefer. Lenient was attractive - children were generally closer to the more indulgent parent, shared their secrets, were not afraid of rejection or reproof. But then there were certain limits where she would certainly not tolerate if they were overstepped, neither by Enric nor his son. Would it work not to adopt a certain kind of mindset but instead switch approaches in accordance with the situation? Could she and Enric swap roles like that? Would the child still take them seriously or be completely confused as he had no idea what to expect from which parent?

Looking down at the absentminded scribblings on her notepad that showed that she had clearly no talent for drawing whatsoever, she wondered whether to send Erbál another message to ask him for advice about the language of his current place of residence. His replies were always without exception charming and obliging, but then he was a diplomat by profession and would not show any irritation. Maybe she would wait another few days before trying his patience anew.

A knock at her study door made her look up. Gerit and Leris had all but snatched Vedric out of her arms after breakfast and declared that they would take him with them while they had a look at Gerit's future home. Enric had declared the location safe enough for the three of them to satisfy their curiosity.

"Come on," she called out and one of their servants opened the door with her shoulder due to holding a rather large, flat box in her hands.

"Lady Eryn," the young woman said by way of a greeting and then entered, close behind her Ram'kel, Ambassador to Anyueel. Oh no, she had completely forgotten that she had something scheduled with him today! She was not at all in the mood for being provoked and teased right now. And he just entered right behind the servant girl without waiting to be announced and invited in! This was a breach of the etiquette of good manners, and she was absolutely certain that this was no mere oversight - he was doing it on purpose.

Her look of dismay at his sight just made him smile. Why exactly did he delight in trying her patience?

But then he was not the only one enjoying that particular pastime, was he? The King, too, liked to put her on edge. Yet lately he was more concerned with somewhat gently encouraging her to do his bidding than playing his little games with her. She wasn't sure if this was more or less perturbing.

"Ambassador Ram'kel, how delightful to see you," she said with a waxen smile that was meant to show him exactly how little she appreciated his company right now. There were gloomy thoughts to be pursued, and he was disturbing her in a rather reflective mood.

"Lady Eryn of House Vel'kim, every time I lay eyes upon you, my day becomes a little brighter," he reciprocated and took her hand to kiss it while the servant seemed slightly uneasy and hurried to deposit what she was carrying on the desk and get out of the study as quickly as she could without making it appear as the escape it essentially was. Eryn couldn't blame her.

Ram'kel appeared unperturbed by her evident displeasure at seeing him and took a seat on the sofa instead of at her desk, making himself comfortable. Unasked.

"I will have whatever tea you have available. It is a little chillier outside than I am accustomed to dealing with. Our nights at home are considerably cooler than our days, as you know, yet these temperatures are something I have yet to get used to - especially during the day."

She got up from her seat and went to her little bar to take out a cup, herbal powder and a water carafe to mix and heat him his beverage. Where did he think he was - in some teahouse? He could at least have waited until she offered him something to drink. She would have done that soon enough. Well, eventually. Probably.

She handed him his drink and felt how her eyes were drawn to the box that had been delivered and that now sat on her desk, beckoning her to look inside.

"Go on, my dear, satisfy your curiosity. I do not mind at all. The shape of the box suggests that it might be a book, and you are known for your fondness of those."

Eryn smiled thinly and went on to prepare a drink for herself. She had no particular wish to share a cosy drink with him, but she had learned that a glass, cup or whatever in her hand was a convenient means of buying time. One could take a sip instead of answering right away and use the seconds that this simple action bought to organise one's thoughts or consider whether the satisfaction of insulting the person in front of you was worth it when set against bearing the consequences of such an insult. Unfortunately those tended to outlast the pleasure... Not in Ram'kel's case, though. He appeared to like it when she was brusque with him. Where his brother was obliging and careful, he was provocative and mischievous. Maybe that was why he liked visiting her - he didn't have to deny his true nature in her presence. If he used diplomacy with her, it was only to cleverly hide a spike.

She felt her gaze inadvertently returning to the box. He was right, the shape did indeed indicate that a book might be within. It might be from Valrad - some book on healing he thought would interest her. Maybe something on herbs?

Or something Vern had found in the medical library that he considered useful for the trainees here?

Ram'kel grinned widely. "On you go, open it. You will not be able to concentrate on anything I say as long as you keep asking yourself what is in there."

"No, thank you, I am quite able to restrain myself," she smiled back and took a seat opposite him, intentionally ignoring the custom from his home country where people preferred not to do that for friendly conversations. It tended to come across as a mite... hostile.

The ambassador noted this, of course, but again it did nothing more than to amuse him. Eryn wondered what it would take to make him really angry. Maybe she would make it a game to find out.

"So," she began, her eyes darting back to the crate on her desk for only a brief moment before she forced herself to face her visitor, "Darnet is on his way to Takhan together with Iklan and Sarol. I'm glad the Triarchy granted his transfer into Iklan's competent care."

"Because you feel that a man who professes that you are capable of killing a man without mercy must be so much out of touch with reality that it clearly shows his need of medical treatment? What a noble disposition, my Lady. A lesser person would have wanted to exact revenge nevertheless and see him rot in a dungeon."

Eryn gave him a lazy smile that showed too many teeth, then leaned back. "Or maybe I wanted him gone from here because his accusations were a lot closer to the truth than I felt comfortable with..." She saw the quick flicker of unease in his eyes and thought: Ha! Got you!

But he recovered in a remarkably short time and chuckled. "No, I think not. Or you would hardly be admitting this to me, would you?"

She shrugged and nodded at her study door. "Who says you will ever make it out that door alive? I'm stronger than you and I happen to be a trained warrior." That last part was stretching things to the point of fantasy, but compared to him she'd at least had several months of training in combat, strategy, deceit and similar.

Ram'kel nodded without seeming the least bit perturbed by what may or may not have been a genuine death threat. "Stronger you are, though the fact that you were among the first to be removed from the game where Lord Tyront was injured makes me doubt that your fellow magicians in this Kingdom would count you among the more... proficient of fighters, if you will forgive me for saying something as ungallant as that."

Sure, she thought sourly, why not pretend that we aim to be civil?

"And you would not want to upset my poor brother by killing off his only sibling, would you? You and he have had to overcome so many obstacles to arrive finally at this relatively stable state of being friends, so I trust that you would not wish to risk that on my account." His eyes glinted humorously when he caught her looking at the box on the desk once again. "Are you completely sure you do not wish to have a look inside? I would be most delighted to end your suffering."

"No, thank you so much, I'm comfortable leaving it," she replied, but it came out a lot more disgruntled than she had intended. A gentleman would have pretended not to notice. "Additionally, I had the impression that seeing me suffer is something you rather enjoyed."

Ram'kel touched his hand to his heart with such a sincere display of devastation that she might even have believed him had the circumstances been different. So he was a good actor; that was something to be mindful of.

"What a cruel thing to say!" he cried out, his wide brown eyes looking up pleadingly from his fallen face.

She rolled her eyes. He didn't even bother saying that it wasn't true. Well, at least they were being honest with each other.

"I heard that Darnet himself was also rather enthusiastic about being sent away," he said, returning to their prior topic. "It seems he saw it a sign of how dangerous the Order considered him, that they went to such great lengths - even having him banished from the country - as executing him would just aid what he saw as his noble cause and result in his followers making him a martyr."

Heard that, had he? she thought sourly. She knew of that as well, only that she was in a position to peruse confidential files on the topic that contained Iklan's reports. He was not. Or at least he shouldn't have been. She ground her teeth. Another who had access to information that was none of his business, and he didn't even mind admitting it, not in the least.

"I hear there is reason to congratulate House Arbil on their forthcoming heir," she said, by way of changing the topic. "So you are about to become an uncle." She suppressed a shiver at the thought of what this man might teach an impressionable child. Maybe it was not such a bad thing that he was far away from his family right now... Even though he was a trial for her nerves, he at least couldn't corrupt his niece or nephew quite that easily.

She forced her eyes straight ahead when they felt a need to wander back to her desk.

A warm smile spread over his face, the first heartfelt expression she had seen on it so far today. "Yes, and I am very much looking forward to that. It is a while since there have been children running through the Arbil gardens. It will be good to see the residence filled with life and noise again." Then he returned to his former demeanour and said, "And I am glad he has found Valcredy. They are both very practical about this arrangement, and I assume that Ram'an will at least have fun with her on occasion. She used to be Lord Enric's lover before, was she not? That would imply that she is skilled bed-partner or she would not have managed to secure his attentions for more than a few hours."

Oh no, he didn't! He was not Sanaf, so he knew exactly that this was a highly inappropriate topic in more than one regard. Talking about sexual intercourse so openly might be acceptable in the Western Territories, but confronting a woman with her companion's former lover was considered tasteless on both sides of the sea. She closed her eyes and exhaled.

When she opened them again, she saw him grimace. "I apologise, that was uncalled for. Let me make up for that by freeing you from this unnecessary uncertainty and restraint on your very apparent inquisitiveness you are making yourself suffer right now." He placed his cup on the small table in front of him and stood up to step over to her desk.

"What?" she exclaimed and followed suit. "You want to make up for your indelicacy by opening my package? How is that any less inappropriate? Stop that right now or I will decide to forget that you are entitled to being treated as a representative of a friendly country! Right now you rather resemble an invading agent!"

He ignored her and stepped towards her desk where he removed the thick cord from around the parcel and then opened the lid to reveal a rectangular item wrapped in brown paper.

Eryn pushed him aside none too gently and was about the slap the lid shut angrily, but... well, it was basically open now, wasn't it? She resisted only for another moment, then sighed and pulled aside the paper. There was another protective layer, this time it was a length of sturdy cloth. When she removed that, too, she held a large, heavy book bound in something that clearly wasn't leather, but equally robust. She had no idea, if the brown colour was the material's natural shade or a dye.

Dark red letters embossed on the binding spelled the words The Book of Pleasure, and next to a name she had never heard or read before there was another one that was familiar, very much so: Illustrated by Vern.

Ram'kel looked over her shoulder, then started laughing.

She turned to him, angry at him, though not sure what for. Was it because he seemed to ridicule what looked like another precious gift from Vern? Or because he probably knew something she wasn't aware of and that caused him such merriment?

"What?" she barked at him and hugged the book protectively to her chest. "Is there something wrong?"

He shook his head. "Nothing wrong, not at all," he assured her when his flurry of hoots had died down to a chuckle. "This is a precious gift indeed. This book is... well, let us call it a piece of my own and essentially also your own culture. Though probably not one you would want to show to your guests here when inviting them to one of those charming social evening gatherings imbued with so much decorum that people here are so very fond of."

Eryn gave him a puzzled look, then opened the book at a page randomly to try and discern what he was talking about. Her eyes needed a few moments to identify precisely what the illustration before her eyes was depicting. The drawing was done extremely well, just like everything Vern produced; yet the shock of seeing something such as this in an actual book seemed to shut down her thought processes for a few moments.

Two naked figures, one male, the other female, very obviously enjoying themselves and each other. Rather a lot. The man was lying, bedded with a heap of cushions against his back, while the woman sitting on top of him was bracing her hands on his knees behind her while arching her spine. Both of them were having a very good time it would appear.

She slammed the book shut with a horrified expression. She was standing in her study looking at a picture of naked people performing athletic sex - with Ram'kel of House Arbil standing beside her.

His wide grin displayed his bright, evenly-spaced teeth. Yet again he was revelling in her discomfort.

"Go away," she growled. "This instant!"

The ambassador nodded and retreated slowly, though not without teasing her further. "I have heard of your prudery, but seeing it with my own eyes is a lot more entertaining. Why, if you are not even blushing!"

And indeed she felt heat rising to her cheeks, though there was not only embarrassment, but also fury involved with her current facial shade.

"Out!" she barked and was glad that he obeyed. The door was almost closed behind him and she was about to exhale, when he opened it a crack and said, "Have a look at number eighty-three. It is a general favourite, even though I myself am rather more fond of number fifty-six."

Only then did she hear the sound that finally released her from his annoying presence. She felt like throttling Vern. Though it was of course not his fault that Ram'kel had been present when the delivery arrived.

She sighed heavily and put the book down on her desk to turn back to the crate to look for some kind of message that had to be in the package somewhere. She found it little later, between the folds of cloth the book had been wrapped in.

Dear Eryn, I hope my gift reaches you soon - I'm eager to learn how you like it. When Vran'el saw what I was drawing, he insisted I make two more, one for him and another to sell. You won't believe how much they were willing to pay for it! My drawing class at the academy now want to learn how to draw naked people properly. You know how I didn't find adapting to this very open way of dealing with sexuality difficult when I came here, yet the thought of gathering around a naked person to draw him or her makes me a little uneasy. What if they turn out to be attractive women and, well, you know how men react in such a case, naturally! I'll have to sort out something here. Maybe I can shut the blood vessels down there so no blood can enter? I seriously hope I wouldn't do any lasting damage with that - and I don't want to ask my healer colleagues for advice. That would be so embarrassing. And I don't want to ask Valrad because he considers me as some kind of prodigy and this might make him think that I'm actually little more than a superficial idiot. Whatever advice you have would be very much appreciated. As for the book: I'm told there is some or other version of it in most households in the Western Territories. It used to be forbidden about two-hundred years back, but is now considered a piece of instructive literature that is even given to young people when they are on the verge of engaging in that pastime. Being such an important member of Takhan society, I decided that you needed one as well to better fit in. I look forward to hearing from you! By the way, I'm told number eighty-three is very popular among the locals here. I tried it, and I can't deny that it has its merits. Your friend Vern.

Eryn let the letter sink and wasn't sure whether to laugh or cry. He had sent her what was obviously an immensely valuable gift that would fetch a high price if she ever decided to put it on the market. For a joke. A book on what was a collection of instructions with very helpful illustrations. She had seen only one so far, and that one had already made her ears burn. And here he was, asking her how to avoid getting an erection while using naked people as models for teaching his students. Could this become any wilder?

She froze when she heard the entrance door closing, and shot up from the sofa to run to the desk, pick up the book and hastily wrap it in the cloth with clumsy fingers. If this were Gerit, Plia or Leris, she would never be able to look them in the eyes again should they find her with a book such as that in her study. They would probably think Eryn had locked herself in here to...

A knock sounded at her study door, and she clutched the book to her chest. Relax, she told herself. None of them could force her to show them what she was holding in her arms. She had magic, they did not. If need be, she could raise a shield, open the window, jump out and... She halted the runaway thoughts and exhaled. Panic was not helpful when it came to thinking straight.

The door opened and Enric stood in the doorway, surprised to see her standing there with eyes widened, her arms wrapped around what looked like a half-covered book. Eryn released her breath, relieved. So there was no need to escape through the window like a complete and utter idiot. That was a comfort.

"Hello, you. Why didn't you answer?" he asked. "I just saw Ram'kel walking away, and he seemed in a very good mood, which surely means as far as you are concerned, the opposite is the case." He nodded at her arms. "What do you have here?"

"Close the door, will you?"

He noted her exasperation, felt it through the mind bond and did as he was told. "What's the matter, my love?"

She swallowed. "I assume you have heard about what people call The Book of Pleasure?" A book that was obviously that popular couldn't possible have gone unnoticed by him.

"Certainly I have," he confirmed and pointed at the book in her arms. "Is that a copy?"

"Yes, and not just any," she sighed and pushed it into his hands.

He pulled away the cloth, read the names and laughed. "Vern illustrated one? Just look at that!" He took the book over to a sofa and opened it on his lap, turning the pages with a wide grin on his face that suggested that there was more than mere appreciation for the artist's talent involved in his enjoyment of the illustrations.

Eryn watched him for a while with folded arms, then asked, "Why did you never mention to me that a book of that kind is obviously so very common in the Western Territories?"

"You never were very comfortable talking about the topic of sexuality openly, so I didn't think you would be interesting in that kind of... literature," he shrugged.

"I might have been with you. You think I am prude, then? Maybe even boring?"

He looked up at the quiet tone and saw the worried frown on her forehead. "Come here, my love," he said and took her hand to pull her onto his lap after first putting the book aside. "I'm absolutely and utterly happy with how things are between us in the bedroom. I never felt any need for improvement in that area. And no, I consider you neither prudish nor a boring partner. You just prefer to treat that particular topic as a private one and struggle with a culture that laughs at you because of that attitude. I don't. If you would rather not keep the book because it makes you feel uneasy or awkward, we can return it to Vern and tell him that we appreciate his generosity, but would rather have a different piece in exchange."

Eryn smiled faintly and pushed her forehead against his tenderly, feeling safe and relieved the way he understood her so well.

"So you would really give the book back?"

"I would, definitely. With a heavy heart, because the drawings are really top grade and people will envy us. Hugely."

She chuckled. "Envy? Since when has that been so important to you?"

"Envy is one proof of success. Pity and sympathy you generally get for free, they are bestowed upon those we look down upon. Envy, though, is something you need to earn. We envy those we consider above us in some or other way. Achievements amount to little if there aren't those around to make us feel that we did well. And the most reliable proof is this very emotion that is always a painful and also by definition, an honest one: envy. Praise results more often than not from politeness or political consideration, or stems from the wish not to hurt those who are close to us. Not so with envy."

Eryn furrowed her brow, not too comfortable with the notion of using other people's negative feelings towards herself as an indicator of success. Moreover, discussing this with a warrior was futile. They were raised to be competitive - winning, being better, prevailing in a real fight meant surviving, after all.

"Being given the book shows no great achievements or success on our part, we were mere recipients of a gift. How does this situation fit your concept?"

"We, or rather you, discovered and nurtured his talent. Or he would never have started pursuing drawing seriously. That is an accomplishment," he countered. "So, would you like to give it back now or shall we keep it?"

She looked at the book thoughtfully, then bit her lip. "Give me a bit more time to decide. First I want to look at why there is such a fuss about number eighty-three."

*   *   *

Eryn went through her notes while trying to keep abreast with Enric as he made his way to the palace. She had spent several days preparing for the Council meeting today, and she was determined to induce them to cooperate. She had arguments, and good ones that would not fail to make them listen, of that she was sure. The lists she had cut into smaller slips of paper easily fit into her pockets, and now she wanted to make sure that nothing essential had slipped her mind. She couldn't afford to muddle this up today - if there were too many failed attempts at getting them to listen to her, soon nobody would take her seriously. The last time she failed to gain proper attention was at the previous meeting, and today she needed to show them that she was not somebody to be ignored just like that - if need be, she would have to remind them that people who provoked or otherwise angered an Aren woman were in great danger of being buried under several tons of roof material. Malhora had been right - collapsing the odd building was a handy way of reminding people that sometimes shutting up or simply nodding in agreement was the healthier alternative.

She wouldn't really collapse the Council hall, of course. Apart from the fact that the King would not at all be happy about her laying waste to any part of his Palace, it would also harm her reputation more than she could afford. It wouldn't do to be considered out of control and a slave to her impulses and emotions - but using the threat to remind them that it still was theoretically an option she harboured might help. And it would remind them that she was strong - stronger than almost any of them. Not many magicians were capable of collapsing a building without resorting to throwing bolts of energy; just charging the air around them with so much energy that the inert substance of walls and roofs started dancing and vibrating until the building lost its structural integrity was quite a feat - especially with high-ceilinged halls such as the Senate building in Takhan. Or the Council hall here in Anyueel...

She had first seen a hint of it when Enric had made motes of dust dislodge from the ceiling during their first visit in Takhan when he wanted to let the Senate know that Eryn's moving in at the Arbil residence for the duration of the proceedings was not something he was at all comfortable with. They had understood right away that it had to require immense magical strength to influence the building's substance from such a distance and had resulted in their being swift to accommodate him in that regard.

At that time Eryn hadn't known that she had enough strength to do that as well. She wouldn't even have known how to go about it, but when Legara had enraged her at that one Senate meeting she had found out two things: firstly, that she indeed possessed the considerable strength that was necessary for making a roof cave in, and secondly, that very strong emotions in combination with a lot of unrestrained magic charged the air enough to cause immense damage.

She had practised Enric's little trick from back then a little yesterday afternoon. She had not wanted to risk accidentally collapsing a building, but had gone down to the river to practice with trees. A few of them had some meagre, dried up leaves on the verge of dropping still attached to their twigs. Those she had tried to shake loose. She had found it immensely hard without the aid of strong emotions. She had thought back to Legara and the day at the Senate, and that was when she first managed to cause a reaction and make a few brown flakes gently drift down from above. Without recalling feelings of anger it was considerably harder to do, so she had decided to commence by letting them aid her in her endeavours for now. She had stopped abruptly when the top of one tree had burst into flames.

It was probably shrewder to do this with non-flammable objects, she decided then and there, and returned home. Enric had already been awaiting her, wanting to know why he had felt anger through the mind bond when she had told him that she just wanted to take a walk through the city.

Enric's arm clutching hers and pulling her out of the way of a cart brought her back to the here and now. Reading while walking was maybe not such a bright idea. Her steps had led her towards the middle of the street, decidedly not a safe place to be on bustling Kingsway.

"Eryn, put your notes away," he scolded her. "You'll get run over by a horse if you don't pay attention to your surroundings."

Even though she obeyed immediately and tucked her papers away, he held on to her upper arm until they reached the Palace gates. Eryn felt like she was being dragged along like a sullen child, which was also very likely the impression the people around them were getting. Yet in this case it was unjustified, because she was both nervous and eager to talk to the Council.

When they had entered the Palace precincts, they took off their cloaks and each draped them over one arm before walking towards the Council hall. Eryn adjusted her robe and checked with a few quick touches that her braid still felt orderly without too many strands standing out or if she had to redo it. It seemed to be satisfactory.

She fell back a few steps during her examination and ran to catch up again with Enric. He looked so immensely different in his blue robes, like a different person. Official, demanding, strict, the strategic thinker and superior who used his piercing blue eyes as his most formidable weapon. His imposing stature, which made him tower above most other men, surely helped to cement that impression. And now that Junar had altered all his robes, they accentuated his impressive build instead of mostly concealing it as it had before. A few skilled stitches had turned his attire from one-design-fits-no-one to something that actually looked good.

He turned to her and raised his brow. "What's the matter? Why are you examining me?"

"I was enjoying the view, Order Lord. Junar did a remarkable job with your robes. You should encourage Tyront to follow your example and have his altered as well. It would set an example."

"It's not the robe that makes the view so pleasant, my love. It takes all its elegance from what's underneath," he explained with complete and utter lack of modesty. "And can I suggest you pose that to Tyront himself? When did I become your messenger boy?"

"I was told that the ability and the willingness to delegate are important preconditions for being an effective leader," she explained.

"Yes, I know. I was the one to impart that wisdom to you. Though I seem to have omitted the fact that delegation doesn't work in both directions. You can't delegate things to your superiors, it's the wrong direction in the command chain. Though as you only have two superiors in the entire Order, that shouldn't be too much of a problem. There are plenty of magicians who have to do your bidding."

"I'd rather have you doing my bidding," she grinned.

He bent down to her ear and whispered, "Not as long as I'm wearing the robe, my love. It is meant to show to the world - and that includes you - that I am in charge."

She nodded thoughtfully. "That essentially means I'm subordinated to your robe."

Enric was glad when the doors to the Council hall came into sight. "If that idea helps you to grasp the principle of following my commands, I'd better start wearing them at home from now on."

Eryn refrained from chuckling as they had almost reached the hall and she wanted to make a business-like, no-nonsense impression on her colleagues today. Being seen to enjoy herself wouldn't aid her to appear adamant, strict and in control.

Tyront strolled towards them.

"Enric wants me to tell you that your robe is shapeless and in dire need of improvement and that you should be a role model for the rest of the Council members by demonstrating that you embrace the new while at the same time holding on to useful achievements from the past," Eryn told him quietly even before he had a chance to greet them.

The Order's leader stared at her for a moment, then his gaze wandered to Enric. "What was that?"

Enric sighed deeply and shook his head at his companion. "Very funny."

Eryn pulled up her brow in mock astonishment. "I'm just following your orders, as is due and proper as long as you are wearing your robe. At least that is what I was told is expected of me."

Tyront looked from one to the other and couldn't help feeling that he was missing out on a private witticism. "Did you tell her to say that now or not?"

Eryn lifted her arm and offered, "I can prove that he did - I herewith agree to a truth block. Ask me whether or not Enric wanted me to tell you about your robe."

Enric pushed her arm down again. "You are so going to pay for that later. Now off you go and let me explain this to Tyront before he despatches me on stable duty." He waited until Eryn strode off towards her seat before turning back to his superior. "She wanted me to suggest that your robe might profit from a few alterations. I instructed her to do that herself instead of using me as her messenger boy. So she was right that I wanted her to tell you herself, but she made it sound as if what she was professing just now was my opinion instead of hers."

Tyront smiled and shook his head. "Nicely played, though. And the way she phrased it not even a truth block would have uncovered her little lie. I'll have to keep in mind that she is getting better at spinning untruths."

It didn't take long until all Council members and the King's observer had arrived and taken their seats.

Tyront waited until all eyes were on him before saying, "A good morning to you, my Lords and my Lady. There are two major issues we wish to take care of today. The first is questioning Onil as several of you have requested, and the second is a number of matters Lady Eryn would like to discuss with us today."

That earned her several glances - a few curious, others sceptical, two of them decidedly unfriendly. She met them all with the same unperturbed half-smile.

Upon Tyront's signal the guards opened the doors to admit Onil, who was looking pale and nervous. He glanced at his father once and then made sure to keep his gaze elsewhere. Eryn gave him an encouraging smile and wished she could tell him not to worry, that everything would be in order. But then she had no idea what her colleagues were up to, if they really only wanted to ask him a few questions or if some of them were looking for someone to blame for what had happened now that Darnet had been declared officially insane and she herself had been cleared. It was never a good thing when bad things happened and there was nobody to pin blame on. It made people restless and they started looking for a convenient candidate so they could push responsibility on them with a clear conscience, believing that justice must have been served as somebody was being sent to the dungeons.

She balled her fists with grim determination. If this is what they thought they could try with Onil today, they would soon find themselves in trouble with her. She wouldn't watch this, and neither would Lord Poron, his immediate superior. Tyront, too, would hardly condone such an act - had he wanted to put somebody behind bars and walls, then he wouldn't have ensured that Darnet received treatment in Takhan. And then there was Enric, who might be a ruthless fellow when it suited his purposes, but who still wouldn't waste a man just like that, sacrifice him in order to appease a few Council members.

Onil stopped a few paces before the table and bowed to the assembled magicians.

Tyront addressed him first, and Eryn was grateful that he kept his voice friendly to calm the healer. "Onil, I suppose you have a basic idea why we summoned you before us today. I want you to know that no charges have been laid against you. This is merely to discover more about a point that concerns us considerably, as you surely will understand." He waited for the younger man to nod before continuing with his first question, "Is there an organised underground resistance within the Order?"

Onil shook his head quickly. "No, my Lord. Not to my knowledge."

"Very well, so it has not yet progressed so far as that. That is good to hear. But I assume I would be right in assuming that there is a… What shall we call it? Let us say: a group of like-minded magicians who sometimes meet informally for a drink or two and happen to discuss what they would wish to be different in the Order?"

The healer swallowed once, then nodded without looking at anyone. "Yes, my Lord, that assumption is correct."

Eryn saw the Council members exchanging glances, though this revelation couldn't have been much of a surprise for them.

"Are you the leader of this... casual circle?" Tyront asked on.

Onil shook his head again. "There is no such thing as a leader, my Lord. As you said, we are nothing more than a few people meeting occasionally to talk about ideas."

Lord Aldon spoke up before Tyront could ask his next question. "You are obviously not aware, young man, that this is exactly how organised efforts at overthrowing governing structures begin. First you start meeting as a group of friends that just so happen to think similarly, and at one point there are so many of you that you start wondering if your numbers alone don't entitle you to take control."

"Thank you very much for that, Lord Aldon," Tyront said with a look that conveyed clearly how little he appreciated being interrupted. "Onil, when you say a few people, how many are we talking about here exactly?"

"Shouldn't we apply a truth block?" Lord Aldon interrupted again. "He might be leading us astray on purpose."

Tyront shot him another look. "I will apply a truth block afterwards and ask him to verify that all his answers were true. And now I would appreciate if you held back with your comments until I have completed asking my questions, Lord Aldon."

The Lord leaned back and folded his arms with a disgruntled expression. It wasn't hard to see that he didn't appreciate being put in his place like that in front of his colleagues and a man he considered a criminal.

When Onil was again the centre of attention, he cleared his throat and answered the question he had been asked. "I would say we are now about twenty people. Twenty-five at the most."

"For how long has this been going on? Your casual meetings, I mean."

"For about six months, I think."

Six months, Eryn thought. That was shortly after she and Orrin had left for Takhan with their families. When four members of the Order had been granted permission to escape the restrictions of the Order for months at a time and Enric had even left the Order altogether.

"How did this commence?" Tyront continued his enquiries.

"First it was just two people, friends, discussing things. Then somehow each of them mentioned a few tidbits of that conversation to others, and after a while it turned out that there were a fair few people who thought the same way. We ended up bringing friends with us, then those friends themselves invited others... It wasn't planned, it just somehow happened. Every time we got together, there were at least one or two new faces."

A group of twenty-five people that had several months ago started as nothing more than two friends having a conversation. That was not a good sign. That was about one sixth of the magicians, not counting the children. Erbál's warning before his departure for Pirinkar had been well-founded. A pity that Tyront had ignored it in favour of waiting.

"Darnet's attack on me..." The Order's leader began, and for the first time Onil interrupted him.

"I swear to you, my Lord, we had nothing to do with that, and neither were we aware of what he was planning! We would never have agreed to such a thing as that. Quite the opposite - had we known, we would have done all we could to impede him!" He turned to the other Council members. "His actions now pose a danger to us because we are now considered a threat by you, something that needs to be dealt with. We don't want to be dealt with, it's not necessary!"

"What is it you want?" Tyront asked calmly.

"We want to be allowed to voice our discontent, share it and see that we are not alone. And at one point many of us were hoping that somebody will listen to what we have to say."

"What if nobody would listen to you? What would be your next step in that case?"

The healer blinked as if surprised by the question. "We never really considered that likelihood, to be honest. Lady Eryn is known to share many of our sentiments, so we knew that there was a good chance that at least one Council member would listen to what we had to say."

"You asked Lady Eryn to assist you in the Council," Tyront pointed out. "What..."

There was a commotion outside the doors of the Council hall that made them all pause. First there were loud words muffled through the doors and almost impossible to understand. Then the doors themselves opened and a number of magicians in brown robes entered.

The Council members all came to their feet within seconds to face the uninvited newcomers.

Eryn's heart pounded while she let her gaze wander over the group of magicians. About twenty, she reckoned at first glance. Their age ranged between twenty and forty she guessed quickly. One of them seemed even younger, about Vern's age. That wasn't at all good. Young people tended to overreact in critical situations, more so than their veteran colleagues. She would have to keep an extra keen eye on that one.

They didn't look like a group of revolutionaries bent on overthrowing the Council, but a number of people who had assembled arbitrarily and had probably needed a little alcohol and a lot of encouragement to storm that meeting.

Tyront stepped forward, his posture non-threatening, but still authoritative. "Gentlemen, we are in the middle of something here. However, your rather dramatic entry clearly shows that there must be something important you wish to make known. Speak out, then."

Eryn nodded almost imperceptibly to herself. She liked how he had reacted. There was more than a hint of his disapproval at their unannounced appearance visible in his frown and the narrowed eyes, but he was nevertheless offering to listen.

One of the group, who Eryn believed to be one of the teachers present when Vern had been stabbed by accident with a table leg more than two years ago, spoke up.

"We are here to tell you that we will not let you banish Onil from the Kingdom! He did nothing whatever to deserve that, and if you send him off, you need to do the same with every single one of us here!"

Tyront exhaled and pinched the bridge of his nose. His voice sounded tired when he asked, "What would give you the idea that Onil is about to be exiled? You think that just because we have contact with another country now we are starting getting rid of people - just like that?"

"You did with Darnet," another voice piped up.

That was good, Eryn thought. One of them doing all the talking would imply that they had a spokesperson, something like a leader, but that didn't seem to be the case. Not yet at least.

"Darnet," Tyront explained patiently, "was not sent to the Western Territories to banish him from the Kingdom for his deeds, but to offer him the chance of treatment of his condition. We are not equipped to provide such treatment here, and our friends in the west offered their help. This, gentlemen, was his only alternative to being locked up in the dungeons. We have so far not been able to discern any tell-tale signs of Onil's suffering from a similar condition, so you may rest assured that there are currently no plans to ship him off to Takhan as well," he concluded dryly.

"You won't send him away, then?" a man in his early thirties asked, wanting confirmation.

"That's what I said," Tyront confirmed.

Eryn watched the assembled intruders exchanging glances. It seemed they were a little baffled. They were probably still trying to decide if they had reached their goal rather more speedily and with less resistance than they had expected, or if they had just interrupted a Council meeting unnecessarily.

"There is more," ventured a fourth voice, belonging to a man of Rolan's age.

Several of his fellow magicians turned to him, a look of dismay on their faces. Ah yes, Eryn thought sourly, that is the disadvantage of being a disorganised group of like-minded people - if one of them said something he was not supposed to, it would be considered the entire group's opinion. And as there was no leader to make sure only the things meant to be uttered at this point in time would be shared, there was no way of controlling what would be said.

"Yes?" Tyront asked warily.

"There are things we want you to know, that we are not willing to go on just accepting as they are!" the same man exclaimed vigorously.

Eryn saw how a few of them closed their eyes at this ill-timed announcement.

"Yes, I gathered that much," the Order's leader replied coolly. "I don't think that this is the right framework to share your grief."

"I told you they wouldn't listen!" a sharp whisper was audible from the group. Eryn guessed that the speaker had either underestimated the excellent acoustics in the hall or didn't care if their words were heard.

"I merely said that this is not the right time to talk about this - we are in the middle of something here, as I told you before," Tyront thundered, and made both the intruders and the several of the Council members flinch. "And I will thank you for not putting words in my mouth! If you want to be listened to, you come to me in a manner that suggests that I am not dealing with a mob, but with considerate people who have given some thought to what they want to tell me." His cold, blue eyes fixed the group, took in all of their faces. "You don't come to my Council unannounced, interrupt it in such a manner and then demand to be heard! You will make an appointment, select a few people to represent your cause and then talk to me properly! Have I made myself understood?" The last sentence resonated through the hall. He had not shouted, but somehow he had changed his voice just enough to make it seem that way, letting the architecture do the work for him.

The magicians nodded hastily, suddenly appearing a lot less adventurous and righteous, but rather eager to retreat and get out of Tyront's sight. Eryn sighed with relief. It looked as if this incident was now over without any major damage being done.

That was the moment when armed men spilled in through the still open doors to the corridors. Men in identical Palace guard uniforms with drawn swords started to fill the rear of the room, blocking the exit. Eryn's eyes widened. She couldn't believe what she was seeing - twenty, thirty, forty... fifty men finally lined up. She was barely able to avoid slapping the flat of her hand against her forehead. What complete imbecile had decided that sending in fifty non-magicians against more than twenty magicians was a workable idea? Tyront alone could have stood his ground against the intruding magicians easily, more so if Enric and Orrin had joined him. Now it looked like the Council had called for reinforcements - however useless they would prove in any struggle. Even Eryn without much enthusiasm or talent when it came to fighting could have held them off easily by doing nothing more than raising a shield. And if she wanted to get rid of them, she would send weak bolts through her shield to make them collapse.

She could see Tyront's face. It didn't look happy, and neither did Enric's. This ill-advised action had made the situation a lot more difficult right now.

The magicians who were now stuck between the Council members and the guards looked panicky. A moment ago it had seemed as if they were being dismissed only to find themselves now surrounded. If they decided that they were willing to defend their freedom and avoid being locked up unjustly, they would plough like a hot knife through butter through the guards blocking the exit.

They had already proved that they were not organised as such, so nobody knew what kind of casualties a frightened group of uncoordinated magicians might cause among non-magicians. If they hurt one of the guards somehow, there would be a whole new set of troubles to deal with, as magicians didn't get away lightly with injuring those who couldn't defend themselves.

"Your little plan didn't unfold quite the way you intended, eh, Lady Eryn? Having a bunch of easily impressionable fools rush in to your minion's defence like that..." Lord Aldon's voice rose above the commotion.

Eryn's head slowly turned in his direction. What was that? Had the situation not be that serious, she would have laughed. Had somebody knocked him on the head or something? Maybe they should send him off to Takhan to give him treatment...

While her reaction to the absurd accusation was amusement, Enric's was clearly not. His loud voice thundered through the hall when he snarled with his index finger lifted in Lord Aldon's direction, "You should be very careful with what you say, or there will be consequences! Baseless accusations cannot be tolerated, and a Council member should know better than to display such flagrant disregard for our rules!"

"Defending your companion is truly more important than stopping this upheaval here, Lord Enric?" Lord Aldon spat back. "I shudder at your priorities!"

"Then you may just as well shudder at your own, as accusing my companion was to you obviously of greater importance than taking care of the situation at hand!" Enric retorted. "You and I will have a little talk when this is over!"

Eryn's head reeled. This had to be some kind of stunt. They were not truly snapping at each other while mayhem could break out any moment now if only one person lost it and did something rash under the stress and caused the entire Council hall to be a mess of bolts being hurled around and possibly even swords sticking out of bodies.

"Eryn," she heard Onil's desperate plea, "please do something before someone gets hurt! I implore you!"

Eryn swallowed. What in the world made him think that she was in a position to take care of this? There were two magicians present higher up than her - why didn't he appeal to them?

She felt fingers close around her upper arm and turned to look at Tyront. She hadn't even noticed that he had crossed the hall. His expression was grim and determined.

"Onil is right. You are the one both sides will listen to, at least for a while. Those magicians consider the Council their enemies, but not you. I want you to take care of this situation without escalating it. Do you hear me?"

Eryn nodded, a lump in her throat. Wasn't that just splendid. He had truly taken this whole pandemonium in front and around them, wrapped it into a neat little package and put it in her hands.

She breathed in and out a few times, closing her eyes to reach that place of peace and quiet she retreated to when she was healing patients. When she opened them again, the situation had not changed, there were still about one hundred men in the Council hall, all tense, a few probably on the verge of violence.

A shrill whistle echoed painfully through the chamber, reflected back to them and making several people flinch. When Eryn removed her fingers from her mouth, all eyes were upon her. She changed the quality of the air around her slightly to lend her voice more volume, make it more impressive. This was an institution that ran on authority, so that was exactly what she had to impersonate.

"You!" her voice boomed while her finger pointed to the assembled guards. "Out! You are not needed here."

The men exchanged puzzled glances with their colleagues. This was a perilous situation, and it was their job to assist in such things, wasn't it? Being sent away just like that was not within their frame of reference.

"Now!" Eryn barked and that one word delivered with menace finally made them move, out the door and along the corridor. She waited until all of them were gone, then stepped forward to glare at the group of brown-robed magicians. So far the men around her were either astonished or curious enough to focus on her instead of the other group. Her taking control despite the fact that two higher ranking magicians were present was undoubtedly a surprise to all of them. Maybe this was something Tyront had counted on, she mused, while letting the intruders become really uneasy under her stare. She wanted them to wish that they could get out of here quickly and be grateful when she finally granted them that desire.

"You," she finally said and made sure to meet every single pair of eyes, "follow me."

They parted hastily when she stepped forward, clearing the way in a hurry. She turned to look at Tyront, who nodded back once to give her permission to lead them away, leaving the rest solely to her discretion. She saw how Enric took a step in her direction, but stopped when Orrin turned up next to her. So he didn't want her to be alone with the intruders but accepted that Orrin would, if necessary, protect her as fiercely as he himself would. This meant Tyront and Enric would take care of the Council while she and Orrin would handle the intruders.

She marched ahead and out the Council hall, deliberately not turning back to see if they were following her. Turning back would only demonstrate uncertainty, and she needed to show them confidence. Confidence that they were not so imprudent as to ignore her command. And indeed she heard the shuffling of feet only a second later when they turned to walk after her.

She exhaled and walked on, increasing the distance between the rebelling magicians and the Council with every step. Eryn felt that breathing had become a little easier now. The immediate danger was over. There had been no escalation, nobody was hurt, there was nothing that would stand in the way of dealing with this issue in a civilised fashion. Neither group had any reason to seek chastisement or retribution. The only thing that was now important was distance to allow frayed tempers to become soothed again.

* * *

Enric watched the group of men retreating, Orrin the last one to step outside, closing the doors behind him. A powerful surge of pride went through him. Eryn had handled the situation extremely well. She had been quick, decisive and forbidding. It thrilled him to see her like that - in control, powerful, formidable. He wondered if Tyront had felt like that when Enric had first shown that he was slowly growing into his leadership role.

He exchanged a look with Tyront, who appeared eagerly pleased, but made sure not to make that too obvious. Right now, there were still the Council members to deal with.

And sure enough, the first complaint came swiftly.

"You are letting them walk away just like that? They all but stormed the Council!" Lord Remdel cried out indignantly.

"The only thing we can accuse them of is having bad manners," Enric said calmly. "There is no law against interrupting Council meetings, or we would regularly have to discipline messengers or those who sent them."

Lord Seagon was the next to speak. "Why did you let her handle this? Or rather, why did you order her to do it - unless I'm very much mistaken. It may now seem to our magicians that our two leaders felt unable to deal with this situation themselves."

Tyront sighed. "That is just one way of looking at it, Lord Seagon. Another one would be that I did not judge the situation to be dire enough to require my personal intervention. A third way might be that I decided to test our newest and youngest member to see how she managed to resolve a tense standoff. Though the reason that truly made me delegate this matter to her is the answer to a very simple question: Who do you think was the most likely person in that room our visitors would trust enough to follow out of here and turn their unprotected backs to people that might or might not have turned out to be enemies?"

"Certainly, she probably is the leader they claim not to have," Lord Aldon murmured resentfully.

Enric's eyes narrowed and restraint and fury fought a vicious battle for dominance inside him. It took them about two seconds to strike a compromise: Enric was allowed to give in to his urge to demonstrate his disapproval, but only very briefly and without resorting to violence.

He closed the distance between himself and Lord Aldon, grabbed his astounded colleague by the collar and pulled him up slightly so that he came to stand on his toes.

"Let me warn you once more," he growled with clenched teeth, "that I will not tolerate your slandering my companion! If you have evidence suggesting that Lady Eryn is in league with Order magicians who are aiming to overthrow the Council, then present it! If not, you'd better shut your mouth or I promise I will do it for you. This is the last warning you will receive about this. Don't test me, Lord Aldon. I will gladly accept whatever punishment Lord Tyront sees fit to mete out to me for manhandling a subordinate."

He then released his colleague, watching how he staggered backward a few steps before he became steady on his feet again. Then he smiled happily and suggested, "Well, I suggest we return to questioning Onil, who is surely eager to get all this behind him. Shall we?"

* * *

Eryn waited until all of them had filed into the large meeting room before she raised her hand to indicate the square table, which was large enough to accommodate all of them easily. "Have a seat."

They quietly followed her instruction and sat down without a word to wait for her to speak again.

Eryn decided to remain standing. It would not only give her the advantage of being in a position where they had to look up at her, but also enable her to express her dissatisfaction better.

"You complete and utter morons," she started calmly with her hands on her back. She caught a glance of Orrin who was leaning against a column to her right with arms folded and barely managing to contain the smile his lips wanted to express.

The assembled magicians looked at her with an array of looks upon their faces that ranged from surprised to embarrassed.

"What exactly did you hope to accomplish by storming in there like that? I suppose we may thank our stars you decided to leave the pitchforks at home! If the Council truly had wanted to send Onil off to Takhan - which is not an option on the table, believe me - you wouldn't have had the ghost of a chance of changing their mind with the ridiculous performance you just gave. Do you think they would ever agree to anything you demanded in such a manner? Think! What precedent would that set? It would be like cordially inviting every idiot to try the very same thing the next time they are unhappy about something. You were lucky Lord Tyront kept you from voicing your demands in there! It would have been an effective way of making sure the Council was unable to be seen ever agreeing to a single one of them." She paused to breathe out audibly and give her words a little time to sink in. Then she went on, seemingly addressing the words more to herself than to her audience, "How is it possible that there was not a single person in this group of more than twenty who remembered how to use their brain? I was taught these subjects for little more than a year, but in my case it was enough to let me recognise utter stupidity when it is before me." She looked back at them. "Have you ever even heard of tactics, or strategy? Whatever were you thinking?"

One man hesitantly raised his voice, "There is so much that..."

"Shut up," Eryn snapped at him. "That was a rhetorical question, I don't need an answer to that. The evidence I saw suggests that there was not much thinking involved." She leaned forward and placed both palms on the smooth, cold stone surface of the table, her stare searing. "Let me tell you a little something about what my own plans for this Council meeting were today." She pulled out her notes and tossed them onto the table, causing them to slide halfway across and spread out. Most of them tried to decipher what was on the papers, but none of them dared to reach out and pull one towards them. "After Onil's interrogation I would have presented to the Council a few ideas that I strongly suspect go in the direction you were wishing. I would have suggested an increase in the quota of healers being trained. My next move would have been to introduce my colleagues to the idea of sending fully trained healers out to work in other cities, towns and villages. Some of you may know that Lord Enric owns ships that transfer the Kingdom's goods to Takhan at regular intervals. As the barrier in the sea requires magic to get across, he is forced to hire magicians from Takhan so at least one is aboard every ship. This would have been an opportunity to try and convince the Council to reconsider the Order's current approach when it comes to excluding magicians from all professions that not involving fighting or healing. This might have been an chance to open new doors for all of us in the long run - enabling us all to travel, choose a place to live outside the city, take over family businesses." She pursed her lips. "How many eldest sons or only children do we have here?"

Six of them raised their hands.

"Congratulations." Her voice had regained its calm. "You just successfully thwarted my attempts to enable you one day to continue what your family started."

Not a single one of them met her eyes. They stared either at the table, at their hands or at her notes.

"And now I will not only not be able to present what took me days to prepare, but also miss the rest of Onil's interrogation. I wanted to be there so he knows he has a friend in that hall with him, so that I can make sure everything is done the way it should be. But instead I'm here with you to educate you on your own stupidity, on how you managed to hinder my pursuing your interests with your unthinking, ill-advised actions!" She slapped her flat palm on the table, making them recoil. "Thank you so much!"

She straightened and closed her eyes for a moment. When she looked back at them, she almost felt pity at their wretched expressions. Almost, but not quite.

"I want you to listen to me, and I want you to do it carefully. You will leave the Palace at a leisurely pace that will not make any guard around here suspect that you are escaping and induce them valiantly to try to stop you. Should you decide to provoke a single one of them into attacking you so you have a chance to get rid of your frustration, you will have to face me, and let me promise you that you wouldn't like that. You will not meet anymore for the time being. You won't need me to tell you that there will be plenty of agents around who have an eye on every single one of you now that you have so conveniently made your identities known to the Council." She omitted the fact that most of the Council members had certainly been aware of that already, that was beside the point. "Don't do a single thing that would make the Council think that exercising lenience in this matter is unjustified. And now get out of my sight!"

Chairs scratched over the floor when the men hurriedly got up to do as they were told. Less than a minute later she was alone with Orrin.

"Look at you," the warrior grinned and pushed away from his column. "You certainly cut them down to size." He strolled over to the table and picked up her notes, scanning the sheets. Then he whistled through his teeth. "They really managed to pick the right meeting for their little riot. I hope this will not doom your efforts to failure."

Eryn accepted the papers when he handed them to her and shook her head, smiling. "No, I don't think so. Despite my rather harsh words I will be able to use the incident today to aid me in my endeavours. Dissatisfied magicians who can rise up any moment are no longer just a theory or an outside chance, but have turned out to be a real thing. Certainly, this just now was an unorganised attempt at being heroic, but it is just a matter of time until others join them, both magicians and non-magicians. I can now argue that there is the threat of instability that might split the Order unless we show at least some goodwill and make changes rather sooner than later. And then there is the danger that Vedric will very probably be next in line to take over the Order one day unless we change the practice of assigning ranks due to magical strength." She grinned broadly. "There is little I dare rely on when it comes to the Council, but I'm absolutely positive that the idea of having my son on top is not one that gives them joy. I'll do my best to fan that flame and turn it into fear, and then we can start working together to provide for a better future."

Orrin slung an arm around her shoulders and pressed her close. "Nicely done. I'm proud of you. Seriously."

Eryn accepted the compliment with a regal nod and they left the meeting room, heading in unspoken agreement to Tyront's quarters.

* * *

Eryn and Orrin had taken a seat in Tyront's parlour with their superior's companion. Vyril had opened the door for them, surprised at seeing them at her doorstep when she knew that a Council meeting was in progress. Eryn vaguely mentioned that she and Orrin had to leave somewhat earlier and now needed to wait for their superior to report to him. She wasn't sure how much Tyront wanted to shelter his companion from the Order's business.

Vyril had just nodded towards the sofas and told them to make themselves comfortable while she prepared drinks for them.

They had then talked about how well the orphanage under Vyril's care funded by Enric - and lately by bored aristocratic ladies who needed an excuse for elaborate dinner parties - was doing. The younger children had generally adapted to the changes easily and welcomed the regular meals, warm clothes, proper shoes, toys and comfortable living surroundings. The older ones who had been used to fending for themselves and considered the world an unfriendly place full of enemies had not all taken well to being made to adhere to rules in exchange for a safe, warm and clean place, and nourishing food. The teaching that had been irregular at best before was now a permanent fixture in the orphanage, so that reading, writing and arithmetic were now only the start, not the full extent of what was possible. That had also met with a measure of resistance from a few of the orphanage's residents.

But Vyril was not one to be easily fazed. She was able to preserve her polite smile and inform her conversation partners about their options and what consequences each decision would entail. It was not hard to make her young charges understand that everything had its price. Living in relative comfort, receiving food, clothes, toys and education required them in turn to follow rules. No more beating each other up, stealing, peddling forbidden substances but instead adhering to the curfew, helping to keep the house clean and sitting down to practise whatever task their teachers had set them.

Vyril also told Eryn that Plia came by regularly to help with whatever needed to be done, be it helping the younger children with their exercises or providing herbs when somebody was ill. Eryn swallowed. Plia worked hard at the clinic; she was more often than not the last one to leave the building. A young woman of fifteen should not have quite that much on her plate, and yet it was admirable that she had, after taking the chance to improve her own living circumstances so energetically, not forgotten where she came from.

She saw how Orrin's expression softened at that as well.

Little more than half an hour later the entrance door opened and Tyront and Enric stepped inside. Neither of them seemed in the least surprised to find the other two magicians in Vyril's company.

Once Enric had closed the study door behind them, Tyront turned to Eryn and put both his hands on her shoulders.

"You did extremely well today. The entire case might have ended a lot less peacefully had it been handled without enough care. Come and sit down. Tell me what happened after you led them out of the Council hall."

Eryn smiled and sank onto the sofa next to Enric. Tyront sat on the chair next to her while Orrin again opted for standing, and leaned against the bookshelves that stretched from floor to ceiling.

"There isn't much to be told. I led them to a meeting room, explained to them why their course of action was not the smartest and advised them to stay out of trouble," Eryn summarised.

Orrin chuckled. "You repeatedly told them that they were idiots and that they had managed to stop you from acting in their interests by forcing you to leave the Council in order to scold them when instead you should have been presenting your suggestions. I pity that poor son of yours when he is up before you for a proper talking-to one day. Never before have I seen a group of mostly grown men lower their eyes and accept that they are to be treated like inconsiderate children. Who would have thought you had that talent?"

"Impressive motherly qualities," Enric grinned.

"Maybe we should despatch you to teach the more difficult classes now and again," Tyront suggested. "After a lesson with you they might be grateful to have their regular teachers back."

"Oh, shut up, the three of you," Eryn sighed tiredly.

"You can't tell me to shut up," Tyront reminded her in a seemingly relaxed manner, although there was a tiny, hardly discernible, spike in his tone.

"As long as I'm willing to bear the consequences, I can tell you whatever I want," she gave back. "What I can't do is make you act on it."

"You might want to consider that I am, in contrast to yourself, in a position to make you act. Specifically to carry out whatever punishment I consider fit for disrespectful remarks," he warned.

Eryn swallowed her remark that she was by now pretty good when it came to cleaning stables, in fact almost longed for the duty as it provided for some variety. He might be good-natured at the moment because she had managed to avert a fight in the Council hall, but clearly not grateful enough to let her get away with brazen cheek.

She nodded at him once to acknowledge the warning and then asked, "Now, how did the rest of the meeting go?"

"There was nothing spectacular after you left," her companion explained. "We finished questioning Onil. He told us there had been talk of doing something, pursuing their goals more actively for a while, but after Darnet attacked Tyront, that was no longer a way forward. Nobody wanted to be associated with such behaviour. And they had not considered doing anything of that kind, but rather wanted to withhold their labour for a day to get the Council's attention for a start. At the end we applied a truth block to make sure that all his answers were honest. They were."

Tyront smiled thinly. "You forgot to mention a little detail, my friend. One I bet your companion would love to hear about." He looked at Eryn. "Enric collared Lord Aldon and threatened him with violence if he wasn't more careful what he said about you."

She laughed and put both hands on her heart. "You threatened him just for me? Oh, that's so sweet!"

He reached over to take her hand and kiss her knuckles. "What can I say? I'm an old-fashioned romantic. Somebody speaks ill of my lady and I shall rush to defend her honour."

Tyront leaned back in his chair. "I'm feeling generous today, Eryn. Is there something I can grant you in recompense?"

Her face went blank before she said, "Yes, there is one thing I have wanted for a long time now: make me the Head of the clinic."

Her superior stared at her for a few moments, then covered his eyes with his hands. "Eryn, please, you know that this would be…"

She interrupted him with a laugh, "Don't worry, this was a put-on. I think Lord Poron is doing a marvellous job, and I'll be off to Takhan again in three months, so it would hardly make sense."

He gave her a disgruntled look. "That's what I get for trying to be nice to you."

"Speaking of Lord Poron - you could tell me what in the name of all that is good and decent has possessed him to agree to putting Loft in charge of the clinic's administration? Did he have the feeling that things were running too smoothly and thought that hiring somebody to irritate the staff as much as possible was the only solution to that?"

Tyront shrugged. "I can't speak for Lord Poron and Rolan - who agreed to it as well, by the way - but I can tell you that the choice is not such a bad one. I never liked Loft particularly myself and I know that you have ample reason to dislike him as well, yet the fact remains that he is an able and experienced organiser. His notions are not always the most… public-spirited ones and he is not a person to adapt to modern ideas easily, but these are not character traits that are important for the position of administrative head, are they? Quite the opposite: he is not the individual who is supposed to come up with revolutionary new concepts, now that things are running smoothly the way Rolan has established them. Working with two Kings has made Loft good at one thing: following orders. And as he

525

will in this position be subordinated to Lord Poron, you may depend on these orders being sensible ones."

Eryn sighed and nodded. So it seemed she was stuck with him. Well, at least she only had to deal with him for six months at a time. And she would just have to get used to going to Lord Poron if there was some problem and asking him to deal with Loft. She would miss Rolan, she was sure of that. After all they had gone through with each other, their aggravations and troubles, to reach this state of mutual respect where they could now rely on each other, it felt to her as if everything had been in vain now that he would soon be relocating to Takhan just like that. That was all Pe'tala's fault, of course. Typical.

"What are we to do with our overzealous magicians?" Enric asked.

"Keep them informed, I would say," Eryn suggested. "They know that I intend to convince the Council to agree to my ideas, so let's invite one of them to those meetings where they are discussed. I would pick Onil for that if he agrees. He can inform his comrades about progress - provided there is some. And even if there is none, he can at least tell them that we are discussing the issues."

Orrin nodded. "I like it. Punishing them would give the wrong message. So far they have been merely impolite by interrupting the meeting and a bit forward in trying to save Onil from a fate that was never on the cards."

"Alright," Tyront said, "then I will let Onil and the Council know that there will be an observer at certain meetings from now on." He looked at Eryn. "Well, that means we had better schedule another one soon so you can finally tell us how we can make the Order and the Kingdom a superior place. Better make it convincing, do you hear me?"

"I'll try," she promised.

CHAPTER 31

A Favour

Eryn walked across the parlour with Vedric on her hip and Urban following behind. They had just returned from visiting Junar and Orrin. It was unusually quiet in the house despite the fact that she saw there was light in Enric's study. He didn't usually work at this late an hour, even less often now that his sister was in the city. Maybe Leris was out with Gerit and he wanted to use the time until his family returned to catch up on some work.

She reached the open door and was surprised to see that he was not alone as the peace would suggest, but with his sister. Enric was sitting behind his desk, staring ahead gloomily, holding a glass of what looked like strong spirits in his hand. Interesting, Eryn thought. It was not often that she saw him drink anything more intoxicating than wine, and that he usually did only when they had company or had been invited somewhere.

Leris was lying slouched on the settee to the left of his desk; she was clutching the same kind of glass as well.

"Is this a sibling-bonding thing where you get companionably tipsy?" Eryn asked lightly. "That should be a lot more fun, as I recall."

Two pairs of eyes sent her a look that conveyed beyond a doubt how little they appreciated her attempts to make light of their mood right now.

She sighed and entered the room. "What's happened?"

"Mother happened," Leris growled.

"Could I have some more details here or would you like to make a guessing game out of this?" Eryn asked, feeling how the mood in the room began to affect her as well. In a few minutes she would maybe be as upset as those two without even knowing why.

Enric twirled the liquid in his glass and stared at the oily film that clung to the sides. "The Palace contacted mother today. She is to go there in two days and either deliver good reasons for leaving her companion, agree to return to him, pay the fine or be sent to prison. Despite the fact that she has good reason, she can't prove that Anwin was unfaithful."

Ah, yes, now she understood. "And Gerit still has no intention of letting you pay the fine but insists on going to prison, which the two of you do not approve of at all."

Enric's expression was pained. "She is my mother! Asking me to watch her being sent to prison and thus be made to suffer punishment for a completely reasonable decision is a bit much to ask. Especially as the amount to be paid to keep her out of it is nothing to speak of."

"Yet still more than she possesses, I assume?" his companion asked carefully.

"But not more than either Enric or me can easily afford," Leris growled. "She is so incredibly stubborn! How hard can it be to accept some money from her own children?"

Eryn raised her brow at that statement. She would have expected Leris of all people to understand about pride. But this was probably not a character trait she associated with her mother.

"Considering that she has accepted being given a house by her son already, I would think that it is only natural that she doesn't want to be a burden on her children - irrespective of the fact that you wouldn't regard her as just that," Eryn explained carefully. "She has just freed herself very bravely from a companion she was financially dependent on. I can't imagine that the idea of now depending on her children instead is very pleasant for her. If going to prison regularly for a while gives her the feeling that she is in a position to pay the price for her own independence - who are you to deny her that?"

Enric placed his glass on the table and shook his head. "We are talking about a long time here, Eryn. The dissolution of the commitment will only be granted without Anwin's consent if she is willing to either pay the fine every two months for two years - or alternatively spend two out of every eight weeks in prison! That's six months in total that she has to spend behind bars!" He closed his eyes. "She might at one point decide that this is more than she can bear and rather return to Anwin than endure this for two years."

His companion rolled her eyes. "That is how little you think of your mother? You think she would just give up like that? Every two weeks in prison will be followed by six she spends in her own house here, where she can do whatever she pleases. I have been to the place your father calls his home, and I am convinced that I'd rather have occasional stays at a prison for quite even longer than two years if the alternative were going back there."

Enric sighed. "That's you, Eryn. Were you in her place, I wouldn't be worrying much. You are strong, determined and proud. You proved very impressively that being kept a prisoner didn't manage to subdue your spirit. But mother is different. All her life she has traded her freedom for protection from the outside world, where she didn't have to deal with the harshness of everyday life. She didn't have a happy life with Anwin, but he never raised his hand against her and at least provided a clean and secure living environment. A golden cage, if you so want. Prison is less comfortable than that. Have you ever been inside a dungeon cell? They are not exactly cosy."

"Of course I was inside a dungeon cell before!" she snapped at him. "I happened to wake up in one after we first met and you knocked me out. That's where they took me afterwards. You remember? It was that charming summer's day when you managed to rob me of my conscience twice in one day - first at the Palace gates and then a few hours later at the testing."

Leris' eyes widened. "You did that? Really?" She turned to Eryn. "And you still became his companion? That is a very twisted thing between the two of you, but, well - that's none of my business."

He gripped his glass once again and downed the content in one go before saying, "You really are resentful, you know that? That was ages ago."

"Two years and a couple of months is not ages," Eryn retorted. "You'll be hearing about that for quite a while yet, that's a promise. And as regards your mother's prison sentences - you may not have been able to get her out of that, but I'm very confident that your influence will help to make her stays as pleasant as possible with warm blankets, proper food and books and needlework, or whatever else she wants to pass the time at her disposal."

"You don't understand this," Leris grumbled. "She's not your mother, after all."

"No," Eryn agreed with a thin smile, "that I can't deny. Were she my mother, I would be delighted to see her go to prison."

Enric's sister scowled at her. "That's an immensely unkind thing to say!"

"You wait till you have met my mother, then we will talk again." Eryn gently freed her braid from her son's greedy fingers and pressed the boy into his aunt's arms. "You mind him for a while." Then she pointed at Enric. "You go and cook dinner. It will do you good to do something instead of just sitting here, brooding. Send a message to the clinic to have Plia return at a civilised time for a change so that we can all eat together."

"And what will you be doing, if you don't mind my asking?" Leris enquired, obviously more than half surprised that she was being asked to babysit so abruptly.

"I'll be taking a relaxing bath after a long day and enjoying the thought that my son is in good hands and that there will be a meal waiting for me when I'm finished."

Saying that, Eryn turned and left the room, smiling to herself when she heard Leris ask her brother, "And since when have you cooked?"

* * *

Plia walked around the strange-looking object or rather composition of rather strange-looking objects on the desk in Eryn's study, a confused expression on her pretty face.

"What exactly is this supposed to do again?"

Eryn eyed the apparatus equally doubtful and compared it to the sketches on the paper in her hand. "It's meant to produce sounds."

"Are you sure you put that together correctly?" the girl enquired. "It really should look like that?"

Eryn nodded hesitantly. "I think so, yes. I mean, it was almost completely assembled when I got it, there are just a few more parts to be attached. Let's go through it once again, shall we? The horn goes on that hole here. That should be right, I think, considering that the two parts fit together so neatly." She rattled the funnel lightly to make sure it was fixed the way it was meant to be. Then she consulted the sheet with the instructive drawings again. "Then the crank is supposed to go... here." She pointed to another spot at what looked to be the rear end of the machine. "It's the only hole small enough to accommodate that thingy, so I would say that should be right."

Plia rummaged about in the crate in which the mysterious machine had been delivered little more than half an hour ago.

"There is something else," she said and pulled a little box out from between the load of crumpled paper that had been added to keep the contents from being damaged, whatever blows the crate had to endure on its trip.

Eryn took it from her and opened it. She compared the little pointed component with her drawings.

"Ah yes, that is supposed to go here. It needs to be fixed to the underside of that round part here, the one that is connected to the bit where the horn is attached."

Gently and carefully she pulled and squeezed until the round metal component could be moved in a way that made fixing the needle possible.

"Well, that leaves only one more item to be added," Eryn nodded and indicated another, larger wooden box made of dark wood with a single drawer. She pulled it open and looked down at six cylindrical metal objects with so many tiny grooves around them that they were impossible to count.

"What are they?" Plia whispered in awe as if afraid that a loud noise could damage them.

Eryn took in their sleek, silvery forms that reflected the light. She lifted another sheet from her desk and scanned the lines next to the picture.

"They are the carriers of the sound information," she murmured.

"What's that supposed to mean?" Plia frowned and eyed the objects suspiciously.

"I have no idea," Eryn confessed and looked at the device with both interest and a certain dread. She was impatient to find out what it could do, but was reluctant to touch it in case she broke something. It would be nigh on impossible to find somebody in the Kingdom to fix it for her.

Erbál had sent it to her, together with a number of sheets explaining how to fix the parts together which had been disassembled to make the transport safer. The sheets featured drawings and detailed instructions. He didn't say exactly what it would do, just that she would find it useful for her studies of the Pirinkar language.

She needed to get this thing working before Enric returned, or he would simply push her aside and play with it himself. He loved working out puzzles. But that was her toy. She wanted to be the one to make it work. So far it resembled the picture on the sheet of paper in her hand. The only thing that was still missing was the cylinder.

Eryn handed the letter to Plia and instructed her, "Read that to me step by step, will you?"

The girl hesitantly took the piece of paper and cleared her throat. "Dislodge the clasp holders on each side of the cylinder socket by unwinding the screws."

The healer groaned. "What?"

Plia consulted the paper and the drawings next to the text once again before pointing her finger to two little screws on either side of what looked to be the place where the cylinder needed to be fixed. "Turn them until they are open, I think."

Eryn carefully tried twisting them and breathed a sigh of relief when they did indeed turn. "If I go on, they will come off," she warned.

"That's fine, they need to come off. Do that with all four screws. Now lift the clasps."

"I suppose that's where the cylinder goes in?"

Plia nodded. "Exactly. It says here to handle them with care and avoid any dirt getting into the grooves, as that might cause the sound experience to suffer. Whatever that is supposed to mean."

"Hm, then maybe I should not grab it with my bare hand. Or I'll make sure not to touch the part in the middle and just hold it with these knobs on both ends." She bent down to the cylinders in the drawer to take a closer look. "They look sturdy. Does it say anything about whether they can be cleaned? And if so, how to best go about it?"

The girl read through the page quickly, then picked up another one. Luckily they were numbered, or by now they would have got badly mixed up.

"It says here that a soft brush can be used to remove dirt and dust from the cylinders."

Eryn nodded, safe in the knowledge that even if she somehow managed to touch them the wrong way, they wouldn't be impaired forever. She reached inside the drawer and carefully lifted the first cylinder out. It was lighter than she had expected. Maybe it was not solid, but hollow on the inside.

She placed the two knobs in the notches and put the clasps back in place, securing them with the screws she had removed before.

"It says here that it's now ready to be put into operation," Plia explained. "That crank to the left side of the box - it needs to be turned exactly thirteen times. Hold the box to steady it, then turn it until the position of that little handle is on top, then slowly push it away from you."

They counted aloud and listened to whatever was going on inside that wooden box. It sounded as if tiny metal parts were suffering.

"Thirteen," Eryn announced as another strange sound, louder than its predecessors was audible. Eryn was about to ask if that meant that she had broken something, but a moment later the cylinder suddenly began to rotate and there was a scratching sound coming from the horn that soon turned into something different. Words!

Plia's eyes went wide.

Eryn's mouth went slack. This was Erbál's voice! It sounded a little rasping and slightly slurred by the scratching of the needle on the cylinder, but it was unmistakably him.

"Hello Eryn. If you can hear this message you have managed to make the sound device work without breaking it. Congratulations. I thought that this little gift might help you to improve your language studies. After arriving here I soon realised that there is quite a difference between what the language looks like written down and what it sounds like. I have put together a little collection of what I have found to be very common sounds and words. It would not make sense just to be able to read the language without understanding the sound of words when actually hearing it used. When next we meet I intend to put your skills to the test. It was not easy to get permission to have this sent to you, so you had better make good use of it."

"This is incredible," Eryn breathed, staring at the appliance. "How can I listen to this again?"

Plia blinked a few times, and when she managed to overcome her astonishment, she looked at the sheet in her hand anew. "Something about putting the needle back to the beginning of the cylinder. And turning the handle again."

Eryn knelt on the floor to get a closer look. "If I just drag it back, it might scratch the cylinder and make it useless." She tried to tilt the horn a little and laughed triumphantly when the needle tilted with it.

They listened to the message once more, and then a third time before smiling at each other in both pride that they had managed to make it work and joy at the unexpected discovery of that wondrous thing.

"You know," Eryn said thoughtfully, "I wish he had managed to send two of them. Then I could take one of them apart and see how the things work. And eventually, maybe have more of them built." She grimaced. "I fear that if the Order learns of this they might want me to give it up so they can try to determine just that."

Plia bit her lip. "Can't you keep it a secret? Hide it from them?"

"With all those spies snooping around? No chance. I would have to look myself inside a light-tight and soundproof closet every time I want to use it."

The girl shrugged. "If that's what it takes to keep it, why not?"

Eryn smiled without joy. "Light-tight is no problem, but the issue of soundproof is more difficult. I would have to raise a shield for that, and they run out of air pretty quickly. And then the Order would know that I tried to hide it from them. No. I'll have to tell Lord Tyront and kindly let him know that he had better keep his hands off my apparatus if he wants me to play nicely. It's mine."

* * *

Enric stared out into the rain while leaning against the door frame of the entrance door of his house. His sister stood behind him with an equally disgruntled look on her face.

Their eyes were focussed on the back of the woman who was retreating with quick steps, her silhouette getting fainter until she turned a corner and was gone from their field of vision.

"She could have permitted me to accompany her. With a shield over her head she would at least have arrived warm and dry," Enric grumbled, displeased with the world in general and his stubborn mother in particular.

He had tried for further two hours to persuade her to let him pay the fine for her instead of letting herself be locked up, but she had insisted. His and Leris' joint efforts hadn't managed to make her cave in. He had tried to get Eryn to talk to her as well, but his companion had just given him one of her pointed looks and walked away. She had already told him several times that she understood Gerit perfectly well and would have done the very same thing in her place. Pride was something she understood, his Eryn. And normally he respected that, but in this case it would have been more helpful to have her on his side.

"Close the door, will you?" Eryn said from the sofa, where she was sitting with Vedric on her lap. She didn't look particularly happy either, but Enric couldn't tell if he was the cause or the situation was making her so.

He obeyed and gently closed the door even though he would rather have given it a proper heft and delighted in the slam. But that would just alarm his son, and as a parent he had to consider things like that now. Rage was nowadays something that needed to be planned. Just like most other things in his life lately that required a much more organised approach. Like being intimate with his companion or taking a bath. Even cooking dinner needed to be coordinated, since one had to look after the baby. They had got used to his mother taking some of the burden off their shoulders in these last weeks. They would have to return to managing on their own for a good while.

"You were able to talk to the guards, weren't you?" Leris asked for what had to be the fourth time now. "They will let her use her own blanket and pillow? And not take away her books and needlework? And you arranged for her to have proper meals from the Palace kitchen, not the usual prison fare?"

"Yes, yes, all that is taken care of," he sighed wearily. He had bribed the guards, and not just a little. He briefly wondered if he should allow himself a drink. He decided against it. The time when he most needed one was not a prudent one to indulge himself. It might happen that he wouldn't stop at one. And when things were difficult it was more judicious to keep a clear head.

"Don't worry too much," Eryn said from the sofa. "We will visit her every day and see how she is doing. I'm sure she will be fine. And the guards are hardly likely to disobey mighty Lord Enric after taking his money."

Leris let herself fall into a chair, her arms limply hanging over the rests. "I need to leave tomorrow. Ardegen told me to take as much time as I need, but I can't leave him alone with the business and the children any longer. And it's not as if there is anything I can do here."

"You did enough by coming here," Eryn said calmly while wiping Vedric's nose with a soft cloth and removing drool from her shoulder. "It was a great comfort to her that you two had a chance to make up. For this and for getting rid of Anwin she has gladly gone to prison. That's what she told me."

"She was Anwin's and Noren's door mat for so many years - I mean, as if it wasn't enough to be treated like a piece of furniture by her own companion, she also endured it from her son! And from his dim-witted companion who thinks being cheated on is the way the world rolls along."

"I need a drink," Leris growled and looked at her brother. "Where do you keep the good stuff?"

"I don't buy any bad stuff," Enric replied wearily and pointed to a glass cabinet. "But if you are looking for the more potent spirit, that's over there. Go easy on it if you really want to travel tomorrow. I don't know if Eryn is willing to heal away the aftereffects of your overindulgence and I am not able to do it."

"If I drink, I will bear the consequences," his sister snapped at him and selected a glass to fill it with something clear and slightly reddish. She tilted back her head and downed the contents of her glass with a few gulps, her face still straight when she lowered her head again. Eryn's brow went up. She herself would probably have doubled over to cough and gasp for air by now. That woman was either a seasoned drinker or a damn good actress. Or she had an iron throat and stomach to match.

Eryn tried to start a conversation several times and finally got up to take Vedric to bed. It was a little early for him, but she found sitting with the two of them a strain and decided to try if her son could be persuaded to sleep. Maybe she would bath him. That usually made him tired.

She was about to climb the stairs, when there was a knock at the door and Enric rose dutifully to answer. Eryn waited to see who visited them that late in the evening. No bad news, she hoped.

Enric pulled the door open and stiffened with surprise. "Mother?"

Leris jumped up as well and Eryn returned to the parlour. It was indeed Gerit who was standing in front of the door, her hair dripping wet as she had either forgotten to put on her hood or for some reason decided against it.

Leris pulled her mother inside and took the oilskin cape off her shoulders to hand to Enric. Then she smiled and pulled her mother into a hug. "I knew you'd change your mind and let us pay the fine for you! Honestly, this was the right decision. And it makes leaving Anwin no less of an accomplishment."

Enric stepped behind his mother and touched her head lightly, making the dampness from her hair rise up into the air until a few moments later she was completely dry again.

"It wasn't me... I didn't..." Gerit stammered and looked strangely helpless. Eryn started to suspect that she had indeed forgotten to put on her hood on account of being shocked or confused. What was going on here?

"What happened?" Eryn asked, slightly worried by now.

"They just sent me back again, saying I didn't need to stay because everything was taken care of," the older woman said.

Only now Enric noted the envelope in her hand.

"May I?" he asked gently and took it when his mother didn't resist. He opened it and pulled out a sheet of paper that had remained dry despite its journey through the rain just now. The oilskin cape must have protected it. His eyes wandered over the lines, then his brow shot up in utter astonishment.

"What?" Leris and Eryn asked in unison, both impatient to learn what was going on.

Enric shook his head and let the paper sink to a nearby table. "The commitment is dissolved with immediate effect. Mother," he said and took both her cold hands into his large, warm ones and squeezed them, looking into her eyes, "you are free now. Completely. There will be no more prison sentence to serve or fines to pay. From now on you can do what you want. You no longer have to answer to Anwin or anybody else."

He pulled his mother close when silent tears began to run down her cheek, bedding her head onto his chest and rocking her slowly.

Eryn picked up the sheet from the table and read the few lines. At the bottom of the official dissolution paper was the seal. The Royal seal. Signed by His Majesty King Folrin of Anyueel. Oh dear. Was that good or bad?

Leris snapped the paper out of her hand so quickly that Eryn worried for a moment that she might tear it.

"The King himself did it?" Leris whispered in awe and looked at Enric. "You really are bloody well important, aren't you?" Then she started laughing, the contrast to the softly sobbing woman in Enric's arms feeling strange. "And there isn't a thing Anwin can do about this! There is no appeal against the King's edict!" She pulled Gerit out of Enric's embrace and into her own. "Dry your tears, mother! You are free! This is not something to be unhappy about - this is something to celebrate with gusto!"

She pulled her mother to a sofa and then went to the glasses cabinet to fetch another glass and a bottle, her steps light and happy.

While Leris tended to Gerit, Eryn turned to her companion. "Will this be a problem? Do we owe him some favour now? Can he make us do things by threatening to make the dissolution somehow invalid?"

Enric smiled and shook his head. "No, rest assured - there is nothing to worry about, my love. The dissolution is official, invalidating it wouldn't be good for his public standing after granting it outside the usual administrative channels. If he had wanted something in return, he wouldn't have done it like that. He would have offered it to us a week ago and made us agree to whatever he wanted before granting it."

"So he just wanted - what? Make us happy?" She shook her head. That sounded wrong. He wasn't the type to grant generous gifts without a catch.

"Not us, but me. You forgave him for what he did back then pretty quickly, but he knows that I still hold a grudge against him for shackling and kissing you. This," he said and pointed to the document on the table, "is to get me back on his side again - especially now that things are about to take place within the Council and subsequently the Order as a whole. And then it wouldn't look too good if he sent Vedric's grandmother to prison only after taking over the role as his guardian, would it? If being in the King's favour didn't hold any advantages, people might start wondering if trying to win his good opinion was a quest worth pursuing. And a King whose subjects try to please him holds more power, after all."

Now, Eryn, too, smiled - finally daring to be happy about that marvellous turn of events. She pressed her son into Enric's hands and got a glass herself before she joined the other two women.

"Fill me up, ladies! We have something to celebrate. Good thing I'm not nursing anymore, so Enric will mind Vedric."

Enric just shook his head with a wide grin when the three most important women in his life lifted their glasses to drink to the King's health. And then to every single misfortune they could wish upon Anwin.

* * *

Enric took her hand when they walked back from the Palace towards their house. Tyront walked by his other side, seemingly enjoying the walk in the cold air.

Eryn was displeased, very much so. Enric couldn't blame her for it. The Council meeting had not gone particularly well, even though she had been well-prepared. She had painted them a picture of a dark future with young, inexperienced magicians on top since the new generation would be immensely strong and thus entitled to leading the Order under the current system. She had furthermore used the incident from the last meeting to make them see that dissatisfaction was not merely something that was shared over a civilised glass of expensive wine with a lot of nodding of heads, but had progressed into something that made people take action. She had showed them figures that indicated that there would be quite a rise in the number of magicians in the years to come now that the barrier in the head had been removed and the gift was being passed on more frequently now. And that this meant that there would soon be a lot of magicians needing to be kept busy somehow. Her next argument had been that they could just as well be kept busy by allowing them to use whatever talents and skills they had - outside healing and fighting.

Enric knew that she had managed to make many of them think, but just as the King had warned her, there were alliances to be protected and maintained. Though Eryn's speech had managed something she would hopefully be able to realise was a very positive thing: they had not rejected her ideas right away but merely held back from supporting them. That meant that these topics would be discussed in the weeks and months - maybe even years - ahead.

He cast a glance at her angrily furrowed brow and her lips that were pressed tightly together. At least she had managed to keep her aggravation inside until they were in a place where she could vent it safely. In the Council hall she had retained her calm, had answered questions in an unperturbed manner that didn't even give away a hint at the turmoil he could feel through the mind bond.

Now that they had left the Palace she allowed her face to express a little of her discontentment.

They rounded the last corner that brought them in view of the house. The buildings with the high wall between them lay quietly amidst the grey and wintry surroundings. Several of the windows shone with a soft, warm glow from lamps and showed that people were inside. Both buildings had smoke curling upwards from the chimney, a sure sign that whatever was going on inside, it would be cosy.

Enric opened the door to let his companion and his superior enter first, then followed them inside.

And true enough, the first thing Eryn did as soon as she was hidden from the world outside was to throw her arms up and exclaim, "Why? Why me? Why do I have to deal with all this folly? Did you hear Lord Remdel's objection about how safe that method of determining magical potential in babies really could be? That we have only been using it for a few months here and therefore could not possibly say whether or not it is reliable? Idiot! They have been doing this in the Western Territories for, what - two-hundred years? That's not reliable enough for him?"

Tyront and Enric both watched her with indulgent expressions. They were more than willing to let her rant a bit considering that she had held back admirably in the Council meeting.

"And Lord Seagon! I ask you: how blind can any man be? He may no longer consider me the ultimate evil sent by the stars to destroy all that he values, but while blood flows in my veins, his obviously enclose fluid tradition! Never before have I encountered a man that averse to change! Unless I can prove to him that there will be an improvement he is unwilling to consider it! How am I to prove something that has not even been done?"

She covered her eyes with both hands. "I won't even start on Lord Woldarn and Lord Aldon. They didn't even listen properly and then asked questions that I had already answered! How embarrassing is that? If children behaved like that in class we would scold them - but for the mighty Council members I just repeat the very same thing in short words and at a slow rate." She closed her eyes and exhaled.

When she remained silent, Enric asked, "Better?"

Eryn nodded. "Thank you, yes." Then she looked at Tyront. "Before the two of you retreat to Enric's study, there is something I'd better show you before your spies tell you about it and you rebuke me for keeping it to myself."

Both men followed her to her study and entered. Their eyes were immediately drawn to the unfamiliar object on the right side of her desk.

Enric tilted his head, curiosity sparkling in his eyes. "That looks like something I would guess was sent from Pirinkar, unless I'm very much mistaken?"

"Yes, it's a gift from Ambassador Erbál. It's a device that reproduces sound."

Tyront shook his head in incomprehension. "What kind of sound?"

"Any, I would suspect. But I'm not an expert." She stepped towards the apparatus and wound the crank thirteen times as per Erbál's instructions. Moments later his voice came out of the horn, once again congratulating her on not breaking the device and informing her, that he intended to test her language skills at their next encounter.

Tyront's eyes had widened into saucers, but he didn't speak. He stepped closer and eyed the machine from all sides without touching it.

Enric stood at her other side and whistled through his teeth. "When did you get that?"

"It was delivered yesterday morning while you were gone."

"Why didn't you tell me about it?"

She shrugged. "You were pretty upset because your mother was about to be sent to prison. It didn't seem appropriate to show you my new fancy toy then. And in the evening, when we learned of the dissolution of her commitment, I simply forgot to."

"And today in the morning?" he wanted to know.

"I'm not a morning person, Enric, as well you know. And between feeding your son, getting dressed, mentally preparing for the Council meeting and struggling to show up there in time there was simply no time."

Tyront was still absorbed in the inspection of the unfamiliar device and didn't seem to listen to them.

"How does this work?" he murmured.

Eryn bent forward so her face was close to the device. She lifted a finger and pointed to the crank. "This here turns something inside the box that in turn makes the cylinder rotate. This little needle here directly under the horn follows the grooves in the cylinder. That's where the sound is somehow stored. Then the sound must travel from the needle up to the horn somehow. The needle and the horn move along the cylinder while it turns. When they reach the end of the cylinder, you can lift the needle like this and listen to it again."

Enric pursed his lips and thought back to his own visit in the city of Kar several months ago. Things he had seen in shop windows where he'd had not the faintest idea what they might have been. And he thought back to how carefully they protected their knowledge. It had taken masses of paperwork for him to get permission for taking the three books for Eryn and the toy for his son with him - and even that had only been possible because they felt they had to make amends for Malriel's having been tricked and almost convicted.

"It can't have been easy for Erbál to persuade his hosts to let him send that. I bet it required quite a lot of effort," he remarked.

Eryn sighed. "I suppose. And the fact that there is next to no chance that he will be able to send another one frustrates me. My fingers itch to dismantle and it and determine how this works. I mean - imagine if we, too, could store sounds like that! We could send cylinders to Takhan and the recipient could listen to messages in the sender's actual voice!" She gestured agitatedly. "We could have cylinders to document important speeches that could then be stored in the library and be listened to by students in the years to come." She stared down at the machine. "I wonder if this would also work with music... Imagine if we could just play a cylinder and enjoy music without actually having musicians in the room! Wouldn't that be terrific?"

Enric smiled at that, marvelling at that spirit of discovery that was so typical for her. He wondered how long the toy he had bought in Kar for Vedric would survive in her eager hands before being disassembled into its component parts. He had no idea how skilled Eryn was when it came to mechanical things. Maybe it was another one of her talents. For now it was probably safer to keep the toy out of her reach. If she truly dismantled it and didn't manage to put it back together, his son would only have a collection of complicated parts to play with one day. No, he decided - he had given Eryn the books. She needed to keep her hands off the other gift.

Tyront eyed the device with increasing interest. "We could have a blacksmith and a goldsmith take a closer look at this. Maybe they have a basic idea how it works."

Eryn's smile was more of a revealing of teeth when she said, "Or we could just leave it here in my study as this was a gift to me and I would not take kindly to having it sequestered."

"Alright, then," Tyront sighed, "I'm not an unreasonable man. I'll buy it from you. Name your price."

"Do I look like I need your money? I'm not selling it! And if it goes missing, I'll know exactly where to start looking, so no funny business, do you hear me?"

Her superior gave her a testing look at the accusation that he might be willing to steal it from her.

"Who says the King won't have it taken from you?"

She sneered. "He won't. It would upset me, and by implication Enric. And for now he is trying to make Enric happy. The fact that he dissolved Gerit's companionship shows that clearly enough."

"You might be stopping us from reckoning how it works."

Eryn folded her arms. "Is that so? I'd rather have thought that I'm your best chance at working out how it works considering that I'm the one with regular contact to Pirinkar."

"So you refuse to share your device?"

"Absolutely," she confirmed with emphasis.

"You should really reconsider your approach to negotiation, Eryn," Tyront frowned.

"I'm not negotiating. I'm simply telling you No. It's mine. Keep your hands off it."

His eyes narrowed. "I could order you to give it up."

She folded her arms. "I wouldn't recommend that. You want me to play nice with the Council and get it to work with me to ensure the Order's survival. This would not exactly motivate me to aid you in your endeavours. I might just as well lean back and bide my time until the Order dissolves into chaos and mayhem in several years' time. That should make it easier for me to get out of it."

The Order's leader ground his teeth at the frivolous way she talked about the demise of the institution he had served almost all his life. And it irked him that she still seemed eager to get out of it.

Tyront smiled faintly, his eyes narrowed. "There might be a grain of truth in what you say, but you are not quite as powerful as you think, my dear girl. If I want that machine, I will get it, you may rely on that. I would prefer, however, not to endanger our harmonious relationship by taking it from you. I'll make you an offer instead, and I trust that you will find it a reasonable one."

Eryn caught Enric's cautioning look and motioned for the older man to go on. "I'm listening."

"I'll let you play around with it for a while, let's say three months." He pointed to the cylinders. "Listen to whatever the ambassador has sent you as often as you want. As soon as you arrive in Takhan, however, you will dedicate your time to determining how it works. Enrol the assistance of craftspeople, if you wish. If you don't manage to work out the functional principle by the time of your return here six months later, you'll surrender it willingly and let others take their chances."

He refrained from voicing what would be the consequence of her refusal: he would just take it away as it pleased him. She thought for several moments, reluctant to agree to that. This wasn't fair, it was hers! She shouldn't have to fight for it like that and accept conditions simply to be allowed to hold on to it!

Enric hadn't spoken a single word during her discussion with Tyront, but he caught her eye and nodded slowly.

She exhaled and rolled her eyes. "Very well, I agree. But I'll have you know that I don't approve of your coercing me through taking away my property."

"Duly noted," Tyront nodded graciously. "I'm confident that your eagerness to hold on to your apparatus will motivate to do your best to find out about its workings."

Enric cleared his throat. "Tyront, shall we go to my study now to discuss the Council's objections?" He needed to get his superior out of here, and quickly. Eryn was not happy, and he felt through the bond that she was holding back her temper. Moreover, if Tyront kept on patronising her, there was no saying how long she could manage to keep her tongue in check.

He was glad when Tyront agreed and followed him out of the room.

CHAPTER 32

An Old Fool

Pe'tala didn't wait for Eryn to invite her in but entered immediately after knocking at the treatment room door. She let herself fall into the patient chair opposite her sister.

"I cannot believe how many stupid injuries happen around here at this time of the year. People slip all the time - as if they were not used to slippery streets in winter! I mean, it is the same every year, is it not? How can it be such a great surprise that running on the slick cobblestones ends with falling over?"

Eryn stretched and covered her mouth with her fist while yawning, then said, "What can I tell you? People are odd."

"Speaking of odd people - your house guest has left again, has she not?"

"If you mean Enric's sister, then yes she has. She returned to her family yesterday afternoon. Gerit will soon be gone from our house as well. Her own place will be ready to move into in a few weeks. She is currently taking care of the interior, so that decorating and furnishing the rooms will happen in a matter of days after the construction work is finished," Eryn explained.

Pe'tala nodded. "Things are progressing, then. Good thing she does not have to go to prison. Not a good time of the year to spend in a cold, damp dungeon. Not that it is a particularly pleasant place to spend time in at any other time of the year, mind you." She leaned forward. "So, when are you going to show it to me?"

Eryn looked at her, confused. "Show you what?"

The younger healer rolled her eyes. "The book of course! I am told that the pictures are extremely well done. But then one would not expect anything else from Vern."

"Oh, no! I should have known that it would be impossible to keep this private! How did you learn about it? Vran'el or Ram'kel?"

"Both, actually. Vran wrote me that Vern was working on the book for you and that he persuaded him to make two more, one for him and one to sell. And Ram'kel told me that he was present when the delivery arrived and you opened it. Your uneasiness really amused him."

Eryn raised one eyebrow. "I wasn't aware that you and Ram'kel are such great chums. Isn't this a bit strange considering that his brother dumped you?"

Pe'tala shrugged. "I do not hold a grudge against him because of what his family members did. It was not his doing, was it? And he told me that he regretted his brother's decision to engage in an unpromising fight for your hand instead of making me his. That earned him a few points with me. And besides, we are the same age, grew up in the same city and move in the same circles. He is a smart one; I like that in a person."

"He keeps teasing and annoying me! I find that highly inappropriate considering his position. A position I obtained for him."

"He does it only in private, so there is no danger of your reputation suffering. He is not stupid, as I said. Never has been. Though a bit of a scoundrel, I will give you that. Ram'kel asked me to invite you to my place and tell you to bring the book. He would then join us. He is really keen to see it. He said he saw only one picture when you opened the book at random, but that was astonishing work already."

Eryn groaned. "What? You want me to look at pictures of people engaging in sex - with another man? Why don't you just kill me now? Because that's what will happen if Enric learns about this. He is adaptable when it comes to treating this field just like any other polite conversation topic, but a little private showing of this kind of pictures with a man that's not him he won't take at all well, honestly."

Pe'tala grinned evilly. "I could ask Rolan to join us. That would be hilarious. He is even more of a prude than you are."

"This is getting better and better," Eryn growled. "I'm surely not going to be looking at pictures of copulating people with two other men. If you want to see the bloody book, you will have to come to my place and do it there. I'm certainly not taking it anywhere. Imagine somebody seeing me with it!"

"Worried about your reputation, sister?" Pe'tala sneered. "This is hilarious coming from a woman who took a man to bed without even seeing his face at that frolicsome occasion you have here once a year." Then her expression became more thoughtful. "That is something I have been wondering about since I first heard about it. How could you not have known that it was Enric? There are quite a few well-built men around, which is not a surprise in a place where warriors are trained, but not many of them are that tall. And what about his voice? Shouldn't you have recognised that? He did talk to you before, did he not? Is it possible that you knew it was him but did not want to admit that you found him appealing because your pride would never have permitted it?"

Eryn exhaled and shook her head wearily. "I can't believe I'm really having this conversation with you. No, I truly had no inkling of who he was, disregarding the fact that he was tall. This is a place with only fair-haired people! Slap on a mask and they all look pretty much the same! And no, our conversations were not quite that frequent back then, so I had no particularly clear memory of his voice. His voice is not especially distinctive. Had it been Lord Tyront's deep rumble, I dare say I would have recognised that one." She stopped when Pe'tala chuckled and narrowed her eyes. "Are you teasing me?"

"I was at first, but now I cannot help but wonder why you have to defend yourself quite that fiercely if there is nothing to it."

Eryn sighed tiredly and lifted her hand to point at the door. "Go away, evil spirit. Wait, one more thing: Enric wants to take Urban hunting one of these days and wonders if Rolan wants to join him."

Pe'tala rose obediently. "I will pass that on. Rolan will get in contact with Enric and let him know."

"Thank you. Now you can go away."

At that moment the door pushed open and Lebern called out, "Lord Aldon has been attacked! They are bringing him in right now."

Eryn jumped to her feet, the weariness from a few moments ago was gone. "Bring him in here," she instructed and stepped aside when a moment later two men carried in the Council member. It seemed they had planned on bringing him to her anyway. She pushed aside the thoughts of who and why and the possible consequences of the attack and instead focussed on the man they placed on the day bed.

Blood was streaming from wounds on his face, he looked like he had just returned from a battle. But then head wounds tended to bleed heavily, even if the injury was minor since the head was well-supplied with blood vessels on account of the brain needing so much nourishment.

"This looks probably worse than it is," Pe'tala confirmed her thoughts. She pointed at herself while looking at her sister, "Body", then at Eryn, "Head".

Eryn nodded and they both stepped to the quietly whimpering man. "Lebern, you stay and watch. The rest of you get out," she instructed and turned to place her hand on Lord Aldon's head without bothering to check if her orders were carried out.

She breathed a sigh of relief when the damage to his head turned out to be easily mendable. It must have been a rather heavy blow that had left him not only with impressive and copious bleeding from wounds but also with a very small fracture to his skull. The brain did not seem to have suffered any damage. She repaired the injury, starting with a shield around the wound to stop the bleeding, then continued with the bone before she fixed the tissue on the outside.

When she opened her eyes, Pe'tala was already waiting.

"Report," Eryn instructed curtly.

"Minor damage to the shin and knee, a few bumps to the shoulder, but nothing major."

She nodded and then pointed to Lebern. "Come here. Carry out a full body check to see if there are any remaining injuries that escaped our attention. Pe'tala, you run and fetch Lord Poron, then send word to Lord Tyront."

Eryn exhaled and leaned against a wall with a grim expression. She would do this here right, there would be no chance anybody would try to pin this here on her. She would make sure that the healing Lord Aldon received was beyond reproof - have it checked by her colleague. She informed the right people, did the right things and made sure that this was written down and made official.

There was little doubt in her mind that Pe'tala and herself had done thorough work with healing their patient. Having Lebern check it was little more than a precaution. If she had to heal somebody who was known to be her opponent in the Council after what had been an attack on him, it needed to be absolutely clear that she had acted in accordance with her profession's ethical code and treated him as best she could. And the fact that the second healer to work with her on this patient was her own sister was not exactly an advantage, either. Family was expected to cover up inconvenient facts, so whatever she said in Eryn's favour would be treated with particular caution.

The door pushed open without anyone knocking and Lord Poron stepped in just as Lebern had finished his examination.

"Everything looks fine. I couldn't detect any residual damage at all," Lebern said and waited for further instructions.

"Good," Lord Poron nodded, his expression serious. "Then go and fetch a bowl of water and two clean towels for Lord Aldon to clean himself. Pe'tala, I want you to wait outside and bring Lord Tyront here as soon as he arrives."

Both healers nodded to acknowledge their orders and left the room, leaving Eryn and Lord Poron alone with the patient.

"How are you feeling, Lord Aldon?" Lord Poron asked and stepped towards the day bed. "Any dizziness or headache?" When the other man shook his head, he further enquired, "And how about the rest of you - any pain or difficulties when you move?"

Lord Aldon slowly sat up and accepted the older man's help in getting to his feet. He walked a few careful steps and returned to the day bed to sit down again.

"Everything seems in order, as far as I can tell," the patient spoke for the first time since his arrival.

"Very good. I would like to make sure of that from a healer's point of view as well, if you don't mind," the Head of Healers smiled and didn't wait for permission before stepping closer and placing a hand on Lord Aldon's shoulder to send an impulse inside that would provide him with the information he needed.

Eryn kept her face carefully blank, hiding the gratified smile that would otherwise have appeared on her face. Cautious Lord Poron. Even though Lebern had already said that there were no areas of oversight, he wanted to be able to swear before the Council under the influence of a truth block if necessary, that truly everything was as it should be. So he also wanted to be prepared in case Eryn was yet again accused of attacking a member of the Council.

"Yes, everything looks totally acceptable," Lord Poron finally confirmed.

"I was walking along the river when they came at me," Lord Aldon started. "Three of them, and..."

"Why don't you first wash off the blood and wait with your narrative until Lord Tyront arrives? That way you won't have to repeat yourself," Lord Poron suggested gently.

As if on cue, Lebern pushed open the door with his shoulder carrying in the requested basin with water and two towels.

Lord Aldon stepped towards the desk where the healer had placed the washing supplies and then started to clean himself. A few minutes later both the water and the towels were coloured red, but Lord Aldon looked reasonably well again - if one didn't let the gaze wander any further south than his face. The collar of his brown robe was blotted through with his blood.

Pe'tala knocked and led Tyront in before wordlessly picking up the bloody water and towels to remove them.

Eryn pushed herself away from the wall and made to follow her sister out of the room, but Tyront lifted a hand and just said, "Stay."

She suppressed a sigh. So healing the man was obviously not where it ended for her. By making her listen to his account of the attack she was now involved in this whole mess in her function as Council member now that her work as a healer was over. She knew that after Darnet's attack on Tyront and the fact that her acquittal had not been unanimous this was a show of trust. He didn't do this to annoy her, she knew. But still... She would much rather have walked away from this and let others handle it.

Tyront took a seat in Eryn's chair and looked at Lord Aldon. "What happened?" he asked gently.

"It was an ambush! They were lying in wait for me and then three men attacked me just like that! It was those rebels, I'm absolutely sure of it!"

The Order's leader didn't show any reaction whatsoever to this accusation, but remained unruffled and just said, "Start at the beginning, if you would."

Lord Aldon nodded and took a few moments to calm down again before he began in a more composed manner, "I have adopted the habit of taking walks after lunch. I was told it is beneficial for the health as it aids the digestion. And I find it a very good opportunity to contemplate matters of importance in peace, a chance for undisturbed introspection, if you like."

Eryn groaned to herself. That was certainly the beginning, but in a lot more detail than she cared to hear about right now. Why didn't he move on to the relevant part and focus on that instead?

It seemed her posture had given away her impatience somehow, because Tyront flashed her a quick look that might or might not have been a warning.

"Go on," Tyront encouraged his colleague.

"So, just as every day, I started my walk at my house, past the warriors' quarters, until I reached the river. There I turned left and continued towards the bridge to walk to the port. I first noticed the three men when I reached the trees next to the river. They were leaning against a house wall and casting seemingly disinterested glances in my direction. This was the first time I suspected that something odd was going on."

Eryn's upper lip wanted to curl in disdain. Sure, suddenly he had known all along that something was wrong. Didn't he realise that saying things like that just made him look more like a dolt than a keen observer because he hadn't acted on whatever suspicions he claimed he'd had? Move on, she urged him silently, talk about the relevant part, for goodness' sake!

"They must have followed me, because when I was about to walk up to the bridge to cross it, they sprung out at me. They bashed and kicked me repeatedly, causing the injuries which I was brought here with."

"You said it was those rebels, if I remember correctly," Lord Poron noted. "What makes you think that? Did you recognise any of them?"

"No, of course not! They would hardly go and do the dirty work themselves and risk being identified, would they? They must have paid those goons to do it for them. I heard one of them say: That should teach him a lesson. Let's see if he continues to hold proceedings back from now on. That makes it pretty obvious who sent them, wouldn't you say?"

Eryn bit her lip, not sure if she were allowed to ask any questions here as Lord Poron was or if she were merely supposed to be quiet, watch and learn.

"Yes?" Tyront asked and looked at her with an encouraging expression. Alright, so she was allowed to speak. Good.

"You are saying that you didn't recognise them, which would imply that they are not members of the Order. Otherwise you would very probably have seen them before. The Order has no more than about one hundred and forty members, so you would likely have encountered them before at some or other ceremony or function."

Lord Aldon nodded slowly, obviously not too happy about her being in a position to contribute anything to this conversation among adults.

"This would mean that they were non-magicians. It was quite a risk for them to attack a magician, even though they outnumbered you," she ventured. "Even though we are not allowed to strike with magic, we are permitted to shield against them. Why didn't you keep them off you with a barrier?"

"I was attacked from behind," he huffed, "I don't know if you have ever been a victim of an attack like that, but it is quite a disturbing situation."

He had to be joking! "You remember the last execution? The apothecaries? Then you may also remember that their attack on me was the reason there were beheaded," she snapped. "So yes, it so happens that I was indeed the victim of a similar attack in the past. Though the reason why I didn't protect myself was that I was unconscious after the first hit. Why didn't you raise a shield? Disturbing situation or not, the Order trains its warriors to be ready to fight for defence of the Kingdom - I think that you would have been able to defend yourself against non-magician attackers."

Lord Aldon's face contorted into a furious expression as he rose from his chair to walk up to her. "Are you implying, Lady Eryn, that I failed to defend myself on purpose for a particular reason? Is there any accusation you wish to put forward at this point? Is this an awkward and shoddy attempt to cover up for your own involvement in this affair - directing the attention away from you and making up stories about my somehow being responsible for the attack on myself?"

And there we go again! Eryn thought wearily, not sure whether to laugh or cry. She didn't reply to his accusation but just sent him a dark look and folded her arms. What could she say, anyway? Accuse him right back or defend herself? Neither would make sense at this point.

"Lord Aldon," Tyront said with emphasis, "please return to your seat. Lady Eryn's question is not entirely without justification. You were trained in fighting over several decades. If your inability to defend yourself against weaker opponents is the result of a flaw in said training, we might wish to reconsider our teaching methods. But for now we shall grant you that you felt under considerable duress and were reluctant to risk harming non-magicians and thereby break the law, shall we? Were there any witnesses to the attack?"

Lord Aldon's eyes lit up in triumph and he sent Eryn a look of contempt before he said, "Indeed there were! The two men who brought me here saw everything. Had they not started running towards us, who knows what those rogues would have done to me? I'm telling you - it was those rebels! Now that we have young Onil watch the Council meetings, he doubtlessly reports to his friends that I am the greatest danger to their unreasonable demands, that I am a respected member of this Council. My colleagues respect my opinion and think about what I say instead of mindlessly agreeing to whatever Lady Eryn wants to push through for them. They think if they sweep me out of the way, there will be no further obstacles!"

Eryn carefully avoided slapping her palm against her face at this delusion of grandeur. He really thought a lot of himself. Her own picture of him was certainly not that of a powerful opposition leader, but rather one of a nuisance who stood against any changes or new ideas on principle. A man who lacked the required foresight to see a problem even if it was jumping up and down right in front of him with arms waiving and shouting loudly. An overgrown child with stubborn disregard for reality, determined to keep within his own little bubble of the world as he wanted it.

"Do you need me here any longer or do I have your permission to leave and return to my patients?" she asked her superior very politely, sending him with her eyes a very clear signal that if he made her stay in the same room with this man any longer, she would probably end up throttling him.

"I would ask you to stay for a little longer, Lady Eryn," Tyront replied. "Lord Aldon, thank you for your account. We will have to ask you to share all this once more with the entire Council as this is a matter of great importance that needs careful consideration."

Lord Aldon's chest inflated a little at that, clearly pleased that this incident received the attention it was due. "Of course, my Lord."

He bowed to his leader and then he strolled out of the room with his head held high.

When the door was closed, Eryn exhaled and let her head loll back to stare at the white ceiling. She wondered if she was the only one uncomfortable with the story they had just been told. Why would the group of dissatisfied magicians unthinkingly attack a Council member who worked against them? They would be the first ones to be suspected, and whether or not it could be proved, it would prejudice the Council against them. This could only cause harm to themselves. Some of the magicians might be too forward, too eager, too impatient, but they also had shrewd people among them, thinkers like Onil. And now Eryn herself was once again suspected of attacking somebody she considered inconvenient. Why did she even bother anymore? Being cleared from one accusation just seemed to lead to the exact same one little later.

Her head snapped back in surprise when she heard Lord Poron sigh, "What a simpleton. But with matters developing the way they are, it was probably only a question of time until he did something rash."

Tyront shook his head. "True enough. I wouldn't have thought that he would be quite that dim-witted about it, though. I don't know whether to be angry about his disregard for the values he is supposed to uphold or insulted because he thinks we are quite that gullible."

Eryn stared at both of them alternately. What were they talking about now?

Lord Poron registered her confusion and smiled thinly. "I think we should fill her in, Tyront. She seems a little lost."

Eryn noted how her colleague had just addressed the Order's leader without his title. She hadn't been aware that those two were that close.

Tyront nodded and explained, "We strongly suspect that Lord Aldon arranged for this little attack himself. There are a few clues that would support that suspicion. Firstly, he gave more details than I asked for. That is not reliable proof that he was lying in itself, but considering that he is not generally known as such a conscientious man with quite that much love for detail, it stands out. The next issue you yourself pointed out - he could have defended himself easily against non-magicians. It might be that he was shocked at first, but then he as a trained fighter should have been able to keep them at bay. Even you raised a shield in your defence when you were first brought here - and did that even though you had no idea how to do it. It's an instinct, especially when there was training. Not raising a shield during an attack would require consciously avoiding following that instinct."

Lord Poron nodded approvingly. "I agree. He wanted to be attacked, and he wanted to be harmed. If you wanted to attack somebody, Eryn, would you do it in the middle of the day, in broad daylight and in a place as open as the river promenade where it is basically impossible not to be observed? I dare say you would not. It would be a most senseless thing to do for an attacker, but a way to make sure that there were much-needed witnesses around."

Eryn exhaled as their words sank in. "So... you think he did this himself? You don't suspect I arranged this to eliminate my most formidable opponent?"

Both men laughed at that.

"That's quite an opinion he has of himself, isn't it?" Tyront chuckled. "No, we don't think that was you. And neither do we blame our rebellious friends for it. I will of course have to question every single one of them under the influence of a truth block - just for the record. Poron, you and I will take care of that. Not a word of this to anyone."

She looked at both men. "And what will happen now? Do we accuse him openly at the next Council meeting? Force him to submit to a truth reading?"

"No," Tyront shook his head. "That wouldn't go down well. I can't coerce him into agreeing to a thing like that when he is allegedly the victim in the case."

"We will have to trick him somehow," Lord Poron agreed. "This shouldn't be too hard. He never was the sharpest sword in the rack. I should know - I had the misfortune of teaching him when he was a boy. A terrible know-it-all who never bothered checking his facts before opening his mouth. I just had to let him talk; it was only a matter of time until he contradicted himself."

Eryn shook her head in amazement. Hearing Lord Poron talk ill of somebody was a rare thing. He had to be really upset with Lord Aldon.

"Why is he in the Council, then? I thought Council members were selected not because of their strength but because they are astute, experienced and level-headed," Eryn remarked.

Tyront sighed and looked a bit ill at ease. "Well, that's what we try very hard to make people think at least. It's theoretically what we strive for in our Council, yet we are limited to a certain degree. The first five ranks in the Order are required to join the Council, that is written in the regulations. Fortunately, the current arrangement of members in top ranks is a very good one, the best we've had in a while now. Every one of you is intelligent and reasonable. Earlier, though, we occasionally had very strong but less prudent people on top. The other seats in the Council we try to award to suitable candidates. This does, however, not always work out as we would wish."

"Such as in Lord Aldon's case?" Eryn probed.

"Exactly. I had only been in charge of the Order for two or three years back then, still struggling to get people to follow my orders and establish myself as an authority. That was when one Council member died, meaning a position became available. King Folrin's father back then approached me and recommended Lord Aldon. He wanted to do a friend a favour and getting his son into the Council seemed like a generous gesture to him. And the fact that Lord Aldon was forever grateful to the old King for his help made him more or less the monarch's mouthpiece. I was young and thought that having the King on my side would help me, but the opposite was the case. Several of the Council members resented me for this decision, and I've had to struggle with him ever since. I'm all for having to live with one's mistakes as it enables us to learn from them, but I feel that two decades of that are more than I deserved."

Lord Poron smiled thinly. "Then this might be your chance finally to correct that mistaken judgement of long ago. If we manage to prove that he arranged this attack himself so as to incriminate others, you could expel him from the Council. The regulations provide for this prospect, even though it has never been done so far."

Tyront steepled his fingers, deep in thought. "Yes," he said slowly. "I could do that, couldn't I... and we wouldn't even have to replace him as we currently have thirteen members and the regulations stipulate that there need to be twelve."

"How sure are you that it was really him?" Eryn insisted. This sounded too good to be true.

"Virtually sure," Tyront replied. "Though virtually sure is not enough, of course. We need absolute certainty. A confession would be the most convenient way here, but I don't really see how he would voluntarily subject himself to a truth block. So we will have to try and do it by digging through his financial records, see if we can determine who he paid, look for the people he hired..."

Eryn interrupted him when an idea began to form in her head. "Wait. When you questioned Onil you didn't do it under the influence of a truth block, did you? You merely applied one afterwards when you asked him to confirm that all his answers were true."

Both men nodded and waited for her to continue.

"He is rather eager to share his little story with the Council, isn't he? So if we let him tell it and make sure not to ask him questions that would let him suspect what we think - we could then ask him to agree to a truth block to confirm that what he said was true. The facts that he was attacked while taking a walk, that witnesses came running and took him to the clinic and that he was injured are all true.

He would surely not object to confirming them, would he? And while he is under the influence of the truth block, well, then suddenly there is another question that comes to mind... Such as: Were you involved in the attack in any way?"

Lord Poron pursed his lips and looked out the window while contemplating this idea. Tyront propped up his chin on his braided fingers while thinking.

For more than a minute nobody spoke, then Tyront said, "Yes, we could do this. We need to consider who should apply the truth block. It shouldn't be myself or Enric... this should be a Council effort. Lord Remdel or Lord Seagon, I would think. It will work even better if it is done by somebody who has been known to cooperate with him occasionally."

"I opt for Lord Seagon," Lord Poron suggested. "He has a better standing in the Council than Lord Remdel, who is considered little too... weak-minded at times."

No wonder, Eryn thought, with a companion such as Inad this might be a survival skill...

"I agree. Lord Seagon it is then. He will apply the truth block and you will ask the questions, Poron." Tyront rubbed his hands. "Then let's get to work! We still need to question the magicians to be absolutely sure they weren't involved before we confront Lord Aldon at the next meeting. We don't want to look like fools in the unlikely case that we are wrong. Eryn - not a word to anyone about this. With the exception of Enric, of course. When you tell him, make sure you have a soundproof barrier in place, even at your home."

She looked around, suddenly uneasy. "It could already be too late for that. There was no shield in place just now! With all these spies around, who knows - we might have been overheard!" Damn - how could all three of them be that negligent? Enric kept impressing on her how important safeguarding confidential information was, but somehow she thought of this only afterwards.

Tyront smiled as he rose. "No, you may rest assured that this conversation was confidential. Agents, you see, can not only be used to procure information. Some of them also specialise in making sure that your information is safe from others by keeping other agents off your trail."

Eryn blinked in surprise. Oh dear. Now there were different kinds of spies. And none of them would be necessary if people just respected each other's privacy. She kept her mouth shut, though. These were just naive country-girl thoughts, unfit for the big city and the high circles she moved in now.

She thought back to the little village where she had grown up. People there hadn't exactly respected each other's secrets and wish for privacy, any more than in the city, but they had at least resorted to the traditional way of collecting information: peeking out from behind curtains or listening to gossip. These were not really pleasant things to do, but at least people didn't have to worry about spies searching their study at night. In the countryside keeping a secret wasn't always easy, either, it just required more care. In the city keeping information confidential was a matter of employing a minor army of people who were scuttling around.

In moments such as that the idea of sneaking away from the city and living somewhere deserted seemed immensely appealing. But instead it was soundproof barriers, spies and political games. Just fabulous.

*　*　*

Eryn read the letter Enric had left on her desk. It was from Malhora with a status report on how their residence was coming along. The structure as such was already complete, now the fixtures and fittings such as windows, flooring, doors, lamps, plumbing and similar needed to be taken care off. Her grandmother was confident that everything would be ready for them to move in when they arrived in about two months. The only thing that would not be much to look at by that time would be the garden. That would take a while yet. But there was a good chance that Valrad would take pity on them. Or maybe also Pe'tala had a hand for plants and felt like gardening.

She wiggled her toes slightly and enjoyed the warmth. Urban was asleep under her desk and she had pushed her cold toes underneath the cat's body.

Her gaze wandered across to the sound machine Erbál had sent her. Tyront really had a nerve to try and take it away from her. Enric had told her that his offer was actually quite a generous one, that he could easily have commandeered it from her there and then, confiscated for the good of the Order.

She decided to accept that. At the moment she was inclined to be more gracious. Tyront had in these last months turned out to be a valuable ally in all these issues that kept emerging. As well as a supportive leader. He had stood by her when she had been accused of trying to kill him. Certainly, she'd had nothing to do with it, yet he could have made her life a lot harder by insisting that, until the end of the proceedings, she was not allowed to work with patients, putting her under a curfew or the like - things which several Council members would have supported. He was also supporting her with all the things she wanted to change. There would be a few minor details where he could probably not agree quite so wholeheartedly, but all in all he was willing to at least listen to what she proposed.

She looked up when there was a light knock at the door she had left ajar. Plia gently pushed it open and smiled when she noted the quietly snoring baby in his crib.

"Hello you," Eryn said. "You are back unusually early. Don't tell me you are actually starting to keep civilised hours for a change?"

The girl shrugged and blushed slightly. "I'm trying to. There is a boy who I meet sometimes, so..."

"That is excellent motivation." Eryn was glad that Plia was seeing people outside the clinic. The girl had seemed disappointed when Vern hadn't returned from Takhan, and as far as Eryn knew there was no correspondence between the two of them. She wondered if Plia was a little dejected because of it. It wouldn't have made things easier for her if she had learned about Vern's amorous adventures as well. But now she was showing interest in another young man. That could only be good. Though...

"Do you need me to, you know, help you protect yourself from unwanted consequences?"

Plia smiled shyly. "Such as getting pregnant? No, thank you. Onil was so kind and helped me with that little point. And we've not yet progressed quite that far..."

"You asked Onil for help in this? I'm a little surprised that you didn't come to me. And feeling a bit snubbed, to be honest. I would like to think that I was the first one you confided in."

The girl waved her off. "There is no need to be jealous - you are still my number one healer. Well, at least while you are staying in the country you are. Onil just happened to watch when my... friend picked me up from work. Next morning he visited me in the laboratory and gave me a lecture on the dangers of unprotected sex. I gave in and let him do something to my reproductive organs just to keep him from nagging. He was a lot more relaxed after."

Eryn couldn't help but smile at that. She knew that Onil had two younger sisters, so playing a big brother was obviously ingrained in him. And for Plia it was excellent that somebody cared for her like that, worried about her for no selfish reason.

The girl bent down to look under the desk. "Are you using a grown mountain cat to warm your feet? Now I've seen everything."

The woman shrugged. "Why not? She doesn't mind it and my toes are grateful. Say, there is something I've been considering. How would you like accompanying us to Takhan for a short time? Maybe for a month for a start and then we could see if you like it."

Plia's eyes went wide, but Eryn couldn't say if this was excitement or shock.

"That is a very generous offer, Eryn, and I hope you don't consider me ungrateful... But I would rather not go away from here for the time being. Maybe next year. The apothecaries are rather troublesome at the moment, and I wouldn't want to leave without anybody to take over my work."

Eryn nodded. And then, of course, there was her new love interest she wouldn't want to abandon. "Of course, no problem. I just wanted you to know that staying here alone is not your only choice, it's just one of two. We would be delighted to have you with us, keep the family together."

She could see a trace a wet glint in one corner of Plia's eyes at that last bit.

"Thank you. That means a lot to me," the girl whispered.

* * *

"Lord Enric?"

Enric smiled when he saw Plia standing in his doorway, and beckoned her in. No matter how often he told her that she didn't need to use the title considering that they were living under the same roof, she still insisted on holding on to the custom.

"What can I do for you?" he asked and leaned back in his chair, watching her come closer until she stood in front of his desk.

She pulled a small brown pouch out of her pocket and counted out four gold pieces. "You have always showed me kindness, my Lord. You let me move into your new house when I wouldn't have had any other place to stay after quitting my apprenticeship at the Palace. This was incredibly generous of you, especially as you and Eryn would surely have preferred your privacy after you had been joined not long before." She cleared her throat. "I earn my own money now, and I want to contribute something."

Enric's face darkened when she held out the gold coins on her flat palm.

"Put that away again," he instructed her calmly.

"I know it's not much," Plia went on quickly, "certainly not what accommodation of this quality is worth, but..."

"Plia," he interrupted her, "I'm not accepting any money from you. Rather save it. I don't know if you are aware of this," he added dryly, "but I am rather wealthy."

The girl looked at him with a pleading expression, clearly uneasy, but determined to see this through and not give in. "I would feel a lot better if you permitted me to contribute something instead of making me accept charity. I earn money, I can pay at least a little! I'm not a beggar," she said with her chin raised high and defiance dancing in her eyes.

Enric stared at her for some time, impressed that she had overcome her awe of him enough to actually defy him like that. Eryn truly had been quite a role model for that girl who had hardly dared to meet his eyes one and a half years ago.

Without moving a muscle he raised a shield in front of the girl and pushed her backwards and out his study door. She stood in front of the door, staring at him incredulously.

"That was a No, in case you were wondering," he said helpfully and produced with the swish of his hand an air blast that closed the door in her face.

The girl shook her head and groaned.

"What's going on here?" Eryn asked when she came out of her study. "I'll have you know that Vedric is asleep, so be a bit more mindful when you slam the doors shut, will you?" Then she frowned as she came nearer. "Is that a shield in front of his door?"

Plia nodded with a sorrowful expression. "He pushed me out and then shielded his door. I just wanted to ask something of him, and he just..." She pointed to the door, helpless.

Eryn ground her teeth. That was not a particularly nice thing to do, not to mention impolite. She motioned for Plia to step back. Chances were that he had not made the barrier particularly strong as a non-magician wouldn't be able to get through it anyway.

She fired two strikes in quick succession, satisfied when the shield flickered and died. Without knocking she opened the door and strolled inside, her arms akimbo when she stopped in front of her companion, looking down at him with a stern expression.

"What do you mean by locking her out like that when she wants to talk to you? That's not particularly grown-up behaviour! You of all people should know that brute force is not the way to enforce your opinion, but listening to people and encour..."

"She wanted to pay her back rent," Enric interrupted her.

Eryn blinked, then rolled her eyes, raised a shield to block the doorway once again and closed Enric's door, though with her hand to keep the noise down.

Enric grinned widely at that. He loved it when they were on the same side.

"You can't do this!" Plia's indignant voice came from the parlour, muffled through the door. "I'm sure that's inappropriate use of magic against non-magicians!"

Eryn let herself fall down on the sofa and called back, "No, it's not - trust me. My mighty rank of number three in the Order makes me kind of a guardian of all these rules. We are totally allowed to raise shields to keep you away when you are a nuisance."

"You can't do this! This just isn't fair!" Plia wailed in desperation. "You can't just forbid me to contribute something!"

At that moment they heard a long-drawn-out, high-pitched cry from above.

"We wouldn't dream of forbidding you that," Eryn called back. "You can go upstairs and take Vedric. Thanks to you he is awake one hour too early, which means that you will entertain him now."

They heard Plia shuffle away from the door.

Eryn looked at her companion with a wide smile. "That was fun. I think we are naturally born parents: strict, yet supportive, fair, but firm."

Enric nodded. "I agree. We are doing a very good job here. So good, in fact, that I was wondering..."

"No," she cut him off. She had a very clear idea where this was going. "One is enough. I distinctly remember telling you that I have no intention to have another child." She groaned. "Why don't you just give up and accept my decision? Why?"

He sighed and played with a pen, twirled it between his fingers. "I love you. And I love to see you with Vedric. You are a beautiful mother, and I enjoy being a father. Well, most of the time I do," he amended. "I think with our moving so frequently between the two countries, a sibling would also be a good thing for Vedric. They could play together, grow up together. Vedric would be a big brother, like I was for Leris or like Vran for Tala..."

Eryn's eyes narrowed. "You want a girl. That's why you keep mentioning sisters. You forgot to mention your sister's children - how much little Dorn adores his sister." She sighed and closed her eyes. "I see you with little girls, and how they adore you. And you them. But even if we had another child, there is no guarantee that it would be a girl." She got up, too agitated to sit. "And even if I agreed to have another child and it truly turned out to be a girl - can you imagine what battles Malriel would fight to get her hands on a daughter of ours? Not only an heir for the next generation, but also somebody to provide the family with descendants from her direct bloodline who would be in charge of her House?" She shook her head vehemently. "No thank you. You'll have to learn to be content with being adored by your nieces." With this she turned and left his study.

Perfect, Enric thought, and ground his teeth... so glad we talked about this. And again he had managed to turn a relaxed conversation into an argument with only a few sentences.

He looked at the two letters that had arrived over the course of the last few days. The Houses in Takhan kept contacting him to offer business opportunities and generous gifts if he could manage to persuade Eryn to enter into a companionship agreement for Vedric. By now it was common knowledge that approaching Eryn in this regard was futile. She simply ignored the letters. Yet many of the Houses were eager to have a chance to join their daughters with Vedric - no matter which House he would ultimately belong with, he would one day be a Head of House in one or the other.

Enric understood why this competition for the most promising companion that started after the children were born repulsed Eryn. And she was right, after all - Malriel's granddaughter would be a prize the Houses would fight over. Firstly, Vran'el and Malriel would both want her for their own House because her children would secure the next generation of power in the family, and secondly most other Houses would try to join their sons with her.

He himself didn't worry too much about this. It was just another political game, little different from the ones he had been playing for these last fifteen years. The playing field was a little different, but nothing he considered beyond his abilities.

If he had a little girl one day, she would not be pushed or forced into any commitment, position as Head of House or whatever else - he would make sure of that. The same went for Vedric. He wondered if convincing Eryn that he could protect their children would make her reconsider her resolve not to have another one.

He wondered if her anger at his repeated attempts would be worth it.

*   *   *

Enric noticed his mother carrying her new suitcase down the stairs and hurried toward her to take it off her. She acknowledged it with a smile.

Good. It meant she was no longer upset because he got rid of her old one, which had more or less fallen apart, and replaced it with another. Only this morning had she discovered it and they had been discussing for a while until she had reluctantly accepted it. He suspected that it had been his argument that she would need a proper one anyway when she would visit Leris and her family, since her old suitcase was neither sturdy nor capacious enough for a lengthy trip.

He wondered a little about his mother's disinclination to accept gifts from him. He had bought a house for her, paid for the reconstruction work, furnished it... and now a minor thing like a suitcase was a problem?

Eryn had explained it to him very patiently when there was a quiet minute after his mother had taken Vedric for a walk. She told him that accepting little gifts became a lot more painful after accepting such an immensely generous one first. And that his mother had surely not expected ever to rely on Enric to take care of her. Parents were supposed to be the ones taking care of their children, not the other way round. It happened, of course, that sometimes a widow depended on her children to take her in after her companion's death, but as Anwin was not a poor man, that problem would not have arisen in her case. After his death she would have been entitled to a part of his fortune, large enough to settle her comfortably for the rest of her own life. To her it probably felt that she was swapping dependency on her companion for dependency on her son.

Enric had pointed out that buying her a house was supposed to give her independence, not make her dependent on him. Eryn had kindly patted his arm and told him that his point of view was not the only one, however rational it might appear to him. She had advised him to apply in Gerit's case what she as his companion appreciated as well: having her wishes respected, even if he didn't always understand them. Then she had turned to return to her study and work on her translations.

"Are you ready to take possession of your new home officially, mother?" he asked and put down the suitcase next to the door to help her into her cloak. Eryn had decided that this was a mother-son moment and visited Junar. He regretted that a little. He would have loved to have her with him for this.

"Yes. A little nervous, though, I have to admit. I have never before in my life lived completely alone. But I'm determined to keep myself too busy to become bored." She looked around. "Where is Eryn?"

"Visiting her friend Junar. She didn't want to disturb this family moment."

"Foolish girl," Gerit sighed and shook her head, making Enric smile. He shared the sentiment.

When they stepped out into the street, the first snowflakes started dancing through the crispy air, whirling around on air currents. Not many people were out today and the few he could see were wrapped in several layers of clothing. Enric sniffed with an expression of distaste. The wind came from the south and carried the stink of numerous chimneys in their direction. He thought longingly of the heat in Takhan. In only a few more weeks they would be returning there and enjoying balmy evenings on their new terrace with a mild breeze playing around them. Strange, how the thought of Takhan glowed in his heart, how the place had turned into something very close to home. He had friends and business interests there, and now even his own residence. Yet at the same time it saddened him to think of everything he would be leaving behind here in Anyueel. Plia, who was for him a strange blend between younger sister and daughter; Tyront, who had redeemed himself again; Orrin, who had turned into a friend; and now his mother.

He knew that he would be looking forward to returning here in six months' time, eager to embrace that other place in his life that was a part of him. He wondered if Eryn felt the same.

"You seem thoughtful, my boy," Gerit remarked while walking next to him.

"I was thinking that it's not long now until I'll return to Takhan. And that I'm sorry to leave you here alone for several months only after I managed to persuade you to stay in the city."

His mother squeezed his arm and smiled. "You will be back in half a year again, and we'll write each other. Having you six out of every twelve months is a lot more than I've had since you were sent here as a boy after your magic was discovered. And I'll not be alone. Inad keeps trying to persuade me to accompany her to her evening invitations, and I think I will give in some time soon. It will do me good to get in contact with people." She paused and then frowned. "The girl, Plia. Who will be taking care of her while you are away? She had to stay alone at your place for several months last time, didn't she? I know she is not like the spoilt children from wealthier families considering that she had to grow up from an early age, yet I can't help thinking that it wouldn't hurt if somebody looked after her every now and then."

Enric waited for her to go on, a faint smile on his lips. He had a feeling where this would go.

"So I was thinking about inviting her to stay with me instead of alone at your house," she said carefully, looking up at her son to see whether he approved.

"Replacing Vedric with a stand-in grandchild as long as we are in Takhan, are you?" he teased her.

"Nonsense, Enric! What a cruel thing to say," she huffed, but sighed when she saw the humour in her eyes.

"I think this is a superb idea. It would take a burden off my shoulders. Eryn offered Plia to come to Takhan with us, but she wants to stay here. It would be a great relief for me if the two of you kept an eye on each other."

"I am fifty-five years old, Enric! I surely don't need anyone to look after me!" she protested.

"Whatever you say, mother," he grinned and put an arm around her shoulders. "After my last conversation with Plia she is probably even eager to move out."

Gerit looked at him. "Why would she?"

"I locked her out of my study with a shield. She tried to pay me rent."

His mother laughed at that. "The poor girl. An attempt condemned to failure."

* * *

Eryn worked hard at keeping her face expressionless when she would rather have glared at Lord Aldon. Tyront and Lord Poron had been busy this last week interviewing every single magician who had invaded that one Council meeting the day Onil was being questioned. And just as they had expected, none of them was involved in this strange attack on Lord Aldon.

Enric accompanied her to her chair right next to Orrin's. The warrior waited until Enric had left to round the table to get to his own seat and then leaned towards her to murmur, "What's going on here?"

Eryn feigned mild surprise. "What do you mean?"

"There is something in the air. I know there was this attack on Lord Aldon and that we will talk about it today, but there is more... I can't put my finger on it, but there is a certain tension. Enric is stony-faced, as he is every time he knows more than the rest of us. Lord Tyront over is there pretending to read something so he doesn't have to talk to anyone, and Lord Poron is trying very hard to appear particularly harmless today. And then there is you."

"Me?"

"Yes. Your face is a mask of pretend calm, but your eyes seem grim. Somebody is in trouble. And I'm pretty sure it's not me. It could be you, though." Then his eyes narrowed. "No, you are neither stupid enough to attack the old fart, nor would it be your style. But you know who did it, don't you?"

Eryn pressed her lips together and looked straight ahead. She wouldn't lie to him. It wouldn't make sense; he knew that something was about to happen. But neither could she tell him about it right now. Somebody might be listening in - and this was a realistic chance in a room that was slowly filling with magicians. Some of them had to be aware how to manipulate air streams to eavesdrop from afar. Her not responding to his question would tell him plainly enough that she wasn't in a position to share right now.

"Wait for it," she just whispered.

A little later all the Council members had arrived and taken their seats. Eryn turned her head to look at the King's observer. The monarch tended to be present in person when interesting things were about to happen, so he either had no idea what would happen today or was considerate enough to stay away to avoid any premature suspicions from Lord Aldon's side. Knowing him, it was probably the latter. Good manners were not exactly his most prominent character trait, but far more likely than his being unaware of what was going on.

Tyront lowered the papers in front of him and the hall fell silent immediately.

"I trust that most if not all of you have heard what happened to Lord Aldon several days ago. Some of you might wonder why it has taken me quite so long to call for a meeting to discuss this. Let me assure you that it was no disregard for the importance of the case but time I needed to consider the possible consequences of it. Lord Aldon, would you please rise and describe to the Council what exactly transpired on that day. As usual, I shall ask you to keep the account rather general as we will let you know if we require more details."

Lord Aldon regally rose from his chair, taking his time as if he enjoyed the attention. He stood with his fingers interlocked and looked up at the ceiling with an air of serious contemplation as if considering how best to start. Eryn forced her foot to remain still when it wanted to tap the floor impatiently. She bet he had rehearsed what he was about to tell them several times.

"It was eight days ago that I set forth to enjoy a leisurely walk along the river, as I am known to do after lunch almost every day," he finally started.

As I am known to do, Eryn went over again in her head, wanting to grind her teeth. As if he were a person of such great importance that everyone took an interest in his unspectacular little habits.

"I took the same route as usual, the one that led me past the Palace and warriors' quarters down to the river promenade and then towards the bridge. I had almost reached the bridge when suddenly there were three men attacking me from behind."

Ah yes, Eryn thought, he left off repeating what he had told them at the clinic: that he had spotted the three suspiciously disinterested looking figures as soon as he had reached the river. So he wanted to avoid inconvenient questions such as why he had not shielded himself if he had noticed the men before. The argument that he had been too surprised to do so was not quite that credible in that case.

Lord Aldon shook his head as if remembering the cruelty and pain of it all with dread. "They struck me with their fists and kicked me repeatedly until I was lying on the ground, bleeding and injured. I was reluctant to defend myself with a shield. When magicians use magic, there is always the danger of whether they can manage to keep it strictly defensive."

Listen to that, Eryn thought, he had explained away that little catch very neatly. The well-trained warrior who didn't trust himself enough to restrain himself when resorting to magical measures, being so eager to uphold the law, that he willingly accepted the injury he had to suffer. Admirably heroic.

And he had even managed to phrase it generally enough so that it was not technically a lie.

She saw on a few faces around her subtle hints that this was not exactly consistent with what they knew of their colleague, but nobody spoke up.

"Two men came running to intervene. Luckily, they were close enough to witness the whole affair and didn't hesitate to come to my aid. They managed to drive my attackers away and then were so kind as to take me to the clinic where my injuries were taken care of. There was one thing, though, I heard them exchange when I was lying on the ground: That will teach him a lesson. He won't be such a trouble in the future."

"Did you recognise any of the attackers?" Lord Remdel enquired.

"No, I don't recall encountering the men before."

"I take it you do not think that you were a random victim?" Lord Seagon then queried.

Lord Aldon shook his head gravely. "Certainly not. I was wearing my robe, you see, so I was recognisable as a magician. And considering what I heard them say I would suggest that they knew exactly who I am."

"This sounds as if you had a suspicion who might be behind this," Orrin remarked, whereupon Eryn kicked him hard under the table. They needed to avoid asking him any questions that might induce him to lie and then cause him to refuse the truth block to avoid being found out. Orrin didn't show any outward sign of pain or surprise but said quickly, "But of course you do, please forgive the stupid question. The evidence seems to point to those whose interests run contrary to your convictions."

Relief rushed through her. Good thing Orrin was a quick thinker. She looked at Tyront, hoping that he would move on quickly before anybody else wanted to put any further inconvenient questions.

Lord Poron was the next to speak. "Lady Eryn, you were the one to heal Lord Aldon together with Lady Pe'tala. Would you be so good as to elaborate on his injuries?"

Eryn nodded. "Of course. Lord Aldon was carried into my treatment room by two men, who I was informed were the witnesses to the attack. I took care of the head injuries consisting of a minor skull fracture and a wound which was bleeding, Pe'tala healed the other, less severe damage to his shin, knees and shoulder."

"You were the one to heal him?" Lord Woldarn asked suspiciously.

"Yes, my Lord," Eryn growled, "and before you even think of wondering aloud if this was a wise idea, I invite you to consult Lebern or Lord Poron who both checked on him afterwards to ascertain that the healing met the clinic's standards."

"You know the procedure, Lady Eryn," Lord Seagon said. "Statements given under circumstances such as this one are generally verified with the aid of a truth block."

Eryn rose instead of replying and walked over to him, holding out her arm for him to take. This was incredibly convenient - now that he had more or less volunteered to test the truth of her words, it would not even be necessary for Tyront to appoint him to do it. It would be the most natural thing in the world for him to also apply the second truth block on Lord Aldon.

Lord Seagon rose and took her arm, releasing a stream of magic into her arm. "Can you confirm that everything you said in connection with Lord Aldon's injuries is the truth?"

"Yes."

"And you healed Lord Aldon just the way you would have treated any other patient, despite the tension between the two of you on account of his point of view being opposed to your own?"

"Yes," she replied with one eyebrow raised.

"One final question," Lord Seagon continued, "were you involved in the attack on Lord Aldon in any way - be it that you knew of it before, planned it, hired the men to carry it out or provided the funds for paying these men?"

She rolled her eyes, displaying her annoyance at being suspected yet again a bit more prominently than she felt it. He was actually doing her a favour with this chance to acquit herself before any official accusations or less official speculations started.

"No, I was not involved in the attack on Lord Aldon in any other way than healing the injuries resulting thereof afterwards."

Tyront nodded and then asked, "Lord Aldon, I assume you, too, have no objections confirming that your account of your story was accurate under a truth block? It's a mere formality, as you know."

Eryn smiled when he nodded. Now that she had agreed to subject herself to a truth read first, it would seem really strange if he refused. Lord Seagon had unwittingly helped this matter along rather splendidly.

"Lord Seagon, take care of this for us, will you?" Tyront requested and leaned back. He seemed relaxed, but Eryn could see how the gaze from under his half-closed lids sharpened. Now the delicate part began.

She watched how Lord Seagon's hand closed around Lord Aldon's bare lower arm.

"Lord Aldon, can you confirm to us that the attack on you happened the way you have described it just now?"

"Yes, that I can," Lord Aldon declared grandly. "Every word I said is true."

Lord Poron opened his mouth and was about to speak, but Lord Seagon was faster and said with a chuckle, "I assume I don't really need to ask you whether or not you were involved in the planning of the attack on yourself, do I?"

Eryn stared at the two men standing not far from her. Could they really be that lucky? They had been worried about the timing, that Lord Poron might not manage to ask this very question in time before the truth block was released, but having Lord Seagon himself do it was more than anyone had dared to hope for.

There was quietly amused laughter from a few sides, but that died down in an instant when Lord Aldon stared at his colleague with wide eyes that shone with panic.

"Lord Aldon?" Lord Seagon asked calmly but with a frown. "Now I can't help but wonder if that question shouldn't be asked anyway." When his colleague didn't answer but just swallowed, he looked at his leader for guidance.

Tyront rose very slowly. Eryn admired his flair for dramatic gestures. He placed his flat palms on the table on both sides of him and pushed himself up, his bright blue eyes focussed on Lord Aldon with a dangerous expression.

"Answer the question," he rumbled. "Were you involved in the planning of the attack on yourself so you could try to lay the blame on someone else?"

It was such a hush within the large Council hall that the drop of a pin would have produced a clearly audible sound.

"Answer!" Tyront barked into the silence, making several people, Eryn included, flinch when the sound was reflected to and fro.

Lord Seagon held on to his colleague when he wanted to free himself from his grip and from the truth block.

"Yes," Lord Aldon finally whispered and closed his eyes.

"Yes, you planned the attack to blame somebody else?" Lord Seagon repeated and added, "Such as for example the group of magicians, who interrupted the meeting in order to make their discontent known to us?"

"Yes," growled Lord Aldon, suddenly no longer resigned and desperate, but instead angry. "I was trying to protect our traditions! To hold on to what has made us successful over these last three hundred years! You fools were about to throw all this away, to turn away from the values we have all sworn to protect! I wanted to open your eyes - these rebels would have done something like that sooner or later, there can be little doubt about that!"

Tyront's lip curled in distaste. "I wasn't aware that you possessed the gift to see into the future, Lord Aldon. We would have looked like fools if you had succeeded with that scheme of yours. Lord Poron and I have questioned every single one of the men who came here that day, and the few more who occasionally joined their meetings. We applied a truth block, so we are certain that none of them was involved. Incriminating innocent people is not how we lead this institution!" The last sentence was a fraction louder than those before. He immediately lowered his voice again. "You are a disgrace to the Order, to the values you claim you want to protect but instead befoul. And you have brought dishonour to this Council, whose responsibility it is to lead those under our care fairly and justly."

Eryn's heart beat faster. She knew what was about to come and was anxious how the other Council members would react to it.

"Lord Aldon, I herewith decree that you are expelled from this Council with immediate effect. The title of Lord shall no longer be applied to you. Your actions have marked you as a traitor to the Order. As the membership in the Order is compulsory for magicians, I do not have the liberty of barring you from it as well, but you will be stripped of your rank and all monetary benefits. You will be assigned a humble position that won't require the ethical standards you have today proven yourself unworthy of." Tyront turned and looked at every single Council member with an expression that made it very clear that he wouldn't take well to opposition on this - despite his next question. "Are there any objections?"

None dared speak.

"Excellent. Guards!" he called out and waited until the large double doors were pushed open and two uniformed Palace guards entered and awaited his instructions.

"Lord Orrin will accompany you, together with former Council member Aldon. He is to be put in golden manacles and locked in a dungeon cell for the next days."

Orrin rose and his hand closed around the upper arm of the man formerly known as Lord Aldon to make sure he posed no danger to their non-magician escort.

All eyes were on Tyront, when the four men had left and the doors closed again.

"The next Council meeting will be in one week. The number of members is again twelve as is the required minimum. This means there will not need to be a replacement. You are all dismissed."

Eryn was the first to stand, working hard at keeping to herself her relief and joy at the smooth conclusion of the case. The men around her stood about, mostly still aghast, with Lord Woldarn shaking his head repeatedly in confounded disbelief at what just had happened.

One week till the next meeting. Time to start preparing.

CHAPTER 33

Breakthrough

Eryn took a deep breath and raised her hand to the iron door knocker of Gerit's entrance door. A moment before the heavy ring would have connected with the wood, she stilled. Once again she asked herself if this really made sense. If putting herself through that ordeal would really bring the result she was hoping for. No, she reproached herself, no retreat - she would face the enemy bravely and endure the agonies to serve her home land. Well, one of them.

Counting to three, she lifted her hand once again to the knocker, grabbed it with determination and pounded it twice against the brand-new door.

It didn't take long until a servant pulled it open, bowed to her and stepped aside to let her enter. Eryn handed over her cloak and held on to her basket carrying the wine bottles.

"Gerit is in the parlour," the servant informed her. Eryn nodded and turned left into the first room.

Enric's mother rose from one of two identical pale green sofas in front of the hearth that sported a cosy fire. On the other sofa the enemy in her dark gold dress squealed with delight at the arrival of the visitor.

"Lady Eryn! What an immensely pleasant surprise!"

Eryn made herself smile and accepted Gerit's hug before turning to Inad.

"Good evening, Inad. I apologise for turning up unannounced like this and disturbing you, but I just wanted to deliver a little something. I will be off again shortly."

"Nonsense!" Inad exclaimed, clearly horrified at the notion that Eryn might feel unwelcome. "You must stay and sit with us for a little while at least - it has been ages since I last saw you at a dinner or banquet."

Eryn's smile turned genuine at that thought. Yes, she truly had managed to wriggle herself free of these occasions quite effectively. Having a small child at home and insisting on raising it on her own had been a useful move, at least in this regard.

"If you don't consider me an unwanted intruder, I would be happy to stay for a short while," she nodded and handed Gerit the basket.

566

"Enric sends these. He says we don't need that much wine at home as we will soon be leaving for Takhan and he thinks you might need it for receiving guests." She grinned. "And as you know he only lays down the good stuff. Mostly the one he himself produces somewhere down south."

Enric's mother nodded and accepted the bottles. "Take a seat, my dear. What would you like to drink? Inad and I just opened a bottle of wine, if you would like a glass?"

"Sure, why not?" Eryn agreed and took a seat on the sofa Gerit had just stood up from.

"Isn't this case with Lord Aldon... Aldon, I should say now, a great shame?" Inad exclaimed with gleeful joy.

"That was a very regrettable turn of events, yes," Eryn consented.

"Did you know that this was the first time ever a member has been expelled from the Council? And rightly so - what an abominable deed!"

Eryn smiled politely. This either meant all and any Council members who had done something forbidden had either been more skilled when it came to hiding it or it had been condoned as crimes committed by rich and mighty people were never quite as despicable when compared to less affluent culprits. But putting words to this would not aid her in her efforts. This would lead to the wrong kind of discussion just now.

Instead she sighed. "Though his actions were most appalling, I can't help but pity him."

"Ah, Lady Eryn," Inad smiled beatifically, "you and your big heart!"

"Well, he was misguided, and the punishment truly is a severe one. Being stripped of his rank, his income, his influence... Imagine if something like that happened to you." She smiled gratefully when Gerit handed her a glass of wine.

"A dreadful fate indeed," Inad assented, clearly safe in the knowledge that nothing of that sort could ever happen to the likes of her.

"And yet a tangible danger to all of us, when you look at the circumstances," Eryn said and took a sip from her wine, giving her words time to sink in.

Inad looked at her, taken aback. "I certainly wouldn't think that! Or are you assuming that all of the Council members are criminals and might at one point be found out to be stripped of everything?"

"Or course not," Eryn assured her quickly. "I would never say a thing like that. I'm sure that my colleagues in the Council are honourable and trustworthy people and that the issue with Aldon was one bad apple in the box. I merely wanted to indicate that there are two very likely scenarios, unless the Order considers a few changes. The first one would be that the magicians who stormed the Council will manage to gather even more supporters and at one point may even be numerous enough and powerful enough to overthrow the Council if we don't change some rules to accommodate their demands. That would without a doubt mean that the current Council would either be dissolved or the members exchanged. The other even more likely prospect is that things remain as they are for the next two decades until the newly-born magicians that have already shown a considerable increase in strength take over the Order. The way things appear right now, my own son will be the next leader of the Order, as you no doubt have heard. As he is not the only extremely strong magician to be born here so far, the Order would in a number of years be in the hands of people who are little more than children. You may remember when Enric was made to take over his position of second in command at the age of twenty-two - a lazy mischief-maker with little interest in or understanding of what was going on. Nonetheless, he was the only young, inexperienced member of the Council and Lord Tyront was a strong and exacting mentor who managed to form him into another person entirely. Imagine the same situation with a whole group of young, disinterested people with no-one above them..." She shook her head with a sad sigh. "I don't think many of the current members of the Council would be able to retain their status and incomes..."

"But that is terrible!" Inad exclaimed wide-eyed, her palm resting over her heart. "Something can be done to avoid this, surely! You said changing a few rules to make the dissatisfied magicians happy could halt them, didn't you?"

Eryn nodded with a mournful smile. "Yes, that would certainly be a start. Yet the Council's willingness to embrace a few slightly more modern concepts is not exactly massive. I fear that their respect for their traditions and history is stronger than their courage to change a few things to preserve the institution as such." Yes, she decided, that sounded satisfactory. She couldn't insult the Council members - and among them Inad's companion Lord Remdel - by calling them old-fashioned idiots with outdated notions that did more harm than good.

"How short-sighted!" Inad cried out desperately. Eryn wondered if that woman had ever managed to speak a sentence without some kind of emotional weighting.

"I try my best, but I'm only one person, and as the newest and youngest member my arguments are considered little more than funny little ideas that should better be ignored. But then this would only have been a delay, anyway - the inevitable change in the power structure of the Order would still be only a matter of about twenty years. To avoid this and keep the experienced and honourable members of the Council in charge of the Order, there would need to be a change in the way power is granted. And that is such a fundamental change that I'm not sure the Council could ever agree upon it." Eryn wondered if she should once again point out that being a Council member equalled holding on to power and a generous income, but then Inad knew very well where the money that kept her well situated came from.

"No, Lady Eryn," Inad exclaimed with utter conviction, "I cannot believe that the Council would be as short-sighted as that! I know that Remdel is one who prefers to hold on what has proved itself in practice, but I'm sure that once he has been made to understand the true impact of rejecting your ideas, he will reconsider his position at once! Leave this to me, Lady Eryn - I shall have a lengthy conversation with him as soon as I return home tonight!"

Eryn mustered all her acting skills to keep the triumphant laugh at bay that wanted to escape and instead tone it down to a modestly hopeful smile. "Ah, I wish we had more women in the Council, and especially such insightful ones as yourself who are so quick on the uptake."

Inad straightened, immensely pleased with the praise. "Yes, we women understand each other, don't we? What would our companions do without us?"

Eryn picked up her glass and drained the rest of the wine. "They would be completely lost, of course. So, the two of you need to excuse me now. I'm expected back home. Vedric needs to be bathed, and I try to do that myself as often as I can. They grow up so quickly and I want to enjoy as much of it as I can."

"Of course you do," Inad nodded sagely, as if she herself had raised her children herself instead of delegating this task to a number of servants. "It was a great pleasure to see you tonight, Lady Eryn. I very much hope that I will meet you again soon."

"So do I," Eryn smiled broadly, making the words come out as sincerely as she could.

"I will see you to the door," Gerit, who had all this time just been sitting next to Eryn without uttering a single word, offered and got to her feet. When they were out in the hallway, Enric's mother whispered, "That's why you wanted me to tell you when Inad was next due for a visit! You wanted to manipulate her into making her companion vote with you!"

Eryn bit her lip. There was little use in denying it. Gerit was a lot smarter than her cousin.

"Are you mad at me now?"

Gerit sighed and then slowly shook her head. "No, not mad. But I'm a little embarrassed on Inad's behalf. After coming here to use my guest for your own purpose like that I feel that it shouldn't have been quite that easy for you."

The younger woman grinned at that. "To be honest, I was prepared to put a lot more effort into it, but what can I do if she is so very desperate to preserve her lifestyle?"

Then Gerit narrowed her eyes. "And I gave Vedric a bath only yesterday, so there is no need to do so again today. This was just a lie to get away from here! Inad enjoys your company very much and you owe her something for using her like that. You could at least stay for an hour and make amends for your unscrupulous games with her!"

Eryn grimaced and quickly slipped into the cloak the servant handed her. "I'm sure I'll have to pay the price for her help one way or another, so please spare me for tonight, will you?"

Gerit sighed and waved her off. "Go home to your family then, my child. And don't you dare decline my invitation for dinner when it comes."

Eryn nodded obediently and then slipped out into the cold, dark evening. Gerit and her sense for justice. How inconvenient.

* * *

Enric had just finished sharing a rather messy dinner with his son when the front door opened and Eryn came in from her visit.

"You look very pleased with yourself," he commented when she entered the dining room, grin wide on her face.

"I know that self-adulation is not very attractive, but I have to say that I did rather well," she nodded and waited until Enric had cleaned their son up enough for her to lift him into her arms without spreading the remainders of his meal on her clothes. "Though, as your mother rightly pointed out, Inad didn't make it too hard for me to convince her that aiding me ultimately means aiding herself."

"My little manipulator," Enric teased her. "So glad to see that you are slowly adapting to the ways of the big city." He smiled at the look that earned him. She didn't want to think that she was slowly turning into a conniving politician and resented every comment that suggested just that.

"I'm not a manipulator," she gave back sullenly.

"But of course you are. But draw comfort from the fact that you in contrast to pretty much everyone else here do it not for selfish reasons but for the common good. You know that there is the prevailing point of view among the rich and powerful that the end justifies the means?"

"I don't share that view," she replied darkly. "It's little more than an attempt to justify their atrocities. As long as you claim that it was done for the greater good, no deed seems too gruesome. That's certainly not what I did today. I merely helped Inad realise what dangers we all may be faced with in the future. It was her decision alone to aid me in my endeavours, I'll have you know."

Enric nodded solemnly and stopped himself from mentioning that using Inad was not a deed worth condemning as such, yet not quite the direct approach she would have chosen a year ago. But that they both knew well enough.

"Am I interrupting something?" Plia's voice came from the doorway to the parlour.

"No, nothing I would want to discuss at any greater length," Eryn sighed and waved the girl in with her free hand.

"There is something I wanted to tell you." The girl took a deep breath, clearly gathering all her courage. "Gerit has invited me to move in with her. She said that the house is a little too large for her on her own and that she would appreciate the company very much. And that she would feel a lot better if I didn't remain alone here in your house as soon as you leave for Takhan."

"And you accepted?" Eryn asked, making herself smile despite the lump in her throat. She didn't want to make this any harder for the girl than necessary.

When Plia nodded hesitantly, Enric cleared his throat. "I think this will be an excellent arrangement. I admit that I was also a little worried about leaving you alone for such a long time. I know that you are neither helpless nor prone to getting yourself into trouble, but I feel a lot better knowing that my mother will be keeping an eye on you. She won't hold back when she thinks that you are working too much or not eating properly."

"Yes," Eryn agreed, "that's quite a load off my shoulders, too. Even though your new beau seems to give you a reason to return from work rather earlier than before, I think having a pair of eyes on you is a good thing. And Gerit isn't used to living alone, so you can take care of each other."

Plia exhaled with relief. "I'm so glad you aren't angry. I thought you might consider me ungrateful after everything you have done for me..."

"You think we assumed some kind of ownership over you because we gave you a job and a place to stay?" Eryn laughed. "No, it was only a matter of time until you moved on to live your own life. Quite a bit sooner than I expected, I'll admit, but at least I don't have to feel bad for leaving you alone here for such a long time every year anymore. Can I persuade you to stay with us until we leave in a few weeks?"

The girl nodded enthusiastically. "Of course, I would have done that anyway." Then she swallowed. "I want you to know that I will always be grateful for what you did for me. For everything that..."

"Shut up," Eryn said gently. "I'm a selfish creature, so whatever I do is mainly aimed at making me happy. You were just lucky."

"Sure," Plia smiled, then changed the topic. "How did your visit go? Did you manage to make Inad yield to your wish?"

"I did. Beautifully so, even if I say it myself. Of course it remains to be seen if Lord Remdel truly acts the way his companion wishes him to."

"Does that mean you can finally make the changes you want?" the girl asked.

"Let's say it means that there is next to no chance that they will be rejected by a majority. Now that Aldon has left the Council and only twelve members remain, I'll have six votes in my favour if I count my own and Lord Remdel's. I need one more for a majority. That means there is at least one more Lord I need to convince that supporting me is a splendid idea. I thought of Lord Seagon. Now that he no longer dislikes me owing to my being a disruptive influence on common decency, he might be willing to listen to me. And he was really helpful when it came to making Aldon confess what he did."

Enric smiled to himself and nodded. "Yes, that is a good choice. I think you will find a private conversation with him most... insightful."

Eryn frowned. "What do you mean? What do you know that I don't?"

He laughed and rose from his chair. Then he kissed her on the forehead before he said, "Plenty, my love."

"Will you be visiting Lord Seagon tonight? Do you want me to mind Vedric while you are gone?" Plia offered.

Eryn shook her head. "No, I'll have to ask him for an appointment first. Just showing up on his doorstep unannounced wouldn't look good. I'll do it tomorrow."

Enric looked at the girl. "I'll be out hunting with Rolan tomorrow night, so if you are free I would very much appreciate your looking after Vedric. If you are busy with something else, I'll ask my mother."

"No, no," Plia assured him hastily, "I'm free. I think it's not too prudent to be always available, anyway. It's not good if a boy thinks everything revolves around him."

Eryn snorted. "Good luck with that. I have been trying to impress that on Enric for a while now, but despite being a smart man in general he proves resistant in that area."

He nodded. "True. And I intend to continue that resistance. One of these days, my love, you will surely comprehend that everything in your life does revolve around me. Or at least that's how it should be."

Eryn gave the girl a pained look. "You go on and teach your young friend that lesson as thoroughly as you can, or you'll end up exactly like me."

Plia raised one eyebrow. "Joined with the richest man in the Kingdom and with a beautiful baby boy? Is that a promise?"

Enric laughed and patted the girl's head. "I like her."

* * *

Eryn noticed that her steps were gradually slowing the closer she came to Lord Seagon's door. She listened to the staccato clack! of her heels on the smooth stone floor of the Palace corridor.

Lord Seagon had responded promptly when she sent him a message in the morning and invited her to take a drink with him in the evening.

When she reached the door to his quarters, she took a deep breath and knocked. Lord Seagon himself answered it and stepped aside to let her in.

"Good evening, Lady Eryn. Do come in and let me take your cloak."

Eryn stepped inside and found herself in the kind of parlour that was typical of magicians' quarters at the Palace. The same size, outline and even preference for dark wood and elegant furnishings.

The fabrics on the settees were dark blue with silver curly patterns, the carpet and curtains dark grey. This should have created a gloomy mood, but flowers arranged in numerous vases spread throughout the room countered the effect and turned the ambience into something more appealing.

"Take a seat, Lady Eryn. May I offer you a glass of wine?"

"Thank you, that would be nice," Eryn replied and sat on a chair. She wondered if she should have worn her robe for this. She was not here in her official capacity, yet she wanted to talk about something that concerned the Order. But then neither was Lord Seagon himself wearing his robe tonight, so forgoing her own was probably acceptable. It was the first time ever she saw him without his official robe. He liked to dress in rather simple garments with hardly any embroidery, yet well-tailored. She was surprised to see her own and also Enric's preferences reflected in his attire. The few Council members she had seen without their robes so far had adopted a more elaborate style. Not to mention their companions' flamboyant dresses that seemed to be designed to do little more than scream rich woman with every bit of fabric, frill, embroidery, ruffle and whatever other means of adornment had been employed by their adventurous tailors.

Lord Seagon placed a glass of red wine before her and took a seat on a large, comfortable looking wing chair, crossing his legs and looking at her with polite interest.

Eryn took a sip of wine to buy another few moments and thought back to what she had prepared for this occasion. She needed to avoid statements he might consider efforts at flattering him. Somehow she doubted that he would appreciate that.

"It's no secret that there are several things in the Order I find outdated, unnecessary or just in need of change," she started. "I see that many of you might consider this an assault on your values, on guidelines that have served you well in the past. Yet there were so many changes recently, changes that have had an impact on people in general, but also concern the Order. I realise that the preservation of traditions and values has for a long time been more important than making changes. But those changes are happening nevertheless, and I'm convinced that the Order needs to react to them, to adapt and shape them before it becomes overwhelmed by the consequences of ignoring them. You might consider that, as the one whose fault those changes basically are, I am not the most suitable advocate for..." She stopped when Lord Seagon lifted a hand to silence her. He was shutting her up already? Not encouraging, she thought.

"Why did you want to see me, Lady Eryn?" he asked calmly.

So he didn't really feel like listening to the speech she had prepared. Pity. She had worked on it so carefully, avoided potentially offensive statements, explained the situation and how everyone would benefit from her ideas.

"I was hoping for your support in the Council", she said stiffly, forcing down the meekness that wanted to creep into her voice.

"Why would you come to me, of all people?"

Eryn mulled that question over. How to answer it without making it seem like the flattery she wanted to avoid at all costs?

"Because even though you are a traditionalist, you don't let it prevent you from using your brain. It wouldn't make sense for me to try and get somebody on my side who is more easily impressionable, because he might just as quickly be persuaded by someone else to support a different idea. Your colleagues in the Council respect you, and if you consider my plans worth pursuing, it will make the others think instead of rejecting them outright." She breathed out steadily, looking at him and waiting for his reaction to her words.

"Why would you be so optimistic as to think that you could convince me to assist you?" Lord Seagon asked. Did she imagine it or did he seem a trifle amused right now?

"I was hoping that now that you are aware I didn't intentionally cause the trouble with your nephew and Enric back then, you would be more neutrally disposed towards me. I know, of course, that the role you played in the matter with Lo... Aldon", she corrected herself quickly, "can't have been too pleasant for you, yet I trust that you are not holding a grudge against me because of it."

Now he smiled openly. "You have learned a lot since you joined the Order, I'll give you that. I remember that naive, overly volatile person you were when you came here. You didn't really act in accordance with your age, if you ask me. But then I suppose one has to give it to you that you grew up far away from all this here, from the need to prevail, to be persuasive, to find allies instead of revelling in the idea of being the only truly noble one fighting against the rest. But as I said, you have developed admirably. Yet there still is one thing that you lack: experience. Lord Tyront is not exactly someone we would call a particularly lenient leader, as your frequent excursions to the horse stables should have taught you. And his expelling a member of the Council for the first time in the history of the Order is another impressive proof of that. So you see, under normal circumstances he would not have let me ask you whether you were involved in the attack on Aldon. It meant accusing you without any other reason than my personal difficulties with you. This Lord Tyront wouldn't have condoned had it not aided his own aims. It suited him extremely well that I proved you innocent in front of the Council, despite the fact that I overstepped a boundary. This was the moment when I knew for sure what I had until then merely suspected: Aldon was guilty and the people aware of it were very carefully trying to make him reveal it."

Eryn stared at him. "You knew?"

He chuckled and shook his head at her. "So you actually thought the timing of my questions was merely fortunate instead of intentional? You commended me on using my brain, yet are surprised when you turn out to be right."

Lord Seagon was right, she realised with resignation. No matter how well she thought she could navigate through this political jungle around her, her lack of experience still made it hard to identify and combine the tell-tale signs around her into a picture. But that didn't make hearing him say it like that any more bearable. Nonetheless there was little she could or rather should remark upon. Not if she wanted to get him to work with her.

She looked at him, unsure of how to proceed now. But he seemed pleased enough with how the conversation was going and nodded to her.

"I'm aware that your intentions of changing the Order, society and whatever other ambitious goals you have are aimed at improvement. And I know that something has to be done in the years to come, both with regard to the higher levels of strength in upcoming magicians and their increased numbers thanks to female ones we are to welcome into our midst." He smiled. "Talk to me. Let me hear why your ideas are the right ones for making this all work. Convince me to support you."

Eryn took another sip from her glass, noting that half was already gone. If she wanted to keep a clear head, she needed to slow down her consumption of the wine. She felt relief at his willingness to listen to her. It meant that he was not in principle opposed to working with her and would very likely support her if she furnished him with reasonable arguments. Straightening, she smiled at him. Reasonable arguments she could offer quite a few.

*   *   *

Enric looked up from his half-sitting, half-lying position on one of the sofas as Eryn breezed in through the entrance door. He caught her attention and touched his index finger to his lips to urge her to be quiet.

Her eyes fell on the baby sleeping on his father's chest.

Quickly she put down her cloak and came closer.

"Tough day?" she asked sympathetically.

Enric nodded. "Yes. I didn't get any work done. Ten minutes ago he fell asleep for the first time so far. I suspect that his teeth are troubling him. He chews on anything he manages to grab at."

Eryn smiled. "You can catch up on your work tomorrow when I mind him. Junar has asked me to look after Téa for an hour or two as she has to meet one of your fabric merchants. It will probably be a bit noisy for a while, but then you can always raise a soundproof barrier in front of your study door."

"That will be a busy time for you with two of them", he remarked. "Téa is already pretty mobile, isn't she?"

She grimaced. "Yes, she moves around on all fours and even pulls herself up into a standing position when she can hold on to something. But you know what? It offers a glimpse of what we can expect soon. It's always useful to be able to practise on other people's children, isn't it?"

He laughed quietly. "An interesting attitude. Not one, I trust, Junar is aware of?"

"Of course not. Though she is glad enough that I'm one of very few people Téa actually accepts being left alone with for a while, so she'd probably condone it."

In surprise Enric lifted his brow. "You are? That is a first - a little girl who actually likes you."

Eryn grinned. "I know! And I'm as perplexed as you are. Even Gara, Junar's sister, has trouble keeping the little one quiet. Last time I visited Orrin, Téa even stretched out her arms towards me."

"Amazing. Maybe she knows deep inside her that she was named after you and that getting on your right side will prove useful in the future. Presently you are the only female, fully-grown magician in the Kingdom, the only one she can turn to for guidance in certain things."

"Well, if she has realised this already, she really is a bright kid."

"Just like her older brother", Enric nodded. "How was your meeting with Lord Seagon? You look satisfied enough, and I didn't catch anything worrying through the mind bond."

"It was an interesting visit; I'm happy to say that it went better than I dared hope. Though he does like to show me that he his is more skilled than me in that bloody political gambit, just like the rest of you lot. It's like everyone enjoys showing me time and again that my high rank is nothing more than a matter of chance. Which, I admit, is not exactly false, but it's not as if I was pretending otherwise. Did you know, that he exposed Aldon on purpose that day? His questions were no fluke, he knew exactly what he was doing!" She looked at Enric's chest when Vedric stirred. That last sentence had been a bit too emotional and raised in volume.

Enric sighed when the blueish-brown eyes opened and moments later their son started to whimper. "Well done, you. Here, your turn now. You woke him - you rock him to keep him happy."

Eryn nodded and plucked Vedric from his father's chest, not at all disappointed that he was awake. She had spent the entire day first at the clinic treating patients and then at Lord Seagon's. Spending a little waking time with him was absolutely fine for her.

Enric returned to the topic they were discussing before. "I suspected that Lord Seagon was not completely unaware of what was going on. This is why Tyront would have chosen him for the truth block anyway even if he hadn't volunteered. So, did he agree to support you?"

"In the end he did. But not without first having me reiterate all the reasons I'd already given them at the Council meetings and then asking me questions as if I was a school girl he was quizzing."

"Well, you were the one coming to him to ask for his support."

"I know", she sighed. "That's why I indulged him. In the end he commended me on my nice presentation. I half expected him to pat me on the head."

Enric had to grin at that picture. A man foolish enough truly to take that liberty with her was in serious danger of losing his hand.

Vedric started to whimper louder and Eryn got up from her chair to start walking up and down the parlour, which calmed him immediately.

"So now you have Lords Seagon and Remdel on your side in addition to Tyront, Orrin, Lord Poron and me. Counting your own vote as well you now have the required majority. Congratulations, my love."

"Thanks", she snorted. "And all it took was sucking up to people, just the kind of thing I like to do."

"That's the way it works, both here and in Takhan."

"Yes, tell me", she said and rolled her eyes. She remembered well enough how her own brother had used her to get Ram'an's vote in the Senate some time back. Little had she known back then that Ram'an had been counting on that very thing and made use of the situation to get her to not only make up with him again, but also subject herself to being kissed. Well, at least they had reconciled with each other then. And Ram'an admitting this to Enric afterwards had probably been the start of the two men's tentative relationship that had started as little more than a truce.

"The Council next meets in five days' time", Enric said and interrupted her trail of thought. "That means that you will then have another month and a half to make sure things will be handled as they should before we are off to Takhan again." He smiled and folded his arms. "I intend to have our third level bond renewed immediately after our arrival there. I have been waiting for that for quite some time now."

Eryn shifted Vedric in her arms. "Immediately? So we will essentially stumble off the ship and into the waiting arms of whoever agrees to renew the bond?"

"Not quite like that, but I asked Valrad and Malriel to arrange for it to be performed the day after our arrival. Just we two and the few people required for providing the magical strength necessary for it. And after this has been taken care of, we can concentrate all our efforts on the preparation for Tala's and Rolan's ceremony a few days later."

"Everything planned out it seems, eh?" she smiled, slightly lopsidedly. It amused her that he was still so very eager to re-establish the bond. And at the same time it was both touching and a relief. He wanted her bound to him as tightly as possible and was not in the least reluctant to share his feelings with her on the immensely private level that the mind bond demanded. He loved her as much as he was capable of loving, and he wanted to share it with her, considering the mind bond a privilege where other couples had experienced it as a curse.

"With you, being well-prepared is a survival skill", he joked.

Plia came down the stairs, the mountain cat trailing on her heels, and nodded to Eryn. "Hello, I thought I heard your voice. Did you tame Lord Seagon?"

"He turned out to be fairly much on my side already, so there was not much taming involved, but rather catering to his delight in lecturing me. But all in all I consider the visit a success."

The girl smiled. "Well done, then."

Urban sauntered over to Eryn, lifting her cheek to have it scratched before flopping to the floor and spreading herself lazily on the carpet with a toothy yawn.

"I suppose so, though I didn't really do much", Eryn shrugged and suppressed a yawn herself. "Time to go to bed, I've had a long day. Maybe I can persuade Vedric to fall asleep before me."

Enric snorted. "Good luck there, then."

*　*　*

Enric squeezed Eryn's hand that clutched his in a firm grip while walking along the Palace corridors towards the Council hall.

"Stay calm and cool, my love. You will do fine. I know it", he encouraged her.

She just nodded, both dreading and awaiting the meeting ahead of her impatiently. This might turn out to be the most important Council meeting she had ever been to. One that might change history. If she didn't mess it up, dread threw in without much consideration for her efforts to get to a more positive mindset.

Enric stopped and turned her to face him, placed both his hands on her shoulders.

"Breathe evenly," he instructed.

She obeyed and followed his lead. In moments like this here it was helpful that he had access to her emotions, she couldn't help but feel. She didn't know if she would have managed to make herself admit to experiencing quite such a high level of tension, but the mind bond obviated the need for that. She briefly wondered if that wasn't a bit of a stumbling block for her personal development, if learning to overcome this reluctance didn't benefit her more than having this openness forced upon her by the mind bond.

"You are distracted, your breathing isn't regular", Enric scolded her mildly. "Look at me. Imagine the meeting is over. You are exiting the Council hall. Everything went exactly the way you wanted it, they agreed on everything you proposed." He shook his head when she opened her mouth. "No, listen. Observe yourself coming out of the hall. Think of what you feel after you have finally managed to get them to work with you after all this time. After reaching this immensely impressive goal. Two years of struggling with them, and you have overcome their short-sightedness, their fear of anything new and unknown, their distrust of you. Imagine that feeling."

She closed her eyes and created that scene in her head. The phantom of a smile played around her lips. If only this wasn't a mere construction in her head but the thing itself.

"What are you feeling?" he asked quietly.

"Joy. Triumph. Relief. Power." She opened her eyes again and grinned. "And smugness, I have to admit."

"Alright. Hold on to that. Borrow against it, make it aid you in your endeavours."

She released a long breath, and when her eyes met his again, the expression in them was less troubled. "Thank you. I'm ready. Let's do this."

The next corner brought the doors to the Council hall in sight. They stood wide open, revealing that the majority of the Council members had already arrived. They were milling together in small groups as they tended to, talking amongst themselves in a leisurely manner.

Her gaze wandered to the throne to one side. It was an exact replica of the original one in the throne room as far as she could tell. It was probably a smart thing not to settle for a more modest version when dealing with magicians. It surely paid to remind them who really was in charge, no matter how important and powerful they saw themselves. The smaller and almost unassuming chair next to it, which was reserved for the King's observer when the big man himself did not feel the need to be present, was unoccupied. That in itself was a rather reliable sign that King Folrin would appear. Otherwise the observer would already have arrived. He tended to get in early, probably to try and catch snippets of conversations and gauge the general mood before a meeting. The King himself would, of course, not wait for anyone; he was the sovereign making others wait.

Several of the magicians nodded at them as she and Enric entered, among them Orrin who was almost the only person standing alone instead of conversing with colleagues. The warrior preferred to observe matters to being in their midst.

Tyront was in a conversation with Lord Remdel and Lord Woldarn, and Eryn murmured, "We shouldn't have come so early. Now I'll just have to stand around waiting until everyone has arrived."

Enric looked around. "Most of us are here already, and there are Lord Seagon and Lord Poron."

Tyront as well noted that the Council was complete and slowly guided the assembled participants towards the oval stone table.

When all of them had gathered and were about to sit, sounds of approaching steps from the corridor resounded, audible through the still open doors. The King was about to arrive.

King Folrin marched in, Marrin at his side and proceeded towards his throne without breaking his stride. Only when he was comfortably seated, did he acknowledge the magicians who had bent the upper half of their bodies forward in a bow.

"Your Majesty", said Tyront, greeting him on behalf of the Council.

"My Lords", he replied and then added, "and, of course, My Lady."

They all sat down. Eryn desperately tried to hold on to the emotions which Enric had guided her towards on their way here. Happy feelings that would relax her enough so her nervousness wouldn't cause her to lose herself and become fuddled. She basically already had all the votes she needed, she reminded herself. If she didn't make a complete mess of this, she would in addition win over a few of the remaining sceptics.

Despite the King's presence, Tyront didn't bother with any particular formality when opening the meeting. "Gentlemen, you all know why we are here today. No matter how this meeting ends, we are about to write a new page in our history. Let's make sure to choose a wise path for it. Lady Eryn, please let us hear your proposals."

Eryn decided to do this standing up. She had briefly considered remaining seated, but she felt she needed freedom to move, to use gestures without accidentally striking Orrin next to her.

Slowly she pushed her seat back, flinching slightly at the scratching sound the heavy wooden chair made on the polished stone floor. Had it always been that loud?

"My Lords, Your Majesty, I thank you very much for the opportunity to introduce to you a number of... adaptations in the Order that will better enable us to deal with the changes we see happening around us. I trust that you are all aware that there are some we cannot reverse, even if many of you might prefer doing just that." She made herself smile. "Some of them, admittedly, I was not entirely innocent in triggering. But whether or not you consider this newfound relationship with the Western Territories and this new field of healing positive developments or not, they still need to be handled one way or another. They won't go away again, and even if they did, I'm convinced that they would leave a void for many of us." Some of them nodded almost imperceptibly, she noted, others just waited for her to go on. "The recent incidents have shown us that there is insecurity, fear and at times helplessness in dealing with all that. This the Order needs to address. We need to help our fellow magicians find their place in this changing society, become role models. They look to us for guidance, but we have not yet managed to give them what they need. The attack on Lord Tyront, the incident with the magicians storming this very room not long ago, and even Aldon's misguided attempt at holding on to what he considered proper values show that something needs to be done."

She noted with relief that the knot in her stomach had loosened since she had started talking. The words were coming as they should, no stuttering or overlong breaks to hunt for phrases prepared and since forgotten. So far, so good.

"There are three great challenges we are facing already or will have to deal with in the years ahead. Firstly, our magicians see the privileges and opportunities our fellow magic users in the Western Territories enjoy. Opportunities such as choosing a profession in line with their leanings and talents, taking over family businesses and also relocating to a place of their own choice. These are substantial freedoms, ones which every non-magician here has as well. Magicians were raised in the belief that not being as free was the price for being born with magic, and now they see that this is not a law derived from nature, but of man." She lifted her head. "And they are right in challenging it! Why would we restrain ourselves and each other in such a way? There might have been good reasons to do this in the past, but now there are even better ones to reconsider this approach in favour of a system that not only imposes no limit our personal freedom, but also allows living up to our potential in so many possible areas. Vern, with his immense artistic talent, is the most impressive example, yet he is not the only person. Each of the healers we have started training has proven to be suited for the profession. Being healers gives them more joy than being a warrior ever could have."

"What exactly is it you are leading up to here, Lady Eryn?" Lord Poron asked.

Eryn swallowed. That was a pretty clear sign that she was talking too much.

"I propose to lift the restrictions on magicians and allow them to pursue whatever profession they consider attractive," she replied with as much dignity as she could muster.

"I would think that many craftspeople would strongly object to having magicians in the same line of work as themselves. They might consider it an unfair advantage," Lord Woldarn said.

She nodded. "At first thought maybe, but it also would open up new potential. In those professions where magical abilities might indeed be an advantage - such as in carpentry, construction or other areas where strength or manipulation of materials is necessary - there could be partnerships undertaken for mutual benefit. Magicians could learn the craft from non-magicians and then keep on working with them. Or there could be specialists for products that can only be provided with the aid of magic, areas which wouldn't be possible for non-magicians anyway. As we are continuously extending our trade with the Western Territories, such products manufactured by magician craftspeople are bound to turn up here sooner or later, anyway. So banning magicians from the professions here in Anyueel wouldn't be a reliable way of avoiding the competition in any event."

Enric's faint smile told her that she had answered the question well, and she felt proud, as if she were a schoolgirl being praised by a particularly exacting teacher.

When nobody else wished to comment on the subject, she returned to her presentation. "The second challenge we have to face is the matter of increased strength in the new generation of magicians who will have been born after the removal of the barrier in the brain. As long as the Order's only task remained defence, magical strength might have been an understandable way of assigning power, but now that the institution is in charge of governing at least one additional field of expertise, namely healing, this needs to be changed for more reasons than one. You all know the report Pe'tala and I wrote on the increasing number of extraordinarily strong babies in this city alone. In twenty years from now, the Order will potentially be being led by a group of barely mature magicians with no experience in leadership, organisation or diplomacy. I shudder at the thought of being bound to follow their commands. Granting power should under these circumstances no longer merely depend on a coincidence - namely that of being born with considerable magical strength - but on criteria that are more suitable for all our needs and aim to ensure the Order's continued existence."

Their expressions showed her that every single one of the men in that room shared that sentiment at least. Nobody wanted to be ordered about by magicians who might be young enough to be their grandchildren.

"Another consequence, the third one I wanted to talk to you about, is the increase in magicians due to the fact that the barrier has not only opened the doors to more magical strength, but also to female magicians. How many warriors could the Order and subsequently the Crown really sustain? Warriors, useful as they may be, do not generate any income as such. Non-magician fighters are in a position to work as guards and earn their keep, but not the Order's warriors."

"So you are suggesting we make ourselves useful instead of being a drain on public funds?" Orrin asked mildly. The remark earned him a few appreciative laughs.

Eryn shook her head. "I would never dare suggesting that you and your warriors were useless, Lord Orrin," she said softly. "But the question is how many more warriors we can afford. This, Gentlemen, is another argument in favour of enabling magicians to choose a profession different from that of warrior or administrator. Well, and lately, healer. In order to do this, however, we first need to allow magicians to live outside the city. Otherwise we will soon be overcrowded with magicians here. You all know of my endeavours to make relocation possible for healers, so that not only may people here in the city benefit from their services, but even those in more remote places. And not all magicians appreciate being separated from their families. Some of them would have taken over family businesses, if they hadn't turned out to be gifted with magic."

Lord Seagon cleared his throat. "You are basically proposing releasing magicians from the Order's control, if I understand you correctly."

Eryn shook her head emphatically. "Not at all, my Lord. Quite the opposite. I'm a firm believer in holding people accountable for their deeds, no matter if they are magicians or not. As non-magicians have little chance of restraining or punishing a magician, this would clearly need to remain the Order's responsibility." She took a few moments to think, then continued, "I have no experience when it comes to keeping magicians under control or maintaining discipline, but in time we might have to consider erecting outposts to keep in contact with our magicians out there - and to provide a place to go for people who wish for the Order to take action against misuse of magic somewhere."

That earned her several stares, yet she couldn't say if the men were appalled or simply surprised by the novel concept. She looked at Enric, whose expression she could normally read better than other people's. He was looking at the ceiling, letting his eyes wander, as he did when he was pondering something. So it seemed that he, at least, considered the suggestion something worthy of further thought.

"Like a magistrate just for magicians?" Tyront now asked, though she wasn't sure whether he was talking to her or to himself. He seemed thoughtful, too.

"Well, yes," she agreed carefully, "that would be one way of looking at it, I suppose." She returned her attention to all of the men around her. It was time to come to an end. "What I'm trying to get over here, what I wish for all of us, for this country, is for us to make use of what we have and do it in a way that benefits us all. You may still consider me a foreigner, but this is not how I see myself. I'm a citizen of this Kingdom, even though my ancestors were not. And as such I wish to see us grow, I wish to be proud of my country. The Western Territories are amiable and helpful, but apart from our superior skills in combat, they look down on us - and with good reason, too. We are backward in many areas, and we shouldn't be!" She slapped her hand, palm downwards, on the table in front of her. "They came here after the war and took away our knowledge to make use of it, leaving us with little more than snippets to remember. Back then, this Kingdom was superior to their country in more than one way - they learned from us about magical music, made use of our expertise in architecture, and even the discipline of healing had been discovered here before it was banished from our realm. It's time for us to show them - and ourselves - that we aren't to be pitied or given a comforting pat on the head, but that these last centuries have comprised nothing more than a break, during which we collected our resources to be all the more formidable now!"

Eryn stopped, blinking in surprise at that last bit. Oh dear, it seemed like Pe'tala's and Vran'el's little jibes must have irked her more than she had realised.

She cast a surreptitious glance at the King, who was regarding her with one eyebrow raised in what looked like a mix of fascination and appreciation.

Now that she was done, she felt strangely empty - as if all her energy was spent. With little ceremony she just sank back on her chair, not sure how things were supposed to progress from here.

Tyront raised his voice. "Thank you, Lady Eryn, for these... interesting insights. My Lords, a member of our circle has made a motion for extensive changes. A motion that requires a response. Allow me to summarise what we were being asked to consider just now. The first two points pertain to permitting magicians to choose a profession outside the ones the Order is offering at the moment and permitting them to relocate to places outside the city. The third point concerns the mode of granting power based on magical strength." He looked at Eryn again. "Your arguments, my Lady, were very powerful indeed. You painted us a picture of a city overcrowded with magicians in the years to come, a considerable burden to our financial resources and an institution in the hands of little more than adolescents. I admit that these are not particularly appealing prospects, and that your arguments are reasonable enough, backed by statistics you yourself collected and forwarded to us in the past. Yet it is not just me you need to convince, but the Council in its entirety." His gaze wandered over the assembled magicians. "There can be no definitive decisions in these points here and now, but what we need to determine here and now is whether or not we agree to act. The first matter I invite you to vote upon is the one of letting magicians choose their profession in accordance with their inclinations. Show hands if you are in favour."

Eryn held her breath and closed her eyes. After three seconds she forced herself to open them again and took in the hands raised to support her first proposal - ten!

"Thank you," Tyront continued. "Then we will return to this point for further consideration. The second point of permitting magicians to relocate outside the city - raise your hands if you support that suggestion."

Eight hands this time. Still more than enough.

"And, finally, the last point of reconsidering our current mode of appointing the top leaders in the Order. Show hands if you think our current approach is in need of reform."

Eryn exhaled in utter relief when eleven hands - all except Lord Woldarn's - went up to indicate support.

Lord Remdel's hand had been raised for every single one of the three votes - Inad had made good on her promise to talk to her companion. There might be quite a few things which could be said about that woman, but her being unreliable was certainly not one of them.

She had really done it. After struggling for two years, after all these setbacks, her quarrels with a number of the Council members, her scrapes with the King, everything that had happened with the Western Territories, she had finally managed to effect the start of a change so considerable that it would alter the nature of the Order as an institution.

Thoughts of her father - or rather her first father, Ved'al, the man who had raised her - emerged. She imagined how he would be proud of her. She had fought for the ideals he had taught her as a child - and prevailed.

Enric watched her from the other side of the table, feeling the mix of emotions through their bond. There was triumph, immense relief, and a hint of melancholy. He wondered whether she was for some reason mourning the end of her long struggles with the Order or thinking of her father. The latter, probably. She had just managed to smooth the way for the Order to turn into the kind of institution Ved'al of House Vel'kim might have found acceptable.

The magicians at the table had started muttering amongst themselves, and Tyront cleared his throat to silence them. "I'm glad to see that the results show a clear preference for taking an active role in dealing with the challenges we are about to face. Our next step must be to determine a sensible course of action for implementing each of them. For this I suggest forming working groups. Each of them need to contain at least one member of the Council, one of the magicians who were so eager to protect Onil from a cruel fate, and whichever other specialists from inside or outside the Order are required. Lord Enric and Lady Eryn will be leaving for Takhan soon, so it makes little sense to include them in this process. The rest of you I shall ask to take an active role in all this and let me know which of the three areas you wish to contribute your time and efforts to. I now declare this meeting closed and shall look forward to hearing from you within the next three days."

Eryn remained seated when all the others around her got up to leave. She would need another minute or so.

Orrin squeezed her shoulder without saying anything before he turned to follow his colleagues out the Council hall. A little later, only Enric, Tyront and the King and his advisor were left.

"You did it", Tyront smiled from across the table while he steepled his fingers. "I'm proud of you."

"Patronising me?" Eryn smiled weakly, too happy to truly bother about it.

Her superior shrugged. "I thought you might be in a mood to tolerate it presently."

Now the King rose from his throne and approached the table, pulling out the chair next to Eryn's before sitting down on it. Eryn blinked. That was an uncharacteristically pally thing to do for him.

"I agree with Lord Tyront, my Lady. I particularly admired the part where you appealed to their sense of nationality when pointing out that the Western Territories consider us somewhat backward." He crossed his legs. "Let's hope you just fuelled the Council's eagerness to compete with them by enabling development, and not inspired them to prepare for war to pay them back for their arrogance."

Eryn flashed him a dark look. He had a way of dousing a joyous mood.

"I was joking, my dear Lady. I truly am very satisfied with how you handled this. Well done indeed. A pity you will not be here in the months ahead to guide the putting into action of the changes you set in motion so impressively. But then I would think that it won't hurt if the Council is seen to be taking care of these concerns without you in charge. This will make it seem more like joint effort than solely yours."

"Pity," Eryn smiled without joy. "You could have tried to get my brother to let me stay here for a while longer."

King Folrin shook his head. "And deprive you of the chance to work on your relationship with your mother? I wouldn't be that cruel."

Enric got up from his chair and walked around the table to stand next to Eryn.

"I wish to grant you a favour," the monarch smiled. "Your efforts and the success they were crowned with have put me in a generous mood."

Eryn grinned. "I want you to dispense with sending us off with a ball this time. Or find another reason to have a ball before we leave here. Basically, just don't have any ball I'm expected to attend."

Enric and Tyront exchanged a look and each hid a smile. A wish as typical for Eryn as the braid she wore every day.

"Granted," King Folrin nodded with little surprise. "No ball for now it is. You realise that this does not keep me from welcoming you back with one as soon as you return in a few months, don't you?"

She nodded. "Certainly. But by then I might have achieved another impressive feat that might make you grant me another favour."

She smiled as he laughed at her reply. Then he rose. "I shall wish you a pleasant day, Lady Eryn. Celebrate your triumph, one which is richly deserved." He took her hand to kiss it, then turned around and left, Marrin one step behind.

"You know, I think, that he is right," Eryn mused. "This really does warrant a celebration, doesn't it? This is the day I tamed the Order, after all!" She beamed when Tyront rolled his eyes.

"You'd better be careful, or I'll have you cleaning out the horse stables one final time before you leave here," he threatened without any barb.

She laughed. "You know something? I'll take that over attending a ball any time."

Enric pulled her to her feet. It was time to leave. "Come, my love. Let's pick up Vedric from my mother's place and then invite a few people for tonight to celebrate your glorious victory over everything that is stuffy and old-fashioned."

Grinning, she pulled her arm through his. "I like it!"

Epilogue

Eryn looked around the spacious Vel'kim gardens, holding on to her glass of sweet white wine. The ceremony had been beautiful, touching and intimate, just the way Pe'tala had intended it. So her little sister was now well and truly joined with Rolan.

The guests were dispersed, mostly sitting on cushions that were spread far and wide amongst the numerous spots where Valrad grew his herbs, a few were wandering through the garden, conversing with somebody.

Eryn lifted her nose into the air, enjoying the mix of scents the light evening breeze carried towards her from the garden. Lanterns were placed on the ground in regular intervals, lending the surroundings a gentle glow that illuminated just enough to be neither gloomy nor harshly bright.

She felt a tickle of amusement and looked over to the terrace, where Enric was standing with Ram'an and Valcredy, whose belly was not exactly bulging, but already well-rounded with the next heir to House Arbil. Eryn pushed aside the feeling of annoyance at seeing Enric's former lover standing so close to him. Enric was laughing at something she was saying, which didn't make things any better. Still she had to smile at the faint echo of his merriment in her head.

The mind bond had returned to her mere hours after the renewal of their third level commitment bond. Iklan told her that he suspected that this was because the connection was already there, and had just been interrupted for a time.

She remembered the sensation of having somebody else's feelings distract her from what she herself was experiencing, but had yet to get used to it again. Four days had not yet managed that.

At that moment Enric looked in her direction and saw her thoughtful gaze rest on him. She watched how he excused himself from the party and walked over to her.

"Hi there," he said and stopped one step below her on the terraces stairs. That way he was only marginally taller than her. "What is a beautiful girl like you doing here all alone?"

She smiled and lifted her wrist that shone with the commitment symbols, newly re-emerged, on her skin. They gave a slight glow when he was that close. His own symbols were not visible with his long sleeves.

"Careful, stranger. I'm a happily joined woman, and my companion is not only immensely jealous, but also a fearsomely powerful magician."

Enric laughed quietly and moved closer. "Is he now? Well, I would say that a woman like yourself is certainly worth risking a little danger."

Their lips touched for a stretched moment, and he tasted the wine she had been sipping while standing here.

"Why don't you come over and join us? I think that way we could get rid of that flicker of jealousy I received from you just now."

She gave in and let herself be pulled towards the group that was standing right under a gorgeously blooming tree.

Valrad was just handing his grandson over to Malriel, who placed him on her hip with an ease that Eryn felt should not look quite so practised. Seeing Malriel as a loving grandmother, no matter that now she at least almost looked old enough to be one, just didn't fit the picture in Eryn's head.

Ram'an placed an arm around Eryn's shoulders and pushed Enric aside with a wink. "Stop monopolising her, Order Lord! It is that time of the year where you have to share her with friends and family for a few months."

Enric gave the Head of House Arbil a token scowl. Under different circumstances he would just have reciprocated by pulling Ram'an's companion closer, but not in that particular case.

"Tala," he said instead and turned to the happy couple. "How are things between you and Vran now? He still seems a little tense around you, even though he has been making efforts to hide it today."

Pe'tala grimaced. "A wee bit tense, as you said. I suppose it will take a while yet before he forgives me for moving in with you. Or you for letting me move in, for that matter."

"Do not worry, my child," Valrad said with a reassuring smile, "he will get over it eventually. And it is not as if he had to live here all alone as long as Vern remains in Takhan. The fact that he is glad to have both his sisters back in Takhan for now already makes it hard for him to stay angry at you."

Vran'el and Vern approached from the terrace door, each of them carrying two bottles of wine. Urban trailed behind Vran'el, happy to be reunited with him in that mischievous attachment cats form with people who are uneasy around them.

"Oh my," Rolan murmured, "it seems they have big plans for tonight."

When the three of them had joined them, Vern placed his two bottles in the grass behind him and grinned at Eryn. Even before he started talking, she knew that she wouldn't appreciate whatever would come out of his mouth.

"So, you never told me how you liked the gift I sent you. Have you tried number eighty-three yet?"

"That's none of your business," she growled, none too happy about the knowing sniggers around her. "Ram'kel was present when it was delivered, and he had a splendid time teasing me about it."

Ram'an nodded. "He wrote to me about that. He said you even blushed." He shook his head. "A grown woman, happily joined to a man, and even with a child, is still shy when talking about such things. I shudder at such prudery. And opening a gift like that in my brother's presence was probably not the smartest thing you could have done."

"I didn't open it! He did! He simply went to my desk and opened it just like that!" she protested.

"You did not answer the question," Tala cut in, her smile beaming across her face. "Have you tried number eighty-three now or not?"

Eryn closed her eyes, wondering what had to go wrong with a culture to consider intimate physical relationships a topic that could be discussed openly just like that.

"You should," her brother now threw in. "I myself am a great fan of number eighty-three."

She stared at him. "You are? But... how?"

Vran'el sighed and shook his head. "Sweetness, this requires nothing more than shifting the angle a few degrees, then two men can do it just as straightforwardly."

Eryn grimaced. "Thank you. What more can a girl want than picturing her brother in such a position. Can we please change the topic? You could at least grant me a week or two to re-acclimatise to your peculiar ways before tormenting me."

"Would you mind terribly, if I sat down?" Valcredy asked. "I tire more easily these days."

Ram'an was at her side in an instant. "Of course, forgive me my thoughtlessness." He held her hand while she sank down onto a nearby cushion." Then he looked over at Eryn, clearing his throat. "There was a little something I wanted to discuss with you, my dear. I do not know if you have heard, but my child will be a girl."

Eryn smiled. "Congratulations! Did you agree on a name?"

"We are still in the process of selecting one," he replied politely, obviously eager to talk about something different. "I was wondering if you and I could take tea together tomorrow?"

She frowned. "What do you want to talk about?" She watched how Ram'an's gaze flickered to Vedric in Malriel's arms, then she sucked in an angry breath. "You must be joking! No!"

Ram'an lifted both palms to placate her. "Look, why do we not just sit..."

"Ram'an," Eryn growled and gave him a murky, hostile look, "there is no way I'll enter into a companionship agreement for our children with you. What in the world makes you think I'd be willing to do a thing like that? And why ever would you be willing to after everything the two of us went through because of the one our idiot parents signed?"

She ignored Malriel's very pointed coughing at idiot parents.

The people around them exchanged awkward glances, and Eryn growled, "Yes, sure, now you are embarrassed - but when I'm invited to openly discuss my sex life, that's completely normal." She pushed her empty glass towards her brother. "Here, top me up, will you?"

Vran'el uncorked one of the bottles and filled the glasses around him, starting with Eryn's. When he came to Pe'tala, she quickly covered the top of her glass.

"No, thank you. One glass will do it for me."

"Come on, Tala, if this is no occasion that warrants celebration, which is?" laughed Vern.

Pe'tala smiled and exchanged a tell-tale look with Rolan, taking his hand in hers before she turned to her guests. "There is another occasion to celebrate, though one that rather prevents me from doing so with alcohol."

Realisation dawned on those around her and exclamations of joy filled the air, while Pe'tala was embraced, kissed and felicitated. Valrad had tears in his eyes as he pressed his youngest daughter close, and gave Rolan a hearty slap on his back.

Eryn's gaze fell on Malriel and the quiet, immensely satisfied smile that curved her lips while she was rocking her grandson on her hip. Their eyes met, and Eryn gulped, feeling for Enric's hand. She felt the urge to walk those five steps and wrestle her mother for Vedric to get him out of her reach.

She looked up at Enric, who looked resigned and squeezed her fingers.

"You tamed the Order, my love, remember?" he whispered and pressed a kiss onto her temple, "How hard can dealing with Malriel be after all that?"

Eryn sighed, feeling his unease through the mind bond and thus knowing exactly that he wasn't quite as optimistic as he was pretending.

Pe'tala's being pregnant was the official start signal. Thanks to House Vel'kim now having another potential heir on the way, the struggle for whose House Vedric would belong to had just begun. Bloody brilliant.

>>><<<

www.ingramcontent.com/pod-product-compliance
Lightning Source LLC
Chambersburg PA
CBHW070537030726
47505CB00001B/72